SMOLLETT, T. (TOBIAS), 172
THE ADVENTURES OF
FERDINAND COUNT FATHOM /
C1988.
37565009120113   CENT

THE WORKS OF TOBIAS SMOLLETT

The Adventures of Ferdinand Count Fathom

THE WORKS OF TOBIAS SMOLLETT

Jerry C. Beasley, General Editor
University of Delaware

O M Brack, Jr., Textual Editor
Arizona State University

Jim Springer Borck, Technical Editor
Louisiana State University

This edition includes all of the works by which Tobias Smollett was best known in his own day and by which he most deserves to be remembered. The edition conforms to the highest standards of textual and editorial scholarship. Individual volumes provide carefully prepared texts together with biographical and historical introductions and extensive explanatory notes.

EDITORIAL BOARD

Hugh Amory, Harvard University
Martin C. Battestin, University of Virginia
Paul-Gabriel Boucé, Université de Paris
James L. Clifford (1901–1978)
Francis M. Cowe, Berwick-upon-Tweed
Robert Adams Day, City University of New York
Byron Gassman, Brigham Young University
Duncan Isles, University College of Wales, Aberystwyth
Lewis M. Knapp (1894–1976)
William Kupersmith, University of Iowa
Louis Landa, Princeton University
Thomas R. Preston, North Texas State University
John V. Price, University of Edinburgh
D. H. Stefanson, Miles College
Albrecht B. Strauss, University of North Carolina at Chapel Hill
William B. Todd, University of Texas at Austin
Mary Wagoner, University of New Orleans
Ian Watt, Stanford University
Curt Zimansky (1913–1973)

Portrait of Smollett by William Verelst, c. 1756.
(National Galleries of Scotland, courtesy of Major Patrick Telfer Smollett.)

The Adventures of Ferdinand Count Fathom

TOBIAS SMOLLETT

Introduction and Notes by
JERRY C. BEASLEY

The Text Edited by
O M BRACK, JR.

The University of Georgia Press
Athens and London

© 1988 by the University of Georgia Press
Athens, Georgia 30602
All rights reserved

Set in Linotron 202 Janson
The paper in this book meets the guidelines for permanence
and durability of the Committee on Production Guidelines for
Book Longevity of the Council on Library Resources.

Printed in the United States of America

96 95 94 93 92   C   6 5 4 3 2
96 95 94 93 92   P   5 4 3 2 1

Library of Congress Cataloging in Publication Data

Smollett, Tobias George, 1721–1771.
The adventures of Ferdinand Count Fathom/introduction and notes
by Jerry C. Beasley; the text edited by O M Brack, Jr.
        p.   cm.—(The works of Tobias Smollett)
                    Includes index.
            ISBN 0-8203-1010-7 (alk. paper)
        ISBN 0-8203-1435-8 (pbk.: alk. paper)
I. Beasley, Jerry C. II. Brack, O M. III. Title. IV. Series:
Smollett, Tobias George, 1721–1771. Works. 1988.
PR3694.A3 1988
823'.6—dc19   87-26368
                                                CIP

British Library Cataloging in Publication Data available

NOTE

The editors wish to thank Hugh Amory, Paul-Gabriel Boucé, Melvyn New, and Pat Rogers for calling to their attention certain misprints, omissions, and other inaccuracies in the original clothbound edition of *Ferdinand Count Fathom*. These have been corrected for the present edition. A table of page and line references for all corrections, together with a record of additions to the original list of emendations and historical collation, may be found at the end of the volume, on pages 481–482.

J.C.B.
OMB., Jr.
November 1991

CONTENTS

Contents

ILLUSTRATIONS

The plates are by Thomas Stothard and his disciple Luke Clennell. Stothard illustrated *Ferdinand Count Fathom* in 1782 for the *Novelist's Magazine* (vol. 7, no. 4), Clennell in 1810 for a collection entitled *British Novelists* (vol. 2, no. 2). The titles for the illustrations are the editor's.

PREFACE

The Adventures of Ferdinand Count Fathom has never before been adequately edited or annotated. The early reputation of the novel was such that it did not particularly engage the attention of nineteenth-century Smollett enthusiasts like Robert Chambers, whose *Smollett: His Life and a Selection from His Writings* (London and Edinburgh: W. and R. Chambers, 1867) initiated the modern scholarly enterprise of identifying the historical allusions in the novels. Chambers was followed by David Herbert, editor of a one-volume selective collection, *The Works of Tobias Smollett* (Edinburgh: William P. Nimmo, 1870). Herbert omitted *Ferdinand Count Fathom* and *Sir Launcelot Greaves* from his edition but included a lengthy introduction analyzing all of the novels and explaining a good many of their references to actual places and people. Like Chambers before him, Herbert was most interested in illuminating the background of *Humphry Clinker*; his introduction treats *Roderick Random* and *Peregrine Pickle* lightly and scarcely discusses *Ferdinand Count Fathom* and *Sir Launcelot Greaves* at all. More than a century after Chambers and Herbert, *Ferdinand Count Fathom* was selected for inclusion in the Oxford English Novels series (London: Oxford University Press, 1971), in an edition prepared by Damian Grant. Modestly annotated, as befits the series to which it belongs, this edition nevertheless represents the first attempt ever to provide anything like a scholarly text of Smollett's third novel.

The present edition is properly much more ambitious. It draws very generally upon the contributions of Grant, and to a lesser extent upon those of Chambers and Herbert; it draws much more heavily upon four major twentieth-century biographical and critical studies that have done so much to revive and then to perpetuate interest in Smollett's life and writings: Louis L. Martz, *The Later Career of Tobias Smollett* (New Haven: Yale University Press, 1942); George M. Kahrl, *Tobias Smollett: Traveler-Novelist* (Chicago: University of Chicago Press, 1945); Lewis M. Knapp, *Tobias Smollett: Doctor of Men and Manners* (Princeton: Princeton University Press, 1949); and Paul-Gabriel Boucé, *The Novels of Tobias Smollett* (London: Longman, 1976). There are debts to the work of other scholars, too numerous to mention here. The notes to the introduction and text will have to suffice as grateful acknowledgment.

This new edition of *Ferdinand Count Fathom* is heavily annotated, and the notes are intended to assist the serious reader or student who wishes to understand Smollett's novel as fully as possible. More precisely described, the notes are designed to illuminate the text itself; they do not seek to provide histories of or elaborate commentaries upon the subject matter of the work, whether literary or historical. Frequent references to primary and secondary sources should enable the interested reader to pursue any topic beyond the boundaries imposed by the ideals of concise and appropriate annotation, which the editor has always tried to honor. Many notes contain cross-references to other notes, to related portions of the text, or to both; these cross-references, especially when used in conjunction with the index found at the end of the volume, should make it possible to trace the recurrence of certain important matters—names, topics, and the like—through the work as a whole.

Obscure or archaic words are defined in the notes, usually on first occurrence; words clearly defined in context are normally not annotated unless Smollett's usage possesses some peculiar historical or literary interest. Proverbs are explained and dated by reference to one or more standard sources. Literary allusions to poems, plays, novels, and other works are identified by name of author (if known) and by lines, acts, scenes, chapter numbers, page numbers (as appropriate), or other conventional means. Quotations from Greek and Latin authors follow the translations in the Loeb Classical Library; quotations from Shakespeare have been checked against *The Riverside Shakespeare*, ed. G. Blakemore Evans et al. (Boston: Houghton Mifflin, 1974).

Many of the notes treat Smollett's topographical allusions. With a few exceptions, large cities and other very familiar places named in the text receive no comment, on the assumption that they need none even for the modern reader. References to less familiar places, whether provinces, cities or towns, quarters or hundreds, streets or buildings, have been explained as fully as the context seemed to require. *Ferdinand Count Fathom* is rich in historical as well as topographical allusions. Every reference to a specific event or person is explained in sufficient detail to account for its importance and its relevance to Smollett's narrative; the explanations regularly cite other contemporary works, including Smollett's own writings in several forms, as sources of important supporting or qualifying evidence.

The editor's introduction requires a brief comment. Its purpose is to furnish a broad background of information thought to be helpful to the reader who wishes to take up *The Adventures of Ferdinand Count Fathom*. In separate sections, the introduction places the novel within the context of its author's career as a writer, traces the history of its composition, printing, and early reception, and discusses its more important uses of contemporary materials. The introduction develops no deliberate line of critical argument, though some readers will doubtless catch the editor in the expression of certain biases he could not completely disguise and still remain faithful to his own privileged experience of Smollett's novel.

ACKNOWLEDGMENTS

Many people have rendered invaluable assistance toward the preparation of this edition. I am grateful to them all. The following friends and colleagues have furnished incidental information for the annotations—often at moments of the greatest exasperation for me, and sometimes without quite knowing that they were helping at all: James G. Basker, Paul-Gabriel Boucé, D. Heyward Brock, Joan Brown, Michael Crump, Jack Ellis, Bradley Howard, Robert D. Hume, Stephen Lukashevich, Corinne Matrat, Donald Mell, Julie Mody, Wocjiech Nowicki, Bonnie Robb, Catherine Sharrock, Simon Varey, Alfred Wedel. Others have aided me in specific ways too varied to enumerate, but they will all know precisely why I have listed their names here: Major Patrick Telfer Smollett, David Daiches, Jack Howells, Ronald Paulson, O M Brack, Jr., Thomas R. Preston, Robert Adams Day, Byron Gassman, Jim Springer Borck, Elizabeth Reynolds.

Numerous librarians have given generously of their time and expertise. I want especially to mention members of the staff at the British Library, who were always prompt with the information I asked for, the books I needed, and the courtesy I appreciated so much. I must note, too, the helpful people at the Historical Medical Museum of the Wellcome Institute, the Bodleian Library of Oxford University, the Glasgow University Library, Princeton University Library, and the libraries of the University of Pennsylvania and the University of Delaware. For their kind assistance with the identification, location, and preparation of the illustrations I want particularly to thank Donald Anderle and Bob Dumont of the New York Public Library, Phil Lapsansky of the Library Company of Philadelphia, Kathleen Reed of the Van Pelt Library at the University of Pennsylvania, Charles E. Greene of the Princeton University Library, John Hayes and Sarah Wimbush of the National Portrait Gallery, Kenneth A. Lohf of the Columbia University Library, and Leonard N. Beck of the Library of Congress.

I wish to express my appreciation to the administration of the University of Delaware for the award of a sabbatical leave, which allowed me to spend the autumn months of 1982 in London, carrying out necessary research. The University of Delaware has also been generous with grants to defray some of the costs of completing the edition. To Brad Howard, who twice proofread the text with an unfailing eye for error, I want to extend special thanks. I shall always be grateful to Rita Beasley for her wizardry at the word processor, her scrupulous attention to the requirements of accuracy, and her astonishing patience.

ABBREVIATIONS

Barrow

J. Barrow, *Dictionarium Medicum Universale: or, A New Medicinal Dictionary* (London, 1749).

Complete History

Tobias Smollett, *A Complete History of England*, 4 vols. (London, 1757–58).

Cunnington and Cunnington

C. Willett Cunnington and Phillis Cunnington, *Handbook of English Costume in the Eighteenth Century*, 3d ed. (London: Faber and Faber, 1964).

Henderson

Nicholas Henderson, *Prince Eugen of Savoy: A Biography* (London: Weidenfeld and Nicolson, 1964).

Knapp

Lewis Mansfield Knapp, *Tobias Smollett: Doctor of Men and Manners* (Princeton: Princeton University Press, 1949).

Letters

The Letters of Tobias Smollett, ed. Lewis M. Knapp (Oxford: Clarendon Press, 1970).

ODEP

Oxford Dictionary of English Proverbs, 3d ed., rev. F. P. Wilson (Oxford: Clarendon Press, 1970).

OED

Oxford English Dictionary.

PMLA

PMLA: Publications of the Modern Language Association of America.

Present State

Tobias Smollett, ed., *The Present State of All Nations*, 8 vols. (London, 1768–69).

Strutt

Joseph Strutt, *The Sports and Pastimes of the People of England*, 1801; rev. J. Charles Cox (London: Methuen, 1903).

Timbs

John Timbs, *Curiosities of London*, 2 vols. (London: David Bogue, 1855).

Travels

Tobias Smollett, *Travels through France and Italy*, ed. Frank Felsenstein (Oxford: Oxford University Press, 1979).

Turberville   A. S. Turberville, ed., *Johnson's England: An Account of the
                     Life and Manners of His Age*, 2 vols. (Oxford: Clarendon
                     Press, 1933).

Williams   Basil Williams, *The Whig Supremacy 1714–1760*, 2d ed.,
                     rev. C. H. Stuart (Oxford: Clarendon Press, 1962).

INTRODUCTION

On or about 15 February 1753, a little more than a month before his thirty-third birthday, Tobias Smollett published his newest novel, *The Adventures of Ferdinand Count Fathom*, in two duodecimo volumes.[1] This work followed *The Adventures of Peregrine Pickle* by almost exactly two years, and it came half a decade after its author's only real literary triumph to date, *The Adventures of Roderick Random*.[2] Neither Smollett's second novel nor his third caused much of a stir. *Ferdinand Count Fathom* in particular suffered neglect at the hands of readers and reviewers; and Smollett, after two comparative failures in a row, wrote no more fiction for seven years.[3]

Now it is true that *Ferdinand Count Fathom* has always been considered one of its author's lesser achievements. Ralph Griffiths, in the only contemporary review of the work, judged it a mixed and finally unsatisfying piece of business; George Saintsbury, writing years afterward in 1895, called it clumsy and characterized it as Smollett's "least good novel."[4] It is a matter for some debate whether *Ferdinand Count Fathom* is indeed inferior to any of Smollett's novels except his first and his last, *Roderick Random* and *Humphry Clinker*. Putting that question aside, the issue of the work's merit probably had little to do with its initial reception. Lewis M. Knapp has ventured one plausible explanation for its failure. Smollett's criminal "hero," says Knapp, was perhaps "too complete a monster" to appeal to the tastes of his readers, who were also very likely disappointed that the story "lacked the comic humor of *Roderick Random* and *Peregrine Pickle*."[5]

But the popular fiction of the mid-century years was full of rogues and villains, sentiment and melodrama. Knapp's explanation, therefore, will not quite do, though the undeniably experimental qualities of *Ferdinand Count Fathom* may have puzzled those readers who had formed their ideas of proper novelistic composition upon the foundation of recent works like Samuel Richardson's *Pamela* and *Clarissa*, Henry Fielding's *Joseph Andrews*, *Tom Jones*, and *Amelia*, and Smollett's own two earlier narratives. We should remember, however, that this same public was quick to applaud that most eccentrically experimental of eighteenth-century novels, Laurence Sterne's *Tristram Shandy*, whose several volumes began to appear within a few years' time. If we are to account for the virtual silence and the almost complete indifference that greeted *Ferdinand Count Fathom* from the day of its publication, we shall have to focus attention upon Smollett's activities and his less-than-happy position in literary and professional circles during the period from about 1749 to 1753.

BIOGRAPHICAL BACKGROUND

After the great success of *Roderick Random*—general critical approval and three editions numbering some 6,500 copies within twenty-two months of its original publication date—Smollett very likely felt that he had truly arrived upon the London literary scene. A medical man by profession, he had opened a surgical practice in Downing Street sometime during the year 1744. He had never managed to thrive in his chosen profession, possibly in large part because his real ambitions lay in the world of letters. His two verse satires, *Advice* (September 1746) and *Reproof* (January 1747), brought him little recognition; his lyrical *Tears of Scotland* (composed in 1746), though set to music by James Oswald and thereafter widely sung and admired, did almost nothing to increase his reputation as a writer. *Roderick Random*, however, made Smollett something of a celebrity, and shortly after its appearance his fine translation of Le Sage's *Histoire de Gil Blas de Santillane* (dated 1749, but published in October 1748) gave the public additional reason to applaud him.[6] At about this same time Smollett began a translation of *Don Quixote*, surely in the sanguine hope that it would further enhance his new stature. But his Spanish was not good and he was unable to complete this ambitious project until 1755. In the early weeks of 1749 he undertook proposals to publish by subscription his unactable tragedy, *The Regicide*, cause of so much grief during his earliest days in London and the reason for his bitter aspersions against the theatrical and patronage establishments in the Melopoyn episode (chapters 61–63) of his first novel.[7]

His play at last in print (it came out in May 1749), handsomely done up on royal paper and generously praised in a lengthy review by John Cleland,[8] Smollett turned his hand to a comedy, *The Absent Man*, and to an opera-masque-tragicomedy called *Alceste*, which he wrote in collaboration with Handel. Both David Garrick and George Lyttelton, Fielding's patron, had encouraged Smollett with his comedy, while John Rich had given his promise that *Alceste* would be staged at Covent Garden during the season of 1749–50. Neither of these works ever went into production; and Smollett, surely disillusioned and probably angry, appears to have simply abandoned them.[9] With these misfortunes, the mercurial pattern of his entire literary career was firmly established. From the heights of his acceptance as the talented young author of *Roderick Random*, Smollett had now fallen once again into the depths of rejection and frustration. He did not quickly forget about his new failures to earn recognition as a playwright. Garrick and Lyttelton are among the numerous people savaged in the pages of *Peregrine Pickle*, the first volume of which was very likely written quite early in 1750, before Smollett's visit to Paris during the summer of that year and while the memory of his two aborted theatrical projects was still painfully fresh.[10]

Just prior to this trip Smollett had moved to commodious quarters at Monmouth House in Old Chelsea, probably because he liked the healthful suburban air—he had been living for two years in Beaufort Street, near Somerset House—and because he thought the new environment might make it easier for him to pursue both his medical career and his ambitions as a writer. He enjoyed the conviviality of Chelsea, which was at the time a center of scientific and intellectual activity (Samuel Richardson's distinguished friend and physician, Dr. George Cheyne, lived there). Almost simultaneously with his move in June, he purchased a medical degree from Aberdeen University and became "Dr." Smollett. The practice he followed in acquiring his degree was common enough in his day, though it usually proscribed complete admission to the London medical establishment, which was in any case very exclusive. Smollett was friendly with a number of important figures in contemporary medical circles, among them Dr. William Smellie, whose pioneering three-volume work on obstetrics and midwifery he edited for publication.[11] But he seems never to have felt accepted as a doctor, and he certainly held strong opinions concerning the incompetence and quackery of so many of his fellow practitioners. He had already made physicians, surgeons, and apothecaries the subject of satiric attacks in *Roderick Random*; and in both *Peregrine Pickle* and *Ferdinand Count Fathom* he would renew these attacks, surely at the cost of his estrangement from many colleagues in the profession.

Peregrine Pickle, to be sure, had many other targets as well: lawyers, politicians, military men, and, of course, numerous people of theatrical and literary prominence. Garrick and Lyttelton have already been mentioned, and they were joined as objects of Smollett's virulence by the actor James Quin, the capricious patron Chesterfield, the poet and physician Mark Akenside, and the novelist and magistrate Henry Fielding. The personal satire against these and other leaders of the London cultural elite was heartfelt, in almost every instance a response to some injury Smollett fancied he had received. We know very little of how his victims responded, but doubtless they were alienated by such rough treatment. Smollett believed that a cabal of enemies forestalled his chances of popular success with *Peregrine Pickle* by preventing reviews and blocking opportunities for reprinting. In the "Advertisement" to the second edition of the novel (1758), he stated these suspicions openly, alluding to the "art and industry" turned upon his brainchild at its birth by "certain booksellers and others, who were at uncommon pains to misrepresent the work and calumniate the author."[12] Knapp discovered a number of years ago that Smollett had indeed angered London booksellers, among them Fielding's publisher Andrew Millar, by daring to preserve to himself the exclusive copyright of *Peregrine Pickle* at the time of its original publication.[13] In other words, there were many people who had reason to wish that this novel might be ignored, and Smollett may have been right to think that at least some of them had gathered together in an effective conspiracy against it.[14]

During the months following the appearance of *Peregrine Pickle*, Smollett entangled himself in several angry controversies. His next novel, *Ferdinand Count Fathom*, very possibly would have been the object of another conspiracy, if conspiracy there was, even had Smollett done nothing in it to revive old antagonisms. But in this new work he chose not to suppress his satiric instincts, and his implacability no doubt contributed to the book's failure. He muted the personal satire against leaders of the literary world, with the exception of Lyttelton, whom he vilified in more than one strongly worded passage.[15] Instead, he turned his heaviest artillery yet upon the professions of medicine and the law, in the process—we may be sure—adding wholesale to the numbers of those enlisted in the camp of his enemies. A letter by Smollett himself gives evidence of the hostility of one eminent attorney, Alexander Hume Campbell, who took particular umbrage at certain of *Ferdinand Count Fathom*'s aspersions against his colleagues at the bar.[16] The case prompting the sneers Campbell found so insulting certainly could have done Smollett's public reputation little good, and it must have hardened him in his already harsh estimate of the fraternity of lawyers. Smollett had lent money to Peter Gordon, a worthless hack and hanger-on who then refused to pay him back. In a fit of rage over this abuse of his generosity, Smollett ambushed Gordon and his landlord Edward Groom in Westminster on 2 November 1752, and then thrashed them both. They sued him for a total of £1,500, a sum he could ill afford to lose. He was eventually acquitted of all criminal charges, though he was required to pay damages and costs in excess of £20. The whole matter was not resolved until Smollett had waited through nearly three months of infuriating delays and legal maneuverings. If he offended the legal establishment in *Ferdinand Count Fathom*, he had reason to feel that the offense was just.[17]

Smollett's still more vigorous campaign against the medical profession in the novel was likewise preceded by some straining of his real-life relations with it. To the broad slurs conveyed in the pages of *Peregrine Pickle* (especially chapters 46–70) he added a quite specific attack, in the form of a pamphlet entitled *An Essay on the External Use of Water*, against the orthodoxies supporting the practice of medicine at Bath and other spas. In these fashionable places many important doctors promoted the use of mineral waters as a miraculous cure-all for a host of diseases. Smollett's *Essay*, published early in March 1752,[18] seriously questioned such treatment, suggesting instead the benefits of cold and hot baths in plain, nonmineral water. In the course of his argument Smollett revealed his violent disgust at the filth of the Bath waters, which (he thought) posed great hazards for those who bathed in them—not to mention those who drank them. It was a subject he would return to in *Ferdinand Count Fathom*,[19] and again with even greater stridency and more graphic detail in *Humphry Clinker*, where an outraged Matthew Bramble lingers over his revulsion at the sickening putridness of the waters into which visitors at Bath immersed their diseased and often cankered bodies.[20] The *Essay* also undertook a bold defense of Archibald Cleland, surgeon to the General Hospital at Bath, who had been dismissed in 1743 on false charges of moral turpitude, apparently because he had dared to propose changes in methods of patient care. The controversy over Cleland had raged for some years, and in renewing it Smollett impugned not only the integrity of the Bath Corporation and the medical men who ran its hospital, but also the judgment and the fair-mindedness of some of the city's leading citizens—among them William Warburton, bishop of Gloucester, and Ralph Allen, owner of Prior Park, friend of Pope and Fielding, and the model for Squire Allworthy in *Tom Jones*.[21]

The tone of Smollett's *Essay*, especially those pages devoted to the argument in behalf of Cleland, is sharp enough to have wounded its intended victims. Many of these people were sufficiently prominent outside medical circles to have had some effect upon the fortunes of the author's next venture into the world of literature, which came with the appearance of *Ferdinand Count Fathom*. But the *Essay* was hardly so venomous or offensive as the inflammatory pamphlet Smollett seems to have published on 15 January 1752, *A FAITHFUL NARRATIVE of the base and inhuman Arts that were lately practised upon the Brain of Habbakkuk Hilding*. This malicious and unjustified attack on Henry Fielding and George Lyttelton has not been certainly attributed to Smollett, but there are good reasons to believe it is his. Fielding, whom Smollett had previously made a target in *Peregrine Pickle*, had mildly depreciated that novel and *Roderick Random* in the pages of his *Covent-Garden Journal* for 7 January 1752. *Habbakkuk Hilding*, in its turn, portrayed Fielding as a sycophant of Lyttelton (thus repeating a charge made in *Peregrine Pickle*), as a hypocritical fool who took his cook-maid for a second wife, as a man deservedly ill in consequence of his former life of abandonment, and—more to the point here than anything else—as a plagiarist who had stolen his ideas for Partridge (in *Tom Jones*) and Miss Mathews (in *Amelia*) from Smollett's own characters of Strap and Nancy Williams in *Roderick Random*. A minor but quite nasty paper war flurried briefly over the conflicts between Smollett and Fielding,[22] and it could hardly have gone unnoticed among members of the literary establishment, which was in any case generally more partial to the distinguished novelist, journalist, and magistrate than to the blustering maverick Scotsman. *Habbakuk Hilding* must surely have hindered Smollett in his desires for acceptance in the world of contemporary letters, whether he wrote the pamphlet or not.

It seems safe to say that when Smollett finally was ready to send the manuscript of *Ferdinand Count Fathom* to the press in late December 1752 or early January 1753, he could have had little expectation of its critical or popular success. Many of those he had already offended were certain to be offended again; there were few influential friends, either literary or professional, to promote the work; the booksellers could have felt little enthusiasm for another novel by the author of *Peregrine Pickle*. Judging from the very candid dedication to himself prefixed to his new story, Smollett recognized that his irascibility had of late cost him much in the way of happiness, tranquility, and prospects. And although the dedication says nothing directly about the likely reception of the narrative it introduces, its general defensiveness suggests an awareness that the nature of the work—as satirical as it was experimental for its time—might provoke something less than an eager response from readers. "We live in a censorious age," Smollett observes, "and an author cannot take too much precaution to anticipate the prejudice, misapprehension and temerity of malice, ignorance and presumption." He closes in tones combining somberness and whimsy, assuring himself of the continued favor of the person he addresses, "whatever" (he says) "may be my fate with the public."

COMPOSITION, PRINTING, AND RECEPTION

Little is known about the composition of *Ferdinand Count Fathom*, except that Smollett must have begun it sometime after March 1752, by which date his active involvement in the imbroglios described above was over and his time free for so extended a project.[23] His surviving letters tell nothing of his work on the book; the manuscript disappeared long ago, and there are no printer's records to provide clues as to how or when he wrote it. The echoes of his anxiety over the protracted lawsuit in the Gordon affair probably mean that he was at some stage of revision during the period from early November 1752 to January 1753.

Ferdinand Count Fathom, at approximately 155,000 words, is only two-thirds as long as *Roderick Random* and not even half the length of the massive *Peregrine Pickle*. It is a substantial novel nonetheless, and Smollett must have written with some haste, perhaps now and again even improvising incidents or descriptions as he went along. He could hardly have managed to devote to it much more time than the "Compass of Eight months" within which, as he explained in a letter to his friend Alexander Carlyle, he completed *Roderick Random*.[24] Like Smollett's first novel, *Ferdinand Count Fathom* contains some infelicities of style, and there are several instances of carelessness in the handling of plot details.[25] But, also like *Roderick Random*, the work as it was printed after such hurried composition is a remarkably finished product. It is furthermore a deliberately experimental narrative, not quite like anything its author (or anybody else) had written before, and the crafting of it in so brief a period represents no small achievement.

Facts about the printing of Smollett's third novel are nearly as scarce as those concerning its composition. Probably the work was done in the shop of William Strahan, who had printed *Roderick Random* and (perhaps) *Peregrine Pickle*. The bookseller, according to the title page, was William Johnston, "at the Golden Ball in St. Paul's Churchyard," from whom Strahan purchased a one-third share in *Ferdinand Count Fathom* on 8 November 1752.[26] A piracy printed for one "T. Johnson," who used the same London address as the prominent and respected Johnston, followed quickly upon the original printing of the work. Meanwhile a Dublin edition was issued under an arrangement between Johnston and the bookseller Robert Main, who had also been responsible for the first Dublin edition of *Peregrine Pickle* in 1751.[27] No records remain to indicate the number of copies of *Ferdinand Count Fathom* printed for Johnston, "Johnson," or Main. It is thus impossible to determine how widely the work circulated, although something may be conjectured from the usual practice of London booksellers at the time, which was to publish novels by more or less established authors in editions of 1,000 to 1,250 copies. If Smollett's novel came out in editions of this quantity, and if all or even most copies were sold, then several thousand people must have read it in England. By any measure, however, the numbers were dismayingly small in comparison with the throngs who by 1753 had enjoyed *Roderick Random*, not to mention Fielding's hugely popular *Tom Jones*, which ran to four editions totaling ten thousand copies within a year of its initial publication date in February 1749.

Smollett, so far as is known, altogether avoided comment on his novel's commercial failure, and he was equally silent about the critics' nearly total disregard for it. The one published notice in which his work was discussed, that by Ralph Griffiths in the *Monthly Review* for March 1753, could hardly have pleased him with its reservations concerning the propriety of the character of Fathom and with its very cautious praise of other effects. After the Griffiths review, *Ferdinand Count Fathom* was not again mentioned anywhere in print until 1760, when George Colman named it, along with *Roderick Random* and *Peregrine Pickle*, in a long list of popular circulating-library titles included in the preface to his "dramatick novel," *Polly Honeycombe*.[28] Only Mrs. Mary Delany among the voluminous novel-reading correspondents of the mid-century years seems to have taken up *Ferdinand Count Fathom*, and she did not like it. It is "a very indifferent affair," she wrote to her friend Mrs. Dewes in 1753; and though "there are some things very interesting, and the whole well-intended," the story and its characters are "none of them" to be "named in a day with our good friend Richardson."[29]

Oddly, and sadly for its author's sake, Smollett's novel fared better after his death. Its scenes of terror and gloom in forest and graveyard (chapters 20–21, 62–63) were frequently mentioned in reviews of Gothic romances as providing a standard of excellence.[30] In 1771 Johnston, who also published *Humphry Clinker* that very year, at last brought out a second edition of *Ferdinand Count Fathom*. The work was included in *The Entertaining Museum; or Complete Circulating Library* in 1780, and two years later Harrison added it to his popular *Novelist's Magazine*, with illustrations by Thomas Stothard. Altogether there were some eleven separate reprintings of Smollett's third novel between 1771 and the end of the eighteenth century, counting probable piracies but not counting its appearance in the editions of Smollett's collected works published by Robert Anderson (1796) and Dr. John Moore (1797). Meanwhile it was translated into German (twice, in 1770–71 and 1799), Italian (1791), French (1798, in an abridged version entitled *Fathom et Melvil*), and Dutch (1798). *Ferdinand Count Fathom* deserved at least this measure of popularity from the moment of its original publication, and one can only regret on Smollett's behalf that circumstances partly of his own making seem to have persuaded those readers who mattered most to ignore it.[31]

SMOLLETT'S CONTEMPORARY MATERIALS

Notwithstanding its qualities as an experimental novel, a subject we shall come to presently, *Ferdinand Count Fathom* was very much in the mainstream of popular fiction during the mid-century years. The work should have had little difficulty in pleasing its audience. It tells an interesting, fast-moving story that borrows freely from the familiar traditions of rogue and criminal narrative, balanced by an almost equal emphasis upon echoes of the conventional fable of virtue tested and triumphant. Smollett's novel scatters allusions to the drama over its pages, and it bears strong resemblances to many of the travel books so widely enjoyed in its day; it introduces an elaborate pattern of references to recent and contemporary history and to real people whose characters or exploits were known to almost everyone; it makes political and especially social commentary an essential part of its method and effects, so that the often closely detailed character portraits and intensive representations of the variety of human nature are projected as serving some genuine moral purpose.

Described in this way, *Ferdinand Count Fathom* appears to be a work carefully contrived by its author to suit the tastes of contemporary readers, while still allowing free play to his own fertile imagination. Smollett was indeed alert to what was going on around him in the world of popular fiction. He was as ready as his fellow storytellers Richardson and Fielding to give the public what it wanted, and as eager as they to elevate prose fiction to respectability through participation in the development of what Richardson called "a new species of writing."[32] By 1753, Richardson, Fielding, and Smollett himself had all made valuable—if very different—contributions toward the establishment of that "new species." Ingeniously conventional in their uses of materials from many kinds of narrative, these writers also vigorously promoted originality and seriousness of moral and aesthetic purpose. We can hardly think of Richardson, Fielding, and Smollett, rivals all, as brothers in a convivial guild of crusading novelists. But it is important to remember that each thought of himself as an experimental writer, a conscious innovator in the art of fiction.[33]

The dedication to *Ferdinand Count Fathom* contains Smollett's only fully articulated statement of a theory of novelistic composition. This statement— a single paragraph in length—is brief enough to make one wish for more, yet it furnishes an exact definition of the kind of narrative he always attempted to write. "A Novel," Smollett proclaims, is "a large diffused picture" of life. These carefully chosen, emphatic words focus attention directly upon the

spaciousness of their author's canvases and upon the variegated structures of
his stories. A Smollett novel typically progresses from episode to episode in
an apparently disjointed fashion, accumulating its intensely pictorial and dramatic representations of people and circumstances, until finally the reader's
eye is drawn irresistibly to a moral center and resolution is possible. As a
painter of verbal pictures, Smollett had learned much from his contemporary
Hogarth; as a novelist who had originally aspired to celebrity in the world of
the stage, he had learned just as much from Shakespeare and the other theatrical geniuses whose works he had studied so well—Sophocles, Ben Jonson, William Congreve, Thomas Otway, Richard Steele. It was no accident
that in filling out his statement on the art of fiction Smollett went on to
develop twin analogies to painting and to the drama.[34] Nor was it any accident that later in the dedication, when defending his potentially disunifying
focus upon the character of the virtuous Renaldo in a story so conspicuously
preoccupied with the roguish adventures of Fathom, Smollett wrote of his
desire to form a "striking" and dramatic "contrast" that would "heighten the
expression" of his work and "give a *Relief* to the moral of the whole."[35]

Smollett's novels, even his masterpiece *Humphry Clinker*, have always suffered by comparison of their erratic and uneven textures with the smooth
regularities of Fielding's performances. There is no denying that his stories,
like those of Defoe, lack the organic consistency so prized by Fielding's fellow
Augustans. But Smollett was in fact little interested in the orthodoxy of
organic structure. The dedication to *Ferdinand Count Fathom* declares his preference for other kinds of structures and makes clear his claim to independence as an innovator in prose fiction. The narrative that occasioned the
dedication is proof of the claim. *Ferdinand Count Fathom* offers more, of
course, than just an object lesson in Smollett's theory and practice of the
novelist's craft. Some of the work's most original attractions arise out of its
adaptations from established narrative conventions. Paul-Gabriel Boucé has
suggested that *Don Quixote* exerted probably the most important formative
influence upon Smollett's literary understanding and his sensibilities,[36] and
indeed Smollett himself pays high tribute to the "inimitable" Cervantes in the
preface to *Roderick Random*. No doubt the episodic form of *Don Quixote* had its
impact on the imagination of the younger writer, who also admired—and
nearly as much—the great examples and adaptations of another invention of
Spanish literary culture, the picaresque romance. In his early novels at least,
Smollett reveals a profound interest in the character of the rogue or criminal
and in the quality and meaning of his experience in a changing world.
Roderick Random and *Peregrine Pickle* represent Smollett's moralized versions of

the picaresque, and the careers of his heroes in these works are as mercurial and almost as brutal as those of the most wayward Spanish adventurers. *Roderick Random* takes as its immediate model for adaptation Le Sage's brilliantly conceived French re-creation of the picaresque, *Gil Blas*, a work Smollett respected hugely and that he was shortly to celebrate in his own new and very loving translation.[37]

Both *Don Quixote* and *Gil Blas* were enormously popular among English readers of the first half of the eighteenth century, and they were widely imitated. Smollett's admiration for these two great works was genuine, but it was also decidedly convenient for his purposes as the hopeful author of *Roderick Random* and *Peregrine Pickle*. *Ferdinand Count Fathom*, in its story of a relentlessly mischievous and aberrant character, emphatically renews the expression of Smollett's affinities with the picaresque tradition, which this new work specifically calls to mind by its pointed references to several of the most important examples of the type, including *Gil Blas*.[38] But *Ferdinand Count Fathom* goes beyond the boundaries of mere roguish adventure and develops a full and detailed portrait of a criminal in action. Smollett was not the first writer to do such a thing, of course; the criminal narrative is very old, and the early eighteenth century abounds in popular versions of it, many of them gritty and sensational accounts of real thieves and murderers who had prowled the streets and highways of London and its environs.[39] Daniel Defoe's *Moll Flanders* is a splendid adaptation from this species of low-life biography, as is Fielding's satiric and parodic *Life of Mr. Jonathan Wild the Great*. The Lovelace portions of Richardson's *Clarissa* provide yet another instance of criminal portraiture, perhaps the best and most powerful example of its kind the period has to offer.

Ferdinand Count Fathom has often been compared with *Moll Flanders* and especially with *Jonathan Wild* and found wanting. The comparison is actually quite inappropriate, for neither Defoe nor Fielding attempted to write precisely the kind of thoroughgoing study of the criminal life undertaken in Smollett's work. Moll is a retrospective moralist, while Wild is conspicuously the object of his narrator's self-conscious irony. Fathom is something else again, a serious and unblinking representation of remorseless (at least until the end) villainy. Smollett was the first English novelist of major talent to venture such a portrait, if we except Richardson and his partial focus upon a vile, demonic libertine; and Smollett was likewise the first to devote a whole novel to the subject. It was a timely enterprise, given the popularity of rogue narrative generally and the intense, fearful, and growing preoccupation of the contemporary public with the inescapable realities of crime in daily life. It was, besides, something of a bold and perhaps risky experiment, as Smollett seems to have known when he devoted much of the last section of his dedication to an explanation and defense of what he had done.

The several paragraphs of this defense further underscore their author's interest in the drama, which he had already identified as a source of his inspiration when stating the theory supporting the composition of his novel. The drama, says Smollett, often portrays objects of our "detestation and abhorrence" as a means toward development of a moral purpose. Nobody is troubled by the presence of such figures on the stage, he observes, and so why should similar representations be judged offensive in a work of fiction? A story showing the "disgrace and discomfiture of vice" may create a "deep impression of terror," promoting those "impulses of fear" which leave the most lasting of all effects upon an audience, whether in the theater or in the closet; and therefore tales of villainy may do more than any other kind to serve the cause of "morality and virtue."[40] With these words Smollett places the genre of prose fiction on a footing with the drama, affirming an equality between the two, and he simultaneously hints obliquely at the episodes of Gothic melodrama that are to follow in his novel. The last of these episodes, containing the graveyard scenes at the tomb of the supposedly dead Monimia, actually borrows directly from a popular play by Congreve, *The Mourning Bride* (1697).[41]

Smollett's general indebtedness to the theater has been so well documented that little need be said of it here.[42] But two or three particular points about *Ferdinand Count Fathom* may be worth pausing over. The character of Monimia, Renaldo's beloved and the sentimental heroine of the tale, is shamelessly adapted from the identically named heroine of Otway's *The Orphan* (1680), a verse tragedy frequently performed in London theaters throughout the first half of the eighteenth century. At times, Fathom resembles one of the usurping villains in a historical play by Shakespeare; at other times (in chapter 45, for example) his relations with Renaldo parallel the scheming Iago's manipulations of Othello. Characters like Sir Giles Squirrel and Sir Stentor Stile draw unmistakably upon the conventions of the dandy and the bumpkin in Restoration comedy. Smollett's language is often blatantly theatrical, especially in his comic scenes, and individual episodes usually develop as little pictorial dramas. Allusions to Shakespeare and other playwrights abound.

The echoes of the drama in *Ferdinand Count Fathom* are both plentiful and deliberate—as they are, of course, in so many other stories of the day, including Smollett's own earlier works and the novels of Fielding and Richardson besides. Smollett's dramatic contrivances, it must be added, are on the whole handled with adroit originality; they are varied, they are interesting, and they contribute importantly to the overall effects of the novel. No reasonably alert person among the few who bothered to read *Ferdinand Count Fathom* when it first came out could have failed to recognize such contrivances for what they were, and the most sophisticated readers must surely have appreciated the success with which they are usually employed.

Smollett's framework for carrying out his design of dramatic and pictorial episodes in *Ferdinand Count Fathom* displays his interest in yet another popular form, the narrative of travel. There is, of course, a natural connection between the literature of roguery and the literature of travel. Smollett was equally interested in both kinds of writing, as all of his early novels make clear. In *Ferdinand Count Fathom* the hero-villain enters the world in motion, so to speak, for he is born in a wagon as it passes over the border between Holland and Flanders. Following some early military adventures, he moves on to Vienna, Paris, London, Bath, Bristol Springs, Tunbridge Wells, and many other places, visiting some of them on more than one occasion. His almost incessant movement reflects a restless energy; there is no particular logic to the routes he takes, except that he conceives very early a desire to get to England, land of his ancestors and a bountiful country that he judges ripe for plunder.

The idea of travel figures in all of Smollett's novels, early and late alike, and indeed it seems to have transfixed his imagination. In this he differed little from perhaps the majority of contemporary storytellers, including Defoe and Fielding.[43] As Smollett saw it, the journey—with its usually erratic pattern of odd turnings and surprising encounters—furnished a metaphor for life itself and for growth into self-knowledge or moral maturity. His own journey down from Scotland to London in 1739, and shortly thereafter his voyage aboard the *Chichester* during the Carthagena expedition of 1741, surely helped to establish his lifelong fascination with the notion of travel itself and with the prodigious quantity of literature it generated.[44] Smollett became an avid reader of travel books, or so it appears. Beginning in May 1753 (or some three months after the publication of *Ferdinand Count Fathom*) he served as editor of a massive *Compendium of Authentic and Entertaining Voyages*, which ran to seven volumes when it finally appeared in April 1756.[45] His *Travels through France and Italy*, published almost exactly a decade later, must be counted one of the half-dozen finest among the many hundreds of travel books produced in his century.

In *Roderick Random* and *Peregrine Pickle*, and with even greater insistence—and success—in *Humphry Clinker*, Smollett made the devices of the travel narrative central to a conception involving the gradual definition of the relations between character and environment. These novels, especially *Humphry Clinker*, frequently represent places with almost the same intensity of feeling they devote to character portraiture. Matt Bramble's descriptions of Bath, already mentioned, join his similarly precise and idiosyncratic reflections of London as perhaps the most memorable performances of their kind in all of his author's fiction, but they typify Smollett's usual approach to the imaginative re-creation of the settings in which his always mobile personages find themselves. *Ferdinand Count Fathom*, however, contains little in the way of such reflective writing, except in the melodramatic forest and graveyard scenes, where Smollett obviously had some different purposes in mind. George M. Kahrl has observed that, for all the constant movement of Fathom himself, the idea of travel exerted "only a secondary and desultory influence" upon Smollett's conception of his novel as a whole. Fathom drifts all over the European continent and rambles widely through England; and yet, "though localities are often specified, there is, with a few exceptions, a total absence of distinguishing features of geography or society." In "none of his novels," Kahrl concludes, "did Smollett have such varied opportunities for contrasting one nationality with another, and in none did he have less to say on the subject."[46]

If we assume that Smollett knew what he was doing when he wrote *Ferdinand Count Fathom*, then he must have had reasons for leaving things so completely generalized as Kahrl rightly judges them to be. One reason seems clear enough: in developing his focus upon the conduct of Fathom, Smollett located the absolute center of the world's threats to order and virtue in the character of the hero-villain himself, and not (as was the case in his other novels) primarily in the external environment. Fathom's own character, of course, is in many important respects a reflection of the reality around him, which is by and large as wicked as he is. But it is the perspective Smollett created that is crucial. To his wily practitioner of the arts of deception and plunder, human society is everywhere very much the same. The German may be a boor, the Frenchman a fop, the Dutchman a greedy glutton, the Spaniard a jealous man of passion, the Englishman a snob. But no nationality has a monopoly on any particular human vice or folly. The English people, inhabitants of Fathom's ancestral land, may differ from the French or the Hungarians in such national traits as excessive xenophobia, but in Fathom's mind the only important distinguishing characteristic is what he conceives to be their special vulnerability to his superior and quite evil genius.

Smollett's energetic rogue, like Peregrine Pickle before him, is an initiator of action and almost never a passive agent in the procession of his own experience. It is plain, however, that Fathom utterly lacks the redeeming quality of fundamental good nature that makes Perry, and the Juvenalian autobiographer Roderick Random as well, a moralistic judge of the follies and the vices of his fellow creatures. Fathom ridicules and exposes, but he is driven by his ambitions and his appetites rather than by indignation. In other words, he is an instrument of satire, but he is neither its voice nor the consciousness that determines its meaning. His role is in some measure dictated and defined by the completeness of his villainy, perhaps in larger measure by the manner of the narration itself. From the first-person immediacy of *Roderick Random* and the limited omniscience of the narrator in *Peregrine Pickle*, Smollett turned to a more generalized omniscience in his third novel, allowing for much greater distancing in the representation of his materials than he had ever before attempted. He is just as panoramic in this work as in his earlier stories, though the effect of the techniques of distancing is to flatten out his canvas in a certain way. Distinctions among places, customs, and manners simply matter less in *Ferdinand Count Fathom* than they do in *Roderick Random* or *Peregrine Pickle*. Distinctions among characters, however, matter very much indeed, and the same types, vividly pictured, appear again and again wherever Fathom goes. The sharper, the *miles gloriosus*, the shrew, the lustful matron, the libertine, the quack, the charlatan, and the hypocritical lawyer may be encountered in almost any place; and people exemplifying the qualities of honest humility, fidelity, benevolence, chastity, and righteous integrity are very scarce, though they do survive in Fathom's world.

Much the same might be said of the varied casts of characters in *Roderick Random* and *Peregrine Pickle*, or for that matter in Fielding's *Joseph Andrews* and *Tom Jones*, except that in these novels attention is fixed from the beginning upon the protagonists as real or potential victims of particular circumstances that threaten to wreck their chances of attaining any kind of personal equilibrium or happiness. *Ferdinand Count Fathom* defines no discernible progress toward equilibrium. There is only the sudden reformation that comes at the end; and it is preceded by portrait upon portrait of common or universal character types, each portrait occasioned by the presence of Fathom—himself a type—and filled out by the details of his usually predatory advances against the figure or figures represented. Time seems as irrelevant as place in this novel. Fathom is born and he grows up, but beyond this simple fact there is no real sense of the passing of days or weeks or years. It is as though Smollett conceived his work as a large, still picture intended to be seen all at once, the individual characters in the foreground enlivened by the striking suggestions of their unmistakably human attributes, but seen against a background partially blurred as to historical moment and setting.

All of this is true even though *Ferdinand Count Fathom* shares with most other novels of its time a habit of regular and specific allusion to topical subject matter. If Smollett was interested in the display of universal character types in his narrative, he wished to provide for them a recognizable context. References to real people and events therefore almost inevitably figure in his account of Fathom's adventures, from the War of the Spanish Succession in the early years of the century, to the bloody conflagration that erupted in the 1740s over the vexing question of the Austrian Succession, to the controversy that was swirling around the coming legislation to naturalize the Jews at the very time Smollett was readying his novel for the press. These references are all accounted for at length in the explanatory notes accompanying the text, and there is no reason to labor over them here.[47] It will be helpful to note in a general way, however, that such references occur in a pattern and by a method rather unlike what we ordinarily find in Smollett's other novels, and very different from what may usually be observed in the works of his contemporaries.

Fathom's life begins in 1711, while the War of the Spanish Succession is drawing slowly to a close; as a child and then as a youth he is seen in the midst of two other European conflicts, the Austrian campaign against the Turks (1716–18) and the War of the Polish Succession (1733–35). In chapters 1 through 28, it appears that Smollett intends the reader to interpret Fathom's experience at least in part as it is illuminated by the genius and the bravery of great generals like the duke of Marlborough and Prince Eugene of Savoy. But chapter 29 introduces something new into the novel's fabric of topical allusions when Fathom, barely out of his adolescence, is mistaken for Prince Charles Edward Stuart almost immediately upon his arrival in England. The fictional time of this incident must be set at a period no later than 1735 or 1736, some ten years earlier than the spectacular but failed Jacobite Rebellion led by the glamorous Young Pretender, whose mysterious escape from would-be captors actually sparked the kinds of suspicions now leveled at Fathom. Such an anachronism surprises to say the least, and one at first suspects inattentiveness or hasty improvisation on the author's part. There may be a degree of both, but the evidence of the remainder of the novel suggests that Smollett was deliberately experimenting with some unconventional relations between fiction and the historical reality it reflects. A novel, this evidence seems unmistakably to say, represents an exertion of the artist's creative powers upon the observed actualities of life, but it is not obliged to follow any exact rules of literalness.

In chapters 39–42, when Fathom (now in his mid-twenties, at most) finds himself in prison for the first time, Smollett brings together a sizable cluster of references to persons and issues whose claim on the attention of the public dates from the late 1740s and early 1750s. Among the characters met in this extended episode are Theodore de Neuhoff, deposed king of Corsica, who had been thrown into debtors' prison at the King's Bench in 1749, and Sir Mungo Barebones, a parodic portrait of the bogus theologian John Hutchinson, whose attacks on Newtonian physics had lately raised a storm of controversy in the popular press. Near the beginning of Fathom's time in prison, one of his fellow inmates offers the loan of his personal library, which is made up almost entirely of novels and tales of roguish adventuring published since 1750. Smollett's later pattern of allusions to the War of the Austrian Succession (beginning in chapter 57) has already been noted, as has his introduction (in chapter 47) of the benevolent moneylender Joshua Manasseh, whose presence brings to mind what was familiarly known in 1753 as the "Jew bill." There are numerous other anachronisms of several kinds in *Ferdinand Count Fathom*, and in every instance Smollett seems to have used historical circumstance to further his definition of Fathom's character. Such purposefulness could hardly have been accidental, the result of mere carelessness. Instead, Smollett's practice stamps his novel as an innovative, if not entirely successful, attempt to discover new ways in which the writer of prose fiction might incorporate facts of real life in creating an imaginative configuration that is actually the product of an act of historical interpretation.

Smollett certainly knew the difference between fiction writing, which gives license to the powers of invention, and the process of recording history, with its principles of fidelity to the march of events through time. "I look upon the Historian who espouses a Faction, who strains Incidents or willfully suppresses any Circumstances of Importance that may tend to the Information of the Reader, as the worst of Prostitutes." So wrote Smollett to his friend William Huggins on 2 July 1758, just six months after the final volume of his new *Complete History of England* had made its appearance in print.[48] But a novel is very different from a work of history. *Ferdinand Count Fathom* "strains Incidents" in its treatment of the past, not suppressing any "Circumstances of Importance" but instead borrowing those deemed relevant from several periods of recent memory, withdrawing them from their temporal limitations, and re-creating them within the context of a new fictional "factuality." For Smollett the artist, as opposed to Smollett the chronicler of public events, the historical moment itself was critical—in or out of its time— because of what it could reveal about the permanent truths of human nature and human experience.

Ferdinand Count Fathom is Smollett's most adventurous experiment with the novelistic uses of history, and indeed in no other work did he take so many liberties with the circumstantial facts of real life. But he always valued history for what it could contribute to the creation of significance in an invented narrative. Not surprisingly, then, he employed an anachronistic method in all of his novels, which strive for wholeness and simultaneity of effect through the accumulation of assorted imaginary and historical episodes, or "moments," reflecting the timeless variety of life. By introducing the literal and then subordinating it to the demands of the imagination, Smollett made history serve fiction. *Ferdinand Count Fathom* helps to clarify the principles and the means by which he achieved this careful balance, so necessary to the successful practice of the novelist's craft as he understood it.

Notes

1. The *Public Advertiser* announced publication of the work on 14 February 1753, the *London Daily Advertiser* a day later. Some five weeks before, on 8 January 1753, the *Public Advertiser* had alerted its readers to the novel's imminent appearance, and the notice was repeated on 9, 12, and 13 January. For full details of the printing and publishing history of *Ferdinand Count Fathom* see below, the textual commentary.

2. *Peregrine Pickle* was published on 25 February 1751, *Roderick Random* on 21 January 1748.

3. His next novel was *The Adventures of Sir Launcelot Greaves*, which ran serially from January 1760 until December 1761 in the *British Magazine, or Monthly Repository*, which Smollett himself edited. The novel was not a success, although it did appear in book form in March 1762. Another long hiatus followed before Smollett's last and best work, *The Expedition of Humphry Clinker*, came out in June 1771.

4. Griffiths, "*The adventures of* Ferdinand *count* Fathom. *By the author of* Roderick Random," *Monthly Review* 8 (March 1753): 203–14; Saintsbury, introduction to *The Adventures of Ferdinand Count Fathom, The Works of Tobias Smollett* (London: Gibbings, 1895), 8:xviii. Twentieth-century criticism has frequently echoed the sentiments of Griffiths and Saintsbury, though sometimes qualifying the echoes with praise. See Robert Giddings, *The Tradition of Smollett* (London: Methuen, 1967), 125–26, for a sharp judgment against Smollett's lack of a unified plan in *Ferdinand Count Fathom*. Other critics have raised the same objection, in some instances softening it by reference to Smollett's pursuit of thematic rather than structural unity. See M. A. Golberg, *Smollett and the Scottish School: Studies in Eighteenth-Century Thought* (Albuquerque: University of New Mexico Press, 1959), chap. 4; Alan Dugald McKillop, *The Early Masters of English Fiction* (Law-

rence: University of Kansas Press, 1956), 164–66; Ronald Paulson, *Satire and the Novel in Eighteenth-Century England* (New Haven: Yale University Press, 1967), especially 165–66; T. O. Treadwell, "The Two Worlds of *Ferdinand Count Fathom*," in *Tobias Smollett: Bicentennial Essays Presented to Lewis M. Knapp*, ed. George S. Rousseau and Paul-Gabriel Boucé (New York: Oxford University Press, 1971), 131–53; Boucé, *The Novels of Tobias Smollett* (London: Longman, 1976), chap. 3; David K. Jeffrey, "'Ductility and Dissimulation': The Unity of *Ferdinand Count Fathom*," *Tennessee Studies in Literature* 23 (1978): 47–60; and K. G. Simpson, "Tobias Smollett: The Scot as English Novelist," in *Smollett: Author of the First Distinction*, ed. Alan Bold (London: Vision, 1982), 64–105. Smollett's experiments with intensive language in the development of his plot and his character portraits in *Ferdinand Count Fathom* have received a large measure of praise, always mixed with reservations provoked by his perceived lack of consistency and his awkwardness when dealing with sentimental subjects. See Albrecht B. Strauss, "On Smollett's Language: A Paragraph in *Ferdinand Count Fathom*," in *Style in Prose Fiction: English Institute Essays 1958*, ed. Harold C. Martin (New York: Columbia University Press, 1959), 25–54; D. W. Jefferson, "Speculations on Three Eighteenth-Century Prose Writers," in *Of Books and Humankind: Essays and Poems Presented to Bonamy Dobrée*, ed. John Butt et al. (London: Routledge and Kegan Paul, 1964), 81–91; and Damian Grant, *Tobias Smollett: A Study in Style* (Manchester: Manchester University Press, 1977), 65–67, 195–99.

5. Knapp, 158.
6. The four parts of *Gil Blas* were published in the original French between 1715 and 1735, and were already available in more than one translation by 1748. Smollett's new English version came out anonymously, but it was widely known to be his. In 1750 he published another translation from Le Sage, *The Devil upon Crutches*. See Knapp, 104.
7. Smollett arrived in London in 1739 with *The Regicide* in hand, but was unable to persuade anyone to produce it. *Roderick Random* attacks patrons, managers, and actors—the fourth earl of Chesterfield, John Rich and James Lacy, David Garrick and James Quin—for their part in the rejection of the play. Before publishing *The Regicide*, Smollett added a preface in which he repeated some of these same attacks.
8. *Monthly Review* 1 (May 1749): 72–79. The imprint on the title page of *The Regicide* reads "*Printed by Subscription, for the Benefit of the* AUTHOR," but the volume contains no list of subscribers. Within a month the same sheets were issued with a revised imprint, "*Printed for* J. OSBORN, *in Pater-noster Row, and* A. MILLAR, *in the Strand*."
9. The manuscripts of both works have been lost, and so we have no clear idea of what they were like. Some of the lyrics from *Alceste* have survived; see Knapp, 91–92, and Otto Erich Deutsch, "Poetry Preserved in Music: Bibliographical Notes on Smollett and Oswald, Handel, and Haydn," *Modern Language Notes* 63

(1948): 73–88. A. D. McKillop has discovered an auction catalogue from 1752 listing *The Absent Man* as Smollett's; see "Smollett's First Comedy," *Modern Language Notes* 45 (1930): 396–97.

10. Howard Swazey Buck, *A Study in Smollett, Chiefly Peregrine Pickle* (New Haven: Yale University Press, 1925), 2.

11. Each volume bore a different title, and publication of the entire work took more than a dozen years. The individual titles and dates are: *A Treatise on the Theory and Practice of Midwifery*, 1751; *A Collection of Cases and Observations in Midwifery*, 1754; *A Collection of Preternatural Cases and Observations in Midwifery*, 1764.

12. The "Advertisement" was included at the beginning of volume 1 of the second edition. In this revised *Peregrine Pickle*, Smollett shortened his novel somewhat, polished some of its rougher passages, and softened or eliminated most of his personal attacks on contemporaries.

13. Knapp, 118–19. Millar had participated in publication of the reissue of Smollett's *The Regicide*; see above, n. 8.

14. The "Memoirs of a Lady of Quality" included in chapter 88 of *Peregrine Pickle* attracted a good deal of attention, but there were very few serious commentaries on the novel as a whole. John Cleland treated it favorably and at length in the *Monthly Review* 4 (March 1751): 355–64, and there were briefer notices in the *Royal Magazine, or Quarterly Bee* 2 (January–March 1751): 396–97, in the *Magazine of Magazines* 1 (April 1751): 287, and in the *Journal Britannique* 4 (April 1751): 429–30.

15. See the dedication, p. 3 and n. 3; and chap. 1, p. 10 and n. 21.

16. *Letters*, 21–26.

17. Alexander Hume Campbell was one of the attorneys for Gordon and Groom. According to Smollett's letter, directed to Campbell himself and dated 23 February 1753 (but probably never sent), Campbell had opened the trial in the King's Bench by quoting from chapter 37 of *Ferdinand Count Fathom* a passage particularly severe against lawyers. Did "any part" of the satirical passage in question "come home to your own conscience?" Smollett asks, or "did you resent it as a sarcasm levelled at the whole Bench without distinction? I take it for granted this must have been the origin of your enmity to me because I can recollect no other circumstance in my conduct, by which I could incur the displeasure of a man whom I scarce knew by sight, and with whom I never had the least dispute" (*Letters*, 25). It is unclear how Campbell could have seen a copy of *Ferdinand Count Fathom* before his address in court, since the case appears to have concluded on or about 12 February—that is, several days before the novel's publication. See below, chap. 37, p. 175 and n. 10. For a more detailed summary of what is known about the Gordon case and trial, see Knapp, 151–53, 156–57; see also H. P. Vincent, "Tobias Smollett's Assault on Gordon and Groom," *Review of English Studies* 16 (1940): 183–88, and Alice Parker, "Tobias Smollett and the Law," *Studies in Philology* 39 (1942): 545–58.

18. It was announced in the *General Advertiser* on 6 March.

19. See especially chap. 35.
20. Matthew Bramble to Dr. Lewis, Bath, April 28 and May 8.
21. Knapp, 146–49, gives a full account of the *Essay* and its contents, purposes, and reception. The work is available to modern readers in an edition prepared by Claude E. Jones (Baltimore: Johns Hopkins University Press, 1935).
22. See Knapp, 131–32.
23. Knapp, 154, fixes on March 1752 because a possible source for the character of Joshua Manasseh, Christian Gellert's *Das Leben der Schwedischen Gräfin von G****, was published in translation during that month. Smollett probably would have known of Gellert's work from the rather enthusiastic recommendation it received in the *Monthly Review* 6 (March 1752): 231–32.
24. *Letters*, 8. The letter is dated 7 June 1748.
25. See, for example, chap. 4, pp. 19–20 and n. 11; chap. 46, p. 217 and n. 3; chap. 48, p. 231 and n. 3; and chap. 67, p. 348 and n. 4.
26. See Lewis M. Knapp, "Smollett's Works as Printed by William Strahan," *Library*, 4th ser., 13 (1932): 282–91. See also Albert Smith, "The Printing and Publication of Smollett's *Peregrine Pickle*," *Library*, 5th ser., 26 (1971): 39–52; and see below, the textual commentary.
27. Strahan's printing ledgers, under the account for William Johnston, include the following undated notation entered sometime between late April 1753 and the end of the year: "For ⅓ of Fathom money from Main £5–5–0." This is slight evidence, but enough to make it probable that the Dublin edition of *Ferdinand Count Fathom*, unlike so many other English works as reprinted in that city at the time, was not a piracy but an authorized version. See below, the textual commentary; and see Robert Harlan, "William Strahan: Eighteenth Century London Printer and Publisher" (Ph.D. diss., University of Michigan, 1960), 68. The very name "T. Johnson," commonly seen on the title pages of pirated works from about 1715 through the 1750s, identifies the third of the 1753 editions of *Ferdinand Count Fathom* as unauthorized. Donald D. Eddy, through O M Brack, Jr., has passed along the suggestion that this Johnson may not even have existed, despite the familiarity of his name to eighteenth-century buyers of books. If there was such a person, he was much more ubiquitous upon the London bookselling scene than the usual publisher, pirate or otherwise.
28. Colman's allusion to *Ferdinand Count Fathom* is curious and difficult to explain. A second edition of the novel had been announced in the *London Chronicle* for 29–31 May 1760, but no copies have been traced. It is possible that unsold copies of the first edition had been bought by the proprietor of a London circulating library, of which there were several by the late 1750s.
29. Quoted in Fred W. Boege, *Smollett's Reputation As a Novelist* (Princeton: Princeton University Press, 1947), 15–16.
30. See, for example, the review of *Radzivil, a Romance*, in *Critical Review* 69 (January 1790): 118; and the review of *The Romance of the Cavern*, in *Critical Review*, 2d ser., 10 (March 1794): 349.

31. During the early decades of the nineteenth century, *Ferdinand Count Fathom* enjoyed a modestly favorable reputation. Sir Walter Scott, in his "Prefatory Memoir" to *The Novels of Tobias Smollett*, vol. 1 of *Ballantyne's Novelist's Library* (London: Hurst, Robinson, 1821), particularly praised the work for the effectiveness of its forest and graveyard episodes. Coleridge, Hazlitt, Keats, Byron, Lamb, and Scott's distinguished biographer Lockhart read all of Smollett's novels with genuine enthusiasm, as did Bulwer and Dickens. See Boege, *Smollett's Reputation*, 90–93. With the general decline of Smollett's fortunes during the reign of Queen Victoria, *Ferdinand Count Fathom* sank into near oblivion, though of course it was included in most editions of the collected works that came out over those many years. When the novel was mentioned at all by the critics it was typically in tones of dismissal, so that it is not surprising at the end of this long period to find the magisterial George Saintsbury poised in readiness to toss *Ferdinand Count Fathom* away as the most reckless and vulgar, and therefore the most forgettable, of its author's performances.

32. *Selected Letters of Samuel Richardson*, ed. John Carroll (Oxford: Clarendon Press, 1964), 41. Richardson used this phrase in a letter to his friend Aaron Hill (January 1741) describing his purposes in *Pamela*.

33. For extended discussion of the relationships between these three major novelists and the background of contemporary popular fiction, see Jerry C. Beasley, *Novels of the 1740s* (Athens: University of Georgia Press, 1982). See also two essays by William Park, "Fielding *and* Richardson," *PMLA* 81 (1966): 381–88, and "What Was New About the 'New Species of Writing'?" *Studies in the Novel* 2 (1970): 112–30.

34. Alan Dugald McKillop was the first important critic to notice the purposefulness of Smollett's analogies; see *The Early Masters*, 164–65. See also Jerry C. Beasley, "Smollett's Novels: *Ferdinand Count Fathom* for the Defense," *Papers on Language and Literature* 20 (1984): 165–84; and John F. Sena, "Fathoming Fathom: Smollett's Count as Malevolent Artist," *Forum for Modern Language Studies* 16 (1980): 1–11.

35. Smollett never added anything of significance to the explanation of his craft introduced into the dedication of *Ferdinand Count Fathom*. Only once did he raise the subject again for discussion at any length, and then he simply repeated himself. The occasion was his review of a novel written in flattering (but not very successful) imitation of his own manner, *The Peregrinations of Jeremiah Grant, Esq., The West Indian* (London, 1763). Smollett's review appeared in the *Critical Review* 15 (January 1763): 13–21.

36. See Boucé, *The Novels of Tobias Smollett*, chap. 3.

37. The subject of *Roderick Random's* connections with the picaresque has been vigorously discussed in Smollett scholarship. Some of this discussion is summarized in Jerry C. Beasley, "*Roderick Random*: The Picaresque Transformed," *College Literature* 6 (1979): 211–20. See also Paul-Gabriel Boucé, "'Snakes in Iceland': The 'Picaresque' in Smollett's *Roderick Random* (1748)," *Caliban* 20 (1983): 29–39. In his book-length study entitled *Tobias George Smollett* (New York: Twayne, 1968),

Robert Donald Spector begins from the premise that the picaresque was central not only in *Roderick Random* and Smollett's other early novels but in the later novels (*Sir Launcelot Greaves* and *Humphry Clinker*) as well.

38. Smollett mentions both *Gil Blas* and *Guzman de Alfarache* (1599–1602), by Mateo Alemán, within a single paragraph of chapter 1 (see pp. 9–10 and nn. 12 and 15). Much later, in chapter 39 (see p. 185 and n. 27), he alludes directly to *La Vida de Lazarillo de Tormes* (1554), the earliest known picaresque tale and the prototype of the form. Frank McCombie, "Count Fathom and El Buscón," *Notes & Queries*, n.s., 7 (1960): 297–99, has suggested a very specific source for Smollett's novel in a popular narrative by Francisco Gómez de Quevedo, *La Vida del Buscon* (1626). Smollett nowhere mentions Quevedo's work in *Ferdinand Count Fathom*, and there is no real evidence to support McCombie's claim.

39. See Beasley, *Novels of the 1740s*, chap. 4.

40. Thomas R. Preston is one critic who has taken seriously Smollett's emphasis on the power of fear to effect a moral response from readers; see "Disenchanting the Man of Feeling: Smollett's *Ferdinand Count Fathom*," in *Quick Springs of Sense: Studies in the Eighteenth Century*, ed. Larry S. Champion (Athens: University of Georgia Press, 1974), 223–39. For a hostile answer to Preston, see Joel J. Thomas, "Smollett and Ethical Sensibility: *Ferdinand Count Fathom*," *Studies in Scottish Literature* 14 (1979): 145–64.

41. See chap. 62, pp. 312–13 and n. 5; and chap. 63, p. 318 and n. 1.

42. See, for example, Lee Monroe Ellison, "Elizabethan Drama and the Works of Smollett," *PMLA* 44 (1929): 842–62; George M. Kahrl, "The Influence of Shakespeare on Smollett," in *Essays in Dramatic Literature: The Parrott Presentation Volume*, ed. Hardin Craig (Princeton: Princeton University Press, 1935), 399–420; Thomas R. Preston, "The 'Stage Passions' and Smollett's Characterization," *Studies in Philology* 71 (1974): 105–25.

43. In his exhaustive study entitled *Travel Literature and the Evolution of the Novel* (Lexington: University Press of Kentucky, 1983), Percy G. Adams has shown conclusively that travel and its literature helped in crucial ways to shape the thinking and the writing of eighteenth-century novelists. According to Adams, the two forms of prose fiction and travel narrative were often so close as to be almost indistinguishable, and he takes Smollett's own *Travels* as an exemplary instance of this intermingling.

44. The Carthagena expedition furnished the firsthand experience upon which Smollett drew for the naval episodes in chapters 24–37 of *Roderick Random*. See George M. Kahrl, *Tobias Smollett: Traveler-Novelist* (Chicago: University of Chicago Press, 1945), chap. 2.

45. For discussion of Smollett's work on this huge project, see Louis L. Martz, *The Later Career of Tobias Smollett* (New Haven: Yale University Press, 1942), 23–64. The *Compendium* grew as much from Smollett's need for money as from his love for its subject. He was paid little—about £155 (Knapp, 159–60); and he was left exhausted by the labor.

46. Kahrl, *Tobias Smollett: Traveler-Novelist*, 54.

47. Detailed discussion of Smollett's uses of recent and contemporary history in the development of his overall design may be found in Beasley, "Smollett's Novels."

48. *Letters*, 69; and see below, chap. 1, p. 7 and n. 2. The first three quarto volumes of the *Complete History* were published in April 1757, the fourth and last volume in January 1758 (Knapp, 186–87).

The Adventures of
Ferdinand Count Fathom

VOLUME ONE

THE

ADVENTURES

O F

Ferdinand Count Fathom.

By the Author of RODERICK RANDOM,

——————Materiam rifus, invenit ad omnes
Occurfus hominum. ———— ————
Ridebat curas, nec non et gaudia vulgi;
Interdum et lachrymas fundebat. ————

IN TWO VOLUMES.

VOL. I.

LONDON:
Printed for W. JOHNSTON, at the Golden Ball.
in St. Paul's Church-yard,
MDCCLIII.

Title Page of First Edition, Volume 1, 1753.
(Special Collections, Van Pelt Library, University of Pennsylvania.)

T O

D O C T O R * * * * * *1

You and I, my good friend, have often deliberated on the difficulty of writing such a Dedication as might gratify the self-complacency of a patron, without exposing the author to the ridicule or censure of the public; and I think we generally agreed that the task was altogether impracticable—Indeed, this was one of the few subjects on which we have always thought in the same manner: for notwithstanding that deference and regard which we mutually pay to each other, certain it is, we have often differed, according to the predominancy of those different passions, which frequently warp the opinion, and perplex the understanding of the most judicious.

In Dedication as in Poetry, there is no medium: for, if any one of the human virtues be omitted in the enumeration of the patron's good qualities; the whole address is construed into an affront, and the writer has the mortification to find his praise prostituted to very little purpose.

On the other hand, should he yield to the transports of gratitude or affection which is always apt to exaggerate, and produce no more than the genuine effusions of his heart, the world will make no allowance for the warmth of his passion, but ascribe the praise he bestows, to interested views and sordid adulation.

Sometimes too, dazzled by the tinsel of a character which he has no opportunity to investigate, he pours forth the homage of his admiration, upon some false Mæcenas,2 whose future conduct gives the lie to his eulogium, and involves him in shame and confusion of face. Such was the fate of a late ingenious* author, who was so often put to the blush for the undeserved incense he had offered, in the heat of an enthusiastic disposition, misled by popular applause, that he had resolved to retract in his last will, all the encomiums which he had thus prematurely bestowed, and stigmatize the unworthy by name: a laudable scheme of poetical justice, the execution of which was fatally prevented by untimely death.

Whatever may have been the fate of other Dedicators, I, for my own part, sit down to write this address, without any apprehension of disgrace or disappointment; because I know you are too well convinced of my affection and sincerity to repine at what I shall say touching your character and conduct:

---

*The author of the SEASONS.3

and you will do me the justice to believe, that this public distinction is a testimony of my particular friendship and esteem.

Not that I am either insensible of your infirmities, or disposed to conceal them from the notice of mankind. There are certain foibles which can only be cured by shame and mortification; and whether or not yours be of that species, I shall have the comfort to think my best endeavours were used for your reformation.

Know then, I can despise your pride, while I honour your integrity; and applaud your taste, while I am shocked at your ostentation.—I have known you trifling, superficial and obstinate in dispute; meanly jealous and aukwardly reserved; rash and haughty in your resentments; and coarse and lowly in your connexions.—I have blushed at the weakness of your conversation, and trembled at the errors of your conduct.—Yet, as I own you possess certain good qualities, which over-balance these defects, and distinguish you on this occasion, as a person for whom I have the most perfect attachment and esteem, you have no cause to complain of the indelicacy with which your faults are reprehended: and as they are chiefly the excesses of a sanguine disposition and looseness of thought, impatient of caution or controul; you may, thus stimulated, watch over your own intemperance and infirmity, with redoubled vigilance and consideration, and for the future profit by the severity of my reproof.[4]

These, however, are not the only motives that induce me to trouble you with this public application. I must not only perform my duty to my friends, but also discharge the debt I owe to my own interest. We live in a censorious age; and an author cannot take too much precaution to anticipate the prejudice, misapprehension and temerity of malice, ignorance and presumption.

I therefore think it incumbent upon me, to give some previous intimation of the plan which I have executed in the subsequent performance, that I may not be condemned upon partial evidence; and to whom can I with more propriety appeal in my explanation, than to you, who are so well acquainted with all the sentiments and emotions of my breast?

A Novel is a large diffused picture, comprehending the characters of life, disposed in different groupes, and exhibited in various attitudes, for the purposes of an uniform plan, and general occurrence,[5] to which every individual figure is subservient. But this plan cannot be executed with propriety, probability or success, without a principal personage to attract the attention, unite the incidents, unwind the clue of the labyrinth, and at last close the scene by virtue of his own importance.[6]

Almost all the heroes of this kind, who have hitherto succeeded on the

English stage, are characters of transcendent worth, conducted through the vicissitudes of fortune, to that goal of happiness, which ever ought to be the repose of extraordinary desert.—Yet the same principle by which we rejoice at the remuneration of merit, will teach us to relish the disgrace and discomfiture of vice, which is always an example of extensive use and influence, because it leaves a deep impression of terror[7] upon the minds of those who were not confirmed in the pursuit of morality and virtue, and while the balance wavers, enables the right scale to preponderate.

In the Drama, which is a more limited field of invention, the chief personage is often the object of our detestation and abhorrence; and we are as well pleased to see the wicked schemes of a RICHARD blasted, and the perfidy of a MASKWELL exposed, as to behold a BEVIL happy, and an EDWARD[8] victorious.

The impulses of fear which is the most violent and interesting of all the passions, remain longer than any other upon the memory; and for one that is allured to virtue, by the contemplation of that peace and happiness which it bestows, an hundred are deterred from the practice of vice, by that infamy and punishment to which it is liable, from the laws and regulations of mankind.

Let me not therefore be condemned for having chosen my principal character from the purlieus of treachery and fraud, when I declare my purpose is to set him up as a beacon for the benefit of the unexperienced and unwary, who from the perusal of these memoirs, may learn to avoid the manifold snares with which they are continually surrounded in the paths of life; while those who hesitate on the brink of iniquity, may be terrified from plunging into that irremeable[9] gulph, by surveying the deplorable fate of FERDINAND Count FATHOM.[10]

That the mind might not be fatigued, nor the imagination disgusted by a succession of vitious objects, I have endeavoured to refresh the attention with occasional incidents of a different nature; and raised up a virtuous character, in opposition to the adventurer, with a view to amuse the fancy, engage the affection, and form a striking contrast which might heighten the expression, and give a *Relief* to the moral of the whole.

If I have not succeeded in my endeavours to unfold the mysteries of fraud, to instruct the ignorant, and entertain the vacant; if I have failed in my attempts to subject folly to ridicule, and vice to indignation; to rouse the spirit of mirth, wake the soul of compassion, and touch the secret springs that move the heart; I have at least, adorned virtue with honour and applause; branded iniquity with reproach and shame, and carefully avoided every hint or expression which could give umbrage to the most delicate reader:[11] circumstances which (whatever may be my fate with the public) will with you always operate in favour of

Dear Sir,

Your very affectionate

friend and servant,

The AUTHOR.

THE
ADVENTURES
OF
Ferdinand Count Fathom.

CHAPTER I.

Some sage observations that naturally introduce
our important history.

Cardinal de Retz[1] very judiciously observes, that all historians must of
necessity, be subject to mistakes, in explaining the motives of those actions they record, unless they derive their intelligence from the candid confession of the person whose character they represent; and that, of consequence, every man of importance ought to write his own memoirs, provided
he has honesty enough to tell the truth, without suppressing any circumstance, that may tend to the information of the reader. This, however, is a
requisite that, I am afraid, would be very rarely found among the number of
those who exhibit their own portraits to the public: indeed, I will venture to
say, that how upright soever a man's intentions may be, he will, in the performance of such a task, be sometimes misled by his own phantasy, and represent objects, as they appeared to him, through the mists of prejudice and
passion.[2]

An unconcerned reader, when he peruses the history of two competitors,
who lived two thousand years ago, or who, perhaps, never had existence,
except in the imagination of the author, cannot help interesting himself in the
dispute, and espousing one side of the contest, with all the zeal of a warm
adherent. What wonder then, that we should be heated in our own concerns,
review our actions with the same self-approbation that they had formerly
acquired, and recommend them to the world with all the enthusiasm of paternal affection?

Supposing this to be the case, it was lucky for the cause of historical truth, that so many pens have been drawn by writers, who could not be suspected of such partiality; and that many great personages, among the ancients as well as moderns, either would not, or could not entertain the public with their own memoirs. From this want of inclination or capacity to write, in our hero himself, the undertaking is now left to me, of transmitting to posterity, the remarkable adventures of FERDINAND Count FATHOM; and by that time the reader shall have glanced over the subsequent sheets, I doubt not, but he will bless God, that the adventurer was not his own historian.

This mirrour of modern chivalry was none of those who owe their dignity to the circumstances of their birth, and are consecrated from the cradle for the purposes of greatness, meerly because they are the accidental children of wealth. He was heir to no visible patrimony, unless we reckon a robust constitution, a tolerable appearance, and an uncommon capacity, as the advantages of inheritance: if the comparison obtains in this point of consideration, he was as much as any man, indebted to his parents; and pity it was, that in the sequel of his fortune, he never had an opportunity of manifesting his filial gratitude and regard. From this agreeable act of duty to his sire, and all those tendernesses that are reciprocally enjoyed betwixt the father and the son, he was unhappily excluded by a small circumstance; at which, however, he was never heard to repine. In short, had he been brought forth in the fabulous ages of the world, the nature of his origin might have turned to his account; he might, like other heroes of antiquity, have laid claim to divine extraction, without running the risque of being claimed by any earthly father; not that his parents had any reason to disown or renounce their offspring, or that there was any thing preternatural in the circumstances of his generation and birth; on the contrary, he was from the beginning, a child of promising parts, and in due course of nature, ushered into the world, amidst a whole cloud of witnesses: but, that he was acknowledged by no mortal sire, solely proceeded from the uncertainty of his mother, whose affections were so dissipated among a number of admirers, that she could never pitch upon the person from whose loins our hero sprung.[3]

Over and above this important doubt, under which he was begotten, other particularities attended his birth, and seemed to mark him out as something uncommon among the sons of men. He was brought forth in a waggon, and might be said to be literally a native of two different countries; for, though he first saw the light in Holland, he was not born till after the carriage arrived in Flanders; so that all these extraordinary circumstances considered, the task of determining to what government he naturally owed allegiance, would be at least as difficult, as that of ascertaining the so much contested birth-place of Homer.[4]

Certain it is, the count's mother was an Englishwoman, who, after having been five times a widow in one campaign, was, in the last year of the renowned Marlborough's command,[5] numbered among the baggage of the allied army, which she still accompanied, through pure benevolence of spirit, supplying the ranks with the refreshing streams of choice geneva,[6] and accommodating individuals with clean linnen, as the emergency of their occasions required: Nor was her philanthropy altogether confined to such ministration: she abounded with "the milk of human kindness,"[7] which flowed plentifully among her fellow-creatures; and to every son of Mars who cultivated her favour, she liberally dispensed her smiles, in order to sweeten the toils and dangers of the field.

And here it will not be amiss to anticipate the remarks of the reader, who, in the chastity and excellency of his conception, may possibly exclaim, "Good Heaven! will these authors never reform their imaginations, and lift their ideas from the obscene objects of low life? Must the publick be again disgusted with the groveling adventures of a waggon?[8] Will no writer of genius draw his pen in the vindication of taste, and entertain us with the agreeable characters, the dignified conversation, the poignant repartee, in short, the genteel comedy of the polite world?"

Have a little patience, gentle, delicate, sublime, critic; you, I doubt not, are one of those consummate connoisseurs, who in their purifications, let humour evaporate, while they endeavour to preserve decorum, and polish wit, until the edge of it is quite wore off: or, perhaps of that class, who, in the sapience of taste, are disgusted with those very flavours, in the productions of their own country, which have yielded infinite delectation to their faculties, when imported from another clime; and damn an author in despite of all precedent and prescription; who extol the writings of Petronius Arbiter,[9] read with rapture the amorous sallies of Ovid's pen,[10] and chuckle over the story of Lucian's ass;[11] yet, if a modern author presumes to relate the progress of a simple intrigue, are shocked at the indecency and immorality of the scene: who delight in following Guzman d'Alfarache,[12] thro' all the mazes of squalid beggary; who with pleasure accompany Don Quixote and his squire,[13] in the lowest paths of fortune; who are diverted with the adventures of Scarron's ragged troop of strollers,[14] and highly entertained with the servile situations of Gil Blas;[15] yet, when a character in humble life occasionally occurs in a performance of our own growth, exclaim with an air of disgust, "Was ever any thing so mean! Sure, this writer must have been very conversant with the lowest scenes of life:" who, when Swift or Pope[16] represents a coxcomb in the act of swearing, scruple not to laugh at the ridiculous execrations; but in a less reputed author, condemn the use of such profane expletives: who eagerly explore the jakes of Rabelais,[17] for amusement, and even extract humour from the dean's description of a lady's dressing-room:[18] yet, in a production of these days, unstampt with such venerable names, will stop their noses with all the signs of loathing and abhorrence, at a bare mention of the china chamber-pot:[19] who applaud Catullus, Juvenal, Persius and Lucan,[20] for their spirit in lashing the greatest names of antiquity; yet, when a British satirist, of this generation, has courage enough to call in question the talents of a Pseudo-patron,[21] in power, accuse him of insolence, rancour and scurrility.

If such you be, courteous reader, I say again, have a little patience; for your entertainment we are about to write. Our hero shall, with all convenient dispatch, be gradually sublimed, into those splendid connexions of which you are enamoured; and God forbid, that in the mean time, the nature of his extraction should turn to his prejudice, in a land of freedom like this, where individuals are every day ennobled in consequence of their own qualifications, without the least retrospective regard to the rank or merit of their ancestors.[22] Yes, refined reader, we are hastening to that goal of perfection, where satire dares not shew her face; where nature is castigated, almost even to still life; where humour turns changeling, and slavers in an insipid grin; where wit is volatilized into a meer vapour; where decency, divested of all substance, hovers about like a fantastic shadow; where the salt of genius, escaping, leaves nothing but pure and simple phlegm; and the inoffensive pen for ever drops the mild manna of soul-sweetning praise.[23]

CHAPTER II.

A superficial view of our hero's infancy.

Having thus bespoke the indulgence of our guests, let us now produce the particulars of our entertainment, and speedily conduct our adventurer through the stage of infancy, which seldom teems with interesting incidents.

As the occupations of his mother would not conveniently permit her to suckle this her first-born at her own breast, and those happy ages were now no more, in which the charge of nursing a child might be left to the next goat or she-wolf, she resolved to improve upon the ordinances of nature, and foster him with a juice much more energic than the milk of goat, or wolf, or woman; this was no other than that delicious nectar, which, as we have already hinted, she so cordially distributed from a small cask that hung before her, depending from her shoulders by a leathern zone.[1] Thus determined, 'ere he was yet twelve days old, she enclosed him in a canvas knapsack, which being adjusted to her neck, fell down upon her back, and balanced the cargo that rested on her bosom.

There are not wanting those who affirm, that while her double charge was carried about in this situation, her cag[2] was furnished with a long and slender flexible tube, which, when the child began to be clamorous, she conveyed into his mouth, and strait he stilled himself with sucking; but this we consider as an extravagant assertion of those, who mix the marvellous in all their narrations, because we cannot conceive how the tender organs of an infant, could digest such a fiery beverage, which never fails to discompose the constitutions of the most hardy and robust: we therefore conclude, that the use of this potation was more restrained, and that it was with simple element,[3] diluted into a composition adapted to his taste and years. Be this as it will, he certainly was indulged in the use of it to such a degree, as would have effectually obstructed his future fortune, had not he been happily cloyed with the repetition of the same fare, for which he conceived the utmost detestation and abhorrence, rejecting it with loathing and disgust, like those choice spirits, who, having been crammed with religion in their childhood, renounce it in their youth, among other absurd prejudices of education.

While he thus dangled in a state of suspension, a German trooper[4] was transiently smit with the charms of his mother, who listened to his honourable addresses, and once more received the silken bonds of matrimony; the ceremony having been performed as usual at the drum-head.[5] The lady had no sooner taken possession of her new name, than she bestowed it upon her son, who was thenceforward distinguished by the appellation of Ferdinand de Fadom;[6] nor was the husband offended at this presumption in his wife, which he not only considered as a proof of her affection and esteem, but also as a compliment, by which he might in time acquire the credit of being the real father of such an hopeful child.

Notwithstanding this new engagement with a foreigner, our Hero's mother still exercised the virtues of her calling among the English troops, so much was she biassed by that laudable partiality, which, as Horace observes, the *natale solum*[7] generally inspires: indeed this inclination was enforced by another reason, that did not fail to influence her conduct in this particular; all her knowledge of the high Dutch language consisted in some words of traffic, absolutely necessary for the practice of her vocation; together with sundry oaths and terms of reproach, that kept her customers in awe; so that, except among her own countrymen, she could not indulge that propensity to conversation, for which she had been remarkable from her earliest years. Nor did this instance of her affection fail of turning to her account in the sequel: She was promoted to the office of cook to a regimental mess of officers; and before the peace of Utrecht,[8] was actually in possession of a suttling-tent,[9] pitched for the accommodation of the gentlemen in the army.

Mean while, Ferdinand improved apace in the accomplishments of infancy; his beauty was conspicuous, and his vigour so uncommon, that he was with justice likened unto Hercules in the cradle: the friends of his father-in-law, dandled him on their knees, while he played with their whiskers, and before he was thirteen months old, taught him to suck brandy impregnated with gun-powder, through the touch-hole of a pistol. At the same time, he was caressed by divers serjeants of the British army, who severally and in secret contemplated his qualifications with a father's pride, excited by the artful declaration, with which the mother had flattered each apart.

Soon as the war was (for her unhappily) concluded, she, as in duty bound, followed her husband into Bohemia;[10] and his regiment being sent into garrison at Prague, she opened a cabaret[11] in that city, which was frequented by a good many guests of the Scotch and Irish nations, who were devoted to the exercise of arms, in the service of the emperor.[12] It was by this communication, that the English tongue became vernacular to young Ferdinand, who, without such opportunity, would have been a stranger to the language of his forefathers, in spite of all his mother's loquacity and elocution: though it must be owned, for the credit of her maternal care, that she let slip no occasion of making it familiar to his ear and conception; for, even at those intervals in which she could find no person to carry on the altercation, she used to hold forth in earnest soliloquies upon the subject of her own situation, giving vent to many opprobrious invectives against her husband's country, between which and old England she drew many odious comparisons; and prayed without ceasing that Europe might speedily be involved in a general war, so as that she might have some chance of reinjoying the pleasures and emoluments of a Flanders campaign.

The Hero's Mother and Her Cargo, by Clennell.
(Library Company of Philadelphia.)

*He is initiated in a military life, and has the
good fortune to acquire a generous patron.*

While she wearied Heaven with these petitions, the flame of war broke out betwixt the houses of Ottoman and Austria, and the emperor sent forth an army into Hungary, under the auspices of the renowned prince Eugene.[1] On account of this expedition, the mother of our hero gave up housekeeping, and chearfully followed her customers and husband into the field; having first provided herself with store of those commodities, in which she had formerly merchandized. Although the hope of profit might in some measure affect her determination, one of the chief motives for her visiting the frontiers of Turkey, was the desire of initiating her son in the rudiments of his education, which she now thought high time to inculcate, he being, at this period, in the sixth year of his age; he was accordingly conducted to the camp, which she considered as the most consummate school of life, and proposed for the scene of his instruction; and in this academy he had not continued many weeks, when he was an eye-witness of that famous victory, which, with sixty thousand men, the imperial general obtained over an army of one hundred and fifty thousand Turks.[2]

His father in law was engaged, and his mother would not be idle on this occasion: she was a perfect mistress of all the camp qualifications, and thought it a duty incumbent on her, to contribute all that lay in her power, towards distressing the enemy:[3] with these sentiments, she hovered about the skirts of the army, and the troops were no sooner employed in the pursuit, than she began to traverse the field of battle with a poignard[4] and a bag, in order to consult her own interest, annoy the foe, and exercise her humanity at the same time. In short, she had with amazing prowess, delivered some fifty or threescore disabled mussulmen[5] of the pain under which they groaned, and made a comfortable booty of the spoils of the slain, when her eyes were attracted by the rich attire of an imperial officer, who lay bleeding on the plain, to all appearance in the agonies of death.

She could not, in her heart, refuse that favour to a friend and christian, she had so compassionately bestowed upon so many enemies and infidels, and therefore drew near with the sovereign remedy, which she had already administred with such success. As she approached this deplorable object of pity, her ears were surprized with an ejaculation in the English tongue, which he fervently pronounced, though with a weak and languid voice, recommending his soul to God, and his family to the protection of Heaven. Our amazon's purpose was staggered by this providential incident; the sound of her native language, so unexpectedly heard, and so pathetically delivered, had a surprising effect upon her imagination; and the faculty of reflexion did not forsake her in such emergency: though she could not recollect the features of this unhappy officer, she concluded from his appearance, that he was some person of distinction in the service, and foresaw greater advantage to herself in attempting to preserve his life, than she could possibly reap from the execution of her first resolve. "If (said she to herself) I can find means of conveying him to his tent, alive, he cannot but in conscience acknowledge my humanity with some considerable recompence; and should he chance to survive his wounds, I have every thing to expect from his gratitude and power."

Fraught with these prudential suggestions, she drew near the unfortunate stranger, and in a softened accent of pity and condolance, questioned him concerning his name, condition, and the nature of his mischance, at the same time making a gentle tender of her service. Agreeably surprized to hear himself accosted in such a manner, by a person whose equipage seemed to promise far other designs, he thanked her in the most grateful terms for her humanity, with the appellation of kind countrywoman; gave her to understand that he was colonel of a regiment of horse; that he had fallen in consequence of a shot he received in his breast, at the beginning of the action; and finally intreated her to procure some carriage on which he might be removed to his tent. Perceiving him faint and exhausted with loss of blood, she raised up his head, and treated him with that cordial which was her constant companion: at that instant, espying a small body of hussars[6] returning to the camp with the plunder they had taken, she invoked their assistance, and they forthwith carried the officer to his own quarters, where his wound was dressed, and his preserver carefully tended him until his recovery was compleated.

In return for these good offices, this gentleman, who was originally of Scotland, rewarded her for the present, with great liberality, assured her of his influence in promoting her husband, and took upon himself the charge of young Ferdinand's education; the boy was immediately taken into his protection, and entered as a trooper in his own regiment; but his good intentions towards his father-in-law, were frustrated by the death of the German, who in a few days after this disposition, was shot in the trenches before Temiswaer.[7]

This event, over and above the conjugal affliction with which it invaded the lady's quiet, would have involved her in infinite difficulty and distress, with regard to her temporal concerns, by leaving her unprotected in the midst of strangers, had not she been thus providentially supplied, with an effectual patron in the colonel, who was known by the appellation of count Melvil.[8] He no sooner saw her, by the death of her husband, detached from all personal connexions with a military life, than he proposed that she should quit her occupation in the camp, and retire to his habitation in the city of Presburg,[9] where she would be entertained in ease and plenty, during the remaining part of her natural life: with all due acknowledgments of his generosity, she begged to be excused from embracing his proposal, alledging she was so much accustomed to her present way of life, and so much devoted to the service of the soldiery, that she should never be happy in retirement, while the troops of any prince of Christendom kept the field.

The count finding her determined to prosecute her scheme, repeated his promise of befriending her upon all occasions; and in the mean time, admitted Ferdinand into the number of his domestics, resolving that he should be brought up in attendance upon his own son, who was a boy of the same age. He kept him, however, in his tent, until he should have an opportunity of revisiting his family in person; and before that occasion offered, two whole years elapsed, during which, the illustrious prince Eugene gained the celebrated battle of Belgrade,[10] and afterwards made himself master of that important frontier.

CHAPTER IV.

His mother's prowess and death; together with some instances of his own sagacity.

It would have been impossible for the mother of our adventurer, such as she hath been described, to sit quietly in her tent, while such an heroic scene was acting. She was no sooner apprised of the general's intention to attack the enemy, than she, as usual, packed up her moveables in a waggon, which she committed to the care of a peasant in the neighbourhood, and put herself in motion with the troops; big with the expectation of re-acting that part, in which she had formerly acquitted herself so much to her advantage. Nay, she by this time looked upon her own presence as a certain omen of success to the cause which she espoused; and in their march to battle, actually encouraged the ranks with repeated declarations, importing, that she had been eyewitness of ten decisive engagements, in all of which her friends had been victorious, and imputing such uncommon good fortune to some supernatural quality inherent in her person.

Whether or not this confidence contributed to the fortune of the day, by inspiriting the soldiers to an uncommon pitch of courage and resolution, I shall not pretend to determine: but, certain it is, the victory began from that quarter in which she had posted herself; and no corps in the army behaved with such intrepidity as that, which was manifested by those who were favoured with her admonitions and example; for, she not only exposed her person to the enemy's fire, with the indifference and deliberation of a veteran, but she is said to have atchieved a very conspicuous exploit by the prowess of her single arm: the extremity of the line to which she had attached herself, being assaulted in flank by a body of the spahis,[1] wheeled about, in order to sustain the charge, and received them with such a seasonable fire, as brought a great number of turbans to the ground; among those who fell, was one of the chiefs, or aga's, who had advanced before the rest, with a view to signalize his valour.

Our English Penthesilea[2] no sooner saw this Turkish leader drop, than, struck with the magnificence of his own and horse's trappings, she sprung forward to seize them as her prize, and found the aga not dead, though in a good measure disabled by his misfortune, which was intirely owing to the weight of his horse, that, having been killed by a musket-ball, lay upon his leg, so that he could not disingage himself. Nevertheless, perceiving the virago approach with fell intent, he brandished his scymitar, and tried to intimidate his assailant with a most horrible exclamation; but, it was not the dismal yell of a dismounted cavalier, though enforced with a hideous ferocity of countenance, and the menacing gestures with which he waited her approach, that could intimidate such an undaunted she-campaigner; she saw him writhing in the agonies of a situation from which he could not move; and, running towards him with the nimbleness and intrepidity of a Camilla,[3] described a semicircle in the progress of her assault, and attacking him on one side, plunged her well-tried dagger in his throat: the shades of death encompassed him, his life-blood issued at the wound, he fell prone upon the earth, he bit the dust, and having thrice invoked the name of Allah! straight expired.

While his destiny was thus fulfilled, his followers began to reel; they seemed dismayed at the fate of their chief, beheld their companions drop like the leaves in autumn, and suddenly halted in the midst of their career. The Imperialists observing the confusion of the enemy, redoubled their fire; and raising a dreadful shout, advanced in order to improve the advantage they

Our English Penthesilea, by Stothard.
(General Research Division, The New York Public Library—
Astor, Lenox and Tilden Foundations.)

had gained: the spahis durst not wait the shock of such an encounter; they wheeled to the right about, and clapping spurs to their horses, fled in the utmost disorder.[4] This was actually the circumstance that turned the scale of battle: the Austrians pursued their good fortune with uncommon impetuosity, and in a few minutes, left the field clear for the mother of our hero, who was such an adept in the art of stripping, that in the twinkling of an eye, the bodies of the aga and his Arabian, lay naked to the skin. It would have been happy for her, had she been contented with these first-fruits, reaped from the fortune of the day, and retired with her spoils, which were not inconsiderable; but, intoxicated with the glory she had won, inticed by the glittering caparisons[5] that lay scattered on the plain, and without doubt, prompted by the secret instinct of her fate, she resolved to seize opportunity by the forelock, and once for all indemnify herself for the many fatigues, hazards and sorrows she had undergone.

Thus determined, she reconnoitred the field, and practised her address so successfully, that in less than half an hour, she was loaded with ermin and embroidery, and disposed to retreat with her burden, when her regards were sollicited by a splendid bundle, which she descried at some distance lying on the ground. This was no other than an unhappy officer of hussars; who, after having had the good fortune to take a Turkish standard, was desperately wounded in the thigh, and obliged to quit his horse; finding himself in such an helpless condition, he had wrapped his acquisition round his body, that whatever might happen, he and his glory should not be parted; and thus shrouded among the dying and the dead, he had observed the progress of our heroine, who stalked about the field, like another Atropos,[6] finishing, wherever she came, the work of death: he did not at all doubt, that he himself would be visited in the course of her peregrinations, and therefore provided for her reception, with a pistol ready cock'd in his hand, while he lay perdue,[7] beneath his covert,[8] in all appearance bereft of life. He was not deceived in his prognostic; she no sooner eyed the golden crescent,[9] than inflamed with curiosity or cupidity, she directed thitherward her steps, and discerning the carcase of a man, from which, she thought, there would be a necessity for disengaging it, she lifted up her weapon, in order to make sure of her purchase; and in the very instant of discharging her blow, receiv'd a brace of bullets in her brain.

Thus ended the mortal pilgrimage of this modern amazon; who, in point of courage, was not inferior to Semiramis, Tomyris, Zenobia, Thalestris,[10] or any boasted heroine of antient times. It cannot be supposed, that this catastrophe made a very deep impression upon the mind of young Ferdinand, who had just then attained the ninth year of his age,[11] and been for a considerable time, weaned from her maternal caresses; especially, as he felt no wants nor grievances in the family of the count, who favoured him with a particular share of indulgence, because he perceived in him, a spirit of docility, insinuation,[12] and sagacity, far above his years. He did not, however, fail to lament the untimely fate of his mother, with such filial expressions of sorrow, as still more intimately recommended him to his patron; who being, himself, a man of extraordinary benevolence, looked upon the boy as a prodigy of natural affection, and foresaw in his future services a fund of gratitude and attachment, that could not fail to render him a valuable acquisition to his family.

In his own country he had often seen connections of that sort, which having been planted in the infancy of the adherent, had grown up to a surprising pitch of fidelity and friendship, that no temptation could biass, and no danger dissolve. He therefore rejoiced in the hope of seeing his own son accommodated with such a faithful attendant, in the person of young Fathom, on whom he resolved to bestow the same education he had planned for the other, though conveyed in such a manner as should be suitable to the sphere in which he was ordained to move. In consequence of these determinations, our young adventurer led a very easy life, in quality of page to the count, in whose tent he lay upon a pallet, close to his field-bed, and often diverted him with his childish prattle in the English tongue, which the more seldom his master had occasion to speak, he the more delighted to hear. In the exercise of his function, the boy was incredibly assiduous and alert; far from neglecting the little particulars of his duty, and embarking in the mischievous amusements of the children belonging to the camp, he was always diligent, sedate, agreeably officious and anticipating; and in the whole of his behaviour, seemed to express the most vigilant sense of his patron's goodness and generosity: nay, to such a degree had these sentiments, in all appearance, operated upon his reflexion, that one morning while he supposed the count asleep, he crept softly to his bedside, and gently kissing his hand, which happened to be uncovered, pronounced, in a low voice, a most fervent prayer in his behalf, beseeching Heaven to shower down blessings upon him, as the widow's friend and the orphan's father: this benediction was not lost upon the count, who chanced to be awake and heard it with admiration; but, what rivetted Ferdinand in his good graces, was a discovery that our youth made, while his master was upon duty in the trenches before Belgrade.

Two foot-soldiers standing centry near the door of the tent, were captivated with the sight of some valuable moveables belonging to it; and supposing, in their great wisdom, that the city of Belgrade was too well fortified to be taken during that campaign, they came to a resolution of with-drawing themselves from the severe service of the trenches, by deserting to the enemy, after they should have rifled count Melvil's tent, of the furniture by which they were so powerfully allured: the particulars of this plan were concerted in the French language, which, they imagined, would screen them from all risk of being detected, in case they should be overheard, though, as there was no living creature in sight, they had no reason to believe, that any person was privy to their conversation. Nevertheless, they were mistaken in both these conjectures. The conference reached the ears of Fathom, who was at the other end of the tent, and had perceived the eager looks, with which they considered some parts of the furniture: he had penetration enough to suspect their desire, and alarmed by that suspicion, listened attentively to their discourse, which from a slender knowledge in the French tongue, he had the good fortune partly to understand.

This important piece of intelligence he communicated to the count at his return, and measures were immediately taken to defeat the design, and make an example of the authors, who being permitted to load themselves with the booty, were apprehended in their retreat, and punished with death according to their demerits.

CHAPTER V.

A brief detail of his education.

Nothing could have more seasonably happened, to confirm the good opinion which the colonel entertained of Ferdinand's principles: his intentions towards the boy grew every day more and more warm; and immediately after the peace of Passarowitz,[1] he retired to his own house at Presburg, and presented young Fathom to his lady, not only as the son of a person to whom he owed his life, but also as a lad, who merited his peculiar protection and regard by his own personal virtue. The countess, who was an Hungarian, received him with great kindness and affability, and her son was ravished with the prospect of enjoying such a companion: in short, fortune seemed to have provided for him an asylum, in which he might be safely trained up, and suitably prepared for more important scenes of life, than any of his ancestors had ever known.

He was not, in all respects, entertained on the footing of his young master;

yet he shar'd in all his education and amusements, as one whom the old gentleman was fully determined to qualify for the station of an officer in the service; and if he did not eat with the count, he was every day regaled with choice bits from his table; holding, as it were, a middle place between the rank of a relation, and favoured domestic. Although his patron maintained a tutor in the house, to superintend the conduct of his heir, he committed the charge of his learning to the instructions of a public school; where, he imagined, the boy would imbibe a laudable spirit of emulation among his fellows, which could not fail of turning out to the advantage of his education. Ferdinand was entered in the same academy; and the two lads proceeded equally in the paths of erudition; a mutual friendship and intimacy soon ensued, and notwithstanding the levity and caprice commonly discernible in the behaviour of such boys, very few, or rather no quarrels happened in the course of their communication. Yet their dispositions were altogether different, and their talents unlike. Nay, this dissimilarity was the very bond of their union; because it prevented that jealousy and rivalship which often interrupts the harmony of two warm cotemporaries.

The young count made extraordinary progress in the exercises of the school, though he seemed to take very little pains in the cultivation of his studies; and became a perfect hero in all the athletic diversions of his fellow-scholars; but, at the same time, exhibited such a bashful appearance and uncouth address, that his mother despaired of ever seeing him improved into any degree of polite behaviour. On the other hand, Fathom, who was in point of learning a meer dunce, became, even in his childhood, remarkable among the ladies for his genteel deportment and vivacity; they admired the proficiency he made, under the directions of his dancing master, the air with which he performed his obeisance at his entrance and exit; and were charmed with the agreeable assurance and lively sallies of his conversation; while they expressed the utmost concern and disgust at the boorish demeanour of his companion, whose extorted bows resembled the pawings of a mule, who hung his head in silence, like a detected sheep-stealer, who sat in company under the most aukward expressions of constraint, and whose discourse never exceeded the simple monosyllables of negation and assent.

In vain did all the females of the family propose to him young Fathom, as a pattern and reproach: he remained unaltered by all their efforts and expostulations, and allowed our adventurer to enjoy the triumph of his praise, while he himself was conscious of his own superiority in those qualifications which seemed of more real importance than the meer exteriors and forms of life. His present ambition was not to make a figure at his father's table, but to eclipse his rivals at school, and to acquire an influence and authority among these confederates. Nevertheless, Fathom might possibly have fallen under his displeasure or contempt, had not that pliant genius found means to retain his friendship by seasonable compliances and submission; for, the sole study, or at least the chief aim of Ferdinand, was to make himself necessary and agreeable to those on whom his dependance was placed: his talent was in this particular suited to his inclination; he seemed to have inherited it from his mother's womb; and without all doubt, would have raised upon it, a most admirable superstructure of fortune and applause, had not it been insepara-bly yoked with a most insidious principle of self-love, that grew up with him from the cradle, and left no room in his heart for the least particle of social virtue. This last, however, he knew so well how to counterfeit, by means of a large share of ductility and dissimulation, that, surely, he was calculated by nature, to dupe even the most cautious, and gratify his appetites by levying contributions on all mankind.

So little are the common instructors of youth, qualified to judge the capacities of those who are under their tutelage and care, that Fathom, by dint of his insinuating arts, made shift to pass upon the schoolmaster, as a lad of quick parts, in despite of a natural inaptitude to retain his lessons, which all his industry could never overcome. In order to remedy, or rather to cloak this defect in his understanding, he had always recourse to the friendship of the young count, who freely permitted him to transcribe his exercises, until a small accident happened, which had well-nigh put a stop to these instances of his generosity.—The adventure, inconsiderable as it is, we shall record, as the first overt-act of Ferdinand's true character, as well as an illustration of the opinion we have advanced, touching the blind and injudicious decisions of a right pedagogue.[2]

Among other tasks imposed by the pedant, upon the form to which our two companions belonged, they were one evening ordered to translate a chapter of Cæsar's commentaries. Accordingly the young count went to work, and performed the undertaking with great elegance and dispatch: Fathom having spent the night in more effeminate amusements, was next morning so much hurried for want of time, that in his transcription, he ne-glected to insert a few variations from the text; these being the terms on which he was allowed to use it: so that it was verbatim a copy of the original. As those exercises were always delivered in a heap, subscribed with the sev-eral names of the boys to whom they belonged; the schoolmaster chanced to peruse the version of Ferdinand, before he looked into any of the rest, and could not help bestowing upon it particular marks of approbation: the next

that fell under his examination was that of the young count, when he immediately perceived the sameness, and far from imputing it to the true cause,
upbraided him with having copied the exercise of our adventurer, and insisted upon chastising him upon the spot, for his want of application.

Had not the young gentleman thought his honour was concerned, he
would have submited to the punishment without murmuring; but he inherited from his parents the pride of two fierce nations, and being overwhelmed
with reproaches, for that which he imagined, ought to have redounded to his
glory, he could not brook the indignity, and boldly affirmed, that he himself
was the original, to whom Ferdinand was beholden for his performance. The
schoolmaster, nettled to find himself mistaken in his judgment, resolved that
the count should have no cause to exult in the discovery he had made, and
like a true flogger,[3] actually whipt him for having allowed Fathom to copy his
exercise. Nay, in the hope of vindicating his own penetration, he took an
opportunity of questioning Ferdinand in private, concerning the circumstances of the translation; and our hero perceiving his drift, gave him such
artful and ambiguous answers, as persuaded him, that the young count had
acted the part of a plagiary, and that the other had been restrained from doing
himself justice, by the consideration of his own dependance.

This profound director did not fail, in honour of his own discernment, to
whisper about the misrepresentation, as an instance of the young count's
insolence, and Fathom's humility and good sense. The story was circulated
among the servants, especially the maids belonging to the family, whose
favour our hero had acquired by his engaging behaviour; and at length it
reached the ears of his patron, who incensed at his son's presumption and
inhospitality, called him to a severe account, when the young gentleman absolutely denied the truth of the allegation, and appealed to the evidence of
Fathom himself. Our adventurer was accordingly summoned by the father,
and encouraged to declare the truth, with an assurance of his constant protection; upon which, Ferdinand very wisely fell upon his knees, and while the
tears gushed from his eyes, acquitted the young count of the imputation, and
expressed his apprehension, that the report had been spread by some of his
enemies, who wanted to prejudice him in the opinion of his patron.

The old gentleman was not satisfied of his son's integrity, by this declaration; being naturally of a generous disposition, highly prepossessed in favour
of the poor orphan, and chagrined at the unpromising appearance of his heir,
he suspected that Fathom was over-awed by the fear of giving offence, and
that notwithstanding what he had said, the case really stood as it had been
represented. In this persuasion, he earnestly exhorted his son to resist and

combat with any impulse he might feel within himself, tending to selfishness, fraud or imposition; to encourage every sentiment of candour and benevolence, and to behave with moderation and affability to all his fellow-creatures. He laid upon him strong injunctions, not without a mixture of threats, to consider Fathom as the object of his peculiar regard; to respect him as the son of the count's preserver, as a Briton, a stranger, and above all, an helpless orphan, to whom the rights of hospitality were doubly due.

Such admonitions were not lost upon the youth, who under the rough husk of his personal exhibition, possessed a large share of generous sensibility: without any formal professions to his father, he resolved to govern himself according to his remonstrances; and far from conceiving the least spark of animosity against Fathom, he looked upon the poor boy as the innocent cause of his disgrace, and redoubled his kindness towards him, that his honour might never again be called in question, upon the same subject. Nothing is more liable to misconstruction than an act of uncommon generosity; one half of the world mistake the motive, from want of ideas to conceive an instance of beneficence, that soars so high above the level of their own sentiments; and the rest suspect it of something sinister or selfish, from the suggestions of their own sordid and vicious inclinations. The young count subjected himself to such misinterpretation, among those who observed the increased warmth of civility and complaisance in his behaviour to Ferdinand: they ascribed it to his desire of still profiting by our adventurer's superior talents, by which alone they supposed him enabled to maintain any degree of reputation at school; or to the fear of being convicted by him of some misdemeanour of which he knew himself guilty. These suspicions were not effaced by the conduct of Ferdinand, who, when examined on the subject, managed his answers in such a manner, as confirmed their conjectures, while he pretended to refute them, and at the same time acquired to himself credit for his extraordinary discretion and self-denial.

If he exhibited such a proof of sagacity in the twelfth year of his age, what might not be expected from his finesse, in the maturity of his faculties and experience? Thus secured in the good graces of the whole family, he saw the days of his puerility[4] glide along in the most agreeable elapse of caresses and amusement. He never fairly plunged into the stream of school education; but, by floating on the surface, imbibed a small tincture of those different sciences, which his master pretended to teach; in short, he resembled those vagrant swallows that skim along the level of some pool or river, without venturing to wet one feather in their wings, except in the accidental pursuit of an inconsiderable fly. Yet, though his capacity or inclination was unsuited for studies of this kind, he did not fail to manifest a perfect genius in the acquisition of other more profitable arts. Over and above the accomplishments of address, for which he hath been already celebrated, he excelled all his fellows in his dexterity at fives[5] and billiards; was altogether unrivalled in his skill at draughts[6] and backgammon; began even at these years, to understand the moves and schemes of chess; and made himself a meer adept[7] in the mystery of cards, which he learned in the course of his assiduities and attention to the females of the house.

CHAPTER VI.

He meditates schemes of importance.

It was in these parties, that he attracted the notice and friendship of his patron's daughter, a girl by two years older than himself, who was not insensible to his qualifications, and looked upon him with the most favourable eyes of prepossession. Whether or not he at this period of his life, began to project plans for availing himself of her susceptibility, is uncertain; but without all doubt, he cultivated her esteem with as obsequious and submissive attention, as if he had already formed the design which in his advanced age, he attempted to put in execution.

Divers circumstances conspired to promote him in the favour of this young lady; the greenness of his years, secured him from any suspicion of sallacious aim; so that he was indulged in frequent opportunities of conversing with his young mistress, whose parents encouraged this communication, by which they hoped she would improve in speaking the language of her father. Such connexions naturally produce intimacy and friendship. Fathom's person was agreeable, his talents calculated for the meridian of those parties, and his manners so engaging, that there would have been no just subject for wonder, had he made an impression upon the tender unexperienced heart of Mademoiselle de Melvil, whose beauty was not so attractive as to extinguish his hope, in raising up a number of formidable rivals; though her expectations of fortune were such as commonly lend additional lustre to personal merit.

All these considerations were so many steps towards the success of Ferdinand's pretensions; and though he cannot be supposed to have perceived them at first, he in the sequel, seemed perfectly well apprized of his advantages, and used them to the full extent of his faculties. Observing that she delighted in music, he betook himself to the study of that art, and by dint of application and a tolerable ear, learned of himself to accompany her with a german flute,[1] while she sung and played upon the harpsichord. The count seeing his inclination, and the progress he had made, resolved that his capacity should not be lost for want of cultivation; and accordingly provided him with a master, by whom he was instructed in the principles of the art, and soon became a proficient in playing upon the violin.

In the practice of these improvements and avocations, and in attendance upon his young master, whom he took care never to disoblige or neglect, he attained to the age of sixteen, without feeling the least abatement in the friendship and generosity of those upon whom he depended; but, on the contrary, receiving every day fresh marks of their bounty and regard. He had before this time, been smit with the ambition of making a conquest of the young lady's heart; and foresaw manifold advantages to himself, in becoming son in law to count Melvil, who, he never doubted, would soon be reconciled to the match, if once it could be effectuated without his knowledge. Altho' he thought he had great reason to believe that Mademoiselle looked upon him with an eye of peculiar favour, his disposition was happily tempered with an ingredient of caution, that hindered him from acting with precipitation, and he had discerned in the young lady's deportment certain indications of lofti-ness and pride, which kept him in the utmost vigilance of circumspection; for, he knew that by a premature declaration, he should run the risque of forfeiting all the advantages he had gained, and blasting those expectations that now blossomed so gaily in his heart.

Restricted by these reflections, he acted at a wary distance, and deter-mined to proceed by the method of sap,[2] and summoning all his artifice and attractions to his aid, employed them under the insidious cover of profound respect, in order to undermine those bulwarks of haughtiness or discretion, which, otherwise, might have rendered his approaches to her impracticable. With a view to inhance the value of his company, and sound her sentiments at the same time, he became more reserved than usual, and seldomer engaged in her parties of music and cards; yet in the midst of his reserve he never failed in those demonstrations of reverence and regard, which he knew perfectly well how to express; but devised such excuses for his absence, as she could not help admitting. In consequence of this affected shyness, she more than once, gently chid him for his neglect and indifference, observing, with an ironical air, that he was now too much of a man to be entertained with such effeminate diversions; but her reproofs were pronounced with too much ease and good humour to be agreeable to our hero, who desired to see her ruffled and chagrined at his absence, and to hear himself rebuked with an angry affectation of disdain. This effort, therefore, he reinforced with the most captivating carriage he could assume, in those hours which he now so sparingly bestowed upon his mistress; he regaled her with all the entertaining stories he could learn or invent, particularly such as he thought would justify and recommend the levelling power of love, that knows no distinctions of fortune. He sung nothing but tender airs and passionate complaints, composed by desponding or despairing swains; and to render his performances of this kind the more pathetic, interlarded them with some seasonable sighs, while the tears which he had ever at command, stood collected in either eye.

It was impossible for her to overlook such studied emotions; she in a jocose manner, taxed him with having lost his heart, rallied the excess of his passion, and in a merry strain undertook to be an advocate for his love. Her behaviour was still wide of his wish and expectation: he thought she would, in consequence of her discovery, have betrayed some interested symptom; that her face would have undergone some favourable suffusion; that her tongue would have faultered, her breast heaved, and her whole deportment betokened internal agitation and disorder; in which case, he meant to profit by the happy impression, and declare himself before she could possibly recollect the dictates of her pride.[3] Baffled however in his endeavours, by the serenity of the young lady, which he still deemed equivocal, he had recourse to another experiment, by which he believed, he should make a discovery of her sentiments, beyond all possibility of doubt. One day, while he accompanied Mademoiselle in her exercises of music, he pretended all of a sudden, to be taken ill, and counterfeited a swoon in her apartment. Surprised at this accident, she screamed aloud, but far from running to his assistance, with the transports and distraction of a lover, she ordered her maid, who was present, to support his head, and went in person to call for more help: he was accordingly removed to his own chamber, where, willing to be still more certified of her inclinations, he prolonged the farce, and lay groaning under the pretence of a severe fever.

The whole family was alarmed upon this occasion; for as we have already observed, he was an universal favourite. He was immediately visited by the old count and his lady, who expressed the utmost concern at his distemper, ordered him to be carefully attended, and sent for a physician, without loss of time. The young gentleman would scarce stir from his bed-side, where he ministred unto him with all the demonstrations of brotherly affection; and miss exhorted him to keep up his spirits, with many expressions of unreserved sympathy and regard: nevertheless, he saw nothing in her behaviour, but what might be naturally expected from common friendship, and a compassionate disposition, and was very much mortified at his disappointment.

Whether the miscarriage actually affected his constitution, or the doctor happened to be mistaken in his diagnostics, we shall not pretend to determine; but the patient was certainly treated Secundum Artem,[4] and all his complaints in a little time realized; for the physician, like a true graduate,[5] had an eye to the apothecary, in his prescriptions;[6] and such was the concern and scrupulous care with which our hero was attended, that the orders of the faculty were performed with the utmost punctuality. He was blooded, vomited, purged and blistered in the usual forms,[7] (for the physicians of Hungary are generally as well skilled in the arts of their occupation, as any other leeches under the sun) and swallowed a whole dispensary of bolusses, draughts and apozems,[8] by which means he became fairly delirious in three days, and so untractable, that he could be no longer managed according to rule; otherwise in all likelihood, the world would never have enjoyed the benefit of these adventures. In short, his constitution, though unable to cope with two such formidable antagonists, as the doctor, and the disease he had conjured up, was no sooner rid of the one, than it easily got the better of the other, and though Ferdinand after all, found his grand aim unaccomplished, his malady was productive of a consequence, which though he had not foreseen it, he did not fail to convert to his own use and advantage.

CHAPTER VII.

Engages in partnership with a female associate, in
order to put his talents in action.

While he displayed his qualifications in order to intrap the heart of his young mistress, he had unwittingly enslaved the affections of her maid. This attendant was also a favourite of the young lady, and though her senior by two or three good years at least, unquestionably her superior in point of personal beauty; she moreover possessed a good stock of cunning and discernment, and was furnished by nature with a very amorous complexion. These circumstances being premised, the reader will not be surprised to find her smitten by those uncommon qualifications which we have celebrated in young Fathom. She had in good sooth, long sighed in secret, under the powerful influence of his charms, and practised upon him all those little arts, by which a woman strives to attract the admiration and ensnare the heart of a man she loves; but, all his faculties were employed upon the plan which he had already projected; that was the goal of his whole attention, to which all his measures tended; and whether or not he perceived the impression he had made upon Teresa, he never gave her the least reason to believe he was conscious of his victory, until he found himself baffled in his design upon the heart of her mistress. She therefore persevered in her distant attempts to allure him, with the usual coquetries of dress and address, and in the sweet hope of profiting by his susceptibility, made shift to suppress her feelings, and keep her passion within bounds; until his supposed danger alarmed her fears, and raised such a tumult within her breast, that she could no longer conceal her love, but gave a loose to her sorrow in the most immoderate expressions of anguish and affliction, and while his delirium lasted, behaved with all the agitation of a despairing shepherdess.

Ferdinand was, or pretended to be, the last person in the family, who understood the situation of her thoughts; when he perceived her passion, he entered into deliberation with himself, and tasked his reflexion and foresight, in order to discover how best he might convert this conquest to his own advantage. Here, then, that we may neglect no opportunity of doing justice to our hero, it will be proper to observe, that howsoever unapt his understanding might be to receive and retain the usual culture of the schools, he was naturally a genius self-taught, in point of sagacity and invention. He dived into the characters of mankind, with a penetration peculiar to himself, and had he been admitted as a pupil in any political academy, would have certainly become one of the ablest statesmen in Europe.

Having revolved all the probable consequences of such a connexion, he determined to prosecute an amour with the lady whose affection he had subdued; because he hoped to interest her as an auxiliary in his grand scheme upon Mademoiselle, which he did not as yet think proper to lay aside; for, he was not more ambitious in the plan, than indefatigable in the prosecution of it. He knew it would be impossible to execute his aims upon the count's daughter, under the eye of Teresa, whose natural discernment would be whetted with jealousy, and who would watch his conduct, and thwart his progress with all the vigilance and spite of a slighted maiden. On the other hand, he did not doubt of being able to bring her over to his interest, by the influence he had already gained, or might afterwards acquire over her passions; in which case, she would effectually espouse his cause, and employ her good offices with her mistress, in his behalf: besides, he was induced by another motive, which though secondary, did not fail in this case to have an effect upon his determination. He looked upon Teresa with the eyes of appetite, which he longed to gratify: for he was not at all dead to the instigations of the flesh, though he had philosophy enough to resist them, when he thought they interfered with his interest. Here the case was quite different: his desire happened to be upon the side of his advantage, and therefore, resolving to indulge it, he no sooner found himself in a condition to manage such an adventure, than he began to make gradual advances in point of warmth and particular complacency to the love-sick maid.

He first of all, thanked her in the most grateful terms, for the concern she had manifested at his distemper, and the kind services he had received from her, during the course of it; he treated her upon all occasions, with unusual affability and regard, assiduously courted her acquaintance and conversation, and contracted an intimacy that, in a little time, produced a declaration of love. Although her heart was too much intendered[1] to hold out against all the forms of assault, far from yielding at discretion, she stood upon honourable terms, with great obstinacy of punctilio, and while she owned he was master of her inclinations, gave him to understand with a peremptory and resolute air, that he should never make a conquest of her virtue: observing, that if the passion he professed was genuine, he would not scruple to give such a proof of it, as would at once convince her of his sincerity; and that he could have no just cause to refuse her that satisfaction, she being his equal in point of birth and situation: for, if he was the companion and favourite of the young count, she was the friend and confidante of Mademoiselle.

He acknowledged the strength of her argument, and that her condescension was greater than his deserts; but objected against the proposal, as infinitely prejudicial to the fortunes of them both. He represented the state of dependance in which they mutually stood; their utter incapacity to support one another, under the consequences of a precipitate match, clandestinely made, without the consent and concurrence of their patrons: he displayed, with great eloquence, all those gay expectations they had reason to entertain, from that eminent degree of favour which they had already secured in the family; and set forth, in the most alluring colours, those enchanting scenes of pleasures they might enjoy, in each other, without that disagreeable consciousness of a nuptial chain, provided she would be his associate in the execution of a plan, which he had projected for their reciprocal convenience.

Having thus inflamed her love of pleasure and curiosity, he, with great caution, hinted his design upon the young lady's fortune, and perceiving her listening with the most greedy attention, and perfectly ripe for the conspiracy, he disclosed his intention at full length, assuring her, with the most solemn protestations of love and attachment, that could he once make himself legal possessor of an estate which Mademoiselle inherited, by the will of a deceased aunt, his dear Teresa should reap the happy fruits of his affluence; and wholly engross his time and attention.

Such a base declaration our hero would not have ventured to make, had he not implicitly believed the damsel was as great a latitudinarian[2] as himself in point of morals and principle; and been well assured that though he should be mistaken in her way of thinking, so far as to be threatned with a detection of his purpose, he would always have it in his power to refute her accusation as meer calumny, by the character he had hitherto maintained, and the circumspection of his future conduct.

He seldom or never erred in his observations on the human heart. Teresa, instead of disapproving, relished the plan in general, with demonstrations of singular satisfaction: she, at once conceived all the advantageous consequences of such a scheme, and perceived in it, only one flaw, which, however, she did not think incurable. This defect was no other than a sufficient bond of union, by which they might be effectually tied down to their mutual interest. She foresaw that in case Ferdinand should obtain possession of the prize, he might, with great ease, deny their contract, and disavow her claim of participation. She therefore demanded security, and proposed as a preliminary of the agreement, that he should privately take her to wife, with a view to dispel all her apprehensions of his inconstancy or deceit, as such a previous engagement would be a check upon his behaviour, and keep him strictly to the letter of their contract.

He could not help subscribing to the righteousness of this proposal, which, nevertheless, he would have willingly waved, on the supposition that they could not possibly be joined in the bands of wedlock, with such secrecy as the nature of the case absolutely required. This would have been a difficulty soon removed, had the scene of the transaction been laid in the metropolis of England, where passengers are plied in the streets by clergymen, who prostitute their characters and consciences for hire, in defiance of all decency and law;[3] but in the kingdom of Hungary, ecclesiastics are more scrupulous in the exercise of their function, and the objection was, or supposed to be altogether insurmountable; so that they were fain to have recourse to an expedient, with which, after some hesitation, our she-adventurer was satisfied. They joined hands in the sight of Heaven, which they called to witness, and to judge the sincerity of their vows, and engaged in a voluntary oath to confirm their union by the sanction of the church, whenever a convenient opportunity for so doing, should occur.

The scruples of Teresa being thus removed, she admitted Ferdinand to the privileges of a husband, which he enjoyed in stolen interviews; and readily undertook to exert her whole power in promoting his suit with her young mistress, because she now considered his interest as inseparably connected with her own. Surely nothing could be more absurd or preposterous, than the articles of this covenant, which she insisted upon with such inflexibility. How could she suppose, that her pretended lover would be restrained by an oath, when the very occasion of incuring it, was an intention to act in violation of all laws human and divine; and yet such ridiculous conjuration is commonly the cement of every conspiracy, how dark, how treacherous, how impious soever it may be. A certain sign that there are some remains of religion left in the human mind, even after every moral sentiment hath abandoned it; and that the most execrable ruffian finds means to quiet the suggestions of his conscience, by some reversionary hope of heaven's forgiveness.[4]

CHAPTER VIII.

Their first attempt; with a digression which some Readers may think impertinent.

Be this as it will, our lovers, though real voluptuaries, amidst the first transports of their enjoyment, did not neglect the great political aim of their conjunction. Teresa's bed-chamber, to which our hero constantly repaired at midnight, was the scene of their deliberations, and there it was determined, that the damsel, in order to avoid suspicion, should feign herself irritated at the indifference of Ferdinand, her passion for whom, was by this time no secret in the family; and that with a view to countenance this affectation, he should upon all occasions treat her with an air of loftiness and disdain.

So screened from all imputation of fraud, she was furnished by him with artful instructions, how to sound the inclinations of her young mistress; how to recommend his person and qualifications by the sure methods of contradiction, comparison, revilings and reproach; how to watch the paroxysms of her disposition, inflame her passions, and improve, for his advantage, those moments of frailty, from which no woman is exempted. In short, this consummate politician taught his agent to poison the young lady's mind with insidious conversation, tending to inspire her with the love of guilty pleasure, to debauch her sentiments, and confound her ideas of dignity and virtue. After all, the task is not difficult to lead the unpractised heart astray, by dint of those opportunities her seducer possessed. The seeds of insinuation seasonably sown upon the warm, luxuriant soil of youth, could hardly fail of shooting up into such intemperate desires as he wanted to produce; especially when cultured and cherished in her unguarded hours, by that stimulating discourse which familiarity admits, and the looser passions ingrafted in every breast, are apt to relish and excuse.

Fathom had previously reconnoitred the ground, and discovered some marks of inflammability in Mademoiselle's constitution; her beauty was not such as to engage her in those gaieties of amusement, which could flatter her vanity, and dissipate her ideas; and she was of an age, when the little loves and young desires take possession of the fancy; he therefore concluded, that she had the more leisure to indulge those inticing images of pleasure that youth never fails to create, particularly in those who, like her, were addicted to solitude and study.

Teresa, full fraught with the wily injunctions of her confederate, took the field, and opened the campaign with such remarkable sourness in her aspect, when Ferdinand appeared, that her young lady could not help taking notice of her affected chagrin, and asked the reason of such apparent alteration in her way of thinking. Prepared for this question, the other replied in a manner calculated for giving Mademoiselle to understand, that whatever impressions Ferdinand might have formerly made on her heart, they were now altogether effaced by the pride and insolence with which he had received her advances; and that her breast now glowed with all the revenge of a slighted lover.

To evince the sincerity of this declaration, she bitterly inveighed against him, and even affected to depreciate those talents, in which she knew his chief merit to consist; hoping by these means to interest Mademoiselle's candour in his defence. So far the train succeeded: that young lady's natural love for truth was offended at the calumnies that were vented against Ferdinand in his absence. She chid her woman for the rancour of her remarks, and undertook to refute the articles of his dispraise: Teresa supported her own assertions with great obstinacy, and a dispute ensued, in which her mistress was heated into some extravagant commendations of our adventurer.

His supposed enemy did not fail to make a report of her success, and to magnify every advantage they had gained; believing in good earnest, that her lady's warmth was the effect of a real passion for the fortunate Mr. Fathom: but he himself viewed the adventure in a different light; and rightly imputed the violence of Mademoiselle's behaviour to the contradiction she had sustained from her maid; or to the fire of her natural generosity, glowing in behalf of innocence traduced. Nevertheless, he was perfectly well pleased with the nature of the contest; because, in the course of such debates, he foresaw that he should become habitually her hero, and that, in time, she would actually believe those exaggerations of his merit, which she herself had feigned for the honour of her own arguments.

This presage, founded upon that principle of self-respect, without which no individual exists, may certainly be justified by manifold occurrences in life: we ourselves have known a very pregnant example, which we shall relate, for the emolument of the reader. A certain needy author having found means to present a manuscript to one of those sons of fortune, who are dignified with the appellation of patrons, instead of reaping that applause, and advantage, with which he had regaled his fancy, had the mortification to find his performance treated with infinite irreverence and contempt: and in high dudgeon and disappointment appealed to the judgment of another critic, who, he knew, had no veneration for the first.

This common consolation, to which all baffled authors have recourse, was productive of very happy consequences to our bard: for though the opinions of both judges, concerning the piece, were altogether the same, the latter, either out of compassion to the appellant, or desire of rendering his rival ridiculous in the eye of taste, undertook to repair the misfortune, and in this manner executed the plan, in a meeting of literati, to which both these wits belonged; he who had espoused the poet's cause, having previously desired another member to bring his composition on the carpet, no sooner heard it mentioned, than he began to censure it with flagrant marks of scorn, and with an ironical air looking at its first condemner, observed that he must be furiously infected with the rage of patronizing, who could take such a deplorable performance into his protection: the sarcasm took effect.

The person against whom it was levelled, taking umbrage at his presumption, assumed an aspect of disdain, and replied with great animosity, that nothing was more easily supported than the character of a Zoilus,[1] because no production was altogether free from blemishes, and any man might pronounce against any piece by the lump, without interesting his own discernment: but to perceive the beauties of a work, it was requisite to have learning, judgment and taste; and therefore he did not wonder that the gentleman had overlooked a great many in the composition which he so contemptuously decried. A rejoinder succeeded this reply, and produced a long train of altercation, in which the gentleman who had formerly treated the book with such disrespect, now professed himself its passionate admirer, and held forth in praise of it with great warmth and elocution.[2]

Not contented with having exhibited this instance of regard, he next morning sent a message to the owner, importing that he had but superficially glanced over the manuscript, and desiring the favour of perusing it a second time; being indulged in this request, he recommended it in terms of rapture, to all his friends and dependants, and by dint of unwearied sollicitation, procured a very ample subscription for the author.[3]

But, to resume the thread of our story: Teresa's practices were not confined to simple defamation: her reproaches were contrived so as to imply some intelligence in favour of the person she reviled. In exemplifying his pertness and arrogance, she repeated his witty repartee; on pretence of blaming his ferocity, she recounted proofs of his spirit and prowess; and in explaining the source of his vanity, gave her mistress to understand, that a certain young lady of fashion was said to be enamoured of his person. Nor did this well-instructed understrapper omit those other parts of her cue, which the principal judged necessary for the furtherance of his scheme. Her conversation became less guarded, and took a freer turn than usual: she seized all opportunities of introducing little amorous stories, the greatest part of which were invented for the purposes of warming her passions, and lowering the price of chastity in her esteem; for, she represented all the young lady's cotemporaries in point of age and situation, as so many sensualists, who without scruple indulged themselves in the stolen pleasures of youth.

Mean while Ferdinand seconded these endeavours with his whole industry and address: he redoubled, if possible, his deference and respect, wheted his assiduity to the keenest edge of attention; and in short, regulated his dress, conversation and deportment, according to the fancy, turn, and prevailing humour of his young mistress. He moreover attempted to profit by her curiosity, which he knew to be truly feminine, and having culled from the library of his patron, certain dangerous books, calculated to debauch the minds of young people,[4] left them occasionally upon the table in his apartment, after having directed Teresa to pick them up, as if by accident, in his absence, and carry them off for the entertainment of Mademoiselle; nay, this crafty projector found means to furnish his associate with some mischievous preparations,[5] which were mingled in her chocolate, tea or coffee, as provocations to warm her constitution: yet, all these machinations, ingenious as they were, failed, not only in fulfilling their aim, but even in shaking the foundations of her virtue or pride, which stood their assaults, unmoved, like a strong tower built upon a rock, impregnable to all the tempestuous blasts of heaven.

Not but that the conspirators were more than once mistaken in the effects of their artifices, and disposed to applaud themselves on the progress they had made. When at any time she expressed a desire to examine those performances which were laid before her as snares to entrap her chastity, they attributed that, which was no other than curiosity, to a looseness of sentiment; and when she discovered no aversion to hear those anecdotes concerning the frailty of her neighbours, they imputed to abatement of chastity, that satisfaction which was the result of self-congratulation on her own superior virtue.

So far did the treacherous accomplice of Fathom presume upon these misconstructions, that she at length divested her tongue of all restraint, and behaved in such a manner, that the young lady confounded and incensed at her indecency and impudence, rebuked her with great severity, and commanded her to reform her discourse, on pain of being dismissed with disgrace from her service.

CHAPTER IX.

The confederates change their battery; and atchieve a remarkable adventure.

Thunderstruck at this disappointment, the confederates held a council, in order to deliberate upon the next measures that should be taken; and Ferdinand, for the present, despairing of accomplishing his grand aim, resolved to profit in another manner, by the conveniency of his situation. He represented to his help-mate, that it would be prudent for them to make hay while the sun shone,[1] as their connexion might be sooner or later discovered, and an end put to all those opportunities which they now so happily enjoyed. All principles of morality had been already excluded from their former plan; consequently, he found it an easy task to interest Teresa in any other scheme tending to their mutual advantage, howsoever wicked and perfidious it might be. He therefore, persuaded her to be his auxiliary in defrauding Mademoiselle at play, and gave her suitable directions for that purpose; and even tutored her how to abuse the trust reposed in her, by embezzling the young lady's effects, without incurring the suspicion of dishonesty.

On the supposition that every servant in the house, was not able to resist such temptation, the purse of her mistress (to which the maid had always access) was dropped in a passage, which the domestics had occasion to frequent, and Fathom posted himself in a convenient place, in order to observe the effect of his strategem. Here he was not disappointed in his conjecture. The first person who chanced to pass that way, was one of the chambermaids, with whom Teresa had lived, for some time, in a state of inveterate enmity, because the wench had failed in that homage and respect which was paid to her by the rest of the servants.

Ferdinand had in his heart espoused the quarrel of his associate, and longed for an occasion to deliver her from the malicious observance of such an antagonist; when he therefore, saw her approach, his heart throbbed with joyful expectations; but, when she snatched up the purse, and thrust it in her bosom, with all the eagerness and confusion of one determined to appropriate the windfall to her own use, his transports were altogether unspeakable. He traced her to her own apartment, whither she immediately retreated with great trepidation, and then communicated the discovery to Teresa, together with instructions how to behave in the sequel.

In conformity with these lessons, she took the first opportunity of going to Mademoiselle, and demanding money for some necessary expence, that the loss might be known, before the finder could have leisure to make any fresh conveyance of the prize; and in the mean time, Ferdinand kept a strict eye upon the motions of the chambermaid. The young lady having rummaged her pockets in vain, expressed some surprize at the loss of her purse, upon which her attendant gave indications of extreme amazement and concern; she said, it could not possibly be lost; intreated her to search her escrutore,[2] while she herself ran about the room, prying into every corner, with all the symptoms of fear and distraction. Having made this unsuccessful inquiry, she pretended to shed a flood of tears, bewailing her own fate, in being near the person of any lady, who met with such a misfortune, by which, she observed, her character might be called in question: she produced her own keys, and begged upon her knees, that her chamber and boxes might be searched without delay.

In a word, she demeaned herself so artfully, upon this occasion, that her mistress, who never entertained the least doubt of her integrity, now looked upon her as a miracle of fidelity and attachment, and was at infinite pains to console her for the accident which had happened; protesting that for her own part, the loss of the money should never affect her with a moment's uneasiness, if she could retrieve a certain medal which she had long kept in her purse, as a remembrance of her deceased aunt, from whom she received it in a present.

Fathom entered accidentally in the midst of this well-acted scene, and perceiving the agitation of the maid, and the concern of the mistress, desired, in a respectful manner, to know the cause of their disorder. Before the young lady had time to make him acquainted with the circumstances of the case, his accomplice exclaimed in an affected passion, "Mr. Fathom, my lady has lost her purse; and as no persons in the family are so much about her, as you and I, you must give me leave in my own justification, to insist upon Mademoiselle's ordering the apartments of us both to be searched without loss of time: here are my pockets and my keys, and you cannot scruple to give her the same satisfaction; for innocence has nothing to fear."

Miss Melvile reprimanded her sharply for her unmannerly zeal; and Ferdinand eying her with a look of disdain, "Madam," said he, "I approve of your proposal; but before I undergo such mortification, I would advise Mademoiselle to subject the two chambermaids to such inquiry: as they also have access to the apartments, and are, I apprehend, as likely as you or I, to behave in such a scandalous manner."

The young lady declared that she was too well satisfied of Teresa's honesty and Ferdinand's honour, to harbour the least suspicion of either, and that she would sooner die than disgrace them so far as to comply with the proposal the former had made; but as she saw no reason for exempting the inferior servants from that examination, which Fathom advised, she would forthwith put it in execution. The chambermaids being accordingly summoned, she calmly asked if either of them had accidentally found the purse she had dropped, and both replying in the negative, she assumed an air of severity and determination, and demanding their keys, threatned to examine their trunks on the instant.

The guilty Abigail,[3] who, though an Hungarian, was not inferior, in point of effrontery, to any one of the sisterhood in England, no sooner heard this menace, than she affected an air of affronted innocence, thanked God she had lived in many reputable families, and been trusted with untold gold; but was never before suspected of theft; that the other maid might do as she should think proper, and be mean-spirited enough to let her things be tumbled topsy-turvy and exposed; but, for her own part, if she should be used in that inhuman and disgraceful manner, she would not stay another hour in the house; and in conclusion said, that Mademoiselle had more reason to look sharp after those who enjoyed the greatest share of her favour, than believe their malicious insinuations against innocent people whom they were well known to hate and defame.

This declaration implying an hint to the prejudice of Teresa, far from diverting miss Melvile from her purpose, served only to inhance the character of the accused in her opinion, and to confirm her suspicion of the accuser, of whom she again demanded her keys, protesting, that should she prove refractory, the count himself should take cognizance of the affair, whereas if she would deal ingenuously, she should have no cause to repent of her confession. So saying, she desired our adventurer to take the trouble of calling up some of the men servants; upon which the conscious criminal began to tremble, and falling upon her knees, acknowledged her guilt, and implored the forgiveness of her young mistress.

Teresa seizing this occasion to signalize her generosity, joined in the request, and the offender was pardoned, after having restored the purse, and promised in the sight of Heaven, that the devil should never again intice her to the commission of such a crime. This adventure fully answered all the purposes of our politician; it established the opinion of his fellow-labourer's virtue, beyond the power of accident or information to shake, and set up a false beacon to mislead the sentiments of Mademoiselle, in case she should for the future meet with the like misfortune.

CHAPTER X.

*They proceed to levy contributions with great success,
until our hero sets out with the young count for
Vienna, where he enters into league with another
adventurer.*

Under this secure cover, Teresa levied contributions upon her mistress with great success. Some trinket was missing every day; the young lady's patience began to fail, the faithful attendant was overwhelmed with consternation, and with the appearance of extreme chagrin, demanded her dismission, affirming that these things were certainly effected by some person in the family, with a view of murthering her precious reputation. Miss Melvile, not without difficulty, quieted her vexation with assurances of inviolable confidence and esteem, until a pair of diamond ear-rings vanished, when Teresa could no longer keep her affliction within bounds. Indeed this was an event of more consequence, than all the rest which had happened, for the jewels were valued at five hundred florins. [1]

Mademoiselle was accordingly alarmed to such a degree, that she made her mother acquainted with her loss, and that good lady, who was an excellent œconomist, did not fail to give indications of extraordinary concern. She asked, if her daughter had reason to suspect any individual in the family, and if she was perfectly confident of her own woman's integrity: upon which Mademoiselle, with many encomiums on the fidelity and attachment of Teresa, recounted the adventure of the chambermaid, who immediately underwent a strict enquiry, and was even committed to prison, on the strength of her former misdemeanour. Our adventurer's mate insisted upon undergoing the same tryal with the rest of the domesticks, and as usual comprehended Fathom in her insinuations; while he seconded the proposal, and privately counselled the old lady to introduce Teresa to the magistrate of the place. By these pre-concerted recriminations, they escaped all suspicion of collusion. After a fruitless inquiry, the prisoner was discharged from her confinement, and turned out of the service of the count, in whose private opinion the character of no person suffered so much, as that of his own son, whom he suspected of having embezzled the jewels, for the use of a certain Inamorata, who, at that time, was said to have captivated his affections.

The old gentleman felt upon this occasion, all that internal anguish which a man of honour may be supposed to suffer, on account of a son's degeneracy; and without divulging his sentiments, or even hinting his suspicions to the youth himself, determined to detach him at once from such dangerous connexions, by sending him forthwith to Vienna, on pretence of finishing his exercises at the academy, [2] and ushering him into acquaintance with the great world. Though he would not be thought by the young gentleman himself, to harbour the least doubt of his morals, he did not scruple to unbosom himself on that subject to Ferdinand, whose sagacity and virtue he held in great veneration. This indulgent patron, expressed himself in the most pathetic terms, on the untoward disposition of his son; he told Fathom that he should accompany Renaldo (that was the youth's name) not only as a companion, but a preceptor and pattern; conjured him to assist his tutor in superintending his conduct, and to reinforce the governor's precepts, by his own example; to inculcate upon him, the most delicate punctilio's of honour, and decoy him into extravagance, rather than leave the least illiberal sentiment in his heart.

Our crafty adventurer, with demonstrations of the utmost sensibility, acknowledged the great goodness of the count in reposing such confidence in his integrity; which, as he observed, none but the worst of villains could abuse; and fervently wished that he might no longer exist, than he should continue to remember and resent[3] the obligations he owed to his kind benefactor. While preparations were making for their departure, our hero held a council with his associate, whom he enriched with many sage instructions touching her future operations; he at the same time disburthened her of all or the greatest part of the spoils she had won, and after having received divers marks of bounty from the count and his lady, together with a purse from his young mistress, he set out for Vienna in the eighteenth year of his age, with Renaldo and his governor, who were provided with letters of recommendation to some of the count's friends belonging to the imperial court.

Such a favourable introduction could not fail of being advantageous to a youth of Ferdinand's specious accomplishments; for he was considered as the young count's companion, admitted into his parties, and included in all the entertainments to which Renaldo was invited. He soon distinguished himself by his activity and address, in the course of those exercises that were taught at the academy of which he was pupil; his manners were so engaging as to attract the acquaintance of his fellow-students, and his conversation being sprightly and inoffensive, grew into very great request; in a word, he and the young count formed a remarkable contrast, which in the eye of the world, redounded to his advantage.

They were certainly, in all respects, the reverse of each other. Renaldo, under a total defect of exterior cultivation, possessed a most excellent understanding, with every virtue that dignifies the human heart; while the other, beneath a most agreeable outside, with an inaptitude and aversion to letters, concealed an amazing fund of villainy and ingratitude. Hitherto, his observation had been confined to a narrow sphere, and his reflections, though surprizingly just and acute, had not attained to that maturity, which age and experience give: but now, his perceptions began to be more distinct, and extended to a thousand objects which had never before come under his cognizance.

He had formerly imagined, but was now fully persuaded, that the sons of men preyed upon one another, and such was the end and condition of their being. Among the principal figures of life, he observed few or no characters that did not bear a strong analogy to the savage tyrants of the wood. One resembled a tyger in fury and rapaciousness; a second prowled about like an hungry wolf, seeking whom he might devour;[4] a third acted the part of a jackall, in beating the bush for game to his voracious employer; and a fourth imitated the wily fox, in practising a thousand crafty ambuscades for the destruction of the ignorant and unwary. This last was the department of life for which he found himself best qualified, by nature and inclination, and he accordingly resolved that his talent should not rust in his possession.[5] He was already pretty well versed in all the sciences of play; but, he had every day, occasion to see these arts carried to such a surprising pitch of finesse and dexterity, as discouraged him from building his schemes on that foundation.

He therefore determined to fascinate the judgment, rather than the eyes of his fellow-creatures, by a continual exercise of that gift of deceiving, with which he knew himself endued to an unrivalled degree; and to acquire un-bounded influence with those who might be subservient to his interest, by an assiduous application to their prevailing passions. Not that play was alto-gether left out in the projection of his œconomy: though he engaged himself very little in the executive part of gaming,[6] he had not been long in Vienna, when he entered into league with a genius of that kind, whom he distin-guished among the pupils of the academy, and who indeed, had taken up his habitation in that place, with a view to pillage the provincials on their first arrival in town, before they could be armed with proper circumspection to preserve their money, or have time to dispose of it in any other shape.

Similar characters naturally attract each other, and people of our hero's principles are, of all others, the most apt to distinguish their own likeness wheresoever it occurs; because they always keep the faculty of discerning in full exertion. It was in consequence of this mutual alertness, that Ferdinand and the stranger, who was a native of Tyrol,[7] perceived themselves reflected in the dispositions of each other, and immediately entered into an offensive and defensive alliance: our adventurer undertaking for the articles of intelli-gence, countenance and counsel; and his associate charging himself with the risque of execution.

CHAPTER XI.

Fathom makes various efforts in the world of gallantry.

Thus connected they began to hunt in couples; and Fathom in order to profit by the alliance, with a good grace, contrived a small scheme that succeeded to his wish. Renaldo being one night intoxicated in the course of a merry-making with his fellow pupils, from which Fathom had purposely ab-sented himself, was by the Tyroleze so artfully provoked to play, that he could not resist the temptation, but engaged at pass-dice[1] with that fell adversary, who in less than an hour, stripped him of a pretty round sum. Next day, when the young gentleman recovered the use of his reflection, he was sensibly chagrin'd at the folly and precipitation of his own conduct, an account of which he communicated in confidence to our hero, with demonstrations of infinite shame and concern.

Ferdinand having moralized upon the subject with great sagacity, and sharply inveighed against the Tyroleze, for the unfair advantage he had taken, retired to his closet and wrote the following billet, which was immediately sent to his ally.

"The obligations I owe, and the attachments I feel to the count de Melvile, will not suffer me to be an idle spectator of the wrongs offered to his son, in the dishonourable use, I understand, you made last night of his unguarded hours: I therefore insist upon your making immediate restitution of the booty which you so unjustly got; otherwise I expect you will meet me upon the ramparts, near the bastion de la Port-Neuve, to-morrow morning at daybreak, in order to justify with your sword, the finesse you have practised upon the friend of

FERDINAND de FATHOM."[2]

The gamester no sooner received this intimation, than according to the plan which had been preconcerted betwixt the author and him, he went to the apartment of Renaldo, and presenting the sum of money which he had defrauded him of, the preceding night, told him with a stern countenance, that though it was a just acquisition, he scorned to avail himself of his good fortune against any person who entertained the smallest doubt of his honour.

The young count, surprized at this address, rejected his offer with disdain, and desired to know the meaning of such an unexpected declaration. Upon which, the other produced Ferdinand's billet, and threatned in very high terms, to meet the stripling according to his invitation, and chastise him severely for his presumption. The consequence of this explanation is obvious. Renaldo imputing the officiousness of Fathom to the zeal of his friendship, interposed in the quarrel, which was amicably compromised, not a little to the honour of our adventurer, who thus obtained an opportunity of displaying his courage and integrity, without the least hazard to his person; while at the same time, his confederate recommended himself to the esteem of the young count, by his spirited behaviour on this occasion; so that Renaldo being less shy of his company for the future, the Tyroleze had the fairer opportunities to prosecute his designs upon the young gentleman's purse.

It would be almost superfluous to say that these were not neglected. The son of count Melvile was not deficient in point of penetration: but, his whole study was at that time, engrossed by the care of his education; and he had sometimes recourse to play, as to an amusement by which he sought to unbend the severity of his attention: no wonder then, that he fell a prey to an artful gamester, who had been regularly trained to the profession, and made it the sole study of his life; especially as the Hungarian was remarkable for a warmth of temper, which a knight of the post[3] always knows how to manage for his own advantage.

In the course of these operations, Fathom was a very useful correspondent; he instructed the Tyroleze in the peculiarities of Renaldo's disposition, and made him acquainted with the proper seasons for profiting by his dexterity. Ferdinand, for example, who by the authority derived to him from the injunctions of the old count, sometimes took upon himself the office of an adviser, cunningly chose to counsel the son, at those conjunctures, when he knew him least able to bear such expostulation. Advice improperly administred, generally acts in diametrical opposition to the purpose for which it is supposed to be given: at least this was the case with the young gentleman, who inflamed by the reproof of such a tutor, used to obey the dictates of his resentment, in an immediate repetition of that conduct which our adventurer had taken the liberty to disapprove; and the gamester was always at hand, to minister unto his indignation. By these means he was disencumbered of divers considerable remittances, with which his father chearfully supplied him, on the supposition that they were spent with taste and liberality, under the direction of our adventurer.

But Ferdinand's views were not confined to the narrow field of this alliance: he attempted divers enterprizes in the world of gallantry, conscious of his own personal qualifications, and never doubting that he could insinuate himself into the good graces of some married lady about court, or lay an opulent dowager under contribution. But he met with an obstacle in his endeavours of this kind, which all his art was unable to surmount. This was no other than the obscurity of his birth, and the want of a title, without which no person in that country lays claim to the privileges of a gentleman. Had he foreseen this inconvenience, he might have made shift to obviate the consequences, by obtaining permission to appear in the character of the count's kinsman: though, in all probability, such an expedient would not have been extremely agreeable to the old gentleman, who was very tenacious of the honour of his family: nevertheless, his generosity might have been prevailed upon, to indulge Fathom with such a pretext, in consideration of the youth's supposed attachment, and the obligations for which he deemed himself indebted to his deceased mother.

True it is, Ferdinand, upon his first arrival at Vienna, had been admitted into fashionable company, on the footing of Renaldo's companion, because no body suspected the defect of his pedigree; and even after a report had been circulated to the prejudice of his extraction, by the industry of a lacquey who attended the young count, there were not wanting many young people of distinction, who still favoured him with their countenance and correspondence: but, he was no longer invited to private families, in which only he could expect to profit by his address among the ladies, and had the mortification of finding himself frequently excepted from parties which were expresly calculated for the entertainment of the young count. Luckily, his spirit was so pliant as to sustain these slights, without being much dejected: instead of repining at the loss of that respect which had been paid to him at first, he endeavoured with all his might, to preserve the little that still remained, and resolved to translate into an humbler sphere, that gallantry which he had no longer opportunities of displaying in the world of rank and fashion.

CHAPTER XII.

*He effects a lodgment in the house of a rich
Jeweller.*

In consequence of this determination, he to the uttermost exerted his good humour among the few friends of consequence his fortune had left, and even carried his complaisance so far, as to become the humble servant of their pleasures; while he attempted to extend his acquaintance in an inferior path of life, where he thought his talents would shine more conspicuous than at the assemblies of the great, and conduce more effectually to the interest of all his designs. Nor did he find himself disappointed in that expectation, sanguine as it was. He soon found means to be introduced to the house of a wealthy bourgeois, where every individual was charmed with his easy air and extraordinary qualifications. He accommodated himself surprisingly to the

humours of the whole family; smoaked tobacco, swallowed wine and discoursed of stones with the husband, who was a rich jeweller; sacrificed himself to the pride and loquacity of the wife, and played upon the violin, and
sung alternately, for the amusement of his only daughter, a buxom lass,
nearly of his own age, the fruit of a former marriage.

It was not long before Ferdinand had reason to congratulate himself on the
footing he had gained in this society. He had expected to find, and in a little
time actually discovered that mutual jealousy and rancour, which almost always subsist between a daughter and her step-dame, inflamed with all the
virulence of female emulation; for the disparity in their ages, served only to
render them the more inveterate rivals in the desire of captivating the other
sex. Our adventurer having deliberated upon the means of converting this
animosity to his own advantage, saw no method for this purpose so feasible as
that of making his approaches to the hearts of both, by ministring to each in
private, food for their reciprocal envy and malevolence: because he well knew
that no road lies so direct and open to a woman's heart, as that of gratifying
her passions of vanity and resentment.

When he had an opportunity of being particular with the mother, he expressed his concern for having unwittingly incurred the displeasure of Mademoiselle, which, he observed, was obvious in every circumstance of her behaviour towards him; protesting he was utterly innocent of all intention of
offending her; and that he could not account for his disgrace, any other way,
than by supposing she took umbrage at the direction of his chief regards
towards her mother-in-law, which, he owned, was altogether involuntary,
being wholly influenced by that lady's superior charms and politeness.

Such a declaration was perfectly well calculated for the meridian of a dame
like her, who with all the intoxication of unenlightened pride, and an increased appetite for pleasure, had begun to find herself neglected, and even to
believe that her attractions were actually in the wane. She very graciously
consoled our gallant for the mishap of which he complained; representing
Wilhelmina (that was the daughter's name) as a pert, illiterate, envious baggage, of whose disgust he ought to make no consideration; then she recounted
many instances of her own generosity to that young lady, with the returns of
malice and ingratitude she had made; and lastly, enumerated all the imperfec-
tions of her person, education, and behaviour; that he might see with what
justice the gypsy pretended to vye with those who had been distinguished by
the approbation, and even gallantry of the best people in Vienna.

Having thus established himself her confident and gossip, he knew his next
step of promotion would necessarily be to the degree of her lover; and in that

belief, resolved to play the same game with Mademoiselle Wilhelmina, whose complexion was very much a-kin to that of her step-mother: indeed they resembled each other too much to live upon any terms of friendship or even decorum. Fathom, in order to enjoy a private conversation with the young lady, never failed to repeat his visit every afternoon, 'till at length, he had the pleasure of finding her disengaged, the jeweller being occupied among his workmen, and his wife gone to assist at a lying-in.

Our adventurer and the daughter had already exchanged their vows, by the expressive language of the eyes; he had even declared himself in some tender ejaculations which had been softly whispered in her ear, when he could snatch an opportunity of venting them, unperceived; nay, he had upon divers occasions, gently squeezed her fair hand, on pretence of tuning her harpsichord, and been favoured with returns of the same cordial pressure: so that instead of accosting her with the fearful hesitation and reserve of a timid swain, he told her, after the exercise of the doux-yeux,[1] that he was come to confer with her upon a subject that nearly concerned her peace; and asked if she had not observed of late, an evident abatement of friendship in her mother's behaviour to him, whom she had formerly treated with such marks of favour and respect. Mademoiselle would not pay so ill a compliment to her own discernment as to say she had not perceived the alteration, which, on the contrary, she owned was extremely palpable; nor was it difficult to divine the cause of such estranged looks. This remark was accompanied with an irresistible glance, she smiled inchanting, the colour deepened on her cheeks, her breast began to heave, and her whole frame underwent a most agreeable confusion.

Ferdinand was not a man to let such a favourable conjuncture pass unregarded. "Yes, charming Wilhelmina!" exclaimed the politician in an affected rapture, "the cause is as conspicuous as your attractions. She hath in spite of all my circumspection, perceived that passion which it is not in my power to conceal, and in consequence of which, I now declare myself your devoted adorer; or, conscious of your superior excellence, her jealousy hath taken the alarm, and though stung with conjecture only, repines at the triumph of your perfections. How far this spirit of malignity may be inflamed to my prejudice, I know not: perhaps as this is the first, it may be also the last opportunity, I shall have of avowing the dearest sentiments of my heart, to the fair object that inspired them; in a word, I may be for ever excluded from your presence. Excuse me then, divine creature! from the practice of those unnecessary forms, which I should take pride in observing, were I indulged with the ordinary privileges of an honourable lover; and once for all, accept the homage of an heart overflowing with love and admiration. Yes, adorable

Wilhelmina! I am dazzled with your supernatural beauty; your other accomplishments strike me with wonder and awe. I am enchanted by the graces of your deportment, ravished with the charms of your conversation; and there is a certain tenderness of benevolence in that endearing aspect, which, I trust will not fail to melt with sympathy at the emotions of a faithful slave like me."

So saying, he threw himself upon his knees, and seizing her plump hand, pressed it to his lips with all the violence of real transport. The nymph, whose passions nature had filled to the brim, could not hear such a rhapsody unmoved: being an utter stranger to addresses of this kind, she understood every word of it, in the literal acceptation; she believed implicitly in the truth of the encomiums he had bestowed, and thought it reasonable he should be rewarded for the justice he had done to her qualifications, which had hitherto been almost altogether over-looked: in short, her heart began to thaw, and her face to hang out the flag of capitulation, which was no sooner perceived by our hero, than he renewed his attack with redoubled fervour, pronouncing in a most vehement tone, "Light of my eyes, and empress of my soul! behold me prostrate at your feet, waiting with the most pious resignation, for that sentence from your lips, on which my future happiness and misery must altogether depend. Not with more reverence does the unhappy bashaw[2] kiss the Sultan's letter that contains his doom, than I will submit to your fatal determination. Speak then, angelic sweetness! for, never, ah never will I rise from this suppliant posture, until I am encouraged to live and hope. No! if you refuse to smile upon my passion, here shall I breathe the last sighs of a despairing lover: here shall this faithful sword do the last office to its unfortunate master, and shed the blood of the truest heart that ever felt the cruel pangs of disappointed love."

The young lady, well nigh overcome by this effusion, which brought the tears into her eyes, "Enough, enough," cried she, interrupting him, "sure you men were created for the ruin of our sex." "Ruin," re-echoed Fathom, "talk not of ruin and Wilhelmina! let these terms be for ever parted, far as the east and west asunder! let ever smiling peace attend her steps, and love and joy still wanton in her train! Ruin indeed, shall wait upon her enemies, if such there be, and those love-lorn wretches who pine with anguish under her disdain: grant me, kind Heaven a more propitious boon: direct her genial regards to one whose love is without example, and whose constancy is unparalleled: bear witness to my constancy and faith, ye verdant hills, ye fertile plains, ye shady groves, ye purling streams: and if I prove untrue, ah! let me never find a solitary willow or a bubling brook, by help of which I may be enabled to put a period to my wretched life."[3]

Here this excellent actor began to sob most piteously, and the tender-

hearted Wilhelmina, unable longer to withstand his moving tale, with a repetition of the interjection ah! gently dropp'd into his arms. This was the
beginning of a correspondence that soon rose to a very interesting pitch; and
they forthwith concerted measures for carrying it on, without the knowledge
or suspicion of her mother-in-law. Nevertheless the young lady, vanquished
as she was, and unskilled in the ways of men, would not all at once yield at
discretion; but insisted upon those terms, without which no woman's reputation can be secured. Our lover far from seeking to evade the proposal, assented to it in terms of uncommon satisfaction, and promised to use his
whole industry in finding a priest, upon whose discretion they could rely;
nay, he certainly resolved to comply with her request in good earnest, rather
than forfeit the advantages which he foresaw in their union. His good fortune, however, exempted him from the necessity of taking such a step, which
at best must have been disagreeable: for so many difficulties occurred in the
enquiry which was set on foot, and so artfully did Fathom in the mean time
manage the influence he had already gained over her heart, that before her
passion could obtain a legal gratification, she surrendered to his wish, without any other assurance, than his solemn profession of sincerity and truth, on
which she reposed herself with the most implicit confidence and faith.

CHAPTER XIII.

*He is exposed to a most perilous incident in the
course of his intrigue with the daughter.*

He was rejoiced to find her so easily satisfied in such a momentous concern: for the principal aim of the intrigue was to make her necessary to
his interested views, and even, if possible, an associate in the fraudulent
plans he had projected upon her father; consequently he considered this relaxation in her virtue, as an happy omen of his future success. All the obstacles to their mutual enjoyment being thus removed, our adventurer was by
his mistress, indulged with an assignation in her own chamber, which,
though contiguous to that of her step-mother, was provided with a door that
opened into a common stair-case, to which he had access at all hours of the
night.
He did not neglect the rendezvous, but, presenting himself at the appointed time, which was midnight, made the signal they had agreed upon,

and was immediately admitted by Wilhelmina, who waited for him with a lover's impatience. Fathom was not deficient in those expressions of rapture, that are current on such occasions; but, on the contrary, became so loud in the transports of self-congratulation, that his voice reached the ears of the vigilant step-mother, who wakening the jeweller from his first nap, gave him to understand that some person was certainly in close conversation with his daughter; and exhorted him to rise forthwith, and vindicate the honour of his family.

The German, who was naturally of a phlegmatic habit,[1] and never went to bed without a full dose of the creature,[2] which added to his constitutional drowsiness, gave no ear to his wife's intimation, until she had repeated it thrice, and used other means to rouse him from the arms of slumber. Mean while, Fathom and his inamorata overheard her information, and our hero would have made his retreat immediately, through the port by which he entered, had not his intention been over-ruled by the remonstrances of the young lady, who observed that the door was already fast bolted, and could not possibly be opened without creating a noise that would confirm the suspicion of her parents; and that over and above this objection, he would, in sallying from that door, run the risque of being met by her father, who in all probability, would present himself before it, in order to hinder our hero's escape: she therefore conveyed him softly into her closet, where she assured him he might remain with great tranquillity, in full confidence that she would take such measures, as would effectually screen him from detection.

He was fain to depend upon her assurance, and accordingly insconced himself behind her dressing table; but he could not help sweating with apprehension, and praying fervently to God for his deliverance, when he heard the jeweller thundring at the door, and calling to his daughter for admittance. Wilhelmina, who was already undressed, and had purposely extinguished the light, pretended to be suddenly waked from her sleep, and starting up, exclaimed in a tone of surprize and affright, "Jesu, Maria! what is the matter?" "Hussey!" replied the German in a terrible accent, "open the door this instant, there is a man in your bed-chamber; and by the lightning and thunder! I will wash away the stain he has cast upon my honour with the schellum's[3] heart's-blood."

Not at all intimidated by this boisterous threat, she admitted him without hesitation, and with a shrillness of voice peculiar to herself, began to hold forth upon her own innocence and his unjust suspicion, mingling in her harangue, sundry oblique hints against her mother in law, importing that some people were so vitiously inclined by their own natures, that she did not won-

der at their doubting the virtue of other people; but that these people despised the insinuations of such people, who ought to be more circumspect in
their own conduct, lest they themselves should suffer reprisals from those
people whom they had so maliciously slandered.

Having uttered these flowers of rhetoric, which were calculated for the
hearing of her step-dame, who stood with a light at her husband's back, the
young lady assumed an ironical air, and admonished her father to search
every corner of her apartment; she even affected to assist his inquiry; with
her own hands pulled out a parcel of small drawers, in which her trinkets
were contained; desired him to look into her needle case and thimble, and
seeing his examination fruitless, earnestly intreated him to rummage her
closet also, saying with a sneer, that in all probability, the dishonourer would
be found in that lurking-place. The manner in which she pretended to
ridicule his apprehensions, made an impression upon the jeweller, who was
very well disposed to retreat into his own nest, when his wife, with a certain
slyness in her countenance, besought him to comply with his daughter's request, and look into that same closet; by which means Wilhelmina's virtue
would obtain a compleat triumph.

Our adventurer, who overheard the conversation, was immediately seized
with a palsy of fear: he trembled at every joint, the sweat trickled down his
forehead, his teeth began to chatter, his hair to stand on end, and he in his
heart, bitterly cursed the daughter's petulance, the mother's malice, together
with his own precipitation, by which he was involved in an adventure so
pregnant with danger and disgrace. Indeed, the reader may easily conceive
his disorder, when he heard the key turning in the lock, and the German
swearing that he would make him food for the beasts of the field and the
fowls of the air.[4]

Fathom had come unprepared with weapons of defence, was naturally an
œconomist of his person, and saw himself on the brink of forfeiting not only
the promised harvest of his double intrigue, but also the reputation of a man
of honour, upon which all his future hopes depended: his agony was therefore unspeakable, when the door flew open, and it was not till after a considerable pause of recollection, that he perceived the candle extinguished by
the motion of the air produced from the German's sudden irruption. This
accident, which disconcerted him so much as to put a full stop to his charge,
was very favourable to our hero, who summoning all his presence of mind,
crept up into the chimney, while the jeweller stood at the door, waiting for
his wife's return with another light; so that when the closet was examined,
there was nothing found to justify the report which the step-mother had

made; and the father, after having made a slight apology to Wilhelmina, for
his intrusion, retired with his yoke-fellow into their own chamber.

The young lady who little thought that her papa would have taken her at
her word, was overwhelmed with confusion and dismay, when she saw him
enter the closet, and had her lover been discovered, would in all probability
have been the loudest in his reproach, and perhaps, have accused him of an
intention to rob the house: but, she was altogether astonished when she
found he had made shift to elude the inquiry of her parents, because she
could not conceive the possibility of his escaping by the window, which was
in the third story, at a prodigious distance from the ground; and how he could
conceal himself in the apartment, was a mystery which she could by no
means unfold. Before her father and mother retired, she lighted her lamp, on
pretence of being afraid to be in the dark, after the perturbation of spirits she
had undergone, and her room was no sooner evacuated of such troublesome
visitants, than she secured the doors, and went in quest of her lover.

Accordingly, every corner of the closet underwent a new search, and she
called upon his name with a soft voice, which she thought no other person
would overhear: but Ferdinand did not think proper to gratify her impatience, because he could not judge of the predicament in which he stood by
the evidence of all his senses, and would not relinquish his post, until he
should be better certified that the coast was clear. Mean while, his Dulcinea[5]
having performed her inquiry to no purpose, imagined there was something
preternatural in the circumstance of his vanishing so unaccountably, and began to cross herself with great devotion. She returned to her chamber, fixed
the lamp in the fire-place, and throwing herself upon the bed, gave way to the
suggestions of her superstition, which were reinforced by the silence that
prevailed, and the gloomy glimmering of the light. She reflected upon the
trespass she had already committed in her heart, and in the conjectures of her
fear, believed that her lover was no other than the devil himself, who had
assumed the appearance of Fathom, in order to tempt and seduce her virtue.

While her imagination teemed with those horrible ideas, our adventurer
concluding from the general stillness, that the jeweller and his wife were at
last happily asleep, ventured to come forth from his hiding-place, and stood
before his mistress, all begrimed with soot. Wilhelmina lifting up her eyes,
and seeing this sable apparition, which she mistook for Satan in propria persona,[6] instantly screamed, and began to repeat her Pater-noster with an audible voice: upon which Ferdinand, fore-seeing that her parents would be
again alarmed, would not stay to undeceive her, and explain himself; but
unlocking the door with great expedition, ran down stairs, and luckily ac-

complished his escape. This was undoubtedly the wisest measure he could have taken: for, he had not performed one half of his descent toward the street, when the German was at his daughter's bed-side, demanding to know the cause of her exclamation: she then gave him an account of what she had seen, with all the exaggerations of her own fancy, and after having weighed the circumstances of her story, he interpreted the apparition into a thief, who had found means to open the door that communicated with the stair, but having been scared by Wilhelmina's shriek, had been obliged to retreat before he could execute his purpose.

Our hero's spirits were so woefully disturbed by this adventure, that for a whole week he felt no inclination to visit his inamorata, and was not without apprehension that the affair had terminated in an explanation very little to his advantage. He was, however, delivered from this disagreeable suspence, by an accidental meeting with the jeweller himself, who kindly chid him for his long absence, and entertained him in the street, with an account of the alarm which his family had sustained, by a thief who broke into Wilhelmina's apartment. Glad to find his apprehension mistaken, he renewed his correspondence with the family, and in a little time, found reason to console himself for the jeopardy and panic he had undergone.

CHAPTER XIV.

He is reduced to a dreadful dilemma, in consequence of an assignation with the wife.

Nor was his whole care and attention engrossed by the execution of this scheme upon the daughter. While he managed his concerns in that quarter, with incredible ardour and application, he was not the less indefatigable in the prosecution of his design upon the mother-in-law, which he forwarded with all his art, during those opportunities he enjoyed in the absence of Wilhelmina, who was frequently called away by the domestic duties of the house. The passions of the jeweller's wife were in such a state of exaltation as exempted our hero from the repulses and fatigue attending a long siege.

We have already observed how cunningly he catered for the gratification of her ruling appetite,[1] and have exhibited pregnant proofs of his ability in gaining upon the human heart; the reader will not therefore be surprized at the rapidity of his conquest over the affections of a lady whose complexion was perfectly amorous, and whose vanity laid her open to all the attempts of adulation. In a word, matters were quickly brought to such a mutual understanding, that one evening, while they amused themselves at lansquenet,[2] Fathom conjured her to give him the rendezvous next day, at the house of any third person of her own sex, in whose discretion she could confide; and after a few affected scruples on her side, which he well knew how to surmount, she complied with his request, and the circumstances of the appointment were settled accordingly. After this treaty, their satisfaction rose to such a warmth, and the conversation became so reciprocally endearing, that our gallant expressed his impatience of waiting so long for the accomplishment of his wishes; and with the most eager transport, begged she would, if possible, curtail the term of his expectation, that his brain might not suffer by his standing so many tedious hours on the giddy verge of rapture.

The dame, who was naturally compassionate, sympathized with his condition, and unable to resist his pathetic supplications, gave him to understand that his desire could not be granted, without subjecting them both to some hazard, but that she was disposed to run any risque in behalf of his happiness and peace. After this affectionate preamble, she told him that her husband was then engaged in a quarterly meeting of the jewellers,[3] from whence he never failed to return quite over-whelmed with wine, tobacco, and the phlegm of his own constitution; so that he would fall fast asleep as soon as his head should touch the pillow; and she be at liberty to entertain the lover without interruption, provided he could find means to deceive the jealous vigilance of Wilhelmina, and conceal himself in some corner of the house, unsuspected and unperceived.

Our lover remembring his adventure with the daughter, would have willingly dispensed with this expedient, and began to repent of the eagerness with which he had preferr'd his sollicitation; but, seeing there was now no opportunity of retracting with honour, he affected to enter heartily into the conversation, and after much canvassing, it was determined that while Wilhelmina was employed in the kitchen, the mother should conduct our adventurer to the outward door, where he should pay the compliment of parting, so as to be overheard by the young lady, but in the mean time, glide softly into the jeweller's bed-chamber, which was a place they imagined least liable to the effects of a daughter's prying disposition; and conceal himself in a large press or wardrobe, that stood in one corner of the apartment. The scene was immediately acted with great success, and our hero cooped up in his cage, where he waited so long, that his desires began to subside, and his imagination to aggravate the danger of his situation.

"Suppose," said he to himself, "this brutal German, instead of being stupified with wine, should come home inflamed with brandy, to the use of which he is sometimes addicted; far from feeling any inclination to sleep, he will labour under the most fretful anxiety of watching, every irascible particle in his disposition will be exasperated: he will be offended with every object that may present itself to his view, and if there is the least ingredient of jealousy in his temper, it will manifest itself in riot and rage. What if his frenzy should prompt him to search his wife's chamber for gallants? this would certainly be the first place to which he would direct his inquiry; or, granting this supposition chimerical, I may be seized with an irresistible inclination to cough, before he is oppressed with sleep: he may be waked by the noise I shall make in disengaging myself from this embarrassed situation; and finally, I may find it impracticable to retire unseen or unheard, after every thing else shall have succeeded to my wish."

These suggestions did not at all contribute to the quiet of our adventurer, who, having waited three whole hours in the most uncomfortable suspence, heard the jeweller brought into the room in that very condition which his fears had prognosticated. He had, it seems, quarrelled over his cups with another tradesman, and received a salutation on the forehead with a candlestick, which, not only left an ignominious and painful mark upon his countenance, but even disordered his brain to a very dangerous degree of delirium: so that, instead of allowing himself quietly to be undressed and put to bed by his wife, he answered all her gentle admonitions and caresses, with the most opprobrious invectives and obstreperous behaviour; and though he did not tax her with infidelity to his bed, he virulently accused her of extravagance and want of œconomy, observed her expensive way of living would bring him to a morsel of bread, and unfortunately recollecting the attempt of the supposed thief, started up from his chair, swearing by God's mother, that he would forthwith arm himself with a brace of pistols, and search every apartment of the house. "That press," said he with great vociferation, "may for aught I know, be the receptacle of some ruffian."

So saying, he approached the ark in which Fathom was embarked, and exclaiming, "Come forth, Satan," applied his foot to the door of it, with such violence as threw him from the centre of gravity, and laid him sprawling on his back. This address made such an impression upon our adventurer, that he had well nigh obeyed the summons, and burst from his concealment, in a desperate effort to escape, without being recognized by the intoxicated German: and indeed had the application been repeated, he in all likelihood would have tried the experiment; for, by this time, his terrors had waxed too strong

to be much longer suppressed: from this hazardous enterprize, he was however exempted by a lucky accident that happened to his disturber, whose
head chancing to pitch upon the corner of a chair, in his fall, he was immediately lulled into a trance; during which, the considerate lady guessing the
disorder of her gallant, and dreading further interruption, very prudently
released him from his confinement, after she had put out the light, and in the
dark conveyed him to the door, where he was comforted with the promise
that she would punctually remember the rendezvous of next day.

She then invoked the assistance of the servants, who being waked for the
purpose, lifted up their master, and tumbled him into bed, while Ferdinand
hied him home in an universal sweat, blessing himself[4] from any future
atchievement of that sort, in an house, where he had been twice in such
imminent danger of life and reputation. Nevertheless, he did not fail to honour the assignation, and avail himself of the disposition his mistress manifested, to make him all the recompence in her power, for the disappointment
and chagrin which he had undergone.

CHAPTER XV.

But at length succeeds in his attempts upon both.

Having thus gained a compleat victory over the affections of these two
ladies, he began to convert his good fortune to the purposes of that
principle, from which his view was never, no not for a moment, detached. In
other words, he used them as ministers and purveyors to his avarice and
fraud. As for the mother-in-law, she was of herself so liberal as to anticipate
the wishes of any moderate adventurer, and presented him with sundry valuable jewels, as memorials of her esteem; nor was the daughter backward in
such expressions of regard; she already considered his interest as her own,
and took frequent opportunities of secreting for his benefit, certain stray trinkets that she happened to pick up in her excursions within doors.

All these gratifications he received with demonstrations of infinite constraint and reluctance, and in the midst of his rapacious extortion, acted so
cunningly as to impose himself upon both, for a miracle of disinterested integrity. Yet not contented with what he thus could earn, and despairing of
being able to steer the bark of his fortune for any length of time, between two
such dangerous quicksands, he resolved to profit by the occasion while it

lasted, and strike some considerable stroke at once. A plan was formed in consequence of this determination, and at an appointment with the mother, in the house of their female friend, our adventurer appeared with an air of dejection, which he veiled with a thin cover of forced pleasantry, that his mistress might suppose he endeavoured to conceal some mortal chagrin that preyed upon his heart.

The stratagem succeeded to his wish: she observed his countenance between whiles over-cast, took notice of the involuntary sighs he heaved; and with the most tender expressions of sympathy, conjured him to make her acquainted with the cause of his affliction. Instead of gratifying her request immediately, he evaded her questions with a respectful reserve, implying, that his love would not suffer him to make her a partner in his sorrow; and this delicacy on his part, whetted her impatience and concern to such a degree, that rather than keep her in such an agony of doubt and apprehension, he was prevailed upon to tell her, that he had been the preceding night, engaged with a company of his fellow-students, where he had made too free with the champaigne, so that his caution forsook him, and he had been decoyed into a play by a Tyroleze gamester, who stripped him of all his ready money, and obtained from him, an obligation for two hundred florins,[1] which he could not possibly pay, without having recourse to his relation the count de Melvile, who would have just cause to be incensed at his extravagance.

This information he concluded, by declaring, that cost what it would, he was resolved to make a candid confession of the truth, and throw himself entirely upon the generosity of his patron, who could inflict no other punishment than that of discarding him from his favour and protection: a misfortune, which how grievous soever it might be, he should be able to sustain with fortitude, could he fall upon some method of satisfying the Tyrolese, who was very importunate and savage in his demand. His kind mistress no sooner found out the source of his inquietude, than she promised to dry it up, assuring him that next day at the same hour, she would enable him to discharge the debt; so that he might set his heart at ease, and recollect that gaiety which was the soul of her enjoyment.

He expressed the utmost astonishment at this generous proffer, which, however, he declined with an affected earnestness of refusal, protesting that he should be extremely mortified, if he thought she looked upon him as one of those mercenary gallants, who could make such a sordid use of a lady's affection. "No madam," cried our politician in a pathetic strain, "whatever happens, I shall never part with that internal consolation that conscious honour never fails to yield in the deepest scenes of solitary distress: the attachment I have the honour to profess for your amiable person, is not founded on such inglorious motives; but, is the genuine result of that generous passion, which none but the noble-minded feel, and the only circumstance of this misfortune, that I dread to encounter, is, the necessity of withdrawing myself for ever, from the presence of her whose genial smiles could animate my soul against all the persecution of adverse fortune."

This declamation, accompanied with a profound sigh, served only to inflame her desire of extricating him from the difficulty in which he was involved. She exhausted all her eloquence in attempting to persuade him that his refusal was an outrage against her affection: he pretended to refute her arguments, and remained unshaken by all the power of her sollicitations; until she had recourse to the most passionate remonstrances of love, and fell at his feet in the posture of a forlorn shepherdess. What he refused to her reason, he granted to her tears, because his heart was melted by her affliction, and next day, condescended to accept of her money, out of pure regard to her happiness and peace.

Encouraged by the success of this atchievement, he resolved to practise the same experiment upon Wilhelmina, in hope of extracting an equal share of profit from her simplicity and attachment; and at their very next nocturnal rendezvous in her chamber, re-acted the farce already rehearsed; with a small variation, which he thought necessary to stimulate the young lady in his behalf. He rightly concluded, that she was by no means mistress of such a considerable sum as he had already extorted from her mother; and therefore thought proper to represent himself in the most urgent predicament, that her apprehension, on his account, might be so alarmed, as to engage her in some enterprize for his advantage, which, otherwise, she would never have dreamed of undertaking. With this view, after having described his own calamitous situation, in consequence of her pressing intreaties, which he affected to evade, he gave her to understand that there was no person upon earth, to whom he would have recourse in this emergency; for which reason, he was determined to rid himself of all his cares at once, upon the friendly point of his own faithful sword.

Such a dreadful resolution could not fail to operate upon the tender passions of his Dulcinea; she was instantly seized with an agony of fear and distraction: her grief manifested itself in a flood of tears, while she hung round his neck, conjuring him in the most melting terms, by their mutual love, in which they had been so happy, to lay aside that fatal determination, which would infallibly involve her in the same fate; for, she took Heaven to witness, that she would not one moment survive the knowledge of his death.

He was not deficient in expressions of reciprocal regard: he extolled her love and tenderness with a most extravagant eulogium; and seemed wrung with mortal anguish at the prospect of parting for ever from his lovely Wilhelmina; but his honour was a stern and rigid creditor, that could not be appeased, except with his blood; and all the boon she could obtain, by dint of the most woeful supplication, was a promise to defer the execution of his baleful purpose, for the space of four and twenty hours, during which, she hoped, Heaven would compassionate her sufferings, and inspire her with some contrivance for their mutual relief. Thus he yielded to her fervent request, rather with a view to calm the present transports of her sorrow, than with any expectation of seeing himself redeemed from his fate, by her interposition; such at least were his professions, when he took his leave, assuring her, that he would not quit his being, before he should have devoted a few hours to another interview with the dear object of his love.

Having thus kindled the train,[2] he did not doubt that the mine of his craft[3] would take effect, and repaired to his own lodging, in full persuasion of seeing his aim accomplished, before the time fixed for their last assignation. His prognostic was next morning verified by the arrival of a messenger, who brought to him a small parcel, to which was cemented with sealing-wax, the following epistle.

"Jewel of my soul!

Scarce had you, last night, quitted my disconsolate arms, when I happily recollected that there was in my possession, a gold chain, of value more than sufficient to answer the exigence of your present occasions: it was pledged to my grandfather for two hundred crowns,[4] by a knight of Malta, who soon after perished in a sea-engagement with the enemies of our faith;[5] so that it became the property of our house, and was bequeathed to me by the old gentleman, as a memorial of his particular affection. Upon whom can I more properly bestow it, than him who is already master of my heart! receive it, therefore, from the bearer of this billet, and convert it without scruple to that use which shall be most conducive to your ease and satisfaction; nor seek, from a too romantic notion of honour, which I know you entertain, to excuse yourself, from accepting this testimony of my affection: for, I have already sworn before an image of our blessed lady, that I will no longer own you as the sovereign of my heart, nor even indulge you with another interview, if you reject this mark of tenderness and concern, from your ever faithful

WILHELMINA."

The heart of our adventurer began to bound with joy, when he surveyed the contents of this letter; and his eyes sparkled with transport at sight of the chain, which he immediately perceived to be worth twice the sum she had mentioned. Nevertheless, he would not avail himself without further question of her generosity; but, that same night, repairing to her apartment at the usual hour of meeting, he prostrated himself before her, and counterfeiting extreme agitation of spirit, begged in the most urgent terms, not even unaccompanied with tears, that she would take back the present which he tendered for her acceptance; and spare him the most insufferable mortification of thinking himself exposed to the imputation of being mercenary in his love. Such, he said, was the delicacy of his passion, that he could not possibly exist under the apprehension of incurring a censure so unworthy of his sentiments; and he would a thousand times, sooner undergo the persecution of his rancorous creditor, than bear the thought of being in the smallest consideration lessened in her esteem: nay, so far did he carry his pretensions to punctilio, as to protest that should she refuse to quiet the scruples of his honour, on this score, her unyielding beneficence would serve only to hasten the execution of his determined purpose, to withdraw himself at once from a life of vanity and misfortune.

The more pathetically he pleaded for her compliance, the more strenuously did she resist his remonstrances. She advanced all the arguments her reason, love and terror could suggest, reminded him of her oath, from which, he could not suppose she would recede, whatever the consequence might be; and in conclusion, vowed to Heaven with great solemnity and devotion, that she would not survive the news of his death. Thus the alternative she offered, was either to retain the chain and be happy in her affection, or forfeit all title to her love, and die in the conviction of having brought his innocent mistress to an untimely grave.

His fortitude was not proof against this last consideration: "My savage honour," said he, "would enable me to endure the pangs of eternal separation, in the confidence of being endowed with the power of ending these tortures by the energy of my own hand; but, the prospect of Wilhelmina's death, and that too occasioned by my inflexibility, disarms my soul of all her resolution, swallows up the dictates of my jealous pride, and fills my bosom with such a gush of tenderness and sorrow, as overwhelms the whole œconomy of my purpose! Yes, inchanting creature! I sacrifice my glory to that irresistible reflection: and rather than know myself the cruel instrument of robbing the world of such perfection, consent to retain the fatal testimony of your love."

So saying, he pocketed the chain, with an air of ineffable mortification, and was rewarded for his compliance with the most endearing caresses of his

Dulcinea, who amidst the tumults of her joy, ejaculated a thousand acknowledgments to Heaven, for having blessed her with the affection of such a man,
whose honour was unrivalled by any thing but his love.

CHAPTER XVI.

*His success begets a blind security, by which he is
once again well nigh entrapped in his Dulcinea's
apartment.*

In this manner did the crafty Fathom turn to account those ingratiating
qualifications he inherited from nature; and maintain with incredible assiduity and circumspection, an amorous correspondence with two domestic
rivals, who watched the conduct of each other, with the most indefatigable
virulence of envious suspicion, until an accident happened, which had well-
nigh overturned the bark of his policy, and induced him to alter the course,
that he might not be shipwrecked on the rocks that began to multiply in the
prosecution of his present voyage.

The jeweller, who, as a German, wanted neither pride nor ostentation,
never failed to celebrate the anniversary of his birth, by an annual feast
granted to his neighbours and friends; and on these occasions, was accustomed to wear that chain, which though bequeathed to his daughter, he
considered as an ornament appertaining to the family, whereof he himself
was head: accordingly, when the time of this festival revolved, he as usual,
ordered Wilhelmina to surrender it for the day. This injunction, the reader
will perceive, our young lady was in no condition to obey; she had, however,
foreseen the demand, and contrived a scheme of behaviour, for the occasion,
which she forthwith put in execution.

With an air of uncommon chearfulness purposely assumed, she retired to
her closet, on pretence of complying with his desire, and having employed a
few minutes in rummaging her drawers, and disordering her moveables, uttered a loud shriek, that brought her father instantly into the apartment,
where he found his daughter tossing about her cloaths and trinkets, with
violent demonstrations of disorder and affright, and heard her in a lamentable strain declare, that she was robbed of her chain, and for ever undone.
This was so far from being an agreeable intimation to the jeweller, that he
was struck dumb with astonishment and vexation, and it was not till after a

long pause, that he pronounced the word Sacrament! with an emphasis, denoting the most mortifying surprize.

Soon as that exclamation escaped from his lips, he flew to the scrutore[1] as if instinctively, and joining Wilhelmina in her occupation, tumbled its whole contents upon the floor, in a trice.

While he was thus employed, in the most expressive silence, the wife of his bosom chanced to pass that way, and seeing them both occupied, with such violence and trepidation, believed at first, that they were certainly actuated by the spirit of frenzy; but when she interposed, by asking with great earnestness, the cause of such transports and distracted behaviour; and heard her husband reply with an accent of despair, "The chain! the chain of my forefathers is no more." She immediately justified his emotion, by undergoing the same alarm, and without further hesitation, engaged herself in the search, beginning with a song, which might be compared to the hymn of battle among the Greeks, or rather more aptly, to that which the Spartan females sung round the altar of Diana, surnamed Orthian:[2] for, it was attended with strange gesticulations, and in the course of utterance, became so loud and shrill, that the guests, who were by this time partly assembled, being confounded at the clamour, rushed towards the place from whence it seemed to proceed, and found their landlord, with his wife and daughter in the attitudes of distraction and despair.

When they understood the nature of the case, they condoled the family on their misfortune, and would have retired, on the supposition that it would defeat the mirthful intent of their meeting; but the jeweller mustering up his whole temper and hospitality, intreated them to excuse his disorder, and favour him with their company, which, he observed, was now more than ever wanted, to dispel the melancholy ideas inspired by his loss. Notwithstanding this apology, and the efforts he made in the sequel, to entertain his friends with jollity and good humour, his heart was so linked to the chain, that he could not detach himself from the thoughts of it, which invaded him at short intervals, in such qualms as effectually spoiled his appetite and hindered his digestion.

He revolved within himself, the circumstances of his disaster, and in canvassing all the probable means, by which the chain could be stolen, concluded that the deed must have been done by some person in the family, who, in consequence of having access to his daughter's chamber, had either found the drawer left open by her carelessness and neglect, or found means to obtain a false key, by some waxen impression: for, the locks of the escritore were safe and uninjured. His suspicion being thus confined within his own house, sometimes pitched upon his workmen, and sometimes upon his wife, who, he thought, was the more likely to practise such finesse, as she considered Wilhelmina in the light of a daughter-in-law, whose interest interfered with her own, and who had often harangued to him in private, on the folly of leaving this very chain in the young lady's possession.

The more he considered this subject, he thought he saw the more reason to attribute the damage he had sustained, to the machinations of his spouse, who, he did not doubt, was disposed to feather her own nest,[3] at the expence of him and his heirs, and who, with the same honest intention had already secreted for her private use, those inconsiderable jewels which of late had at different times, been missing. Arroused by these sentiments, he resolved to retaliate her own schemes, by contriving means to visit her cabinet in secret, and if possible, to rob the robber, of the spoils she had gathered to his prejudice, without coming to any explanation, which might end in domestic turmoils and eternal disquiet.

While the husband exercised his reflection in this manner, his innocent mate did not allow the powers of her imagination to rest in idleness and sloth. Her observations touching the loss of the chain were such, as a suspicious woman, biassed by hatred and envy, would naturally make. To her it seemed highly improbable, that a thing of such value, so carefully deposited, should vanish without the connivance of its keeper, and without much expence of conjecture, divined the true manner in which it was conveyed. The sole difficulty that occurred in the researches of her sagacity, was to know the gallant, who had been favoured with such a pledge of Wilhelmina's affection; for as the reader will easily imagine, she never dreamed of viewing Ferdinand in that odious perspective. In order to satisfy her curiosity, discover this happy favourite, and be revenged on her petulant rival, she prevailed upon the jeweller to employ a scout, who should watch all night upon the stair, without the knowledge of any other person in the family, alledging, that in all likelihood, the house-maid gave private admittance to some lover, who was the author of all the losses they had lately suffered, and that they might possibly detect him in his nocturnal adventures; and observing that it would be imprudent to intimate their design to Wilhelmina, lest through the heedlessness and indiscretion of youth, she might chance to divulge the secret, so as to frustrate their aim.

A Swiss, in whose honesty the German could confide, being hired for this purpose, was posted in a dark corner of the stair-case, within a few paces of the door, which he was directed to watch, and actually stood centinel three nights, without perceiving the least object of suspicion; but on the fourth, the evil stars of our adventurer conducted him to the spot, on his voyage to the apartment of his Dulcinea, with whom he had pre-concerted the assignation. Having made the signal, which consisted of two gentle taps on her door, he was immediately admitted, and the Swiss, no sooner saw him fairly housed, than he crept softly to the other door, that was left open for the purpose, and gave immediate intimation of what he had perceived: this intelligence, however, he could not convey so secretly, but the lovers, who were always vigilant upon these occasions, overheard a sort of commotion in the jeweller's chamber, the cause of which their apprehension was ingenious enough to comprehend.

We have formerly observed, that our adventurer could not make his retreat by the door, without running a very great risque of being detected, and the expedient of the chimney he had no inclination to repeat; so that he found himself in a very uncomfortable dilemma, and was utterly abandoned by all his invention and address; when his mistress in a whisper, desired him to begin a dialogue, aloud, in an apology, importing, that he had mistaken the door; and that his intention was to visit her father, touching a ring belonging to the young count Melvile, which, she knew, Fathom had put into his hands, in order to be altered.

Ferdinand seizing the hint, availed himself of it, without delay, and unbolting the door, pronounced in an audible voice, "Upon my honour, Mademoiselle, you wrong my intention, if you imagine I came hither with any disrespectful or dishonourable motive: I have business with your father, which cannot be delayed till to-morrow, without manifest prejudice to my friend and myself; therefore I took the liberty of visiting him at these untimely hours; and it has been my misfortune to mistake the door in the dark. I beg pardon for my involuntary intrusion; and again assure you, that nothing was farther from my thoughts, than any design to violate that respect, which I have always entertained for you and your father's family."

To this remonstrance, which was distinctly heard by the German and his wife, who by this time, stood listening at the door, the young lady replied in a shrill accent of displeasure, "Sir, I am bound to believe that all your actions are conducted by honour; but, you must give me leave to tell you, that your mistake is a little extraordinary, and your visit even to my father at this time of the night, altogether unseasonable, if not mysterious. As for the interruption I have suffered in my repose, I impute it to my own forgetfulness, in leaving my door unlocked, and blame myself so severely for the omission that I shall tomorrow put it out of my own power to be guilty of the like for the future, by ordering the passage to be nailed up; mean while, if you would persuade me of your well-meaning, you will instantly withdraw, lest my reputation should suffer by your continuance in my apartment."

"Madam," answered our hero, "I will not give you an opportunity to repeat the command, which I shall forthwith obey, after having intreated you once more, to forgive the disturbance I have given." So saying, he gently opened the door, and at sight of the German and his wife, who, he well knew, waited for his exit, started back, and gave tokens of confusion which was partly real and partly affected. The jeweller fully satisfied with Fathom's declaration to his daughter, received him with a complaisant look, and in order to alleviate his concern, gave him to understand that he already knew the reason of his being in that apartment, and desired to be informed of what had procured him the honour to see him at such a juncture.

"My dear friend," said our adventurer, pretending to recollect himself with difficulty, "I am utterly ashamed and confounded to be discovered in this situation; but as you have overheard what past between Mademoiselle and me, I know you will do justice to my intention and forgive my mistake. After begging pardon for having intruded upon your family at these hours, I must now tell you, that my cousin count Melvile was sometime ago so much mis-represented to his mother, by certain malicious informers, who delight in sowing discord in private families, that she actually believed her son an ex-travagant spendthrift, who had not only consumed his remittances in the most riotous scenes of disorder, but also indulged a pernicious appetite for gaming to such a degree, that he had lost all his cloaths and jewels at play. In consequence of such false information, she expostulated with him in a severe letter, and desired he would transmit to her that ring which is in your custody, it being a family stone, for which she expressed an inestimable value. The young gentleman, in his answer to her reproof, endeavoured to vindicate himself from the aspersions which had been cast upon his charac-ter, and with regard to the ring, told her it was at present in the hands of a jeweller, in order to be new set, according to her own directions, and that whenever it should be altered, he would send it home to her by some safe conveyance. This account the good lady took for an evasion, and upon that supposition, has again written to him, in such a provoking stile, that although the letter arrived but half an hour ago, he is determined to dispatch a courier before morning with the mischievous ring, for which, in compliance with the impetuosity of his temper, I have taken the freedom to disturb you at this unseasonable hour."

The German paid implicit faith to every circumstance of this story, which indeed could not well be supposed to be invented extempore; the ring was immediately restored, and our adventurer took his leave, congratulating himself upon his signal deliverance from the snare in which he had fallen.

CHAPTER XVII.

*The step-dame's suspicions being awakened, she lays
a snare for our adventurer, from which he is
delivered by the interposition of his good genius.*

Though the husband swallowed the bait, without further inquiry, the penetration of the wife was not so easily deceived: that same dialogue in Wilhelmina's apartment, far from allaying, rather inflamed her suspicion, because in the like emergency, she herself had once profited by the same, or nearly the same contrivance. Without communicating her doubts to the father, she resolved to double her attention to the daughter's future conduct, and keep such a strict eye over the behaviour of our gallant, that he should find it very difficult, if not impossible, to elude her observation. For this purpose, she took into her pay an old maiden, of the right sour disposition, who lived in an house opposite to her own, and directed her to follow the young lady in all her out-goings, whenever she should receive from the window a certain signal, which the mother-in-law agreed to make for the occasion. It was not long before this scheme succeeded to her wish: the door of communication, betwixt Wilhelmina's apartment and the stair-case, being nailed up, by the jeweller's express order, our adventurer was altogether deprived of those opportunities he had hitherto enjoyed; and was not at all mortified to find himself so restricted, in a correspondence which began to be tiresome and disagreeable: but the case was far otherwise with his Dulcinea, whose passion, the more it was thwarted, raged with greater violence, like a fire, that from the attempts that are made to extinguish it, gathers greater force, and flames with double fury.

Upon the second day of her misfortune, she had written a very tender billet, lamenting her unhappiness, in being deprived of those meetings which constituted the chief joy of her life, and intreating him to contrive some means of renewing the delicious commerce in an unsuspected place. This intimation she proposed to convey privately into the hand of her lover, during his next visit to the family; but both were so narrowly eyed by the mother, that she found the execution of her design impracticable; and next forenoon, on pretence of going to church, repaired to the house of a companion, who being also her confidante, undertook to deliver the billet with her own hand.

The she-dragon employed by her mother, in obedience to the sign, which was displayed from the window, immediately put on her veil, and followed Wilhelmina at a distance, until she saw her fairly housed: she would not even then, return from her excursion, but hovered about in sight of the door, with a view of making further observations: in less than five minutes after the young lady disappeared, the scout perceived her coming out, accompanied by her comrade, from whom she instantly parted, and bent her way towards the church in good earnest, while the other steered her course in another direction. The duenna,[1] after a moment's suspence and consideration, divined the true cause of this short visit, and resolved to watch the motions of the confidante, whom she traced to the academy in which our hero lodged, and from which she saw her return, after the supposed message was delivered.

Fraught with this intelligence, the rancorous understrapper, hied her home to the jeweller's wife, and made a faithful recital of what she had seen; communicating, at the same time, her own conjectures on the subject. Her employer was equally astonished and incensed at this information: she was seized with all that frenzy which takes possession of a slighted woman, when she finds herself supplanted by a detested rival; and in the first transports of her indignation, devoted them as sacrifices to her vengeance: nor was her surprize so much the effect of his dissimulation, as of his want of taste and discernment. She inveighed against him, not as the most treacherous lover, but as the most abject wretch, in courting the smiles of such an aukward dowdy, while he enjoyed the favours of a woman, who had numbered princes in the train of her admirers. For the brilliancy of her attractions, such as they at present shone, she appealed to the decision of her minister, who consulted her own satisfaction and interest, by flattering the other's vanity and resentment: and so unaccountable did the depravity of our hero's judgment appear to this conceited dame, that she began to believe there was some mistake in the person, and to hope that Wilhelmina's gallant was not in reality her professed admirer Mr. Fathom, but rather one of his fellow lodgers, whose passion he favoured with his mediation and assistance.

On this notion, which nothing but meer vanity could have inspired, in opposition to so many more weighty presumptions, she took the resolution of bringing the affair to a fuller explanation, before she would concert any measures to the prejudice of our adventurer, and forthwith dispatched her spy

back to his lodgings to sollicit on the part of Wilhelmina an immediate answer
to the letter he had received. This was an expedition with which the old
maiden would have willingly dispensed, because it was founded upon an
uncertainty, which might be attended with troublesome consequences; but
rather than be the means of retarding a negociation, so productive of that sort
of mischief which is particularly agreeable to all of her tribe, she undertook to
manage and effect the discovery, in full confidence of her own talents and
experience.

With such a fund of self-sufficiency and instigation, she repaired to the
academy on the instant, and inquiring for Mr. Fathom, was introduced to his
apartment, where she found him in the very act of writing a billet to the
jeweller's daughter. The artful agent having asked, with the mysterious air of
an expert go-between, if he had not lately received a message from a certain
young lady; and being answered in the affirmative, gave him to understand,
that she herself was a person favoured with the friendship and confidence of
Wilhelmina, whom she had known from her cradle, and often dandled on her
knee; then in the genuine stile of a pratling dry-nurse, she launched out in
encomiums on his Dulcinea's beauty and sweetness of temper, recounting
many simple occurrences of her infancy and childhood; and finally, desiring a
more circumstantial answer to that which she had sent to him by her friend
Catherina. In the course of her loquacity, she had also, according to her instructions, hinted at the misfortune of the door; and on the whole, performed
her cue with such dexterity and discretion, that our politician was actually
over-reached, and having finished his epistle, committed it to her care, with
many verbal expressions of eternal love and fidelity to his charming Wilhelmina.

The messenger doubly rejoiced at her atchievement, which not only recommended her ministry, but also gratified her malice, returned to her principal with great exultation, and delivering the letter, the reader will easily conceive the transports of that lady, when she read the contents of it in these
words.

"Angelic Wilhelmina!

To forget those extatic scenes we have enjoyed together, or even live without the continuation of that mutual bliss, were to quit all title to perception,
and resign every hope of future happiness. No! my charmer, while my head
retains the least spark of invention, and my heart glows with the resolution of
a man, our correspondence shall not be cut off by the machinations of an

envious step-mother, who never had attractions to inspire a generous passion, and now that age and wrinkles have destroyed what little share of beauty she once possessed, endeavours, like the fiend in paradise, to blast those joys in others, from which she is herself eternally excluded. Doubt not, dear sovereign of my soul! that I will study with all the eagerness of desiring love, how to frustrate her malicious intention, and renew those transporting moments, the remembrance of which now warms the breast of your ever constant

Fᴀᴛʜᴏᴍ."

Had our hero murdered her father, or left her a disconsolate widow, by effecting the death of her dear husband, there might have been a possibility of her exerting the christian virtues of resignation and forgiveness; but such a personal outrage as that contained in this epistle, precluded all hope of pardon, and rendered penitence of no signification. His atrocious crime being now fully ascertained, this virago gave a loose to her resentment, which became so loud and tempestuous, that her informer shuddered at the storm she had raised, and began to repent of having communicated the intelligence which seemed to have such a violent effect upon her brain.

She endeavoured, however, to allay the agitation, by flattering her fancy with the prospect of revenge, and gradually soothed her into a state of deliberate ire; during which she determined to take ample vengeance on the delinquent. In the zenith of her rage, she would have had immediate recourse to poison or steel, had she not been diverted from her mortal purpose, by her counsellor, who represented the danger of engaging in such violent measures, and proposed a more secure scheme, in the execution of which she would see the perfidious wretch sufficiently punished, without any hazard to her own person or reputation. She advised her to inform the jeweller of Fathom's efforts, to seduce her conjugal fidelity, and impart to him a plan, by which he would have it in his power, to detect our adventurer in the very act of practising upon her virtue.

The lady relished her proposal, and actually resolved to make an assignation with Ferdinand, as usual, and give notice of the appointment to her husband, that he might personally discover the treachery of his pretended friend, and inflict upon him such chastisement, as the German's brutal disposition should suggest, when inflamed by that species of provocation. Had this project been brought to bear, Ferdinand in all likelihood, would have been disqualified from engaging in any future intrigue; but fate ordained, that the design should be defeated, in order to reserve him for more important occasions.

Before the circumstances of the plan could be adjusted, it was his good fortune to meet his Dulcinea in the street, and in the midst of their mutual condolance on the interruption they had suffered in their correspondence, he assured her, that he would never give his invention respite, until he should have verified the protestations contained in the letter he had delivered to her discreet agent. This allusion to a billet she had never received, did not fail to alarm her fears, and introduce a very mortifying explanation, in which he so accurately described the person of the messenger, that she forthwith comprehended the plot, and communicated to our hero her sentiments on that subject.

Though he expressed infinite anxiety and chagrin at this misfortune, which could not fail to raise new obstacles to their love, his heart was a stranger to the uneasiness he affected; and rather pleased with the occasion, which would furnish him with pretences to withdraw himself gradually, from an intercourse by this time become equally cloying and unprofitable. Being well-acquainted with the mother's temperament, he guessed the present situation of her thoughts, and concluding she would make the jeweller a party in her revenge, he resolved from that moment to discontinue his visits, and cautiously guard against any future interview with the lady, whom he had rendered so implacable.

It was well for our adventurer that his good fortune so seasonably interposed; for that same day, in the afternoon, he was favoured with a billet from the jeweller's wife, couched in the same tender stile she had formerly used, and importing an earnest desire of seeing him next day, at the wonted rendezvous. Although his penetration was sufficient to perceive the drift of this message; or at least, to discern the risque he should run, in complying with her request, yet he was willing to be more fully certified of the truth of his suspicion, and wrote an answer to the billet, in which he assured her, that he would repair to the place of appointment, with all the punctuality of an impatient lover. Nevertheless, instead of performing this promise, he, in the morning, took post in a public house opposite to the place of assignation, in order to reconnoitre the ground, and about noon had the pleasure of seeing the German wrapped in a cloak, enter the door of his wife's she-friend, though the appointment was fixed at five in the evening. Fathom blessed his good angel, for having conducted him clear of this conspiracy, and kept his station with great tranquillity, till the hour of meeting, when he beheld his enraged Thalestris take the same route, and enjoyed her disappointment with ineffable satisfaction.

Thus favoured with a pretext, he took his leave of her, in a letter, giving her to understand, that he was no stranger to the barbarous snare she had laid for him; and upbraiding her with having made such an ungrateful return for all his tenderness and attachment. She was not backward in conveying a reply to this expostulation, which seemed to have been dictated in all the distraction of a proud woman who sees her vengeance baffled, as well as her love disdained. Her letter was nothing but a succession of reproaches, menaces, and incoherent execrations. She taxed him with knavery, insensibility and dissimulation; imprecated a thousand curses upon his head, and threatned not only to persecute his life with all the arts that hell and malice could inspire, but also to wound him in the person of her daughter-in-law, who should be inclosed for life in a convent, where she would have leisure to repent of those loose and disorderly practices, which he had taught her to commit, and of which she could not pretend innocence, as they had it in their power to confront her with the evidence of her lover's own confession. Yet all this denunciation was qualified with an alternative, by which he was given to understand, that the gates of mercy[2] were still open, and that penitence was capable of washing out the deepest stain of guilt.

Ferdinand read the whole remonstrance with great composure and moderation, and was content to incur the hazard of her hate, rather than put her to the trouble of making such an effort of generosity, as would induce her to forgive the heinous offence he had committed; nor did his apprehension for Wilhelmina in the least influence his behaviour on this occasion: so zealous was he for her spiritual concerns, that he would have been glad to hear she had actually taken the veil; but he knew such a step was not at all agreeable to her disposition, and that no violence would be offered to her inclinations on that score, unless her step-mother should communicate to the father that letter of Fathom's which she had intercepted, and by which the German would be convinced of his daughter's backsliding; but this measure, he rightly supposed, the wife would not venture to take, lest the husband, instead of taking her advice, touching the young lady, should seek to compromise the affair, by offering her in marriage to her debaucher; a proffer, which, if accepted, would overwhelm the mother with vexation and despair. He therefore chose to trust to the effects of lenient time, which he hoped would gradually weaken the resentment of this Penthesilea, and dissolve his connexion with the other parts of the family, from which he longed to be totally detached.

How well soever he might have succeeded in his attempts to shake off the yoke of the mother, who by her situation in life was restrained from prosecuting those measures her resentment had planned against his fortitude and indifference; he would have found greater difficulty than he had foreseen, in disengaging himself from the daughter, whose affections he had won under the most solemn professions of honour and fidelity; and who, now she was debarred of his company and conversation, and in danger of losing him for ever, had actually taken the resolution of disclosing the amour to her father, that he might interpose in behalf of her peace and reputation, and secure her happiness by the sanction of the church.

CHAPTER XVIII.

Our hero departs from Vienna, and quits the domain
of Venus for the rough field of Mars.

Luckily for our adventurer, before he adhered to this determination, the young count de Melvile was summoned to Presburg by his father, who desired to see him, before he should take the field, in consequence of a rupture between the emperor and the French king;[1] and Fathom of course, quitted Vienna, in order to attend his patron, after he and Renaldo had resided two whole years in that capital, where the former had made himself perfect in all the polite exercises, become master of the French tongue, and learned to speak the Italian with great facility; over and above those other accomplishments in which we have represented him as an inimitable original.

As for the young count, his exteriors were so much improved by the company to which he had access, since his departure from his father's house, that his parents were equally surprised and overjoyed at the alteration. All that aukwardness and rusticity, which hung upon his deportment, was, like the rough coat of a diamond, polished away; the connexion and disposition of his limbs seemed to have been adjusted anew; his carriage was become easy, his air perfectly genteel, and his conversation gay and unrestrained. The merit of this reformation was in a great measure ascribed to the care and example of Mr. Fathom, who was received by the old count and his lady with marks of singular friendship and esteem; nor was he over-looked by Mademoiselle, who still remained in a state of celibacy, and seemed to have resigned all hope of altering her condition; she expressed uncommon satisfaction at the return of her old favourite, and re-admitted him into the same degree of familiarity with which he had been honoured before his departure.

The joy of Teresa was so excessive at his arrival, that she could scarce suppress her raptures, so as to conceal them from the notice of the family; and our hero, upon this occasion, performed the part of an exquisite actor, in dissembling those transports which his bosom never knew. So well had this pupil retained the lessons of her instructor, that in the midst of those fraudulent appropriations, which she still continued to make, she had found means to support her interest and character with Mademoiselle, and even to acquire such influence in the family, that no other servant male or female, could pretend to live under the same roof, without paying incessant homage to this artful waiting-woman, and yielding the most abject submission to her will.

The young gentlemen having tarried at Presburg about six weeks, during which a small field equipage was prepared for Renaldo, they repaired to the camp at Heilbron,[2] under the auspices of count Melvile, in whose regiment they carried arms, as volunteers, with a view to merit promotion in the service, by their own personal behaviour. Our adventurer would have willingly dispensed with this occasion of signalizing himself, his talents being much better adapted to another sphere of life; nevertheless, he affected uncommon alacrity at the prospect of gathering laurels in the field, and subscribed to his fortune with a good grace; forseeing that even in a campaign, a man of his art and ingenuity, might find means to consult his corporal safety, without any danger to his reputation. Accordingly, before he had lived full three weeks in camp, the damp situation and sudden change in his way of life, had such a violent effect upon his constitution, that he was deprived of the use of all his limbs, and mourned without ceasing, his hard fate, by which he found himself precluded from all opportunity of exerting his diligence, courage and activity, in the character of a soldier, to which he now aspired.

Renaldo, who was actually enamoured of a martial life, and missed no occasion of distinguishing himself, consoled his companion, with great cordiality, encouraged him with the hope of seeing his constitution familiarized to the inconveniences of a camp, and accommodated him with every thing which he thought would alleviate the pain of his body, as well as the anxiety of his mind. The old count, who sincerely sympathized with his affliction, would have persuaded him to retire into quarters, where he could be carefully nursed, and provided with every thing necessary to a person in his condition; but, such was his desire of glory, that he resisted his patron's importunities, with great constancy, till at length, seeing the old gentleman obstinately determined to consult his health, by removing him from the field, he gradually suffered himself to recover the use of his hands, made shift to sit up in his bed, and amuse himself with cards or back-gammon, and notwithstanding the feeble condition of his legs, ventured to ride out on horseback, to visit the lines; though the count and his son would never yield to his sollicitations so far, as to let him accompany Renaldo in those excursions and reconnoitring parties by which a volunteer inures himself to toil and peril, and acquires that knowledge in the operations of war, which qualifies him for a command in the service.

Notwithstanding this exemption from all duty, our adventurer managed matters so as to pass for a youth of infinite mettle, and even rendered his backwardness and timidity subservient to the support of that character, by expressing an impatience of lying inactive, and a desire of signalizing his prowess, which even the disabled condition of his body could scarce restrain. He must be a man of very weak nerves and excessive irresolution, who can live in the midst of actual service, without imbibing some portion of military fortitude; danger becomes habitual, and loses a great part of its terror; and as fear is often caught by contagion, so is courage communicated among the individuals of an army. The hope of fame, desire of honours and preferment, envy, emulation, and the dread of disgrace, are motives which co-operate in suppressing that aversion to death or mutilation, which nature hath implanted in the human mind; and therefore, it is not to be wondered at, if Fathom, who was naturally chicken-hearted, gained some advantages over his disposition, before the end of the campaign, which happened to be neither perilous nor severe.[3]

During the winter, while both armies remained in quarters, our adventurer attended his patron to Presburg, and before the troops were in motion, Renaldo obtained a commission, in consequence of which, he went into garrison at Philipsburg,[4] whither he was followed by our hero, while the old count's duty called him to the field in a different place. Ferdinand, for some time had no reason to be dissatisfied with this disposition, by which he was at once delivered from the fatigues of a campaign, and the inspection of a severe censor, in the person of count Melvile; and his satisfaction was still increased by an accidental meeting with the Tyrolese, who had been his confederate at Vienna, and now chanced to serve in garrison, on the same footing with himself. These two knights-errant renewed their former correspondence, and as all soldiers are addicted to gaming, levied contributions upon all those officers who had money to lose, and temerity to play.

However they had not long pursued this branch of traffic, when their success was interrupted by a very serious occurrence, that for the present intirely detached the gentlemen in the garrison from such amusements. The French troops invested fort Kehl,[5] situated on the Rhine, opposite to Strasburg, and the Imperialists dreading that the next storm would fall upon Philipsburg, employed themselves with great diligence, to put that important fortress in a proper posture of defence. If the suspension of play was displeasing to our hero, the expectation of being besieged was by no means more agreeable. He knew the excellence of the French engineers, the power of their artillery, and the perseverance of their general: he felt, by anticipation, the toils of hard duty upon the works, the horrors of night-alarms, cannonading, bombardment, sallies and mines blown up; and deliberated with himself, whether or not he should privately withdraw, and take refuge among the besiegers; but, when he reflected that such a step, besides the infamy that must attend it, would be like that of running upon Scylla, seeking to avoid Charybdis,[6] as he would be exposed to more danger and inconvenience in the trenches, than he could possibly undergo in the town, and after all run the risque of being taken and treated as a deserter; upon these considerations, he resolved to submit himself to his destiny, and endeavoured to mitigate the rigour of his fate, by those arts he had formerly practised with success. He accordingly found means to enjoy a very bad state of health during the whole siege, which lasted about six weeks after the trenches were opened; and then the garrison marched out by capitulation, with all the honours of war.[7]

CHAPTER XIX.

He puts himself under the guidance of his associate,
and stumbles upon the French camp, where he
finishes his military career.

Nothing else of moment was transacted during that campaign; and in the winter, our adventurer, with the young count, and his friend the Tyrolese, were disposed in quarters of cantonment,[1] where Ferdinand made himself amends for the chagrin he had undergone, by the exercise of those talents in which he excelled. Not that he was satisfied with the sphere of life in which he acted; though he knew himself consummate in the art of play, he was not at all ambitious of a gamester's name; nor did he find himself disposed to hazard those discoveries and explanations to which heroes of that class are sometimes necessarily exposed. His aim was to dwell among the tents of civil life, undisturbed by quarrels and the din of war, and render mankind subservient to his interest, not by strategems which irritate, but by that suppleness of insinuation, which could not fail to sooth the temper of those on whom he meant to prey.

He saw that all his expectations of count Melvile's future favour, were connected with his choice of a military life; and that his promotion in the service would, in a great measure, depend upon his personal behaviour in such emergencies as he did not at all wish to encounter. On the other hand, he confided so much in his own dexterity and address, that he never doubted of being able to rear a splendid fortune for himself, provided he could once obtain a fixed and firm foundation. He had in fancy, often enjoyed a prospect of England, not only as his native country, to which, like a true citizen, he longed to be united; but also as the land of promise, flowing with milk and honey,[2] and abounding with subjects on which he knew his talents would be properly exercised.

These reflections never occurred, without leaving a strong impression upon the mind of our adventurer, which influenced his deliberations, in such a manner, as at length amounted to a perfect resolution of withdrawing himself privately from a service that teemed with disagreeable events; and of transporting himself into the country of his ancestors, which he considered as the Canaan[3] of all able adventurers. But, previous to his appearance on that stage, he was desirous of visiting the metropolis of France, in which he hoped to improve himself in the knowledge of men and things, and acquire such intelligence as would qualify him to act a more important part upon the British scene. After having for sometime indulged these prospects in secret, he determined to accommodate himself with the company and experience of the Tyrolese, whom, under the specious title of an associate, he knew he could convert into a very serviceable tool, in forwarding the execution of his own projects.

Accordingly, the inclination of this confederate, was sounded by distant hints, and being found apt, our hero made him privy to his design of decamping without beat of drum;[4] though, at the same time, he begged his advice, touching the method of their departure, that he might retire with as much delicacy as the nature of such a step would permit. Divers consultations were

held upon this subject, before they adhered to the resolution of making their
escape from the army, after it should have taken the field in the spring; because, in that case, they would have frequent opportunities of going abroad
on foraging parties, and during one of these excursions, might retire in such a
manner as to persuade their companions, that they had fallen into the enemy's hands.

Agreeable to this determination, the camp was no sooner formed in Alsace,[5] than our associates began to make preparations for their march, and
had already taken all the previous measures for their departure, when an
accident happened, which our hero did not fail to convert to his own advantage: this was no other than the desertion of Renaldo's valet, who, in consequence of a gentle chastisement, which he had richly merited, thought
proper to disappear, after having plundered his master's portmanteau, which
he had forced open for the purpose. Ferdinand, who was the first person that
discovered the theft, immediately comprehended the whole adventure, and
taking it for granted, that the delinquent would never return, resolved to
finish what the fugitive had imperfectly performed.

Being favoured with the unreserved confidence of the young count, he
instantly had recourse to his bureau, the locks of which, he found means to
burst open, and examining a private drawer contrived with great art to conceal Renaldo's jewels and cash, made himself master of the contents without
hesitation; then cutting open his cloak bag, and strewing the tent with his
linnen and cloaths, began to raise his voice, and produce such a clamour as
alarmed the whole neighbourhood, and brought a great many officers into
the tent.

He on this, as on all other occasions, performed his cue to a miracle, expressing confusion and concern so naturally, in his gestures and exclamation,
that no man could possibly suspect his sincerity; nay, to such a degree of
finesse did his cunning amount, that when his friend and patron entered, in
consequence of an intimation he soon received of his loss, our adventurer
exhibited undoubted signs of distraction and delirium, and springing upon
Renaldo with all the frantic fury of a bedlamite,[6] "Villain!" cried he, "restore
the effects you have stole from your master, or you shall be immediately
committed to the care of the prévot."[7] However mortified M. de Melvile
might be, at his own misfortune, the condition of his friend seemed to touch
him more nearly; he undervalued his own loss, as a trifle that could be easily
repaired, said every thing which he thought would tend to sooth and compose the agitation of Ferdinand, and finally prevailed upon him to retire to
rest. The calamity was wholly attributed to the deserter, and Renaldo, far
from suspecting the true author, took occasion, from his behaviour on this

emergency, to admire him as a mirrour of integrity and attachment; in such an exquisite manner did he plan all his designs, that almost every instance of his fraud furnished matter of triumph to his reputation.

Having thus profitably exercised his genius, this subtle politician, thought it high time to relinquish his military expectations, and securing all his valuable acquisitions about his own person, rode out with his understrapper, in the midst of fifty dragoons who went in quest of forage. While the troopers were employed in making up their trusses,[8] the two adventurers advanced towards the skirt of a wood, on pretence of reconnoitring, and the Tyroleze, who undertook to be our hero's guide, directing him to a path which led towards Strasburg, they suddenly vanished from the eyes of their companions, who in a few minutes hearing the report of several pistols, which the confederates purposely fired, conjectured that they had fallen in with a party of French, by whom they were made prisoners of war.

The Tyroleze had over-rated his own knowledge, when he took upon himself the charge of conducting our hero; for, upon their arrival at a certain place, where two roads crossed each other, he chanced to follow that which not only frustrated their intention, but even led them directly to the French camp: so that in the twilight they fell in upon one of the out-guards, before they were aware of their mistake. Whatever confusion and perplexity they might undergo, when they heard themselves questioned by the centinel on the advanced post, certain it is, they betrayed no symptoms of fear or disorder; but while Ferdinand endeavoured to recollect himself, his fellow-traveller, with the appearance of admirable intrepidity and presence of mind, told the soldier, that he and his companion were two gentlemen of family, who had quitted the Austrian army, on account of having sustained some ill-usage, which they had no opportunity of resenting in any other way; and that they were come to offer their services to the French general, to whose quarters they desired to be immediately conveyed.

The centinel, to whom such an instance of desertion was neither rare, nor indeed uncommon, directed them without scruple to the next post, where they found a serjeant's party, from which, at their request, they were transmitted to the officer of the grand guard, and by him, next morning, introduced to count Coigny,[9] who very politely received them as volunteers in the army of France. Though this translation was not at all to our hero's liking, he was forced to acquiesce in his fate, glad to find himself, on these terms, in possession of his effects, of which he would otherwise have been infallibly rifled.

This campaign, however, was the most disagreeable period of his whole life; because the manner in which he had entered into the service, subjected him to the particular observation and notice of the French officers; so that he was obliged to be very alert in his duty, and summon all his fortitude to maintain the character he had assumed. What rendered his situation still more unpalatable, was the activity of both armies in the course of this season, during which, over and above sundry fatiguing marches and counter-marches, he was personally engaged in the affair of Hallch,[10] which was very obstinate, where being in the skirts of the detachment, he was actually wounded in the face by the sword of an hussar; but this was, luckily for him, the last time he found himself under the necessity of exerting his military prowess; for a cessation of arms was proclaimed, before he was cured of his wound, and peace concluded about the end of the campaign.

During his sojourn in the French camp, he assumed the character of a man of family, who being disgusted at some supercilious treatment he had met with, in the German service, and at the same time ambitious of carrying arms under the banners of France, took the opportunity of retreating by stealth from his friends, accompanied only by one with whom he could entrust his intention. In this capacity, he had managed his matters to such advantage, that many French officers of rank were very well disposed to contribute their interest in his behalf, had his inclination verged towards promotion in the army; but he thought proper to conceal his real design, under the specious pretext of longing to see the metropolis of France, that centre of pleasure and politeness, in which he proposed to spend some time for the improvement of his address and understanding. These were motives too laudable to be opposed by his new patrons, some of whom furnished him with letters of recommendation to certain noblemen of the first rank at the court of Versailles, for which place he and his companion set out from the banks of the Rhine, very well satisfied with the honourable dismission they had obtained from a life of inconvenience, danger and alarm.

CHAPTER XX.

*He prepares a strategem, but finds himself
countermined; proceeds on his journey, and is
overtaken by a terrible tempest.*

In the course of this journey, Ferdinand, who was never deficient in his political capacity, held a secret conclave with his own thoughts, not only touching the plan of his own future conduct, but also concerning his associate, of whose fidelity and adherence he began to entertain such doubts as discouraged him from the prosecution of that design, in which the Tyroleze had been at first included: for, he had lately observed him practise the arts of his occupation among the French officers, with such rapacity and want of caution, as indicated a dangerous temerity of temper, as well as a furious rage of acquiring, which might be sometime or other, satiated upon his own friends. In other words, our adventurer was afraid that his accomplice would profit by his knowledge of the road and countries through which they travelled, and after having made free with his most valuable effects, in consequence of the familiarity subsisting between them, leave him some morning without the ceremony of a formal adieu.

Arroused by this suspicion, he resolved to anticipate the supposed intention of the Tyroleze, by taking his own departure in the same abrupt manner; and this scheme he actually put in execution, upon their arrival in Bar le duc,[1] where it was agreed they should spend a day to repose and refresh themselves from the fatigue of hard riding. Ferdinand, therefore, taking the advantage of his companion's absence, for the Tyroleze had walked abroad to view the town, found means to hire a peasant, who undertook to conduct him through a bye-road, as far as Chalons,[2] and with this guide, he accordingly set out on horseback, after having discharged the bill, left a blank paper sealed up in form of a letter, directed to his friend, and secured behind his own saddle, a pair of leathern bags in which his jewels and cash were usually contained. So eager was our hero to leave the Tyroleze at a considerable distance behind, that he rode all night at a round pace, without halting, and next morning, found himself at a village distant thirteen good leagues,[3] from any part of the route, which he and his companion had at first resolved to pursue.

Here thinking himself safely delivered from the cause of all his apprehension, he determined to lie incognito for a few days, so as that he might run no risque of an accidental meeting upon the road, with the person whose company he had forsaken; and accordingly he took possession of an apartment, in which he went to rest, desiring his guide to wake him, when dinner should be ready. Having enjoyed a very comfortable refreshment of sleep, with his bags under his pillow, he was summoned according to his direction, and ate a very hearty meal with great tranquillity and internal satisfaction. In the afternoon, he amused himself with happy presages, and ideal prospects of his future fortune, and in the midst of these imaginary banquets was seized with an inclination of realizing his bliss, and regaling his eye-sight with the fruits of that success, which had hitherto attended his endeavours. Thus inflamed, he opened the repository, and O reader! what were his reflections, when in lieu of mademoiselle Melvile's earrings and necklace, the German's golden chain, divers jewels of considerable value, the spoils of sundry dupes, and about two hundred ducats[4] in ready money, he found neither more nor less than a parcel of rusty nails, disposed in such a manner as to resemble in weight and bulk the moveables he had lost.

It is not to be supposed, our adventurer made this discovery without emotion. If the eternal salvation of mankind could have been purchased for the tenth part of his treasure,[5] he would have left the whole species in a state of reprobation, rather than redeem them at that price, unless he had seen in the bargain, some evident advantage to his own concerns: one may therefore easily conceive with what milkiness[6] of resignation, he bore the loss of the whole, and saw himself reduced from such affluence, to the necessity of depending upon about twenty ducats, and some loose silver which he carried in his pocket, for his expence upon the road. However bitter this pill might be in swallowing, he so far mastered his mortification, as to digest it with a good grace: his own penetration at once, pointed out the canal through which this misfortune had flowed upon him; he forthwith placed the calamity to the account of the Tyroleze, and never doubting that he had retired with the booty across the Rhine, into some place to which he knew Fathom would not follow his footsteps, he formed the melancholy resolution of pursuing with all dispatch, his journey to Paris, that he might with all convenient expedition, indemnify himself for the discomfiture he had sustained.

With regard to his confederate, his conjecture was perfectly right; that adventurer, though infinitely inferior to our hero in point of genius and invention, had manifestly the advantage of him, in the articles of age and experience; he was no stranger to Fathom's qualifications, the happy exertion of which he had often seen. He knew him to be an œconomist of the most frugal order, consequently concluded his finances were worthy of examination; and upon the true principles of a sharper, eased him of the incumbrance, taking it for granted, that in so doing, he only precluded Ferdinand from the power of acting the same tragedy upon him, should ever opportunity concur with his inclination. He had therefore concerted his measures with the dexterity of an experienced conveyancer, and snatching the occasion, while our hero traveltainted,[7] lay sunk in the arms of profound repose, he ript up the seams of the leathern depository, withdrew the contents, introduced the parcel of nails, which he had made up for the purpose, and then repaired the breach with great deliberation.

Had Fathom's good genius prompted him to examine his effects next morning, the Tyroleze, in all probability, would have maintained his acquisition by force of arms; for his personal courage was rather more determined than that of our adventurer, and he was conscious of his own ascendancy in this particular; but, his good fortune prevented such explanation. Immediately after dinner, he availed himself of his knowledge, and betaking himself to a remote part of the town, set out in a post-chaise for Luneville,[8] while our hero was meditating his own escape.

Fathom's conception was sufficient to comprehend the whole of this adventure, as soon as his chagrin would give his sagacity fair play; nor would he allow his resolution to sink under the trial; on the contrary, he departed from the village, that same afternoon, under the auspices of his conductor, and found himself benighted in the midst of a forest far from the habitations of men; the darkness of the night, the silence and solitude of the place, the indistinct images of the trees that appeared on every side, "stretching their extravagant arms athwart the gloom,"[9] conspired with the dejection of spirits occasioned by his loss to disturb his fancy, and raise strange phantoms in his imagination.[10] Although he was not naturally superstitious, his mind began to be invaded with an awful horror, that gradually prevailed over all the consolations of reason and philosophy; nor was his heart free from the terrors of assassination. In order to dissipate these disagreeable reveries, he had recourse to the conversation of his guide, by whom he was entertained with the history of divers travellers, who had been robbed and murdered by ruffians, whose retreat was in the recesses of that very wood.

In the midst of this communication, which did not at all tend to the elevation of our hero's spirits, the conductor made an excuse for dropping behind, while our traveller jogged on in expectation of being joined again by him in a few minutes: he was however disappointed in that hope: the sound of the other horse's feet, by degrees, grew more and more faint, and at last, altogether died away. Alarmed at this circumstance, Fathom halted in the middle of the road, and listened with the most fearful attention; but his sense of hearing was saluted with nought but the dismal sighings of the trees, that seemed to foretell an approaching storm; accordingly the Heavens contracted a more dreary aspect, the lightning began to gleam, the thunder to roll, and the tempest raising its voice to a tremendous roar, descended in a torrent of rain.

In this emergency, the fortitude of our hero was almost quite overcome; so many concuring circumstances of danger and distress, might have appalled the most undaunted breast; what impression then must they have made upon the mind of Ferdinand, who was by no means a man to set fear at defiance! indeed, he had well nigh lost the use of his reflection, and was actually invaded to the skin, before he could recollect himself so far as to quit the road, and seek for shelter among the thickets that surrounded them. Having rode some furlongs[11] into the forest, he took his station under a tuft of tall trees, that screened him from the storm, and in that situation called a council within himself, to deliberate upon his next excursion. He persuaded himself that his guide had deserted him for the present, in order to give intelligence of a traveller, to some gang of robbers with whom he was connected; and that he must of necessity fall a prey to those banditti, unless he should have the good fortune to elude their search, and disentangle himself from the mazes of the wood.

Harrowed with these apprehensions, he resolved to commit himself to the mercy of the hurricane, as of two evils the least, and penetrate streight forwards through some devious opening, until he should be delivered from the forest. For this purpose, he turned his horse's head in a line, quite contrary to the direction of the high-road which he had left, on the supposition, that the robbers would pursue that tract in quest of him, and that they would never dream of his deserting the highway, to traverse an unknown forest, amidst the darkness of such a boisterous night. After he had continued in this progress, thro' a succession of groves, and bogs, and thorns and brakes, by which, not only his cloaths, but also his skin suffered in a grievous manner, while every nerve quivered with eagerness of dismay; he at length reached an open plain, and pursuing his course, in full hope of arriving at some village, where his life would be safe, he descried a rush light[12] at a distance, which he looked upon as the star of his good fortune, and riding towards it at full speed, arrived at the door of a lone cottage, into which he was admitted by an old woman, who understanding he was a bewildered traveller, received him with great hospitality.

When he learned from his hostess, that there was not another house within three leagues, that she could accommodate him with a tolerable bed, and his horse with lodging and oats, he thanked Heaven for his good fortune in stumbling upon this homely habitation, and determined to pass the night under the protection of the old cottager, who gave him to understand that her husband, who was a faggot-maker,[13] had gone to the next town to dispose of his merchandize, and that in all probability, he would not return till next morning, on account of the tempestuous night. Ferdinand sounded the beldame with a thousand artful interrogations, and she answered with such appearance of truth and simplicity, that he concluded his person was quite secure; and after having been regaled with a dish of eggs and bacon, desired she would conduct him into the chamber where she proposed he should take his repose. He was accordingly ushered up by a sort of ladder, into an apartment furnished with a standing-bed, and almost half filled with trusses of straw. He seemed extremely well pleased with his lodging, which in reality exceeded his expectation, and his kind landlady cautioning him against letting the candle approach the combustibles, took her leave, and locked the door on the outside.

CHAPTER XXI.

He falls upon Scylla, seeking to avoid Charybdis.

Fathom, whose own principles taught him to be suspicious, and ever upon his guard against the treachery of his fellow-creatures, could have dispensed with this instance of her care in confining her guest to her chamber, and began to be seized with strange fancies, when he observed that there was no bolt on the inside of the door, by which he might secure himself from intrusion. In consequence of these suggestions, he proposed to take an accurate survey of every object in the apartment, and in the course of his inquiry, had the mortification to find the dead body of a man, still warm, who had been lately stabbed, and concealed beneath several bundles of straw.

Such a discovery could not fail to fill the breast of our hero, with unspeakable horror; for he concluded that he himself would undergo the same fate before morning, without the interposition of a miracle in his favour. In the first transports of his dread, he ran to the window with a view to escape by that outlet, and found his flight effectually obstructed by divers strong bars of iron. Then his heart began to palpitate, his hair to bristle up, and his knees to totter; his thoughts teemed with presages of death and destruction; his conscience rose up in judgment against him, and he underwent a severe paroxysm of dismay and distraction. His spirits were agitated into a state of fermentation that produced a species of resolution a-kin to that which is inspired by brandy or other strong liquors, and by an impulse that seemed supernatural, he was immediately hurried into measures for his own preservation.

What upon a less interesting occasion his imagination durst not propose, he now executed without scruple or remorse: he undressed the corpse that lay bleeding among the straw, and conveying it to the bed in his arms, deposited it in the attitude of a person who sleeps at his ease; then he extin-

guished the light, took possession of the place from whence the body had
been removed, and holding a pistol ready cocked in each hand, waited for the
sequel with that determined purpose, which is often the immediate production of despair. About midnight he heard the sound of feet ascending the
ladder, the door was softly opened, he saw the shadow of two men stalking
towards the bed, a dark lanthorn being unshrouded, directed their aim to the
supposed sleeper, and he that held it, thrust a poignard to his heart; the force
of the blow made a compression on the chest, and a sort of groan issued from
the windpipe of the defunct; the stroke was repeated, without producing a
repetition of the note, so that the assassins concluded the work was effectually done, and retired for the present, with a design to return and rifle the
deceased at their leisure.

Never had our hero spent a moment in such agony, as he felt during this
operation; the whole surface of his body was covered with a cold sweat, and
his nerves were relaxed with an universal palsy: in short, he remained in a
trance that, in all probability, contributed to his safety; for, had he retained
the use of his senses, he might have been discovered by the transports of his
fear. The first use he made of his retrieved recollection was to perceive that
the assassins had left the door open in their retreat; and he would have instantly availed himself of this their neglect, by sallying out upon them, at the
hazard of his life, had not he been restrained by a conversation he overheard
in the room below, importing that the ruffians were going to set out upon
another expedition, in hopes of finding more prey: they accordingly departed, after having laid strong injunctions upon the old woman, to keep the
door fast locked during their absence; and Ferdinand took his resolution
without farther delay. So soon as by his conjecture, the robbers were at a
sufficient distance from the house, he rose from his lurking-place, moved
softly towards the bed, and rummaging the pockets of the deceased, found a
purse well stored with ducats, of which, together with a silver watch and a
diamond ring, he immediately possessed himself without scruple; then descending with great care and circumspection, into the lower apartment, stood
before the old beldam, before she had the least intimation of his approach.

Accustomed as she was to the trade of blood, the hoary hag did not behold
this apparition without giving signs of infinite terror and astonishment, believing it was no other than the spirit of her second guest who had been
murdered; she fell upon her knees, and began to recommend herself to the
protection of the saints, crossing herself with as much devotion, as if she had
been intitled to the particular care and attention of Heaven. Nor did her
anxiety abate, when she was undeceived in this her supposition, and under-

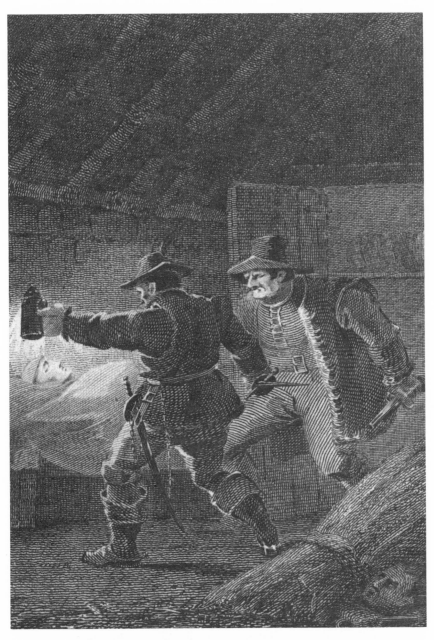

The Assassins Stalking Toward the Bed, by Clennell.
(Library Company of Philadelphia.)

stood it was no phantom, but the real substance of the stranger, who without staying to upbraid her with the enormity of her crimes, commanded her on pain of immediate death to produce his horse, to which being conducted, he set her upon the saddle without delay, and mounting behind, invested her with the management of the reins, swearing in a most peremptory tone, that the only chance she had for her life, was in directing him safely to the next town; and that so soon as she should give him the least cause to doubt her fidelity in the performance of that task, he would, on the instant, act the part of her executioner.

This declaration had its effect upon the withered Hecate,[1] who, with many supplications for mercy and forgiveness, promised to guide him in safety, to a certain village at the distance of two leagues, where he might lodge in security, and be provided with a fresh horse, or other convenience, for pursuing his intended route. On these conditions, he told her, she might deserve his clemency, and they accordingly took their departure together, she being placed astride upon the saddle, holding the bridle in one hand, and a switch in the other; and our adventurer sitting on the crupper,[2] superintending her conduct, and keeping the muzzle of a pistol close at her ear. In this equipage, they travelled across part of the same wood, in which his guide had forsaken him; and it is not to be supposed, that he passed his time in the most agreeable reverie, while he found himself involved in the labyrinth of those shades, which he considered as the haunts of robbery and assassination.

Common fear was a comfortable sensation to what he felt in this excursion. The first steps he had taken for his preservation, were the effects of meer instinct, while his faculties were extinguished or suppressed by despair; but, now as his reflection began to recur, he was haunted by the most intolerable apprehensions. Every whisper of the wind through the thickets, was swelled into the hoarse menaces of murder, the shaking of the boughs was construed into the brandishing of poignards, and every shadow of a tree, became the apparition of a ruffian eager for blood. In short, at each of these occurrences, he felt what was infinitely more tormenting than the stab of a real dagger; and at every fresh filip[3] of his fear, he acted as remembrancer to his conductress, in a new volley of imprecations, importing that her life was absolutely connected with his opinion of his own safety.

Human nature could not long subsist under such complicated terror: at last he found himself clear of the forest, and was blessed with the distant view of an inhabited place: he then began to exercise his thoughts upon a new subject. He debated with himself, whether he should make a parade of his intrepidity and public spirit, by disclosing his atchievement and surrendring his guide to the penalty of the law; or leave the old hag and her accomplices to the remorse of their own consciences, and proceed quietly on his journey to Paris, in undisturbed possession of the prize he had already obtained. This last step he determined to take, upon recollecting that in the course of his information, the story of the murdered stranger would infallibly attract the attention of justice, and in that case, the effects he had borrowed from the defunct, must be refunded for the benefit of those who had a right to the succession. This was an argument which our adventurer could not resist; he foresaw that he should be stript of his acquisition, which he looked upon as the fair fruits of his valour and sagacity; and moreover, be detained as an evidence against the robbers, to the manifest detriment of his affairs: perhaps too, he had motives of conscience that dissuaded him from bearing witness against a set of people, whose principles did not much differ from his own.

Influenced by such considerations, he yielded to the first importunity of the beldam, whom he dismissed at a very small distance from the village, after he had earnestly exhorted her to quit such an atrocious course of life, and attone for her past crimes, by sacrificing her associates to the demands of justice. She did not fail to vow a perfect reformation, and to prostrate herself before him, for the favour she had found; then she betook herself to her habitation, with full purpose of advising her fellow-murderers to repair with all dispatch to the village, and impeach[4] our hero, who wisely distrusting her professions, staid no longer in the place, than to hire a guide for the next stage, which brought him to the city of Chalons sur Marne.

CHAPTER XXII.

He arrives at Paris, and is pleased with his reception.

He was not so smitten with the delightful situation of this ancient town, but that he abandoned it as soon as he could procure a post-chaise, in which he arrived at Paris, without having been exposed to any other troublesome adventure upon the road. He took lodgings at a certain hotel in the Fauxbourg de St. Germain,[1] which is the general rendezvous of all the strangers that resort to this capital; and now sincerely congratulated himself upon his happy escape from his Hungarian connections, and from the snares of the banditti; as well as upon the spoils of the dead body, and his arrival at Paris, from whence there was such a short conveyance to England, whither he was attracted by far other motives than that of filial veneration for his native soil.

He suppressed all his letters of recommendation, which he justly concluded, would subject him to a tedious course of attendance upon the great, and lay him under the necessity of solliciting preferment in the army, than which nothing was farther from his inclination; and resolved to make his appearance in the character of a private gentleman, which would supply him with opportunities of examining the different scenes of life in such a gay metropolis, so as that he should be able to chuse that sphere in which he could move the most effectually to his own advantage. He accordingly hired an occasional domestick, and under the denomination of count Fadome, which he had retained since his elopement from Renaldo, repaired to dinner at an ordinary,[2] to which he was directed as a reputable place frequented by fashionable strangers of all nations.

He found this piece of information perfectly just; for he no sooner entered the apartment, than his ears were saluted with a strange confusion of sounds, among which he at once distinguished the high and low Dutch, barbarous French, Italian and English languages. He was rejoiced at this occasion of displaying his own qualifications; took his place at one of three long tables, betwixt a Westphalian count, and a Bolognian marquis,[3] insinuated himself into the conversation with his usual address, and in less than half an hour, found means to accost a native of each different country, in his own mother tongue.

Such extensive knowledge did not pass unobserved. A French abbé, in a provincial dialect, complimented him upon his retaining that purity in pronunciation, which is not to be found in the speech of a Parisian. The Bolognian mistaking him for a Tuscan, "Sir," said he, "I presume you are from Florence: I hope the illustrious house of Lorrain leaves you gentlemen of that famous city, no room to regret the loss of your own princes."[4] The castle of Versailles becoming the subject of conversation, monsieur le Comte appealed to him as to a native German, whether it was not inferior in point of magnificence to the Chateau of Grubenhagen:[5] the Dutch officer addressing himself to Fathom, drank to the prosperity of Faderland, and asked if he had not once served in garrison at Schenkenschans;[6] and an English knight swore with great assurance, that he had frequently rambled with him at midnight, among the hundreds of Drury.[7]

To each person he replied in a polite, tho' mysterious manner, which did not fail to inhance their opinion of his good breeding and importance; and long before the desert appeared, he was by all the company supposed to be a personage of great consequence, who for some substantial reasons, found it convenient to keep himself incognito. This being the case, it is not to be doubted that particular civilities were poured upon him from all quarters: he perceived their sentiments, and encouraged them, by behaving with that sort of complaisance which seems to be the result of engaging condescension in a character of superior dignity and station. His affability was general; but his chief attention limited to those gentlemen already mentioned, who chanced to sit nearest him at table; and he no sooner gave them to understand that he was an utter stranger in Paris, than they unanimously begged to have the honour of making him acquainted with the different curiosities peculiar to that metropolis.

He accepted of their hospitality, accompanied them to a coffee-house in the afternoon, from whence they repaired to the opera, and afterwards adjourned to a noted hotel, in order to spend the remaining part of the evening. It was here that our hero secured himself effectually in the footing he had gained in their good graces: he in a moment saw through all the characters of the partie, and adapted himself to the humour of each individual; without descending from that elevation of behaviour, which, he perceived, would operate among them in his behalf. With the Italian he discoursed on musick, in the stile of a connoisseur; and indeed had a better claim to that title than the generality of those upon whom it is usually conferred; for he understood the art in theory as well as in practice, and would have made no contemptible figure among the best performers of the age.

He harangued upon taste and genius, to the abbé, who was a wit and critic, ex officio, or rather ex vestitu:[8] for, a young pert Frenchman, the very moment he puts on the petit collet,[9] or little band, looks upon himself as an inspired son of Apollo; and every one of the fraternity thinks it incumbent upon him to assert the divinity of his mission: in a word, the abbés are a set of people, that bear a strong analogy to the templars in London.[10] Fools of each fabric, sharpers of all sorts, and dunces of every degree, profess themselves of both orders: the templar is, generally speaking a prig, so is the abbé: both are distinguished by an air of petulance and self-conceit, which holds a middle rank betwixt the insolence of a first rate buck,[11] and the learned pride of a supercilious pedant. The abbé is supposed to be a younger brother in quest of preferment in the church: the temple is considered as a receptacle or seminary for younger sons, intended for the bar; but a great number of each profession turn aside into other paths of life, long before they reach these proposed goals: an abbé is often metamorphosed into a foot soldier; a templar sometimes sinks into an attorney's clerk: the gallies of France abound with abbés; and many templars may be found in our American plantations; not to mention those who have made a public exit nearer home.[12] Yet, I would not have it thought that my description includes every individual of those societies. Some of the greatest scholars, politicians, and wits that ever Europe produced, have wore the habit of an abbé; and many of our most noble families in England derive their honours from those who have studied law in the temple: the worthy sons of every community shall always be sacred from my censure and ridicule; and while I laugh at the folly of particular members, I can still honour and revere the institution.

But, let us return from this comparison, which some readers may think impertinent and unseasonable; and observe that the Westphalian count, Dutch officer, and English knight, were not excepted from the particular regard and attention of our adventurer: he pledged the German in every bumper; flattered the Hollander with complements upon the industry, wealth and policy of the seven United Provinces;[13] but he reserved his chief battery for his own countryman, on the supposition that he was, in all respects, the best adapted for the purposes of a needy gamester: him, therefore, he cultivated with extraordinary care, and singular observance; for he soon perceived him to be an humourist,[14] and from that circumstance derived an happy presage of his own success. The baronet's disposition seemed to be cast in the true English mould.[15] He was sour, silent and contemptuous; his very looks indicated a consciousness of superior wealth, and he never opened his mouth, except to make some dry, sarcastic, national reflection: nor was his behaviour free from that air of suspicion which a man puts on, when he believes himself in a croud of pickpockets whom his caution and vigilance set at defiance: in a word, though his tongue was silent on the subject, his whole demeanour was continually saying, "You are all a pack of poor, lousy rascals, who have a design upon my purse: 'tis true, I could buy your whole generation; but, I wont be bubbled, d'ye see; I am aware of your flattery, and upon my guard against all your knavish pranks; and I come into your company, for my own amusement only."

Fathom having reconnoitred this peculiarity of temper, instead of treating him with that assiduous complaisance, which he received from the other gentlemen of the party, kept aloof from him in the conversation, with a remarkable shyness of distant civility, and seldom took notice of what he said, except with a view to contradict him, or retort some of his satyrical observations. This he conceived to be the best method of acquiring his good opinion; because the Englishman would naturally conclude he was a person who could have no sinister views upon his fortune, else he would have chosen quite a different manner of deportment. Accordingly, the knight seemed to bite at the hook: he listened to Ferdinand with uncommon regard; he was even heard to commend his remarks; and at length drank to their better acquaintance.

CHAPTER XXIII.

Acquits himself with address in a nocturnal riot.

The Italian and the Abbé were the first who began to grow whimsical under the influence of the Burgundy; and in the heat of their elevation, proposed that the company should amuse themselves during the remaining part of the night, at the house of an obliging dame, who maintained a troop of fair nymphs, for the accommodation of the other sex. The proposal was approved by all, except the Hollander, whose œconomy the wine had not as yet invaded; and while he retreated soberly to his own lodgings, the rest of the society adjourned in two coaches, to the temple of love, where they were received by the venerable priestess, a personage turned of seventy, who seemed to exercise the functions of her calling, in despight of the most cruel ravages of time: for age had bent her into the form of a Turkish bow:[1] her head was agitated by the palsy, like the leaf of the poplar-tree, her hair fell down in scanty parcels, as white as the driven snow: her face was not simply wrinkled, but ploughed into innumerable furrows: her jaws could not boast of one remaining tooth; one eye distilled a large quantity of rheum,[2] by virtue of the fiery edge that surrounded it, the other was altogether extinguished, and she had lost her nose[3] in the course of her ministration. The Delphic sibyl[4] was but a type of this hoary matron, who by her figure might have been mistaken for the consort of chaos, or mother of time.[5] Yet there was something meritorious in her appearance, as it denoted her an indefatigable minister to the pleasure of mankind; and as it formed an agreeable contrast with the beauty and youth of the fair damsels that wantoned in her train. It resembled those discords in musick, which properly disposed, contribute to the harmony of the whole piece: or those horrible giants who in the world of romance, used to guard the gates of the castle, in which the inchanted damsel was confined.

This Urganda[6] seemed to be aware of her own importance, and perfectly well acquainted with the human appetite; for she compelled the whole company to undergo her embrace; then a lacquey in magnificent livery, ushered them into a superb apartment, where they waited some minutes, without being favoured with the appearance of the ladies, to the manifest dissatisfaction of the abbé, who sending for the gouvernante, reprimanded her severely for her want of politesse. The old lady, who was by no means a patern of patience and submission, retorted his reproaches with great emphasis and vivacity: her eloquence flowed altogether in the Covent-garden strain; and I question whether the celebrated mother D--gl--s herself could have made such a figure in extemporaneous altercation.[7]

After having bestowed upon the abbé the epithets of saucy insignificant pimp, she put him in mind of the good offices which he had received at her hands; how she had supplied him with bed, board, and bedfellow, in his greatest necessity; sent him abroad with money in his pockets, and in a word, cherished him in her bosom, when his own mother had abandoned him to distress: she then reviled him for presuming to affront her before strangers, and gave the company to understand that the young ladies would wait upon them, as soon as they could be confessed and receive absolution from a worthy cordelier,[8] who was now employed in performing that charitable office. The gentlemen were satisfied with this remonstrance, which argued the old lady's pious concern for the souls that were under her care, and our adventurer proposed an accommodation betwixt her and the abbé, who was prevailed upon to ask her pardon, and received her blessing upon his knees.

This affair had not been long adjusted, when five damsels were introduced in a very gay dishabille, and our hero was complimented with the privilege of chusing his Amanda[9] from the whole bevy: when he was provided, the others began to pair themselves, and unhappily, the German count chanced to pitch upon the same nymph who had captivated the desires of the British knight: a dispute immediately ensued, for the Englishman made his addresses to the lady, without paying the least regard to the priority of the other's claim; and she being pleased with his attachment, did not scruple to renounce his rival, who swore by the thunder, lightning and sacrament, that he would not quit his pretensions for any prince in Christendom, much less for a little English chevalier,[10] whom he had already honoured too much in condescending to be his companion.

The knight, provoked at this stately declaration, which was the immediate effect of anger and ebriety,[11] eyed his antagonist with a most contemptuous aspect, and advised him to avoid such comparisons for the future: "We all know," said he, "the importance of a German count; I suppose your revenue amounts to three hundred rixdollars;[12] and you have a chateau that looks like the ruins of an English gaol. I will bind myself to lend you a thousand pounds upon a mortgage of your estate (and a bad bargain I am sure I should have) if I do not in less than two months, find a yeoman of Kent, who spends more in strong ale, than the sum total of your yearly income; and were the truth known, I believe that lace upon your coat, is no better than tinsel, and those fringed ruffles with fine Holland sleeves,[13] tacked to a shirt of brown canvas, so that were you to undress yourself before the lady, you would only expose your own poverty and pride."

The count was so much enraged at these sarcastic observations, that his faculty of speech was overwhelmed by his resentment; though in order to acquit himself of the Englishman's imputation, he forthwith pulled off his cloaths with such fury, that his brocard[14] waistcoat was tore from top to bottom. The knight mistaking his meaning, considered this demeanour as a fair challenge, to try which was the better man in the exercise of boxing; and on that supposition, began to strip in his turn, when he was undeceived by Fathom, who put the right interpretation upon the count's behaviour, and begged that the affair might be compromised. By this time the Westphalian recovered the use of his tongue, and with many threats and imprecations, desired they would take notice how falsly he had been aspersed, and do him justice in espousing his claim to the damsel in question.

Before the company had time or inclination to interest themselves in the quarrel, his opponent observed that no person who was not a meer German, would ever dream of forcing the inclinations of a pretty girl, whom the accidents of fortune had subjected to his power: that such compulsion was equivalent to the most cruel rape that could be committed; and that the lady's aversion was not at all surprising; for, to speak his own sentiments, were he a woman of pleasure, he would as soon grant favours to a Westphalian hog,[15] as to the person of his antagonist. The German enraged at this comparison, was quite abandoned by his patience and discretion: he called the knight an English clown, and swearing he was the most untoward beast of a whole nation of mules, snatched up one of the candlesticks which he launched at him with such force and violence, that it sung through the air, and winging its flight into the anti-chamber, encountered the skull of his own valet, who with immediate prostration received the message of his master.

The knight, that he might not be behind hand with the Westphalian, in point of courtesy, returned the compliment with the remaining chandelier, which also missed its mark, and smiting a large mirrour that was fixed behind them, emitted such a crash as one might expect to hear if a mine were sprung beneath a manufacture of glass. Both lights being thus extinguished, a furious combat ensued in the dark; the Italian scampered off with infinite agility, and as he went down stairs, desired that nobody would interpose, because it was an affair of honour, which could not be made up. The ladies consulted their safety in flight; count Fathom slily retired to one corner of the room, while the abbé having upon him the terrors of the commissaire,[16] endeavoured to appease and part the combatants, and in the attempt, sustained a random blow upon his nose, which sent him howling into the other chamber, where finding his band besmeared with his own blood, he began to caper about the apartment, in a transport of rage and vexation.

Mean while, the old gentlewoman being alarmed with the noise of the battle, and apprehensive that it would end in murder, to the danger and discredit of herself and family, immediately mustered up her myrmidons,[17] of whom she always retained a formidable band, and putting herself at their head, lighted them to the scene of uproar: Ferdinand, who had hitherto observed a strict neutrality, no sooner perceived them approach, than he leaped in between the disputants, that he might be found acting in the character of a peace-maker; and indeed, by this time, victory had declared for the baronet, who had treated his antagonist with a cross-buttock,[18] which laid him almost breathless on the floor. The victor was prevailed upon, by the intreaties of Fathom, to quit the field of battle, and adjourn into another room, where in less than half an hour, he received a billet from the count, defying him to single combat on the frontiers of Flanders, at an appointed time and place. The challenge was immediately accepted by the knight, who being flushed with conquest, treated his adversary with great contempt.

But, next day, when the fumes of the Burgundy were quite exhaled, and the adventure recurred to his remembrance and sober reflection, he waited upon our adventurer at his lodgings, and sollicited his advice in such a manner, as gave him to understand that he looked upon what had happened, as a drunken brawl, which ought to have no serious consequences. Fathom foreseeing that the affair might be managed for his own interest, professed himself of the baronet's opinion; and without hesitation, undertook the office of a mediator, assuring his principal, that his honour should suffer no stain in the course of his negotiation.

Having received the Englishman's acknowledgments for this instance of friendship, he forthwith set out for the place of the German's habitation, and understanding he was still asleep, insisted upon his being immediately waked, and told, that a gentleman from the chevalier, desired to see him, upon business of importance which could not be delayed. Accordingly, his valet de chambre pressed by Fathom's importunities and remonstrances, ventured to go in and shake the count by the shoulder; when this furious Teutonian, still agitated by the fever of the preceding night, leaped out of bed in a frenzy, and seizing his sword that lay upon a table, would have severely punished the presumption of his servant, had not he been restrained by the entrance of Ferdinand, who with a peremptory countenance, gave him to understand that the valet had acted at his immediate instigation; and that he was come, as the Englishman's friend, to concert with him proper measures for keeping the appointment they had made at their last meeting.

This message effectually calmed the German, who was not a little mortified to find himself so disagreeably disturbed. He could not help cursing the impatience of his antagonist, and even hinting that he would have acted more like a gentleman and good christian, in expressing a desire of seeing the affair accommodated, as he knew himself to be the aggressor, consequently the first offender against the laws of politeness and good fellowship. Fathom finding him in a fit temper of mind, took the opportunity of assenting to the reasonableness of his observation: he ventured to condemn the impetuosity of the baronet, who, he perceived, was extremely nice and scrupulous in the punctilios of honour; and said it was pity that two gentlemen should forfeit each other's friendship, much less expose their lives for such a frivolous cause. "My dear count!" cried the Westphalian, "I am charmed to find your sentiments so conformable to my own: in an honourable cause, I despise all danger; my courage, thank Heaven! has been manifested in many public engagements as well as in private rencounters; but, to break with my friend, whose eminent virtues I admire, and even to seek his life, on such a scandalous occasion, for a little insignificant whore, who, I suppose, took the advantage of our intoxication, to foment the quarrel: by Heaven! my conscience cannot digest it."

Having expressed himself to this purpose, he waited impatiently for the reply of Ferdinand, who after a pause of deliberation, offered his services in the way of mediation; though he observed, it was a matter of great delicacy, and the event altogether uncertain. "Nevertheless," added our adventurer, "I will strive to appease the knight, who, I hope will be induced by my remonstrances to forget the unlucky accident, which hath so disagreeably interrupted your mutual friendship." The German thanked him for this proof of his regard, which yielded him more satisfaction on account of the chevalier than of himself: "For, by the tombs of my fathers!" cried he, "I have so little concern for my personal safety, that if my honour were interested, I durst oppose myself singly to the whole ban of the empire;[19] and I am now ready, if the chevalier requires it, to give him the rendezvous in the forest of Senlis,[20]

either on horseback or on foot, where this contest may be terminated with
the life of one or both of us."

Count Fathom, with a view to chastise the Westphalian for this rhodomontade,[21] told him with a mortifying air of indifference, that if they were both
bent upon taking the field, he would save himself the trouble of interposing
farther in the affair; and desired to know the hour at which it would suit him
to take the air with the baronet: the other, not a little embarrassed by this
question, said with a faultering tongue, he should be proud to obey the
chevalier's orders; but, at the same time, owned he should be much better
pleased, if our hero would execute the pacific proposal he had made. Fathom,
accordingly promised to exert himself for that purpose, returned to the
knight, with whom he assumed the merit of having tranquillized the rage of
an incensed barbarian, who was now disposed to a reconciliation upon equal
terms: the baronet overwhelmed him with caresses and compliments upon
his friendship and address; the parties met that same forenoon, as if by accident in Fathom's apartment, where they embraced each other cordially, exchanged apologies, and renewed their former correspondence.

Our adventurer thought he had good reason to congratulate himself upon
the part he acted in this pacification: he was treated by both with signal marks
of particular affection and esteem. The count pressed him to accept as a token
of his attachment, a sword of very curious workmanship, which he had received in a present from a certain prince of the empire: the knight forced
upon his finger a very splendid diamond ring, as a testimony of his gratitude
and esteem: but there was still another person to be appeased, before the
peace of the whole company could be established. This was no other than the
abbé, from whom each of the reconciled friends received at dinner a billet
couched in these words.

"I have the honour to lament the infinite chagrin and mortification that
compels me to address myself in this manner to a person of your rank and
eminence, whom I should do myself the pleasure of waiting upon in person;
were I not prevented by the misfortune of my nose, which was last night
most cruelly disarranged, by a violent contusion I had the honour to receive,
in attempting to compose that unhappy *fracas*, at the house of madam la
Maquerelle;[22] and what puts the finishing stroke to my mishap, is my being
rendered incapable of keeping three or four assignations with ladies of fashion, by whom I have the honour to be particularly esteemed. The disfigura-
tion of my nose, the pain I have undergone, with the discomposure of brain
which it produced, I could bear as a philosopher; but the disappointment of
the ladies, my glory will not permit me to overlook: and as you know the

injury was sustained in your service, I have the pleasure to hope you will not refuse to grant such reparation as will be acceptable to a gentleman who has the honour to be with inviolable attachment,

Sir your most devoted slave,

Pepin Clothaire Charlé Henri Louis

Barnabe de Fumier."[23]

This epistle was so equivocal, that the persons to whom it was addressed, did not know whether or not they ought to interpret the contents into a challenge; when our hero observed, that the ambiguity of his expressions, plainly proved there was a door left open for accommodation; and proposed that they should forthwith visit the writer at his own apartment: they accordingly followed his advice, and found the abbé in his morning-gown and slippers, with three huge night-caps on his head, and a crape hat-band tied over the middle of his face, by way of bandage to his nose. He received his visiters with the most ridiculous solemnity, being still a stranger to the purport of their errand; but soon as the Westphalian declared they were come in consequence of his billet, in order to ask pardon for the undesigned offence they had given, his features retrieved their natural vivacity, and he professed himself perfectly satisfied with their polite acknowledgment. Then they condoled him upon the evil plight of his nose, and seeing some marks upon his shirt, asked with seeming concern, if he had lost any blood in the fray. To this interrogation, he replied, that he had still a sufficient quantity left for the occasions of his friends; and that he should deem it his greatest glory, to expend the last drop of it in their service.

Matters being thus amicably adjusted, they prevailed upon him to uncase his nose, which retained no signs of the outrage he had suffered; and the amusements of the day were concerted. It was in consequence of this plan, that after the comedy, they were entertained at the count's lodgings, where quadrille[24] was proposed by the abbé, as the most innocent pastime, and the proposal was immediately embraced by all present, and by none with more alacrity than by our adventurer, who without putting forth a moiety of his terror, went home with twenty louis' clear gain:[25] though, far from believing himself greatly superior to the rest of the party, in the artifices of play, he justly suspected that they had concealed their skill, with a view of stripping him on some other occasion; for he could not suppose, that persons of their figure and character, should be, in reality, such novices as they affected to appear.

CHAPTER XXIV.

He overlooks the advances of his friends, and
smarts severely for his neglect.

Steeled with this cautious maxim he guarded himself from their united
endeavours, in sundry subsequent attacks, by which his first conjecture
was confirmed, and still came off conqueror, by virtue of his unparallelled
finesse and discretion: till at length they seemed to despair of making him
their prey, and the count began to drop some hints, importing a desire of
seeing him more closely united to the views and interest of their triumvirate.
But Ferdinand, who was altogether selfish, and quite solitary in his prospects, discouraged all those advances; being resolved to trade upon his own
bottom only, and to avoid all such connexions with any person or society
whatever; much more, with a set of raw adventurers whose talents he despised. With these sentiments, he still maintained the dignity and reserve of
his first appearance among them, and rather inhanced than diminished that
idea of importance which he had inspired at the beginning; because besides
his other qualifications, they gave him credit for the address with which he
kept himself superior to their united designs.

While he thus enjoyed his pre-heminence, together with the fruits of his
success at play, which he managed so discreetly, as never to incur the reputation of an adventurer; he one day, chanced to be at the ordinary, when the
company was surprised by the entrance of such a figure as had never appeared before in that place.[1] This was no other than a person habited in the
exact uniform of an English jockey.[2] His leathern cap, cut bob, fustian[3] frock,
flannel waistcoat, buff[4] breeches, hunting-boots and whip, were sufficient of
themselves to furnish out a phænomenon for the admiration of all Paris: but
these peculiarities were rendered still more conspicuous by the behaviour of
the man who owned them. When he crossed the threshold of the outward
door, he produced such a sound from the smack of his whip, as equalled the
explosion of an ordinary cohorn;[5] and then broke forth into the hollow of a
foxhunter, which he uttered with all its variations, in a strain of vociferation,
that seemed to astonish and confound the whole assembly, to whom he introduced himself and his spaniel, by exclaiming in a tone something less melo-
dious than the cry of mackarel or live cod.[6] "By your leave, Gentlevolks, I
hope there's no offence, in an honest plain Engishman's coming with money
in his pocket, to taste a bit of your Vrench frigasee and ragooze."[7]

This declaration was made in such a wild, fantastical manner, that the

greatest part of the company mistook him for some savage monster or maniac,[8] and consulted their safety by starting up from table, and drawing their
swords. The Englishman seeing such a martial apparatus produced against
him, recoiled two or three steps, saying, "Waunds,[9] a believe the people are
all bewitched: what do they take me for a beast of prey; is there no body here
that knows Sir Stentor Stile, or can speak to me in my own lingo?" He had no
sooner pronounced these words, than the baronet, with marks of infinite
surprize, ran towards him, crying, "Good Heaven! Sir Stentor, who expected to meet with you in Paris?" Upon which, the other eyeing him very
earnestly, "Odds heartlikens,"[10] cried he, "my neighbour Sir Giles Squirrel,
as I am a living soul!" With these words, he flew upon him like a tyger, kissed
him from ear to ear, demolished his periwig, and disordered the whole
œconomy of his dress, to the no small entertainment of the company.

Having well nigh stifled his countryman with embraces, and besmeared
himself with pulville[11] from head to foot, he proceeded in this manner;
"Mercy upon thee, knight, thou art so transmographied and bedaubed, and
bedizened,[12] that thou mought rob thy own mother without fear of information. Look ye here now, I will be trussed, if the very bitch that was
brought up in thy own bosom, knows thee again. Hey, sweetlips, here hussy,
damn thee tuoad, do'st n't know thy old measter. Ey, ey, thou may'st smell
till Christmas. I'll be bound to be hanged, knight, if the creature's nose an't
foundered by the damned stinking perfumes you have got among you."

These compliments being past, the two knights sat down by one another,
and Sir Stentor being asked by his neighbour, upon what errand he had
crossed the sea, gave him to understand, that he had come to France, in
consequence of a wager with squire Snaffle,[13] who had laid a thousand
pounds, that he, Sir Stentor, would not travel to Paris by himself, and for a
whole month, appear every day at a certain hour, in the public walks, without wearing any other dress, than that in which he saw him. "The fellor has
got no more stuff in his pate," continued this polite stranger, "than a jack-ass,
to think I could not find my way hither, thof I could not jabber your French
lingo. Ecod! the people of this country, are sharp enough to find out your
meaning, when you want to spend any thing among them: and as for the
matter of dress, bodikins![14] for a thousand pounds, I would engage to live in
the midst of them, and shew myself without any cloaths at all. Odd's heart![15]
a true-born Englishman needs not be afeard to shew his face, nor his backside neither, with the best Frenchman, that ever trod the ground. Thof we
Englishmen don't beplaister our doublets[16] with gold and silver, I believe as
how we have our pockets better lined than most of our neighbours; and for all

my bit of a fustian frock, that cost me in all but forty shillings, I believe, between you and me, knight, I have more dust in my fob,[17] than all these powdered sparks put together. But the worst of the matter is this; here is no solid belly timber[18] in this country: one can't have a slice of a delicate sirloin, or nice buttock of beef, for love nor money. Apize upon them![19] I could get no eatables upon the ruoad, but what they call Bully,[20] which looks like the flesh of Pharaoh's lean kine[21] stewed into rags and tatters; and then their peajohn, peajohn, rabbet them![22] one would think every old woman of this kingdom hatched pidgeons from her own body."

It is not to be supposed that such an original sat unobserved. The French and other foreigners, who had never been in England, were struck dumb with amazement, at the knight's appearance and deportment; while the English guests were over-whelmed with shame and confusion, and kept a most wary silence, for fear of being recognized by their countryman. As for our adventurer, he was inwardly transported with joy at sight of this curiosity. He considered him as a genuine, rich country booby, of the right English growth, fresh as imported; and his heart throbbed with rapture, when he heard Sir Stentor value himself upon the lining of his pockets: he foresaw, indeed, that the other knight would endeavour to reserve him for his own game; but he was too conscious of his own accomplishments to think he should find great difficulty in superseding the influence of Sir Giles.

Mean while, the new comer was by his friend, helped to some ragout, which pleased his palate, so well, that he declared he should now make a hearty meal, for the first time, since he had crossed the water; and while his good humour prevailed, he drank to every individual around the table. Ferdinand seized this opportunity of insinuating himself into his favour, by saying in English, he was glad to find there was any thing in France, that was agreeable to Sir Stentor: to this compliment the knight replied with an air of surprize. "Waunds! I find here's another countryman of mine, in this here company. Sir, I am proud to see you with all my heart." So speaking, he thrust out his right hand, across the table, and shook our hero by the fist, with such violence of civility, as proved very grievous to a French marquis, who, in helping himself to soup, was jostled in such a manner, as to overturn the dividing spoon[23] in his own bosom. The Englishman seeing the mischief he had produced, cried, "no offence, I hope," in a tone of vociferation, which the marquis in all probability misconstrued: for he began to model his features into a very sublime and peremptory look, when Fathom interpreted the apology, and at the same time, informed Sir Stentor, that although he himself had not the honour of being an Englishman, he had always entertained a most particular veneration for the country, and learned the language in consequence of that esteem.

"Blood!"[24] answered the knight, "I think myself the more obliged to you for your kind opinion, than if you was my countryman in good earnest: for there be abundance of we English, no offence Sir Giles, that seem to be ashamed of their own nation, and leave their homes to come and spend their fortunes abroad, among a parcel of—you understand me, Sir—a word to the wise, as the saying is—"[25] Here he was interrupted by an article of the second course, that seemed to give him great disturbance: this was a roasted leveret very strong of the fumet,[26] which happened to be placed directly under his nose. His sense of smelling was no sooner encountered by the effluvia of this delicious fare, than he started up from table, exclaiming, "Odd's my liver! here's a piece of carrion, that I would not offer to e'er a hound in my kennel; 'tis enough to make any christian vomit both gut and gall;" and indeed, by the wry faces he made while he ran to the door, his stomach seemed ready to justify this last assertion.

The abbé, who concluded from these symptoms of disgust, that the leveret was not sufficiently stale, began to exhibit marks of discontent, and desired that it might be brought to the other end of the table, for his examination. He accordingly hung over it with the most greedy appetite, feasting his nostrils with the steams of animal putrefaction; and at length declared that the morceau was passable, though he owned it would have been highly perfect, had it been kept another week. Nevertheless, mouths were not wanting to discuss it,[27] insipid as it was: for in three minutes there was not a vestige to be seen of that which had offended the organs of Sir Stentor, who now resumed his place, and did justice to the desert. But what he seemed to relish better than any other part of the entertainment, was the conversation of our adventurer, whom after dinner, he begged to have the honour of treating with a dish of coffee; to the seeming mortification of his brother knight, over which Fathom exulted in his own heart.

In short, our hero, by his affablity and engaging deportment, immediately gained possession of Sir Stentor's good graces: insomuch, that he desired to crack a bottle with him in the evening, and they repaired to an auberge,[28] whither his fellow knight accompanied them, not without manifest signs of reluctance. There the stranger gave a loose to jollity; though at first he damned the Burgundy as a poor, thin liquor, that ran through him in a twinkling, and instead of warming, cooled his heart and bowels: however, it insensibly seemed to give the lie to his imputation; for his spirits rose to a more elevated pitch of mirth and good fellowship; he sung or rather roared the

Early Horn[29] so as to alarm the whole neighbourhood, and began to slabber his companions, with a most bearlike affection. Yet, whatever haste he made to the goal of ebriety, he was distanced by his brother baronet, who from the beginning of the party had made little other use of his mouth, than to receive the glass, and now sunk down upon the floor, in a state of temporary annihilation.

He was immediately carried to bed by the direction of Ferdinand, who now saw himself in a manner possessor of that mine, to which he had made such eager and artful advances. That he might, therefore, carry on the approaches in the same cautious manner, he gradually shook off the trammels of sobriety, gave a loose to that spirit of freedom, which good liquor commonly inspires, and in the familiarity of drunkenness, owned himself head of a noble family of Poland, from which he had been obliged to absent himself on account of an affair of honour, not yet compromised.

Having made this confession, and laid strong injunctions of secresy upon Sir Stentor, his countenance seemed to acquire from every succeeding glass, a new symptom of intoxication: they renewed their embraces, swore eternal friendship from that day, and swallowed fresh bumpers, till both being in all appearance, quite over-powered, they began to yawn in concert, and even nod in their chairs. The knight seemed to resent the attacks of slumber, as so many impertinent attempts to interrupt their entertainment; he cursed his own propensity to sleep, imputing it to the damned French climate, and proposed to engage in some pastime that would keep them awake. "Odd's flesh!"[30] cried the Briton, "when I'm at home, I defy all the devils in hell to fasten my eye-lids together, if so be as I am otherwise inclined. For there's mother and sister Nan, and brother Numps, and I continue to divert ourselves at all fours, brag, cribbidge, tetotum, hussle-cap, and chuck-varthing;[31] and tho'f I say it, that should n't say it, I won't turn my back to e'er a he in England, at any of these pastimes: and so count, if you are so disposed, I am your man, that is in the way of friendship, at which of these you shall please to pitch upon."

To this proposal Fathom replied, he was quite ignorant of all the games he had mentioned; but, in order to amuse Sir Stentor, he would play with him at lansquenet, for a trifle, as he had laid it down for a maxim, to risk nothing considerable at play. "Waunds," answered the knight, "I hope you don't think I come here in quest of money. Thank God! I have a good landed estate worth five thousand a year, and owe no man a halfpenny; and I question whether there be many counts in your nation, no offence, I hope, that can say a bolder word. As for your lambskin net, I know nothing of the matter:

but I will toss up with you for a guinea, cross or pile[32] as the saying is, or if there's such a thing in this country as a box and dice, I love to hear the bones rattle sometimes."

Fathom found some difficulty in concealing his joy, at the mention of this last amusement, which had been one of his chief studies, and in which he had made such progress, that he could calculate all the chances with the utmost exactness and certainty. However, he made shift to contain himself, within due bounds, and with seeming indifference, consented to pass away an hour at hazard,[33] provided the implements could be procured. Accordingly, the landlord was consulted, and their desire gratified; the dice were produced, and the table resounded with the effects of their mutual eagerness. Fortune, at first, declared for the Englishman, who was permitted by our adventurer to win twenty broad pieces; and he was so elated with his success, as to accompany every lucky throw with a loud burst of laughter, and other savage and simple manifestations of excessive joy, exclaiming in a tone something less sweet than the bellowing of a bull; "Now for the main, count,—odd! here they come—here are the seven black stars, i'faith. Come along my yellow-boys—odd's heart! I never liked the face of Lewis[34] before."

Fathom drew happy presages from these boyish raptures, and after having indulged them for some time, began to avail himself of his arithmetic, in consequence of which the knight was obliged to refund the greatest part of his winning: then he altered his note, and became as intemperate in his chagrin, as he had been before immoderate in his mirth. He cursed himself and his whole generation, damned his bad luck, stamped with his feet, upon the floor, and challenged Ferdinand to double stakes. This was a very welcome proposal to our hero, who found Sir Stentor, just such a subject as he had long desired to encounter with; the more the Englishman laid, the more he lost, and Fathom took care to inflame his passions, by certain well-timed sarcasms upon his want of judgment, 'till at length, he became quite outrageous, swore the dice were false, and threw them out at the window; pulled off his periwig, and committed it to the flames, spoke with the most rancorous contempt of his adversary's skill, insisting upon his having stripped many a better man, for all he was a count, and threatning that before they parted, he should not only look like a Pole, but also smell like a pole-cat.

This was a spirit which our adventurer industriously kept up, observing that the English were dupes to all the world; and that in point of genius and address, they were no more than noisy braggadocios. In short, another pair of dice was procured; the stakes were again raised, and after several vicissitudes, fortune declared so much in favour of the knight, that Fathom lost all the money in his pocket, amounting to a pretty considerable sum. By this time, he was warmed into uncommon eagerness and impatience; being equally piqued at the success and provoking exultations of his antagonist, whom he now invited to his lodgings, in order to decide the contest: Sir Stentor complied with his request; the dispute was renewed with various success, till towards day-light, Ferdinand saw this noisy, raw, unexperienced simpleton, carry off all his ready cash, together with his jewels, and almost every thing that was valuable about his person; and to crown the whole, the victor at parting, told him with a most intolerable sneer, that so soon as the count should receive another remittance from Poland, he would give him his revenge.

CHAPTER XXV.

He bears his fate like a philosopher; and contracts acquaintance with a very remarkable personage.

This was a proper subject for our hero to moralize upon; and accordingly, it did not pass without his remarks;[1] he found himself fairly foiled at his own weapons, reduced to indigence in a foreign land, and, what he chiefly regretted, robbed of all those gay expectations he had indulged from his own supposed excellence in the wiles of fraud: for, upon a little recollection, he plainly perceived he had fallen a sacrifice to the confederacy he had refused to join; and did not at all doubt that the dice were loaded for his destruction: but instead of beating his head against the wall, tearing his hair, imprecating vain curses upon himself, or betraying other frantic symptoms of despair, he resolved to accommodate himself to his fate, and profit by the lesson he had so dearly bought.

With this intention, he immediately dismissed his valet, quitted his lodgings, retired to an obscure street, on the other side of the river, and covering one eye with a large patch of black silk, presented himself in quality of a musician, to the director of the opera, who upon hearing a trial of his skill, received him into the band, without further question. While he continued in this situation, he not only improved his taste and execution in musick, but likewise found frequent opportunities to extend his knowledge of mankind; for, besides the employment he exercised in public, he was often concerned in private concerts that were given in the hotels of noblemen; by which means, he became more and more acquainted with the persons, manners and characters of high life, which he contemplated with the most industrious attention, as a spectator, who being altogether unconcerned in the performance, is at more liberty to observe and enjoy the particulars of the entertainment.

It was in one of those assemblies, he had the pleasure of seeing his friend Sir Stentor, dressed in the most fashionable manner, and behaving with all the overstrained politesse of a native Frenchman: he was accompanied by his brother knight and the abbé, and this triumvirate, even in Fathom's hearing, gave a most ludicrous detail of the finesse they had practised upon the Polish count, to their entertainer, who was ambassador from a certain court, and made himself extremely merry with the particulars of the relation. Indeed, they made shift to describe some of the circumstances in such a ridiculous light, that our adventurer himself, smarting as he was with the disgrace, could not help laughing in secret at the account. He afterwards made it his business to enquire into the characters of the two British knights, and understood they were notorious sharpers, who had come abroad for the good of their country,[2] and now hunted in couple among a French pack, that dispersed themselves through the public ordinaries, walks, and spectacles, in order to make a prey of incautious strangers.

The pride of Ferdinand was piqued at this information; and he was even animated with the desire of making reprisals upon this fraternity, from which he ardently longed to retrieve his honour and effects: but, the issue of his last adventure had reinforced his caution; and for the present, he found means to suppress the dictates of his avarice and ambition; resolving to employ his whole penetration in reconnoitring the ground, before he should venture to take the field again. He therefore, continued to act the part of a one-eyed fidler, under the name of Fadini, and lived with incredible frugality, that he might save a purse for his future operations. In this manner had he proceeded for the space of ten months, during which, he acquired a competent knowledge of the city of Paris, when his curiosity was attracted by certain peculiarities in the appearance of a man, who lived in one of the upper apartments belonging to the house, in which he himself had fixed his habitation.

This was a tall, thin, meagre figure, with a long black beard, an aquiline nose, a brown complexion, and a most piercing vivacity in his eyes: he seemed to be about the age of fifty, wore the Persian habit, and there was a remarkable severity in his aspect and demeanour. He and our adventurer had been fellow-lodgers for some time, and, according to the laudable custom of these days, had hitherto remained as much estranged to one another, as if they had lived on opposite sides of the globe; but of late, the Persian seemed to regard our hero with particular attention; when they chanced to meet on the stair-case, or elsewhere, he bowed to Ferdinand with great solemnity, and complimented him with the Pas:[3] he even proceeded in the course of this communication, to open his mouth, and salute him with a good morrow, and sometimes made the common remarks upon the weather. Fathom, who was naturally complaisant, did not discourage these advances: on the contrary, he behaved to him with marks of particular respect, and one day, desired the favour of his company to breakfast.

This invitation the stranger declined with due acknowledgment, on pretence of being out of order;[4] and in the mean time, our adventurer bethought himself of questioning the landlord concerning his outlandish[5] guest. His curiosity was rather inflamed than satisfied with the information he could obtain from this quarter; for, all he learned, was, that the Persian went by the name of Ali Beker, and that he had lived in the house, for the space of four months, in a most solitary and parsimonious manner, without being visited by one living soul; that, for sometime after his arrival, he had been often heard to groan dismally in the night, and even to exclaim in an unknown language, as if he had laboured under some grievous affliction; and though the first transports of his grief had subsided, it was easy to perceive, he still indulged a deep rooted melancholy, for the tears were frequently observed to trickle down his beard. The commissaire of the quarter, had at first ordered this Oriental to be watched in his out-goings, according to the maxims of the French police; but his life was found so regular and inoffensive, that his precaution was soon set aside.

Any man of humane sentiments, from the knowledge of these particulars, would have been prompted to offer his services to the forlorn stranger: but as our hero was devoid of all these infirmities of human nature, it was necessary that other motives should produce the same effect: his curiosity, therefore, joined with the hopes of converting the confidence of Ali to his own emolument, effectually impelled him towards his acquaintance; and in a little time, they began to relish the conversation of each other: for, as the reader may have already observed, Fathom possessed all the arts of insinuation; and had discernment enough to perceive an air of dignity in the Persian, which the humility of his circumstances could not conceal. He was, moreover, a man of good understanding, not without a tincture of letters, perfectly well-bred, though in a ceremonious stile, extremely moral in his discourse, and scrupulously nice in his notions of honour.

Our hero conformed himself in all respects, to the other's opinions, and managed his discretion so as to pass upon him, for a gentleman reduced by misfortunes, to the exercise of an employment which was altogether unsuitable to his birth and quality. He made earnest and repeated tenders of his good offices to the stranger, and pressed him to make use of his purse, with such cordial perseverance, that at length Ali's reserve was overcome, and he condescended to borrow of him a small sum, which, in all probability, saved his life; for he had been driven to the utmost extremity of want before he would accept of this assistance.

Fathom, having gradually stole into his good graces, began to take notice of many piteous sighs that escaped him, in the moments of their intercourse, and seemed to denote an heart fraught with woe; and on pretence of administring consolation and counsel, begged leave to know the cause of his distress; observing that his mind would be disburthened by such communication, and perhaps his grief alleviated by some means which they might jointly concert, and execute in his behalf.

Ali, thus sollicited, would often shake his head with marks of extreme sorrow and despondence, and while the tears gushed from his eyes, declared that his distress was beyond the power of any remedy but death, and that by making our hero his confident, he should only extend his unhappiness to a friend, without feeling the least remission of his own torture. Notwithstanding these repeated declarations, Ferdinand, who was well enough acquainted with the mind of man, to know that such importunity is seldom or never disagreeable, redoubled his instances, together with his expressions of sympathy and esteem, until the stranger was prevailed upon to gratify his curiosity and benevolence. Having therefore, secured the chamber-door, one night, while all the rest of the family was asleep, the unfortunate Hali disclosed himself in these words.

CHAPTER XXVI.

The history of the noble Castilian. [1]

I should be ungrateful as well as unwise, did I longer resist the desire you express to know the particulars of that destiny, which hath driven me to this miserable disguise, and rendered me in all considerations, the most wretched of men. I have felt your friendship, am confident of your honour, and though my misfortunes are such as can never be repaired, because I am utterly cut off from hope, which is the wretch's last comfort, yet I may by your means, be enabled to bear them with some degree of fortitude and resignation.

Know then, my name is not Hali; neither am I of Persian extraction. I had once the honour to own myself a Castilian,[2] and was, under the appellation of Don Diego de Zelos,[3] respected as the head of one of the most ancient families of that kingdom. Judge then how severe that distress must be, which compels a Spaniard to renounce his country, his honours and his name. My youth was not spent in inglorious ease, neither did it waste unheeded in the rolls of fame: before I had attained the age of nineteen, I was twice wounded in battle; I once fortunately recovered the standard of the regiment to which I belonged, after it had been seized by the enemy; and at another occasion made shift to save the life of my colonel when he lay at the mercy of an enraged barbarian.

He that thinks I recapitulate these particulars, out of ostentation, does wrong to the unhappy Don Diego de Zelos, who in having performed these little acts of gallantry, thinks he has done nothing, but simply approved himself worthy of being called a Castilian. I mean only to do justice to my own character, and to make you acquainted with one of the most remarkable incidents of my life. It was my fate, during my third campaign, to command a troop of horse in the regiment of Don Gonzales Orgullo,[4] between whom and my father a family-feud had long been maintained with great enmity; and that gentleman did not leave me without reason to believe he rejoiced at the opportunity of exercising his resentment upon his adversary's son; for he with-held from me that countenance which my fellow officers enjoyed, and found means to subject me to divers mortifications, of which I was not at liberty to complain. These I bore in silence, for some time, as part of my probation in the character of a soldier; resolved nevertheless, to employ my interest at court, for a removal into another corps, and to take some future opportunity of explaining my sentiments to Don Gonzales, upon the injustice of his behaviour.

While I animated myself with these sentiments, against the discouragements I underwent, and the hard duty to which I was daily exposed, it was our fate to be concerned in the battle of Saragossa,[5] where our regiment was so severely handled by the English infantry, that it was forced to give ground with the loss of one half of its officers and men. Don Gonzales, who acted as brigadier in another wing, being informed of our fate, and dreading the disgrace of his corps, which had never turned back to the enemy, put spurs to his horse, and riding across the field at full speed, rallied our broken squadrons, and led us back to the charge, with such intrepidity of behaviour, as did not fail to inspire us all with uncommon courage and alacrity: for my own part, I thought myself doubly interested, to distinguish my valour; not only on account of my own glory, but likewise on the supposition, that as I was acting under the eye of Gonzales, my conduct would be narrowly observed.

I therefore exerted myself with unusual vigour, and as he began the attack with the remains of my troop, fought close by his side, during the rest of the engagement. I even acquired his applause in the very heat of battle: when his hat was struck off, and his horse fell under him, I accommodated and re-mounted him upon my own, and having seized for my own use, another that belonged to a common trooper, attended this stern commander as before, and seconded him in all his repeated efforts: but it was impossible to withstand the numbers and impetuosity of the foe, and Don Gonzales having had the mortification to see his regiment cut in pieces, and the greatest part of the army routed, was fain to yield to the fortune of the day; yet he retired as became a man of honour and a Castilian: that is, he marched off with great deliberation, in the rear of the Spanish troops, and frequently faced about to check the pursuit of the enemy. Indeed, this exercise of his courage had well nigh cost him his life; for, in one of these wheelings, he was left almost alone, and a small party of the Portuguese horse[6] had actually cut off our communication with the retreating forces of Spain.

In this dilemma, we had no other chance for saving our lives and liberty, than that of opening a passage sword in hand; and this was what Gonzales instantly resolved to attempt. We accordingly recommended our souls to God, and charging the line abreast of another, bore down all opposition, and were in a fair way of accomplishing our retreat, without further danger; but the gallant Orgullo, in crossing a ditch, had the misfortune to be thrown from his horse, and was almost the same instant overtaken by one of the Portuguese dragoons, whose sword was already suspended over his head, as he lay half-stunned with his fall; when I rode up, discharged a pistol in the ruffian's brain, and seating my colonel on his horse, had the good fortune to conduct him to a place of safety.

Here he was provided with such accommodation as his case required: for, he had been wounded in the battle, and dangerously bruised by his fall, and when all the necessary steps were taken towards his recovery, I desired to know if he had any further commands for his service, being resolved to join the army without delay. I thought proper to communicate this question, by message, because he had not spoke one word to me, during our retreat, not-withstanding the good office he had received at my hands; a reserve which I attributed to his pride, and resented accordingly. He no sooner understood my intention, than he desired to see me in his apartment, and as near as I can remember spoke to this effect.

"Were your father Don Alonzo alive, I should now, in consequence of your behaviour, banish every suggestion of resentment, and sollicit his friendship, with great sincerity. Yes, Don Diego, your virtue hath triumphed over that enmity I bore your house, and I upbraid myself with the ungenerous treatment you have suffered under my command. But it is not enough for me to withdraw that rigour which it was unjust to exercise, and would be wicked to maintain: I must likewise attone for the injuries you have sustained, and make some suitable acknowledgment for that life which I have twice to-day owed to your valour and generosity. Whatever interest I have at court, shall be employed in your behalf; and I have other designs in your favour, which shall be disclosed in due season. Mean while, I desire you will still add one obligation to the debt which I have already incurred, and carry this billet, in person, to my Estifania, who from the news of this fatal overthrow, must be in despair upon my account."

So saying, he presented a letter, directed to his lady, which I received in a transport of joy, with expressions suitable to the occasion, and immediately set out for his country-house, which happened to be about thirty leagues from the spot. This expedition was equally glorious and interesting: for my thoughts upon the road were engrossed by the hope of seeing Don Orgullo's daughter and heiress Antonia, who was reported to be a young lady of great beauty, and the most amiable accomplishments. However ridiculous it may seem, for a man to conceive a passion for an object which he hath never beheld, certain it is, my sentiments were so much prepossessed by the fame of her qualifications, that I must have fallen a victim to her charms, had they been much less powerful than they were. Notwithstanding the fatigues I had undergone in the field, I closed not an eye, until I arrived at the gate of Gonzales, being determined to precede the report of the battle, that madam d'Orgullo might not be alarmed for the life of her husband.

I declared my errand, and was introduced into a saloon, where I had not waited above three minutes, when my colonel's lady appeared, and in great confusion, received the letter, exclaiming, "Heaven grant that Don Gonzales be well!" In reading the contents, she underwent a variety of agitations; but when she had perused the whole, her countenance regained its serenity, and regarding me with an air of ineffable complacency, "Don Diego," said she, "while I lament the national calamity, in the defeat of our army, I at the same time, feel the most sincere pleasure, in seeing you upon this occasion, and according to the directions of my dear lord, bid you heartily welcome to this house, as his preserver and friend. I was not unacquainted with your character, before this last triumph of your virtue, and have often prayed to Heaven, for some lucky determination of that fatal quarrel, which raged so long between the family of Gonzales and your father's house. My prayers have been heard, the long wished-for reconciliation is now effected, and I hope nothing will ever intervene, to disturb this happy union."

To this polite and affectionate declaration, I made such a reply, as became a young man, whose heart overflowed with joy and benevolence, and desired to know how soon her answer to my commander would be ready, that I might gratify his impatience, with all possible dispatch. After having thanked me for this fresh proof of my attachment, she begged I would retire into a chamber, and repose myself from the uncommon fatigues I must have undergone; but, finding I persisted in the resolution of returning to Don Gonzales, without allowing myself the least benefit of sleep, she left me engaged in conversation with an uncle of Don Gonzales, who lodged in the house, and gave orders that a collation should be prepared in another apartment, while she retired to her closet, and wrote a letter to her husband.

In less than an hour from my first arrival, I was introduced into a most elegant dining-room, where a magnificent entertainment was served up, and where we were joined by Donna Estifania, and her beautiful daughter the fair Antonia, who advancing, with the most amiable sweetness, thanked me in very warm expressions of acknowledgment, for the generosity of my conduct towards her father. I had been ravished with her first appearance, which far exceeded my imagination, and my faculties were so disordered by this address, that I answered her compliment with the most aukward confusion. But this disorder did not turn to my prejudice in the opinion of that lovely creature, who has often told me in the sequel, that she gave herself credit for that perplexity in my behaviour, and that I never appeared more worthy of her regard and affection, than at that juncture, when my dress was discomposed, and my whole person disfigured by the toils and duty of the preceding day; for this very dishabille presented itself to her reflexion as the immediate effect of that very merit by which I was intitled to her esteem.

Wretch that I am! to survive the loss of such an excellent woman, endeared to my remembrance by the most tender offices of wedlock, happily exercised for the space of five and twenty years! Forgive these tears, they are not the drops of weakness, but remorse. Not to trouble you with idle particulars, suffice it to say, I was favoured with such marks of distinction, by madam d'Orgullo, that she thought it incumbent upon her to let me know, she had not overacted her hospitality, and while we sat at table, accosted me in these words: "You will not be surprised, Don Diego, at my expressions of regard, which I own are unusual from a Spanish lady to a young cavalier like you, when I communicate the contents of this letter from Don Gonzales." So saying, she put the billet into my hand, and I read these words, or words to this effect.

"Amiable Estifania,

You will understand, that I am as well as a person can possibly be, who hath this day lived to see the army of his king defeated. If you would know the particulars of this unfortunate action, your curiosity will be gratified by the bearer Don Diego de Zelos, to whose virtue and bravery I am twice indebted for my life. I therefore desire you will receive him with that respect and gratitude, which you shall think due for such an obligation; and in entertaining him, dismiss that reserve, which often disgraces the Spanish hospitality. In a word, let your own virtue and beneficence conduct you upon this occasion, and let my Antonia's endeavours be joined with your own, in doing honour to the preserver of her father. Adieu."

Such a testimonial could not fail of being very agreeable to a young soldier, who by this time, had begun to indulge the transporting hope of being happy in the arms of the adorable Antonia. I professed myself extremely happy in having met with an opportunity of acquiring such a degree of my colonel's esteem, entertained them with a detail of his personal prowess in the battle, and answered all their questions with that moderation which every man ought to preserve in speaking of his own behaviour. Our repast being ended, I took my leave of the ladies, and at parting received a letter from Donna Estifania to her husband, together with a ring of great value, which she begged I would accept, as a token of her esteem. Thus loaded with honour and caresses, I set out on my return for the quarters of Don Gonzales, who could scarce credit his own eyes when I delivered his lady's billet; for he thought it impossible to perform such a journey in so short a time.

When he had glanced over the paper, "Don Diego," said he, "by your short stay, one would imagine you had met with indifferent reception at my house: I hope Estifania has not been deficient in her duty." I answered this question, by assuring him, my entertainment had been so agreeable in all respects, that nothing but my duty to him, could have induced me to give it up so soon. He then turned the conversation upon Antonia, and hinted his intention of giving her in marriage to a young cavalier, for whom he had a particular friend-ship. I was so much affected by this insinuation, which seemed at once to blast all my hopes of love and happiness, that the blood forsook my face; I was seized with an universal trepidation, and even obliged to retire, on pre-tence of being suddenly taken ill.

Though Gonzales seemed to impute this disorder to fatigue and want of rest, he in his heart ascribed it to the true cause, and after having sounded my sentiments to his own satisfaction, blessed me with a declaration, importing that I was the person upon whom he had pitched for a son-in-law. I will not trouble you with a repetition of what passed on this interesting occasion, but proceed to observe, that his intention in my favour was far from being dis-agreeable to his lady; and that, in a little time, I had the good fortune to espouse the charming Antonia, who submitted to the will of her father with-out reluctance.

Soon after this happy event, I was, by the influence of Don Gonzales, joined to my own interest, promoted to the command of a regiment, and served with honour during the remaining part of the war. After the treaty of Utrecht,[7] I was employed in reducing the Catalans to their allegiance,[8] and in an action with these obstinate rebels, had the misfortune to lose my father-in-law, who by that time was preferred to the rank of a major-general. The virtuous Estifania did not long survive this melancholy accident; and the loss of these indulgent parents, made such a deep impression upon the tender heart of my Antonia, that I took the first opportunity of removing her from a place, in which every object served to cherish her grief, to a pleasant villa, near the city of Seville,[9] which I purchased on account of its agreeable situa-tion. That I might the more perfectly enjoy the possession of my amiable partner, who could no longer brook the thoughts of another separation, peace was no sooner re-established, than I obtained leave to resign my commission, and I wholly devoted myself to the joys of a domestic life.

Heaven seemed to smile upon our union, by blessing us with a son, whom, however, it was pleased to recall in his infancy, to our unspeakable grief and mortification; but, our mutual chagrin was afterwards alleviated, by the birth of a daughter, who seemed born with every accomplishment to excite the love and admiration of mankind. Why did nature debase such a master-piece with the mixture of an allay,[10] which hath involved herself and her whole family in perdition? but the ways of Providence are unsearchable. She hath paid the debt of her degeneracy; peace be with her soul! the honour of my family is vindicated; though by a sacrifice which hath robbed me of every thing else that is valuable in life, and ruined my peace past all redemption. Yes, my friend, all the tortures that human tyranny can inflict, would be ease, tranquillity and delight, to the unspeakable pangs and horrors I have felt.

But, to return from this digression: Serafina, which was the name of that little darling, as she grew up, not only disclosed all the natural graces of external beauty, but likewise manifested the most engaging sweetness of disposition, and a capacity for acquiring with ease, all the accomplishments of her sex. 'Tis impossible to convey any adequate idea of a parent's raptures in the contemplation of such a fair blossom; she was the only pledge of our love, she was presumptive heiress to a large fortune, and likely to be the sole representative of two noble Castilian families. She was the delight of all who saw her, and a theme of praise for every tongue. You are not to suppose, that the education of such a child was neglected. Indeed it wholly engrossed the attention of me and my Antonia, and her proficiency rewarded our care. Before she had attained the age of fifteen, she was mistress of every elegant qualification, natural and acquired. Her person was, by that time, the confessed pattern of beauty. Her voice was enchantingly sweet, and she touched the lute with the most ravishing dexterity. Heaven and earth! how did my breast dilate with joy, at the thoughts of having given birth to such perfection! how did my heart gush with paternal fondness, whenever I beheld this ornament of my name! and what scenes of endearing transport, have I enjoyed with my Antonia, in mutual congratulation upon our parental happiness.

Serafina, accomplished as she was, could not fail to make conquests among the Spanish cavaliers, who are famous for sensibility in love. Indeed, she never appeared without a numerous train of admirers, and though we had bred her up in that freedom of conversation and intercourse, which holds a middle space, between the French license and Spanish restraint, she was now so much exposed to the addresses of promiscuous gallantry, that we found it necessary to retrench the liberty of our house; and behave to our male visitants with great reserve and circumspection, that our honour and peace might run no risque from the youth and inexperience of our daughter.

This caution produced overtures from a great many young gentlemen of rank and distinction, who courted my alliance by demanding Serafina in marriage; and from the number, I had actually selected one person, who was in all respects worthy the possession of such an inestimable prize. His name was Don Manuel de Mendoza; his birth was noble, and his character dignified with repeated acts of generosity and virtue. Yet, before I would signify to him my approbation of his suit, I resolved to inform myself, whether or not the heart of Serafina was totally unengaged, and indifferent to any other object, that I might not lay a tyrannical restraint upon her inclinations. The result of my enquiry was a full conviction of her having hitherto been deaf to the voice of love; and this piece of information, together with my own sentiments in his favour, I communicated to Don Manuel, who heard these tidings with transports of gratitude and joy. He was immediately favoured with opportunities of acquiring the affection of my daughter, and his endeavours were at first received with such respectful civility, as might have been easily warmed into a mutual passion, had not the evil genius of our family interposed.

O my friend! how shall I describe the depravity of that unhappy virgin's sentiments! how recount the particulars of my own dishonour! I that am descended from a long line of illustrious Castilians, who never received an injury they did not revenge; but washed away every blemish in their fame, with the blood of those who attempted to stain it. In that circumstance, I have imitated the example of my glorious progenitors; and that consideration alone, hath supported me against all the assaults of despair.

As I grudged no pains and expence in perfecting the education of Serafina, my doors were open to every person who made an extraordinary figure in the profession of those amusing sciences, in which she delighted. The house of Don Diego de Zelos was a little academy for painting, poetry and music; and Heaven decreed that it should fall a sacrifice to its regard for these fatal and delusive arts. Among other preceptors, it was her fate to be under the instruction of a cursed German; who, though his profession was drawing, understood the elements and theory of musick, possessed a large fund of learning and taste, and was a person remarkable for his agreeable conversation. This traitor, who like you, had lost one eye, I not only admitted into my house, for the improvement of my daughter, but even distinguished with particular marks of confidence and favour; little thinking he had either inclination or capacity to debauch the sentiments of my child. I was rejoiced beyond measure, to see with what alacrity she received his lessons, with what avidity she listened to his discourse, which was always equally moral, instructing and entertaining.

Antonia seemed to vie with me, in expressions of regard for this accomplished stranger, whom she could not help supposing to be a person of rank and family, reduced to his present situation, by some unfortunate vicissitude of fate. I was disposed to concur with this opinion, and actually conjured him to make me his confident, with such protestations, as left him no room to doubt my honour and beneficence; but he still persisted in declaring himself the son of an obscure mechanic[11] in Bohemia; an origin to which surely no man would pretend, who had the least claim to nobility of birth. While I was thus undeceived in my conjecture, touching his birth and quality, I was confirmed in an opinion of his integrity and moderation, and looked upon him as a man of honour, in despite of the lowness of his pedigree. Nevertheless he was at bottom, a most perfidious wretch, and all this modesty and self-denial were the effects of the most villainous dissimulation, a cloak under which he unsuspected robbed me of my honour and my peace.

Not to trouble you with particulars, the recital of which would tear my heart-strings with indignation and remorse, I shall only observe, that by the power of his infernal insinuation, he fascinated the heart of Serafina, brought over Antonia herself to the interests of his passion, and at once detached them both from their duty and religion. Heaven and earth! how dangerous, how irresistible is the power of infatuation! while I remained in the midst of this blind security, waiting for the nuptials of my daughter, and indulging myself with the vain prospect of her approaching felicity, Antonia found means to protract the negociation of the marriage, by representing that it would be pity to deprive Serafina of the opportunity she then had of profiting by the German's instructions; and upon that account I prevailed upon Don Manuel to bridle the impatience of his love.

During this interval, as I one evening enjoyed the cool air in my own garden, I was accosted by an old duenna, who had been my nurse, and lived in the family since the time of my childhood. "My duty," said she, "will no longer permit me to wink in silence, at the wrongs I see you daily suffer. Dismiss that German from your house, without delay, if you respect the glory of your name, and the rights of our holy religion: the stranger is an abominable heretic; and, grant Heaven! he may not have already poisoned the minds of those you hold most dear." I had been extremely alarmed at the beginning of this address, but finding the imputation limited to the article of religion, in which, thank God, I am no bigot, I recovered my serenity of disposition, thanked the old woman for her zeal, commended her piety, and encouraged her to persevere in making observations on such subjects as should concern my honour and my quiet.

We live in such a world of wickedness and fraud, that a man cannot be too vigilant in his own defence: had I employed such spies from the beginning, I should, in all probability, have been at this day in possession of every comfort that renders life agreeable. The duenna thus authorized, employed her sagacity with such success, that I had reason to suspect the German of a design upon the heart of Serafina; but, as the presumptions did not amount to conviction, I contented myself with exiling him from my house, under the pretext of having discovered, that he was an enemy to the catholic church; and forthwith appointed a day for the celebration of my daughter's marriage, with Don Manuel de Mendosa. I could easily perceive a cloud of melancholy overspread the faces of Serafina and her mother, when I declared these my resolutions; but, as they made no objection to what I proposed, I did not, at that time, enter into an explanation of the true motives that influenced my conduct. Both parties were, probably, afraid of such expostulation.

Mean while, preparations were made for the spousals of Serafina; and, notwithstanding the anxiety I had undergone, on account of her connexion with the German, I began to think that her duty, her glory, had triumphed over all such low-born considerations, if ever they had been entertained; because she and even Antonia seemed to expect the ceremony with resignation, though the features of both still retained evident marks of concern, which I willingly imputed to the mutual prospect of their separation. This, however, was but a faithless calm, that soon, ah! too soon, brought forth a tempest, which hath wrecked my hopes.

Two days before the appointed union of don Manuel and Serafina, I was informed by the duenna, that while she accompanied Antonia's waiting-maid at church, she had seen her receive a billet from an old woman, who, kneeling at her side, had conveyed it in such a mysterious manner, as wakened the duenna's apprehensions about her young lady; she had therefore hastened home to communicate this piece of intelligence, that I might have an opportunity of examining the messenger before she should have time to deposit her trust. I could not help shivering with fearful presages, upon this occasion, and even abhorring the person to whose duty and zeal I was beholden for the intelligence, even while I endeavoured to persuade myself, that the inquiry would end in the detection of some paultry intrigue, between the maid and her own gallant, I intercepted her in returning from church, and commanding her to follow me to a convenient place, extorted from her by dint of threats, the fatal letter, which I read to this effect.

"The whole business of my life, O divine Serafina! will be to repay that affection I have been so happy as to engage. With what transport then shall I obey your summons, in performing that enterprize, which will rescue you from the bed of a detested rival, and put myself in full possession of a jewel, which I value infinitely more than life. Yes, adorable creature, I have provided every thing for our escape, and at midnight will attend you in your own apartment, from whence you shall be conveyed into a land of liberty and peace, where you will unmolested enjoy the purity of that religion you have espoused, and in full security, bless the arms of your ever faithful

ORLANDO."[12]

Were you a fond parent, a tender husband and a noble Castilian, I should not need to mention the unutterable horrors that took possession of my bosom, when I perused this accursed letter, by which I learned the apostasy, disobedience, and degeneracy of my idolized Serafina, who had overthrown and destroyed the whole plan of felicity which I had erected, and blasted all the glories of my name; and when the wretched messenger, terrified of my menaces and agitation, confessed that Antonia herself was privy to the guilt of her daughter, whom she had solemnly betrothed to that vile German, in the sight of Heaven, and that by her connivance, this Plebeian[13] intended that very night, to bereave me of my child; I was for some moments stupified with grief and amazement, that gave way to an extasy of rage, which had well-nigh terminated in despair and distraction.

I now tremble, and my head grows giddy with the remembrance of that dreadful occasion: behold how the drops trickle down my forehead; this agony is a fierce and familiar visitant, I shall banish it anon. I summoned my pride, my resentment to my assistance; these are the cordials that support me against all other reflections; those were the auxiliaries that enabled me in the day of trial, to perform that sacrifice which my honour demanded, in a strain so loud, as to drown the cries of nature, love and compassion. Yes, they espoused that glory, which humanity would have betrayed, and my revenge was noble, though unnatural.

My scheme was soon laid, my resolution soon taken; I privately confined the wretch who had been the industrious slave of this infamous conspiracy, that she might take no step to frustrate, or interrupt the execution of my design. Then repairing to the house of an apothecary, who was devoted to my service, communicated my intention, which he durst not condemn, and could not reveal, without breaking the oath of secrecy I had imposed; and he furnished me with two vials of poison, for the dismal catastrophe I had planned. Thus provided, I on pretence of sudden business at Seville, carefully avoided the dear, the wretched pair, whom I had devoted to death, that my heart might not relent, by means of those tender ideas, which the sight of them would have infallibly inspired; and when day-light vanished, took my station near that part of the house, through which the villain must have entered, on his hellish purpose. There I stood in a state of horrid expectation, my soul ravaged with the different passions that assailed it, until the fatal moment arrived; when I perceived the traitor approach the window of a lower apartment, which led into that of Serafina, and gently lifting the casement, which was purposely left unsecured, insinuate half of his body into the house: then rushing upon him, in a transport of fury, I plunged my sword into his heart, crying "Villain! receive the reward of thy treachery and presumption."

The steel was so well aimed as to render a repetition of the stroke unnecessary; he uttered one groan, and fell breathless at my feet. Exulting with this first success of my revenge, I penetrated into the chamber, where the robber of my peace was expected by the unhappy Serafina and her mother, who seeing me enter with a most savage aspect, and a sword reeking with the vengeance I had taken, seemed almost petrified with fear. "Behold," said I, "the blood of that base plebeian, who made an attempt upon the honour of my house: your conspiracy against the unfortunate Don Diego de Zelos, is now discovered; that presumptuous slave, the favoured Orlando, is now no more."

Scarce had I pronounced these words, when a loud scream was uttered by both the unhappy victims. "If Orlando is slain," cried the infatuated Serafina, "what have I to do with life? O my dear lord! my husband, and my lover! how are our promised joys at once cut off! here strike, my father, compleat your barbarous sacrifice, the spirit of the murdered Orlando still hovers for his wife." These frantic exclamations, in which she was joined by Antonia, kept up the fury of my resentment, which by meekness and submission might have been weakened and rendered ineffectual. "Yes, hapless wretches," I replied, "ye shall enjoy your wish: the honour of my name requires that both shall die; yet I will not mangle the breast of Antonia, on which I have so often reposed; I will not shed the blood of Zelos, nor disfigure the beauteous form of Serafina, on which I have so often gazed with wonder and unspeakable delight: here is an elixir, to which I trust the consummation of my revenge."

So saying, I emptied the vials into separate cups, and presenting one in each hand, the miserable, the fair offenders, instantly received the destined draughts, which they drank without hesitation: then praying to Heaven for the wretched Don Diego, sunk upon the same couch, and expired without a groan. O well-contrived beverage! O happy composition, by which all the miseries of life are so easily cured!

Such was the fate of Antonia and Serafina; these hands were the instruments that deprived them of life, these eyes beheld them the richest prize that death had ever won. Powers supreme! does Don Diego live to make this recapitulation? I have done my duty; but ah! I am haunted by the furies of remorse: I am tortured with the incessant stings of remembrance and regret; even now the images of my wife and daughter, present themselves to my imagination. All the scenes of happiness I have enjoyed as a lover, husband and parent, all the endearing hopes I have cherished, now pass in review before me, embittering the circumstances of my inexpressible woe; and I consider myself as a solitary outcast from all the comforts of society. But, enough of these unmanly complaints, the yearnings of nature are too importunate.

Having compleated my vengeance, I retired into my closet, and furnishing myself with some ready money and jewels of considerable value, went into the stable, saddled my favourite steed, which I instantly mounted, and before the tumults of my breast subsided, found myself at the town of St. Lucar.[14] There I learned from inquiry, that there was a Dutch bark in the harbour ready to sail; upon which, I addressed myself to the master, who for a suitable gratification, was prevailed upon to weigh anchor that same night; so that embarking without delay, I soon bid eternal adieu to my native country. It was not from reason and reflection, that I took these measures for my personal safety; but in consequence of an involuntary instinct, that seems to operate in the animal machine, while the faculty of thinking is suspended.

To what a dreadful reckoning was I called, when reason resumed her function! you may believe me, my friend, when I assure you, that I should not have outlived those tragedies I acted, had I not been restrained from doing violence upon myself, by certain considerations, which no man of honour ought to set aside. I could not bear the thought of falling ingloriously by the hand of an executioner, and intailing disgrace upon a family that knew no stain; and I was deterred from putting an end to my own misery, by the apprehensions of posthumous censure, which would have represented me as a desponding wretch, utterly destitute of that patience, fortitude and resignation, which are the characteristics of a true Castilian. I was also influenced by religious motives, that suggested to me the necessity of living to attone by my sufferings and sorrow, for the guilt I had incurred, in complying with a savage punctilio, which is, I fear, displeasing in the sight of Heaven.

These were the reasons that opposed my entrance into that peaceful harbour, which death presented to my view; and they were soon reinforced by another principle, that sanctioned my determination, to continue at the servile oar of life. In consequence of unfavourable winds, our vessel for some

COUNT FATHOM.

Stothard del.   *Heath sculp.*

Don Diego Administers the Poison, by Stothard.
(General Research Division, The New York Public Library—
Astor, Lenox and Tilden Foundations.)

days made small progress in her voyage to Holland, and near the coast of Gallicia[15] we were joined by an English ship from Vigo,[16] the master of which gave us to understand, that before he set sail, a courier had arrived from Madrid, at that place, with orders for the corregidor,[17] to prevent the escape of any native Spaniard, by sea, from any port within his district; and to use his utmost endeavours to apprehend the person of Don Diego de Zelos, who was suspected of treasonable practices against the state. Such an order, with a minute description of my person, was at the same time, dispatched to all the sea-ports and frontier places in Spain.

You may easily suppose how I, who was already overwhelmed with distress, could bear this aggravation of misfortune and disgrace: I, who had always maintained the reputation of loyalty, which was acquired at the hazard of my life, and the expence of my blood. To deal candidly, I must own, that this intelligence roused me from a lethargy of grief, which had begun to overpower my faculties. I immediately imputed this dishonourable charge to the evil offices of some villain, who had basely taken the advantage of my deplorable situation, and I was inflamed, inspirited with the desire of vindicating my fame, and revenging the injury. Thus animated, I resolved to disguise myself effectually from the observation of those spies, which every nation finds its account in employing, in foreign countries; I purchased this habit from the Dutch navigator, in whose house I kept myself concealed, after our arrival at Amsterdam, until my beard was grown to a sufficient length to favour my design, and then appeared as a Persian dealer in jewels. As I could gain no satisfactory information touching myself, in this country, had no purpose to pursue, and was extremely miserable among a people, who being mercenary and unsocial, were very ill adapted to alleviate the horrors of my condition; I gratified my landlord for his important services, with the best part of my effects; and having, by his means, procured a certificate from the magistracy, repaired to Rotterdam, from whence I set out in a travelling carriage for Antwerp, on my way to this capital; hoping with a succession of different objects, to mitigate the anguish of my mind, and by the most industrious enquiry, to learn such particulars of that false impeachment, as would enable me to take measures for my own justification, as well as for projecting a plan of revenge against the vile perfidious author.

This, I imagined, would be no difficult task, considering the friendship and intercourse subsisting between the Spanish and French nations, and the communicative disposition, for which the Parisians are renowned; but I have found myself egregiously deceived in my expectation: the officers of the Police in this city are so inquisitive and vigilant, that the most minute action of a stranger, is scrutinized with great severity; and although the inhabitants are very frank in discoursing on indifferent subjects, they are at the same time extremely cautious in avoiding all conversation that turns upon state occurrences and maxims of government. In a word, the peculiarity of my appearance, subjects me so much to particular observation, that I have hitherto thought proper to devour my griefs in silence, and even to bear the want of almost every convenience, rather than hazard a premature discovery, by offering my jewels to sale.

In this emergency, I have been so far fortunate as to become acquainted with you, whom I look upon as a man of honour and humanity. Indeed, I was at first sight, prepossessed in your favour: for notwithstanding the mistakes which men daily commit in judging from appearances, there is something in the physiognomy of a stranger, from which one cannot help forming an opinion of his character and disposition.[18] For once, my penetration hath not failed me; your behaviour justifies my decision, you have treated me with that sympathy and respect which none but the generous will pay to the unfortunate. I have trusted you accordingly: I have put my life, my honour in your power; and I must beg leave to depend upon your friendship, for obtaining that satisfaction, for which alone I seek to live. Your employment engages you in the gay world: you daily mingle with the societies of men; the domestics of the Spanish ambassador will not shun your acquaintance; you may frequent the coffee-houses to which they resort; and in the course of these occasions, unsuspected inform yourself of that mysterious charge which lies heavy on the fame of the unfortunate Don Diego. I must likewise, implore your assistance in converting my jewels into money, that I may breathe independant of man, until Heaven shall permit me to finish this weary pilgrimage of life.

CHAPTER XXVII.

A flagrant instance of Fathom's virtue, in the manner of his retreat to England.

Fathom, who had lent an attentive ear to every circumstance of this disastrous story, no sooner heard it concluded, than with an aspect of generous and cordial compassion, not even unattended with tears, he condoled the lamentable fate of Don Diego de Zelos; deplored the untimely death of the gentle Antonia and the fair Serafina, and undertook the interests of the wretched Castilian with such warmth of sympathizing zeal, as drew a flood from his eyes, while he wrung his benefactor's hand in a transport of gratitude. Those were literally tears of joy, or at least of satisfaction on both sides; as our hero wept with affection and attachment to the jewels that were to be committed to his care: but, far from discovering the true source of his tenderness, he affected to dissuade the Spaniard from parting with the diamonds, which he counselled him to reserve for a more pressing occasion; and in the mean time, earnestly intreated him to depend upon his friendship, for present relief. This generous proffer served only to confirm Don Diego's resolution, which he forthwith executed, by putting into the hands of Ferdinand, jewels to the value of a thousand crowns,[1] and desiring him to detain for his own use, any part of the sum they would raise.

Our adventurer thanked him for the good opinion he entertained of his integrity, an opinion fully manifested in honouring him with such important confidence; and assured him he would transact his affairs with the utmost diligence, caution and dispatch. The evening being by this time almost consumed, these new allies retired separately to rest: though each passed the night without repose, in very different reflections; the Castilian being, as usual, agitated with the unceasing pangs of his unalterable misery, interspersed with gleaming hopes of revenge; and Fathom being kept awake with revolving plans, for turning his fellow-lodger's credulity to his own advantage. From the nature of the Spaniard's situation, he might have appropriated the jewels to himself, and remained in Paris, without fear of a prosecution, because the injured party had, by the above narrative, left his life and liberty at discretion. But he did not think himself secure from the personal resentment of an enraged desperate Castilian; and therefore determined to withdraw himself privately into that country where he had all along proposed to fix the standard of his finesse,[2] which fortune had now impowered him to exercise according to his wish.

Bent upon this retreat, he went abroad in the morning, on pretence of acting in the concerns of his friend Don Diego, and having hired a post-chaise to be ready at the dawn of next day, returned to his lodgings, where he cajoled the Spaniard with a feigned report of his negotiation; then securing his most valuable effects about his person, arose with the cock, repaired to the place, at which he had appointed to meet the postilion with the carriage, and set out for England without further delay; leaving the unhappy Zelos to the horrors of indigence, and the additional agony of this fresh disappointment. Yet he was not the only person affected by the abrupt departure of Fathom, which was hastened by the importunities, threats and reproaches of his landlord's daughter, whom he had debauched under promise of marriage, and now left in the fourth month of her pregnancy.

Notwithstanding the dangerous adventure in which he had been formerly involved by traveling in the night, he did not think proper to make the usual halts on this journey, for sleep or refreshment, nor did he once quit the chaise, till his arrival at Boulogne,[3] which he reached in twenty hours, after his departure from Paris. Here he thought he might safely indulge himself with a comfortable meal; accordingly, he bespoke a poulard[4] for dinner, and while that was preparing, went forth to view the city and harbour. When he beheld the white cliffs of Albion, his heart throbbed with all the joy of a beloved son, who after a tedious and fatiguing voyage, reviews the chimneys of his father's house: he surveyed the neighbouring coast of England, with fond and longing eyes, like another Moses reconnoitring the land of Canaan from the top of mount Pisgah:[5] and to such a degree of impatience was he enflamed by the sight, that instead of proceeding to Calais,[6] he resolved to take his passage directly from Boulogne, even if he should hire a vessel for the purpose. With these sentiments, he inquired if there was any ship bound for England, and was so fortunate as to find the master of a small bark, who intended to weigh anchor for Deal,[7] that same evening at high water.

Transported with this information, he immediately agreed for his passage, sold the post-chaise to his landlord for thirty guineas, as a piece of furniture, for which he could have no further use, purchased a portmanteau, together with some linen and wearing apparel, and at the recommendation of his host, took into his service, an extra-postilion or helper, who had formerly wore the livery of a travelling marquis. This new domestic, whose name was Maurice, underwent with great applause, the examination of our hero, who perceived in him, a fund of sagacity and presence of mind, by which he was excellently qualified for being the valet of an adventurer; he was therefore accommodated with a second-hand suit, and another shirt, and at once listed under the banners of count Fathom, who spent the whole afternoon in giving him proper instructions for the regulation of his conduct.

Having settled these preliminaries to his own satisfaction, he and his baggage were embarked about six o'clock in the month of September, and it was not without emotion, that he found himself benighted upon the great deep, of which, before the preceding day, he had never enjoyed even the most distant prospect. However, he was not a man to be afraid, where there was really no appearance of danger; and the agreeable presages of future fortune supported his spirits, amidst the disagreeable nausea which commonly attends landmen at sea, until he was set ashore upon the beach at Deal, which he entered in good health about seven o'clock in the morning.

Like Cæsar, however, he found some difficulty in landing, on account of the swelling surf,[8] that tumbled about with such violence, as had almost overset the cutter[9] that carried him on shore; and in his eagerness to jump upon the strand, his foot slipped from the side of the boat, so that he was thrown forwards in an horizontal direction, and his hands were the first parts of him that touched the English ground. Upon this occasion, he, in imitation of Scipio's behaviour on the coast of Afric,[10] hailed the omen, and grasping an handful of the sand, was heard to exclaim in the Italian language, "Ah ha, old England, I have thee fast."

As he walked up to the inn, followed by Maurice loaded with his portmanteau, he congratulated himself upon his happy voyage, and the peaceable possession of his spoil, and could not help snuffing up the British air with marks of infinite relish and satisfaction. His first care was to recompence himself for the want of sleep he had undergone, and after he had sufficiently recruited himself with several hours of uninterrupted repose, he set out in a post-chaise for Canterbury, where he took a place in the London stage, which, he was told, would depart next morning, the coach being already full. On this very first day of his arrival, he perceived between the English and the people among whom he had hitherto lived, such essential difference in customs, appearance, and way of living, as inspired him with high notions of that British freedom, opulence, and convenience on which he had often heard his mother expatiate. On the road, he feasted his eye-sight with the verdant hills covered with flocks of sheep, the fruitful vales parcelled out into cultivated inclosures; the very cattle seemed to profit by the wealth of their masters, being large, sturdy and sleek, and every peasant breathed the insolence[11] of liberty and independance. In a word, he viewed the wide extended plains of Kent, with a lover's eye, and his ambition becoming romantic, could not help fancying himself another conqueror of the isle.[12]

He was not, however, long amused by these vain chimeras, which soon vanished before other reflections of more importance and solidity. His imagination, it must be owned, was at all times too chaste, to admit those overweening hopes, which often mislead the mind of a projector. He had studied mankind with incredible diligence, and knew perfectly well how far he could depend on the passions and foibles of human nature. That he might now act consistent with his former sagacity, he resolved to pass himself upon his fellow travellers, for a French gentleman, equally a stranger to the language and country of England, in order to glean from their discourse, such intelligence as might avail him in his future operations; and his lacquey was tutored accordingly.

CHAPTER XXVIII.

Some account of his fellow-travellers.

Those who had taken places for the coach, understanding the sixth seat was engaged by a foreigner, determined to profit by his ignorance; and with that politeness which is peculiar to this happy island, fixed themselves in the vehicle, in such a manner, before he had the least intimation of their design, that he found it barely practicable to insinuate himself sidelong between a corpulent quaker and a fat Wapping-landlady,[1] in which attitude he stuck fast, like a thin quarto between two voluminous dictionaries on a bookseller's shelf: and as if the pain and inconvenience of such compression, was not sufficient matter of chagrin, the greatest part of the company entertained themselves with laughing at his ludicrous station.

The jolly dame at his left hand, observed with a loud exclamation of mirth, that Monsieur would be soon better acquainted with a buttock of English beef; and said by that time they should arrive at their dining place, he might be spitted without larding. "Yes, verily," replied Obadiah,[2] who was a wag in his way, "but the swine's fat will be all on one side." "So much the better for you," cried mine hostess, "for that side is all your own." The quaker was not so much disconcerted by the quickness of this repartee, but that he answered with great deliberation, "I thank thee for thy love, but will not profit by thy loss; especially as I like not the savour of these outlandish fowls; they are profane birds of passage, relished only by the children of vanity, like thee."[3]

The plump gentlewoman took umbrage at this last expression, which she considered as a double reproach, and repeated the words "Children of vanity!" with an emphasis of resentment. "I believe, if the truth were known," said she, "there's more vanity than midriff, in that great belly of yours, for all your pretending to humility and religion. Sirrah! my corporation[4] is made up of good, wholsome English fat; but you are puffed up with the wind of vanity and delusion; and when it begins to gripe your entrails, you pretend to have a motion, and then get up and preach nonsense:[5] yet, you'll take it upon you to call your betters children; marry come up, Mr. Goose-cap,[6] I have got children that are as good men as you, or any hypocritical trembler in England."

A person who sat opposite to the quaker, hearing this remonstrance, which seemed pregnant with contention, interposed in the conversation with a conscious leer, and begged there might be no rupture between the spirit and the flesh. By this remonstrance, he relieved Obadiah from the satire of this female orator, and brought the whole vengeance of her elocution upon his own head. "Flesh!" cried she, with all the ferocity of an enraged Thalestris, "none of your names, Mr. Yellow-chaps.[7] What! I warrant you have an antipathy to flesh, because you yourself are nothing but skin and bone. I suppose you are some poor starv'd journeyman taylor come from France, where you have been learning to cabbage,[8] and have not seen a good meal of victuals these seven years; you have been living upon rye-bread and soup maigre,[9] and now you come over like a walking atomy, with a rat's tail at your wig, and a tinsy jacket;[10] and so forsooth, you set up for a gentleman, and pretend to find fault with a sur-loin of roast beef."

The gentleman heard this address with admirable patience, and when she had rung out her alarm, very coolly replied. "Any thing but your stinking fish, Madam. Since when, I pray, have you travelled in stage-coaches, and left off your old profession of crying oysters in winter, and rotten mackarel in June? You was then known by the name of Kate Brawn, and in good repute among the ale-houses in Thames-street,[11] till that unlucky amour with the master of a corn vessel, in which he was unfortunately detected by his own spouse; but you seem to have risen by that fall; and I wish you joy of your present plight: though considering your education on Bear key,[12] you can give but a sorry account of yourself."

The amazon, though neither exhausted nor dismayed, was really confounded at the temper and assurance of this antagonist, who had gathered all these anecdotes from the fertility of his own invention; after a short pause, however, she poured forth a torrent of obloquy sufficient to overwhelm any person who had not been used to take up arms against such seas of trouble;[13] and a dispute ensued, which would have not only disgraced[14] the best orators on the Thames,[15] but even have made a figure in the celebration of the Eleusinian mysteries,[16] during which the Athenian matrons rallied one another from different waggons, with that freedom of altercation so happily preserved in this our age and country.

Such a redundancy of epithets and variety of metaphors, tropes and figures were uttered between these well-matched opponents, that an epic bard would have found his account in listening to the contest, which, in all probability, would not have been confined to words; had it not been interrupted for the sake of a young woman of an agreeable countenance and modest carriage; who being shocked at some of their flowers of speech, and terrified by the menacing looks and gestures of the firey featured dame, began to scream aloud, and beg leave to quit the coach. Her perturbation put an end to the high debate. The sixth passenger, who had not opened his mouth, endeavoured to comfort her with assurances of protection; the quaker proposed a cessation of arms; the male disputant acquiesced in the proposal, assuring the company he had entered the lists for their entertainment only, without acquiring the least grudge or ill-will to the fat gentlewoman, whom he protested he had never seen before that day, and who, for aught he knew, was a person of credit and reputation. He then held forth his hand in token of amity, and asked pardon of the offended party, who was appeased by his submission; and in testimony of her benevolence, presented to the other female, whom she had discomposed, an Hungary-water bottle[17] filled with cherry-brandy, recommending it as a much more powerful remedy, than the Sal volatile,[18] which the other held to her nose.

Peace being thus re-established in a treaty, comprehending Obadiah and all present, it will not be improper to give the reader some further information touching the several characters assembled in this vehicle. The quaker was a London merchant, who had been at Deal, superintending the repairs of a ship, which had suffered by a storm in the Downs.[19] The Wapping landlady, was on her return from the same place, where she had attended the payment of a man of war, with sundry powers of attorney, granted by the sailors, who had lived upon credit at her house. Her competitor in fame was a dealer in wine, a smuggler of French lace, and a petty gamester just arrived from Paris, in the company of an English barber who sat on his right hand, and the young woman was daughter of a country curate, in her way to London, where she was bound apprentice to a milliner.

Hitherto Fathom had sat in silent astonishment at the manners of his fellow-travellers, which far exceeded the notions he had pre-conceived of English plainness and rusticity: he found himself a monument of that disregard and contempt, which a stranger never fails to meet with from the inhabitants of this island;[20] and saw with surprize, an agreeable young creature sit as solitary and unheeded as himself. He was, indeed, allured by the roses of her complexion, and the innocence of her aspect, and began to repent of having pretended ignorance of the language, by which he was restrained from exercising his eloquence upon her heart; he resolved, however, to ingratiate himself, if possible, by the courtesy and politeness of dumb shew, and for that purpose, put his eyes in motion without farther delay.

CHAPTER XXIX.

Another providential deliverance, from the effects
of the smuggler's ingenious conjecture.

During these deliberations, the wine-merchant, with a view to make a
parade of his superior parts and breeding, as well as to pave the way for
a match at backgammon, made a tender of his snuff-box to our adventurer,
and asked in bad French, how he travelled from Paris. This question produced a series of interrogations, concerning the place of Ferdinand's abode in
that city, and his business in England; so that he was fain to practise the
science of defence, and answered with such ambiguity, as arroused the suspicion of the smuggler, who began to believe our hero had some very cogent
reason, for evading his curiosity: he immediately set his reflection at work,
and after various conjectures, fixed upon Fathom's being the young pretender.[1] Big with this supposition, he eyed him with the most earnest attention, comparing his features with those of the chevalier's portrait, which he
had seen in France, and though the faces were as unlike as any two human
faces could be, found the resemblance so striking as to dispel all his doubts,
and persuade him to introduce the stranger to some Justice on the road: a step
by which he would not only manifest his zeal for the protestant succession,[2]
but also acquire the splendid reward proposed by parliament, to any person
who should apprehend that famous adventurer.[3]

These ideas intoxicated the brain of this man, to such a pitch of enthusiasm, that he actually believed himself in possession of the thirty thousand
pounds, and amused his fancy with a variety of magnificent projects to be
executed by means of that acquisition; until his reverie was interrupted by
the halting of the coach at the inn where the passengers used to eat their
breakfasts. Waked as he was from the dream of happiness, it had made such
impression upon his mind, that seeing Fathom rise up with an intention to
alight, he took it for granted his design was to escape, and seizing him by the
collar, called aloud for assistance, in the king's name.

Our hero, whose sagacity and presence of mind, very often supplied the
place of courage, instead of being terrified at this assault, which might have
disturbed the tranquillity of an ordinary villain, was so perfectly master of
every circumstance of his own situation, as to know at once, that the aggressor could not possibly have the least cause of complaint against him; and
therefore, imputing this violence either to madness or mistake, very deliberately suffered himself to be made prisoner by the people of the house, who

ran to the coach-door, in obedience to the summons of the wine-merchant. The rest of the company were struck dumb with surprize and consternation at this sudden adventure, and the quaker dreading some fell resistance on the side of the outlandish-man, unpinned the other coach-door in the twinkling of an eye, and trundled[4] himself into the mud for safety. The others seeing the temper and resignation of the prisoner, soon recovered their recollection, and began to inquire into the cause of his arrest: Upon which the captor, whose teeth chattered with terror and impatience, gave them to understand that he was a state criminal, and demanded their help in conveying him to justice.

Luckily for both parties, there happened to be at the inn a company of squires just returned from the death of a leash of hares,[5] which they had ordered to be dressed for dinner, and among these gentlemen was one of the Quorum,[6] to whom the accuser had immediate recourse, marching before the captive, who walked very peaceably between the landlord and one of his waiters, and followed by a croud of spectators, some of whom had secured the faithful Maurice, who in his behaviour, closely imitated the deliberation of his master. In this order did the procession advance to the apartment in which the magistrate with his fellows of the chace, sat smoking his morning pipe over a tankard of strong ale; and the smuggler being directed to the right person, "May it please your worship," said he, "I have brought this foreigner before you, on a violent suspicion of his being a proclaimed outlaw, and I desire before these witnesses, that my title may be made good to the reward that shall become due upon his conviction."

"Friend," replied the justice, "I know nothing of you or your titles, but, this I know, if you have any information to give in, you must come to my house when I am at home, and proceed in a lawful way, that is, d'ye mind me, if you swear as how this here person is an outlaw, then if so be as he has nothing to say to the contrary, my clerk shall make out a mittimus;[7] and so to jail with him till next size."[8] "But Sir," answered the impeacher, "this is a case that admits of no delay, the person I have apprehended, is a prisoner of consequence to the state." "How! fellor," cried the magistrate, interrupting him, "is there any person of more consequence than one of his majesty's justices of the peace, who is besides, a considerable member of the landed interest? d'ye know sirrah, who you are talking to? if you don't go about your business, I believe I shall lay you by the heels."

The smuggler fearing his prize would escape, through the ignorance, pride and obstinacy of this country justice, approached his worship, and in a whisper, which was overheard by all the company, assured him, he had indubita-

The Magistrate, by Clennell.
(Library Company of Philadelphia.)

ble reason to believe the foreigner was no other than the pretender's eldest
son. At mention of this formidable name, every individual of the audience
started, with signs of terror and amazement. The justice dropped his pipe,
recoiled upon his chair, and looking most ridiculously aghast, exclaimed,
"Seize him in the name of God and his majesty king George! has he got no
secret arms about him?"

Fathom being thus informed of the suspicion under which he stood, could
not help smiling at the eagerness with which the spectators flew upon him;
and suffered himself to be searched with great composure, well knowing they
would find no moveables about his person, but such as upon examination,
would turn to his account; he, therefore, very calmly presented to the magistrate his purse, and a small box that contained his jewels, and in the French
language, desired they might be preserved from the hands of the mob. This
request was interpreted by the accuser, who at the same time, laid claim
to the booty; the justice took charge of the deposit, and one of his neighbours having undertaken the office of clerk, he proceeded to the examination
of the culprit, whose papers were by this time laid on the table before him.
"Stranger," said he, "you stand charged with being son of the pretender to
these realms: what have you to say in your own defence?" Our hero assured
him in the French language that he was falsely impeached, and demanded
justice on the accuser, who without the least reason, had made such a malicious attack upon the life and honour of an innocent gentleman.

The smuggler, instead of acting the part of a faithful interpreter, told his
worship that the prisoner's answer was no more than a simple denial, which
every felon would make, who had nothing else to plead in his own behalf; and
that this alone was a strong presumption of his guilt; because, if he was not
really the person they suspected him to be, the thing would speak for itself:
for, if he was not the young pretender, who then was he? This argument had
great weight with the justice, who assuming a very important aspect, observed, "Very true, friend, if you are not the pretender, in the name of God
who are you? one may see with half an eye, that he is no better than a
promiscuous fellow."

Ferdinand now began to repent of having pretended ignorance of the English language, as he found himself at the mercy of a rascal, who put a false
gloss upon all his words; and addressed himself to the audience successively
in French, High-Dutch, Italian, and Hungarian Latin, desiring to know if
any person present understood any of these tongues, that his answers might
be honestly explained to the bench. But, he might have accosted them in
Chinese with the same success: there was not one person present tolerably

versed in his mother tongue, much less acquainted with any foreign language, except the wine-merchant, who incensed at this appeal, which he considered as an affront to his integrity, gave the judge to understand that the delinquent, instead of speaking to the purpose, contumaciously insulted his authority, in sundry foreign lingo's, which he apprehended, was an additional proof of his being the chevalier's son, inasmuch, as no person would take the pains to learn such a variety of gibberish, except with some sinister intent.[9]

This annotation was not lost upon the squire, who was too jealous of the honour of his office, to overlook such a flagrant instance of contempt. His eyes glistened, his cheeks were inflated with rage: "The case is plain," said he, "having nothing of signification to offer in his own favour, he grows refectory,[10] and abuses the court in his base Roman catholic jargon: but I'll let you know, for all you pretend to be a prince, you are no better than an outlawed vagrant; and I'll shew you what a thing you are, when you come in composition[11] with an English justice like me, who have more than once extinguished[12] myself in the service of my country. As nothing else accrues,[13] your purse, black box and papers shall be sealed up before witnesses, and sent by express to one of his majesty's secretaries of state; and as for yourself, I will apply to the military at Canterbury, for a guard to conduct you to London."

This was a very unwelcome declaration to our adventurer, who was on the point of harranguing the justice and spectators in their own language, when he was relieved from the necessity of taking that step, by the interposition of a young nobleman just arrived at the inn, who being informed of this strange examination, entered the court, and at first sight of the prisoner, assured the justice he was imposed upon; for, that he himself had often seen the young Pretender in Paris, and that there was no kind of resemblance between that adventurer and the person now before him. The accuser was not a little mortified at his lordship's affirmation, which met with all due regard from the bench; though the magistrate took notice that granting the prisoner was not the young chevalier himself, it was highly probable, he was an emissary of that house, as he could give no satisfactory account of himself, and was possessed of things of such value as no honest man would expose to the accidents of the road.

Fathom having thus found an interpreter, who signified to him in the French tongue, the doubts of the justice, told his lordship that he was a gentleman of a noble house in Germany, who for certain reasons, had come abroad incognito, with a view to see the world; and that although the letters they had seised, would prove the truth of that assertion, he should be loth to expose his private concerns to the knowledge of strangers, if he could possibly be released without that mortification. The young nobleman explained his desire to the court; but, his own curiosity being interested, observed at the same time, that the justice could not be said to have discharged the duty of his station, until he should have examined every circumstance relating to the prisoner: upon which remonstrance, he was requested by the bench to peruse the papers, and accordingly communicated the substance of one letter, to this effect.

"My dear son,

Though I am far from approving the rash step you have taken in withdrawing yourself from your father's house, in order to avoid an engagement, which would have been equally honourable and advantageous to your family, I cannot so far suppress my affection, as to bear the thought of your undergoing those hardships, which for your disobedience, you deserve to suffer. I have therefore, without the knowledge of your father, sent the bearer to attend you in your peregrinations; his fidelity you know hath been tried in a long course of service, and I have entrusted to his care for your use, a purse of two hundred ducats,[14] and a box of jewels to the value of twice that sum, which though not sufficient to support an equipage suitable to your birth, will, at least for some time, preserve you from the importunities of want. When you are dutiful enough to explain your designs and situation, you may expect further indulgence from your too tender and disconsolate mother,

The countess of Fathom."

This letter, which, as well as the others, our hero had forged for the purpose, effectually answered his intent, in throwing dust in the eyes and understanding of the spectators, who now regarded the prisoner with looks of respectful remorse, as a man of quality who had been falsly accused: his lordship to make a parade of his own politeness and importance, assured the bench, he was no stranger to the family of the Fathoms, and with a compliment, gave Ferdinand to understand he had formerly seen him at Versailles. There being no longer room for suspicion, the justice ordered our adventurer to be set at liberty, and even invited him to be seated, with an apology for the rude manner in which he had been treated, owing to the misinformation of the accuser, who was threatned with the stocks for his malice and presumption.

But, this was not the only triumph our hero obtained over the wine-merchant. Maurice was no sooner unfettered, than advancing into the middle of the room; "My lord, (said he, addressing himself in French, to his master's deliverer), since you have been so generous as to protect a noble stranger from the danger of such a false accusation, I hope you will still lay an additional obligation upon the count, by retorting the vengeance of the law upon his perfidious accuser, whom I know to be a trader in those articles of merchandize, which are prohibited by the ordonnances of this nation. I have seen him lately at Bullogne, and am perfectly well acquainted with some persons who have supplied him with French lace and embroidery; and as a proof of what I alledge, I desire you will order him and this barber, who is his understrapper, to be examined on the spot."

This charge, which was immediately explained to the bench, yielded extraordinary satisfaction to the spectators, one of whom, being an officer of the customs, forthwith began to exercise his function upon the unlucky Perruquier,[15] who being stripped of his upper garments, and even of his shirt, appeared like the mummy of an Ægyptian king, most curiously rolled up in bandages of rich, figured gold shalloon,[16] that covered the skirts of four embroidered waistcoats. The merchant seeing his expectation so unhappily reversed, made an effort to retire with a most rueful aspect; but was prevented by the officer, who demanded the interposition of the civil power, that he might undergo the same examination, to which the other had been subjected. He was accordingly rifled without loss of time, and the enquiry proved well worth the care of him who made it; for, a considerable booty of the same sort of merchandize was found in his boots, breeches, hat, and between the buckram and lining of his surtout.[17] Yet not contented with this prize, the experienced spoiler proceeded to search his baggage, and perceiving a false bottom in his portmanteau, detected beneath it a valuable accession to the plunder he had already obtained.

CHAPTER XXX.

The singular manner of Fathom's attack and triumph over the virtue of the fair Elenor.

Proper cognizance being thus taken of these contraband effects, and the informer furnished with a certificate by which he was intitled to a share of the seizure, the coachman summoned his passengers to the carriage; the purse and jewels were restored to count Fathom, who thanked the justice, and his lordship in particular, for the candour and hospitality with which he had been treated, and resumed his place in the vehicle, amidst the congratulations of all his fellow travellers, except the two forlorn smugglers, who instead of reimbarking in the coach, thought proper to remain at the inn, with a view to mitigate, if possible, the severity of their misfortune.

Among those who felicitated Fathom upon the issue of this adventure, the young maiden seemed to express the most sensible pleasure at that event. The artful language of his eyes had raised in her breast certain fluttering emotions, before she knew the value of her conquest; but now that his rank and condition were discovered, these transports were increased by the ideas of vanity and ambition which are mingled with the first seeds of every female constitution. The belief of having captivated the heart of a man who could raise her to the rank and dignity of a countess, produced such agreeable sensations in her fancy, that her eyes shone with unusual lustre, and a continual smile played in dimples, on her rosy cheeks; so that her attractions, though not powerful enough to engage the affection, were yet sufficient to inflame the desire of our adventurer, who very honestly marked her chastity for prey to his voluptuous passion. Had she been well seasoned with knowledge and experience, and completely armed with caution against the artifice and villainy of man, her virtue might not have been able to withstand the engines of such an assailant, considering the dangerous opportunities to which she was necessarily exposed: how easy then must his victory have been over an innocent, unsuspecting country damsel, flushed with the warmth of youth, and an utter stranger to the ways of life.

While Obadiah, therefore, and his plump companion were engaged in conversation, on the strange incidents which had passed, Fathom acted a very expressive pantomime with this fair buxom nymph, who comprehended his meaning with surprizing facility, and was at so little pains to conceal the pleasure she took in this kind of intercourse, that several warm squeezes were interchanged between her and her lover, before they arrived at Rochester,[1] where they proposed to dine. It was during this period, he learned from the answers she made to the inquisitive quaker, that her sole dependance was upon a relation, to whom she had a letter, and that she was a perfect stranger in the great city; circumstances on which he soon formed the project of her ruin.

Upon their arrival at the Black Bull,[2] he for the first time found himself alone with his Amanda,[3] whose name was Elenor, their fellow-travellers being elsewhere employed about their own concerns; and unwilling to lose the precious opportunity, he began to act the part of a very importunate

lover, which he conceived to be a proper sequel to the prelude, which had
been performed in the coach. The freedoms that she, out of pure simplicity
and good humour, permitted him to take with her hand, and even her rosy
lips, encouraged him to practise other familiarities upon her fair bosom,
which scandalized her virtue so much, that in spite of the passion she had
begun to indulge in his behalf, she rejected his advances with all the marks of
anger and disdain; and he found it necessary to appease the storm he had
raised, by the most respectful and submissive demeanour; resolving to
change his operations, and carry on his attacks, so as to make her yield at
discretion, without alarming her religion or pride. Accordingly, when the bill
was called after dinner, he took particular notice of her behaviour, and perceiving her pull out a large leathern purse that contained her money, reconnoitred the pocket in which it was deposited, and while they sat close to each
other in the carriage, conveyed it with admirable dexterity into an hole in the
cushion. Whether the corpulent couple, who sat opposite to these lovers, had
entered into an amorous engagement at the inn, or were severally induced by
other motives, is uncertain; but, sure it is, both left the coach on that part of
the road which lies nearest to Gravesend,[4] and bad adieu to the other pair, on
pretence of having urgent business at that place.

Ferdinand, not a little pleased at their departure, renewed his most pathetic expressions of love, and sung several French songs on that tender subject,
which seemed to thrill to the soul of his beauteous Helen.[5] While the driver
halted at Dartford[6] to water his horses, she was smit with the appearance of
some cheesecakes, which were presented by the landlady of the house, and
having bargained for two or three, put her hand in her pocket, in order to pay
for her purchase; but what was her astonishment, when after having rummaged her equipage, she understood her whole fortune was lost! This mishap was by a loud shriek announced to our hero, who affected infinite amazement and concern; and no sooner learned the cause of her affliction, than he
presented her with his own purse, from which he, in emphatic dumb shew,
begged she would indemnify herself for the damage she had sustained. Although this kind proffer was some alleviation of her misfortune, she did not
fail to pour forth a most piteous lamentation, importing that she had not only
lost all her money, amounting to five pounds, but also her letter of recommendation upon which she had altogether relied for present employment.

The vehicle was minutely searched from top to bottom, by herself and our
adventurer, assisted by Maurice, and the coachman, who finding their inquiry ineffectual, did not scruple to declare his suspicion of the two fat tur-
tles who had deserted the coach in such an abrupt manner. In a word, he

rendered this conjecture so plausible, by wresting[7] the circumstances of their behaviour and retreat, that poor Elenor implicitly believed they were the thieves by whom she had suffered; and was prevailed upon to accept the proffered assistance of the generous count, who seeing her very much disordered by this mischance, insisted upon her drinking a large glass of Canary[8] to quiet the perturbation of her spirits. This is a season, which of all others, is most propitious to the attempts of an artful lover; and justifies the metaphorical maxim of fishing in troubled waters.[9] There is an affinity and short transition betwixt all the violent passions that agitate the human mind: they are all false perspectives, which though they magnify, yet perplex and render indistinct every object which they represent: and flattery is never so successfully administred, as to those who know they stand in need of friendship, assent and approbation.

The cordial she swallowed, far from calming, increased the disturbance of her thoughts, and produced an intoxication; during which, she talked in an incoherent strain, laughed and wept by turns, and acted other extravagancies, which are known to be symptoms of the hysterical affection.[10] Fathom, though an utter stranger to the sentiments of honour, pity and remorse, would not perpetrate his vitious purpose, though favoured by the delirium his villainy had intailed upon this unfortunate young maiden; because his appetite demanded a more perfect sacrifice, than that which she could yield in her present deplorable situation, when her will must have been altogether unconcerned in his success. Determined therefore, to make a conquest of her virtue, before he would take possession of her person, he mimicked that compassion and benevolence, which his heart had never felt, and when the coach arrived at London, not only discharged what she owed for her place, but likewise, procured for her an apartment in the house, to which he himself had been directed for lodgings, and even hired a nurse to attend her, during a severe fever, which was the consequence of her disappointment and despondence. Indeed she was supplied with all necessaries by the generosity of this noble count, who for the interest of his passion, and the honour of his name, was resolved to extend his charity to the last farthing of her own money, which he had been wise enough to secure for this purpose.

Her youth soon got the better of her distemper, and when she understood her obligations to the count, who did not fail to attend her in person with great tenderness, her heart, which had been before prepossessed in his favour, now glowed with all the warmth of gratitude, esteem and affection. She knew herself in a strange place, destitute of all resource but in his generosity: she loved his person, she was dazzled by his rank; and he knew so well

how to improve the opportunities and advantages he derived from her unhappy situation, that he gradually proceeded in sapping[11] from one degree of
intimacy to another, until all the bulwarks of her chastity were undermined,
and she submitted to his desire; not with the reluctance of a vanquished
people, but with all the transports of a joyful city, that opens its gates to
receive a darling prince, returned from conquest: for, by this time, he had
artfully concentred[12] and kindled up, all the inflammable ingredients of her
constitution; and she now looked back upon the virtuous principles of her
education, as upon a disagreeable and tedious dream, from which she had
waked to the fruition of never-fading joy.

CHAPTER XXXI.

*He by accident encounters his old friend, with
whom he holds a conference, and renews a
treaty.*

Our Hero having thus provided himself with a proper subject for his
hours of dalliance, thought it was now high time to study the ground
which he had pitched upon for the scene of his exploits, and with that view
made several excursions to different parts of the town, where there was
ought[1] of entertainment or instruction to be found: yet he always, on these
occasions, appeared in an obscure ordinary dress, in order to avoid singularity, and never went twice to the same coffee-house, that his person
might not be afterwards known, in case he should shine forth to the public, in
a superior sphere. On his return from one of these expeditions, while he was
passing through Ludgate,[2] his eyes were suddenly encountered, by the apparition of his old friend the Tyroleze, who perceiving himself fairly caught in
the toil,[3] made a virtue of necessity, and running up to our adventurer with
an aspect of eagerness and joy, clasped him in his arms, as some dear friend,
whom he had casually found after a most tedious and disagreeable separation.

Fathom, whose genius never failed him in such emergencies, far from receiving these advances with the threats and reproaches which the other had
deserved at his hands, returned the salute with equal warmth, and was really
over-joyed at meeting with a person, who might one way or other make
amends for the perfidy of his former conduct. The Tyroleze, whose name

was Ratchkali, pleased with his reception, proposed they should adjourn to the next tavern, in which they had no sooner taken possession of an apartment, than he addressed himself to his old companion in these words.

"Mr. Fathom, by your frank and obliging manner of treating a man who hath done you wrong, I am more and more confirmed in my opinion of your sagacity, which I have often considered with admiration: I will not therefore, attempt to make an apology for my conduct at our last parting; but only assure you that this meeting may turn out to our mutual advantage, if we now re-enter into an unreserved union, the ties of which we will soon find it our interest and inclination to preserve. For my own part, as my judgment is ripened by experience, so are my sentiments changed since our last association. I have seen many a rich harvest lost, for want of a fellow-labourer in the vineyard; and I have more than once fallen a sacrifice to a combination, which I could have resisted with the help of one able auxiliary. Indeed I might prove what I alledge by mathematical demonstration; and I believe no body will pretend to deny, that two heads are better than one,[4] in all cases that require discernment and deliberation."

Ferdinand could not help owning the sanity of his observations, and forthwith acquiesced in his proposal of the new alliance; desiring to know the character in which he acted in the English stage, and the scheme he would offer for their mutual emolument: at the same time he resolved within himself, to keep such a strict eye over his future actions, as would frustrate any design, he might hereafter harbour, of repeating the prank he had so successfully played upon him, in their journey from the banks of the Rhine.

"Having quitted you at Bar le duc," resumed the Tyroleze, "I travelled without ceasing, until I arrived at Franckfort upon the Maine,[5] where I assumed the character of a French chevalier, and struck some masterly strokes, which you yourself would not have deemed unworthy of your invention; and my success was the more agreeable, as my operations were chiefly carried on against the enemies of our religion:[6] but my prosperity was not of long duration. Seeing they could not foil me at my own weapons, they formed a damned conspiracy, by which I not only lost all the fruits of my industry, but likewise ran the most imminent hazard of my life. I had ordered some of those jewels which I had borrowed of my good friend Fathom, to be new set in a fashionable taste, and soon after had an opportunity to sell one of these at a great advantage, to one of the fraternity,[7] who offered an extraordinary price for the stone, on purpose to effect my ruin. In less than four and twenty hours after this bargain, I was arrested by the officers of justice, upon the oath of the purchaser, who undertook to prove me guilty of a fraud, in selling a Saxon pebble[8] for a real diamond; and this accusation was actually true; for the change had been artfully put upon me, by the jeweller, who was himself engaged in the conspiracy.

Had my conscience been clear of any other impeachment, perhaps, I should have rested my cause upon the equity and protection of the law; but, I foresaw that the trial would introduce an inquiry, to which I was not at all ambitious of submitting, and therefore was fain to compromise the affair, at the price of almost my whole fortune. Yet, this accommodation was not made so secretly, but that my character was blasted, and my credit overthrown; so that I was fain to relinquish my occasional equipage, and hire myself as journeyman to a lapidary,[9] an employment which I had exercised in my youth. In this obscure station, I laboured with great assiduity, until I made myself perfect in the knowledge of stones, as well as in the different methods of setting them off to the best advantage; and having, by dint of industry and address, got possession of a small parcel, set out for this kingdom, in which I happily arrived about four months ago; and surely England is the paradise of artists of our profession.

One would imagine, that nature had created the inhabitants, for the support and enjoyment of adventurers like you and me. Not that these islanders[10] open the arms of hospitality to all foreigners without distinction: on the contrary, they inherit from their fathers, an unreasonable prejudice against all nations under the sun; and when an Englishman happens to quarrel with a stranger, the first term of reproach he uses, is the name of his antagonist's country, characterized by some opprobrious epithet; such as a chattering Frenchman, an Italian ape, a German hog, and a beastly Dutchman; nay, their national prepossession is maintained even against those people with whom they are united, under the same laws and government; for, nothing is more common than to hear them exclaim against their fellow-subjects, in the expressions of a beggarly Scot, and an impudent Irish bog-trotter. Yet, this very prejudice will never fail to turn to the account of every stranger possessed of ordinary talents; for he will always find opportunities of conversing with them in Coffee-houses, and places of public resort, in spite of their professed reserve, which, by the bye, is so extraordinary, that I know some people who have lived twenty years in the same house, without exchanging one word with their next door neighbours; yet, provided he can talk sensibly, and preserve the deportment of a sober gentleman, in those occasional conversations, his behaviour will be the more remarkably pleasing, as it will agreeably disappoint the expectation of the person, who had entertained notions to his prejudice. When a foreigner has once crossed this bar, which perpetually occurs, he sails without further difficulty into the harbour of an Englishman's good will; for the pique is neither personal nor rancorous, but rather contemptuous and national; so that while he despises a people in the lump, an individual of that very community, may be one of his chief favourites.

The English are in general upright and honest, therefore unsuspecting and credulous: they are too much engrossed with their own business, to pry into the conduct of their neighbours, and too indifferent, in point of disposition, to interest themselves, in what they conceive to be foreign to their own concerns. They are wealthy and mercantile, of consequence liberal and adventurous, and so well disposed to take a man's own word for his importance, that they suffer themselves to be preyed upon by such a bungling set of impostors, as would starve for lack of address, in any other country under the sun. This being a true sketch of the British character, so far as I have been able to observe and learn, you will easily comprehend the profits that may be extracted from it, by virtue of those arts by which you so eminently excel; *the great the unbounded prospect lies before me!*[11] Indeed, I look upon this opulent kingdom, as a wide and fertile common, on which we adventurers may range for prey, without let[12] or molestation: for so jealous are the natives of their liberty, that they will not bear the restraint of necessary *Police*, and an able artist may enrich himself with their spoils, without running any risque of attracting the notice of the magistrate, or incuring the least penalty of the law.[13]

In a word, this metropolis is a vast masquerade, in which a man of stratagem may wear a thousand different disguises, without danger of detection. There is a variety of shapes, in which we knights of the industry, make our appearance in London. One glides into a nobleman's house in the capacity of a valet de chambre, and in a few months leads the whole family by the nose. Another exhibits himself to the public, as an empiric or operator for the teeth; and by dint of assurance and affidavits, bearing testimony to wonderful cures that never were performed, whirls himself into his chariot, and lays the town under contribution: a third professes the composition of musick, as well as the performance, and by means of a few *Capriciosos*[14] on the violin, properly introduced, wriggles himself into the management of private and public concerts: and a fourth breaks forth at once in all the splendor of a gay equipage, under the title and denomination of a foreign count. Not to mention those inferior projectors, who assume the characters of dancers, fencing-masters, and French ushers, or by renouncing their religion, seek to obtain a provision for life.

Either of these parts will turn to the account of an able actor; and as you are equally qualified for all, you may choose that which is most suitable to your own inclination: though in my opinion, you was designed by nature, to shine in the great world, which, after all, is the most ample field, for men of genius; because the game is deeper, and people of fashion being, for the most part, more ignorant, indolent, vain and capricious than their inferiors, are of consequence more easily deceived; besides their morals fit generally so loose about them, that when a gentleman of our fraternity is discovered in the exercise of his profession, their contempt of his skill is the only disgrace he incurs."

Our hero was so well pleased with this picture, that he longed to peruse the original, and before these two friends parted, they settled all the operations of the campaign. Ratchkali, that same evening, hired magnificent lodgings for count Fathom, in the court end of the town,[15] and furnished his wardrobe and liveries from the spoils of Monmouth-street;[16] he likewise enlisted another footman and valet de chambre into his service, and sent to the apartments divers large trunks, supposed to be filled with the baggage of this foreign nobleman, though in reality, they contained little else than common lumber.

Next day, our adventurer took possession of his new habitation, after having left to his friend and associate the task of dismissing the unfortunate Ellenor, who was so shocked at the unexpected message, that she fainted away; and when she recovered the use of her senses, so well as to reflect upon her forlorn condition, she was seized with the most violent transports of grief and dismay, by which her brain was disordered to such a degree, that she grew furious and distracted, and was by the advice and assistance of the Tyroleze, conveyed into the hospital of Bethlem;[17] where we shall leave her for the present, happily bereft of her reason.

CHAPTER XXXII.

He appears in the great world with universal applause and admiration.

Mean while, Fathom and his engine[1] were busied in compleating his equipage, so that in a few days, he had procured a very gay chariot, adorned with painting, gilding and a coat of arms according to his own fancy and direction: the first use he made of this vehicle, was that of visiting the young nobleman from whom he had received such important civilities on the road, in consequence of an invitation at parting, by which he learned his title and the place of his abode in London.

His lordship was not only pleased, but proud to see such a stranger at his gate, and entertained him with excess of complaisance and hospitality; insomuch, that by his means our hero soon became acquainted with the whole circle of polite company, by whom he was caressed for his insinuating manners and agreeable conversation. He had thought proper to tell the nobleman at their first interview in town, that his reasons for concealing his knowledge of the English tongue were now removed, and that he would no longer deny himself the pleasure of speaking a language which had been always musick to his ear: he had also thanked his lordship for his generous interposition at the inn, which was an instance of that generosity and true politeness, which are engrossed by the English people, who leave nought to other nations but the meer shadow of these virtues.

A testimony like this, from the mouth of such a noble stranger, won the heart of the peer, who professed a friendship for him on the spot, and undertook to see justice done to his lacquey, who in a short time was gratified with a share of the seisure which had been made upon his information, amounting to fifty or sixty pounds.

Ferdinand put not forth the whole strength of his accomplishments at once, but contrived to spring a new mine of qualification every day, to the surprize and admiration of all his acquaintance. He was gifted with a sort of elocution, much more specious than solid, and spoke on every subject that occurred in conversation, with that familiarity and ease, which, one would think, could only be acquired by long study and application. This plausibility and confidence, are faculties really inherited from nature, and effectually serve the possessor, in lieu of that learning, which is not to be obtained without infinite toil and perseverance: the most superficial tincture of the arts and sciences in such a juggler,[2] is sufficient to dazzle the understanding of half mankind; and if managed with circumspection, will enable him even to spend his life among the literati, without once forfeiting the character of a connoisseur.

Our hero was perfectly master of this legerdemain, which he carried to such a pitch of assurance, as to declare in the midst of a mathematical assembly, that he intended to gratify the publick with a full confutation of Sir Isaac Newton's philosophy,[3] to the nature of which he was as much a stranger as the most savage Hottentot in Afric.[4] His pretensions to profound and universal knowledge, were supported not only by this kind of presumption, but also by the facility with which he spoke so many different languages, and the shrewd remarks[5] he had made in the course of his travels and observation.

Among politicians, he settled the balance of power upon a certain footing, by dint of ingenious schemes, which he had contrived for the welfare of Europe. With officers, he reformed the art of war, with improvements which had occurred to his reflection, while he was engaged in a military life. He sometimes held forth upon painting, like a member of the *Dillettanti* club:[6] the theory of musick was a theme upon which he seemed to expatiate with particular pleasure: in the provinces of love and gallantry, he was a perfect Oroondates:[7] he possessed a most agreeable manner of telling entertaining stories, of which he had a large collection: he sung with great melody and taste, and played upon the violin with surprizing execution. To these qualifications, let us add his affability and pliant disposition, and then the reader will not wonder that he was looked upon as the pattern of human perfection, and his acquaintance courted accordingly.

While he thus captivated the favour and affection of the English nobility, he did not neglect to take other measures in behalf of the partnership to which he had subscribed. This adventure with the two squires[8] at Paris, had weakened his appetite for play, which was not at all restored by the observations he had made in London, where the art of gaming is reduced into a regular system,[9] and its professors so laudably devoted to the discharge of their functions, as to observe the most temperate regimen, lest their invention should be impaired by the fatigue of watching or exercise, and their ideas disturbed by the fumes of indigestion. No Indian Brachman[10] could live more abstemious than two of the pack, who hunted in couple, and kennelled in the upper apartments of the hotel in which our adventurer lived: they abstained from animal food with the abhorrence of Pythagoreans,[11] their drink was the pure, simple element, they were vomited once a week, took physic or a glyster[12] every third day, spent the forenoon in algebraical calculations, and slept from four o'clock till midnight, that they might then take the field with that cool serenity which is the effect of refreshment and repose.

These were terms upon which our hero would not risque his fortune; he was too much addicted to pleasure to forego every other enjoyment but that of amassing; and did not so much depend upon his dexterity in play, as upon his talent of insinuation, which by this time, had succeeded so far beyond his expectation, that he began to indulge the hope of enslaving the heart of some rich heiress, whose fortune would at once raise him above all dependance.

Indeed no man ever set out with a fairer prospect on such an expedition; for, he had found means to render himself so agreeable to the fair sex, that like the boxes of the playhouse, during the representation of a new performance, his company was often bespoke for a series of weeks; and no lady, whether widow, wife or maiden, ever mentioned his name, without some epithet of esteem or affection; such as *the dear Count! the charming Man! the Nonpareil!* or *the Angel!*

While he thus shone in the zenith of admiration, it is not to be doubted, that he could have melted some wealthy dowager or opulent ward: but being an enemy to all precipitate engagements, he resolved to act with great care and deliberation in an affair of such importance, especially as he did not find himself hurried by the importunities of want: for, since his arrival in England, he had rather increased than exhausted his finances, by methods equally certain and secure. In a word, he with the assistance of Ratchkali carried on a traffick, which yielded great profits, without subjecting the trader to the least loss or inconvenience. Fathom, for example, wore upon his finger a large brilliant,[13] which he played to such advantage one night, at a certain nobleman's house, where he was prevailed upon to entertain the company with a solo on the violin, that every body present took notice of it's uncommon lustre, and it was handed about for the perusal of every individual. The water[14] and the workmanship were universally admired; and one among the rest, having expressed a desire of knowing the value of such a jewel, the count seized that opportunity of entertaining them with a learned disquisition into the nature of stones; this introduced the history of the diamond in question, which he said had been purchased of an Indian trader of Fort St. George,[15] at an under price; so that the present proprietor could afford to sell it at a very reasonable rate; and concluded with telling the company, that for his own part, he had been importuned to wear it, by the jeweller, who imagined it would have a better chance for attracting a purchaser on his finger, than while it remained in his own custody.

This declaration was no sooner made, than a certain lady of quality, bespoke the refuse[16] of the jewel, and desired Ferdinand to send the owner next day to her house, where he accordingly waited upon her ladyship with the ring, for which he received one hundred and fifty guineas, two thirds of the sum being clear gain, and equally divided betwixt the associates. Nor was this bargain such as reflected dishonour upon the lady's taste, or could be productive of ill consequences to the merchant: for the method of estimating diamonds is altogether arbitrary; and Ratchkali, who was an exquisite lapidary, had set it in such a manner as would have imposed upon any ordinary jeweller. By these means of introduction, the Tyroleze soon monopolized the custom of a great many noble families, upon which he levied large contributions, without incurring the least suspicion of deceit: he every day out of pure esteem and gratitude for the honour of their commands, entertained them with the sight of some new trinket, which he was never permitted to carry home, unsold; and from the profits of each job, a tax was raised for the benefit of our adventurer.

Yet his indultos[17] were not confined to the article of jewels, which constituted only one part of his revenue: by the industry of his understrapper, he procured a number of old crazy fiddles, which were thrown aside as lumber; upon which he counterfeited the Cremona mark,[18] and otherwise cook'd them up with great dexterity; so that when he had occasion to regale the lovers of musick, he would send for one of these vamped[19] instruments, and extract from it such tones as quite ravished the hearers; among whom there was always some conceited pretender, who spoke in raptures of the violin, and gave our hero an opportunity of launching out in its praise, and declaring it was the best Cremona he had ever touched. This encomium never failed to inflame the desires of the audience, to some one of whom, he was generous enough to part with it at prime cost, that is, for twenty or thirty guineas clear profit; for he was often able to oblige his friends in this manner, because, being an eminent connoisseur, his countenance was solicited by all the musicians, who wanted to dispose of such moveables.

Nor did he neglect the other resources of a skilful virtuoso.[20] Every auction afforded some picture, in which, though it had been over-looked by the ignorance of the times, he recognized the stile of a great master, and made a merit of recommending it to some noble friend. This commerce he likewise extended to medals, bronzes, busts, intaglios[21] and old china, and kept divers artificers continually employed in making antiques for the English nobility. Thus he went on with such rapidity of success in all his endeavours, that he himself was astonished at the infatuation he had produced. Nothing was so wretched among the productions of art, that he could not impose upon the world as a capital performance, and so fascinated were the eyes of his admirers, he could easily have persuaded them that a barber's bason was an Etrurian Patera,[22] and the cover of a copper pot, no other than the shield of Ancus Martius.[23] In short, it was become so fashionable to consult the count in every thing relating to taste and politeness, that not a plan was drawn, not even an house furnished without his advice and approbation; nay, to such a degree did his reputation in these matters excel, that a particular pattern of paper-hangings was known by the name of Fathom; and his hall was every morning crouded with upholsterers and other tradesmen, who came by order of their employers, to learn his choice, and take his directions.

The character and influence he thus acquired he took care to maintain with the utmost assiduity and circumspection: he never failed to appear the chief personage at all public diversions, and private assemblies, not only in conversation and dress, but also in the article of dancing, in which he outstripped all his fellows, as far as in every other genteel accomplishment.

CHAPTER XXXIII.

*He attracts the envy and ill offices of the minor knights
of his own order, over whom he obtains a compleat
victory.*

Such a preheminence could not be enjoyed without exciting the malevolence of envy and detraction, in the propagation of which, none were so industrious as the brethren of his own order, who, had like him, made a descent upon this island, and could not without repining, see the whole harvest in the hands of one man, who with equal art and discretion avoided all intercourse with their society. In vain they strove to discover his pedigree, and detect the particular circumstances of his life and conversation; all their inquiries were bafled by the obscurity of his origin, and that solitary scheme which he had adopted in the beginning of his career. The whole fruit of their investigation, amounted to no more than a certainty that there was no family of any consideration in Europe, known by the denomination of Fathom; and this discovery they did not fail to divulge for the benefit of our adventurer, who had by this time, taken such firm root in the favour of the great, as to set all those little arts at defiance; and when the report reached his ear, actually made his friends merry with the conjectures which had been circulated at his expence.

His adversaries finding themselves disappointed in this effort, held a consultation to devise other measures against him, and came to a resolution of ending him by the sword, or rather of expelling him from the kingdom, by the fear of death, which they hoped he had not courage enough to resist, because his deportment had been always remarkably mild and pacific. It was upon this supposition, that they left to the determination of the dice, the choice of the person who should execute their plan; and the lot falling upon a Swiss, who from the station of a foot-soldier in the Dutch service, out of which he had been drummed for theft, had erected himself into the rank of a self-created chevalier; this hero fortified himself with a double dose of brandy, and betook himself to a certain noted coffee-house, with an intent to affront count Fathom in publick.

He was lucky enough to find our adventurer sitting at a table in conversation with some persons of the first rank; upon which he seated himself in the next box, and after having intruded himself into their discourse, which happened to turn upon the politicks of some German courts; "Count," said he to Ferdinand, in a very abrupt and disagreeable manner of address, "I was last night in company with some gentlemen, among whom a dispute happened about the place of your nativity; pray, what country are you of?" "Sir," answered the other, with great politeness, "I at present have the honour to be of England." "Oho!" replied the chevalier, "I ask your pardon, that is to say, you are incog.[1]—Some people may find it convenient to keep themselves in that situation." "True," said the count, "but some people are too well known to enjoy that privilege." The Swiss being a little disconcerted at this repartee, which extracted a smile from the audience; after some pause, observed, that persons of a certain class, had good reason to drop the remembrance of what they have been; but a good citizen will not forget his country or former condition. "And a bad citizen," saith Fathom, "cannot if he would, provided he has met with his deserts; a sharper may as well forget the shape of a die, or a discarded soldier the sound of a drum."

As the chevalier's character and story were not unknown, this application raised a universal laugh at his expence, which provoked him to such a degree, that starting up, he swore Fathom could not have mentioned any object in nature that he himself resembled so much as a drum, which was exactly typified by his emptiness and sound, with this difference however, that a drum was never noisy till beaten, whereas the count would never be quiet until he should have undergone the same discipline. So saying, he laid his hand upon his sword with a menacing look, and walked out as if in expectation of being followed by our adventurer, who suffered himself to be detained by the company, and very calmly took notice, that his antagonist would not be ill pleased at their interposition. Perhaps he would not have comported himself with such ease and deliberation, had not he made such remarks upon the disposition of the chevalier, as convinced him of his own safety. He had perceived a perplexity and perturbation in the countenance of the Swiss, when he first entered the coffee-room; his blunt and precipitate way of accosting him, seemed to denote confusion and compulsion; and in the midst of his ferocity, this accurate observer discerned the trepidation of fear. By the help of these signs, his sagacity soon comprehended the nature of his schemes, and prepared accordingly for a formal defiance.

His conjecture was verified next morning by a visit from the chevalier, who taking it for granted that Fathom would not face an adversary in the field, because he had not followed him from the coffee-house, went to his lodgings with great confidence, and demanded to see the count upon an affair that would admit of no delay. Maurice, according to his instructions, told him that his master was gone out, but desired he would have the goodness to repose himself in a parlour, till the count's return, which he expected every moment. Ferdinand, who had taken post in a proper place for observation, seeing his antagonist fairly admitted, took the same road, and appearing before him, wrapped up in a long Spanish cloak, desired to know what had procured him the honour of such an early visit. The Swiss raising his voice to conceal his agitation explained his errand, in demanding reparation, for the injury his honour had sustained the preceding day, in that odious allusion to a scandalous report which had been raised by the malice of his enemies; and insisted in a very imperious stile, upon his attending him forthwith to the nursery in Hyde-park.[2] "Have a little patience," said our adventurer with great composure, "and I will do myself the pleasure to wait upon you in a few moments."

With these words, he rung the bell, and calling for a bason of water, laid aside his cloak, and displayed himself in his shirt, with a sword in his right-hand, which was all over besmeared with recent blood, as if he had just come from the slaughter of a foe. This phænomenon made such an impression upon the astonished chevalier, already discomposed by the resolute behaviour of the count, that he became jaundiced with terror and dismay, and while his teeth chattered in his head, told our hero he had hoped from his known politeness, to have found him ready to acknowledge an injury which might have been the effect of anger or misapprehension, in which case the affair might have been compromised to their mutual satisfaction, without proceeding to those extremities, which, among men of honour, are always accounted the last resource. To this representation, Ferdinand answered, that the affair had been of the chevalier's own seeking, inasmuch as he had intruded himself into his company, and treated him with the most insolent and unprovoked abuse, which plainly flowed from a premeditated design against his honour and reputation; he therefore, far from being disposed to own himself in the wrong, would not even accept of a public acknowledgment from him the aggressor, whom he looked upon as an infamous sharper, and was resolved to chastise accordingly.

Here the conversation was interrupted by the arrival of a person who was brought to the door in a chair, and conducted into another apartment, from which a message was brought to the count, importing, that the stranger desired to speak with him, upon business of the last importance. Fathom having chid the servant for admitting people without his order, desired the Swiss to excuse him for a minute longer, and went into the next room; from whence the following dialogue was overheard by this challenger. "Count," said the stranger, "you are not ignorant of my pretensions to the heart of that young lady, at whose house I met you yesterday; therefore you cannot be surprized when I declare myself displeased with your visits and behaviour to my mistress, and demand that you will instantly promise to drop the correspondence." "Else what follows?" answered Ferdinand, with a cool and temperate voice. "My resentment and immediate defiance;" replied the other, "for the only alternative I propose, is to forego your design upon that lady, or to decide our pretensions by the sword."

Our hero having expressed a regard for this visitant, as the son of a gentleman whom he honoured, was at the pains to represent the unreasonableness of his demand, and the folly of his presumption; and earnestly exhorted him to put the issue of his cause upon a more safe and equitable footing. But this admonition, instead of appeasing the wrath, seemed to inflame the resentment of the opponent, who swore he would not leave him until he should have accomplished the purport of his errand. In vain our adventurer requested half an hour for the dispatch of some urgent business, in which he was engaged with a gentleman in the other parlour: this impetuous rival rejected all the terms he could propose, and even challenged him to decide the controversy upon the spot; an expedient to which the other having assented with reluctance, the door was secured, the swords unsheathed, and an hot engagement ensued, to the inexpressible pleasure of the Swiss, who did not doubt that he himself would be screened from all danger by the event of this rencontre: nevertheless, his hope was disappointed in the defeat of the stranger, who was quickly disarmed, in consequence of a wound through the sword arm; upon which occasion Fathom was heard to say, that in consideration of his youth and family, he had spared his life; but he would not act with the same tenderness towards any other antagonist. He then bound up the limb he had disabled, conducted the vanquished party to his chair, rejoined the chevalier with a serene countenance, and asking pardon for having detained him so long, proposed they should instantly set out in an hackney coach, for the place of appointment.

The stratagem thus conducted, had all the success the inventor could desire. The fear of the Swiss had risen almost to an extasy, before the count quitted the room; but after this sham battle which had been preconcerted betwixt our adventurer and his friend Ratchkali, the chevalier's terrors were unspeakable. He considered Fathom as a devil incarnate, and went into the coach as a malefactor bound for Tyburn.[3] He would have gladly compounded for the loss of a leg or arm, and entertained some transient gleams of hope, that he should escape for half a dozen flesh-wounds, which he would have willingly received, as the price of his presumption; but, these hopes were banish'd by the remembrance of that dreadful declaration which he had heard the count make, after having overcome his last adversary; and he continued under the power of the most insupportable pannic, until the carriage halted at Hyde-park-corner,[4] where he crawled forth in a most piteous and lamentable condition; so that when they reached the spot, he was scarce able to stand.

Here he made an effort to speak, and proposed an accommodation upon a new plan, by which he promised to leave his cause to the arbitrement of those gentlemen who were present at the rupture, and to ask pardon of the count, provided he should be found guilty of a trespass upon good manners: but this proposal would not satisfy the implacable Ferdinand, who perceiving the agony of the Swiss, resolved to make the most of the adventure, and giving him to understand he was not a man to be trifled with, desired him to draw without further preamble. Thus compelled, the unfortunate gamester pulled off his coat, and putting himself in a posture, to use the words of Nym, "winked and held out his cold iron."[5]

Our adventurer, far from making a gentle use of the advantages he possessed, fiercely attacked him, while he was incapable of making resistance, and aiming at a fleshy part, ran him through the arm and outside of the shoulder at the very first pass: the chevalier, already stupified with the horror of expectation, no sooner felt his adversary's point in his body, than he fell to the ground, and concluding he was no longer a man for this world, began to cross himself with great devotion, while Fathom walked home deliberately, and in his way sent a couple of chairmen to the assistance of the wounded knight.

This atchievement, which could not be concealed from the knowledge of the publick, not only furnished the character of Fathom with fresh wreaths of admiration and applause, but likewise effectually secured him from any future attempts of his enemies, to whom the Swiss, for his own sake, had communicated such terrible ideas of his valour, as over-awed the whole community.

CHAPTER XXXIV.

He performs another exploit that conveys a true idea of his gratitude and honour.

It was not long after this celebrated victory, that he was invited to spend part of the summer, at the house of a country gentleman, who lived about one hundred miles from London, possessed of a very opulent fortune, the greatest part of which was expended in acts of old English hospitality. He had met with our hero by accident, at the table of a certain great man,[1] and was so struck with his manner and conversation, as to desire his acquaintance and cultivate his friendship; and he thought himself extremely happy in having prevailed upon him to pass a few weeks in his family.

Fathom, among his other observations, perceived that there was a domestic uneasiness, occasioned by a very beautiful young creature, about the age of fifteen, who resided in the house under the title of the gentleman's niece, though she was in reality, his natural daughter, born before his marriage. This circumstance was not unknown to his lady, by whose express approbation he had bestowed particular attention upon the education of the child, whom we shall distinguish by the name of Celinda:[2] their liberality in this particular, had not been misapplied; for she not only gave marks of uncommon capacity, but as she grew up, became more and more amiable in her person, and was now returned from the boarding-school, possessed of every accomplishment that could be acquired by one of her age and opportunities. These qualifications, which endeared her to every other person, excited the jealousy and displeasure of her supposed aunt, who could not bear to see her own children eclipsed by this illegitimate daughter, whom she therefore discountenanced upon all occasions, and exposed to such mortifications as would in all appearance drive her from her father's house. This persecuting spirit was very disagreeable to the husband, who loved Celinda with a truly paternal affection, and produced abundance of family disquiet; but being a man of a peaceable and yielding disposition, he could not long maintain the resolution he had taken in her favour, and therefore he ceased opposing the malevolence of his wife.

In this unfortunate predicament stood the fair bastard, at the arrival of our adventurer, who being allured by her charms, and apprized of her situation at the same time, took the generous resolution to undermine her innocence, that he might banquet his vicious appetite with the spoils of her beauty. Perhaps such a brutal design might not have entered his imagination, if he had not observed in the disposition of this hapless maiden, certain peculiarities from which he derived the most confident presages of success. Besides a total want of experience, that left her open and unguarded against the attacks of the other sex, she discovered a remarkable spirit of credulity and superstitious fear, which had been cherished[3] by the conversation of her school-fellows: she was particularly fond of musick, in which she had made some progress; but so delicate was the texture of her nerves, that one day, while Fathom entertained the company with a favourite air, she actually swooned with pleasure.

Such sensibility, our projector[4] well knew, must be diffused through all the passions of her heart; he congratulated himself upon the sure ascendancy he had gained over her in this particular; and forthwith began to execute the plan he had erected for her destruction. That he might the more effectually deceive the vigilance of her father's wife, he threw such a dash of affectation in his complaisance towards Celinda, as could not escape the notice of that prying matron, though it was not palpable enough to disoblige the young lady herself, who could not so well distinguish between overstrained courtesy and real good breeding: this behaviour screened him from the suspicion of the family, who considered it as an effort of politeness, to cover his indifference and disgust for the daughter of his friend, who had by this time, given some reason to believe she looked upon him with the eyes of affection; so that the opportunities he enjoyed of conversing with her in private, were less liable to intrusion or inquiry. Indeed, from what I have already observed, touching the sentiments of her step-dame, that lady, far from taking measures for thwarting our hero's design, would have rejoiced at the execution of it, and had she been informed of his intent, might have fallen upon some method to facilitate the enterprize; but, as he solely depended upon his own talents, he never dreamed of soliciting such an auxiliary.

Under cover of instructing and accomplishing her in the exercise of musick, he could not want occasions for promoting his aim; when after having soothed her sense of hearing, even to a degree of ravishment, so as to extort from her an exclamation, importing, that he was surely something supernatural! he never failed to whisper some insidious compliment or tale of love, exquisitely suited to the emotions of her soul. Thus was her heart insensibly subdued; though more than half his work was still undone; for, at all times, she disclosed such purity of sentiment, such inviolable attachment to religion and virtue, and seemed so averse to all sorts of inflammatory discourse, that he durst not presume upon the footing he had gained in her affection, to explain the baseness of his desire; therefore applied to another of her passions, that proved the bane of her virtue: this was her timidity, which at first being constitutional, was afterwards increased by the circumstances of her education, and now aggravated by the artful conversation of Fathom, which he checquered with dismal stories of omens, portents, prophecies and apparitions, delivered upon such unquestionable testimony, and with such marks of conviction, as captivated the belief of the devoted Celinda, and filled her imagination with unceasing terrors.

In vain she strove to dispel those frightful ideas, and avoid such topics of discourse for the future: the more she endeavoured to banish them, the more troublesome they became; and such was her infatuation, that as her terrors increased, her thirst after that sort of knowledge was augmented. Many sleepless nights did she pass amidst those horrors of fancy, starting at every noise, and sweating with dreary apprehension, yet ashamed to own her fears, or sollicit the comfort of a bed-fellow, lest she should incur the ridicule and censure of her father's wife; and what rendered this disposition the more irksome, was the solitary situation of her chamber, that stood at the end of a long gallery scarce within hearing of any other inhabited part of the house.

All these circumstances had been duly weighed by our projector, who having prepared Celinda for his purpose, stole at midnight from his apartment, which was in another story, and approaching her door, there uttered a piteous groan; then softly retired to his bed, in full confidence of seeing next day the effect of this operation: nor did his arrow miss the mark: poor Celinda's countenance gave such indications of melancholy and dismay, that he could not omit asking the cause of her disquiet, and she, at his earnest request, was prevailed upon to communicate the dreadful salutation of the preceding night, which she considered as an omen of death to some person in the family, in all probability to herself, as the groan seemed to issue from one corner of her own apartment. Our adventurer argued against this supposition, as contradictory to the common observation of those supernatural warnings, which are not usually imparted to the person who is doomed to die, but to some faithful friend or trusty servant, particularly interested in the event. He therefore supposed that the groans foreboded the death of my lady, who seemed to be in a drooping state of health, and were by her genius conveyed to the organs of Celinda, who was the chief sufferer by her jealous and barbarous disposition; he likewise expressed an earnest desire to be an ear-witness of such solemn communication, and alledging that it was highly improper for a young lady of her delicate feelings, to expose herself alone to such another dismal visitation, begged he might be allowed to watch all night in her chamber, in order to defend her from the shocking impressions of fear.

Though no person ever stood more in need of a companion or guard, and her heart throbbed with transports of dismay at the prospect of night, she rejected his proposal with due acknowledgment, and resolved to trust solely to the protection of Heaven: not that she thought her innocence or reputation could suffer by her compliance with his request; for hitherto, her heart was a stranger to those young desires which haunt the fancy and warm the breast of youth; so that being ignorant of her danger, she saw not the necessity of avoiding temptation: but she refused to admit a man into her bed-chamber, merely because it was a step altogether opposite to the forms and decorum of life. Nevertheless, far from being discouraged by this repulse, he knew her fears would multiply, and reduce that reluctance, which, in order to weaken, he had recourse to another piece of machinery, that operated powerfully in behalf of his design.

Some years ago, a twelve-stringed instrument was contrived by a very ingenious musician, by whom it was aptly intitled the harp of Æolus,[5] because, being properly applied to a stream of air, it produces a wild, irregular variety of harmonious sounds, that seem to be the effect of inchantment, and wonderfully dispose the mind for the most romantic situations. Fathom, who was really a virtuoso in musick, had brought one of those new-fashioned guittarres[6] into the country, and as the effect of it was still unknown in the family, he that night converted it to the purposes of his amour, by fixing it in the casement of a window belonging to the gallery, exposed to the west-wind, which then blew in a gentle breeze. The strings no sooner felt the impression of the balmy zephyr, than they began to pour forth a stream of melody, more ravishingly delightful than the song of Philomel,[7] the warbling brook, and all the concert of the wood. The soft and tender notes of peace and love were swelled up with the most delicate and insensible transition, into a loud hymn of triumph and exultation, joined by the deep-toned organ, and a full choir of voices, which gradually decayed[8] upon the ear, until it died away, in distant sound, as if a flight of angels had raised the song in their ascent to Heaven. Yet the chords hardly ceased to vibrate after the expiration of this overture, which ushered in a composition in the same pathetic stile; and this again was succeeded by a third, almost without pause or intermission, as if the artist's hand had been indefatigable, and the theme never to be exhausted.

His heart must be quite callous, and his ear lost to all distinction, who could hear such harmony without emotion; how deeply then must it have affected the delicate Celinda, whose sensations, naturally acute, were whetted to a most painful keenness, by her apprehension; who could have no previous idea of such entertainment, and was credulous enough to believe the most improbable tale of superstition! She was overwhelmed with awful terror, and never doubting that the sounds were more than mortal, recommended herself to the care of providence in a succession of pious ejaculations.

Our adventurer having allowed some time for the effect of this contrivance, repaired to her chamber-door, and in a whisper conveyed thro' the key-hole, asked if she was awake, begged pardon for such an unseasonable visit, and desired to know her opinion of the strange musick which he then heard. In spite of her notions of decency, she was glad of his intrusion, and being in no condition to observe punctilios, slipped on a wrapper, opened the door, and with a faultering voice, owned herself frightened almost to distraction. He pretended to console her with reflections, importing, that she was in the hands of a benevolent being, who would not impose upon his creatures any task which they could not bear; he insisted upon her returning to bed, and assured her he would not stir from her chamber till day. Thus comforted she betook herself again to rest, while he sat down in an elbow-chair at some distance from the bed-side, and in a soft voice began the conversation with her, on the subject of those visitations from above, which though undertaken on pretence of dissipating her fear and anxiety, was in reality calculated for the purpose of augmenting both.

"That sweet air," said he, "seems designed for soothing the bodily anguish of some saint in his last moments. Hark! how it rises into a more sprightly and elevated strain, as if it were an inspiriting invitation to the realms of bliss! sure he is now absolved from all the misery of this life; that full and glorious concert of voices and celestial harps, betoken his reception among the heavenly choir, who now waft his soul to paradisian joys! this is altogether great, solemn and amazing! the clock strikes one, the symphony hath ceased!"

This was actually the case; for, he had ordered Maurice to remove the instrument at that hour, lest the sound of it should become too familiar, and excite the curiosity of some undaunted domestic, who might frustrate his scheme, by discovering the apparatus. As for poor Celinda, her fancy was, by his musick and discourse, worked up to the highest pitch of enthusiastic terrors; the whole bed shook with her trepidation, the awful silence that succeeded the supernatural musick, threw an additional damp upon her spirits, and the artful Fathom affecting to snore at the same time, she could no longer contain her horror, but called upon his name with a fearful accent, and having owned her present situation insupportable, intreated him to draw near her bed-side, that he might be within touch, on any emergency.

This was a welcome request to our adventurer, who asked pardon for his drowsiness, and taking his station on the side of her bed, exhorted her to compose herself; then locking her hand fast in his own, was again seized with such an inclination to sleep, that he gradually sunk down by her side, and seemed to enjoy his repose in that attitude. Mean while, his tender-hearted mistress, that he might not suffer in his health, by his humanity and complaisance, covered him with the counterpane as he slept, and suffered him to take his rest, without interruption: till he thought proper to start up suddenly, with an exclamation of, "Heaven watch over us!" and then asked with symptoms of astonishment, if she had heard nothing. Such an abrupt address, upon such an occasion, did not fail to amaze and affright the gentle Celinda, who unable to speak sprung towards her treacherous protector; and he catching her in his arms, bad her fear nothing; for he would, at the expence of his life, defend her from all danger.

Having thus, by tampering with her weakness, conquered the first and chief obstacles to his design, he with great art and perseverance improved the intercourse to such a degree of intimacy as could not but be productive of all the consequences which he had foreseen. The groans and musick were occasionally repeated, so as to alarm the whole family, and inspire a thousand various conjectures: he failed not to continue his nocturnal visits and ghastly discourse, until his attendance became so necessary to this unhappy maiden, that she durst not stay in her own chamber without his company, nor even sleep, except in contact with her betrayer.

Such a commerce between two such persons of a different sex, could not possibly be long carried on, without degenerating from the platonic system of sentimental love. In her paroxysms of dismay, he did not forget to breathe the soft inspirations of his passion, to which she listened with more pleasure, as they diverted the gloomy ideas of her fear; and by this time his extraordinary accomplishments had made a conquest of her heart. What therefore could be a more interesting transition, than that from the most uneasy to the most agreeable sensation of the human breast.

This being the case, the reader will not wonder that a consummate traitor, like Fathom, should triumph over the virtue of an artless innocent young creature, whose passions he had entirely under his command. The gradations towards vice are almost imperceptible, and an experienced seducer can strew them with such inticing and agreeable flowers, as will lead the young sinner on insensibly, even to the most profligate stages of guilt. All therefore that can be done by virtue, unassisted with experience, is to avoid every trial with such a formidable foe, by declining and discouraging the first advances towards a particular correspondence with perfidious man, howsoever agreeable it may seem to be: for, here, is no security but in conscious weakness.

Fathom, though possessed of the spoils of poor Celinda's honour, did not enjoy his success with tranquillity. Reflection and remorse often invaded her in the midst of their guilty pleasures, and embittered all those moments they had dedicated to mutual bliss. For the seeds of virtue are seldom destroyed at once: even amidst the rank productions of vice, they regerminate to a sort of imperfect vegetation, like some scattered hyacinths shooting up among the weeds of a ruined garden, that testify the former culture and amenity of the soil: she sighed at the sad remembrance of that virgin dignity which she had lost; she wept at the prospect of that disgrace, mortification and misery she should undergo, when abandoned by this transient lover, and severely reproached him for the arts he had used to shipwreck her innocence and peace.

Such expostulations are extremely unseasonable when addressed to a man well nigh sated with the effects of his conquest; they act like strong blasts of wind applied to embers almost extinguished, which instead of reviving the flame, scatter and destroy every remaining particle of fire. Our adventurer, in the midst of his peculiarities, had inconstancy in common with the rest of his sex. More than half cloyed with the possession of Celinda, he could not fail to be disgusted with her upbraidings; and had she not been the daughter of a gentleman whose friendship he did not think it his interest to forfeit, he would have dropt this correspondence without reluctance or hesitation: but, as he had measures to keep with a family of such consequence, he constrained his inclinations so far, as to counterfeit those raptures he no longer felt, and found means to appease those intervening tumults of her grief.

Foreseeing, however, that it would not be always in his power to console her on these terms; he resolved, if possible, to divide her affection, which now glowed upon him too intensely; and with that view, whenever she complained of the vapours or dejection, he prescribed, and even insisted upon her swallowing certain cordials⁹ of the most palatable composition, without which he never travelled; and these produced such agreeable reveries and flow of spirits, that she gradually became enamoured of intoxication; while he encouraged the pernicious passion, by expressing the most extravagant applause and admiration at the wild, irregular sallies it produced. Without having first made this diversion, he would have found it impracticable to leave the house in tranquillity; but when this bewitching philtre¹⁰ grew into an habit, her attachment to Ferdinand was insensibly dissolved; she began to bear his neglect with indifference, and sequestring herself from the rest of the family, used to sollicit this new ally, for consolation.

Having thus put the finishing stroke to the daughter's ruin, he took leave of the father with many acknowledgments and expressions of gratitude for his hospitality and friendship, and riding cross the country to Bristol, took up his habitation near the Hot-well,[11] where he staid during the remaining part of the season. As for the miserable Celinda, she became more and more addicted to the vices in which she had been initiated by his superlative perfidy and craft; until she was quite abandoned by decency and caution: her father's heart was torn with anguish, while his wife rejoiced in her fall: at length, her ideas were quite debased by her infirmity; she grew every day more and more sensual and degenerate, and contracted an intimacy with one of the footmen, who was kind enough to take her to wife, in hope of obtaining a good settlement from his master; but being disappointed in his aim, he conducted her to London, where he made shift to insinuate himself into another service, leaving to her, the use, and partly the advantage of her own person, which was still uncommonly attractive.

CHAPTER XXXV.

He repairs to Bristol spring, where he reigns Paramount during the whole season.

We shall therefore, leave her in this comfortable situation, and return to our adventurer, whose appearance at Bristol was considered as a happy omen by the proprietor of the hot-well, and all the people who live by the resort of company to that celebrated spring. Nor were they deceived in their prognostic; Fathom, as usual, formed the nucleus or kernel of the beau monde; and the season soon became so crouded, that many people of fashion were obliged to quit the place for want of lodging. Ferdinand was the soul that animated the whole society. He not only invented parties of pleasure, but also, by his personal talents, rendered them more agreeable: In a word, he regulated their diversions, and the master of the ceremonies never would allow the ball to be begun, until the count was seated.

Having thus made himself the object of admiration and esteem, his advice was an oracle to which they had recourse in all doubtful cases of punctilio or dispute, or even of medicine; for among his other accomplishments, his discourse on that subject was so plausible, and well adapted to the understanding of his hearers, that any person who had not actually studied the medical art, would have believed he was inspired by the spirit of Æsculapius.[1] What contributed to the agrandizement of his character in this branch of knowledge, was a victory he obtained over an old physician,[2] who plied at the well, and had one day unfortunately begun to harrangue in the pump-room, upon the nature of the Bristol-water; in the course of this lecture, he undertook to account for the warmth of the fluid; and his ideas being perplexed with a great deal of reading, which he had not been able to digest, his disquisition was so indistinct, and his expression so obscure and unentertaining, that our hero seized the opportunity of displaying his own erudition, by venturing to contradict some circumstances of the doctor's hypothesis, and substituting a theory of his own, which, as he had invented it for the purpose, was equally amusing and chimerical.

He alledged, that fire was the sole vivifying principle that pervaded all nature; that as the heat of the sun concocted the juice of vegetables and ripened those fruits that grow upon the surface of this globe, there was likewise an immense store of central fire reserved within the bowels of the earth, not only for the generation of gems, fossils, and all the purposes of the mineral world; but likewise, for cherishing and keeping alive those plants which would otherwise perish by the winter's cold. The existence of such a fire, he proved from the nature of all those volcanos, which in almost every corner of the earth, are continually vomiting up either flames or smoke. "These," said he, "are the great vents appointed by nature, for the discharge of that rarified air, and combustible matter, which if confined, would burst the globe asunder; but besides the larger outlets, there are some small chimnies through which part of the heat transpires; a vapour of that sort, I conceive, must pass through the bed or channel of this spring, the waters of which, accordingly, retain a moderate warmth."[3]

This account, which totally overthrew the other's doctrine, was so extremely agreeable to the audience, that the testy doctor lost his temper, and gave them to understand without preamble, that he must be a person wholly ignorant of natural philosophy, who could invent such a ridiculous system, and they involved in worse than an Ægyptian fog,[4] that could not at once discern its weakness and absurdity. This declaration introduced a dispute, which was unanimously determined in favour of our adventurer. On all such occasions, the stream of prejudice runs against the physician, even though his antagonist has nothing to recommend himself to the favour of the spectators: and this decision depends upon divers considerations; in the first place, there

is a continual war carried on against the learned professions, by all those
who, conscious of their own ignorance, seek to level the reputation of their
superiors, with their own. Secondly, in all disputes upon physic, that happen
betwixt a person who really understands the art, and an illiterate pretender,
the arguments of the first will seem obscure and unintelligible to those who
are unacquainted with the previous systems on which they are built; while
the other's theory, derived from common notions, and superficial observation, will be more agreeable, because better adapted to the comprehension of
the hearers. Thirdly, the judgment of the multitude is apt to be biassed by
that surprize, which is the effect of seeing an artist foiled at his own weapons,
by one who engages him only for amusement.

Fathom, besides these advantages, was blessed with a flow of language, an
elegant address, a polite and self-denying stile of argumentation, together
with a temper not to be ruffled; so that the victory could not long waver
between him and the physician, to whom he was infinitely superior in every
acquisition but that of solid learning, of which the judges had no idea. This
contest was not only glorious but profitable to our adventurer, who grew into
such request in his medical capacity, that the poor doctor was utterly deserted by his patients, and Fathom's advice sollicited by every valetudinarian
in the place; nor did he forfeit the character he thus acquired,[5] by any miscar-
riages in his practice; being but little conversant with the Materia medica,[6]
the circle of his prescriptions was very small: his chief study was to avoid all
drugs of rough operation, and uncertain effect; and to administer such only
as should be agreeable to the palate, without doing violence to the constitution. Such a physician could not but be agreeable to people of all dispositions;
and as most of the patients were in some shape hypochondriac,[7] the power of
imagination co-operating with his remedies, often effected a cure.

On the whole, it became the fashion to consult the count in all distempers,
and his reputation would have had its run, though the death of every patient
had given the lie to his pretensions. But empty fame was not the sole fruit of
his success. Though no person would presume to affront this noble graduate
with a fee; they did not fail to manifest their gratitude by some more valuable
present: every day some superb piece of china, curious snuff-box or jewel
was pressed upon him; so that at the end of the season, he could almost have
furnished a toy-shop,[8] with the acknowledgments he had received: not only
his avarice but his pleasure was gratified in the course of his medical administration. He enjoyed free access, egress and regress, with all the females at
the well, and no matron scrupled to put her daughter under his care and
direction. These opportunities could not be lost upon a man of his intriguing

genius; though he conducted his amours with such discretion, that during the whole season, no lady's character suffered on his account: yet he was highly fortunate in his addresses; and we may venture to affirm, that the reproach of barrenness was more than once removed by the vigour of his endeavours.

End of the First VOLUME.

The Adventures of
Ferdinand Count Fathom

VOLUME TWO

THE

ADVENTURES

OF

Ferdinand Count Fathom.

By the Author of RODERICK RANDOM.

——— Materiam rifus, invenit ad omnes
Occurfus hominum. ——— ———
Ridebat curas, nec non et gaudia vulgi ;
Interdum et lachrymas fundebat. ———

VOL. II.

LONDON:

Printed for W. JOHNSTON, at the Golden Ball
in St. Paul's Church-yard.

MDCCLIII.

Title Page of First Edition, Volume 2, 1753.
(Special Collections, Van Pelt Library, University of Pennsylvania.)

CHAPTER XXXVI.

He is smitten with the charms of a female adventurer,
whose allurements subject him to a new
vicissitude of fortune.

Among those who were distinguished by his gallantry, was the young wife of an old citizen of London, who had granted her permission to reside at the Hot-well for the benefit of her health, under the eye and inspection of his own sister, who was a maiden of fifty years. The pupil, whose name was Mrs. Trapwell,[1] though low in stature, was finely shaped, her countenance engaging, though her complexion was brown, her hair in colour rivalled the raven's back, and her eyes emulated the lustre of the diamond. Fathom had been struck with her first appearance; but found it impracticable to elude the vigilance of her duenna, so as to make a declaration of his flame; until she herself guessing the situation of his thoughts, and not displeased with the discovery, thought proper to furnish him with the opportunity he wanted, by counterfeiting an indisposition, for the cure of which, she knew his advice would be implored. This was the beginning of an acquaintance, which was soon improved to his wish; and so well did she manage her attractions, as in some measure to fix the inconstancy of his disposition; for, at the end of the season, his passion was not sated; and they concerted the means of continuing their commerce, even after their return to London.

This intercourse effectually answered the purpose of the husband, who had been decoyed into matrimony, by the cunning of his spouse, whom he had privately kept as a concubine before marriage. Conscious of her own precarious situation, she had resolved to impose upon the infirmities of Trap-well, and feigning herself pregnant, gave him to understand she could no longer conceal her condition from the knowledge of her brother, who was an officer in the army, and of such violent passions, that should he once discover her backsliding, he would undoubtedly wipe way the stains of his family-dishonour with her own blood, as well as that of her keeper. The citizen, to prevent such a catastrophe, took her to wife; but soon after perceiving the trick which had been played upon him, set his invention at work, and at length contrived a scheme which he thought would enable him, not only to retrieve his liberty, but also indemnify himself for the mortification he had undergone.

Far from creating any domestic disturbance, by upbraiding her with her finesse, he seemed perfectly well pleased with his acquisition; and as he knew her void of any principle, and extremely addicted to pleasure, he chose proper occasions to insinuate, that she might gratify her own inclination, and at the same time turn her beauty to good account. She joyfully listened to these remonstrances, and in consequence of their mutual agreement, she re-paired to Bristol-spring, on pretence of an ill state of health accompanied by her sister-in-law, whom they did not think proper to intrust with the real motive of her journey. Fathom's person was agreeable, and his finances sup-posed to be in flourishing order; therefore, she selected him from the herd of gallants, as a proper sacrifice to the powers which she adored; and on her arrival in London, made her husband acquainted with the importance of her conquest.

Trapwell overwhelmed her with caresses and praise for her discreet and dutiful conduct, and faithfully promised that she should pocket in her own privy purse, one half of the spoils that should be gathered from her gallant, whom she therefore undertook to betray, after he had swore in the most solemn manner, that his intention was not to bring the affair to a public trial, which would redound to his own disgrace, but to extort a round sum of money from the count, by way of composition. Confiding in this protesta-tion, she in a few days, gave him intelligence of an assignation she had made with our adventurer, at a certain bagnio[2] near Covent-garden; upon which he secured the assistance of a particular friend and his own journeyman, with whom, and a constable, he repaired to the place of rendezvous, where he waited in an adjoining room according to the directions of his virtuous spouse, until she made the preconcerted signal of hemming three times aloud, when he and his associates rushed into the chamber and surprised our hero in bed with his inamorata.

The lady, on this occasion, acted her part to a miracle; she screamed at their approach; and after an exclamation of "ruined and undone!" fainted away in the arms of her spouse, who had by this time seized her by the shoulders, and begun to upbraid her, with her infidelity and guilt. As for Fathom, his affliction was unutterable, when he found himself discovered in that situation, and made prisoner by the two assistants, who had pinioned him in such a manner, that he could not stir, much less accomplish an escape. All his ingenuity and presence of mind, seemed to forsake him in this emergency. The horrors of an English jury overspread his imagination; for he at once perceived that the toil into which he had fallen, was laid for the purpose; consequently he took it for granted, that there would be no deficiency in point of evidence. Soon as he recollected himself, he begged that no violence might be offered to his person, and intreated the husband to favour him with a conference, in which the affair might be compromised, without prejudice to the reputation of either.

At first, Trapwell breathed nothing but implacable revenge, but by the persuasion of his friends, after he had sent home his wife in a chair, he was prevailed upon to hear the proposals of the delinquent, who having assured him, by way of apology, that he had always believed the lady was a widow, made him an offer of five hundred pounds, as an atonement for the injury he had sustained. This being a sum no ways adequate to the expectation of the citizen, who looked upon the count as possessor of an immense estate, he rejected the terms with disdain, and made instant application to a judge, from whom he obtained a warrant for securing his person till the day of trial. Indeed, in this case, money was but a secondary consideration with Trapwell, whose chief aim was to be legally divorced from a woman he detested.[3] Therefore, there was no remedy for the unhappy count, who in vain offered to double the sum: he found himself reduced to the bitter alternative of procuring immediate bail, or going directly to Newgate.[4]

In this dilemma he sent a messenger to his friend Ratchkali, whose countenance fell when he understood the count's condition; nor would he open his mouth in the stile of consolation, until he had consulted a certain sollicitor of his acquaintance, who assured him the law abounded with such resources, as would infallibly screen the defendant, had the fact been still more palpable than it was. He said there was great presumption to believe the count had fallen a sacrifice to a conspiracy, which by some means or other would be detected; and in that case, the plaintiff might obtain one shilling in lieu of damages. If that dependance should fail, he hinted that, in all probability, the witnesses were not incorruptible; or should they prove to be so, one man's oath was as good as another's, and thank Heaven, there was no dearth of evidence, provided money could be found to answer the necessary occasions.

Ratchkali comforted by these insinuations, and dreading the resentment of our adventurer, who in his despair, might punish him severely for his want of friendship, by some precipitate explanation of the commerce they had carried on; moved, I say, by these considerations, and moreover tempted with the prospect of continuing to reap the advantages resulting from their conjunction, he and another person of credit with whom he largely dealt in jewels, condescended to become sureties for the appearance of Fathom, who was accordingly admitted to bail. Not but that the Tyroleze knew Ferdinand too well, to confide in his parole: he depended chiefly upon his ideas of self-interest, which he thought, would persuade him to risk the uncertain issue of a trial, rather than quit the field before the harvest was half over; and he resolved to make his own retreat without ceremony, should our hero be unwise enough to abandon his bail.

Such an adventure could not long lie concealed from the notice of the public, even if both parties had been at pains to suppress the circumstances: but the plaintiff, far from seeking to cover, affected to complain loudly of his misfortune, that he might interest his neighbours in his behalf, and raise a spirit of rancour and animosity, to influence the jury against this insolent foreigner, who had come over into England to debauch our wives and deflower our daughters; while he employed a formidable band of lawyers to support the indictment, which he laid for ten thousand pounds damages.

Mean while, Fathom and his associate did not fail to take all proper measures for his defence; they retained a powerful bar of council, and the sollicitor was supplied with one hundred pounds after another, to answer the expence of secret service; still assuring his clients that every thing was in an excellent train, and that his adversary would gain nothing but shame and confusion of face. Nevertheless, there was a necessity for postponing the trial, on account of a material evidence, who, though he wavered, was not yet quite brought over; and the attorney found means to put off the decision from term to term, until there was no quibble left for further delay.[5] While this suit was depending, our hero continued to move in his usual sphere; nor did the report of his situation at all operate to his disadvantage, in the polite world: on the contrary, it added a fresh plume to his character, in the eyes of all those who were not before acquainted with the triumphs of his gallantry. Notwithstanding this countenance of his friends, he himself considered the affair in a very serious light; and perceiving that at any rate he must be a considerable loser, he resolved to double his assiduity in trade, that he might be the more able to afford the extraordinary expence to which he was subjected.

CHAPTER XXXVII.

Fresh cause for exerting his equanimity and fortitude.

The reader may have observed, that Fathom with all his circumspection, had a weak side, which exposed him to sundry mischances: this was his covetousness, which on some occasions became too hard for his discretion: at this period of time, it was by the circumstances of his situation, inflamed to a degree of rapacity. He was now prevailed upon to take a hand at whist,[1] or piquet,[2] and even to wield the hazard-box;[3] though he had hitherto declared himself an irreconcileable enemy to all sorts of play; and so uncommon was his success and dexterity at these exercises, as to surprize his acquaintance, and arrouse the suspicion of some people, who repined at his prosperity.

But in nothing was his conduct more inexcusable, than in giving way to the dangerous temerity of Ratchkali, which he had been always at pains to restrain, and permitting him to practise the same fraud upon an English nobleman, which had been executed upon himself at Franckfort. In other words, the Tyroleze by the canal[4] of Ferdinand's finger and recommendation, sold a pebble for a real brilliant, and in a few days the cheat was discovered, to the infinite confusion of our adventurer, who nevertheless assumed the guise of innocence, with so much art, and expressed such indignation against the villain, who had imposed upon his judgment and unsuspecting generosity, that his lordship acquitted him of any share in the deceit, and contented himself with the restitution, which he insisted upon making out of his own pocket, until he should be able to apprehend the rogue, who had thought proper to abscond for his own safety. In spite of all this exculpation, his character did not fail to retain a sort of stigma, which indeed the plainest proofs of innocence are hardly able to efface; and his connexion with such a palpable knave as the Tyroleze appeared to be, had an effect to his prejudice, in the minds of all those who were privy to the occurrence.

When a man's reputation is once brought in question, every trifle is by the malevolence of mankind, magnified into a strong presumption against the culprit: a few whispers communicated by the envious mouth of slander, which he can have no opportunity to answer and refute, shall, in the opinion of the world, convict him of the most horrid crimes; and for one hypocrite who is decked with the honours of virtue, there are twenty good men who suffer the ignominy of vice; so well disposed are individuals to trample upon the fame of their fellow-creatures.[5] If the most unblemished merit is not protected from this injustice, it will not be wondered at, that no quarter was given to the character of an adventurer like Fathom, who among other unlucky occurrences, had the misfortune to be recognized about this time, by his two Parisian friends Sir Stentor Stiles and Sir Giles Squirrel.

These worthy knights-errant had returned to their own country, after having made a very prosperous campaign in France, at the end of which, however, they very narrowly escaped the gallies; and seeing the Polish count seated at the head of taste and politeness, they immediately circulated the story of his defeat at Paris, with many ludicrous circumstances of their own invention, and did not scruple to affirm that he was a rank impostor. When the laugh is raised upon a great man, he never fails to dwindle into contempt. Ferdinand began to perceive a change in the countenance of his friends. His company was no longer sollicited with that eagerness which they had formerly expressed in his behalf: even his entertainments were neglected; when he appeared at any private or public assembly, the ladies, instead of glowing with pleasure, as formerly, now tittered or regarded him with looks of disdain; and a certain pert, little, forward coquette, with a view to put him out of countenance by raising the laugh at his expence, asked him one night, at a drum,[6] when he had heard from his relations in Poland? She succeeded in her design upon the mirth of the audience, but was disappointed in the other part of her aim; for, our hero replied without the least mark of discomposure, "They are all in good health at your service, madam; I wish I knew in what part of the world your relations reside, that I might return the compliment." By this answer, which was the more severe, as the young lady was of very doubtful extraction, he retorted the laugh upon the aggressor, though he likewise failed in his attempt upon her temper: for, she was perhaps the only person present, who equall'd himself in stability of countenance.

Notwithstanding this appearance of unconcern, he was deeply touched with these marks of alienation, in the behaviour of his friends, and foreseeing in his own disgrace, the total shipwreck of his fortune, he entered into a melancholy deliberation with himself, about the means of retrieving his importance in the beau-monde, or of turning his address into some other channel, where he could stand upon a less slippery foundation. In this exercise of his thoughts, no scheme occured more feasible, than that of securing the booty he had made, and retiring with his associate, who was also blown,[7] into some other country, where, their names and characters being unknown, they might pursue their old plan of commerce without molestation. He imparted this suggestion to the Tyroleze, who approved the proposal of decamping, though he combated with all his might our hero's inclination to withdraw himself before the trial, by repeating the assurances of the sollicitor, who told him he might depend upon being reimbursed by the sentence of the court, for great part of the sums he had expended in the course of the prosecution.

Fathom suffered himself to be persuaded by these arguments, supported with the desire of making an honourable retreat, and waiting patiently for the day of trouble, discharged his sureties, by a personal appearance in court. Yet this was not the only score he discharged that morning; the sollicitor presented his own bill before they set out for Westminster-hall,[8] and gave the count to understand that it was the custom, from time immemorial, for the client to clear with his attorney before trial. Ferdinand had nothing to object against this established rule, though he looked upon it as a bad omen, in spite of all the sollicitor's confidence and protestations; and he was not a little confounded, when looking into the contents, he found himself charged with 350 attendances. He knew it was not his interest to disoblige his lawyer at such a juncture; nevertheless, he could not help expostulating with him on this article, which seemed to be so falsly stated with regard to the number; when his questions drew on an explanation, by which he found he had incurred the penalty of three shillings and four-pence for every time he chanced to meet the conscientious attorney, either in the park, the coffee-house or the street, provided they had exchanged the common salutation: and he had great reason to believe the sollicitor had often thrown himself in his way, with a view to swell this item of his account.

With this extortion our adventurer was fain to comply, because he lay at the mercy of the caitiff;[9] accordingly, he with a good grace paid the demand, which including his former disbursements, amounted to three hundred and sixty-five pounds eleven shillings three-pence three farthings, and then presenting himself before the judge, quietly submitted to the laws of the realm. His council behaved like men of consummate abilities in their profession; they exerted themselves with equal industry, eloquence and erudition, in their endeavours to perplex the truth, browbeat the evidence, puzzle the judge, and mislead the jury:[10] but the defendant found himself woefully disappointed in the deposition of Trapwell's journeyman, whom the sollicitor pretended to have converted to his interest: this witness, as the attorney afterwards declared, played booty,[11] and the facts came out so clear, that Ferdinand Count Fathom was convicted of criminal conversation with the plaintiff's wife, and cast in fifteen hundred pounds,[12] under the denomination of damages.

He was not so much surprized as afflicted at this decision, because he saw it gradually approaching from the examination of the first evidence: his thoughts were now employed in casting about for some method of deliverance, from the snare in which he found himself intangled. To escape he foresaw it would be impracticable, as Trapwell would undoubtedly be prepared for arresting him before he could quit Westminster-hall; he was too well acquainted with Ratchkali's principles, to expect any assistance from that quarter, in money-matters; and he was utterly averse to the payment of the sum awarded against him, which would have exhausted his whole fortune. He therefore resolved to try the friendship of some persons of fashion, with whom he had maintained an intimacy of correspondence: should they fail him in the day of his necessity, he proposed to have recourse to his former sureties, one of whom he meant to bilk, while the other might accompany him in his retreat: or, should both these expedients miscarry, he determined, rather than part with his effects, to undergo the most disagreeable confinement, in hope of obtaining the jailor's connivance at his escape.

These resolutions being taken, he met his fate with great fortitude and equanimity, and calmly suffered himself to be conveyed to the house of a sheriff's officer, who, as he made his exit from the hall, according to his own expectation, executed a writ against him, at the suit of Trapwell, for a debt of two thousand pounds. To this place he was followed by his sollicitor, who was allured by the prospect of another job, and who with great demonstrations of satisfaction, congratulated him upon the happy issue of the trial; arrogating to himself, the merit of having saved him eight thousand pounds, in the article of damages, by the previous steps he had taken, and the noble defence that he and his friends the council had made for their client: he even hinted an expectation of receiving a gratuity for his extraordinary care and discretion.

Fathom, galled as he was with his misfortune, and enraged at the effrontery of this pettifogger,[13] maintained a serenity of countenance, and sent the attorney with a message to the plaintiff, importing, that as he was a foreigner, and could not be supposed to have so much cash about him, as to spare fifteen hundred pounds from the funds of his ordinary expence, he would grant him a bond payable in two months, during which period, he should be able to procure a proper remittance from his own estate. While the sollicitor was employed in this negociation, he dispatched his valet de chambre to one nobleman, and Maurice to another, with billets, signifying the nature of the verdict which his adversary had obtained, and desiring that each would lend him a thousand pounds upon his parole,[14] until he could negociate bills upon the continent.

His three messengers returned almost at the same instant of time, and these were the answers they brought back.

Trapwell absolutely rejected his personal security; and threatned him with all the horrors of a goal,[15] unless he would immediately discharge the debt, or procure sufficient bondsmen; and one of his quality-friends, favoured him with this reply to his request.

"My dear Count!

I am mortally chagrin'd at the triumph you have furnished to that rascally citizen. By the lard! the judge must have been in the terrors of cuckoldom, to influence the decision; and the jury, a meer herd of horned beasts, to bring in such a barbarous verdict. Egad! at this rate, no gentleman will be able to lie with another man's wife, but at the risk of a cursed prosecution. But, to wave this disagreeable circumstance, which you must strive to forget; I declare my mortification is still the greater, because I cannot at present supply you with the trifle your present exigency requires; for, to tell you a secret, my own finances are in damnable confusion. But a man of count Fathom's figure and address can never be puzzled[16] for the want of such a paultry sum. Adieu, my dear Count! we shall, I suppose, have the pleasure of seeing you to-morrow at White's:[17] Mean while, I have the honour to be with the most perfect attachment,

Yours,

GRIZZLEGRIN."

The other noble peer to whom he addressed himself on this occasion, cherished the same sentiments of virtue, friendship and generosity; but his expression was so different, that we shall, for the edification of the reader, transcribe his letter in his own words.

"Sir,

I was never more astonished than at the receipt of your very extraordinary billet, wherein you sollicit the loan of a thousand pounds, which you desire may be sent with the bearer on the faith of your parole. Sir, I have no money to send you or lend you; and cannot help repeating my expressions of surprize at your confidence in making such a strange and unwarranted demand. 'Tis true, I may have made professions of friendship, while I looked upon you as a person of honour and good morals; but now that you are convicted of such a flagrant violation of the laws of that kingdom where you have been treated with such hospitality and respect, I think myself fully absolved from any such conditional promise, which indeed is never interpreted into any other than a bare compliment. I am sorry you have involved your character and fortune in such a disagreeable affair, and am,

Sir, Yours, &c.

TROMPINGTON."18

Ferdinand was not such a novice in the world as to be disappointed at these repulses; especially as he had laid very little stress upon the application, which was made by way of an experiment upon the gratitude or caprice of those two noblemen, whom he had actually more than once obliged with the same sort of assistance which he now sollicited, though not to such a considerable amount.

Having nothing further to expect from the fashionable world, he sent the Tyroleze to the person who had been bail for his appearance, with full instructions to explain his present occasion in the most favourable light, and desire he would reinforce the credit of the count with his security; but, that gentleman, though he placed the most perfect confidence on the honour of our hero, and would have willingly entered into bonds again for his personal appearance, was not quite so well satisfied of his circumstances, as to become liable for the payment of two thousand pounds, an expence, which in his opinion, the finances of no foreign count were able to defray: he therefore, lent a deaf ear to the most pressing remonstrances of the ambassador, who had recourse to several other merchants, with the same bad success; so that the prisoner despairing of bail, endeavoured to persuade Ratchkali, that it would be his interest to contribute a thousand pounds towards his discharge, that he might be enabled to quit England with a good grace, and execute his part of the plan they had projected.

So powerful was his eloquence on the occasion, and such strength of argument did he use, that even the Tyroleze seemed convinced, though reluctantly, and agreed to advance the necessary sum upon the bond and judgment of our adventurer, who being disabled from transacting his own affairs in person, was obliged to intrust Ratchkali with his keys, papers and power of attorney, under the check and inspection of his faithful Maurice and the sollicitor, whose fidelity he bespoke with the promise of an ample recompence.

CHAPTER XXXVIII.

The biter is bit.

Yet, he had no sooner committed his effects to the care of this triumvirate, than his fancy was visited with direful warnings, which produced cold sweats and palpitations, and threw him into such agonies of apprehension as he had never known before. He remembered the former desertion of the Tyroleze, the recent villainy of the sollicitor, and recollected the remarks he had made upon the disposition and character of his valet, which evinced him a fit companion for the other two.

Alarmed at these reflections, he intreated the bailiff to indulge him with a visit to his own lodgings, and even offered one hundred guineas as a gratification for his compliance. But, the officer, who had formerly lost a considerable sum by the escape of a prisoner, would not run any risque in an affair of such consequence, and our hero was obliged to submit to the tortures of his own presaging fears. After he had waited five hours in the most racking impatience, he saw the attorney enter with all the marks of hurry, fatigue and consternation, and heard him exclaim, "Good God, have you seen the gentleman?"

Fathom found his fears realized in this interrogation, to which he answered in a tone of horror and dismay, "What gentleman? I suppose I am robbed: speak and keep me no longer in suspense." "Robbed!" cried the attorney, "the Lord forbid! I hope you can depend upon the person you impowered to receive your jewels and cash. I must own his proceedings are a little extraordinary: for after he had rummaged your scrutore, from which in presence of me and your servant, he took one hundred and fifty guineas, a parcel of diamond rings and buckles according to this here inventory, which I wrote with my own hand, and East-India bonds[1] to the tune of five hundred more, we adjourned to Garraway's,[2] where he left me alone, under pretence of going to a broker of his acquaintance who lived in the neighbourhood, while the valet, as I imagined, waited for us in the alley. Well, Sir, he stayed so long, that I began to be uneasy, and at length resolved to send the servant in quest of him, but when I went out for that purpose, deuce³ a servant was to be found. Though I in person inquired for him, at every alehouse within half a mile of the place. I then dispatched no less than five ticket porters⁴ upon the scent after them, and I myself by a direction from the bar-keeper, went to signor Ratchkali's lodgings, where, as they told me, he had not been seen since nine o'clock in the morning. Upon this intimation, I came directly hither, to give you timely notice, that you may without delay, take measures for your own security. The best thing you can do, is to take out writs for apprehending him, in the counties of Middlesex, Surry, Kent and Essex, and I shall put them in the hands of trusty and diligent officers, who will soon ferret him out of his lurking-place, provided he sculks within ten miles of the bills of mortality:⁵ to be sure the job will be expensive; and all these runners must be paid before-hand. But, what then? the defendant is worth powder,⁶ and if we can once secure him, I'll warrant the prosecution will quit cost."⁷

Fathom was almost choaked with concern and resentment, at the news of this mischance, so that he could not utter one word until this narrative was finished. Nor was his suspicion confined to the Tyroleze and his own lacquey; he considered the sollicitor as their accomplice and director, and was so much provoked at the latter part of his harangue, that his discretion seemed to vanish, and collaring the attorney, "Villain!" said he, "you yourself have been a principal actor in this robbery;" Then turning to the bystanders, "and I desire in the king's name, that he may be secured, until I can make oath before a magistrate, in support of the charge. If you refuse your assistance in detaining him, I will make immediate application to one of the secretaries of state who is my particular friend, and he will see justice done to all parties."

At mention of this formidable name, the bailiff and his whole family were in commotion, to obstruct the retreat of the lawyer, who stood aghast, and trembled under the grasp of our adventurer: but, soon as he found himself delivered from this embrace, by the interposition of the spectators, and collected his spirits, which had been suddenly dissipated by Fathom's unexpected assault, he began to display one art of his occupation, which he always reserved for extraordinary occasions: this was the talent of abuse, which he poured forth with such fluency of opprobrious language, that our hero smarting as he was, and almost desperate with his loss, deviated from that temperance of behaviour which he had hitherto preserved, and snatching up the poker, with one stroke opened a deep trench upon the attorney's skull, that extended from the hind head, almost to the upper part of the nose, upon each side of which, it discharged a sanguine stream. Notwithstanding the pain of this application, the sollicitor was transported with joy at the sense of the smart, and inwardly congratulated himself upon the appearance of his own blood, which he no sooner perceived, than he exclaimed, "I'm a dead man," and fell upon the floor at full length.

Immediate recourse was had to a surgeon in the neighbourhood, who having examined the wound, declared there was a dangerous depression of the first table of the skull,[8] and that if he could save the patient's life, without the application of the trepan,[9] it would be one of the greatest cures that ever were performed. By this time, Fathom's first transport being overblown, he summoned up his whole resolution, and reflected upon his own ruin, with that fortitude which had never failed him in the emergencies of his fate: little disturbed at the prognostic of the surgeon, which he considered in the right point of view; "Sir," said he, "I am not so unacquainted with the resistance of an attorney's skull, as to believe the chastisement I have bestowed on him, will at all endanger his life, which is in much greater jeopardy from the hands of the common executioner: for, notwithstanding this accident, I am determined to prosecute the rascal for robbery, with the utmost severity of the law; and that I may have a sufficient fund left for that prosecution, I shall not at present throw away one farthing in unnecessary expence, but insist upon being conveyed to prison without farther delay."

This declaration was equally unwelcome to the bailiff, surgeon and sollicitor, who upon the supposition that the count was a person of fortune, and would rather part with an immense sum, than incur the ignominy of a goal, or involve himself in another disgraceful law-suit, had resolved to fleece him to the utmost of their power. But, now the attorney finding him determined to set his fate at defiance, and to retort upon him a prosecution which he had no mind to undergo, began to repent heartily of the provocation he had given, and to think seriously on some method to overcome the obstinacy of the incensed foreigner. With this view, while the bailiff conducted him to bed, in another apartment, he desired the catchpole[10] to act the part of mediator between him and the count, and furnished him with proper instructions for that purpose. Accordingly, the landlord on his return, told Fathom that he was sure the sollicitor was not a man for this world; for that he had left him deprived of his senses, and praying to God with great devotion, for mercy to his murderer: he then exhorted him with many protestations of friendship, to compromise the unhappy affair by exchanging releases with the attorney before his delirium should be known, otherwise he would bring himself into a most dangerous premunire,[11] whether the plaintiff should die of his wound, or live to prosecute him for the assault: "and with regard to your charge of robbery against him," said he, "as it is no more than a bare suspicion, unsupported by the least shadow of evidence, the bill would be thrown out, and then he might sue you for damages. I therefore, out of pure friendship and good nature advise you to compromise the affair, and if you think proper, will endeavour to bring about a mutual release."

Our hero, whose passion was by this time pretty well cooled, saw reason for assenting to the proposal; upon which the deed was immediately executed, the mediator's bill was discharged; and Ferdinand conveyed in an hackney coach to prison, after he had impowered his own landlord to discharge his servants, and convert his effects into ready money. Thus, he saw himself, in the course of a few hours, deprived of his reputation, rank, liberty and friends; and his fortune reduced from two thousand pounds, to something less than two hundred, fifty of which he had carried to goal in his pocket.

CHAPTER XXXIX.

Our adventurer is made acquainted with a new scene of life.

Just as he entered these mansions of misery, his ears were invaded with an hoarse and dreadful voice, exclaiming, "You, Bess Beetle,[1] score a couple of fresh eggs, a pennyworth of butter, and half a pint of mountain[2] to the king; and stop credit till the bill is paid; he is now debtor for fifteen shillings and sixpence, and damn me if I trust him one farthing more, if he was the best king in Christendom: and d'ye hear, send ragged-head with five pounds of potatoes for major Macleaver's supper, and let him have what drink he wants; the fat widow gentlewoman from Pimlico[3] has promised to quit his score. Sir Mungo Barebones may have some hasty pudding[4] and small beer,[5] though I don't expect to see his coin, no more than to receive the eighteen pence I laid out for a pair of breeches to his backside. What then? he's a quiet sort of a body, and a great scholar, and it was a scandal to the place, to see him going about in that naked condition: as for the mad Frenchman with the beard, if you give him so much as a cheese-paring, you b——ch, I'll send you back to the hole, among your old companions; an impudent dog! I'll teach him to draw his sword upon the governor of an English county goal. What! I suppose he thought he had to do with a French hang-tang-dang,[6] rabbit him! he shall eat his white feather before I give him credit for a morsel of bread."[7]

Although our adventurer was very little disposed, at this juncture, to make observations foreign to his own affairs, he could not help taking notice of these extraordinary injunctions; especially those concerning the person who was intitled king, whom, however, he supposed to be some prisoner elected as the magistrate by the joint suffrage of his fellows. Having taken possession of his chamber, which he rented at five shillings a week, and being ill at ease in his own thoughts, he forthwith secured his door, undressed and went to bed, in which, though it was none of the most elegant or inviting couches, he enjoyed profound repose after the accumulated fatigues and mortifications of the day. Next morning after breakfast, the keeper entered his apartment, and gave him to understand, that the gentlemen under his care, having heard of the count's arrival, had deputed one of their number to wait upon him with the compliments of condolance, suitable to the occasion, and invite him to become a member of their society. Our hero could not politely dispense with this instance of civility, and their ambassador being instantly introduced by the name of captain Minikin, saluted him with great solemnity.[8]

This was a person equally remarkable for his extraordinary figure and address; his age seemed to border upon forty, his stature amounted to five feet, his visage was long, meagre and weather-beaten, and his aspect, though not quite rueful, exhibited a certain formality, which was the result of care and conscious importance. He was very little encumbred with flesh and blood; yet, what body he had, was well proportioned, his limbs were elegantly turned, and by his carriage he was well intitled to that compliment which we pay to any person, when we say he has very much the air of a gentleman. There was also an evident singularity in his dress, which tho' intended as an improvement, appeared to be an extravagant exaggeration of the mode, and at once evinced him an original to the discerning eyes of our adventurer, who received him with his usual complaisance, and made a very eloquent acknowledgment of the honour and satisfaction he received from the visit of the representative, and the hospitality of his constituents. The captain's peculiarities were not confined to his external appearance; for his voice resembled the sound of a bassoon, or the aggregate hum of a whole bee-hive, and his discourse was almost nothing else than a series of quotations from the English poets, interlarded with French phrases, which he retained for their significance, on the recommendation of his friends, being himself unacquainted with that or any other outlandish tongue.

Fathom finding this gentleman of a very communicative disposition, thought he could not have a fairer opportunity of learning the history of his fellow-prisoners; and turning the conversation on that subject, was not disappointed in his expectation. "I don't doubt, Sir," said he, with the utmost solemnity of declamation, "but you look with horror upon every object that surrounds you in this uncomfortable place; but nevertheless here are some, who, as my friend Shakespear has it, *have seen better days, and have with holy bell been knolled to church; and sat at good men's feasts, and wiped their eyes of drops that sacred pity hath engendered.*[9] You must know, Sir, that exclusive of the *Canaille*,[10] or the *profanum Vulgus*,[11] as they are stiled by Horace, there are several small communities in the goal, consisting of people who are attracted by the manners and dispositions of each other: for this place, Sir, is quite a *microcosm*, and as the great world, so is this a *Stage, and all the men and women meerly players.*[12] For my own part, Sir, I have always made it a maxim to associate with the best company I can find: not that I pretend to boast of my family or extraction; because you know, as the poet says, *Vix ea nostra voco.*[13] My father, 'tis true, was a man that piqued himself upon his pedigree, as well as upon his politesse and personal merit; for he had been a very old officer in the army, and I myself may say, I was born with a spontoon[14] in my hand. Sir, I have had the honour to serve his majesty these twenty years, and have been bandied about in the course of duty, through all the British plantations, and you see the recompence of all my service. But this is a disagreeable subject, and therefore I shall wave it: however, as Butler observes,

> My only comfort is that now,
> My dubbolt fortune is so low,
> That either it must quickly end,
> Or turn about again and mend.[15]

And now to return from this digression, you will perhaps be surprized to hear that the head or chairman of our club is really a sovereign prince.[16] No less I'll assure you than the celebrated Theodore king of C–rs–ca, who lies in prison for a debt of a few hundred pounds.[17] *Heu! quantum mutatus ab illo.*[18] It is not my business to censure the conduct of my superiors: but I always speak my mind in a cavalier manner, and, as according to the Spectator, talking to a friend is no more than thinking aloud,[19] *entre nous*, his Corsican majesty has been scurvily treated by a certain administration:[20] be that as it will, he is a personage of a very portly appearance, and is quite master of the *bienseance*.[21] Besides, they will find it their interest to have recourse again to his alliance; and in that case, some of us may expect to profit by his restoration: but few words are best.[22]

He that maintains the second rank in our assembly, is one major Macleaver,[23] an Irish gentleman, who has served abroad: a soldier of fortune, Sir, a man of unquestionable honour and courage; but a little over-bearing, in consequence of his knowledge and experience. He is a person of a good address to be sure, and quite free of the *mauvaise honte*;[24] and he may have seen a good deal of service; but what then? other people may be as good as he, though they have not had such opportunities: if he speaks five or six languages, he does not pretend to any taste in the liberal arts, which are the criterion of an accomplished gentleman. The next is Sir Mungo Barebones, the representative of a very ancient family in the North; his affairs are very much *derangée*,[25] but he is a gentleman of great probity and learning, and at present engag'd in a very grand scheme,[26] which, if he can bring it to bear, will render him famous to all posterity: no less than the conversion of the Jews and the Gentiles. The project, I own, looks chimerical to one who has not conversed with the author; but, in my opinion, he has clearly demonstrated from an anagrammatical analysis of a certain Hebrew word, that his present majesty, whom God preserve, is the person pointed at in scripture, as the temporal Messiah of the Jews; and if he could once raise by subscription, such a trifling sum as twelve hundred thousand pounds, I make no doubt but he would accomplish his aim, vast and romantic as it seems to be.

Besides these, we have another messmate, who is a French chevalier, an odd sort of a man, a kind of Lazarillo de Tormes,[27] a Caricatura;[28] he wears a long beard, pretends to be a great poet, and makes a damned *Fracas* with his verses.[29] The king has been obliged to exert his authority over him more than once, by ordering him into close confinement, for which he was so rash as to send his majesty a challenge; but, he afterwards made his submission and was again taken into favour: the truth is, I believe his brain is a little disordered, and he being a stranger we overlook his extravagancies.

Sir, we shall think ourselves happy in your accession to our society: you will be under no sort of restraint: for though we dine at one table, every individual calls and pays for his own mess. Our conversation, such as it is, will not, I hope be disagreeable; and though we have not opportunities of breathing the pure Arcadian air, and cannot 'under the shade of melancholy boughs, lose and neglect the creeping hours of time;'[30] we may enjoy ourselves over a glass of punch or a dish of tea: nor are we destitute of friends who visit us in these shades of distress. The major has a numerous acquaintance of both sexes, among others, a first cousin of good fortune, who with her daughters often chear our solitude; she is a very sensible lady-like gentlewoman, and the young ladies have a certain *degagée*[31] air, that plainly shews they have seen the best company: besides, I will venture to recommend Mrs. Minikin, as a woman of tolerable breeding and capacity, who I hope, will not be found altogether deficient in the accomplishments of the sex. So that we find means to make little parties, in which the time glides away insensibly. Then I have a small collection of books, which are at your service. You may amuse yourself with Shakespear, or Milton, or Don Quixote, or any of our modern authors that are worth reading, such as the adventures of Loveill, Lady Frail, George Edwards, Joe Thompson, Bampfylde More Carew, Young Scarron, and Miss Betsy Thoughtless:[32] and if you have a taste for drawing, I can entertain you with a parcel of prints by the best masters."

A man of our hero's politeness, could not help expressing himself in the warmest terms of gratitude for this courteous declaration. He thanked the captain in particular for his obliging offers, and begged he would be so good as to present his respects to the society of which he longed to be a member. It was determined therefore, that Minikin should return in an hour, when the count would be dressed, in order to conduct him into the presence of his majesty; and he had already taken his leave for the present, when all of a sudden he came back, and taking hold of a waistcoat that lay upon a chair, "Sir," said he, "give me leave to look at that fringe; I think it is the most elegant knitting I ever saw: but pray Sir, are not these quite out of fashion: I thought plain silk, such as this that I wear, had been the mode; with the pockets very low." Before Fathom had time to make any sort of reply, he took notice of his hat and pumps; the first of which he said was too narrow in the brims, and the last an inch too low in the heels; indeed they formed a remarkable contrast with his own:[33] for, exclusive of the fashion of the cock,[34] which resembled the form of a Roman galley, the brim of his hat, if properly spread, would have projected a shade sufficient to shelter a whole file of musqueteers from the heat of a summer's sun; and the heels of his shoes were so high as to raise his feet three inches at least, from the surface of the earth.

Having made these observations for the credit of his taste, he retired, and returning at the time appointed, accompanied Ferdinand to the apartment of the king, at the door of which, their ears were invaded with a strange sound, being that of an human voice imitating the noise of a drum. The captain hearing this alarm, made a full stop, and giving the count to understand that his majesty was busy, begged he would not take it amiss, if the introduction should be delayed for a few moments. Fathom curious to know the meaning of what he had heard, applied to his guide for information, and learned that the king and the major, whom he had nominated to the post of his general in chief, were employed in landing troops upon the Genoese territory: that is, that they were settling before-hand, the manner of their disembarkation.[35]

He then, by the direction of his conductor, reconnoitred them through the key-hole, and perceived the sovereign and his minister sitting on opposite sides of a deal board table,[36] covered with a large chart or map, upon which he saw a great number of muscle and oister-shells, ranged in a certain order, and at a little distance, several regular squares and columns made of cards cut in small pieces. The prince himself, whose eyes were reinforced by spectacles, surveyed this armament with great attention, while the general put the whole in action, and conducted their motions by beat of drum. The muscle-shells, according to Minikin's explanation, represented the transports, the oyster-shells were considered as the men of war that covered the troops in landing, and the pieces of card exhibited the different bodies into which the army was formed upon its disembarkation.

As an affair of such consequence could not be transacted without opposition, they had provided divers ambuscades,[37] consisting of the enemy, whom they represented by grey pease; and accordingly, general Macleaver perceiving the said grey pease marching along shore, to attack his forces before they could be drawn up in battalia,[38] thus addressed himself to the oyster-shells in an audible voice: "You men of war, don't you see the front of the enemy advancing, and the rest of the detachment following out of sight? Arrah![39] the Devil burn you, why don't you come ashore and open your batteries?" So saying, he pushed the shells towards the breach, performed the cannonading with his voice, the grey pease were soon put in confusion, the general was beat, the cards marched forwards in order of battle, and the enemy having retreated with great precipitation, they took possession of their ground without farther difficulty.

CHAPTER XL.

He contemplates majesty and its satellites in eclipse.

This expedition being happily finished, general Macleaver put the whole army, navy, transports and scene of action into a canvas bag, the prince unsaddled his nose,[1] and captain Minikin being admitted, our hero was introduced in form. Very gracious was the reception he met with from his majesty, who with a most princely demeanour, welcomed him to court, and even seated him on his right hand, in token of particular regard. True it is, this presence-chamber was not so superb, nor the appearance of the king so magnificent as to render such an honour intoxicating to any person of our hero's coolness and discretion: in lieu of tapestry the apartment was hung with halfpenny ballads,[2] a truckle-bed[3] without curtains, supplied the place of a canopy, and instead of a crown, his majesty wore a woolen night-cap. Yet, in spite of these disadvantages, there was an air of dignity in his deportment, and a nice physiognomist would have perceived something majestic in the features of his countenance.

He was certainly a personage of a very prepossessing mien, his manners were engaging; his conversation agreeable, and any man whose heart was subject to the meltings of humanity, would have deplored his distress, and looked upon him as a most pathetic instance of that miserable reverse, to which all human grandeur is exposed. His fall was even greater than that of Belisarius,[4] who after having obtained many glorious victories over the enemies of his country, is said to have been reduced to such extremity of indigence, that in his old age, when he was deprived of his eye-sight, he sat upon the high-way like a common mendicant, imploring the charity of passengers, in the piteous exclamation of *Date obolum Belisario*;[5] that is, "Spare a farthing to your poor old soldier Belisarius." I say, this general's disgrace was not so remarkable as that of Theodore, because he was the servant of Justinian,[6] consequently his fortune depended upon the nod of that emperor; whereas the other actually possessed the throne of sovereignty by the best of all titles, namely, the unanimous election of the people over whom he reigned; and attracted the eyes of all Europe, by the efforts he made in breaking the bands of oppression, and vindicating that liberty which is the birthright of man.

The English of former days, alike renowned for generosity and valour, treated those hostile princes whose fate it was to wear their chains, with such delicacy of benevolence, as even dispelled the horrors of captivity; but, their posterity of this refined age, feel no compunction at seeing an unfortunate monarch, their former friend, ally and partizan, languish amidst the miseries of a loathsome gaol, for a paultry debt contracted in their own service.[7] But moralizing apart, our hero had not long conversed with this extraordinary debtor, who in his present condition, assumed no other title than that of Baron, than he perceived in him a spirit of Quixotism, which all his experience, together with the vicissitudes of his fortune, had not been able to overcome; not that his ideas soared to such a pitch of extravagant hope as that which took possession of his mess-mates, who frequently quarrelled one with another, about the degrees of favour to which they should be intitled after the king's restoration; but he firmly believed that affairs would speedily take such a turn in Italy, as would point out to the English court, the expediency of employing him again; and this persuasion seemed to support him against every species of poverty and mortification.

While they were busy in trimming the balance of power on the other side of the Alps, their deliberations were interrupted by the arrival of a scullion,[8] who came to receive their orders touching the bill of fare for dinner, and his majesty found much more difficulty in settling this important concern, than in compromising all the differences between the emperor and the queen of Spain.[9] At length, however, General Macleaver undertook the office of purveyor for his prince; captain Minikin insisted upon treating the count, and in a little time the table was covered with a cloth, which for the sake of my delicate readers, I shall not attempt to describe.

At this period, they were joined by Sir Mungo Barebones, who having found means to purchase a couple of mutton chops, had cooked a mess of broth, which he now brought in a saucepan to the general rendezvous: this was the most remarkable object which had hitherto presented itself to the eyes of Fathom: being naturally of a meagre habit, he was by indigence and hard study wore almost to the bone, and so bended towards the earth, that in walking, his body described at least 150 degrees of a circle. The want of stockings and shoes he supplied with a jockey straight boot[10] and an half jack.[11] His thighs and middle were cased in a monstrous pair of brown trunk breeches,[12] which the keeper bought for his use, from the executor of a Dutch seaman who had lately died in the jail: his shirt retained no signs of its original colour, his body was shrouded in an old greasy tattered plaid night-gown; a blue and white handkerchief surrounded his head, and his looks betokened that immense load of care, which he had voluntarily incurred for the eternal salvation of sinners. Yet this figure, uncouth as it was, made his compliments to our adventurer in terms of the most elegant address, and in the course of conversation, disclosed a great fund of valuable knowledge. He had appeared in the great world, and bore divers offices of dignity and trust, with universal applause: his courage was undoubted, his morals were unimpeached, and his person held in great veneration and esteem; when his evil genius engaged him in the study of Hebrew, and the mysteries of the Jewish religion, which fairly disordered his brain, and rendered him incapable of managing his temporal affairs.[13] When he ought to have been employed in the functions of his post, he was always rapt in visionary conferences with Moses on the Mount;[14] rather than regulate the œconomy of his houshold, he chose to exert his endeavours in settling the precise meaning of the word *Elohim*; and having discovered that now the period was come, when the Jews and Gentiles would be converted, he postponed every other consideration, in order to facilitate that great and glorious event.

By this time, Ferdinand had seen every member of the club, except the French chevalier, who seemed to be quite neglected by the society; for his name was not once mentioned during this communication, and they sat down to dinner, without asking whether he was dead or alive. The king regaled himself with a plate of ox-cheek; the major, who complained that his appetite had forsaken him, amused himself with some forty hard eggs, malaxed[15] with salt butter; the knight indulged upon his soup and bouillé,[16] and the captain entertained our adventurer with a neck of veal roasted, with potatoes;

but before Fathom could make use of his knife and fork, he was summoned to the door, where he found the chevalier in great agitation, his eyes sparkling like coals of fire.

Our hero was not a little surprized at this apparition, who having asked pardon for the freedom he had used, observed, that understanding the count was a foreigner, he could not dispense with appealing to him, concerning an outrage he had suffered from the keeper, who, without any regard to his rank or misfortunes, had been base enough to refuse him credit for a few necessaries, until he could have a remittance from his steward in France; he therefore conjured count Fathom, as a stranger and nobleman like himself, to be the messenger of defiance, which he resolved to send to that brutal gaoler, that for the future he might learn to make proper distinctions in the exercise of his function.

Fathom, who had no inclination to offend this choleric Frenchman, assured him that he might depend upon his friendship; and in the mean time, prevailed upon him to accept of a small supply, in consequence of which, he procured a pound of sausages, and joined the rest of the company without delay; making a very suitable addition to such an assemblage of rarities. Tho' his age did not exceed thirty years, his beard, which was of a brindled hue,[17] flowed down, like Aaron's, to his middle:[18] upon his legs he wore red stockings rolled up over the joint of the knee, his breeches were of blue drab[19] with vellum button-holes,[20] and garters of gold lace, his waistcoat of scarlet, his coat of rusty[21] black cloath, his hair twisted into a ramellie,[22] hung down to his rump, of the colour of jet, and his hat was adorned with a white feather.[23]

This original had formed many ingenious schemes to increase the glory and grandeur of France, but was discouraged by cardinal Fleury,[24] who, in all appearance, jealous of his great talents, not only rejected his projects, but even sent him to prison, on pretence of being offended at his impertinence. Perceiving that, like the prophet, he had no honour in his own country,[25] he no sooner obtained his release, than he retired to England, where he was prompted by his philanthropy, to propose an expedient to our ministry, which would have saved a vast effusion of blood and treasure; this was an agreement between the queen of Hungary and the late emperor, to decide their pretensions by a single combat;[26] in which case he offered himself as the Bavarian champion; but in this endeavour he also proved unsuccessful: then turning his attention to the delights of poetry, he became so enamoured of the muse, that he neglected every other consideration, and she as usual, gradually conducted him to the author's never-failing goal;[27] a place of rest appointed for all those sinners, whom the profane love of poesy hath led astray.

CHAPTER XLI.

One quarrel is compromised; and another decided by unusual arms.

Among other topics of conversation that were discussed at this genial meeting, Sir Mungo's scheme was brought upon the carpet, by his majesty, who was graciously pleased to ask how his subscription filled? To this interrogation, the knight answered, that he met with great opposition from a spirit of levity and self-conceit, which seemed to prevail in this generation; but, that no difficulties should discourage him, from persevering in his duty; and he trusted in God, that in a very little time he should be able to confute and overthrow the false philosophy of the moderns, and to restore the writings of Moses to that pre-eminence and veneration, which is due to an inspired author. He spoke of the immortal Newton with infinite contempt, and undertook to extract from the Pentateuch, a system of chronology, which would ascertain the progress of time since the fourth day of the creation to the present hour with such exactness, that not one vibration of a pendulum should be lost! nay, he affirmed that the perfection of all arts and sciences might be attained by studying those sacred memoirs; and that he himself did not despair of learning from them the art of transmuting baser metals into gold.[1]

The chevalier, though he did not pretend to contradict these assertions, was too much attached to his own religion to acquiesce in the knight's project of converting the Jews and the Gentiles to the protestant heresy, which, he said, God Almighty would never suffer to triumph over the interests of his own holy catholic church. This objection produced abundance of altercation between two very unequal disputants, and the Frenchman finding himself puzzled by the learning of his antagonist, had recourse to the *Argumentum ad hominem*,[2] by laying his hand upon his sword, and declaring that he was ready to lose the last drop of his blood in opposition to such a damnable scheme.

Sir Mungo, though in all appearance, reduced to the last stage of animal existence, no sooner heard this epithet applied to his plan, than his eyes gleamed like lightning; he sprung from his seat, with the agility of a grasshopper, and darting himself out at the door, like an arrow from a bow, reappeared in a moment with a long rusty weapon, which might have been shewn among a collection of rarities, as the sword of Guy earl of Warwick.[3] This implement he brandished over the chevalier's head, with the dexterity

of an old prize-fighter, exclaiming in the French language, "Thou art a pro-
phane wretch marked out for the vengeance of Heaven, whose unworthy
minister I am; and here thou shalt fall by the sword of the Lord and of
Gideon."[4]

The chevalier, unterrified by this dreadful salutation, desired he would
accompany him to a more convenient place; and the world might have been
deprived of one or both these knights-errant, had not general Macleaver, at
the desire of his majesty, interposed, and found means to bring matters to an
accommodation.

In the afternoon, the society was visited by the major's cousin and her
daughters, who no sooner appeared, than they were recognized by our adventurer; and his acquaintance with them renewed in such a manner as
alarmed the delicacy of captain Minikin, who in the evening, repaired to the
count's apartment, and with a very formal physiognomy, accosted him in
these words. "Sir, I beg pardon for this intrusion; but, I come to consult you
about an affair in which my honour is concerned: and a soldier without honour, you know is no better than a body without a soul. I have always admired
that speech of Hotspur, in the first part of Henry the fourth.

> By Heaven, methinks it were an easy leap,
> To pluck bright honour from the pale-fac'd moon;
> Or dive into the bottom of the deep,
> Where fathom line could never touch the ground,
> And pluck up drowned honour by the locks.—[5]

There is a boldness and ease in the expression, and the images are very
pictoresque. But, without any further preamble; pray Sir, give me leave to
ask how long you have been acquainted with those ladies, who drank tea with
us this afternoon? You'll forgive the question Sir, when I tell you that major
Macleaver introduced Mrs. Minikin to them, as to ladies of character; and I
don't know how Sir, I have a sort of *presentiment* that my wife has been imposed upon. Perhaps I may be mistaken, and God grant I may. But there was
a *je ne sçai quoy*[6] in their behaviour to-day, which begins to alarm my suspicion. Sir, I have nothing but my reputation to depend upon; and I hope you
will excuse me, when I earnestly beg to know what rank they maintain in
life."

Fathom, without minding the consequence, told him with a simper,[7] that
he knew them to be very good-natured ladies, who devoted themselves to the
happiness of mankind. This explanation had no sooner escaped from his lips,
than the captain's face began to glow with indignation, his eyes seemed burst-

ing from their spheres, he swelled to twice his natural dimensions, and raising himself on his tiptoes, pronounced in a strain that emulated thunder.
"Blood! Sir, you seem to make very light of the matter; but it is no joke to me,
I'll assure you: and Macleaver shall see that I am not to be affronted with
impunity. Sir, I shall take it as a singular favour, if you will be the bearer of a
billet to him, which I shall write in three words: nay, Sir, you must give me
leave to insist upon it, as you are the only gentleman of our mess, whom I can
intrust with an affair of this nature."

Fathom, rather than run the risque of disobliging such a punctilious warrior, after having in vain attempted to dissuade him from his purpose, undertook to carry the challenge, which was immediately penned in these words.

"Sir,

You have violated my honour, in imposing upon Mrs. Minikin, your pretended cousins, as ladies of virtue and reputation; I therefore demand such
satisfaction as a soldier ought to receive, and expect you will adjust with my
friend count Fathom, the terms upon which you shall be met by the much
injured

GOLIAH MINIKIN."

This morçeau[8] being sealed and directed, was forthwith carried by our
adventurer to the lodgings of the major, who had by this time, retired to rest,
but hearing the count's voice, he got up and opened the door in *cuerpo*,[9] to the
astonishment of Ferdinand, who had never before seen such an Herculean
figure. He made an apology for receiving the count in his birth-day suit,[10] to
which, he said, he was reduced by the heat of his constitution, though he
might have assigned a more adequate cause, by owning that his shirt was in
the hands of his washerwoman; then shrouding himself in a blanket, desired
to know what had procured him the honour of such an extraordinary visit.
He read the letter with great composure, like a man accustomed to such
intercourse; then addressing himself to the bearer, "I will be after diverting
the gentleman," said he, "in any manner he shall think proper: but by Jesus!
this is no place for such amusements; because, as you well know, my dear
count, if both should be killed by the chance of war, neither of us will be able
to escape, and after the breath is out of his body, he will make but a sorry
excuse to his family and friends. But, that is no concern of mine, and therefore I am ready to please him in his own way."

Fathom approved of his remarks, which he reinforced with sundry considerations to the same purpose, and begged the assistance of the major's advice, in finding some expedient to terminate the affair without bloodshed, that no troublesome consequences might ensue either to him or to his antagonist, who in spite of this over-strained formality, seemed to be a person of worth and good-nature. "With all my heart," said the generous Hibernian, "I have a great regard for the little man, and my own character is not to seek at this time of day. I have served a long apprenticeship to fighting, as this same carcass can testify, and if he compels me to run him through the body, by my shoul I shall do it in a friendly manner."

So saying, he threw aside the blanket, and displayed scars and seams innumerable upon his body, which appeared like an old patched leathern doublet. "I remember," proceeded this champion, "when I was a slave at Algiers, Murphy Macmorris and I happened to have some difference in the bagnio;[11] upon which he bad me turn out. 'Arra, for what?' said I, 'here are no weapons that a gentleman can use, and you would not be such a negro[12] as to box like an English carman.'[13] After he had puzzled himself for some time, he proposed that we should retire into a corner, and funk one another[14] with brimstone, 'till one of us should give out. Accordingly we crammed half a dozen of tobacco-pipes with sulphur, and setting foot to foot, began to smoke, and kept a constant fire, until Macmorris dropped down; then I threw away my pipe, and taking poor Murphy in my arms, 'What are you dead,' said I, 'if you are dead, speak.' 'No by Jesus!' cried he, 'I an't dead, but I'm speechless.' So he owned, I had obtained the victory, and we were as good friends as ever. Now if Mr. Minikin thinks proper to put the affair upon the same issue, I will smoke a pipe of brimstone with him to-morrow morning, and if I cry out first, I will be after asking pardon for this supposed affront."

Fathom could not help laughing at the proposal, to which, however, he objected on account of Minikin's delicate constitution, which might suffer more detriment from breathing in an atmosphere of sulphur, than from the discharge of a pistol, or the thrust of a small sword. He therefore suggested another expedient in lieu of the sulphur, namely, the gum called *Assa fœtida*,[15] which though abundantly nauseous, could have no dangerous effect upon the infirm texture of the lieutenant's[16] lungs. This hint being relished by the major, our adventurer returned to his principal, and having repeated the other's arguments against the use of mortal instruments, described the succedaneum,[17] which he had concerted with Macleaver. The captain at first believed this scheme was calculated for subjecting him to the ridicule of his fellow-prisoners, and began to storm with great violence; but by the assurances and address of Fathom, he was at length reconciled to the plan, and preparations were made on each side for this duel, which was actually smoaked next day, about noon, in a small closet, detached from the challenger's apartment, and within hearing of his majesty and all his court, assembled as witnesses and umpires of the contest.

The combatants being locked up together, began to ply their engines with great fury, and it was not long before captain Minikin perceived he had a manifest advantage over his antagonist. For his organs were familiarized to the effluvia of this drug, which he had frequently used in the course of an hypochondriac disorder;[18] whereas Macleaver, who was a stranger to all sorts of medicine, by his wry faces and attempts to puke, expressed the utmost abhorrence of the smell that invaded his nostrils. Nevertheless, resolved to hold out to the last extremity, he continued in action, until the closet was filled with such an intolerable vapour as discomposed the whole œconomy of his intrails, and compelled him to disgorge his breakfast in the face of his opponent, whose nerves were so disconcerted by this disagreeable and unforeseen discharge, that he fell back into his chair in a swoon, and the major bellowed aloud for assistance. The door being opened, he ran directly to a window, to inhale the fresh air, while the captain recovering from his fit, complained of Macleaver's unfair proceedings, and demanded justice of the arbitrators, who decided in his favour; and the major being prevailed upon to ask pardon for having introduced Mrs. Minikin to women of rotten[19] reputation, the parties were reconciled to each other, and peace and concord reestablished in the mess.

Fathom acquired universal applause for his discreet and humane conduct upon this occasion; and that same afternoon had an opportunity of seeing the lady in whose cause he had exerted himself. He was presented to her as the husband's particular friend, and when she understood how much she was indebted to his care and concern for the captain's safety, she treated him with uncommon marks of distinction; and he found her a genteel well-bred woman, not without a good share of personal charms, and a well cultivated understanding.

CHAPTER XLII.

An unexpected rencounter, and an happy revolution
in the affairs of our adventurer.

As she did not lodge within the precincts of this garrison, she was one day, after tea, conducted to the gate by the captain and the count, and just as they approached the turnkey's lodge, our hero's eyes were struck with the apparition of his old companion Renaldo, son of his benefactor and patron the count de Melvile. What were the emotions of his soul, when he saw that young gentleman enter the prison, and advance towards him, after having spoke to the gaoler! He never doubted that being informed of his confinement, he was come to upbraid him with his villainy and ingratitude, and he in vain endeavoured to recollect himself from that terror and guilty confusion which his appearance had inspired; when the stranger lifting up his eyes, started back with signs of extreme amazement, and after a considerable pause, exclaimed, "Heaven and earth! Sure my eyes do not deceive me! is not your name Fathom? it is, it must be my old friend and companion, the loss of whom I have so long regreted!" With these words, he ran towards our adventurer, and while he clasped him in his arms, with all the eagerness of affection, protested that this was one of the happiest days he had ever seen.

Ferdinand, who from this salutation, concluded himself still in possession of Renaldo's good opinion, was not deficient in expressions of tenderness and joy; he returned his embraces with equal ardour, the tears trickled down his cheeks, and that perturbation which proceeded from conscious perfidy and fear, was mistaken by the unsuspecting Hungarian for the sheer effects of love, gratitude and surprize. These first transports having subsided, they adjourned to the lodgings of Fathom, who soon recollected his spirits and invention so well as to amuse the other with a feigned tale of his having been taken by the French, sent prisoner into Champaigne,[1] from whence he had written many letters to count Melvile and his son, of whom he could hear no tidings; of his having contracted an intimacy with a young nobleman of France, who died in the flower of his age, after having in token of friendship, bequeathed to him a considerable legacy; by this he had been enabled to visit the land of his forefathers in the character of a gentleman, which he had supported with some figure, until he was betrayed into a misfortune that exhausted his funds, and drove him to the spot where he was now found: and he solemnly declared, that far from forgetting the obligation he owed to count Melvile, or renouncing the friendship of Renaldo, he had actually resolved to set out for Germany on his return to the house of his patron in the beginning of the week, posterior to that in which he had been arrested.

Young Melvil, whose own heart had never known the instigations of fraud, implicitly believed the story and protestations of Fathom; and tho' he would not justify that part of his conduct by which the term of his good fortune was abridged, he could not help excusing an indiscretion into which he had been hurried by the precipitancy of youth, and the allurements of an artful woman: nay, with the utmost warmth of friendship, he undertook to wait upon Trapwell, and endeavour to soften him into some reasonable terms of composition.

Fathom seemed to be quite overwhelmed with a deep sense of all this goodness, and affected the most eager impatience to know the particulars of Renaldo's fate, since their unhappy separation, more especially his errand to this uncomfortable place which he should henceforth revere as the providential scene of their reunion: nor did he forget to enquire, in the most affectionate and dutiful manner, about the situation of his noble parents and amiable sister.

At mention of these names, Renaldo, fetching a deep sigh, "Alas! my friend, (said he) the Count is no more; and what aggravates my affliction for the loss of such a father, it was my misfortune to be under his displeasure at the time of his death. Had I been present on that melancholy occasion, so well I knew his generosity and paternal tenderness, that sure I am, he would in his last moments have forgiven an only son whose life had been a continual effort to render himself worthy of such a parent, and whose crime was no other than an honourable passion for the most meritorious of her sex. But I was removed at a fatal distance from him, and doubtless my conduct must have been invidiously misrepresented. Be that as it will, my mother has again given her hand in wedlock to Count Trebasi; by whom I have the mortification to be informed that I am totally excluded from my father's succession; and I learn from other quarters, that my sister is barbarously treated by this inhuman father-in-law. Grant, Heaven, I may soon have an opportunity of expostulating with the tyrant upon that subject."

So saying, his cheeks glowed, and his eyes lightened with resentment. Then he thus proceeded.

"My coming hither to-day, was with a view to visit a poor female relation, from whom I yesterday received a letter describing her most deplorable situation, and solliciting my assistance: but the turnkey affirms, that there is no such person in the jail; and I was on my way to consult the keeper, when I was agreeably surprised with the sight of my dear Fathom."

Our adventurer having wiped from his eyes the tears which were produced by the news of his worthy patron's death, desired to know the name of that afflicted prisoner in whose behalf he interested himself so much, and Renaldo produced the letter, subscribed your unfortunate cousin Helen Melvil. This pretended relation, after having explained the degree of consanguinity which she and the Count stood in to each other, and occasionally mentioned some anecdotes of the family in Scotland, gave him to understand, that she had married a merchant of London, who, by repeated losses in trade, had been reduced to indigence, and afterwards confined in prison, where he then lay a breathless coarse,[2] having left her in the utmost extremity of wretchedness and want, with two young children in the small-pox, and an incurable cancer in one of her own breasts. Indeed, the picture she drew was so moving, and her expressions so sensibly pathetic, that no person whose heart was not altogether callous, could peruse it without emotion. Renaldo had sent two guineas by the messenger whom she had represented as a trusty servant, whose fidelity had been proof against all the distress of her mistress: and he was now arrived, in order to reinforce his bounty.

Fathom, in the consciousness of his own practices, immediately comprehended the scheme of this letter, and confidently assured him, that no such person resided in the prison, or in any other place: and when his friend applied for information to the keeper, these assurances were confirmed; and that stern janitor[3] told him, he had been imposed upon by a stale trick which was often practised upon strangers, by a set of sharpers, who make it their business to pick up hints of intelligence relating to private families, upon which they build such superstructures of fraud and imposition.

However piqued the young Hungarian might be to find himself duped in this manner, he rejoiced at the occasion which had thrown Fathom in his way; and, after having made him a tender of his purse, took his leave, on purpose to wait upon Trapwell, who was not quite so untractable as an enraged cuckold commonly is; for, by this time, he had accomplished the best part of his aim, which was to be divorced from his wife, and was fully convinced that the defendant was no more than a needy adventurer, who in all probability would be released by an act of parliament for the benefit of insolvent debtors;[4] in which case, he (the plaintiff) would reap no solid advantage from his imprisonment.

He therefore listened to the remonstrances of the mediator, and after much canvassing[5] agreed to discharge the defendant in consideration of two hundred pounds, which were immediately paid by Count Melvil, who by this deduction was reduced to somewhat less than thirty.

Nevertheless he chearfully beggared himself in behalf of his friend, for whose release he forthwith obtained an order: and next day our adventurer having bid a formal adieu to his fellows in distress, and in particular to his majesty, for whose restoration his prayers were preferred, he quitted the jail, and accompanied his deliverer, with all the outward marks of unutterable gratitude and esteem.

Surely, if his heart had been made of *penetrable stuff*,[6] it would have been touched by the circumstances of this redemption: but, had not his soul been invincible to all such attacks, these memoirs would, possibly, never have seen the light.

When they arrived at Renaldo's lodgings, that young gentleman honoured him with other proofs of confidence and friendship, by giving him a circumstantial detail of all the adventures in which he had been engaged after Fathom's desertion from the imperial camp. He told him, that immediately after the war was finished, his father had pressed him to a very advantageous match, with which he would have complied, though his heart was not at all concerned, had not he been inflamed with the desire of seeing the world before he could take any step towards a settlement for life: that he had signified his sentiments on this head to the Count, who opposed them with unusual obstinacy, as productive of a delay which might be fatal to his proposal: for which reason he had retired *incognito* from his family, and travelled thro' sundry states and countries in a disguise by which he eluded the inquiries of his parents.

That in the course of these peregrinations he was captivated by the irresistible charms of a young lady on whose heart he had the good fortune to make a tender impression: that their mutual love had subjected both to many dangers and difficulties, during which they suffered a cruel separation; after the torments of which, he had happily found her in England, where she now lived entirely cut off from her native country and connexions, and destitute of every other resource but his honour, love, and protection: and, finally, that he was determined to combat his own desires, how violent soever they might be, until he should have made some suitable provision for the consequences of a stricter union with the mistress of his soul, that he might not by a precipitate marriage ruin the person whom he adored.

This end he proposed to attain, by an application to the court of Vienna,[7] which, he did not doubt, would have some regard to his own service and that of his father; and thither he resolved to repair with the first opportunity, now that he had found a friend with whom he could intrust the inestimable jewel of his heart.

He likewise gave our hero to understand, that he had been eight months in England, during which he had lived in a frugal manner, that he might not unnecessarily exhaust the money he had been able to raise upon his own credit; that hitherto he had been obliged to defer his departure for Germany, on account of his attendance upon the mother of his mistress, who was lately dead of sorrow and chagrin; and that since he resided in London, he had often heard of the celebrated Count Fathom, tho' he never imagined that his friend Ferdinand could be distinguished by that appellation.

CHAPTER XLIII.

Fathom justifies the proverb, "What's bred in the bone will never come out of the flesh."[1]

Some circumstances of this conversation made a deep impression upon the mind of our adventurer, who nevertheless concealed his emotions from the knowledge of his friend, and was next day introduced to that hidden treasure of which Renaldo had spoke with such rapture and adoration. It was not without reason he had expatiated upon the personal attractions of this young lady, whom (for the present) we shall call Monimia, a name that implies her orphan situation.[2] When she entered the room, even Fathom, whose eyes had been sated with beauty, was struck dumb with admiration, and could scarce recollect himself so far as to perform the ceremony of his introduction.

She seemed to be about the age of eighteen: her stature was tall; her motion graceful; a knot of artificial flowers restrained the luxuriancy of her fine black hair that flowed in shining ringlets a-down her snowy neck. The contour of her face was oval; her forehead remarkably high; her complexion clean and delicate, tho' not florid; and her eyes were so piercing as to strike the soul of every beholder: yet, upon this occasion, one half of their vivacity was eclipsed by a languishing air of melancholy concern; which, while it in a manner sheathed the edge of her beauty, added a most engaging sweetness to her looks: in short, every feature was elegantly perfect; and the harmony of the whole ravishing and delightful.[3]

It was easy to perceive the mutual sentiments of the two lovers, at meeting, by the pleasure that sensibly diffused itself in the countenances of both. Fathom was received by her as the intimate friend of her admirer, whom she had often heard of in terms of the most sincere affection; and the conversation was carried on in the Italian language, because she was a foreigner who had not as yet made great proficiency in the knowledge of the English tongue. Her understanding was such, as, instead of diminishing, reinforced the prepossession which was inspired by her appearance; and if the sum total of her charms could not melt the heart, it at least excited the appetite of Fathom to such a degree, that he gazed upon her with such violence of desire, as had never transported him before; and instantly began to harbour thoughts not only destructive to the peace of his generous patron, but also to the prudential maxims he had adopted on his first entrance into life.

We have already recorded divers instances of his conduct, to prove that there was an intemperance in his blood, which often interfered with his caution: and although he had found means to render this heat sometimes subservient to his interest; yet, in all probability, Heaven mingled the ingredient in his constitution, on purpose to counteract his consummate craft, defeat the villany of his intention, and, at last, expose him to the justice of the law, and the contempt of his fellow creatures.

Stimulated as he was by the beauty of the incomparable Monimia, he foresaw that the conquest of her heart would cost him a thousand times more labour and address than all the victories he had ever atchieved: for, besides her superior understanding, her sentiments of honour, virtue, gratitude, religion, and pride of birth, her heart was already engaged by the tenderest ties of love and obligation, to a man whose person and acquired accomplishments at least equalled his own; and whose connexion with him was of such a nature, as raised an almost insurmountable bar to his design: because, with what face could he commence rival to the person whose family had raised him from want and servility, and whose own generosity had rescued him from the miseries of a dreary jail?

Notwithstanding these reflections, he would not lay aside an idea which so agreeably flattered his imagination. He, like every other projector in the same circumstances, was so partial to his own qualifications, as to think the lady would soon perceive a difference between him and Renaldo that could not fail to turn to his advantage in her opinion. He depended a good deal on the levity and inconstancy of the sex; and did not doubt, that, in the course of their acquaintance, he should profit by that languor which often creeps upon and flattens the intercourse of lovers cloyed with the sight and conversation of each other.

This way of arguing was very natural to a man who had never known other motives than those of sensuality and convenience; and perhaps, upon these maxims, he might have succeeded with nine tenths of the fair sex: but, for once, he erred in his calculation. Monimia's soul was perfect: her virtue impregnable. His first approaches were, as usual, performed by the method of insinuation, which succeeded so well, that in a few days, he actually acquired a very distinguished share of her favour and esteem: to this he had been recommended in the warmest strain of exaggerating friendship, by her dear Renaldo; so that placing the most unreserved confidence in his honour and integrity, and being almost quite destitute of acquaintance, she made no scruple of owning herself pleased with his company and conversation; and therefore he was never abridg'd in point of opportunity. She had too much discernment to overlook his uncommon talents and agreeable address, and too much susceptibility to observe them with indifference. She not only regarded him as the confident of her lover, but admired him as a person whose attachment did honour to Count Melvil's choice: she found his discourse remarkably entertaining, his politeness dignified with an air of uncommon sincerity; and she was ravished with his skill in musick, an art of which she was deeply enamoured.

While he thus ingratiated himself with the fair Monimia, Renaldo rejoiced at their intimacy, being extremely happy in the thought of having found a friend who could amuse and protect the dear creature in his absence. That she might be the better prepared for the temporary separation which he meditated, he began to be less frequent in his visits, or rather to interrupt by gradual intermissions the constant attendance he had bestowed upon her since her mother's death. This alteration she was enabled to bear by the assiduities of Fathom, when she understood that her lover was indispensibly employed in negotiating a sum of money for the purposes of his intended voyage. This was really the case: for, as the reader hath been already informed, the provision he had made for that emergency was expended in behalf of our adventurer; and the persons of whom he had borrowed it, far from approving of the use to which it was put, and accommodating him with a fresh supply, reproached him with his benevolence as an act of dishonesty to them, and, instead of favouring this second application, threatened to distress him for what he had already received. While he endeavoured to surmount these difficulties, his small reversion was quite exhausted, and he saw himself on the brink of wanting the common necessaries of life.

There was no difficulty which he could not have encountered with fortitude, had he alone been concerned:[4] but his affection and regard for Monimia were of such a delicate nature, that, far from being able to bear the prospect of her wanting the least convenience, he could not endure that she should suspect her situation cost him a moment's perplexity; because he foresaw it would wring her gentle heart with unspeakable anguish and vexation. This therefore he endeavoured to anticipate by expressions of confidence in the emperor's equity,[5] and frequent declarations touching the goodness and security of that credit from which he derived his present subsistence.

CHAPTER XLIV.

Anecdotes of poverty, and experiments for the benefit of those whom it may concern.

His affairs being thus circumstanced, it is not to be supposed that he passed his time in tranquillity. Every day ushered in new demands and fresh anxiety: for, though his œconomy was frugal, it could not be supported without money; and now not only his funds were drained, but also his private friends tired of relieving his domestic necessities: nay, they began to relinquish his company, which formerly they had coveted; and those who still favoured him with their company, embittered that favour with disagreeable advice mingled with impertinent reproof. They loudly exclaimed against the last instance of his friendship for Fathom as a piece of wrongheaded extravagance, which neither his fortune could afford, nor his conscience excuse; and alledged, that such specimens of generosity are vicious in any man, let his finances be never so opulent, if he has any relations of his own who need his assistance; but altogether scandalous, not to say unjust, in a person who depends for his own support upon the favour of his friends.

These expostulations did not even respect the beauteous, the accomplished, the gentle-hearted, the orphan Monimia. Although they owned her perfections, and did not deny that it would be highly meritorious in any man of fortune to make her happy, they disapproved of Renaldo's attachment to the fair beggar, made light of that intimate union of hearts which subsisted between the two lovers, and which no human consideration could dissolve; and some among them, in the consummation of their prudence, ventured to hint a proposal of providing for her in the service of some lady of fashion.

Any reader of sensibility will easily conceive how these admonitions were relished by a young gentleman whose pride was indomitable, whose notions of honour were scrupulously rigid and romantic, whose temper was warm, and whose love was intense. Every such suggestion was as a dagger to his soul; and what rendered the torture more exquisite, he lay under obligations to those very persons, whose selfish and sordid sentiments he disdained: so that he was restricted by gratitude from giving vent to his indignation; and his forlorn circumstances would not permit him to renounce their acquaintance. While he struggled with these mortifications, his wants grew more and more importunate, and his creditors became clamorous.

Fathom, to whom all his grievances were disclosed, lamented his hard hap[1] with all the demonstrations of sympathy which he could expect to find in such a zealous adherent; he upbraided himself incessantly as the cause of his patron's distress; took God to witness, that he would rather have perished in jail, than have enjoyed his liberty, had he known it would have cost his dearest friend and benefactor one tenth part of the anguish he now saw him suffer; and in conclusion, the fervency of his affection glowed to such a degree, that he offered to beg, steal, or plunder on the high way, for Renaldo's assistance.

Certain it is, he might have recollected a less disagreeable expedient than any of these, to alleviate the pangs of this unhappy lover: for, at that very period, he was possessed of money and moveables to the amount of a much greater sum than that which was necessary to remove the severest pangs of the Count's misfortune. But, whether he did not reflect upon this resource, or was willing to let Melvil be better acquainted with adversity, which is the great school of life, I shall leave the reader to determine: yet, so far was he from supplying the wants of the young Hungarian, that he did not scruple to receive a share of the miserable pittance which that gentleman made shift to extort from the complaisance of a few companions, whose countenance he still enjoyed.

Renaldo's life was now become a sacrifice to the most poignant distress: almost his whole time was engrossed by a double scheme comprehending his efforts to render his departure practicable, and his expedients for raising the means of daily bread. With regard to the first, he exerted himself among a set of merchants, some of whom knew his family and expectations; and, for the last, he was fain to depend upon the assistance of a few intimates, who were not in condition to furnish him with sums of consequence. These, however, gradually dropped off, on pretence of friendly resentment for his indiscreet conduct; so that he found himself naked and deserted by all his former companions, except one gentleman, with whom he had lived in the most unreserved correspondence, as with a person of the warmest friendship, and the most unbounded benevolence: nay, he had actually experienced repeated proofs of his generosity; and such were the Count's sentiments of the gratitude, love and esteem which were due to the author of these obligations, that he would have willingly laid down his own life for his interest or advantage. He had already been at different times accommodated by this benefactor, with occasional supplies, amounting in the whole to about forty or fifty pounds; and so fearful was he of taking any step by which he might forfeit the good-will of this gentleman, that he struggled with unparalelled difficulty and vexation, before he could prevail upon himself to put his liberality to another proof.

What maxims of delicacy will not the dire calls of necessity infringe![2] Reduced to the alternative of applying once more to that beneficence which had never failed him, or of seeing Monimia starve, he chose the first, as of two evils the least, and intrusted Fathom with a letter explaining the bitterness of his case. It was not without trepidation that he received in the evening, from his messenger, an answer to this billet: but what were his pangs when he learned the contents? The gentleman, after having professed himself Melvil's sincere well-wisher, gave him to understand, that he was resolved for the future to detach himself from every correspondence which would be inconvenient for him to maintain; that he considered his intimacy with the Count in that light: yet, nevertheless, if his distress was really as great as he had described it, he would still contribute something towards his relief; and accordingly had sent by the bearer five guineas for that purpose: but desired him to take notice, that, in so doing, he laid himself under some difficulty.

Renaldo's grief and mortification at this disappointment were unspeakable: he now saw demolished the last screen betwixt him and the extremity of indigence and woe; he beheld the mistress of his soul abandoned to the bleakest scenes of poverty and want; and he deeply resented the lofty strain of the letter, by which he conceived himself treated as a worthless spendthrift, and importunate beggar. Tho' his purse was exhausted to the last shilling; tho' he was surrounded with necessities and demands, and knew not how to provide another meal for his fair dependant, he, in opposition to all the suggestions and eloquence of Fathom, dispatched him with the money and another billet, intimating in the most respectful terms, that he approved of his friend's new adopted maxim, which, for the future, he should always take care to remember; and that he had sent back the last instance of his bounty, as a proof how little he was disposed to incommode his benefactor.

This letter, tho' sincerely meant, and written in a very serious mood, the gentleman considered as an ungrateful piece of irony, and in that opinion complained to several persons of the Count's acquaintance, who unanimously exclaimed against him, as a sordid, unthankful, and profligate knave that abused and reviled those very people who had generously befriended him, whenever they found it inconvenient to nourish his extravagance with further supplies. Notwithstanding these accumulated oppressions, he still persevered with fortitude in his endeavours to disentangle himself from this maze of misery. To these he was encouraged by a letter which about this time he received from his sister, importing, that she had good reason to believe the real will of her father had been suppressed for certain sinister views; and desiring him to hasten his departure for Hungary, where he would still find some friends who were both able and willing to support his cause. He had some trinkets left; the pawn-broker's shop was still open; and hitherto he made shift to conceal from Monimia the extent of his affliction.

The money-broker whom he employed, after having amused him with a variety of schemes, which served no other purpose than that of protracting his own job, at length undertook to make him acquainted with a set of monied men who had been very adventurous in lending sums upon personal security; he was therefore introduced to their club,[3] in the most favourable manner, after the broker had endeavoured to prepossess them separately, with magnificent ideas of his family and fortune. By means of this anticipation, he was received with a manifest relaxation of that severity, which people of this class mingle in their aspects to the world in general; and they even vied with each other in their demonstrations of hospitality and respect; for every one in particular looked upon him as a young heir, who would bleed freely, and mortgage at cent. per cent.[4]

Renaldo, buoyed up with these exterior civilities, began to flatter himself with hopes of success, which, however, were soon checked by the nature of the conversation; during which the chair-man upbraided one of the members in open club, for having once lent forty pounds upon slight security: the person accused alledged in his own defence, that the borrower was his own kinsman, whose funds he knew to be sufficient; that he had granted his bond, and been at the expence of insuring his life for the money; and, in conclusion, had discharged it to the day with great punctuality. These allegations were not deemed exculpatory by the rest of the assembly, who with one voice pronounced him guilty of unwarrantable rashness and indiscretion, which, in time coming, must undoubtedly operate to the prejudice of his character and credit.

This was a bitter declaration to the young Count, who, nevertheless, endeavoured to improve the footing he had gained among them, by courting their company, conforming to their manners, and attentively listening to their discourse. When he had cultivated them with great assiduity, for the space of some weeks, dined at their houses upon pressing invitations, and received repeated offers of service and friendship, believing that things were now ripe for the purpose, he one day, at a tavern to which he had invited him to dinner, ventured to disclose his situation to him, whose countenance was the least unpromising; and as he introduced the business with a proposal of borrowing money, he perceived his eyes sparkle with a visible alacrity, from which he drew an happy presage. But, alas! this was no more than a transient gleam of sunshine, which was suddenly obumbrated[5] by the sequel of his explanation; insomuch, that, when the merchant understood the nature of the security, his visage was involved in a most disagreeable gloom, and his eyes distorted into a most hideous obliquity of vision: indeed, he squinted so horribly, that Renaldo was amazed and almost affrighted at his looks, until he perceived that this distortion proceeded from concern for a silver tobacco-box which he had laid down by him on the table, after having filled his pipe: as the youth proceeded to unfold his necessities, the other became gradually alarmed for this utensil, to which he darted his eyes askance in this præter-natural direction, until he had slily secured it in his pocket.

Having made this successful conveyance, he shifted his eyes alternately from the young gentleman to the broker, for a considerable pause, during which he in silence reproached the last for introducing such a beggarly varlet[6] to his acquaintance; then taking the pipe from his mouth, "Sir, (said he, addressing himself to the Count) if I had all the inclination in the world to comply with your proposal, it is really not in my power: my correspondents abroad have remitted such a number of bad bills of late, that all my running cash hath been exhausted in supporting their credit. Mr. Ferret,[7] sure I am, you was not ignorant of my situation; and I'm not a little surprized, that you should bring the gentleman to me, on business of this kind: but, as the Wise Man observes, *Bray a fool in a mortar, and he'll never be wise.*"[8] So saying, with a most emphatic glance directed to the broker, he rung the bell, and called for the reckoning; when, finding that he was to be the guest of Renaldo, he thanked him drily for his good chear, and in an abrupt manner took himself away.

Tho' baffled in this quarter, the young gentleman would not despair; but forthwith employed Mr. Ferret in an application to another of the society; who, after having heard the terms of his commission, desired him to tell his principal, that he could do nothing, without the concurrence of his partner, who happened to be at that time in one of our American plantations: a third being sollicited, excused himself on account of an oath which he had lately taken, on the back of[9] a considerable loss: a fourth being tried, made answer, that it was not in his way: and a fifth candidly owned, that he never lent money without proper security.

Thus the forlorn Renaldo tried every experiment without success, and now saw the last ray of hope extinguished. Well nigh destitute of present support, and encompassed with unrelenting duns, he was obliged to keep within doors, and seek some comfort in the conversation of his charming mistress, and his faithful friend: yet, even there, he experienced the extremest rigour of adverse fate. Every rap at the door alarmed him with the expectation of some noisy tradesman demanding payment, when he endeavoured to amuse himself with drawing, some unlucky feature of the occasional portrait, recalled the image of an obdurate creditor, and made him tremble at the work of his own hands. When he fled for shelter to the flattering creation of fancy, some abhorred idea always started up amidst the gay vision, and dissolved the pleasing enchantment. Even the seraphic voice of Monimia had no longer power to compose the anxious tumults of his mind: every song she warbled, every tune she played, recalled to his remembrance some scene of love and happiness elapsed; and overwhelmed his soul with the woful comparison of past and present fate. He saw all that was amiable and perfect in woman, all that he held most dear and sacred upon earth, tottering on the brink of misery, without knowing the danger of her situation, and found himself unable to prevent her fall, or even to forewarn her of the peril: for, as we have already observed, his soul could not brook the thought of communicating the tidings of distress to the tender-hearted Monimia.

CHAPTER XLV.

Renaldo's distress deepens, and Fathom's plot thickens.

Such aggravated misfortune could not fail to affect his temper and deportment: the continual efforts he made to conceal his vexation produced a manifest distraction in his behaviour and discourse. He began to be seized with horror at the sight of poor Monimia, whom he therefore shunned as much as the circumstances of their correspondence would allow; and every evening he went forth alone to some solitary place, where he could unperceived give a loose to the transports of his sorrow, and in silence meditate some means to lighten the burden of his woe. His heart was sometimes so savaged with despair, which represented mankind as his inveterate enemies, that he entertained thoughts of denouncing[1] war against the whole community, and supplying his own wants with the spoils he should win: at other times, he was tempted with the desire of putting an end to his miseries and life together: yet these were but the transitory suggestions of temporary madness, that soon yielded to the dictates of reason. From the execution of the first, he was restrained by his own notions of honour and morality; and from using the other expedient, he was deterred by his love for Monimia, together with the motives of philosophy and religion.

While in this manner he secretly nursed the worm of grief that preyed upon his vitals, the alteration in his countenance and conduct did not escape the eye of that discerning young lady. She was alarmed at the change, yet afraid to inquire into the source of it; for, being ignorant of his distress, she could impute it to no cause in which her happiness was not deeply interested. She had observed his strained complaisance, and extraordinary emotion: she had detected him in repeated attempts to avoid her company, and taken notice of his regular excursions in the dark. These were alarming symptoms to a lover of her delicacy and pride: she strove in vain to put the most favourable construction on what she saw; and finally, imputed the effects of his despondence to the alienation of his heart. Made miserable beyond expression by these suspicions, she imparted them to Fathom, who by this time was in full possession of her confidence and esteem, and implored his advice touching her conduct in such a nice[2] conjuncture.

This artful politician, who rejoiced at the effect of her penetration, no sooner heard himself questioned on the subject, than he gave tokens of surprize and confusion, signifying his concern to find she had discovered what (for the honour of his friend) he wished had never come to light. His behaviour on this occasion confirmed her fatal conjecture; and she conjured him in the most pathetic manner, to tell her if he thought Renaldo's heart had contracted any new engagement. At this question, he started with signs of extreme agitation, and stifling an artificial sigh, "Sure, madam," said he, "you cannot doubt the Count's constancy——I am confident——he is certainly ——I protest, madam, I am so shocked"——

Here he made a full pause, as if the conflict between his integrity and his friendship would not allow him to proceed, and summoned the moisture into either eye—— "Then are my doubts removed," cried the afflicted Monimia: "I see your candour in the midst of your attachment to Renaldo; and will no longer torment you with impertinent interrogations and vain complaints." With these words, a flood of tears gushed from her enchanting eyes, and she instantly withdrew into her own apartment, where she indulged her sorrow to excess. Nor was her grief unanimated with resentment. She was by birth, nature and education inspired with that dignity of pride which ennobles the human heart; and this, by the circumstance of her present dependence, was rendered extremely jealous and susceptible: insomuch that she could not brook the least shadow of indifference, much less an injury of such a nature, from the man whom she had honoured with her affections, and for whom she had disobliged and deserted her family and friends.

Though her love was so unalterably fixed on this unhappy youth, that, without the continuation of reciprocal regard, her life would have become an unsupportable burden, even amidst all the splendour of affluence and pomp; and altho' she foresaw, that when his protection should cease, she must be left a wretched orphan in a foreign land, exposed to all the miseries of want: yet, such was the loftiness of her displeasure, that she disdained to complain, or even demand an explanation from the supposed author of her wrongs.

While she continued undetermined in her purpose, and fluctuating on this sea of torture, Fathom, believing that now was the season for working upon her passions, while they were all in commotion, became, if possible, more assiduous than ever about the fair mourner, modelled his features into a melancholy cast, pretended to share her distress with the most emphatic sympathy, and endeavoured to keep her resentment glowing by cunning insinuations, which, tho' apparently designed to apologize for his friend, served only to aggravate the guilt of his perfidy and dishonour. This pretext of friendly concern, is the most effectual vehicle for the conveyance of malice and slander; and a man's reputation is never so mortally stabbed, as when the assassin begins with the preamble of, "For my own part, I can safely say, that no man upon earth has a greater regard for him than I have; and it is with the utmost anguish and concern that I see him misbehave in such a manner." Then he proceeds to mangle his character, and the good-natured hearers concluding he is even blacker than he is represented, on the supposition that the most attrocious circumstances are softened or suppressed by the tenderness or friendship of the accuser, exclaim, "Good lack! what a wretch he must be, when his best friends will no longer attempt to defend him!" Nay, sometimes these well-wishers undertake his defence, and treacherously betray the cause they have espoused, by omitting the reasons that may be urged in his vindication.

Both these methods were practised by the wily Ferdinand, according to the predominant passion of Monimia: when her indignation prevailed, he expatiated upon his love and sincere regard for Renaldo, which, he said, had grown up from the cradle, to such a degree of fervour, that he would willingly part with life for his advantage. He shed tears for his apostacy; but every drop made an indelible stain upon his character; and, in the bitterness of his grief, swore, notwithstanding his fondness for Renaldo, which had become a part of his constitution, that the young Hungarian deserved the most infamous destiny, for having injured such perfection. At other times, when he found her melted into silent sorrow, he affected to excuse the conduct of his friend. He informed her, that the young gentleman's temper had been uneven from his infancy; that frailty was natural to man; that he might in time be reclaimed by self-conviction; he even hinted, that she might have probably ascribed to inconstancy, what was really the effect of some chagrin, which he industriously concealed from his participation: but, when he found her disposed to listen to this last suggestion, he destroyed the force of it, by recollecting the circumstances of his nocturnal rambles, which, he owned, would admit of no favourable construction.

By these means he blew the coals of her jealousy,[3] and inhanced the value of his own character, at the same time; for she looked upon him as a mirror of faith and integrity, and the mind being overcharged with woe, naturally seeks some confident, upon whose sympathy it can repose itself: indeed, his great aim was, to make himself necessary to her affliction, and settle a gossiping correspondence, in the familiarity of which he hoped his purpose would certainly be answered.

Yet the exertion of these talents was not limited to her alone. While he laid these trains for the hapless young lady, he was preparing snares of another kind for her unsuspecting lover, who (for the completion of his misery) about this time began to perceive marks of disquiet and displeasure in the countenance and deportment of his adored Monimia: for, that young lady, in the midst of her grief, remembered her origin, and over her vexation affected to throw a veil of tranquillity, which served only to give an air of disgust[4] to her internal disturbance.

Renaldo, whose patience and philosophy were barely sufficient to bear the load of his other evils, would have been quite overwhelmed with the additional burthen of Monimia's woe, if it had not assumed this appearance of disesteem, which, as he knew he had not deserved it, brought his resentment to his assistance: Yet this was but a wretched cordial[5] to support him against the baleful reflections that assaulted him from every quarter; it operated like those desperate remedies, which while they stimulate exhausted nature, help to destroy the very fundamentals of the constitution. He reviewed his own conduct with the utmost severity, and could not recollect one circumstance which could justly offend the idol of his soul. The more blameless he appeared to himself in this examination, the less excusable did her behaviour appear: He tasked his penetration to discover the cause of this alteration; he burned with impatience to know it; his discernment failed him, and he was afraid (tho' he knew not why) to demand an explanation. His thoughts were so circumstanced, that he durst not even unbosom himself to Fathom, tho' his own virtue and friendship resisted those sentiments that began to intrude upon his mind, with suggestions to the prejudice of our adventurer's fidelity.

Nevertheless, unable to endure the torments of such interesting suspense, he, at length, made an effort to expostulate with the fair orphan; and in an abrupt address, the effect of his fear and confusion, begged to know if he had inadvertently done any thing to incur her displeasure. Monimia hearing herself bluntly accosted in this unusual strain, after repeated instances of his reserve and supposed inconstancy, considered the question as a fresh insult, and summoning her whole pride to her assistance, replied with affected tranquillity, or rather with an air of scorn, that she had no title to judge, neither did she pretend to condemn his conduct. This answer, so wide of that tenderness and concern which had hitherto manifested itself in the disposition of his amiable mistress, deprived him of all power to carry on the conversation, and he retired with a low bow, fully convinced of his having irretrievably lost the place he had possessed in her affection; for, to his imagination, warped and blinded by his misfortunes, her demeanour seemed fraught, not with a transient gleam of anger, which a respectful lover would soon have appeased, but with that contempt and indifference which denote a total absence of affection and esteem. She, on the other hand, misconstrued his sudden retreat; and now they beheld the actions of each other thro' the false medium of prejudice and resentment. To such fatal misunderstandings, the peace and happiness of whole families often fall a sacrifice.

CHAPTER XLVI.

Our adventurer becomes absolute in his power over
the passions of his friend; and effects one half
of his aim.

Influenced by this dire mistake, the breasts of those unhappy lovers began to be invaded with the horrors of jealousy: the tender-hearted Monimia endeavoured to devour her griefs in silence; she in secret bemoaned her forlorn fate, without ceasing; her tears flowed without intermission from night to morn, and from morn to night: She sought not to know the object for which she was forsaken; she meant not to upbraid her undoer; her aim was to find a sequestered corner, in which she could indulge her sorrow; where she could brood over the melancholy remembrance of her former felicity, where she could recollect those happy scenes she had enjoyed under the wings of her indulgent parents, when her whole life was a revolution of pleasures, and she was surrounded with affluence, pomp and admiration; where she could, unmolested, dwell upon the wretched comparison between her past and present condition, and paint every circumstance of her misery in the most aggravating colours, that they might make the deeper impression upon her mind, and the more speedily contribute to that dissolution for which she ardently wished, as a total release from woe.

Amidst these pinings, she began to loath all sustenance; her cheeks grew wan, her bright eyes lost their splendor, the roses vanished from her lips, and her delicate limbs could hardly support their burthen; in a word, her sole consolation was limited to the prospect of depositing her sorrows in the grave; and her only wish was to procure a retreat in which she might wait with resignation for that happy period. Yet this melancholy comfort she could not obtain without the advice and mediation of Fathom, whom she therefore still continued to see and consult. While these consultations were held, Renaldo's bosom was ravaged with tempests of rage and distraction. He believed himself superseded in the affection of his mistress, by some favoured rival, whose success rankled at his soul; and tho' he scarce durst communicate the suspicion to his own heart, his observation continually whispered to him, that he was supplanted by his friend Fathom; for Monimia was totally detached from the conversation of every other man, and he had of late noted their intercourse with distempered eyes.

These considerations sometimes transported him to such a degree of frenzy, that he was tempted to sacrifice them both as traitors to gratitude, friendship, and love; but such deliriums soon vanished before his honour and humanity. He would not allow himself to think amiss of Ferdinand, until some undoubted mark of his guilt should appear; and this was so far from being the case, that hitherto there was scarce a presumption. On the contrary (said he to himself) I am hourly receiving proofs of his sympathy and attachment: Not but that he may be the innocent cause of my mishap. His superior qualifications may have attracted the eye, and engaged the heart of that inconstant fair, without his being sensible of the victory he has won; or, perhaps, shocked at the conquest he hath unwillingly made, he discourages her advances, tries to reason down her unjustifiable passion, and in the mean time, conceals from me the particulars, out of regard to my happiness and quiet.

Under cover of these favourable conjectures, our adventurer securely prosecuted his scheme upon the unfortunate Monimia. He dedicated himself wholly to her service and conversation, except at those times when his company was requested by Renaldo, who now very seldom exacted his attendance: In his ministry about the person of the beauteous orphan, this cunning incendiary mingled such awful regard, such melting compassion, as effectually screened him from the suspicion of treachery, while he widened the fatal breach between her and her lover, by the most diabolical insinuations. He represented his friend as a voluptuary, who gratified his own appetite without the least regard to honour or conscience; and with a shew of infinite reluctance imparted some anecdotes of his sensuality, which he had feigned for the purpose; then he would exclaim in an affected transport, "Gracious heaven! is it possible for any man who has the least title to perception or humanity to injure such innocence and perfection! for my own part, had I been so undeservedly happy——heaven and earth! Forgive my transports, madam, I cannot help seeing and admiring such divine attractions. I cannot help resenting your wrongs; it is the cause of virtue I espouse; it ought to be the cause of every honest man."

He had often repeated such apostrophes as these, which she ascribed to nothing else than sheer benevolence and virtuous indignation, and actually began to think he had made some impression upon her heart; not that he now entertained the hope of an immediate triumph over her chastity. The more he contemplated her character, the more difficult the conquest seemed to be; he therefore altered his plan, and resolved to carry on his operations, under the shelter of honourable proposals, foreseeing that a wife of her qualifications, if properly managed, would turn greatly to the account of the husband; or if her virtue should prove refractory, that he could, at any time, rid himself of the incumbrance, by decamping without beat of drum, after he should be cloyed with possession.

Elevated by these expectations, he, one day, in the midst of a preconcerted rhapsody, importing, that he could no longer conceal the fire that preyed upon his heart, threw himself on his knees before the lovely mourner, and imprinted a kiss on her fair hand: Tho' he did not presume to take this liberty, till after such preparation as he thought had altogether extinguished her regard for Melvil, and paved the way for his own reception in room of that discarded lover; he had so far overshot his mark, that Monimia, instead of favouring his declaration, started up and retired in silence, her cheeks glowing with shame, and her eyes gleaming with indignation.

Ferdinand no sooner recovered from the confusion produced by this unexpected repulse, than he saw the necessity of coming to a speedy determination, lest the offended fair one should appeal to Renaldo, in which case they might be mutually undeceived, to his utter shame and confusion; he therefore resolved to deprecate[1] her anger, by humble supplications, and by protesting, that whatever tortures he might suffer by suppressing his sentiments, she should never again be offended with a declaration of his passion.

Having thus appeased the gentle Monimia, and discovered, that in spite of her resentment, his friend still kept possession of her heart, he determined to work an effectual separation, so as that the young lady being utterly deserted by Melvil, should be left altogether in his power. With this christian intention he began to sadden his visage with a double shade of pensive melancholy, in the presence of Renaldo, to stifle a succession of involuntary sighs, to answer from the purpose, to be incoherent in his discourse, and in a word, to act the part of a person wrapt up in sorrowful cogitation.

Count Melvil, soon as he perceived these symptoms, very kindly enquired into the cause of them, and was not a little alarmed to hear the artful and evasive answers of Ferdinand, who without disclosing the source of his disquiet, earnestly begg'd leave to retire into some other corner of the world. Roused by this intreaty, the Hungarian's jealousy awoke, and with violent agitation he exclaimed: "Then are my fears too true! my dear Fathom, I comprehend the meaning of your request. I have for some time perceived an host of horrors approaching from that quarter. I know your worth and honour. I depend upon your friendship, and conjure you by all the ties of it, to free me at once from the most miserable suspense, by owning you have involuntarily captivated the heart of that unhappy maiden."

To this solemn interrogation he made no reply; but shedding a flood of tears (of which he had always a magazine[2] at command) he repeated his desire of withdrawing, and took God to witness, that what he proposed was solely for the quiet of his honoured patron and beloved friend. "Enough (cried the unfortunate Renaldo) the measure of my woes is now filled up." So saying, he fell backwards in a swoon, from which he was with difficulty recovered to the sensation of the most exquisite torments. During this paroxysm, our adventurer nursed him with infinite care and tenderness; he exhorted him to summon all his fortitude to his assistance; to remember his fore-fathers, and exert himself in the imitation of their virtues; to fly from those bewitching charms which had enslaved his better part, to retrieve his peace of mind, by reflecting on the inconstancy and ingratitude of woman, and amuse his imagination in the pursuit of honour and glory.

After these admonitions, he abused his ears with a forged detail of the gradual advances made to him by Monimia, and the steps he had taken to discourage her addresses, and re-establish her virtue; poisoning the mind of that credulous youth to such a degree, that in all probability he would have put a fatal period to his own existence, had not Fathom found means to allay the rage of his extasy, by the cunning arrangement of opposite considerations. He set his pride against his love, he opposed his resentment to his sorrow, and his ambition to his despair. Notwithstanding the ballance of power, so settled among these antagonists, so violent were the shocks of their successive conflicts, that his bosom fared like a wretched province harrassed, depopulated, and laid waste, by two fierce contending armies. From this moment, his life was nothing but an alternation of starts and reveries; he wept and raved by turns, according to the prevailing gust of passion; food became a stranger to his lips, and sleep to his eye-lids; he could not support the presence of Monimia; her absence increased the torture of his pangs; and when he met her by accident, he started back with horror, like a traveller who chances to tread upon a snake.

The poor afflicted orphan, worn to a shadow with self-consuming anguish, eager to find some lowly retreat, where she could breathe out her soul in peace, and terrified at the frantic behaviour of Renaldo, communicated to Fathom her desire of removing, and begged that he would take a small picture of her father, decorated with diamonds, and convert them into money for the expence of her subsistence. This was the last pledge of her family, which she had received from her mother, who had preserved it in the midst of numberless distresses; and no other species of misery, but that which she groaned under, could have prevailed upon the daughter to part with it: But exclusive of other motives, the very image itself, by recalling to her mind the honours of her name, upbraided her with living in dependence upon a man, who had treated her with such indignity and ingratitude; besides, she flattered herself with the hope that she should not long survive the loss of this testimonial.

Our adventurer, with many professions of sorrow and mortification at his own want of capacity, to prevent such an alienation, undertook to dispose of it to the best advantage, and to provide her with a cheap and retired apartment, to which he would conduct her in safety, tho' at the hazard of his life. In the mean time, however, he repaired to his friend Renaldo; and after having admonished him to arm his soul with patience and philosophy, declared that Monimia's guilty passion for himself, could no longer be kept within bounds: that she had conjured him, in the most pressing manner, to assist her in escaping from an house which she considered as the worst of dungeons, because she was in it daily exposed to the sight and company of a man whom she detested; and that she had bribed him to compliance with her request, not only with repeated promises of eternal love and submission, but also with the picture of her father set with diamonds, which she had hitherto reserved as the last and greatest testimony of her affection and esteem.

With these words, he presented the fatal pledge[3] to the eyes of the astonished youth, upon whom it operated like the poisonous sight of the basilisk;[4] for, in an instant, the whole passions of his soul were in the most violent agitation. "What! (cried he, in an extasy of rage) is she so abandoned to perfidy, so lost to shame, so damned to constancy, to gratitude and virtuous love, as to meditate the means of leaving me without decency, without remorse! to forsake me in my adversity, when my hapless fortune can no longer flatter the pride and vanity of her expectation! O woman! woman! woman! what simile shall I find to illustrate the character of the sex; but I will not have recourse to vain complaints and feeble exclamations. By heaven! she shall not scape; she shall not triumph in her levity—she shall not exult in my distress: No! I will rather sacrifice her to my just resentment, to the injured powers of love and friendship. I will act the avenging minister of heaven![5] I will mangle that fair bosom which contains so false an heart! I will tear her to pieces, and scatter those beauteous limbs, as a prey to the beasts of the field, and the fowls of the air!"[6]

Fathom, who expected this storm, far from attempting to oppose its progress, waited with patience until its first violence was overblown, then assuming an air of condolance, animated with that resolution which a friend ought to maintain on such occasions: "My dear count (said he) I am not at all surprized at your emotion, because I know what an heart, susceptible as yours, must feel, from the apostacy of one who has reigned so long the object of your love, admiration, and esteem. Your endeavours to drive her from your thoughts, must create an agony much more severe, than that which divorces the soul from the body. Nevertheless, I am so confident of your virtue and your manhood, as to foresee that you will allow the frail Monimia to execute that resolution which she hath so unwisely taken to withdraw herself from your love and protection. Believe me, my best friend and benefactor, this is a step, in consequence of which you will infallibly retrieve your peace of mind. It may cost you many bitter pangs, it may probe your wounds to the quick; but those pangs will be soothed by the gentle and salutary wing of time, and that probing will rouse you to a due sense of your own dignity and importance, which will enable you to convert your attention to objects far more worthy of your contemplation. All the hopes of happiness you had cherished in the possession of Monimia, are now irrecoverably blasted; her heart is now debased beneath your consideration; her love is, without all doubt, extinguished, and her honour irretrievably lost; insomuch, that were she to profess sorrow for her indiscretion, and implore your forgiveness, with the most solemn promises of regarding you for the future with unalterable fidelity and affection, you ought not to restore her to that place in your heart which she hath so meanly forfeited; because you could not at the same time reinstate her in the possession of that delicate esteem without which there is no harmony, no rapture, no true enjoyment in love. No, my dear Renaldo, expel the unworthy tenant from your bosom; allow her to fill up the measure of her ingratitude, by deserting her lover, friend and benefactor. Your glory demands her dismission; the world will applaud your generosity, and your own heart approve of your conduct: So disincumbered, let us exert ourselves once more in promoting your departure from this island, that you may revisit your father's house, do justice to your self and amiable sister, and take vengeance on the author of your wrongs; then dedicate yourself to glory, in imitation of your renowned ancestors, and flourish in the favour of your imperial patron."

These remonstrances had such effect upon the Hungarian, that his face was lighted up with a transient gleam of satisfaction; he embraced Ferdinand with great ardour, calling him his pride, his Mentor,[7] his good genius, and intreated him to gratify the inclination of that fickle creature, so far as to convey her to another lodging, without loss of time, while he would, by absenting himself, favour their retreat.

Our hero having obtained this permission, went immediately to the skirts[8] of the town, where he had previously bespoke a small, tho' neat apartment, at the house of an old woman, widow of a French refugee: he had already reconnoitred the ground, by sounding his landlady, from whose poverty and complaisance he found reason to expect all sorts of freedom and opportunity for the accomplishment of his aim upon Monimia's person. The room being prepared for her reception, he returned to that disconsolate beauty, to whom he presented ten guineas, which he pretended to have raised by pledging the picture; though he himself acted as the pawn-broker on this occasion, for a very plain and obvious reason.

The fair orphan was overjoyed to find her wish so speedily accomplished: she forthwith packed up her necessaries in a trunk; and an hackney-coach was called in the dusk of the evening, in which she imbarked with her baggage and conductor.

Yet she did not leave the habitation of Renaldo without regret. In the instant of parting, the idea of that unfortunate youth was associated with every well known object that presented itself to her eyes; not as an inconstant, ungenerous and perjured swain, but as the accomplished, the virtuous, the melting lover, who had captivated her virgin heart. As Fathom led her to the door, she was met by Renaldo's dog, which had long been her favourite, and the poor animal fawning upon her as she passed, her heart was overwhelmed with such a gush of tenderness, that a flood of tears streamed down her cheeks, and she had well nigh sunk upon the floor.

Ferdinand considering this emotion as the last tribute she would pay to Renaldo, hurried her into the coach, where she soon recovered her composure; and in a little time he ushered her into the house of madam la Mer,⁹ by whom she was received with great cordiality, and conducted to her apartment, with which she found no other fault, but that of its being too good for one in her forlorn situation: here, while the tear of gratitude started in either eye, she thanked our adventurer for his benevolence and kind concern, assuring him, that she would not fail daily to beseech the Most High to shower down blessings upon him, as the orphan's friend and protector.

Fathom was not deficient in those expressions that were best adapted to her present turn of mind: he observed, that what he had done, was in obedience to the dictates of common humanity, which would have prompted him to assist any fellow-creature in distress; but that her peculiar virtue and qualifications were such as challenged the utmost exertion of his faculties in her service: he said, that surely Heaven had not created such perfection in vain; that she was destined to receive as well as to communicate happiness; and that the Providence which she so piously adored, would not fail, in due season, to raise her from distress and affliction, to that honour and felicity for which she was certainly ordained: in the mean time he intreated her to depend upon his service and fidelity, and the article of her board being settled, he left her to the company and consolation of her discreet hostess, who soon insinuated herself into the good opinion of her beauteous lodger.

While our hero was employed in this transaction, Renaldo sallied forth in a sort of intoxication, which Fathom's admonitions had inspired; and repairing to a certain noted coffee-house,¹⁰ engaged at chess with an old French refugee, that his attention, by being otherwise employed, might not stray towards that fatal object which he ardently wished to forget. But, unluckily for him, he had scarce performed three moves of the game, when his ears were exposed to a dialogue between two young gentlemen; one of whom asked the other if he would go and see the Orphan acted at one of the theatres; observing, as a farther inducement, that the part of Monimia would be performed by a young gentlewoman who had never appeared on the stage.[11] At mention of that name Renaldo started: for, tho' it did not properly belong to his orphan, it was the appellation by which she had been distinguished ever since her separation from her father's house; and therefore, it recalled her to his imagination in the most interesting point of view. Though he endeavoured to expel the image, by a closer application to his play, every now and then it intruded upon his fancy, and at each return made a stronger impression; so that he found himself in the situation of an unfortunate bark stranded upon some hidden rock, which, when the wind begins to blow, feels every succeeding wave more boisterous than the former, until, with irresistible fury, they surmount her decks, sweep every thing before them, and dash her all to pieces.

The refugee had observed his first emotion, which he attributed to an unforeseen advantage he himself had gained over the Hungarian: but seeing him, in the sequel, bite his lip, roll his eyes, groan, writhe his body, ejaculate incoherent curses, and neglect his game, the Huguenot[12] concluded, that he was mad; and, being seized with terror and dismay, got up and scampered off without ceremony or hesitation.

Melvil, thus left to the horrors of his own thought, which tortured him with the apprehension of losing Monimia for ever, could no longer combat that suggestion, but ran homewards with all the speed he could exert, in order to prevent her retreat. When he crossed the threshold, he was struck with such a damp[13] of presaging fear, that he durst not in person approach her apartment, nor even, by questioning the servant, inform himself of the particulars he wanted to know: yet his suspence becoming more insupportable than his fear, he rushed from room to room in quest of that which was not to be found; and, seeing Monimia's chamber-door open, entered the deserted temple in a state of distraction, calling aloud upon her name. All was silent, solitary, and woful, "She is gone—(he cried, shedding a flood of tears)—she is for ever lost; and all my hopes of happiness are fled!"

So saying, he sunk upon that couch on which Monimia had oft reposed, and abandoned himself to all the excess of grief and despondence. In this deplorable condition he was found by our adventurer, who gently chid him for his want of resolution, and again repelled his sorrow, by arousing his resentment against the innocent cause of his disquiet, having before hand forged the particulars of provocation. "Is it possible," said he, "that Renaldo can still retain the least sentiment of regard for a fickle woman, by whom he has been so ungratefully forsaken and so unjustly scorned? Is it possible he

can be so disturbed by the loss of a creature who is herself lost to all virtue
and decorum?—Time and reflection, my worthy friend, will cure you of that
inglorious malady: and the future misconduct of that imprudent damsel will,
doubtless, contribute to the recovery of your peace. Her behaviour at leaving
the house where she had received so many marks of the most delicate affection, was in all respects so opposite to honour and decency, that I could
scarce refrain from telling her I was shocked at her deportment, even while
she loaded me with protestations of love. When a woman's heart is once
depraved, she bids adieu to all restraint;—she preserves no measures. It was
not simply contempt which she expressed for Renaldo; she seems to resent
his being able to live under her disdain; and that resentment stoops to objects
unworthy of indignation. Even your dog was not exempted from the effects
of her displeasure: for, in her passage to the door, she kicked the poor animal
as one of your dependants; and in our way to the apartment I had provided
for her, she entertained me with a ludicrous comment upon the manner in
which you first made her acquainted with your passion. All that modesty of
carriage, all that chastity of conversation, all that dignity of grief, which she
knew so well how to affect, is now entirely laid aside, and when I quitted her,
she seemed the most gay, giddy and impertinent of her sex."

"Gracious powers! (exclaimed Renaldo, starting from the couch) am I under the delusion of a dream; or are these things really so, as my friend has
represented them? Such a total and sudden degeneracy is amazing! is monstrous and unnatural!"——"Such, my dear Count," replied our hero, "is the
caprice of a female heart, fickle as the wind, uncertain as a calm at sea, fixed
to no principle, but swayed by every fantastic gust of passion, or of whim.
Congratulate yourself, therefore, my friend, upon your happy deliverance
from such a domestic plague—upon the voluntary exile of a traitor from your
bosom:—recollect the dictates of your duty, your discretion, and your glory,
and think upon the honours and elevated enjoyment for which you are certainly ordained. To night, let us over a chearful bottle anticipate your success; and tomorrow I will accompany you to the house of an usurer, who, I
am informed, fears no risk, provided twenty *per cent.* be given, and the borrower's life insured."

CHAPTER XLVII.

The art of borrowing further explained; and an
account of a strange phænomenon.

In this manner did the artful incendiary work upon the passions of the credulous unsuspecting Hungarian, who pressed him to his breast with the most cordial expressions of friendship, calling him his guardian, his saviour, his second father, and gave himself up wholly to his advice.

Next morning, according to the plan they had laid over night, they repaired to a tavern in the neighbourhood of the person to whom our adventurer had been directed, and were fortunate enough to find him in the house, transacting a money affair with a young gentleman who treated him with his morning's whet.[1]

That affair being negotiated, he adjourned into another room with Renaldo and his companion, who were not a little surprised to see this minister of Plutus[2] in the shape of a young sprightly beau, trimmed up in all the foppery of the fashion; for they had hitherto always associated with the idea of an usurer, old age and rusty apparel. After divers modish congees,[3] he begged to know to what he should attribute the honour of their message; when Ferdinand, who acted the orator, told him, that his friend Count Melvil, having occasion for a sum of money, had been directed to a gentleman of his name, "and I suppose," added he, "you are the son of the person with whom the affair is to be negotiated."

"Sir," said this *petit maitre*,[4] with a smile, "I perceive you are surprised to see one of my profession in the appearance of a gentleman; and perhaps your wonder will not cease, when I tell you, that my education was liberal, and that I once had the honour to bear a commission in the British army. I was indeed a first lieutenant of marines, and will venture to say, that no officer in the service was more delicate than myself, in observing all the punctilios of honour. I entertained the utmost contempt for all the trading part of the nation, and suffered myself to be run through the body in a duel, rather than roll[5] with a brother-lieutenant who was a broker's son: but, thank Heaven! I have long ago conquered all those ridiculous prejudices. I soon observed, that without money there was no respect, honour, or convenience to be acquired in life; that wealth amply supplied the want of wit, merit and pedigree, having influence and pleasure ever at command; and that the world never failed to worship the flood of affluence, without examining the dirty channels thro' which it commonly flowed.

At the end of the war, finding my appointments reduced to two shillings and four-pence *per* day, and being addicted to pleasures which I could not possibly purchase from such a fund, I sold my half-pay[6] for two hundred pounds, which I lent upon bond to a young officer of the same regiment, on condition that he should insure his life, and restore one fourth part of the sum by way of premium. I happened to be lucky in this first essay: for the borrower, having in six weeks expended the money, made an excursion on the high-way, was apprehended, tried, convicted of felony, and cut his own throat, to prevent the shame of a public execution; so that his bond was discharged by the insurers.

In short, gentlemen, when I engaged in this business, I determined to carry it on with such spirit, as would either make my fortune, or entirely ruin me in a little time; and hitherto my endeavours have been tolerably successful:[7] nor do I think my proceedings a whit more criminal or unjust, than those of other merchants, who strive to turn their money to the best account. The commodity I deal in is cash; and it is my business to sell it to the best advantage. A London factor sends a cargo of goods to market, and if he gets two hundred *per cent.* upon the sale, he is commended for his industry and address. If I sell money for one fourth part of that profit, certain persons will be so unjust, as to cry, Shame upon me, for taking such advantage of my neighbour's distress: not considering, that the trader took four times the same advantage of those people who bought his cargo, tho' his risque was not half so great as mine; and although the money I sold, perhaps retrieved the borrower from the very jaws of destruction: for example, it was but yesterday I saved a worthy man from being arrested for a sum of money, for which he had bailed a friend who treacherously left him in the lurch: as he did not forsee what would happen, he had made no provision for the demand, and his sphere of life secluding him from all sorts of money'd intercourse, he could not raise the cash by his credit in the usual way of borrowing; so that, without my assistance, he must have gone to jail; a disgrace which would have proved fatal to the peace of his family, and utterly ruined his reputation.—Nay, that very young gentleman from whom I just now parted, will, in all probability, be indebted to me for a very genteel livelihood. He had obtained the absolute promise of being provided for, by a great man, who sits at the helm of affairs in a neighbouring kingdom; but being destitute of all other resources, he could not have equipped himself for the voyage, in order to profit by his lordship's intention, unless I had enabled him to pursue his good fortune."

Renaldo was not a little pleased to hear this harrangue, to which Fathom replied with many florid encomiums upon the usurer's good sense and humane disposition: then he explained the errand of his friend, which was to borrow three hundred pounds, in order to retrieve his inheritance, of which he had been defrauded in his absence.

"Sir, (said the lender, addressing himself to Count Melvil), I pretend to have acquired by experience some skill in physiognomy; and tho' there are some faces so deeply disguised as to baffle all the penetration of our art, there are others, in which the heart appears with such nakedness of integrity, as at once to recommend it to our good will.—I own your countenance prepossesses me in your favour; and you shall be accommodated, upon those terms from which I never deviate, provided you can find proper security, that you shall not quit the British dominions, for that, with me, is a condition *sine qua non*."[8]

This was a very disagreeable declaration to Renaldo, who candidly owned, that as his concerns lay upon the continent, his purpose was to leave England without delay. The usurer professed himself sorry that it was not in his power to oblige him; and, in order to prevent any farther importunity, assured them, he had laid it down as a maxim, from which he would never swerve, to avoid all dealings with people whom (if need should be) he could not sue by the laws of this realm.

Thus the intervention of one unlucky and unforeseen circumstance blasted, in an instant, the budding hopes of Melvile, who, while his visage exhibited the most sorrowful disappointment, begged to know, if there was any person of his acquaintance, who might be less scrupulous in that particular.

The young gentleman directed them to another member of his profession, and wishing them success, took his leave with great form and complaisance. This instance of politeness was, however, no more than a shift to disingage himself the more easily from their intreaties: for, when the case was opened to the second usurer, he blessed himself[9] from such customers, and dismissed them with the most mortifying and boorish refusal. Notwithstanding these repulses, Renaldo resolved to make one desperate push; and, without allowing himself the least respite, sollicited, one by one, not fewer than fifteen persons who dealt in this kind of traffic, and his proposals were rejected by each. At last, fatigued by the toil, and exasperated at the ill success of his expedition; and half mad with the recollection of his finances, which were now drained to half a crown, "Since we have nothing to expect," cried he, "from the favour of christians, let us have recourse to the descendants of Judah.[10] Tho' they lie under the general reproach of nations, as a people dead to virtue and benevolence, and wholly devoted to avarice, fraud, and extortion,[11] the most savage of their tribe cannot treat me with more barbarity of indifference, than I have experienced among those who are the authors of their reproach."

Although Fathom looked upon this proposal as an extravagant symptom of despair, he affected to approve of the scheme, and encouraged Renaldo with the hope of succeeding in another quarter, even if this expedition should fail: for, by this time, our adventurer was half resolved to export him at his own charge, rather than he should be much longer restricted in his designs upon Monimia.

Mean while, being resolved to try the experiment upon the children of Israel, they betook themselves to the house of a rich Jew, whose wealth they considered as a proof of his rapaciousness; and, being admitted into his compting-house, they found him, in the midst of half a dozen clerks, when Renaldo, in his imagination, likened him unto a minister of darkness surrounded by his familiars, and planning schemes of misery to be executed upon the hapless sons of men. In spite of these suggestions, which were not at all mitigated by the forbidding aspect of the Hebrew, he demanded a private audience; and, being ushered into another apartment, he explained his business with manifest marks of disorder and affliction. Indeed his confusion was in some measure owing to the looks of the Jew, who in the midst of his exordium pulled down his eye-brows, which were surprisingly black and bushy, so as, in appearance, totally to extinguish his vision, tho' he was all the time observing our youth from behind those almost impenetrable thickets.

Melvil having signified his request, "Young gentleman, (said the Israelite, with a most discordant voice), what in the name of goodness, could induce you to come to me, upon such an errand? Did you ever hear that I lent money to strangers, without security?" "No," replied Renaldo; "nor did I believe I should profit by my application: but my affairs are desperate; and my proposals having been rejected by every Christian to whom they were offered, I was resolved to try my fate among the Jews, who are reckoned another species of men."

Fathom, alarmed at this abrupt reply, which he supposed could not fail to disgust the merchant, interposed in the conversation, by making an apology for the plain dealing of his friend, who, he said, was soured and ruffled by his misfortunes: then exerting that power of eloquence which he had at command, he expostulated upon Renaldo's claim and expectations, described the wrongs he had suffered, extolled his virtue, and drew a most pathetic picture of his distress.

The Jew listened attentively for some time; then his eye-brows began to rise and fall alternately; he cough'd, sneez'd, and winking hard, "I'm plagued," said he, "with a salt rheum that trickles from my eyes without intermission."[12] So saying, he wiped the moisture from his face, and proceeded in these words: "Sir, your story is plausible; and your friend is a good advocate: but, before I give an answer to your demand, I must beg leave to ask if you can produce undeniable evidence of your being the identical person you really assume. If you are really the Count de Melvil, you will excuse my caution: we cannot be too much on our guard against fraud; tho' I must own you have not the air of an impostor."

Renaldo's eyes began to sparkle at this preliminary question; to which he replied, that he could procure the testimony of the Emperor's minister, to whom he had occasionally paid his respects since his first arrival in England.

"If that be the case," said the Jew, "take the trouble to call here to-morrow morning at eight o'clock, and I will carry you in my own coach to the house of his excellency, with whom I have the honour to be acquainted; and, if he has nothing to object against your character, or pretensions, I will contribute my assistance towards your obtaining justice at the imperial court."

The Hungarian was so much confounded at this unexpected reception, that he had not power to thank the merchant for his promised favour, but stood motionless and silent, while the streams of gratitude ran down his cheeks. This genuine emotion of the heart was of more weight with the Jew, than the eloquent acknowledgment which Ferdinand took the opportunity of making for his friend; and he was fain to dismiss them a little abruptly, in order to prevent a second discharge of that same rheum of which he had already complained.

Melvil recollected all that had happened as a dream, which had no foundation in truth, and was all day long in a sort of delirium, produced by the alternate gusts of hope and fear that still agitated his bosom: for he was not yet without apprehension of being again disappointed by some unlucky occurrence.

He did not, however, fail to be punctual to the hour of his appointment, when the Jew told him, there would be no occasion for visiting the ambassador, because Renaldo had been, the preceding day, recognised by one of the clerks who had been employed as a purveyor in the imperial army; and who, knowing his family, confirmed every thing he had alledged. "After breakfast," continued this benevolent Israelite, "I will give you an order upon my banker for five hundred pounds, that you may be enabled to appear at Vienna, as the son and representative of Count Melvil; and you shall also be furnished with a letter of recommendation to a person of some influence at that court, whose friendship and countenance may be of some service to your suit: for I am now heartily engaged in your interest, in consequence of the fair and unblemished character which I find you have hitherto maintained."

The reader must appeal to his own heart, to acquire a just idea of Renaldo's feelings, when every tittle of these promises was fulfilled, and the merchant refused to take one farthing by way of premium, contenting himself with the slender security of a personal bond. He was, in truth, overwhelmed with the obligation, and certainly disposed to believe, that his benefactor was something more than human. As for Fathom, his sentiments took a different turn; and he scrupled not to impute all this kindness to some deep-laid interested scheme, the scope of which he could not at present comprehend.

After the tumults of the young gentleman's joy had subsided, and he found himself eased of that burthensome poverty, under which he had groaned so long; his thoughts, which before were dissipated upon the various circumstances of distress, began to collect themselves in a body, and to resume their deliberations upon a subject which they had been long accustomed to consider; this was no other than the forlorn Monimia, whose idea now emerged in his bosom, being disencumbered of one part of the load by which it had been depressed. He mentioned her name to Fathom, with marks of the most melting compassion, deplored her apostasy; and, while he protested that he had divorced her for ever from his heart, expressed an inclination to see her once more, before his departure, that he might in person exhort her to penitence and reformation.

Our adventurer, who dreaded such an interview as the infallible means of his own ruin, resisted the proposal with the whole power of his elocution. He affirmed, that Renaldo's desire was a manifest proof that he still retained part of the fatal poison which that inchantress had spread within his veins, and that the sight of her, softened by his reproaches into tears and affected contrition, would dispel his resentment, disable his manhood, and blow the embers of his former passion to such a rage, as would hurry him on to a reconciliation, which would debase his honour, and ruin his future peace. In a word, Ferdinand described the danger that would attend the meeting, in such emphatic terms, that the Hungarian started with horror at the picture which he drew, and in this particular conformed with the admonition of his friend.

One hundred pounds of the Jew's money was immediately appropriated for the payment of his most urgent debts; the like sum he presented to his friend Fathom, with a solemn promise of sharing with him whatever good fortune might await him in Germany: and tho' Monimia had forfeited all title to his regard, so ill could he bear the prospect of her distress, that he entrusted his dear companion with the half of what remained, to be expended for her use, fully resolving to screen her from the shocks and temptations of want, as the circumstances of his future fate would allow.

Fathom, far from opposing, applauded his generosity with marks of extreme wonder and admiration, assuring him, that she should be put in possession of his bounty, immediately after his departure, he being unwilling to make her acquainted with her good fortune before that period, lest finding his affairs in a fair way of being retrieved, she should be base enough to worship his returning prosperity, and, by false professions, and artful blandishments, seek to ensnare his heart anew.

CHAPTER XLVIII.

Count Fathom unmasks his battery; is repulsed;
and varies his operations without effect.

Every necessary preparation being made, Renaldo, accompanied by our adventurer, took the road to Dover, where he embarked in a packet boat for Calais, after having settled a correspondence with his dear Ferdinand, from whom he did not part without tears. He had before sollicited him to be his fellow-traveller, that he might personally enjoy the benefit of his conversation, and superior sagacity; but these intreaties he strenuously opposed, on pretence of his being determined to push his fortune in England, which he considered as his native country, and as the land in which (of all others) a man of merit has the best encouragement. Such were the reasons he alledged, for refusing to attend his benefactor, who was himself eagerly desirous of attaining a settlement in the island of Great Britain: but our hero's real motives for staying were of a very different complexion.—The reader is already informed of his aim upon the fair orphan, which, at present, was the chief spring of his conduct: he may also recollect such passages of his life, as were sufficient to deter him from re-appearing at Presburg or Vienna: but, besides these reflexions, he was detained by a full persuasion that Renaldo would sink under the power and influence of his antagonist, consequently be rendered incapable to provide for his friends; and that he himself, fraught with wiles and experience, as he was, could not fail to make himself amends for what he had suffered among a people equally rich and unthinking.

Melvil having embraced our adventurer, and with a deep sigh bid him take care of the unfortunate Monimia, committed himself to the sea, and, by the assistance of a favourable gale, was, in four hours, safely landed on the French shore; while Fathom took post-horses for London, where he arrived that same night, and next day, in the forenoon, went to visit the beauteous mourner, who had as yet received no intimation of Renaldo's departure or design. He found her in the attitude of writing a letter to her inconstant lover, the contents of which the reader will be acquainted with in due time. Her countenance, notwithstanding the veil of melancholy by which it was overcast, seemed altogether serene and composed; she was the picture of pious resignation, *and sat like* PATIENCE *on a monument, smiling at grief.*[1] After having paid the compliment of the morning, Fathom begged pardon for having omitted to visit her during three days, in which, he said, his time had been wholly engrossed in procuring a proper equipage for Count Melvil, who had at last bid an eternal adieu to the island of Great Britain.

At this information the hapless Monimia fell back in her chair, and continued some minutes in a swoon; from which being recovered, "Excuse me, Mr. Fathom (cried she, with a deep sigh); this, I hope, is the last agony I shall feel from my unhappy passion."—Then wiping the tears from her lovely eyes, she retrieved her tranquillity, and desired to know by what means Renaldo had been enabled to undertake his journey into the empire. Our hero, upon this occasion, assumed the whole merit of having promoted the interest of his friend, by giving her to understand, that he, in consequence of an unforeseen windfall had defrayed the expence of the Count's equipment; though he observed, that it was not without reluctance he saw Renaldo make a wrong use of his friendship.

"Although I was happy (proceeded this artful traitor) in being able to discharge my obligations to the house of Melvil, I could not help feeling the most sensible[2] chagrin, when I saw my assistance rendered subservient to the triumphs of the youth's baseness and infidelity; for he chose, as the companion of his travels, the abandoned woman, for whom he had forsaken the all-perfect Monimia, whose virtue and accomplishments did not preserve her sacred from his ungrateful sarcasms and unmannerly ridicule. Believe me, madam, I was so shocked at his conversation on that subject, and so much incensed at his want of delicacy, that my temper was scarce sufficient for the ceremony of parting: and now that my debt to his family is overpaid, I have solemnly renounced his correspondence."

When she heard that, instead of betraying the least symptom of regret or compassion for her unhappy fate, the perfidious youth had exulted over her fall, and even made her a subject for his mirth, the blood revisited her faded cheeks, and resentment restored to her eyes that poignancy which sorrow had before overcome. Yet she scorn'd to give speech to her indignation; but, forcing a smile, "Why should I repine," said she, "at the mortifications of a life which I despise, and from which, I hope, Heaven will speedily set me free!"

Fathom, fired by her emotion, which had recalled all the graces of her beauty, exclaimed in a rapture, "Talk not so contemptuously of this life, which hath still a fund of happiness in store for the amiable, the divine Monimia. Though one admirer hath proved an apostate to his vows, your candour will not suffer you to condemn the whole sex. Some there are, whose bosoms glow with passion equally pure, unalterable and intense. For my own part, I have sacrificed to a rigid punctilio of honour the dearest ideas of my heart. I beheld your unrivalled charms, and deeply felt their power: yet, while a possibility of Melvil's reformation remained, and while I was restrained by my niggard fortune, from making a tender worthy of your acceptance, I combated with my inclinations, and bore without repining the pangs of hopeless love. But, now that my honour is disengaged, and my fortune rendered independent, by the last will of a worthy nobleman, whose friendship I was favoured with in France, I presume to lay myself at the feet of the adorable Monimia, as the most faithful of admirers, whose happiness or misery wholly depends upon her nod. Believe me, Madam, these are not the professions of idle gallantry—I speak the genuine, though imperfect, language of my heart: words even the most pathetic cannot do justice to my love. I gaze upon your beauty with ravishment; but, I contemplate the graces of your soul with such awful veneration, that I tremble while I approach you, as if my vows were addressed to some superior being."

During this declaration, which was pronounced in the most emphatic manner, Monimia was successively agitated with shame, anger and grief; nevertheless, she summoned her whole philosophy to her aid, and with a tranquil, though determined air, begged he would not diminish the obligations he had already conferred, by disturbing with such unseasonable addresses, a poor unhappy maid, who had detached all her thoughts from earthly objects, and waited impatiently for that dissolution which alone could put a period to her misfortunes.

Fathom, imagining that these were no other than the suggestions of a temporary disappointment and despondence, which it was his business to oppose with all his eloquence and art, renewed his theme with redoubled ardour, and at last became so importunate in his desires, that Monimia, provoked beyond the power of concealing her resentment, said, she was heartily sorry to find herself under the necessity of telling him, that, in the midst of her misfortunes, she could not help remembering what she had been. Then rising from her seat with all the dignity of displeasure, "Perhaps," added she, "you have forgot who was the father of the once happy Monimia."[3]

With these words she retired into another chamber, leaving our adventurer confounded by the repulse he had sustained. Not that he was discouraged from prosecuting his aim: on the contrary, this rebuff seemed to add fresh vigour to his operations. He now thought it high time to bring over Madam la Mer to his interest; and, to facilitate her conversion, took an opportunity of bribing her with some inconsiderable presents, after having amused her with a plausible tale of his passion for Monimia, with whom she undertook the office of his mediatrix, on the supposition that his intentions were honourable and highly advantageous to her lodger.[4]

She was, first of all, invested with the office of obtaining pardon for the offence he had given; and in this negotiation she succeeded so well, as to become an advocate for his suit: accordingly, she took all occasions of magnifying his praise. His agreeable person was often the subject of her discourse to the fair mourner: her admiration dwelt upon his politeness, good sense and winning deportment: and she every day retailed little stories of his benevolence and greatness of soul. The defect in his birth she represented as a circumstance altogether foreign from the consideration of his merit; especially in a nation where such distinctions are as little respected as they will be in a future state. She mentioned several persons of note,[5] who basked in the sun-shine of power and fortune, without having enjoyed the least hereditary assistance from their fore-fathers. One, she said, sprung from the loins of an obscure attorney, another was the grandson of a valet de chambre, a third was the issue of an accomptant, and a fourth the offspring of an woolen-draper: all these were the children of their own good works, and had raised themselves upon their personal virtues and address; a foundation certainly more solid and honourable, than a vague inheritance derived from ancestors, in whose deserts they could not be supposed to have bore the least share.

Monimia listened to all these arguments with great patience and affability, though she at once dived into the source from which all such insinuations flowed: she joined in the commendations of Fathom, and owned herself a particular instance of that benevolence which the old lady had so justly extolled; but, once for all, to prevent the supplication which Madam la Mer was about to make, she solemnly protested, that her heart was altogether shut against any other earthly engagement; and that her thoughts were altogether employed upon her eternal salvation.

The assiduous landlady perceiving the steadiness of her disposition, thought proper to alter her method of proceeding, and, for the present suspended that theme by which she found her fair lodger disobliged. Resolved to reconcile Monimia to life, before she would again recommend Ferdinand to her love, she endeavoured to amuse her imagination, by recounting the occasional incidents of the day, hoping gradually to decoy her attention to those sublunary objects from which it had been industriously weaned: she seasoned her conversation with agreeable sallies; enlarged upon the different scenes of pleasure and diversion appertaining to this great metropolis; practised upon her palate, with the delicacies of eating; endeavoured to shake her temperance with repeated proffers and recommendations of certain cordials and restoratives which she alledged were necessary for the recovery of her health; and pressed her to make little excursions into the fields that skirt the town, for the benefit of air and exercise.

While this auxiliary plied the disconsolate Monimia on one hand, Fathom was not remiss on the other: he now seemed to have sacrificed his passion to her quiet; his discourse turned upon more indifferent subjects; he endeavoured to dispel her melancholy with arguments drawn from philosophy and religion: on some occasions, he displayed all his fund of good humour, with a view to beguile her sorrow; he importuned her to give him the pleasure of 'squiring her to some place of innocent entertainment; and, finally, insisted upon her accepting a pecuniary reinforcement to her finances, which he knew to be in a most consumptive condition.[6]

CHAPTER XLIX.

Monimia's honour is protected by the interposition of Heaven.

With that complacency and fortitude which were peculiar to herself, this hapless stranger resisted all those artful temptations. Her sustenance was barely such as exempted her from the guilt of being accessory to her own death; her drink was the simple element: she encouraged no discourse but that which turned upon the concerns of her immortal part; she never went abroad except in visits to a French chapel in the neighbourhood; she refused the proffered assistance of our adventurer with equal obstinacy and politeness, and with pleasure saw herself wasting towards that period of mortality which was the consummation of her wish. Yet her charms, far from melting away with her constitution, seemed to triumph over the decays of nature: her shape and features still retained that harmony for which they had always been distinguished: a mixture of majesty and sweetness diffused itself in her looks, and her feebleness added to that soft and feminine grace which attracts the sympathy, and engages the protection of every humane beholder. The associates, thus baffled in their attempts to excite her ideas of pleasure, again shifted their plan, and resolved to attack this forlorn beauty, on the side of fear and mortification.

Our adventurer became less frequent in his visits, and more indifferent in his language and deportment; while Madam la Mer gradually relaxed in that complacency and respect with which she had hitherto behaved towards her fair lodger. She even began to drop hints of disapprobation and reproach against this pattern of innocence and beauty, and at length grew bold enough to tell her, that her misfortunes could be attributed to nothing but her own obstinacy and pride; that she had been at great pains to disoblige the only person who was able and willing to raise her above dependance, and that if his protection should be withdrawn, she must be exposed to the utmost extremity of distress.

These insinuations, instead of producing the desired effect, inflamed the indignation of Monimia, who, in a most dignified stile of rebuke, chid her for her indelicacy and presumption, observing, that she could have no title to take such freedoms with lodgers, whose punctuality and regular deportment left her no room to complain. Notwithstanding this animated reply, she underwent the most deplorable anguish, when she reflected upon the insolence of this woman, from whose barbarity she had no resource; and seeing no other possibility of redress, than that of appealing to the good offices of Fathom, she conquered her reluctance so far, as to complain to him of Madam la Mer's incivility.

Pleased with this application, he gave her to understand, with very little ceremony or preamble, that it wholly depended upon herself, whether she should continue to be wretched, or be delivered at once from all her cares and perplexity; that, notwithstanding the disdain with which she had treated his addresses, he was still ready to lay himself and his fortune at her feet; and that if she should again reject the disinterested proposal, the whole world, and her own conscience, would charge upon herself, whatever calamities she might be subjected to in the sequel. Interpreting into a favourable hesitation her silence, which was the result of wrath and amazement, he proceeded to throw himself at her feet, and utter a romantic rhapsody, in the course of which, laying aside all that restraint which he had hitherto preserved, he seized her delicate hand, and pressed it to his lips; nay, so far did he forget himself on this occasion, that he caught the fair creature in his arms, and rudely ravished a kiss from those lips which he had before contemplated with the most distant reverence of desire.

Having thus broken down the fences of decorum, and being heated with transport, he, in all probability, would have acted the part of young Tarquin,[1] and violated, by force, that sacred shrine of honour, beauty, and unblemished truth, had not the wrath kindled by such an unexpected outrage, inspired her with strength and spirits sufficient to protect her virtue, and intimidate the ruffian who could offer violence to such perfection. She broke from his detested embrace, with surprising agility, and called aloud to her landlady for assistance; but that discreet matron was resolved to hear nothing, and Fathom's appetite being whetted to a most brutal degree of eagerness, "Madam, (said he) all opposition is vain: what you have refused to my intreaties, you shall yield to my power; and I am determined to force you to your own advantage."

So saying, he sprung towards her, with the most savage and impious intent, when this amiable heroine snatching up his sword, which lay upon a by-table, and unsheathing it instantaneously, presented the point to his breast,[2] and while her eyes glanced with intolerable keenness, "Villain! (cried she) the spirit of my father animates my bosom, and the vengeance of heaven shall not be frustrated." He was not so much affected by his bodily danger, as awe-struck at the manner of her address, and the appearance of her aspect, which seemed to shine with something supernatural, and actually disordered his whole faculties, insomuch that he retreated without attempting to make the least reply; and she having secured the door after his departure, sat down to ponder upon this shocking event.

Words are wanting to describe the accumulated horrors that took possession of her mind, when she thus beheld all her presaging fears realized, and found herself at the mercy of two wretches, who had now pulled off the mask, after having lost all sentiments of humanity. Common affliction was an agreeable reverie to what she suffered, deprived of her parents, exiled from her friends and country, reduced to the brink of wanting the most indispensable necessaries of life, in a foreign land, where she knew not one person to whose protection she could have recourse, from the inexpressible woes that environed her: she complained to heaven, that her life was protracted, for the augmentation of that misery which was already too severe to be endured; for she shuddered at the prospect of being utterly abandoned in the last stage of mortality, without one friend to close her eyes, or do the last offices of humanity to her breathless coarse. These were dreadful reflections to a young lady who had been born to affluence and splendor, trained up in all the elegance of education, by nature fraught with that sensibility which refines the sentiment and taste, and so tenderly cherished by her indulgent parents, that *they suffered not the winds of heaven to visit her face too roughly.*[3]

Having passed the night in such agony, she rose at day-break, and hearing the chapel bell toll for morning prayers, resolved to go to this place of worship, in order to implore the assistance of heaven: she no sooner opened her chamber door, with this intent, than she was met by Madam la Mer, who after having professed her concern for what had happened over night, and imputed Mr. Fathom's rudeness to the spirit of intoxication, by which she had never before seen him possessed, she endeavoured to dissuade Monimia from her purpose, by observing, that her health would be prejudiced by the cold morning air; but finding her determined, she insisted upon accompanying her to chapel, on pretence of respect, though, in reality, with a view to prevent the escape of her beauteous lodger. Thus attended, the hapless mourner entered the place, and according to the laudable hospitality of England, which is the only country in Christendom, where a stranger is not made welcome to the house of God;[4] this amiable creature, emaciated and enfeebled as she was, must have stood in a common passage, during the whole service, had not she been perceived by a humane gentlewoman, who, struck with her beauty and dignified air, and melted with sympathy, at the ineffable sorrow which was visible in her countenance, opened the pew in which she sat, and accommodated Monimia and her attendant: if she was captivated by her first appearance, she was not less affected by the deportment of her fair guest, which was the pattern of genuine devotion.

In a word, this good lady, who was a merchant's widow in opulent circumstances, was inflamed with a longing desire to know and befriend the amiable stranger, who, after service, turning about to thank her for her civility, Madam Clement,[5] with that frankness which is the result of true benevolence, told her, she was too much prepossessed in her favour, to let slip this opportunity of craving her acquaintance, and of expressing her inclination to alleviate (if possible) that affliction which was manifest in her looks.

Monimia, overwhelmed with gratitude and surprize, at this unexpected address, gazed upon the lady in silence, and when she repeated her tenders of service, could make no other reply to her goodness, than by bursting into a flood of tears: this was a species of eloquence, which did not pass unregarded by Madam Clement, who, while her own eyes were bedewed with the drops of sympathy and compassion, took the lovely orphan by the hand, and led her, without further ceremony, to her own coach, that stood waiting at the door, whither they were followed by Mrs. La Mer, who was so much confounded at the adventure, that she made no objections to the proposal of the lady who handed her lodger into the carriage; but retired, with all possible dispatch, to make Fathom acquainted with this unforeseen event.

Mean while, the agitation of Monimia, at this providential deliverance, was such as had well nigh destroyed her tender frame: the blood flushed and forsook her cheeks by turns; she trembled from head to foot, notwithstanding the consolatory assurances of Madam Clement, and, without being able to utter one word, was conducted to the house of that kind benefactress, where the violence of her transports overpowered her constitution, and she sunk down upon a couch in a swoon, from which she was not easily recovered. This affecting circumstance augmented the pity, and interested the curiosity of Madam Clement, who concluded there was something very extraordinary in the case of the stranger, to produce these agonies; and grew impatient to hear the particulars of her story.

Monimia no sooner retrieved the use of her faculties, than looking around, and observing with what humane concern her new hostess was employed in effecting her recovery, "Is this (said she) a flattering illusion of the brain? or am I really under the protection of some beneficent being, whom heaven hath inspired with generosity, to rescue an hapless stranger from the most forlorn state of misery and woe?" Her voice was, at all times, ravishingly sweet; and this exclamation was pronounced with such pathetic fervour, that Madam Clement clasped her in her arms, and kissing her with all the eagerness of maternal affection, "Yes, (cried she) fair creature, heaven hath bestowed upon me an heart to compassionate, and power, I hope, to lighten the burthen of your sorrows."

She then prevailed upon her to take some nourishment, and afterwards to recount the particulars of her fate; a task she performed with such accuracy and candour, that Madam Clement, far from suspecting her sincerity, saw truth and conviction in every circumstance of her tale; and having condoled her misfortunes, entreated her to forget them, or, at least, look upon herself as one sheltered under the care and tuition of a person, whose study it would be to supply her want of natural parents. This would have been an happy vicissitude of fortune, had it not arrived too late; but such a sudden and unlooked-for transition, not only disordered the faculties of poor Monimia's mind, but also overpowered the organs of her body, already fatigued and enfeebled by the distresses she had undergone; so that she was taken ill of a fever that same night, and became delirious before morning, when a physician was called to her assistance.

While this gentleman was in the house, Madam Clement was visited by

Fathom, who after having complained, in the most insinuating manner, that she had encouraged his wife to abandon her duty, told her a plausible story of his first acquaintance with Monimia, and his marriage at the Fleet,[6] which, he said, he was ready to prove, by the evidence of the clergyman who joined them, and that of Mrs. la Mer, who was present at the ceremony. The good lady, although a little staggered at the genteel appearance, and engaging address of this stranger, could not prevail upon herself to believe that she had been imposed upon by her fair lodger, who, by this time, had given too convincing a proof of her sincerity; nevertheless, in order to prevent any dispute that might be prejudicial to the health or recovery of Monimia, she gave him to understand, that she would not, at present, enter upon the merits of the cause, but only assure him, that the young lady was actually bereft of her senses, and in imminent danger of her life: for the truth of which assertions she would appeal to his own observation, and the opinion of the physician, who was then employ'd in writing a prescription for the cure of her disease.

So saying, she conducted him into the chamber, where he beheld the hapless virgin stretched upon a sick bed, panting under the violence of a distemper too mighty for her weakly frame, her hair dishevelled, and discomposure in her looks; all the roses of her youth were faded, yet all the graces of her beauty were not fled: she retained that sweetness and symmetry, which death itself could not destroy; and though her discourse was incoherent, her voice was still musical, resembling those feathered songsters who *warble their native wood-notes wild.*[7]

Fathom, as upon all other occasions, so on this, did behave like an inimitable actor; he ran to the bed-side, with all the trepidation of a distracted lover; he fell upon his knees, and while the tears rolled down his cheeks, imprinted a thousand kisses on the soft hand of Monimia, who regarding him with a lack lustre, and undistinguishing eye, "Alas! Renaldo, (said she) we were born to be unhappy." "Would to heaven! (cried Ferdinand, in a transport of grief) the wretch Renaldo had never been born! that is the villain who seduced the affection of this unfortunate woman. I admitted the traitor into my friendship and confidence, relieved him in his necessities; and, like the ungrateful viper, he hath stung the very bosom that cherished him in his distress." Then he proceeded to inform Madam Clement, how he had delivered that same Renaldo from prison, maintained him afterwards at a great expence, and, at length, furnished him with a sum of money, and proper credentials to support his interest at the court of Vienna.

Having finished this detail, he asked the physician's sentiments of his wife's distemper, and being told, that her life was in extreme jeopardy, begged he would use his utmost endeavours in her behalf, and even made him a tender of an extraordinary fee; which was refused: he also thanked Madam Clement for her charity and benevolence towards a stranger, and took his leave, with many polite professions of gratitude and esteem. He had no sooner quitted the house, than the physician, who was a humane man, and a foreigner, began to caution the lady against his insinuations, observing, that some circumstances of the story concerning Renaldo, were, to his particular knowledge, contrary to truth: for that he himself had been applied to, for letters of recommendation, in behalf of count Melvil, by a Jew merchant of his acquaintance, who had supplied the young gentleman with money sufficient for his occasions, in consequence of a minute inquiry he had made into the character of Renaldo, who was, by all reports, a youth of strict honour, and untainted morals.

Madam Clement, thus cautioned, entered into deliberation with her own thoughts, and comparing the particulars of this account with those of Monimia's own story, she concluded, that Fathom was the very traitor he himself had described; and that he had, by abusing the confidence of both, effected a fatal breach between two innocent and deserving lovers. She accordingly looked upon him with horror and detestation; but, nevertheless resolved to treat him with civility in the mean time, that the poor young lady might not be disturbed in her last moments; for she had now lost all hopes of her recovery. Yet the fever abated, and in two days she retrieved the use of her reason: though the distemper had affected her lungs, and she was in all appearance doomed to linger a few weeks longer in a consumption.

Fathom was punctual in his visitation, though never admitted into her presence after the delirium vanished; and he had the opportunity of seeing her conveyed in a chariot to Kensington Gravel-pits,[8] a place which may be termed the last stage of many a mortal peregrination. He now implicitly believed, that death would in a few days baffle all his designs upon the unfortunate Monimia; and foreseeing, that, as he had owned himself her husband, he might be obliged to defray the expence incurred by her sickness and burial, he very prudently intermitted in his visits, and had recourse to the intelligence of his auxiliary.

As for Monimia, she approached the goal of life; not simply with resignation, but with rapture: she enjoyed, in tranquillity, the conversation of her kind benefactress, who never stirred from her apartment; she was blessed with the spiritual consolation of a worthy clergyman, who removed all her religious scruples; and she congratulated herself on the near prospect of that land of peace where sorrow is not known.

At length Mrs. la Mer gave notice to our adventurer of this amiable young lady's decease, and the time fixed for the interment: upon which these two

virtuous associates took possession of a place, from whence they could, unperceived, behold the funeral. He must have a hard heart, who, without an
emotion of pity, can see the last offices performed to a young creature cut off
in the flower of youth and beauty, even tho' he knows not her name, and is an
utter stranger to her virtues.—How callous then must the soul of that wretch
have been, who, without a symptom of remorse or concern, saw the sable
hearse adorned with white plumes, as emblems of Monimia's purity, pass
before him, while her incomparable merit stood full in his remembrance, and
he knew himself the wicked cause of her untimely fate!

Perfidious wretch! thy crimes turn out so attrocious, that I half repent me
of having undertaken to record thy memoirs: yet such monsters ought to be
exhibited to public view,[9] that mankind may be upon their guard against
imposture; that the world may see how fraud is apt to overshoot itself: and
that, as virtue, though it may suffer for a while, will triumph in the end; so
iniquity, though it may prosper for a season, will at last be overtaken by that
punishment and disgrace which are its due.

CHAPTER L.

*Fathom shifts the scene, and appears in a new
character.*

Fathom's expectations, with respect to the fair orphan, having thus proved
abortive, he lost no time in bewailing his miscarriage, but had immediate
recourse to other means of improving his small fortune, which, at this period,
amounted to near two hundred pounds. Whatever inclination he had to resume the character he had formerly bore in the polite world, he durst not
venture to launch out again into the expence necessary to maintain that station, because his former resources were now stopt, and all the people of
fashion, by this time, convinced of his being a needy adventurer. Nevertheless, he resolved to sound the sentiments of his old friends at a distance, and
judge, from the reception he should meet with, how far he might presume
upon their countenance and favour: for he rightly supposed, that, if he could
in any shape contribute to their interest or amusement, they would easily
forgive his former pretensions to quality, arrogant as they were, and still
entertain him on the footing of a necessary acquaintance.

With this view, he one day presented himself at court in a very gay suit of
cloaths, and bowed, at a distance, to many of his old fashionable friends of

both sexes, not one of whom favoured him with any other notice, than that of a quarter curt'sy, or slight inclination of the head: for, by this time, the few that remembered him knew from what retirement he now emerged, and avoided him accordingly as the jail infection:[1] but the greater part of those who had cultivated him in the zenith of his fortune, were now utter strangers to his person, which they had actually forgot, amidst the succession of novelties that surrounded them; or, if they did recollect his name, it was remembered as an old fashion which had been many months out of date.

Notwithstanding these mortifying discouragements, our hero, that same evening, effected a lodgement in a certain gaming-house[2] not far from St. James's; and, as he played pretty high, and made a parade of his ready money, he was soon recognized by divers persons of consequence, who cordially welcomed him to England, on pretence of believing he had been abroad, and with great complacency, repeated their former professions of friendship. Though this was a certain way of retaining the favour of those worthies, while his finances continued to flourish, and his payments were prompt, he knew the weakness of his funds too well, to think they could bear the vicissitudes of play; and the remembrance of the two British Knights who had spoiled him at Paris, hung over his imagination with the most frightful presages: besides, he perceived that gaming was now managed in such a manner, as rendered skill and dexterity of no advantage: for the spirit of play having overspread the land, like a pestilence,[3] raged to such a degree of madness and desperation, that the unhappy people who were infected, laid aside all thoughts of amusement, œconomy or caution, and risqued their fortunes upon issues equally extravagant, childish, and absurd.

The whole mystery of the art was reduced to the simple exercise of tossing up a guinea, and the lust of laying wagers, which they indulged to a surprising pitch of ridiculous intemperance. In one corner of the room might be heard a pair of lordlings running their grandmothers against each other, that is, betting sums on the longest liver; in another, the success of the wager depended upon the sex of the landlady's next child; and one of the waiters happening to drop down in an apoplectic fit, a certain noble peer exclaimed, "Dead for a thousand pounds." The challenge was immediately accepted; and when the master of the house sent for a surgeon to attempt the cure, the nobleman who set the price upon the patient's head, insisted upon his being left to the efforts of nature alone, otherwise the wager should be void: nay, when the landlord harped upon the loss he should sustain by the death of a trusty servant, his lordship obviated the objection, by desiring that the fellow might be charged in the bill.

In short, the rage of gaming seemed to have devoured all their other faculties, and to have equalled the rash enthusiasm of the inhabitants of Malacca in the East-Indies,[4] who are so possessed with that pernicious spirit, that they sacrifice to it not only their fortunes, but also their wives and children; and then letting their hair down upon their shoulders, in imitation of the ancient Lacedemonians when they devoted themselves to death, those wretches unsheath their daggers and murder every living creature in their way.[5] In this, however, they differ from the gamesters of our country, who never find their senses, until they have lost their fortune, and beggared their families; whereas, the Malayse never *run a muck*,[6] but in consequence of misery and despair.

Such are the amusements, or rather, such is the continual employment of those hopeful youths who are destined by birth to be the judges of our property, and pillars of our constitution: such are the heirs and representatives of those patriots who planned, and those heroes who maintained the laws and freedom of their country; who were the patrons of merit, the fathers of the poor, the terror of vice and immorality, and, at once, the ornaments and support of an happy nation.

Our adventurer considered all these circumstances with his wonted sagacity, and seeing upon what precarious footing he must stand, should he rank himself with such society, he wisely came to the resolution of descending one step in the degrees of life, and of taking upon him the title of physician, under which he did not despair of insinuating himself into the pockets of his patients, and into the secrets of private families, so as to acquire a comfortable share of practice, or captivate the heart of some heiress or rich widow, whose fortune would, at once, render him independent and happy.

After this determination, his next care was, to concert measures for his first appearance in this new character; well knowing, that the success of a physician, in a great measure, depends upon the external equipage in which he first declares himself an adept in the healing art. He first of all procured a few books on the subject of medicine, which he studied with great attention, during the remaining part of the winter and spring, and repaired to Tunbridge[7] with the first of the season, where he appeared in the uniform of Æsculapius, namely, a plain suit full trimm'd, with a voluminous tye periwig;[8] believing that, in this place, he might glide, as it were, imperceptibly, into the functions of his new employment, and gradually accustom himself to the method and form of prescription.

A man so well known in the gay world could not be supposed to effect such a transformation, without being observed; and therefore, in order to anticipate the censure and ridicule of those who might be tempted to make themselves merry at his expence, he, on his arrival at the wells, repaired to the shop of an apothecary, and, calling for pen, ink and paper, wrote a prescription, which he desired might be immediately made up. While this was doing by the servant, he was invited into a parlour by the master, with whom he entered into conversation, touching the properties of the Tunbridge-water, which seemed to have been his particular study: and indeed he had perused Rouzee's treatise[9] on that subject, with indefatigable assiduity. From this theme, he made digressions into other parts of medicine, upon which he spoke with such plausible elocution, that the apothecary, whose knowledge in that art was not very profound, looked upon him as a physician of great learning and experience, and hinted a desire of knowing his name and situation.

Fathom accordingly gave him to understand, that he had studied physic, and had taken his degrees at Padua,[10] rather for his amusement, than with any view of exercising medicine, as he then could not possibly foresee the misfortunes which had since happened to his family, and by which he was now compelled to have recourse to a profession that was very much beneath the expectations of his birth. Yet he bore his disappointments with resignation, and even good humour, and blessed his stars for having inclined him to the study of any branch of knowledge by which he might be enabled to laugh at the vicissitudes of fortune. He then observed, that he had practised with some applause at the hot-well, near Bristol, before he thought he should be ever reduced to the necessity of taking a fee; and that, in all probability, his metamorphosis, when known, would furnish matter of surprise and merriment to some of his old acquaintance.

The apothecary was equally struck with his polite address, and pleased with his agreeable discourse: he consoled him for the misfortunes of his family, by assuring him, that, in England, nothing could be more honourable, or indeed profitable, than the character of a physician, provided he could once wriggle himself into practice; and insinuated, that, although he was restricted by certain engagements with other persons of the faculty,[11] he should be glad of an opportunity to shew his regard for doctor Fathom. This was a very effectual method which our hero took to intimate his new character to the public. By the industry and communicative disposition of the apothecary, it was circulated in half a day thro' every family in the place; and next morning, when Ferdinand appeared, the company forthwith assembled in separate groups, and from each knot he heard his name reverberated in a whisper.

Having thus announced himself to all whom it might concern, and allowed the ladies two days to discuss the merit of his transfiguration, together with the novelty of the case, he ventured to salute, at a distance, a lady and her

daughter, who had been his patients at the hot-well; and although they honoured his bow with the return of a slight curtsy, they gave him not the least
encouragement to make a nearer approach. Notwithstanding this rebuff, he
concluded, that, should the health of either come in question, they would
renew their application to his skill, and what was refused by their pride,
would be granted by their apprehension. Here, however, he happened to be
mistaken in his conjecture.

The young lady being seized with a violent head-ach and palpitation,[12] her
mother desired the apothecary to recommend a physician; and the person,
with whom he was contracted, being at that time absent, he proposed doctor
Fathom as a man of great ability and discretion: but the good lady rejected
the proposal with disdain, because she had formerly known him in the character of a Count; though that very character was the chief reason that had
then induced her to crave his advice.

Such is the caprice of the world in general, that whatever bears the face of
novelty captivates, or rather bewitches the imagination, and confounds the
ideas of reason and common sense. If, for example, a scullion from the clinking of pewter should conceive a taste for the clinking of rhime, and make shift
to bring together twenty syllables, so as that the tenth and last shall have the
like ending; the composition is immediately extolled as a miracle; and what
appeals to the admiration, is not the wit, the elegance or poetry of the work,
but the uncultivated talent, and humble station of the author. A reader does
not exclaim, "What a delicate sentiment! what a beautiful simile! what easy
and musical versification!" but cries in rapture, "Heavens! what a prodigy! a
poet from the scullery! a muse in livery! or, Apollo with a trowel!"[13]—The
public is astonished into liberality—the scullion eats from those trenchers he
scoured before—the footman is admitted into the coach, behind which he
was wont to stand; and the bricklayer, instead of plaistering walls, bedaubs
his *illustrious part'ner* with the mortar of his praise.[14] Thus, lifted into an
higher sphere, their talents receive cultivation; they become professed bards;
and tho' their subsequent works bear evident marks of improvement, they are
neglected among the rest of their brethren; because that novelty, which recommended them in the beginning, no longer remains.

So it fared with our adventurer in his new occupation. There was something so extraordinary in a nobleman's understanding medicine; and so uncommon in a physician's prescribing gratis, that the curiosity and admiration
of the company at Bristol were engaged, and they followed his advice, as the
direction of some supernatural intelligence: but, now that he professed himself one of the faculty, and might be supposed to have refreshed his memory,
and reinforced his knowledge for the occasion, he was as much over-looked as

any other physician unsupported by interest or cabal; or, at least, the notice he attracted was not at all to the advantage of his character, because it wholly regarded the decline of his fortune, which is a never-failing fund of disgrace.

These mortifications did not overcome the patience and perseverance of Fathom, who foresaw that the soothing hand of time would cast a veil of oblivion over those scenes which were remembered to his prejudice; and that in the mean time, though he was excluded from the private parties of the fair sex, in which his main hope of success was placed, he should be able to insinuate himself into some degree of favour and practice among the male patients; and some lucky cure, properly displayed, might be the means of propagating his fame, and banishing that reserve which at present interfered with his purpose. Accordingly, it was not long before he found means to break that spell of universal prejudice that hedged him in. At the ordinary which he frequented, his polite carriage, facetious remarks, and agreeable stories, soon conciliated the regard of his fellow guests, among whom he sometimes rallied his own transformation with singular good humour and success: he was even witty upon his want of employment; and used to observe, that a physician, without practice, had one comfort to which his brethren were strangers, namely, that the seldomer he had occasion to prescribe, the less he had upon his conscience on account of being accessory to the death of his fellow-creatures.

Nothing so effectually blunts the shafts of ridicule, and defeats the aims of slander, as this method of anticipation. In spite of the arrows that were levelled against his reputation from every tea-table at Tunbridge, he made his party good among almost all the gay young gentlemen that frequented the place: far from avoiding his company, they began to court his conversation, and he was commonly seen in the walks, surrounded with a group of admirers.

Having thus paved the way for a total removal of the invidious prepossession that obstructed his views, he, one night, while every person was lulled in the arms of repose, and universal silence prevailed, tuned his violin, and began to play some masterly airs, in a tone so uncommonly expressive, and with such ravishing dexterity of execution, that a certain lady who lodged in the same house, being waked by the music, and ignorant of the source from which it flowed, listened with rapture, as to the harp of an angel, and wrapping herself in a loose gown, rose and opened her chamber-door, in order to discover in what apartment the musician resided. She no sooner entered the passage, than she found her fellow-lodgers already assembled on the same occasion; and there they remained during the best part of the night, transported by the harmony which our hero produced.

Doctor Fathom was immediately known to be the author of this entertainment; and thus retrieved the benefit of that admiration which he had forfeited by appearing in the shape of a physician. For, as people had formerly wondered to see a Count skilled in medicine; they were now amazed to find a physician such a master in music.

The good effects of this stratagem were almost instantaneous. His performance became the topic of discourse among all the fashionable company: his male friends complimented him from the information of the other sex; and that lady whom he had regaled, instead of that shyness and disdain with which she used to receive his salutation, at their very next meeting in the thoroughfare, returned his bow with marks of profound respect. Nay, at midnight, she, with the rest, took post in the same place where they had been stationed before; and by frequent tittering, and repeated whispers, gave intimation to Fathom, that they would be glad of a second serenade. But he was too well acquainted with the human passions to indulge this their desire: it was his interest to inflame their impatience, rather than to gratify their expectation: and therefore he tantalized them for some hours, by tuning his violin, and playing some flourishes, which, however, produced nothing to fulfil their wishes.

At the ordinary, he was accosted by a gentleman, a lodger in the same house, who assured him, that the ladies would take it as a great favour, if he would let them know when he intended to amuse himself again with his instrument, that they might not, by falling asleep before-hand, deprive themselves of the pleasure of hearing his music. To this message he replied with an air of consequence and reserve, that, though music was not the art he professed, he should be always complaisant enough to entertain the ladies to the utmost of his power, when their commands were signified to him in a manner suited to his character; but that he would never put himself on the footing of an itinerant harper, whose music is tolerated thro' the medium of a board partition. The gentleman having reported this answer to his constituents, they empowered him to invite doctor Fathom to breakfast, and he was next morning introduced with the usual ceremony, and treated with uncommon regard by all the females of the house, assembled for his reception.

Having thus broke the ice of their aversion, in one part, so as that the beams of his personal accomplishments had room to operate, he soon effected a general thaw in his favour, and found himself growing once more into request among the most amiable part of the creation. His company was coveted, and his taste consulted in their balls, concerts, and private assemblies; and he recompenced the regard they paid to him, with an incessant exertion of his agreeable talents, politeness and good humour.

Doctor Fathom Plays the Violin, by Clennell.
(Library Company of Philadelphia.)

CHAPTER LI.

Triumphs over a medical rival.

Yet, in the midst of all this attention, his medical capacity seemed to be quite forgot. They respected his good breeding, were charmed with his voice, and admired the fine touches of his hand upon the violin; but, in cultivating the fidler, they utterly neglected the physician; and in vain did he attempt to divide their regard, by taking all opportunities to turn the conversation into a more interesting channel. It was to little purpose he endeavoured to arrouse the wonder of his audience with frequent descriptions of portentuous maladies and amazing cures he had seen and performed in the course of his study and practice abroad: and to no effect did he publickly busy himself in making experiments on the mineral water, in which he pretended to have made several new and important discoveries. These efforts did not make a lasting impression upon the minds of the company; because they saw nothing surprizing in a physician's being acquainted with all the mysteries of his art; and, as their custom was already bespoke for others of the profession, whom it was their interest to employ, our adventurer might have starved amidst the caresses of his acquaintance, had not he derived considerable advantage from a lucky accident in the course of his expectancy.

A gentlewoman's daughter, of a weakly constitution, by drinking the waters, had so far recovered her health and complexion, as to allure the affection of a young squire in the neighbourhood, who amused her for some time with his addresses, until his heart was seduced by the charms of another young lady lately arrived at the wells. The forsaken nymph, shocked at this disgrace and mortification, relapsed into her former languishing disorder, and was by her mother put under the management and prescription of a physician, who had been an industrious enemy of Fathom, from his first appearance at Tunbridge. The patient, tho' violently chagrined at the levity of her quondam admirer, was not altogether without hope, that the very same inconstancy which had prompted him to leave her, might in time induce him to return, after the novelty of his new passion should be wore off; and this hope served to support her under the sorrow and disgrace of her disappointment. At length, however, the squire and his new mistress disappeared, and some busy body was officious enough to communicate this piece of news to the forlorn shepherdess, with this additional circumstance, that they were gone to a neighbouring parish, to be joined in the bands of wedlock.

These fatal tidings were no sooner imparted to the abandoned Phillis,[1] than she was seized with an hysteric fit; and, what rendered the accident more unfortunate, her physician had been called to the country, and was not expected at Tunbridge 'till next day. The apothecary was immediately summoned; and, being either puzzled by the symptoms, or afraid of encroaching upon the province of his superiors, advised the old lady to send for doctor Fathom without delay. She had no other objection to this expedient, but the enmity which she knew subsisted between the two leeches: yet hearing that her own doctor would not consult with Fathom upon his return, but, perhaps, renounce the patient, by which means her daughter's health might be endangered, she would not sollicit our hero's assistance, until the young lady had remained seven hours speechless and insensible; when her fear prevailing over every other consideration, she implored the advice of our adventurer, who having made the necessary interrogations, and felt the patient's pulse, which was regular and distinct, found reason to conclude, that the fit would not last much longer; and, after having observed, that she was in a very dangerous way, prescribed some medicines for external application; and, to enhance their opinion of his diligence and humanity, resolved to stay in the room, and observe their effect.

His judgment did not fail him on this occasion. In less than half an hour after his embrocations[2] had been applied, she recovered the use of her tongue, opened her eyes, and having in delirious exclamations, upbraided her perfidious lover, became quite sensible and composed; though she continued extremely low and dejected: to remedy these sinkings, certain cordials were immediately administered, according to the prescription of doctor Fathom, upon whom extraordinary encomiums were bestowed by all present, who believed he had actually rescued her from the jaws of death; and as he was, by this time, let into the secrets of the family, he found himself in a fair way of being an egregious favourite of the old gentlewoman; when, unluckily, his brother having dismissed his country patient with uncommon dispatch, entered the apartment, and eyed his rival with looks of inexpressible rage; then surveying the patient, and the vials that stood upon the table, by turns, "What, in the name of God! (cried he) is the meaning of all this trash?"

"Really, doctor, (replied the mother, a little confounded at being thus taken by surprize) Biddy[3] has been taken dangerously ill, and lain seven or eight hours in a severe fit, from which, I am confident, she would never have recovered, without the help of a physician; and as you were absent, we had recourse to this gentleman, whose prescription hath had an happy and surprising effect." "Effect! (cried this offended member of the faculty) pshaw! stuff, who made you judge of effects or causes? (then advancing to the patient) what has been the matter, miss Biddy, that you could not wait till my return?'

Here Fathom interposing, "Sir, (said he) if you will step into the next room, I will communicate my sentiments of the case, together with the method upon which I have proceeded, that we may deliberate upon the next step that is to be taken." Instead of complying with this proposal, he seated himself in a chair, with his back to our adventurer, and while he examined miss Biddy's pulse, gave him to understand, that he should not consult with him about the matter.

Fathom, not in the least disconcerted at this uncivil answer, walked round his antagonist, and placing himself in his front, desired to know his reason for treating him with such supercilious contempt. "I am resolved (said the other) never to consult with any physician who has not taken his degrees at either of the English universities." "Upon the supposition (replied our adventurer) that no person can be properly educated for the profession at any other school." "You are in the right: (answered doctor Looby[4]) that is one of many reasons I have to decline the consultation."

"How far you are in the right, (retorted Fathom) I leave the world to judge, after I have observed, that in your English universities, there is no opportunity of studying the art; no, not so much as a lecture given on the subject: nor is there one physician of note, in this kingdom, who has not derived the greatest part of his medical knowledge, from the instructions of foreigners."[5]

Looby, incensed at this asseveration, which he was not prepared to refute, exclaimed in a most infuriate accent, "Who are you? whence came you? where was you bred? you are one of those, I believe, who graduate themselves, and commence doctors, the Lord knows how: an interloper, who, without license or authority, come hither to take the bread out of the mouths of gentlemen, who have been trained to the business in a regular manner, and bestowed great pains and expence to qualify themselves for the profession: for my part, my education cost me fifteen hundred pounds."

"Never was money laid out to less purpose: (said Ferdinand) for it does not appear, that you have learned so much as the basis of medical acquirements, namely, that decorum and urbanity which ought to distinguish the deportment of every physician: you have even debased the noblest and most beneficial art that ever engaged the study of mankind, which cannot be too much cultivated, and too little restrained, in seeking to limit the practice of it, to a set of narrow-minded illiberal wretches, who, like the lowest handicraftsmen, claim the exclusive privileges of a corporation:[6] had you doubted my ability, you ought to have satisfied yourself in a manner consistent with decency and candour: but your behaviour, on this occasion, is such a malicious outrage upon good manners and humanity, that, were it not for my regard to these ladies, I would chastise you for your insolence, on the spot. Mean while, madam, (addressing himself to the mother) you must give me leave to insist upon your dismissing either that gentleman, or me, without hesitation."

This peremptory language had an instantaneous effect upon the hearers. Looby's face grew pale, and his nether lip began to tremble: the patient was dismayed, and the old gentlewoman concerned and perplexed: she earnestly besought the gentlemen to be reconciled to each other, and enter into a friendly consultation upon her daughter's distemper: but, finding both equally averse to accommodation, and Fathom becoming more and more importunate in his demand, she presented him with a double fee; and giving him to understand, that doctor Looby had long attended the family, and was intimately acquainted with her own and Biddy's constitution, said, she hoped he would not take it amiss, if she retained her old physician.

Though our hero was much mortified at this triumph of his rival, he made a virtue of necessity, and retired with great complaisance, wishing, that Miss Biddy might never again be the subject of such a disagreeable dispute. Whether the patient was frighted at this altercation, or displeased with her mother's decision against an agreeable young fellow, who had, as it were, recalled her from the grave, and made himself master of the secret that rankled at her heart; or the disease had wound up her nerves for another paroxysm; certain it is, she, all of a sudden, broke forth into a violent peal of laughter, which was succeeded by the most doleful cries, and other expressions of grief; then she relapsed into a fit, attended with strong convulsions, to the unspeakable terror of the old gentlewoman, who intreated doctor Looby to be expeditious in his prescription: accordingly, he seized the pen with great confidence, and a whole magazine of anti-hysteric medicines were, in different forms, externally and internally applied.

Nevertheless, either nature was disturbed, in her own efforts, by these applications, or the patient was resolved to disgrace the doctor: for the more remedies that were administered, her convulsions became the more violent; and in spite of all his endeavours, he could not overcome the obstinacy of the distemper. Such a miscarriage upon the back of his rival's success, could not fail to overwhelm him with confusion; especially as the mother baited him with repeated intreaties, to do something for the recovery of her daughter: at length, after having exercised her patience in vain, for several hours, this affectionate parent could no longer suppress the suggestions of her concern, but, in an incoherent strain, told him, that her duty would not suffer her to be longer silent in an affair on which depended the life of her dear child: that she had seen enough, to believe he had mistaken the case of poor Biddy, and he could not justly blame her for recalling doctor Fathom, whose prescription had operated in a miraculous manner.

Looby, shocked at this proposal, protested against it with great vehemence, as an expedient highly injurious to himself. "My remedies (said he) are just beginning to take effect, and, in all probability, the fit will not last much longer; so that by calling in another person, at this juncture, you will defraud me of that credit which is my due, and deck my adversary with trophies, to which he has no pretension." She was prevailed upon, by this remonstrance, to wait another half hour, when perceiving, as yet, no alteration for the better, and being distracted with her fears, which reproached her with want of natural affection, she sent a message to doctor Fathom, desiring to see him with all possible dispatch.

He was not slow in obeying the call, but hastening to the scene of action, was not a little surprised to find Looby still in the apartment. This gentleman, since better might not be, resolved to sacrifice his pride to his interest, and, rather than lose his patient altogether, and run the risque of forfeiting his reputation at the same time, staid with intention to compromise his difference with Fathom, that he might not be wholly excluded from the honour of the cure, in case it could be effected: but he had reckoned without his host, in his calculation of the count's placability; for when he put on his capitulating face, and after a slight apology for his late behaviour, proposed that all animosity should subside in favour of the young lady, whose life was at stake, our hero rejected his advances with infinite disdain, and assured the mother, in a very solemn tone, that, far from consulting with a man who had treated him so unworthily, he would not stay another minute in the house, unless he should see him discarded: a satisfaction barely sufficient to attone for the affront he himself had suffered by the unjust preference she had before given to his rival.

There was no remedy: Looby was obliged to retreat in his turn; then our adventurer approaching the bed-side, reconnoitered the patient, examined the medicines which had been administered, and lifting up his eyes in expressive silence, detached the footman with a new order to the apothecary. It was well the messenger used expedition, otherwise doctor Fathom would have been anticipated by the operation of nature; for, the fit having almost run its carreer, miss Biddy was on the point of retrieving her senses, when the frontal[7] prescribed by Fathom was applied; to the efficacy of this, therefore, was ascribed her recovery, when she opened her eyes, and began to pour forth unconnected ejaculations; and in a few moments after, she was persuaded to swallow a draught prepared for the purpose, her perception returned, and Ferdinand gained the reputation of having performed a second miracle.

But he was furnished with a piece of intelligence, of much more energy than all she had taken, and so soon as he concluded she was capable to bear the news, without any dangerous emotion, he, among other articles of chit-chat, culled for her amusement, took the opportunity of telling the company, that 'squire Stub[8] (the cause of miss Biddy's disorder) had, in his way to matrimony, been robbed of his bride, by a gentleman to whom she had been formerly engaged. He had waited for her, on purpose, at an inn on the road, where he found means to appease her displeasure, which he had, it seems, incurred, and to supersede her new lover, whom she quitted without ceremony; upon which the 'squire had returned to Tunbridge, cursing her levity, yet blessing his good stars for having so seasonably prevented his ruin, which would have infallibly been the consequence of his marrying such an adventurer.

It would be superfluous to observe, that these tidings operated, like an admirable specifick,[9] on the spirits of the young lady, who, while she affected to pity the 'squire, was so much overjoyed at his disappointment, that her eyes began to sparkle with uncommon vivacity, and in less than two hours after the last of those terrible attacks, she was restored to a better state of health than she had enjoyed for many weeks. Fathom was not forgot amidst the rejoicings of the family: besides an handsome gratuity for the effects of his extraordinary skill, the old lady favoured him with a general invitation to her house, and the daughter not only considered him as the restorer of her health, and angel of her good fortune, but also began to discover an uncommon relish for his conversation; so that he was struck with the prospect of succeeding 'squire Stub in her affection: a conquest, which, if sanctioned by the approbation of the mother, would console him for all the disappointments he had sustained; for Miss Biddy was intitled to a fortune of ten thousand pounds, provided she should marry with the consent of her parent, who was the sole executrix of the father's will.

Animated with the hope of such an advantageous match, our adventurer missed no opportunity of improving the lodgement[10] he had made; while the two ladies failed not to extol his medical capacity, among all their female acquaintance. By means of this circulation, his advice was demanded in several other cases, which he managed with such an imposing air of sagacity and importance, that his fame began to spread, and before the end of the season, he had ravished more than one half of the business from his competitor. Notwithstanding these fortunate events, he foresaw, that he should find great difficulty in transplanting his reputation, so as to take root in London, which was the only soil in which he could propose to rise to any degree of prosperity and independance; and this reflection was grounded upon a maxim which universally prevails among the English people, namely, to overlook and wholly neglect, on their return to the metropolis, all the connexions they may have chanced to acquire during their residence at any of the medical wells: and this social disposition is so scrupulously maintained, that two persons who lived in the most intimate correspondence at Bath or Tunbridge, shall, in four and twenty hours, so totally forget their friendship, as to meet in St. James's park, without betraying the least token of recognition; so that one would imagine those mineral waters were so many streams issuing from the river *Lethe*,[11] so famed of old, for washing away all traces of memory and recollection.

Aware of this oblivious principle,[12] doctor Fathom collected all his qualifications, in order to make such an impression upon the heart of Miss Biddy, as would resist all her endeavours to shake him from her remembrance; and his efforts succeeded so well, that 'squire Stub's advances to a reconciliation, were treated with manifest indifference. In all probability, our hero would have made a very advantageous campaign, had not his good fortune been retarded by an obstruction, which (as he did not perceive it) he could not possibly surmount: in displaying his accomplishments to captivate the daughter, he had unwittingly made an absolute conquest of the mother, who superintended the conduct of Miss Biddy, with such jealous vigilance, that he could find no opportunity of profiting by the progress he had made in her heart; for the careful matron would never lose sight of her, no, not for one moment.

Had the old lady given the least intimation to our adventurer, of the sentiments she entertained in his behalf, his complaisance was of such a pliable texture, that he would have quitted his other pursuit, and made her the sole object of his attention: but she either depended upon the effect of his own good taste and discernment, or was too proud to disclose a passion which he had hitherto overlooked.

CHAPTER LII.

Repairs to the Metropolis, and enrols himself among the sons of Pæan.[1]

Before this affair could be brought to a proper explanation, the season being almost ended, the ladies departed from Tunbridge, and in a little time doctor Fathom followed them to London, having previously obtained permission to visit them in that metropolis. He had sollicited the same favour of some other families, in which he hoped to take root, though he knew they were pre-engaged to different physicians; and resolving to make his first medical appearance in London, with some *eclat*, he not only purchased an old chariot, which was new painted for the purpose, but likewise hired a footman, whom he cloathed in laced livery, in order to distinguish himself from the common run of his brethren.

This equipage, though much more expensive than his finances could bear, he found absolutely necessary, to give him a chance for employment; as every shabby retainer to physic, in this capital, had provided himself with a vehicle, which was altogether used by way of a travelling sign post, to draw in customers; so that a walking physician was considered as an obscure pedlar, trudging from street to street, with his pack of knowledge on his shoulders, and selling his remnants of advice by retail. A chariot was not now set up for the convenience of a man sinking under the fatigue of extensive practice, but as a piece of furniture every way as necessary as a large periwig with three tails;[2] and a physician, let his merit, in other respects, be never so conspicuous, can no more expect to become considerable in business, without the assistance of this implement, than he can hope to live without food, or breathe without a windpipe.

This requisite is so well understood, that, exclusive of those who profess themselves doctors, every raw surgeon, every idle apothecary, who can make interest with some foolhardy coachmaker, may be seen dancing the hays[3] in all places of public resort, and grinning to one another from their respective carriages. Hence proceed many of those cruel accidents which are recorded in the daily papers. An apothecary's horses take fright, and run away with his chariot, which is heard of no more: an eminent surgeon being overturned, is so terrified at the thoughts of mutilation, that he resolves to walk on foot all the days of his life; and the coachman of a physician of great practice, having the misfortune to be disabled by a fall from the box, his master can never find another to supply his place.[4]

None of these observations escaped the penetrating eye of Fathom, who, before he pretended to seat himself in his machine, had made proper inquiry into all the other methods practised, with a view to keep the wheels in motion. In his researches, he found that the great world was wholly engrossed by a few practitioners who had arrived at the summit of reputation, consequently, were no longer obliged to cultivate those arts by which they rose; and that the rest of the business was parcelled out into small inclosures, occupied by different groupes of personages, male and female, who stood in rings, and tossed the ball from one to another, there being in each department two sets, the individuals of which relieved one another occasionally. Every knot was composed of a waiting woman, nurse, apothecary, surgeon and physician, and, sometimes, a midwife was admitted into the partie; and in this manner the farce was commonly performed.[5]

A fine lady, fatigued with idleness, complains of the vapours, is deprived of her rest, tho' not so sick as to have recourse to medicine: her favourite maid, tired with giving her attendance in the night, thinks proper, for the benefit of her own repose, to complain of a violent head-ach, and recommends to her mistress a nurse of approved tenderness and discretion; at whose house (in all likelihood) the said chamber-maid hath oft given the rendezvous to a male friend. The nurse, well skilled in the mysteries of her occupation, persuades the patient, that her malady, far from being slight or chimerical, may proceed to a very dangerous degree of the hysterical affection, unless it be nipt in the bud by some very effectual remedy: then she recounts a surprising cure performed by a certain apothecary, and appeals to the testimony of the waiting woman, who being the gossip of his wife, confirms the evidence, and corroborates the proposal. The apothecary being summoned, finds her ladyship in such a delicate situation, that he declines prescribing, and advises her to send for a physician without delay. The nomination, of course, falls to him, and the doctor being called, declares the necessity of immediate venæsection,[6] which is accordingly performed by the surgeon of the association.

This is one way of beginning the game: tho' the commencement often varies, and sometimes the apothecary, and sometimes the physician opens the scene; but, be that as it will, they always appear in a string, like a flight of wild geese, and each confederacy maintains a correspondence with one particular undertaker. Fathom, upon these considerations, set up his rest[7] in the first floor of an apothecary in the neighbourhood of Charing-cross,[8] to whom he was introduced by a letter from a friend at Tunbridge, and who being made acquainted with his ability and scheme, promised to let slip no opportunity of serving him; and, indeed, seemed to espouse his interest with great alacrity. He introduced him to some of his patients, on the strength of a gratis visit, sounded forth his praise among all the good women of his acquaintance; and even prevailed upon him to publish advertisements, importing, that he would, every day, at a certain time and place, give his advice to the poor for nothing; hoping, that, by means of some lucky cure, his fame might be extended, and his practice grow into request.

In the mean time, his chariot rolled along thro' all the most frequented streets, during the whole forenoon, and, at the usual hour, he never failed to make his appearance at the medical coffee-house,[9] with all that solemnity of feature and address, by which the modern sons of *Pæan* are distinguished; not but that he was often puzzled about the decision of his diurnal route: for the method of driving up one street, and down another, without halting, was become such a stale expedient, that the very 'prentices used to stand at the shop doors, and ridicule the vain parade. At length, however, he perused the map of London with great diligence, and having acquired a distinct idea of its topography, used to alight at the end of long narrow thorough-fares, and paved courts, where the chariot was ordered to wait till his return; and walking with great gravity thro' the different turnings of these alleys, regain his carriage by another passage, and resume his seat with an air of vast importance. With a view to protract the time of his supposed visits, he would, at one place, turn aside to the wall; at another, cheapen an urinal;[10] at a third corner, read a quack advertisement, or lounge a few minutes in some bookseller's shop; and, lastly, glide into some obscure coffeehouse, and treat himself with a dram of usquebaugh.[11]

The other means used to force a trade, such as ordering himself to be called from church, alarming the neighbourhood with knocking at his door in the night, receiving sudden messages in places of resort, and inserting his cures by way of news in the daily papers, had been so injudiciously hackneyed by every desperate sculler[12] in physick, that they had lost their effect upon the publick, and therefore were excluded from the plan of our adventurer, whose scheme, for the present, was to exert himself in winning the favour of those sage Sybils,[13] who keep, as it were, the temple of medicine, and admit the young priest to the service of the altar; but this he considered as a temporary project only, until he should have acquired interest enough to erect an hospital, lock,[14] or infirmary, by the voluntary subscription of his friends; a scheme which had succeeded to a miracle, with many of the profession, who had raised themselves into notice, upon the carcases of the poor.

Yet, even this branch was already over-stocked, insomuch that almost every street was furnished with one of these charitable receptacles, which, instead of diminishing the taxes for the maintenance of the poor, encouraged the vulgar to be idle and dissolute, by opening an asylum to them, and their families, from the diseases of poverty and intemperance: for it remains to be proved, that the parish rates are decreased, the bills of mortality lessened, the people more numerous, or the streets less infested with beggars, notwithstanding the immense sums yearly granted by individuals for the relief of the indigent.[15]

But, waving these reflections, doctor Fathom hoped, that his landlord would be a most useful implement for extending his influence, and, for that reason, admitted him into a degree of partnership, after being fully convinced, that he was not under articles to any other physician. Nevertheless, he was very much mistaken in reckoning on the importance of this new ally, who was, like himself, a needy adventurer, settled upon credit, and altogether unemployed, except among the very refuse of the people, whom no other person would take the trouble to attend: so that our hero got little else than experience and trouble, excepting a few guineas, which he made shift to glean among sojourners, with whom he became occasionally acquainted, or young people, who had been unfortunate in their amours.[16]

In the midst of these endeavours, he did not omit his duty to the old gentlewoman, whose daughter he had cured at Tunbridge; and was always received with particular complacency, which, perhaps, he, in some measure, owed to his genteel equipage, that gave credit to every door before which it was seen; yet Miss Biddy was as inaccessible as ever, while the mother became more and more warm in her civilities, 'till at length, after having prepared him with some extraordinary compliments, she gave him to understand, that Biddy was no better than a giddy-headed girl, far from being unexceptionable in her moral character, and particularly deficient in duty and gratitude to her, who had been always a tender and indulgent parent; she was therefore determined to punish the young minx, for her levity, and want of natural affection, by altering her own condition, could she find a worthy and agreeable man, on whom she could bestow her hand and fortune without a blush.

The film was instantly removed from Fathom's eyes by this declaration, which she uttered with such a significancy of look, as thrilled to his soul with joyful presage, while he replied, it would, indeed, be a difficult task to find a man who merited such happiness and honour; but, surely, some there were, who would task their faculties to the uttermost, in manifesting their gratitude, and desire of rendering themselves worthy of such distinction. Though this answer was pronounced in such a manner as gave her to understand he had taken the hint, she would not cheapen her condescension so much as to explain herself further at that juncture, and he was very well contented to wooe her on her own terms; accordingly he began to season his behaviour with a spice of gallantry, when he had opportunities of being particular with this new inamorata, and, in proportion to the returns she made, he gradually detached himself from Miss Biddy, by intermitting, and, at last, discontinuing those ardent expressions of love and admiration, which he had made shift to convey in private looks and stolen whispers, during the rancorous inspection of her mother.

Such alteration could not long escape the jealous eyes of the young lady, no more than the cause of this alienation, which, in a moment, converted all her love into irreconcilable hate, and filled her whole soul with the most eager desire of vengeance: for she now not only considered him as a mercenary wretch, who had slighted her attractions for the sordid gratifications of avarice, but also as an interloper, who wanted to intercept her fortune, in the odious character of a father-in-law. But, before she could bring her aim to any ripeness of contrivance, her mother having caught cold at church, was seized with a rheumatic fever, became delirious in less than three days, and, notwithstanding all the prescriptions and care of her admirer, gave up the ghost, without having retrieved the use of her senses, or been able to manifest, by will, the sentiments she entertained in favour of her physician, who (as the reader will easily perceive) had more reasons than one, to be mortally chagrined at this event.

Miss Biddy being thus put in possession of the whole inheritance, not only renounced all correspondence with doctor Fathom, by forbidding him the house, but likewise took all opportunities of prejudicing his character, by hinting, that her dear mamma had fallen a sacrifice to his ignorance and presumption.

CHAPTER LIII.

Acquires employment, in consequence of a lucky miscarriage.

These ill offices, however, far from answering her purpose, had a quite contrary effect: for, in consequence of her invectives, he was, in a few days, called to the wife of a merchant, who piously hoped, that his practice would not give Miss Biddy the lie. The patient had long lingered under a complication of distempers, and being in no immediate danger of her life, doctor Fathom was in no hurry to strike a decisive stroke; till the husband growing impatient of delay, and so explicit in his hints, that it was impossible to misapprehend his meaning, our adventurer resolved to do something effectual for his satisfaction, and prescribed a medicine of such rough operation,[1] as he thought, must either oblige his employer, or produce a change in the lady's constitution, that would make a noise in the world, and bring a new accession to his fame.

Proceeding upon these maxims, he could not be disappointed: the remedy played its part with such violence, as reduced the patient to extremity, and the merchant had actually bespoke an undertaker; when, after a series of swoonings and convulsions, nature so far prevailed, as to expel, at once, the prescription and the disease; yet the good-natured husband was so much affected with the agonies to which he saw the wife of his bosom exposed by this specific, that, although the effect of it was her perfect recovery, he never could bear the sight of Fathom, for the future, nor even hear his name mentioned, without giving signs of horror and indignation: nay, he did not scruple to affirm, that had our adventurer been endowed with the least tincture of humanity, he would have suffered the poor woman to depart in peace, rather than restore her to health, at the expence of such anxiety and torture.

On the other hand, this extraordinary cure was blazoned abroad by the good lady, and her gossips, with such exaggerations as roused the astonishment of the publick, and concurred with the report of his last miscarriage, to bring him upon the carpet, as the universal subject of discourse. When a physician becomes the town talk, he generally concludes his business more than half done, even though his fame should wholly turn upon his malpractice; insomuch that some members of the faculty have been heard to complain, that they never had the good fortune to be publickly accused of homicide; and it is well known, that a certain famous empyrick,[2] of our day, never flourished to any degree of wealth and reputation, till after he had been attacked in print, and fairly convicted of having destroyed a good number of the human species. Success raised upon such a foundation, would, by a disciple of Plato, and some modern moralists, be ascribed to the innate virtue and generosity of the human heart, which naturally espouses the cause that needs protection: but I, whose notions of human excellence are not quite so sublime, am apt to believe it is owing to that spirit of self-conceit and contradiction, which is, at least, as universal, if not as natural, as the moral sense so warmly contended for by those ideal philosophers.[3]

The most infamous wretch often finds his account in these principles of malevolence and self-love: for wheresoever his character falls under discussion, there is generally some person present, who, either from an affectation of singularity, or envy to the accusers, undertakes his defence, and endeavours to invalidate the articles of his impeachment, until he is heated by altercation, and hurried into more effectual measures for his advantage. If such benefits accrue to those who have no real merit to depend upon; surely, our hero could not but reap something extraordinary from the debates to which he now gave rise; as by the miraculous cure he had effected, all his patient's friends, all the enemies of her husband, all those who envied his other adversary, were interested in his behalf, exclusive of such admirers as surprize and curiosity might engage in his cause.

Thus wafted upon the wings of applause, his fame soon diffused itself into all the corners of this great capital: the news-papers teemed with his praise; and in order to keep up the attention of the publick, his emissaries, male and female, separated into different coffee-houses, companies, and clubs, where they did not fail to comment upon these articles of intelligence. Such a favourable incident is, of itself, sufficient to float the bark of a man's fortune: he was, in a few days; called to another lady, labouring under the same disorder he had so successfully dispelled, and she thought herself benefited by his advice. His acquaintance naturally extended itself among the visitants and allies of his patients; he was recommended from family to family: the fees began to multiply; a variety of footmen appeared every day at his door; he discontinued his sham circuit, and looking upon the present conjuncture, as that tide in his affairs, which (according to Shakespear) when taken at the full, leads on to fortune,[4] he resolved, that the opportunity should not be lost, and applied himself with such assiduity to his practice, that, in all likelihood, he would have carried the palm from all his contemporaries, had not he split upon the same rock which had shipwrecked his hopes before.

We have formerly descanted upon that venereal appetite, which glowed in the constitution of our adventurer, and which all his philosophy and caution could hardly keep within bounds: the reader, therefore, will not be much surprised, to learn, that, in the exercise of his profession, he contracted an intimacy with a clergyman's wife, whom he attended as a physician, and whose conjugal virtue he subdued by a long and diligent exertion of his delusive arts, while her mind was enervated by sickness, and her husband abroad upon his necessary occasions. This unhappy patient, who was a woman of an agreeable person, and lively conversation, fell a sacrifice to her own security and self-conceit: her want of health had confined her to a sedentary life, and her imagination being active and restless, she had spent those hours in reading, which other young women devote to company and diversion: but, as her studies were not superintended by any person of taste, she had indulged her own fancy without method or propriety. The Spectator taught her to be a critick and philosopher; from plays she learned poetry and wit; and derived her knowledge of life from books of history and adventures. Fraught with these acquisitions, and furnished by nature with uncommon vivacity, she despised her own sex, and courted the society of men, among whom she thought her talents might be more honourably displayed; fully confident of her own virtue and sagacity, which enabled her to set all their arts at defiance.

Thus qualified, she, in an evil hour, had recourse to the advice of our adventurer, for some ailment under which she had long laboured; and found such relief from his skill, as very much prepossessed her in his favour: she was no less pleased with his obliging manners, than with his physick; and found much entertainment in his conversation, so that the acquaintance proceeded to a degree of intimacy; during which, he perceived her weak side, and being enamoured of her person, flattered her out of all her caution. The privilege of his character furnished him with opportunities to lay snares for her virtue, and taking advantage of that listlessness, languor, and indolence of the spirits, by which all the vigilance of the soul is relaxed, he, after a long course of attention and perseverance, found means to make shipwreck of her peace.

Though he mastered her chastity, he could not quiet her conscience, which incessantly upbraided her with breach of the marriage vow; nor did her undoer escape without a share of the reproaches suggested by her penitence and remorse. This internal anxiety co-operating with her disease, and, perhaps, with the medicines he prescribed, reduced her to the brink of the grave; when her husband returned from a neighbouring kingdom, in consequence of her earnest request, joined to the information of her friends, who had written to him an account of the extremity in which she was. The good man was afflicted beyond measure, when he saw himself upon the verge of losing a wife whom he had always tenderly loved: but, what were his emotions, when she, taking the first opportunity of his being alone with her, accosted him to this effect: "I am now hastening towards that dissolution, from which no mortal is exempted; and though the prospect of futurity is altogether clouded and uncertain, my conscience will not allow me to plunge into eternity, without unburthening my mind, and by an ingenuous confession, making all the atonement in my power, for the ingratitude I have been guilty of, and the wrongs I have committed against a virtuous husband, who never gave me cause of complaint. You stand amazed at this preamble; but, alas! how will you be shocked when I own that I have betrayed you in your absence; that I have trespassed against God and my marriage-vow, and fallen from the pride and confidence of virtue, to the most abject state of vice: yes, I have been unfaithful to your bed, having fallen a victim to the infernal insinuations of a villain, who took advantage of my weak and unguarded moments. Fathom is the wretch who hath thus injured your honour, and ruined my unsuspecting innocence. I have nothing to plead in alleviation of my crime, but the most sincere contrition of heart; and though, at any other juncture, I could not expect your forgiveness, yet, as I now touch the goal of life, I trust in your humanity and benevolence, for that pardon which will lighten the sorrows of my soul, and those prayers which I hope will entitle me to favour at the throne of grace."

The poor husband was so much overwhelmed with grief and confusion, at this unexpected address, that he could not recollect himself till after a pause of several minutes, when uttering a hollow groan, "I will not (said he) aggravate your sufferings, by reproaching you with my wrongs; though your conduct hath been but an ill return for all my tenderness and esteem. I look upon it as a trial of my christian patience, and bear my misfortune with resignation: mean while, I forgive you from my heart, and fervently pray, that your repentance may be acceptable to the father of mercy." So saying, he approached her bed-side, and embraced her in token of his sincerity. Whether this generous condescension diffused such a composure upon her spirits, as tended to the ease and refreshment of nature, which had been almost exhausted by disease and vexation; certain it is, that, from this day, she began to struggle with her malady in surprising efforts; and hourly gained ground, until her health was pretty well re-established.

This recovery was so far beyond the husband's expectation, that he began to make very serious reflections on the event, and even to wish he had not been quite so precipitate in pardoning the backslidings of his wife: for, though he could not withhold his compassion from a dying penitent, he did not at all relish the thoughts of co-habiting, as usual, with a wife, self-convicted of the violation of the matrimonial contract: he therefore considered his declaration as no more than a provisional pardon, to take place on condition of her immediate death; and, in a little time, not only communicated to her his sentiments on this subject; but also separated himself from her company, secured the evidence of her maid, who had been confidante in her amour with Fathom, and immediately set on foot a prosecution against our adventurer, whose behaviour to his wife, he did not fail to promulgate, with

all its aggravating circumstances. By these means the doctor's name became
so notorious, that every man was afraid of admitting him into his house, and
every woman ashamed of solliciting his advice.

CHAPTER LIV.

His eclipse, and gradual declination.

Misfortunes seldom come single: upon the back of this hue and cry, he
unluckily prescribed phlebotomy[1] to a gentleman of some rank, who
chanced to expire during the operation; and quarrelled with his landlord the
apothecary, who charged him with having forgot the good offices he had done
him in the beginning of his career; and desired he would provide himself with
another lodging.

All these mishaps treading upon the heels of one another, had a very mortifying effect upon his practice. At every tea-table, his name was occasionally
put to the torture, with that of the vile creature whom he had seduced;
though it was generally taken for granted, by all those female casuists, that
she must have made the first advances; for it could not be supposed, that any
man would take much trouble in laying schemes for the ruin of a person
whose attractions were so slender, especially considering the ill state of her
health, a circumstance that seldom adds to a woman's beauty or good humour; besides, she was always a pert minx, that affected singularity, and a
masculine manner of speaking; and many of them had foreseen, that she
would, some time or other, bring herself into such a præmunire.[2] At all
gossipings, where the apothecary or his wife assisted, Fathom's pride, ingratitude, and mal-practice were canvassed; in all clubs of married men, he
was mentioned with marks of abhorrence and detestation; and every medical
coffee-house rung with his reproach. Instances of his ignorance and presumption were quoted, and many particulars feigned for the purpose of
defamation; so that our hero was exactly in the situation of a horseman, who,
in riding at full speed for the plate,[3] is thrown from the saddle in the middle
of the race, and left without sense or motion upon the plain. His progress,
though rapid, had been so short, that he could not be supposed to have laid
up store against such a day of trouble; and as he still cherished hopes of
surmounting those obstacles which had so suddenly started up in his way, he

would not resign his equipage, nor retrench his expences; but appeared, as usual, in all public places, with that serenity and confidence of feature which he had never deposited;[4] and maintained his external pomp, upon the little he had reserved in the days of his prosperity, and the credit he had acquired by the punctuality of his former payments. Both these funds, however, failed in a very little time: his law-suit was a gulph that swallowed up all his ready money; and the gleanings of his practice were scarce sufficient to answer his pocket expences, which now increased in proportion to the decrease of business; for as he had more idle time, and was less admitted into private families, so he thought he had more occasion to enlarge his acquaintance among his own sex, who alone were able to support him in his disgrace with the other. He accordingly listed himself in several clubs, and endeavoured to monopolize the venereal branch of trade: tho' this was but an indifferent resource; for almost all his patients of this class, were such as either could not, or would not properly recompence the physician.

For some time, he lingered in this situation, without going upwards or downwards, floating like a wisp of straw, at the turning of the tide, until he could no longer amuse the person of whom he had hired his coach horses, or postpone the other demands, which multiplied upon him every day. Then was his chariot overturned with a hideous crash, and his face so much wounded with the shivers of the glass, which went to pieces in the fall, that he appeared in the coffeehouse with half a dozen black patches upon his countenance, gave a most circumstantial detail of the risque he had run, and declared, that he did not believe he should ever hazard himself again in any sort of wheel carriage.

Soon after this accident, he took an opportunity of telling his friends, in the same public place, that he had turned away his footman, on account of his drunkenness, and was resolved, for the future, to keep none but maids in his service, because the men servants are generally impudent, lazy, debauched, or dishonest; and, after all, neither so neat, handy, or agreeable as the other sex. In the rear of this resolution, he shifted his lodgings into a private court, being distracted with the din of carriages, that disturb the inhabitants who live towards the open street; and gave his acquaintance to understand, that he had a medical work upon the anvil, which he could not finish without being indulged in silence and tranquillity. In effect, he gradually put on the exteriors of an author: his watch, with an horizontal movement by Graham,[5] which he had often mentioned, and shewn as a very curious piece of workmanship, began, about this time, to be very much out of order, and was committed to the care of a mender, who was in no hurry to restore it. His tye-wig degenerated into a major;[6] he sometimes appeared without a sword, and was even observed in public with a second day's shirt:[7] at last, his cloaths became rusty, and when he walked about the streets, his head turned round in a surprising manner, by an involuntary motion in his neck, which he had contracted by an habit of reconnoitering the ground, that he might avoid all dangerous or disagreeable encounters.

Fathom, finding himself descending the hill of fortune, with an acquired gravitation, strove to catch at every twig, in order to stop or retard his descent. He now regretted the opportunities he had neglected, of marrying one of several women of moderate fortune, who had made advances to him, in the zenith of his reputation; and endeavoured, by forcing himself into a lower path of life than any he had hitherto trod, to keep himself afloat, with the portion of some tradesman's daughter, whom he meant to espouse. While he exerted himself in this pursuit, he happened, in returning from a place about thirty miles from London, to become acquainted, in the stage coach, with a young woman, of a very homely appearance, whom, from the driver's information, he understood to be the niece of a country justice, and daughter of a soap-boiler,[8] who had lived and died in London, and left her, in her infancy, sole heiress of his effects, which amounted to four thousand pounds. The uncle, who was her guardian, had kept her sacred from the knowledge of the world, resolving to effect a match betwixt her and his own son; and it was with much difficulty he had consented to this journey, which she had undertaken as a visit to her own mother, who had married a second husband in town.

Fraught with these anecdotes, Fathom began to put forth his gallantry and good humour, and, in a word, was admitted by the lady, to the privilege of an acquaintance, in which capacity he visited her during the term of her residence in London; and as there was no time to be lost, declared his honourable intentions: he had such a manifest advantage, in point of personal accomplishments, over the young gentleman who was destined for her husband, that she did not disdain his proposals, and before she set out for the country, he had made such progress in her heart, that the day was actually fixed for their nuptials, on which he faithfully promised to carry her off in a coach and six. How to raise money for this expedition, was all the difficulty that remained: for, by this time, his finances were utterly dried up, and his credit altogether exhausted. Upon a very pressing occasion, he had formerly applied himself to a certain wealthy quack, who had relieved his necessities by lending him a small sum of money, in return for having communicated to him a secret medicine, which he affirmed to be the most admirable specifick that ever was invented. The nostrum had been used, and luckily for him, succeeded in the trial; so that the empyrick, in the midst of his satisfaction, began to reflect, that this same Fathom, who pretended to be in possession of a great many remedies, equally efficacious, would certainly become a formidable rival to him, in his business, should he ever be able to extricate himself from his present difficulties.

In consequence of these suggestions, he resolved to keep our adventurer's head under water, by maintaining him in the most abject dependance; accordingly he had, from time to time, accommodated him with small trifles, which barely served to support his existence, and even for these had taken notes of hand, that he might have a scourge over head, in case he should prove insolent or refractory. To this benefactor, Fathom applied for a reinforcement of twenty guineas, which he sollicited with the more confidence, as that sum would certainly enable him to repay all other obligations. The quack would advance the money upon no other condition, than that of knowing the scheme, which being explained, he complied with Ferdinand's request; but, at the same time, privately dispatched an express to the young lady's uncle, with a full account of the whole conspiracy; so that when the doctor arrived at the inn, according to appointment, he was received by his worship, in person, who gave him to understand, that his niece had changed her mind, and gone fifty miles farther into the country to visit a relation. This was a grievous disappointment to Fathom, who really believed his mistress had forsaken him thro' mere levity and caprice, and was not undeceived till several months after her marriage with her cousin, when, at an accidental meeting in London, she explained the story of the secret intelligence, and excused her marriage, as the effect of rigorous usage and compulsion.

Had our hero been really enamoured of her person, he might have, probably, accomplished his wishes, notwithstanding the steps she had taken: but this was not the case; his passion was of a different nature, and the object of it effectually without his reach. With regard to his appetite for women, as it was an infirmity of his constitution, which he could not overcome, and as he was in no condition to gratify it at a great expence, he had of late chosen an housekeeper from the hundreds of Drury,[9] and to avoid scandal, allowed her to assume his name. As to the intimation which had been sent to the country justice, he immediately imputed it to the true author, whom he marked for his vengeance accordingly, but, in the mean time, suppressed his resentment, because he, in some measure, depended upon him for subsistence. On the other hand, the quack, dreading the forwardness and plausibility of our hero, which might, one time or other, render him independent, put a stop to those

supplies, on pretence of finding them inconvenient; but, out of his friendship
and good will to Fathom, undertook to procure for him such letters of recommendation, as would infallibly make his fortune in the West-Indies, and even
to fit him out in a genteel manner for the voyage. Ferdinand perceived his
drift, and thanked him for his generous offer, which he would not fail to
consider with all due deliberation: though he was determined against the
proposal, but obliged to temporize, that he might not incur the displeasure of
this man, at whose mercy he lay. Mean while the prosecution against him, in
Doctors Commons, [10] drew near a period, and the lawyers were clamorous
for money, without which he foresaw he should lose the advantage which his
cause had lately acquired by the death of his antagonist's chief evidence: he
therefore, seeing every other channel shut up, began to doubt, whether the
risque of being apprehended or slain in the character of an highwayman, was
not over-ballanced by the prospect of being acquitted of a charge which had
ruined his reputation and fortune, and actually entertained thoughts of taking the air on Hounslow Heath, [11] when he was diverted from this expedient
by a very singular adventure.

CHAPTER LV.

*After divers unsuccessful efforts, he has recourse to
the matrimonial noose.*

Chancing to meet with one of his acquaintance at a certain coffeehouse,
the discourse turned upon the characters of mankind, when, among
other oddities, his friend brought upon the carpet a certain old gentlewoman
of such a rapacious disposition, that, like a jack-daw, [1] she never beheld any
metalline substance without an inclination, and even an effort to secrete it for
her own use and contemplation: nor was this infirmity originally produced
from indigence, inasmuch as her circumstances had been always affluent,
and she was now possessed of a considerable sum of money in the funds; [2]
notwithstanding which, the avarice of her nature tempted her to let lodgings,
though few people could live under the same roof with such an original, who,
rather than be idle, had often filched pieces of her own plate, and charged her
servants with the theft, or hinted suspicion of her lodgers. Fathom, struck
with the description, soon perceived how this woman's disease might be converted to his advantage; and after having obtained sufficient intelligence, on

pretence of satisfying his curiosity, he visited the widow, in consequence of a bill at her door, and actually hired an apartment in her house, whither he forthwith repaired with his inamorata. It was not long before he perceived, that his landlady's character had not been misrepresented; he fed her distemper with divers inconsiderable trinkets, such as copper medals, cork screws, odd buckles, and a paultry seal set in silver, which were, at different times, laid as baits for her infirmity, and always convey'd away with remarkable eagerness, which he and his Dulcinea took pleasure in observing from an unsuspected place. Thus confirmed in his opinion, he, at length, took an opportunity of exposing a metal watch that belonged to his mistress, and saw it seized, with great satisfaction, in the absence of his help-mate, who had gone abroad on purpose. According to instruction, she soon returned, and began to raise a terrible clamour about the loss of her watch; upon which she was condoled by her landlady, who seemed to doubt the integrity of the maid, and even proposed, that Mrs. Fathom should apply to some justice of the peace, for a warrant to search the servant's trunk. The lady thanked her for the good advice, in compliance with which, she had immediate recourse to a magistrate, who granted a search warrant, not against the maid, but the mistress; and she, in a little time, returned with the constable at her back.

These precautions being taken, doctor Fathom desired a private conference with the old gentlewoman, in which he gave her to understand, that he had undoubted proofs of her having secreted, not only the watch, but also several other odd things, of less consequence, which he had lost since his residence in her house: he then shewed the warrant he had obtained against her, and asked, if she had any thing to offer, why the constable should not do his duty. Inexpressible were the anguish and confusion of the defendant, when she found herself thus entrapped, and reflected, that she was on the point of being detected of felony; for she at once concluded, that the snare was laid for her, and knew, that the officer of justice would certainly find the unlucky watch in one of the drawers of her scrutore.

Tortured with these suggestions, afraid of public disgrace, and dreading the consequence of legal conviction, she fell on her knees before the injured Fathom, and, after having imputed her crime to the temptations of necessity, implored his compassion, promised to restore the watch, and every thing she had taken, and begged he would dismiss the constable, that her reputation might not suffer in the eye of the world.

Ferdinand, with a severity of countenance purposely assumed, observed, that were she really indigent, he had charity enough to forgive what she had done; but, as he knew her circumstances were opulent, he looked upon this excuse as an aggravation of her guilt, which was certainly the effect of a vicious inclination; and he was therefore determined to prosecute her with the utmost severity of the law, as an example and terror to others, who might be infected with the same evil disposition. Finding him deaf to all her tears and intreaties, she changed the note, and offered him one hundred guineas, if he would compromise the affair, and drop the prosecution, so as that her character should sustain no damage: after much argumentation, he consented to accept of double the sum, which being instantly paid in East-India bonds, doctor Fathom told the constable, that the watch was found; and for once her reputation was patched up. This seasonable supply enabled our hero to stand trial with his adversary, who was nonsuited,[3] and also to mend his external appearance, which of late had not been extremely magnificent.

Soon after this gleam of good fortune, a tradesman, to whom he was considerably indebted, seeing no other probable means to recover his money, introduced Fathom to the acquaintance of a young widow who lodged at his house, and was said to be in possession of a considerable fortune. Considering the steps that were taken, it would have been almost impossible for him to miscarry in his addresses: the lady had been bred in the country, was unacquainted with the world, and of a very sanguine disposition, which her short trial of matrimony had not served to cool. Our adventurer was instructed to call at the tradesman's house, as if by accident, at an appointed time, when the widow was drinking tea with her landlady: on these occasions he always behaved to admiration. She liked his person, and praised his politeness, good humour, and good sense: his confederates extolled him as a prodigy of learning, taste, and good nature: they likewise represented him as a person on the eve of eclipsing all his competitors in physick: an acquaintance and intimacy soon ensued, nor was he restricted in point of opportunity. In a word, he succeeded in his endeavours, and one evening, on pretence of attending her to the play, he accompanied her to the Fleet, where they were married,[4] in presence of the tradesman and his wife, who were of the party.

This grand affair being accomplished to his satisfaction, he, next day, visited her brother, who was a counsellor of the Temple,[5] to make him acquainted with the step his sister had taken; and though the lawyer was not a little mortified, to find she had made such a clandestine match, he behaved civilly to his new brother-in-law, and gave him to understand, that his wife's fortune consisted of a jointure of one hundred and fifty pounds a year, and fifteen hundred pounds bequeathed to her during her widowhood, by her own father, who had taken the precaution of settling it in the hands of trustees, in such a manner as that any husband she might afterwards espouse, should be restricted from encroaching upon the capital, which was reserved for the benefit of her heirs. This intimation was far from being agreeable to our hero, who had been informed, that this sum was absolutely at the lady's disposal, and had actually destined the greatest part of it for the payment of his debts, for defraying the expence of furnishing an elegant house, and setting up a new equipage.

Notwithstanding this disappointment, he resolved to carry on his plan, upon the credit of his marriage, which was published in a very pompous article of the news papers; a chariot was bespoke, a ready furnished house immediately taken, and doctor Fathom began to reappear in all his former splendor.

His good friend the empirick, alarmed at this event, which not only raised our adventurer into the sphere of a dangerous rival, but also furnished him with means to revenge the ill office he had sustained at his hands, on the adventure of the former match; for, by this time, Fathom had given him some hints, importing, that he was not ignorant of his treacherous behaviour: roused, I say, by these considerations, he employed one of his emissaries, who had some knowledge of Fathom's brother-in-law, to prejudice him against our adventurer, whom he represented as a needy sharper, not only overwhelmed with debt and disgrace, but likewise previously married to a poor woman, who was prevented by nothing but want, from seeking redress at law. To confirm these assertions, he gave him a detail of Fathom's incumbrances, which he had learned for the purpose, and even brought the counsellor in company with the person who had lived with our hero before marriage, and who was so much incensed at her abrupt dismission, that she did not scruple to corroborate these allegations of the informer.

The lawyer, startled at this intelligence, set on foot a minute inquiry into the life and conversation of the doctor, which turned out so little to the advantage of his character and circumstances, that he resolved, if possible, to disunite him from his family, and as a previous step, repeated to his sister, all that he had heard to the prejudice of her husband, not forgetting to produce the evidence of his mistress, who laid claim to him by a prior title, which, she pretended, could be proved by the testimony of the clergyman who joined them. Such an explanation could not fail to inflame the resentment of the injured wife, who, at the very first opportunity, giving a loose to the impetuosity of her temper, upbraided our hero with the most bitter invectives for his perfidious dealing.

Ferdinand, conscious of his own innocence, which he had not always to plead, far from attempting to sooth her indignation, assumed the authority and prerogative of an husband, and sharply reprehended her for her credulity and indecent warmth. This rebuke, instead of silencing, gave new spirit and volubility to her reproaches, in the course of which, she plainly taxed him with want of honesty and affection, and said, that though his pretence was love, his aim was no other than a base design upon her fortune.

Fathom, stung with these accusations, which he really did not deserve, replied with uncommon heat, and charged her, in his turn, with want of sincerity and candour, in the false account she had given of that same fortune, before marriage: he even magnified his own condescension, in surrendering his liberty to a woman, who had so little to recommend her to the addresses of the other sex; a reflection which provoked this mild creature to such a degree of animosity, that, forgetting her duty and allegiance, she lent him a box on the ear, with such energy as made his eyes water; and he, for the honour of his manhood and sovereignty, having washed her face with a dish of tea, withdrew abruptly, to a coffee-house in the neighbourhood, where he had not long remained, when his passion subsided, and he then saw the expediency of an immediate reconciliation, which he resolved to purchase, even at the expence of a submission.

It was pity that such a salutary resolution had not been sooner taken: for when he returned to his own house, he understood, that Mrs. Fathom had gone abroad in an hackney coach; and upon examining her apartment, in lieu of her cloaths and trinkets, which she had removed with admirable dexterity and dispatch, he found this billet in one of the drawers of her buroe.[6] "Sir, being convinced that you are a cheat and an impostor, I have withdrawn myself from your cruelty and machinations, with a view to sollicit the protection of the law; and I doubt not but I shall soon be able to prove, that you have no just title to, or demand upon the person or effects of the unfortunate Sarah Muddy."

The time had been when Mr. Fathom would have allowed Mrs. Muddy to resine at her leisure, and blessed God for his happy deliverance; but at present the case was quite altered. Smarting as he was, from the expence of law suits, he dreaded a prosecution for bigamy, which (though he had justice on his side) he knew he could not of himself support: besides, all his other schemes of life were frustrated by this unlucky elopement: he therefore speedily determined to anticipate, as much as in him lay, the malice of his enemies, and to obtain, without delay, authentic documents of his marriage. With this view he hastened to the house of the tradesman, who, with his wife, had been witness to the ceremony and consummation; and, in order to interest them the more warmly in his cause, made a pathetic recital of this unhappy breach, in which he had suffered such injury and insult: but all his rhetoric would not avail; Mrs. Muddy had been beforehand with him, and proved the better orator of the two; for she had assailed this honest couple with such tropes and figures of eloquence, as were altogether irresistible. Nevertheless, they heard our hero, to an end, with great patience: then the wife, who was the common mouth, upon all such occasions, contracting her features into a very formal disposition, "I'll assure you," said she, "doctor Fathom, my husband and I have been in a very great terrification and numb-plush,[7] to hear such bad things of a person, whom, as one may say, we thought a worthy gentleman, and were ready to serve at all times, by day and by night, as the saying is; and besides, for all that, you know, and God knows, as we are dustrious people, and work hard for what we get, and we have served gentlemen to our own harm, whereby my husband was last Tuesday served with a siserary,[8] being that he was bound for an officer that ran away: and I said to my husband, 'Timothy,' says I, "tis a very hard thing for one to ruin one's self for stranger people. There's doctor Fathom,' says I, 'his account comes to nine and forty pounds seven shillings and four-pence half-penny; and you know, doctor, that was before your last bill began: but, howsomever, little did I think, as how a gentleman of your learning, would go to deceive a poor gentlewoman, when you had another wife alive.'"

In vain did our adventurer endeavour to vindicate himself from this aspersion; the good woman, like a great many modern disputants, proceeded with her declamation, without seeming to hear what was said on the other side of the question; and the husband was altogether neutral. At length, Ferdinand finding all his protestations ineffectual, "Well," said he, "though you are resolved, I see, to discredit all that I can say in opposition to that scandalous slander, of which I can easily acquit myself in a court of justice, surely you will not refuse to grant me a certificate, signifying, that you were present at the ceremony of my marriage with this unhappy woman." "You shall excuse us; (replied the female orator) people cannot be too wary in signing their names, in this wicked world; many a one has been brought to ruination by signing his name, and my husband shall not, with my good will, draw himself into such a primmineery."[9]

Fathom, alarm'd at this refusal, earnestly argued against the inhumanity and injustice of it, appealing to their own consciences for the reasonableness of his proposal; but, from the evasive answers of the wife, he had reason to believe, that, long before the time of trial, they would take care to have forgotten the whole transaction.

Though he was equally confounded and incensed at this instance of their
perfidy, he durst not manifest his indignation, conscious of the advantage
they had over him in divers respects; but repaired, without loss of time, to
the lodging of the clergyman who had noosed him, resolved to consult his
register, and secure his evidence. Here too his evil genius had got the start of
him, for the worthy ecclesiastic not only could not recollect his features, or
find his name in the register; but, when importuned by his pressing remonstrances, took umbrage at the freedom of his behaviour, and threatened,
if he would not immediately take himself away, to raise the posse of the
Fleet,[10] for the safety of his own person.

Rather than put the pastor to the trouble of alarming his flock, he retreated
with a heavy heart, and went in quest of his mistress, whom he had dismissed
at his marriage, in hopes of effecting a reconciliation, and preventing her
from joining in the conspiracy against him; but, alas, he met with such a
reception, as he had reason to expect from a slighted woman, who had never
felt any real attachment for his person. She did not upbraid him with his
cruelty, in leaving her as a mistress, but, with a species of effrontery, never
enough to be admired, reproached him with his villainy, in abandoning her,
who was his true and lawful wife, to go and ruin a poor gentlewoman, by
whose fortune he had been allured.

When he attempted to expostulate with this virago, upon the barbarity of
this assertion, she very prudently declined engaging in private conversation
with such an artful and wicked man, and calling up the people of the house,
insisted upon his being conducted to the door.

CHAPTER LVI.

In which his fortune is effectually strangled.

The last resource, and that upon which he least depended, was the advice
and assistance of his old friend the empirick, with whom he still maintained a slight correspondence; and to whose house he steered his course, in
great perplexity and tribulation. That gentleman, instead of consoling him
with assurances of friendship and protection, faithfully recapitulated all the
instances of his indiscretion and misconduct, taxed him with want of sincerity in the West-India affair, as well as with want of honesty in this last

marriage, while his former wife was alive; and finally, reminded him of his notes, which he desired might be immediately taken up, as he (the quack) had present occasion for a sum of money.

Ferdinand seeing it would be impracticable to derive any succour from this quarter, sneaked homewards, in order to hold a consultation with his own thoughts; and the first object that presented itself to his eyes, when he entered his apartment, was a letter from the tradesman, with his account inclosed, amounting to fifty-five pounds, which the writer desired might be paid without delay. Before he had time to peruse the articles, he received a summons, in consequence of a bill of indictment for bigamy, found against him in Hicks's-hall,[1] by Sarah Muddy, widow; and while he was resolving measures to avert these storms, another billet arrived from a certain attorney, giving him to understand, that he had orders from doctor Buffalo, the quack, to sue him for the payment of several notes, unless he would take them up in three days from the date of this letter.

Such a concurrence of sinister events, made a deep impression upon the mind of our adventurer: all his fortitude was insufficient to bear him up against this torrent of misfortunes; his resources were all dried up, his invention failed, and his reflection began to take a new turn. "To what purpose (said he to himself) have I deserted the paths of integrity and truth, and exhausted a fruitful imagination, in contriving schemes to betray my fellow-creatures; if, instead of acquiring a splendid fortune, which was my aim, I have suffered such a series of mortifications, and at last brought myself to the brink of inevitable destruction? By a virtuous exertion of those talents I inherit from nature and education, I might, long before this time, have rendered myself independent, and, perhaps, conspicuous in life: I might have grown up like a young oak, which being firmly rooted in its kindred soil, gradually raises up its lofty head, expands its leafy arms, projects a noble shade, and towers the glory of the plain: I should have paid the debt of gratitude to my benefactors, and made their hearts sing with joy for the happy effects of their benevolence; I should have been a bulwark to my friends, a shelter to my neighbours in distress; I should have run the race of honour, seen my fame diffused like a sweet-smelling odour, and felt the ineffable pleasure of doing good: whereas I am, after a vicissitude of disappointments, dangers and fatigues, reduced to misery and shame, aggravated by a conscience loaded with treachery and guilt. I have abused the confidence and generosity of my patron; I have defrauded his family, under the mask of sincerity and attachment; I have taken the most cruel and base advantages of virtue in distress; I have seduced unsuspecting innocence to ruin and despair;

I have violated the most sacred trust reposed in me by my friend and benefactor; I have betrayed his love, torn his noble heart asunder, by means of the most perfidious slander and false insinuations; and finally, brought to an untimely grave the fairest pattern of human beauty and perfection. Shall the author of these crimes pass with impunity? Shall he hope to prosper in the midst of such enormous guilt? It were an imputation upon providence to suppose it—Ah, no! I begin to feel myself overtaken by the eternal justice of heaven! I totter on the edge of wretchedness and woe, without one friendly hand to save me from the terrible abyss."

These reflections, which, perhaps, the misery of his fellow creatures would never have inspired, had he himself remained without the verge of misfortune, were now produced from the sensation of his own calamities; and, for the first time, his cheeks were bedewed with the drops of penitence and sorrow.[2] Contraries, saith Plato, are productive of each other.[3] Reformation is oftentimes generated from unsuccessful vice; and our adventurer was, at this juncture, very well disposed to turn over a new leaf,[4] in consequence of those salutary suggestions; though he was far from being cured beyond the possibility of a relapse: on the contrary, all the faculties of his soul were so well adapted, and had been so long habituated to deceit, that in order to extricate himself from the evils that environed him, he would not, in all probability, have scrupled to practise it upon his own father, had a convenient opportunity occurred.

Be that as it may, he certainly, after a tedious and fruitless exercise of his invention, resolved to effect a clandestine retreat from that confederacy of enemies which he could not withstand, and once more join his fortune to that of Renaldo, whom he proposed to serve, for the future, with fidelity and affection, thereby endeavouring to attone for the treachery of his former conduct. Thus determined, he packed up his necessaries in a portmanteau, attempted to amuse his creditors with promise of speedy payment, and venturing to come forth in the dark, took a place in the Canterbury stage coach, after having converted his superfluities into ready money. These steps were not taken with such privacy, as to elude the vigilance of his adversaries; for although he had been cautious enough to transport himself and his baggage to the inn, on Sunday evening, and never doubted, that the vehicle, which set out at four o'clock on Monday morning, would convey him out of the reach of his creditors, before they could possibly obtain a writ for securing his person; they had actually taken such precautions as frustrated all his finesse; and the coach being stopt in the Borough of Southwark,[5] doctor Fathom was seized by virtue of a warrant obtained on a criminal indictment, and was forthwith conducted to the prison of the King's Bench; yet not before he had, by his pathetic remonstrances, excited the compassion, and even drawn tears from the eyes of his fellow passengers.

He no sooner recollected himself from the shock which must have been occasioned by this sinister incident, than he dispatched a letter to his brother-in-law the counsellor, requesting an immediate conference, in which he promised to make such a proposal, as would save him all the expence of a lawsuit and trial, and at the same time effectually answer all the purposes of both. He was accordingly favoured with a visit from the lawyer, to whom, after the most solemn protestations of his own innocence, he declared, that, finding himself unable to wage war against such powerful antagonists, he had resolved even to abandon his indubitable right, and retire into another country, in order to screen himself from persecution, and remove all cause of disquiet from the prosecutrix, when he was unfortunately prevented by the warrant which had been executed against him. He said he was still willing, for the sake of his liberty, to sign a formal renunciation of his pretensions to Mrs. Fathom and her fortune, provided the deeds could be executed, and the warrant withdrawn, before he should be detained by his other creditors; and lastly, he conjured the barrister to spare himself the guilt and the charge of suborning evidence for the destruction of an unhappy man, whose misfortune was his only fault.

The lawyer felt the force of his expostulations, and though he would by no means suppose him innocent of the charge of bigamy, yet, under the pretext of humanity and commiseration, he undertook to persuade his sister to accept of a proper release, which he observed would not be binding, if executed during the confinement of Fathom; he therefore took his leave in order to prepare the papers, withdraw the action, and take such other measures as would hinder the prisoner from giving him the slip. Next day he returned with an order to release our hero, who being formally discharged, was conducted, by the lawyer, to a tavern in the neighbourhood, where the releases were exchanged, and every thing concluded with amity and concord. This business being happily transacted, Fathom stept into an hackney coach with his baggage, and was followed by a bailiff, who told him, with great composure, that he was again a prisoner at the suit of doctor Buffalo, and desired the coachman to reconduct him to the lodging he had so lately discharged.

Fathom, whose fortitude had been hitherto of the pagan temper, was now fain to reinforce it with the philosophy of christian resignation, tho' he had not as yet arrived to such a pitch of self-denial, as to forgive the counsellor, to whose double dealing he imputed this new calamity. After having received the compliments of the jailor on his recommitment, he took pen, ink, and paper, and composed an artful and affecting epistle to the empirick, imploring his mercy, flattering his weakness, and demonstrating the bad policy of cooping up an unhappy man in a jail, where he could never have an opportunity of doing justice to his creditors; nor did he forget to declare his intention of retiring into another country, where he might have some chance of earning a subsistence, which he had so long toiled for to no purpose in England. This last declaration he made in consequence of the jealous disposition of the quack, who, he knew, had long looked upon him in the odious light of an interloping rival. However, he reaped no benefit from this supplication, which served only to gratify the pride of Buffalo, who produced the extravagant encomiums which Fathom had bestowed upon him, as so many testimonials of his foe's bearing witness to his virtue.

CHAPTER LVII.

Fathom being safely housed, the reader is entertained with a retrospect.

But now it is high time to leave our adventurer to chew the cud of reflexion and remorse in this solitary mansion, that we may trace Renaldo in the several steps he took to assert his right, and do justice to his family. Never man indulged a more melancholy train of ideas than that which accompanied him in his journey to the Imperial court: for, notwithstanding the manifold reasons he had to expect a happy issue to his aim, his imagination was incessantly infected with something that chilled his nerves, and saddened his heart, recurring, with quick succession, like the unwearied wave that beats upon the bleak, inhospitable Greenland shore. This, the reader will easily suppose, was no other than the remembrance of the forlorn Monimia, whose image appeared to his fancy in different attitudes, according to the prevalence of the passions which raged in his bosom. Sometimes he viewed her in the light of apostacy, and then his soul was maddened with indignation and despair: but these transitory blasts were not able to efface the impressions she had formerly made upon his heart; impressions which he had so often and so long contemplated with inconceivable rapture. These pictures still remained, representing her fair as the most perfect idea of beauty, soft and tender as an angel of mercy and compassion, warmed with every virtue of the heart, and adorned with every accomplishment of human nature: yet the alarming contrast came still in the rear of this recollection; so that his soul was by turns agitated by the tempests of horror, and overwhelmed by the floods of grief.

He recalled the moment on which he first beheld her, with that pleasing regret which attends the memory of a dear deceased friend; then he bitterly cursed it, as the source of all his misfortunes and affliction: he thanked heaven for having blessed him with a friend to detect her perfidy and ingratitude; then ardently wished he had still continued under the influence of her delusion. In a word, the loneliness of his situation aggravated every horror of his reflection; for, as he found himself without company, his imagination was never sollicited, or his attention diverted from these subjects of woe; and he travelled to Brussels in a reverie, fraught with such torments as must have entirely wrecked his reason, had not providence interposed in his behalf. He was, by his postilion, conducted to one of the best inns of the place, where he understood the cloth was already laid for supper, and as the ordinary is open to strangers, in all those houses of entertainment, he introduced himself into the company, with a view to alleviate, in some measure, his sorrow and chagrin, by the conversation of his fellow guests: yet he was so ill prepared to obtain the relief which he courted, that he entered the apartment, and sat down to table, without distinguishing either the number or countenances of those who were present: though he himself did not remain so unregarded. His mein and deportment produced a prepossession in his favour; and the air of affliction, so remarkable in his visage, did not fail to attract their sympathy and observation.

Among the rest, was an Irish officer in the Austrian service,[1] who having eyed Renaldo attentively, "Sir, (said he, rising) if my eyes and memory do not deceive me, you are the count de Melvile, with whom I had the honour to serve upon the Rhine, during the last war."[2] The youth hearing his own name mentioned, lifted up his eyes, and at once recognizing the other to be a gentleman who had been a captain in his father's regiment, ran forwards, and embraced him with great affection.

This was, in divers respects, a fortunate rencounter for young Melvile; as the officer was not only perfectly well acquainted with the situation of the count's family, but also resolved, in a few days, to set out for Vienna, whither he promised to accompany Renaldo, as soon as he understood his route lay the same way. Before the day fixed for their departure arrived, this gentleman found means to insinuate himself so far into the confidence of the count, as to learn the cause of that distress which he had observed in his features at their first meeting; and being a gentleman of uncommon vivacity, as well as sincerely attached to the family of Melvile, to which he had owed his promotion; he exerted all his good humour and good sense, in amusing the fancy, and reasoning down the mortification of the afflicted Hungarian. He, in particular, endeavoured to wean his attention from the lost Monimia, by engaging it upon his domestic affairs, and upon the wrongs of his mother and sister, who, he gave him to understand, were languishing under the tyranny of his father-in-law.

This was a note that effectually roused him from the lethargy of his sorrow; and the desire of taking vengeance on the oppressor, who had ruined his fortune, and made his nearest relations miserable, so intirely engrossed his thoughts, as to leave no room for other considerations. During their journey to Austria, major Farrel (that was the name of his fellow-traveller) informed him of many circumstances touching his father's house, to which himself was an utter stranger.

"The conduct of your mother," said he, "in marrying count Trebasi, was not at all agreeable either to the friends of the count de Melvile, or to her own relations, who knew her second husband to be a man of a violent temper, and rapacious disposition, which the nature of his education and employment, had served rather to inflame than allay; for you well know he was a partizan during the whole course of the late war.[3] They were, moreover, equally surprized and chagrined, when they found she took no step to prevent his seizing upon that inheritance which of right belonged to you, and which, by the laws of Hungary, is unalienable from the heir of blood: nevertheless, they are now fully convinced, that she hath more than sufficiently attoned for her indiscretion, by the barbarity of her husband, who hath not only secluded her from all communication with her friends and acquaintance, but even confined her to the west tower of your father's house, where she is said to be kept close prisoner, and subjected to all sorts of inconvenience and mortification. This severity she is believed to have incurred, in consequence of having expostulated with him upon his unjust behaviour to you and mademoiselle, whom he hath actually shut up in some convent in Vienna, which your relations have not as yet been able to discover: but the memory of your noble father is so dear to all those who were favoured with his friendship; and the sufferings of the countess and mademoiselle have raised such a spirit of resentment against her cruel jailor, that nothing is wanted but your presence, to begin the prosecution, and give a sanction to the measures of your friends, which will, in a little time, restore your family to the fruition of its rights and fortune: for my own part, my dear count, I consider myself as one wholly indebted to your house, for the rank and expectation I now enjoy, and my finances, interest, and person, such as they are, I dedicate to your service."

Renaldo was not slow in making his acknowledgments to this generous Hibernian, whom he informed of his scheme, recounting to him his uncommon transaction with the benevolent Jew, and communicating the letters of recommendation he had received by his means, to some of the first noblemen at the Imperial court. Mean while, he burned with impatience, to chastise count Trebasi for his perfidious conduct to the widow and the fatherless, and would have taken the road to Presburg,[4] without touching at Vienna, in order to call him to a severe account, had not he been strenuously opposed by major Farrel, who represented the imprudence of taking such a step before he had secured a proper protection from the consequences with which it might be attended.

"It is not," said he, "your own life and fortune only which depend upon your behaviour in this emergency, but also the quiet and happiness of those who are most dear to your affection: not you alone, but likewise your mother and sister would infallibly suffer by your temerity and precipitation. First of all, deliver your credentials at court, and let us join our endeavours to raise an interest strong enough to counterbalance that of Trebasi. If we succeed, there will be no necessity for having recourse to personal measures: he will be compelled to yield up your inheritance which he unjustly detains, and to restore your sister to your arms; and if he afterwards refuses to do justice to the countess, you will always have it in your power to evince yourself the son of the brave count de Melvile."

These just and salutary representations had a due effect upon Renaldo, who no sooner arrived at the capital of Austria, than he waited upon a certain prince of distinction, to whose patronage he was commended; and from whom he met with a very cordial reception, not only on account of his credentials, but also for the sake of his father, who was well known to his highness. He heard his complaints with great patience and affability, assured him of his assistance and protection, and even undertook to introduce him to the empress queen,[5] who would not suffer the weakest of her subjects to be oppressed, much less disregard the cause of an injured young nobleman who by his own services and those of his family was peculiarly intitled to her favour.

Nor was he the only person whose countenance and patronage Melvile sollicited upon this occasion; he visited all the friends of his father, and all his mother's relations, who were easily interested in his behalf; while major Far-

rel contributed all his efforts in strengthening the association. So that a law-
suit was immediately commenced against count Trebasi, who on his side was
not idle, but prepared with incredible industry for the assault, resolving to
maintain with his whole power the acquisition he had made.

The laws of Hungary, like those of some other countries I could name,
afford so many subterfuges for the purposes of perfidy and fraud, that it is no
wonder our youth began to complain of the slow progress of his affair; especially as he glowed with the most eager desire of redressing the grievances of
his parent and sister, whose sufferings he did not doubt were doubled since
the institution of his process against their tormentor. He imparted his sentiments on this head to his friend; and, as his apprehension every moment
increased, plainly told him he could no longer live without making some
effort to see those with whom he was so nearly connected in point of blood
and affection: he therefore resolved to repair immediately to Presburg, and
according to the intelligence he should procure, essay to see and converse
with his mother, tho' at the hazard of his life.

CHAPTER LVIII.

Renaldo abridges the proceedings at law, and
approves himself the son of his father.

The major finding him determined, insisted upon attending him in his
expedition, and they set out together for Presburg, where they privately
arrived in the dark, resolving to keep themselves concealed at the house of a
friend, until they should have formed some plan for their future operations.
Here they were informed that count Trebasi's castle was altogether inaccessible; that all the servants who were supposed to have the least veneration or
compassion for the countess, were dismissed; and that since Renaldo was
known to be in Germany, the vigilance and caution of that cruel husband
were redoubled to such a degree, that no body knew whether his unfortunate
lady was actually alive or dead.

Farrel perceiving Melvile exceedingly affected with this intimation, and
hearing him declare that he would never quit Presburg until he should have
entered the house, and removed his doubts on that interesting subject; not
only argued with great vehemence against such an attempt, as equally dangerous and indiscreet, but solemnly swore he would prevent his purpose, by

discovering his design to the family, unless he would promise to listen to a more moderate and feasible expedient. He then proposed that he himself should appear in the equipage of one of those travelling Savoyards[1] who stroll about Europe, amusing ignorant people with the effects of a magic lanthorn,[2] and in that disguise endeavour to obtain admittance from the servants of Trebasi, among whom he might make such inquiries, as would deliver Melvile from his present uneasy suspence.

This proposal was embraced, tho' reluctantly, by Renaldo, who was unwilling to expose his friend to the least danger or disgrace; and the major being next day provided with the habit and implements of his new profession, together with a ragged attendant who preceded him, extorting music from a paultry viole,[3] approached the castle-gate, and proclaimed his shew so naturally in a yell partaking of the scream of Savoy and the howl of Ireland,[4] that one would have imagined he had been conductor to madam Catherina[5] from his cradle. So far his stratagem succeeded: he had not long stood in waiting, before he was invited into the court-yard, where the servants formed a ring, and danced to the efforts of his companion's skill; then he was conducted into the buttery,[6] where he exhibited his figures on the wall and his princess[7] on the floor; and while they regaled him in this manner with scraps and sour wine, he took occasion to inquire about the old lady and her daughter, before whom he said he had performed in his last peregrination. Tho' this question was asked with all that air of simplicity which is peculiar to these people, one of the domestics took the alarm, being infected with the suspicions of his master, and plainly taxed the major with being a spy, threatening at the same time that he should be stripped and searched.

This would have been a very dangerous experiment for the Hibernian, who had actually in his pocket a letter to the countess from her son, which he hoped fortune might have furnished him with an opportunity to deliver. When he therefore found himself in this dilemma, he was not at all easy in his own mind: however, instead of protesting his innocence in an humble and beseeching strain, in order to acquit himself of the charge, he resolved to elude the suspicion by provoking the wrath of his accuser, and putting on the air of vulgar integrity affronted, began to reproach the servant in very insolent terms for his unfair supposition, and undressing himself in a moment to the skin, threw his tattered garments in the face of his adversary, telling him he would find nothing there which he would not be very glad to part with; at the same time raising his voice, he, in the gibberish of the clan he represented, scolded and cursed with great fluency: so that the whole house resounded with the noise. The valet's jealousy,[8] like a smaller fire, was in a trice swallowed up in the greater flame of his rage enkindled by this abrupt address: in consequence of which, Farrel was kicked out at the gate, naked as he was to the waist, after his lanthorn had been broke to pieces on his head; and there he was joined by his domestic, who had not been able to recover his apparel and effect a retreat, without incurring marks of the same sort of distinction.

The major, considering the risk he must have run in being detected, thought himself cheaply quit for this moderate discipline, though he was really concerned for his friend Renaldo, who understanding the particulars of the adventure, determined, as the last effort, to ride round the castle in the open day, on pretence of taking the air, when, peradventure, the countess would see him from the place of her confinement, and favour him with some mark or token of her being alive.

Though his companion did not much relish this plan, which he foresaw would expose him to the insults of Trebasi; yet, as he could not contrive a better, he acquiesced in Renaldo's invention, with the proviso, that he would defer the execution of it until his father-in-law should be absent in the chase, which was a diversion he every day enjoyed.

Accordingly they set a proper watch, and lay concealed until they were informed of Trebasi's having gone forth; when they mounted their horses, and rode into the neighbourhood of the castle. Having made a small excursion in the adjoining fields, they drew nearer the walls, and at an easy pace had twice circled them, when Farrel descried at the top of a tower, a white handkerchief waved by a woman's hand thro' the iron bars that secured the window. This signal being pointed out to Renaldo, his heart began to throb with great violence; he made a respectful obeissance towards the part in which it appeared, and perceiving the hand beckoning him to approach, advanced to the very buttress of the turret; upon which, seeing something drop, he alighted with great expedition, and took up a picture of his father in miniature, the features of which he no sooner distinguished, than the tears ran down his cheeks; he pressed the little image to his lips with the most filial fervour; then conveying it to his bosom, looked up to the hand, which waved in such a manner, as gave him to understand it was high time to retire. Being by this time highly persuaded that his kind monitor was no other than the countess herself, he pointed to his heart, in token of his filial affection, and laying his hand on his sword, to denote his resolution of doing her justice, he took his leave with another profound bow, and suffered himself to be reconducted to his lodging.

Every circumstance of this transaction was observed by the servants of

The White Handkerchief, by Stothard.
(General Research Division, The New York Public Library—
Astor, Lenox and Tilden Foundations.)

count Trebasi, who immediately dispatched a messenger to their lord, with an account of what had happened. Alarmed at this information, from which he immediately concluded that the stranger was young Melvile, he forthwith quitted the chace, and returning to the castle by a private postern,[9] ordered his horse to be kept ready saddled, in hope that his son-in-law would repeat the visit to his mother. This precaution would have been to no purpose, had Renaldo followed the advice of Farrel, who represented the danger of returning to a place where the alarm was undoubtedly given by his first appearance; and exhorted him to return to Vienna for the prosecution of his suit, now that he was satisfied of his mother's being alive: in order to strengthen this admonition, he bad him recollect the signal for withdrawing, which was doubtless the effect of maternal concern, inspired by the knowledge of the count's vigilance and vindictive disposition.

Notwithstanding these suggestions, Melvile persisted in his resolution of appearing once more below the tower, on the supposition that his mother, in expectation of his return, had prepared a billet for his acceptance, from which he might obtain important intelligence. The major seeing him lend a deaf ear to his remonstrances, was contented to attend him in this second expedition, which he pressed him to undertake that same afternoon, as Trebasi had taken care to circulate a report of his having gone to dine at the seat of a nobleman in the neighbourhood. Our knight-errant and his squire, deceived by this finesse, presented themselves again under the prison of the countess, who no sooner beheld her son return, than she earnestly intreated him to be gone, by the same sign which she had before used; and he taking it for granted that she was debarred the use of pen, ink and paper, and that he had nothing more to expect, consented to retire, and had already moved to some distance from the house, when, in crossing a small plantation that belonged to the castle, they were met by count Trebasi and another person on horseback.

At sight of this apparition, the blood mounted into Renaldo's cheeks, and his eyes began to lighten with eagerness and indignation; which was not at all diminished by the ferocious address of the count, who, advancing to Melvile, with a menacing air, "Before you proceed," said he, "I must know with what view you have been twice to-day patroling round my inclosures, and reconnoitring the different avenues of my house: you likewise carry on a clandestine correspondence with some person in the family, of which my honour obliges me to demand an explanation."

"Had your actions been always regulated by the dictates of honour," replied Renaldo, "I should never have been questioned for riding round that castle which you know is my rightful inheritance; or excluded from the sight of a parent who suffers under your tyranny and oppression. It is my part, therefore, to expostulate; and, since fortune hath favoured me with an opportunity of revenging our wrongs in person, we shall not part until you have learned that the family of the count de Melvile is not to be injured with impunity. Here is no advantage on either side, in point of arms or number, you are better mounted than I am, and shall have the choice of the ground on which our difference ought to be brought to a speedy determination."

Trebasi, whose courage was not of the sentimental kind, but purely owing to his natural insensibility of danger, instead of concerting measures coolly for the engagement, or making any verbal reply to this defiance, drew a pistol without the least hesitation, and fired it at the face of Renaldo, part of whose left eye brow was carried off by the ball. Melvile was not slow in returning the compliment, which, as it was deliberate, proved the more decisive: for the shot entering the count's right breast, made its way to the back bone with such a shock, as struck him to the ground; upon which the other alighted, in order to improve the advantage he had gained.

During this transaction, Farrel had well nigh lost his life by the savage behaviour of Trebasi's attendant, who had been a hussar officer,[10] and who thinking it was his duty to imitate the example of his patron on this occasion, discharged a pistol at the major before he had the least intimation of his design. The Hibernian's horse being a common hireling, and unaccustomed to stand fire, no sooner saw the flash of Trebasi's pistol, than starting aside, he happened to plunge into a hole, and was overturned at the very instant when the hussar's piece went off, so that no damage ensued to his rider, who pitching on his feet, flew with great nimbleness to his adversary, then laying hold on one leg, dismounted him in a twinkling, and seizing his throat as he lay, would have soon dispatched him without the use of firearms, had he not been prevented by his friend Renaldo, who desired him to desist, observing that his vengeance was already satisfied, as the count seemed to be in the agonies of death. The major was loth to quit his prey, as he thought his aggressor had acted in a treacherous manner; but recollecting that there was no time to lose, because, in all probability, the firing had alarmed the castle, he took his leave of the vanquished hussar, with a couple of hearty kicks, and mounting his horse, followed Melvile to the house of a gentleman in the neighbourhood, who was kinsman to the countess, and very well disposed to grant him a secure retreat, until the troublesome consequences of this rencounter should be overblown.

Trebasi, though to the young gentleman he seemed speechless and insen-

Count Trebasi Fires upon Renaldo, by Clennell.
(Library Company of Philadelphia.)

sible, had neither lost the use of his reason, nor of his tongue, but affected that extremity, in order to avoid any further conversation with the victor. He was one of those people who never think of death until he knocks at the door, and then earnestly intreat him to excuse them for the present, and be so good as to call another time. The count had so often escaped unhurt, in the course of his campaigns, that he looked upon himself as invulnerable, and set all danger at defiance. Though he had hitherto taken no care of the concerns of his soul, he had a large fund of superstition at bottom; and when the surgeon who examined his wound, declared it was mortal, all the terrors of futurity took hold on his imagination, and all the misdemeanours of his life presented themselves in aggravated colours to his recollection.

He implored the spiritual assistance of a good priest in the neighbourhood, who, in the discharge of his own conscience, gave him to understand, that he had little mercy to expect, unless he would, as much as lay in his power, redress the injuries he had done to his fellow-creatures. As nothing lay heavier upon his soul than the cruelty and fraud he had practised upon the family of count Melvile, he earnestly besought this charitable clergyman to mediate his pardon with the countess, and at the same time desired to see Renaldo before his death, that he might put him in possession of his paternal estate, and sollicit his forgiveness for the offence he had given.

His lady, far from waiting for the priest's intercession, no sooner understood the lamentable situation of her husband, and found herself at liberty, than she hastened to his apartment, expressed the utmost concern for his misfortune, and tended him with truly conjugal tenderness and fidelity. Her son gladly obeyed the summons, and was received with great civility and satisfaction by his father-in-law, who, in presence of the judge and divers gentlemen assembled for that purpose, renounced all right and title to the fortune he had so unjustly usurped; disclosed the name of the convent to which mademoiselle de Melvile had been conveyed, dismissed all the agents of his iniquity, and being reconciled to his son-in-law, began to prepare himself in tranquillity for his latter end.

The countess was overwhelmed with an excess of joy, while she embraced her long lost son, who had proved himself so worthy of his father. Yet this joy was imbittered, by reflecting that she was made a widow by the hands of that darling son: for, though she knew his honour demanded the sacrifice, she could not lay aside that regard and veneration which is attached to the name of husband; and therefore resolved to retire into a monastry, where she could spend the remainder of her life in devotion, without being exposed to any intercourse which might interfere with the delicacy of her sentiments on that subject.

CHAPTER LIX.

He is the messenger of happiness to his sister, who removes the film which had long obstructed his penetration, with regard to count Fathom.

As the most endearing affection had always subsisted between Renaldo and his sister, he would not one moment deny himself the pleasure of flying to her embrace, and of being the glad messenger of her deliverance. Soon, therefore, as he understood the place of her retreat, and had obtained a proper order to the abbess, signed by count Trebasi, he set out post for Vienna, still accompanied by his faithful Hibernian, and arriving at the convent, found the abbess and the whole house so engrossed in making preparations for the ceremony of giving the veil next day to a young woman who had fulfilled the term of her probation, that he could not possibly see his sister with that leisure and satisfaction which he had flattered himself with enjoying at this meeting; and therefore he was fain to bridle his impatience for two days, and keep his credentials until the hurry should be over, that mademoiselle might have no intimation of her good fortune, except from his own mouth.

In order to fill up this tedious interval, he visited his friends at court, who were rejoiced to hear the happy issue of his excursion to Presburg; the prince who was his particular patron desired he would make himself perfectly easy with regard to the death of count Trebasi, for he would take care to represent him in such a light to the empress queen, as would screen him from any danger or prosecution on that account. His Highness, moreover, appointed the following day for performing the promise he had made of presenting him to that august princess, and in the mean time prepossessed her so much in his favour, that when he approached her presence, and was announced by his noble introductor, she eyed him with a look of peculiar complacency, saying, "I am glad to see you returned to my dominions. Your father was a gallant officer, who served our house with equal courage and fidelity; and as I understand you tread in his foot-steps, you may depend upon my favour and protection."

He was so much overwhelmed with this gracious reception, that, while he bowed in silence, the drops of gratitude trickled from his eyes; and her imperial majesty was so well pleased with this manifestation of his heart, that she immediately gave directions for promoting him to the command of a troop of horse.—Thus fortune seemed willing and indeed eager to discharge the debt she owed him for the different calamities he had undergone. And as he looked upon the generous Hebrew to be the sole source of his success, he did not fail to make him acquainted with the happy effects of his recommendation and friendship, and to express, in the warmest terms, the deep sense he had of his uncommon benevolence, which, by the bye, was still greater with regard to Renaldo, than the reader as yet imagines; for he not only furnished him with money for his present occasions, but also given him an unlimited credit on a banker in Vienna to whom one of his letters was directed.

The ceremony of the nun's admission being now performed, and the convent restored to its former quiet, Melvile hasted thither on the wings of brotherly affection, and presented his letter to the abbess, who having perused the contents, by which she learned that the family disquiets of count Trebasi no longer subsisted, and that the bearer was the brother of mademoiselle, she received him with great politeness, congratulated him on this happy event, and begging he would excuse her staying with him in the parlour, on pretence of business, withdrew, saying, she would immediately send in a young lady who would console him for her absence. In a few minutes he was joined by his sister, who, expecting nothing less than to see Renaldo, no sooner distinguished his features, than she shriek'd aloud with surprize, and would have sunk upon the floor, had not he supported her in his embrace.

Such a sudden apparition of her brother at any time, or in any place, after their long separation, would have strongly affected this sensible young lady: but to find him so abruptly in a place where she thought herself buried from the knowledge of all her relations, occasioned such commotion in her spirits as had well nigh endangered her reason: for it was not 'till after a considerable pause, that she could talk to him with connexion or coherence. However, as those transports subsided, they entered into a more deliberate and agreeable conversation; in the course of which, he gradually informed her of what had passed at the castle; and inexpressible was the pleasure she felt in learning that her mother was released from captivity, herself restored to freedom, and her brother to the possession of his lawful inheritance, by the only means to which she had always prayed these blessings might be owing.

As she had been treated with uncommon humanity by the abbess, she would not consent to leave the convent until he should be ready to set out for Presburg; so that they dined together with that good lady, and passed the afternoon in that mutual communication with which a brother and sister may be supposed to entertain themselves on such an occasion. She gave him a detail of the insults and mortifications she had suffered from the brutality of her father-in-law, and told him, that her confinement in this monastry was owing to Trebasi's having intercepted a letter to her from Renaldo, signifying his intention to return to the empire, in order to assert his own right and redress her grievances. Then turning the discourse upon the incidents of his peregrinations, she in a particular manner inquired about that exquisite beauty who had been the innocent source of all his distresses, and upon whose perfections he had often, in his letters to his sister, expatiated with indications of rapture and delight.

This inquiry in a moment blew up that scorching flame which had been well nigh stifled by other necessary avocations. His eyes gleamed, his cheeks glowed and grew pale alternately, and his whole frame underwent an immediate agitation; which being perceived by mademoiselle, she concluded that some new calamity was annexed to the name of Monimia, and dreading to rip up a wound which she saw was so ineffectually closed, she for the present suppressed her curiosity and concern, and industriously endeavoured to introduce some less affecting subject of conversation. He saw her aim, approved of her discretion, and joining her endeavours, expressed his surprize at her having omitted to signify the least remembrance of her old favourite Fathom, whom he had left in England. He had no sooner pronounced this name than she suffered some confusion in her turn; from which, however, recollecting herself, "Brother," said she, "you must endeavour to forget that wretch, who is altogether unworthy of retaining the smallest share of your regard."

Astonished and indeed angry at this expression, which he considered as the effect of malicious misrepresentation, he gently chid her for her credulity in believing the envious aspersion of some person who repined at the superior virtue of Fathom, whom he affirmed to be an honour to the human species.

"Nothing is more easy," replied the young lady, "than to impose upon a person, who, being himself unconscious of guile, suspects no deceit. You have been a dupe, dear brother, not to the finesse of Fathom, but to the sincerity of your own heart. For my own part, I assume no honour to my own penetration in having comprehended the villainy of that impostor, which was discovered in more than one instance by accidents I could not possibly foresee.

You must know that Teresa, who attended me from my childhood, and in whose honesty I reposed such confidence, having disobliged some of the inferior servants, was so narrowly watched in all her transactions, as to be at last detected in the very act of conveying a piece of plate, which was actually found concealed among her cloaths.

You may guess how much I was astonished when I understood this circumstance; I could not trust to the evidence of my own senses, and should have still believed her innocent, in spite of ocular demonstration, had not she, in the terrors of being tried for felony, promised to make a very material discovery to the countess, provided she would take such measures as would save her life.

This request being complied with, she, in my hearing, opened up such an amazing scene of iniquity, baseness and ingratitude, which had been acted by her and Fathom, in order to defraud the family to which they were so much indebted, that I could not have believed the human mind capable of such degeneracy, or that traitor endowed with such pernicious cunning and dissimulation, had not her tale been congruous, consistent and distinct, and fraught with circumstances that left no room to doubt the least article of her confession: on consideration of which, she was permitted to go into voluntary exile."

She then explained their combination in all the particulars, as we have already recounted them in their proper place; and, finally, observed, that the opinion she had hence conceived of Fathom's character, was confirmed by what she had since learned of his perfidious conduct towards that very nun who had lately taken the veil.

Perceiving her brother struck dumb with astonishment, and gaping with the most eager attention, she proceeded to relate the incidents of his double intrigue with the jeweller's wife and daughter, as they were communicated to her by the nun, who was no other than the individual Wilhelmina.[1] After those rivals had been forsaken by their gallant, their mutual animosities and chagrin served to whet the attention and invention of each; so that in a little time the whole mystery stood disclosed to both. The mother had discovered the daughter's correspondence with Fathom, as we have formerly observed, by means of that unfortunate letter which he unwittingly committed to the charge of the old beldame; and as soon as she understood he was without the reach of all sollicitation or prosecution, imparted this billet to her husband, whose fury was so ungovernable, that he had almost sacrificed Wilhelmina with his own hands, especially when terrified by his threats and imprecations, she owned that she had bestowed the chain on this perfidious lover. However, his dreadful purpose was prevented, partly by the interposition of his wife, whose aim was not the death but immurement of his daughter, and partly by the tears and supplication of the young gentlewoman herself, who protested, that, although the ceremony of the church had not been performed, she was contracted to Fathom by the most solemn vows, to witness which, he invoked all the saints in Heaven.

The jeweller, upon cooler consideration, was unwilling to lose the least spark of hope that glittered among the ruins of his despair, and resisted all the importunities of his wife, who pressed him to consult the welfare of his daughter's soul, in the fond expectation of finding some expedient to lure back the chain and it's possessor. In the mean time Wilhelmina was daily and hourly exposed to the mortifying animadversions of her mamma, who, with all the insolence of virtue, incessantly upbraided her with the backslidings of her vicious life, and exhorted her to reformation and repentance. This continual triumph lasted for many months, 'till at length a quarrel happening between the mother and the gossip at whose house she used to give the rendezvous to her admirers, that incensed confidante, in the precipitation of her anger, promulgated the history of those secret meetings, and, among the rest, her interviews with Fathom were brought to light.

The first people who hear news of this sort, are generally those to whom they are most unwelcome. The German was soon apprised of his wife's frailty, and considered the two females of his house as a couple of devils incarnate, sent from hell to exercise his patience: yet, in the midst of his displeasure he found matter of consolation, in being furnished with a sufficient reason for parting with his help-mate, who had for many years kept his family in disquiet. He therefore, without hazarding a personal conference, sent proposals to her by a friend, which she did not think proper to reject: and seeing himself restored to the dominion of his own house, exerted his sway so tyrannically, that Wilhelmina became weary of her life, and had recourse to the comforts of religion, of which she soon became enamoured, and begged her father's permission to dedicate the rest of her life to the duties of devotion. She was accordingly received in this convent; the regulations of which were so much to her liking, that she performed the task of probation with pleasure, and voluntarily excluded herself from the vanities of this life. It was here she had contracted an acquaintance with mademoiselle de Melvile, to whom she communicated her complaints of Fathom, on the supposition that he was related to the count, as he himself had often declared.

While the young lady rehearsed the particulars of this detail, Renaldo sustained a strange vicissitude of different passions. Surprize, sorrow, fear, hope and indignation raised a most tumultuous conflict in his bosom. Monimia rushed upon his imagination in the character of innocence betrayed by the insinuations of treachery. He with horror viewed her at the mercy of a villain, who had broken all the ties of gratitude and honour.

Affrighted at the prospect, he started from his seat, exclaiming in the unconnected strain of distraction and despair: "Have I then nourished a serpent in my bosom! Have I listened to the voice of a traitor who hath murdered my

peace! who hath tore my heart-strings asunder, and perhaps ruined the pattern of all earthly perfection. It cannot be. Heaven would not suffer such
infernal artifice to take effect. The thunder would be levelled against the head
of the accursed projector."

From this transport, compared with his agitation when she mentioned
Monimia, his sister judged that Fathom had been the occasion of a breach
between the two lovers; and this conjecture being confirmed by the disjointed
answers he made to her interrogations upon the affair, she endeavoured to
calm his apprehensions, by representing that he would soon have an opportunity of returning to England, where the misunderstanding might be easily
cleared up; and that, in the mean time, he had nothing to fear on account of
the person of his mistress, in a country where individuals were so well protected by the laws and constitution of the realm.[2] At length he suffered himself to be flattered with the fond hope of seeing Monimia's character triumph
in the inquiry; of retrieving that lost jewel, and of renewing that ravishing
intercourse and exalted expectation which had been so cruelly cut off. He
now wished to find Fathom as black as he had been exhibited, that Monimia's
apostacy might be numbered among the misrepresentations of his treachery
and fraud.

His love, which was alike generous and ardent, espoused the cause, and he
no longer doubted her constancy and virtue: but when he reflected how her
tender heart must have been wrung with anguish at his unkindness and cruelty, in leaving her destitute in a foreign land; how her sensibility must have
been tortured in finding herself altogether dependent upon a ruffian, who
certainly harboured the most baleful designs upon her honour; how her life
must be endangered both by his barbarity and her own despair: I say, when
he reflected on these circumstances, he shuddered with horrour and dismay;
and that very night dispatched a letter to his friend the Jew, intreating him, in
the most pressing manner, to employ all his intelligence in learning the situation of the fair orphan, that she might be protected from the villany of
Fathom, until his return to England.

CHAPTER LX.

He recompenses the attachment of his friend: and receives a letter that reduces him to the verge of death and distraction.

This step being taken, his mind in some measure retrieved its former tranquillity: he soothed himself with the prospect of an happy reconciliation with the divine Monimia, and his fancy was decoyed from every disagreeable presage by the entertaining conversation of his sister, with whom in two days he set out for Presburg, attended by his friend the major, who had never quitted him since their meeting at Brussels. Here they found count Trebasi entirely rid of the fever which had been occasioned by his wound, and in a fair way of doing well; a circumstance that afforded unspeakable pleasure to Melvile, whose manner of thinking was such, as would have made him unhappy, could he have charged himself with the death of his mother's husband, howsoever criminal he might have been.

The count's ferocity did not return with his health: his eyes were opened by the danger he had incurred, and his sentiments turned in a new channel: he heartily asked pardon of mademoiselle for the rigorous usage she had suffered from the violence of his temper; thanked Renaldo for the seasonable lesson he had administered to him; and not only insisted upon being removed from the castle to an house of his own in Presburg, but proffered to make immediate restitution of all the rents which he had unjustly converted to his own use.

These things being settled in the most amicable manner, to the entire satisfaction of the parties concerned, as well as of the neighbouring noblesse, among whom the house of Melvile was in universal esteem, Renaldo resolved to sollicit leave at the Imperial court to return to England, in order to investigate that affair of Monimia, which was more interesting than all the points he had hitherto adjusted: but, before he quitted Presburg, his friend Farrel taking him aside one day, "Count," said he, "will you give me leave to ask, if, by my zeal and attachment for you, I have had the good fortune to acquire your esteem?" "To doubt that esteem," replied Renaldo, "were to suspect my gratitude and honour, of which I must be utterly destitute before I lose the sense of those obligations I owe to your gallantry and friendship: obligations which I long for a proper occasion to repay."

"Well then," resumed the major, "I will deal with you like a downright Swiss,[1] and point out a method by which you may shift the load of obligation from your own shoulders to mine. You know my birth, rank and expectations in the service: but perhaps you do not know, that, as my expence hath always unavoidably exceeded my income, I find myself a little out at elbows in my circumstances, and want to piece them up by matrimony. Of those ladies with whom I think I have any chance of succeeding, mademoiselle de Melvile seems the best qualified to render my situation happy in all respects. Her fortune is more than sufficient to disembarrass my affairs; her good sense will be a seasonable check upon my vivacity; her agreeable accomplishments will engage a continuation of affection and regard: I know my own disposition well enough to think I shall become a most dutiful and tractable husband; and shall deem myself highly honoured in being more closely united to my dear count de Melvile, the son and representative of that worthy officer under whom my youth was formed: if you will therefore sanction my claim, I will forthwith begin my approaches, and doubt not, under your auspices, to bring the place to a capitulation."

Renaldo was pleased with the frankness of this declaration, approved of his demand, and desired him to depend upon his good offices with his sister, whom he sounded, that same evening, upon the subject, recommending the major to her favour, as a gentleman well worthy of her choice. Mademoiselle, who had never been exercised in the coquetries of her sex, and was now arrived at those years, when the vanity of youth ought to yield to discretion, considered the proposal as a philosopher, and after due deliberation, candidly owned she had no objection to the match. Farrel was accordingly introduced in the character of a lover, after the permission of the countess had been obtained; and he carried on his addresses in the usual form, so much to the satisfaction of all concerned in the event, that a day was appointed for the celebration of his nuptials, when he entered into peaceable possession of his prize.

A few days after this joyful occasion, while Renaldo was at Vienna, where he had been indulged with leave of absence for six months, and employed in making preparations for his journey to Britain, he was one evening presented, by his servant, with a pacquet from London, which he no sooner opened, than he found inclosed a letter directed to him, in the hand-writing of Monimia. He was so much affected at sight of those well-known characters, that he stood motionless as a statue, eager to know the contents, yet afraid to peruse the billet. While he hesitated in this suspense, he chanced to cast his eye on the inside of the cover, and perceived the name of his Jewish friend at the bottom of a few lines, importing, that the inclosed was delivered to him by a physician of his acquaintance, who had recommended it in a particular manner to his care. This intimation served only to encrease the mystery, and whet his impatience; and as he had the explanation in his hand, he summoned all his resolution to his aid, and breaking the seal, began to read these words, "Renaldo will not suppose, that this address proceeds from interested motives, when he learns, that, before it can be presented to his view, the unfortunate Monimia will be no more."

Here the light forsook Renaldo's eyes, his knees knocked together, and he fell at full length insensible on the floor: his valet hearing the noise, ran into the apartment, lifted him upon a couch, and dispatched a messenger for proper assistance, while he himself endeavoured to recal his spirits by such applications as chance afforded: but before the count exhibited any signs of life, his brother-in-law entered his chamber by accident, and as soon as he recollected himself from the extreme confusion and concern produced by this melancholy spectacle, he perceived the fatal epistle which Melvile, though insensible, still kept within his grasp; justly suspecting this to be the cause of that severe paroxysm, he drew near the couch, and with difficulty read what is above rehearsed, and the sequel, to this effect.

"Yes, I have taken such measures as will prevent it from falling into your hands, until after I shall have been released from a being imbittered with inexpressible misery and anguish. It is not my intention, once loved, and ah! still too fondly remembered youth, to upbraid you as the source of that un-ceasing woe, which hath been so long the sole inhabitant of my lonely bosom. I will not call you inconstant or unkind. I dare not think you base or dishonourable; yet I was abruptly sacrificed to a triumphant rival, before I had learned to bear such mortification; before I had overcome the prejudices which I had imbibed in my father's house. I was all at once abandoned to despair, to indigence and distress, to the vile practices of a villain, who, I fear, hath betrayed us both. What have not I suffered from the insults and vicious designs of that wretch, whom you cherished in your bosom! yet to these I owe this near approach to that goal of peace, where the canker-worm of sorrow will expire. Beware of that artful traitor; and, oh! endeavour to overcome that levity of disposition, which, if indulged, will not only stain your reputation, but also debauch the good qualities of your heart. I release you, in the sight of heaven, from all obligations: if I have been injured, let not my wrongs be visited on the head of Renaldo, for whom shall be offered up the last fervent prayers of the hapless Monimia."

This letter was a clue to the labyrinth of Melvile's distress: though the major had never heard him mention the name of this beauty, he had received such hints from his own wife, as enabled him to comprehend the whole of the count's disaster. By the administration of stimulating medicines, Renaldo re-covered his perception: but this was a cruel alternative, considering the situa-tion of his thoughts. The first word he pronounced was Monimia, with all the emphasis of the most violent despair: he perused the letter, and poured forth incoherent execrations against Fathom and himself. He exclaimed in a frantic tone, "she is lost for ever! murthered by my unkindness! we are both undone by the infernal arts of Fathom! execrable monster! Restore her to my arms. If thou art not a fiend in reality, I will tear out thy false heart!"

So saying, he sprung upon his valet, who would have fallen a sacrifice to his undistinguishing fury, had not he been saved by the interposition of Far-rel and the family, who disengaged him from his master's gripe by dint of force; yet, notwithstanding their joint endeavours, he broke from this re-straint, leaped upon the floor, and seizing his sword, attempted to plunge it in his own breast. When he was once more overcome by numbers, he cursed himself, and all those who withheld him; swore he would not survive the fair victim who had perished by his credulity and indiscretion; and the agitation of his spirits increased to such a degree, that he was seized with strong con-vulsions, which nature was scarce able to sustain: every medical expedient was used to quiet this perturbation, which at length yielded so far as to subside into a continual fever, and confirmed delirium, during which he ceased not to pour forth the most pathetic complaints[2] touching his ruined love, and to rave about the ill-starred Monimia. The major, half distracted by the calamity of his friend, would have concealed it from the knowledge of his family, had not the physician, by despairing of his life, laid him under the necessity of making them acquainted with his condition.

The countess and mrs. Farrel were no sooner informed of his case, than they hasted to the melancholy scene, where they found Renaldo deprived of his senses, panting under the rage of an exasperated[3] disease. They saw his face distorted, and his eyes glaring with frenzy: they heard him invoke the name of Monimia, with a tenderness of accent, which even the impulse of madness could not destroy. Then with a sudden transition of tone and ges-ture, he denounced vengeance against her betrayer, and called upon the north wind to cool the fervour of his brain. His hair hung in dishevelled parcels, his cheeks were wan, his looks ghastly, his vigour was fled, and all the glory of his youth faded: the physician hung his head in silence, the attendants wrung their hands in despair, and the countenance of his friend was bathed in tears.

Such a picture would have moved the most obdurate heart: what impres-sion then must it have made upon a parent and sister, melting with all the enthusiasm of affection! The mother was struck dumb, and stupified with grief: the sister threw herself on the bed, in a transport of sorrow, caught her loved Renaldo in her arms, and was, with great difficulty, tore from his embrace. Such was the dismal reverse that overtook the late so happy family of Melvile: such was the extremity to which the treachery of Fathom had reduced his best benefactor!

Three days did nature struggle with surprising efforts, and then the constitution seemed to sink under the victorious fever; yet, as his strength diminished, his delirium abated, and on the fifth morning he looked round, and recognized his weeping friends. Though now exhausted to the lowest ebb of life, he retained the perfect use of speech, and his reason being quite unclouded, spoke to each with equal kindness and composure: he congratulated himself upon the sight of shore, after the horrors of such a tempest; called upon the countess and his sister, who were not permited to see him at such a conjuncture, and being apprized by the major, of his reason for excluding them from his presence, he applauded his concern, bequeathed them to his future care, and took leave of that gentleman with a cordial embrace. Then he desired to be left in private with a certain clergyman, who regulated the concerns of his soul; and he being dismissed, turned his face from the light, in expectation of his final discharge: in a few minutes all was still and dreary; he was no longer heard to breathe, no more the stream of life was perceived to circulate; he was supposed to be absolved from all his cares, and an universal groan from the by-standers announced the decease of the gallant, generous, and tender-hearted Renaldo.

"Come hither ye whom the pride of youth and health, of birth and affluence inflames, who tread the flowery maze of pleasure, trusting to the fruition of ever-circling joys: ye who glory in your accomplishments, who indulge the views of ambition, and lay schemes for future happiness and grandeur; contemplate here the vanity of life: behold how low this excellent young man is laid! mowed down even in the blossom of his youth, when fortune seemed to open all her treasures to his worth!"

Such were the reflections of the generous Farrel, who, while he performed the last office of friendship, in closing the eyes of the much-lamented Melvile, perceived a warmth on the skin, which the hand of death seldom leaves unextinguished: this uncommon sensation he reported to the physician, who, though he could feel no pulsation in the heart or arteries, conjectured, that life still lingered in some of its interior haunts, and immediately ordered such applications to the extremities and surface of the body, as might help to concentrate and reinforce the natural heat.

By these prescriptions, which, for some time, produced no sensible effect, the embers were, in all probability, kept glowing, and the vital power revived; for, after a considerable pause, respiration was gradually renewed at long intervals, a languid motion was perceived at the heart, a few feeble and irregular pulsations were felt at the wrist; the clay-coloured livery of death began to vanish from his face; the circulation acquired new force, and he opened his eyes with a sigh, which proclaimed his return from the shades of death.

When he recovered the faculty of swallowing, a cordial was administered; and whether the fever abated, in consequence of the blood's being cooled and condensed during the recess of action in the solids,[4] or nature, in that agony, had prepared a proper channel for the expulsion of the disease; certain it is, he was, from this moment, rid of all bodily pain, he retrieved the animal functions, and nothing remained of his malady but an extreme weakness and languor, the effect of nature's being fatigued in the battle she had won.

Unutterable was the joy that took possession of his mother and sister, when Farrel flew into their apartment, to intimate this happy turn. Scarce could they be restrained from pouring forth their transports in the presence of Renaldo, who was still too feeble to endure such communication: indeed he was extremely mortified and dejected at this event, which had diffused such pleasure and satisfaction among his friends; for though his distemper was mastered, the fatal cause of it still rankled at his heart, and he considered this respite from death as a protraction of his misery.

When he was congratulated by the major, on the triumph of his constitution, he replied, with a groan, "I would to heaven it had been otherwise; for I am reserved for all the horrors of the most poignant sorrow and remorse. O Monimia! Monimia! I hoped, by this time, to have convinced thy gentle shade, that I was, at least intentionally, innocent of that ruthless barbarity which hath brought thee to an untimely grave. Heaven and earth! do I still survive the consciousness of that dire catastrophe! and lives the atrocious villain who hath blasted all our hopes!"

With these last words, the fire darted from his eyes, and his brother, snatching this occasional handle for reconciling him to life, joined in his exclamations against the treacherous Fathom, and observed, that he should not, in point of honour, wish to die, until he should have sacrificed that traitor to the manes[5] of the beauteous Monimia. This incitement acted as a spur upon exhausted nature, causing the blood to circulate with fresh vigour, and encouraging him to take such sustenance as would recruit his strength, and repair the damage which his health had sustained.

His sister assiduously attended him in his recovery, flattering his appetite, and amusing his sorrow at the same time; the clergyman assailed his despondence with religious weapons, as well as with arguments drawn from philosophy; and the fury of his passions being already expended, he became so tractable as to listen to his remonstrances: but notwithstanding the joint endeavours of all his friends, a deep-fixed melancholy remained, after every consequence of his disease had vanished: in vain they assayed to elude[6] his grief by gaiety and diversions; in vain they tried to decoy his heart into some new engagement.

These kind attempts served only to feed and nourish that melancholy which pined within his bosom. Monimia still haunted him in the midst of these amusements, while his reflection whispered to him, "Pleasures like these I might have relished with her participation." That darling idea mingled in all the female assemblies at which he was present, eclipsing their attractions, and inhancing the bitterness of his loss; for absence, enthusiasm, and even his despair had heightened the charms of the fair orphan into something supernatural and divine.

Time, that commonly weakens the traces of remembrance, seemed to deepen its impressions in his breast: nightly, in his dreams, did he converse with his dear Monimia: sometimes on the verdant bank of a delightful stream, where he breathed, in soft murmurs, the dictates of his love and admiration: sometimes reclined within the tufted grove, his arm encircled and sustained her snowy neck, whilst she, with looks of love ineffable, gazed on his face, invoking heaven to bless her husband and her lord: yet, even in these illusions, was his fancy oft alarmed for the ill-fated fair: sometimes he viewed her tottering on the brink of a steep precipice, far distant from his helping hand: at other times she seemed to sail along the boisterous tide, imploring his assistance: then would he start with horror from his sleep, and feel his sorrows more than realized: he deserted his couch: he avoided the society of mankind: he courted sequestered shades, where he could indulge his melancholy; there his mind brooded over his calamity, until his imagination became familiar with all the ravages of death: it contemplated the gradual decline of Monimia's health; her tears, her distress, her despair at his imagined cruelty; he saw thro' that perspective, every blossom of her beauty wither, every sparkle vanish from her eyes: he beheld her faded lips, her pale cheek, and her inanimated features, the symmetry of which, not death itself was able to destroy. His fancy conveyed her breathless corse to the cold grave, o'er which, perhaps, no tear humane was shed, where her delicate limbs were consigned to dust, where she was dished out a delicious banquet to the unsparing worm.

O'er these pictures he dwelt with a sort of pleasing anguish, until he became so enamoured of her tomb, that he could no longer resist the desire which compelled him to make a pilgrimage to the dear hallowed spot, where all his once gay hopes lay buried; that he might nightly visit the silent habitation of his ruined love, embrace the sacred earth with which she was now compounded, moisten it with his tears, and bid the turf lie easy on her breast. Besides the prospect of this gloomy enjoyment, he was urged to return to England, by an eager desire of taking vengeance on the perfidious Fathom, as well as of acquitting himself of the obligations he owed in that kingdom, to those who had assisted him in his distress. He therefore communicated his intention to Farrel, who would have insisted upon attending him in the journey, had not he been conjured to stay and manage Renaldo's affairs in his absence. Every previous step being taken, he took leave of the countess and his sister, who had, with all their interest and elocution, opposed his design, the execution of which, they justly feared, would, instead of dissipating, augment his chagrin; and now, seeing him determined, they shed a flood of tears at his departure, and he set out from Vienna in a postchaise, accompanied by a trusty valet de chambre on horseback.

CHAPTER LXI.

Renaldo meets with a living monument of justice,
and encounters a personage of some note in these
memoirs.

As this domestic was very well qualified for making all the proper dispositions, and adjusting every necessary article on the road, Renaldo totally abstracted himself from earthly considerations, and mused without ceasing on that theme which was the constant subject of his contemplation. He was blind to the objects that surrounded him; he scarce ever felt the importunities of nature; and had not they been reinforced by the pressing entreaties of his attendant, he would have proceeded without refreshment or repose. In this absence of mind did he traverse a great part of Germany, in his way to the Austrian Netherlands,[1] and arrived at the fortress of Luxemburg,[2] where he was obliged to tarry a whole day on account of an accident which had happened to his chaise. Here he went to view the fortifications; and as he walked along the ramparts, his ears were saluted with these words, "Heaven bless the noble count de Melvile! will not he turn the eyes of compassion upon an old fellow-soldier reduced to misfortune and disgrace?"

Surprised at this address, which was attended with the clanking of chains, Renaldo lifted up his eyes, and perceived the person who spoke, to be one of two malefactors shackled together, who had been sentenced for some crime to work as labourers on the fortifications: his face was so covered with hair, and his whole appearance so disguised by the squalid habit which he wore, that the count could not recollect his features, until he gave him to understand that his name was Ratchkali. Melvile immediately recognized his fellow student at Vienna and his brother volunteer upon the Rhine, and expressed equal surprize and concern at seeing him in such a deplorable situation.

Nothing renders the soul so callous and insensible as the searing brands of infamy and disgrace. Without betraying the least symptoms of shame or confusion, "Count," says he, "this is the fate of war, at least of the war in which I have been engaged, ever since I took leave of the imperial army, and retreated with your old companion Fathom. Long life to that original genius! If he is not unhappily eclipsed by some unfortunate interposition, before his terrene parts[3] are purified, I foresee that he will shine a star of the first magnitude in the world of adventure."

At mention of this detested name, Renaldo's heart began to throb with indignation; yet he suppressed the emotion, and desired to know the meaning of that splendid encomium which he had bestowed upon his confederate. "It would be quite unnecessary," replied Ratchkali, "for a man in my present situation to equivocate or disguise the truth: the nature of my disgrace is perfectly well known. I am condemned to hard labour for life; and unless some lucky accident (which I cannot now foresee) shall intervene, all I can expect is some alleviation of my hard lot from the generosity of such gentlemen as you who compassionate the sufferings of your fellow creatures. In order to engage this benevolence the more in my behalf, I shall (if you will give me the hearing) faithfully inform you of some particulars, which it may import[4] you to know, concerning my old acquaintance Ferdinand Count Fathom, whose real character hath perhaps hitherto escaped your notice."

Then he proceeded to give a regular detail of all the strokes of finesse which he, in conjunction with our adventurer, had practised upon Melvile and others, during their residence at Vienna, and the campaigns they had made upon the Rhine: he explained the nature of the robbery which was supposed to have been done by the count's valet, together with the manner of their desertion: he described his separation from Fathom, their meeting at London, the traffic they carried on in copartnership, and the misfortune that reduced Ferdinand to the condition in which he was found by Melvile.

"After having gratified the honest lawyer," said he, "with a share of the unfortunate Fathom's spoils, and packed up all my own valuable effects, my new auxiliary Maurice and I posted to Harwich,[5] embarked in the pacquet-boat,[6] and next day arrived at Helveotsluys;[7] from thence we repaired to the Hague, in order to mingle in the gaities of the place, and exercise our talents at play, which is there cultivated with universal eagerness: but, chancing to meet with an old acquaintance, whom I did not at all desire to see, I found it convenient to withdraw softly to Rotterdam; from whence we set out for Antwerp; and having made a tour of the Austrian Netherlands, set up our rest at Brussels, and concerted a plan for laying the Flemings[8] under contribution.

From our appearance we procured admission into the most polite assemblies, and succeeded to a wonder in all our operations; until our career was unfortunately checked by the indiscretion of my ally, who, being detected in the very act of conveying a card, was immediately introduced to a magistrate; and this minister of justice was so curious, inquisitive, and clear-sighted, that count Maurice, finding it impossible to elude his penetration, was fain to stipulate for his own safety, by giving up his friend to the cognizance of the law. I was accordingly apprehended, before I knew the cause of my arrest; and being unhappily known by some soldiers of the prince's guard, my character turned out so little to the approbation of the inquisitors, that all my effects were confiscated for the benefit of the state, and I was by a formal sentence condemned to labour on the fortifications all the days of my life; while Maurice escaped at the expence of five hundred stripes, which he received in public from the hands of the common executioner.

Thus have I, without evasion or mental reservation, given a faithful account of the steps by which I have arrived at this barrier, which is likely to be the *ne plus ultra*[9] of my peregrinations, unless the generous count de Melvile will deign to interpose his interest in behalf of an old fellow-soldier, who may yet live to justify his mediation."

Renaldo had no reason to doubt the truth of this story, every circumstance of which tended to corroborate the intelligence he had already received touching the character of Fathom, whom he now considered with a double portion of abhorrence, as the most abandoned miscreant that nature had ever produced. Tho' Ratchkali did not possess a much higher place in his opinion, he favoured him with marks of his bounty, and exhorted him, if possible, to reform his heart; but he would by no means promise to interpose his credit in favour of a wretch self-convicted of such enormous villany and fraud. He could not help moralizing upon this rencounter, which inspired him with great contempt for human nature: and next day he proceeded on his journey with a heavy heart, ruminating on the perfidy of mankind, and, between whiles, transported with the prospect of revenging all his calamities upon the accursed author.

While he was wrapped up in these reveries, his carriage rolled along, and had already entered a wood between Mons[10] and Tournay,[11] when his dream was suddenly interrupted by the explosion of several pistols that were fired among the thickets at a little distance from the road. Roused at this alarm, he snatched his sword that stood by him, and springing from the chaise, ran directly towards the spot, being close followed by his valet, who had alighted and armed himself with a pistol in each hand. About forty yards from the high way they arrived in a little glade or opening, where they saw a single man standing at bay against five banditti, after having killed one of their companions, and lost his own horse that lay dead upon the ground.

Melvile seeing this odds, and immediately guessing their design, rushed among them without hesitation, and in an instant ran his sword thro' the heart of one whose hand was raised to smite the gentleman behind, while he was engaged with the rest in front. At the same time the valet disabled another by a shot in the shoulder; so that the number being now equal on both sides, a furious combat ensued, every man being paired with an antagonist, and each having recourse to swords, as all their pieces had been discharged. Renaldo's adversary finding himself pressed with equal fury and skill, retreated gradually among the trees, until he vanished altogether into the thickest of the wood; and his two companions followed his example with great ease, the valet de chambre being hurt in the leg, and the stranger so much exhausted by the wounds he had received before Renaldo's interposition, that when the young gentleman approached to congratulate him on the defeat of the robbers, he, in advancing to embrace his deliverer, dropt down motionless on the grass.

The count, with that warmth of sympathy and benevolence which was natural to his heart, lifted up the wounded cavalier in his arms, and carried him to the chaise, in which he was deposited, while the valet de chambre reloaded his pistols, and prepared for a second attack, as they did not doubt that the banditti would return with a reinforcment. However, before they reappeared, Renaldo's driver disengaged him from the wood, and in less than a quarter of an hour they arrived at a village, where they halted for assistance to the stranger, who, tho' still alive, had not recovered the use of his senses.

After he was undressed and laid in a warm bed, a surgeon examined his body, and found a wound in his neck by a sword, and another in his right side occasioned by a pistol-shot; so that his prognostic was very dubious: mean while, he applied proper dressings to both; and, in half an hour after this administration, the gentleman gave some tokens of perception. He looked around him with a wildness of fury in his aspect, as if he had thought himself in the hands of the robbers by whom he had been attacked: but, when he saw the assiduity with which the by-standers exerted themselves in his behalf, one raising his head from the pillow, while another exhorted him to swallow a little wine which was warmed for the purpose; when he beheld the sympathising looks of all present, and heard himself accosted in the most cordial terms by the person whom he recollected as his deliverer; all the severity vanished from his countenance; he took Renaldo's hand and pressed it to his lips; and while the tears gushed from his eyes, "Praised be God," said he, "that virtue and generosity are still to be found among the sons of men."

Every body in the apartment was affected by this exclamation; and Melvile, above all the rest, felt such emotions as he could scarcely restrain. He intreated the gentleman to believe himself in the midst of such friends as would effectually secure him from all violence and mortification; he conjured him to compose the perturbation of his spirits, and quiet the apprehensions of his mind with that reflection; and protested, that he himself would not quit the house while his attendance should be deemed necessary for the stranger's cure, or his conversation conducive to his amusement.

These assurances, considered with the heroic part which the young Hungarian had already acted in his behalf, inspired the cavalier with such a sublime idea of Melvile, that he gazed upon him with silent astonishment, as an angel sent from heaven for his succour; and in the transport of his gratitude, could not help exclaiming, "Sure Providence hath still something in reserve for this unfortunate wretch, in whose favour such a miracle of courage and generosity hath interposed!"

Being accommodated with proper care and attendance, his constitution in a little time overcame the fever; and at the third dressing, the surgeon declared him out of all danger from his wounds. Then was Renaldo indulged with opportunities of conversing with the patient, and of inquiring into the particulars of his fortune and designs in life, with a view to manifest the inclination he felt to serve him in his future occasions.

The more this stranger contemplated the character of the count, the more his amazement increased, on account of his extraordinary benevolence in favour of a person whose merit he could not possibly know; he even expressed his surprize on this subject to Renaldo, who at length told him, that, altho' his best offices should always be ready for the occasions of any gentleman in distress, his particular attachment and regard to him was improved by an additional consideration: "I am no stranger," said he, "to the virtues and honour of the gallant Don Diego de Zelos."

"Heaven and earth!" cried the stranger, starting from his seat with extreme emotion, "do I then live to hear myself addressed by that long lost appellation! my heart glows at the expression! my spirits are kindled with a flame that thrills thro' every nerve! Say, young gentleman, if you are really an inhabitant of earth, by what means are you acquainted with the unhappy name of Zelos?"

In answer to this eager interrogation, Renaldo gave him to understand, that in the course of his travels, he had resided a short time at Seville, where he had frequently seen Don Diego, and often heard his character mentioned with uncommon esteem and veneration. "Alas!" replied the Castilian, "that justice is no longer done to the wretched Zelos; his honours are blasted, and his reputation canker-bitten by the venomous tooth of slander."

He then proceeded to unfold his misfortunes, as they have already been explained in the first volume of these memoirs; at the recapitulation of which, the heart of Melvile being intendered by his own calamities, was so deeply affected, that he re-echoed the groans of Don Diego, and wept over his sufferings with the most filial sympathy. When he repeated the story of that cruel fraud, which was practised upon him by the faithless Fadini, Melvile, whose mind and imagination teemed with the villanies of Fathom, was immediately struck with the conjecture of his being the knave; because, indeed, he could not believe, that any other person was so abandoned, by principle and humanity, as to take such a barbarous advantage of a gentleman in distress.

CHAPTER LXII.

His return to England, and midnight pilgrimage to Monimia's tomb.

He considered the date of that unparalelled transaction, which agreed with his conjecture, and from the inquiries he made concerning the person of the traitor, gathered reasons sufficient to confirm his supposition. Thus certified, "That is the villain," cried the count, "whose infernal arts have overwhelmed me with such misery as heaven itself hath no remedy to dispel! To revenge my wrongs on that perfidious miscreant, is one of the chief reasons for which I deign to drag about an hateful being. O don Diego! what is life, when all its enjoyments are so easily poisoned by the machinations of such a worm!" So saying, he smote his breast in all the agony of woe, and besought the Spaniard to relate the steps he took in consequence of this disaster.

The Castilian's cheeks reddened at this information, which reinforced his own resentment, and casting up his eyes to heaven, "Sacred powers! (cried he) let him not perish, before you bring him within my reach. You ask me, noble cavalier, what measures I took in this abyss of misery. For the first day, I was tortured with apprehensions for the friendly Fadini, fearing that he had been robbed and murthered for the jewels which he had, perhaps, too unwarily exposed to sale: but this terror soon vanished before the true presages of my fate; when, on the morrow, I found the whole family in tears and confusion, and heard my landlord pour forth the most bitter imprecations against the fugitive who had deflowered his daughter, and even robbed the house. You will ask, which of the passions of my heart were interested on this occasion; they were shame and indignation: all my grief flowed in another channel: I blushed to find my judgment deceived: I scorned to complain; but in my heart denounced vengeance against my base betrayer. I silently retired to my apartment, in order to commune with my own thoughts.

I had bore greater calamities, without being driven to despair: I summoned all my fortitude to my assistance, and resolved to live in spite of affliction. Thus determined, I betook myself to the house of a general officer, whose character was fair in the world; and having obtained admission in consequence of my oriental appearance; "To a man of honour," said I, "the unfortunate need no introduction: my habit proclaims me a Persian; this passport from the States of Holland will confirm that supposition. I have been robbed of jewels, to a considerable value, by a wretch whom I favoured with my confidence; and now, reduced to extreme indigence, I come to offer myself as a soldier in the armies of France. I have health and strength sufficient to discharge that duty: nor am I unacquainted with a military life, which was once my glory and occupation. I therefore sue for your protection, that I may be received, though in the lowest order of them that serve the king; and that your future favour may depend upon my behaviour in that capacity."

The general, surprized at my declaration, surveyed me with uncommon attention; he perused my certificate, asked divers questions concerning the art of war, to which I returned such answers as convinced him that I was not wholly ignorant in that particular. In short, I was inlisted as a volunteer in his own regiment, and soon after promoted to the rank of a subaltern,[1] and the office of equerry[2] to his own son, who, at that time, had attained to the degree of colonel, though his age did not exceed eighteen years.

This young man was naturally of a ferocious disposition, which had been rendered quite untractable by the pride of birth and fortune, together with the licence of his education. As he did not know the respect due to a gentleman, so he could not possibly pay it to those who were unfortunately under his command. Divers mortifications I sustained with that fortitude which became a Castilian who lay under obligations to the father; till at length, laying aside all decorum, he smote me. Sacred heaven! he smote don Diego de Zelos, in presence of his whole houshold.

Had my sword been endowed with sensation, it would of itself have started from the scabbard, at this indignity offered to its master. I unsheathed it without deliberation, saying, "Know, insolent boy, he is a gentleman whom thou hast thus outraged; and thou hast cancelled the ties which have hitherto restrained my indignation." His servants would have interposed, but he commanded them to retire; and flushed with that confidence which the impetuosity of his temper inspired, he drew, in his turn, and attacked me with redoubled rage; but his dexterity being very unequal to his courage, he was soon disarmed and overthrown; when pointing my sword to his breast, "In consideration of thy youth and ignorance," said I, "I spare that life which thou hast forfeited by thy ungenerous presumption."

With these words I put up my weapon, retired through the midst of his domestics, who seeing their master safe, did not think proper to oppose my passage, and mounting my horse, in less than two hours entered the Austrian dominions, resolving to proceed as far as Holland, that I might embark in the first ship for Spain, in order to wash away, with my own blood, or that of my enemies, the cruel stain which hath so long defiled my reputation.

This was the grievance that still corroded my heart, and rendered ineffectual the inhuman sacrifice I had made to my injured honour. This was the consideration that incessantly prompted, and still importunes me to run every risque of life and fortune, rather than leave my fame under such an ignominious aspersion. I purpose to obey this internal call. I am apt to believe it is the voice of heaven; of that providence which manifested its care by sending such a generous auxiliary to my aid, when I was overpowered by banditti, on the very first day of my expedition."

Having in this manner gratified the curiosity of his deliverer, he expressed a desire of knowing the quality of him to whom he was so signally obliged; and Renaldo did not scruple to make the Castilian acquainted with his name and family: he likewise communicated the story of his unfortunate love, with all the symptoms of unutterable woe, which drew tears from the noble-hearted Spaniard, while with a groan that announced the load which over-whelmed his soul, "I had a daughter," said he, "such as you describe the peerless Monimia, had heaven decreed her for the arms of such a lover, I, who am now the most wretched, should have been the most happy parent upon earth."

Thus did these new friends alternately indulge their mutual sorrow, and concert measures for their future operations. Melvile earnestly sollicited the Castilian to favour him with his company to England, where, in all proba-bility, both would enjoy the gloomy satisfaction of being revenged upon their common betrayer Fathom; and as a farther inducement, he assured him, that as soon as he should have accomplished the melancholy purposes of his voy-age, he would accompany don Diego to Spain, and employ his whole interest and fortune in his service. The Spaniard, thunderstruck at the extravagant generosity of this proposal, could scarce believe the evidence of his own senses, and after some pause, replied, "My duty would teach me to obey any command you should think proper to impose; but here my inclination and interest are so agreeably flattered, that I should be equally ungrateful and unwise, in pretending to comply with reluctance."

This point being settled, they moved forwards to Mons, as soon as don Diego was in a condition to bear the shock of such a removal; and there remaining until his wounds were perfectly cured, they hired a post-chaise for Ostend,[3] embarked in a vessel at that port, reached the opposite shore of England, after a short and easy passage, and arrived in London without hav-ing met with any sinister accident on the road.

As they approached this capital, Renaldo's grief seemed to regurgitate with redoubled violence. His memory was waked to the most minute and painful exertion of its faculties; his imagination teemed with the most afflicting im-ages, and his impatience became so ardent, that never lover panted more eagerly for the consummation of his wishes, than Melvile for an opportunity of stretching himself upon the grave of the lost Monimia. The Castilian was astonished, as well as affected at the poignancy of his grief, which, as a proof of his susceptibility and virtue, endeared him still more to his affection; and though his own misfortunes had rendered him very unfit for the office of a comforter, he endeavoured, by soothing discourse, to moderate the excess of his friend's affliction.

Though it was dark when they alighted at the inn, Melvile ordered a coach to be called, and being attended by the Spaniard, who would not be per-suaded to quit him upon such an occasion, he repaired to the house of the generous Jew, whose rheum distilled very plentifully at his approach. The count had already acquitted himself in point of pecuniary obligations to this benevolent Hebrew; and now, after having made such acknowledgments as might be expected from a youth of his disposition, he begged to know by what channel he had received that letter, which he had been so kind as to forward to Vienna.

Joshua, who was ignorant of the contents of that epistle, and saw the young gentleman extremely moved, would have eluded his enquiry, by pretending he had forgot the circumstance; but when he understood the nature of the case, which was not explained without the manifestation of the utmost inquietude, he heartily condoled the desponding lover, telling him he had in vain employed all his intelligence about that unfortunate beauty, in consequence of Melvile's letter to him on that subject; and then directed him to the house of that physician, who had brought the fatal billet which had made him miserable.

No sooner did he receive this information than he took his leave abruptly, with promise of returning next day, and hied him to the lodgings of that gentleman, whom he was lucky enough to find at home. Being favoured with a private audience, "When I tell you," said he, "that my name is Renaldo count de Melvile, you will know me to be the most unfortunate of men. By that letter, which you committed to the charge of my worthy friend Joshua, the fatal veil was removed from my eyes, which had been so long darkened by the artifices of incredible deceit, and my own incurable misery fully presented to my view. If you were acquainted with the unhappy fair, who hath fallen a victim to my mistake, you will have some idea of the insufferable pangs which I now feel in recollecting her fate. If you have compassion for these pangs, you will not refuse to conduct me to the spot where the dear remains of Monimia are deposited; there let me enjoy a full banquet of woe; there let me feast that worm of sorrow that preys upon my heart: for such entertainment have I revisited this (to me) ill-omened isle:[4] for this satisfaction I intrude upon your condescension at these unseasonable hours; for to such a degree of impatience is my affliction whetted, that no slumber shall assail mine eyelids, no peace reside within my bosom, until I shall have adored that earthy shrine where my Monimia lies! Yet would I know the circumstances of her fate. Did heaven ordain no angel to minister to her distress? were her last moments comfortless? ha! was not she abandoned to indigence, to insults; left in the power of that inhuman villain who betrayed us both! Sacred heaven! why did providence wink at the triumph of such consummate perfidy?"

The physician having listened with complacency to this effusion, replied, "It is my profession, it is my nature to sympathize with the afflicted. I am a judge of your feelings, because I know the value of your loss. I attended the incomparable Monimia in her last illness, and am well enough acquainted with her story, to conclude, that she fell a sacrifice to an unhappy misunderstanding, effected and fomented by that traitor who abused your mutual confidence."

He then proceeded to inform him of all the particulars which we have already recorded, touching the destiny of the beauteous orphan, and concluded with telling him he was ready to yield him any other satisfaction which it was in his power to grant. The circumstances of the tale had put Renaldo's spirits into such commotion, that he could utter nothing but interjections and unconnected words. When Fathom's behaviour was described, he trembled with fierce agitation, started from his chair, pronouncing, "Monster! fiend! but we shall one day meet."

When he was made acquainted with the benevolence of the French lady, he exclaimed, "O heaven-born charity and compassion! sure that must be some spirit of grace sent hither to mitigate the tortures of life! where shall I find her, to offer up my thanks and adoration?" Having heard the conclusion of the detail, he embraced the relater, as the kind benefactor of Monimia, shed a flood of tears in his bosom, and pressed him to crown the obligation, by conducting him to the solitary place where now she rested from all her cares.

The gentleman perceiving the transports of his grief were such as could not be opposed, complied with his request, attended him in the vehicle, and directed the coachman to drive to a sequestered field, at some distance from the city, where stood the church, within whose awful isle this scene was to be acted. The sexton being summoned from his bed, produced the keys, in consequence of a gratification, after the physician had communed with him apart, and explained the intention of Renaldo's visit.

During this pause, the soul of Melvile was wound up to the highest pitch of enthusiastic sorrow.[5] The uncommon darkness of the night, the solemn silence, and lonely situation of the place, conspired with the occasion of his coming, and the dismal images of his fancy, to produce a real rapture of gloomy expectation, which the whole world would not have persuaded him to disappoint. The clock struck twelve, the owl screeched from the ruined battlement, the door was opened by the sexton, who, by the light of a glimmering taper, conducted the despairing lover to a dreary isle, and stamped upon the ground with his foot, saying, "Here the young lady lies interred."

Melvile no sooner received this intimation, than falling on his knees, and pressing his lips to the hallowed earth: "Peace," cried he, "to the gentle tenant of this silent habitation." Then turning to the bystanders, with a bloodshot eye, said, "Leave me to the full enjoyment of this occasion: my grief is too delicate to admit the company even of my friends: the rites to be performed require privacy: adieu then, here must I pass the night alone."

The doctor, alarmed at this declaration, which he was afraid imported some resolution fatal to his own life, began to repent of having been accessary to the visit, attempted to dissuade him from his purpose, and finding him obstinately determined, called in the assistance of the sexton and coachman, and sollicited the aid of don Diego, to force Renaldo from the execution of his design.

The Castilian, knowing his friend was then very unfit for common altercation, interposed in the dispute, saying, "You need not be afraid that he will obey the dictates of despair: his religion, his honour will baffle such temptations: he hath promised to reserve his life for the occasions of his friend; and he shall not be disappointed in his present aim." In order to corroborate this peremptory address, which was delivered in the French language, he unsheathed his sword, and the others retreating at sight of his weapon, "Count," said he, "enjoy your grief in full transport: I will screen you from interruption, though at the hazard of my life; and while you give a loose to sorrow, within that ghastly vault, I will watch till morning in the porch, and meditate upon the ruin of my own family and peace."

He accordingly prevailed upon the physician to retire, after he had satisfied the sexton, and ordered the coachman to return by break of day.

Renaldo thus left alone, prostrated himself upon the grave, and poured forth such lamentations as would have drawn tears from the most savage hearer. He called aloud upon Monimia's name, "Are these the nuptial joys to which our fate hath doomed us? Is this the fruit of those endearing hopes, that intercourse divine, that raptured admiration, in which so many hours insensibly elapsed! where now are those attractions, to which I yielded up my captive heart? quenched are those genial eyes that gladdened each beholder, and shone the planets of my happiness and peace! cold! cold and withered are those lips that swelled with love, and far out-blushed the damask rose! and ah! for ever silenced is that tongue, whose eloquence had power to lull the pangs of misery and care! no more shall my attention be ravished with the music of that voice, which used to thrill in soft vibrations to my soul! O sainted spirit! O unspotted shade of her whom I adored; of her whose memory I shall still revere with ever-bleeding sorrow and regret; of her whose image will be the last idea that forsakes this hapless bosom! now art thou conscious of my integrity and love; now dost thou behold the anguish that I feel. If the pure essence of thy nature will permit, wilt thou, ah! wilt thou indulge this wretched youth with some kind signal of thy notice, with some token of thy approbation? wilt thou assume a medium of embodied air, in semblance of that lovely form, which now lies mouldering in this dreary tomb, and speak the words of peace to my distempered soul! Return, Monimia! appear, though but for one short moment, to my longing eyes! vouchsafe one smile; Renaldo will be satisfied; Renaldo's heart will be at rest; his grief no more will overflow its banks, but glide with equal current to his latest hour! Alas! these are the ravings of my delirious sorrow! Monimia hears not my complaints; her soul, sublimed far, far above all sublunary cares, enjoys that felicity, of which she was debarred on earth. In vain I stretch these eyes, environed with darkness undistinguishing and void: no object meets my view; no sound salutes mine ear, except the noisy wind that whistles through these vaulted caves of death."

In this kind of exclamation did Renaldo pass the night, not without a certain species of woful enjoyment, which the soul is often able to conjure up from the depths of distress; insomuch, that when the morning intruded on his privacy, he could scarce believe it was the light of day, so fast had fleeted the minutes of his devotion.

His heart being thus disburthened, and his impatience gratified, he became so calm and composed, that don Diego was equally pleased and astonished at the air of serenity with which he came forth, and embraced him with warm acknowledgments of his goodness and attachment: he frankly owned, that his mind was now more at ease then he had ever found it, since he first received the fatal intimation of his loss; that a few such feasts would entirely moderate the keen appetite of his sorrow, which he would afterwards feed with less precipitation.

He also imparted to the Castilian, the plan of a monument, which he had designed for the incomparable Monimia; and don Diego was so much struck with the description, that he solicited his advice in projecting another, of a different nature, to be erected to the memory of his own ill-fated wife and daughter, should he ever be able to re-establish himself in Spain.

CHAPTER LXIII.

He renews the rites of sorrow, and is entranced.

While they amused themselves with this sort of conversation, the physician returned with the coach, and accompanied them back to their inn, where he left them to their repose, after having promised to call again at noon, and conduct Renaldo to the house of madame Clement, the benefactress of Monimia, to whom he eagerly desired to be introduced.

The appointment was observed with all imaginable punctuality on both sides. Melvile had arrayed himself in a suit of deep mourning, and he found the good lady in the like habit, assumed upon the same occasion: the goodness of her heart was manifest in her countenance; the sensibility of the youth discovered itself in a flood of tears, which he shed at her appearance. His sensations were too full for utterance; nor was she, for some time, able to give him welcome: while she led him by the hand to a seat, the drops of sympathy rushed into either eye; and at length she broke silence, saying, "Count, we must acquiesce in the dispensations of providence; and quiet the transports of our grief, with a full assurance that Monimia is happy."

This name was the key that unlocked the faculty of his speech. "I must strive," said he, "to ease the anguish of my heart with that consolation. But say, humane, benevolent lady, to whose compassion and generosity that hapless orphan was indebted for the last peaceful moment she enjoyed upon earth; say, in all your acquaintance with human nature, in all your intercourse with the daughters of men, in all the exercise of your charity and beneficence, did you ever observe such sweetness, purity, and truth; such beauty, sense, and perfection, as that which was the inheritance of her whose fate I shall for ever deplore?" "She was indeed," replied the lady, "the best and fairest of our sex."

This was the beginning of a conversation touching that lovely victim, in the course of which, he explained those wicked arts which Fathom practised to alienate his affections from the adorable Monimia; and she described the cunning hints and false insinuations by which that traitor had aspersed the unsuspecting lover, and soiled his character in the opinion of the virtuous orphan. The intelligence he obtained, on this occasion, added indignation to his grief: the whole mystery of Monimia's behaviour, which he could not before explain, now stood disclosed before him: he saw the gradual progress of that infernal plan, which had been laid for their mutual ruin; and his soul was inflamed with such desire of vengeance, that he would have taken his leave abruptly, in order to set on foot an immediate enquiry about the perfidious author of his wrongs, that he might exterminate such a monster of iniquity from the face of the earth; but he was restrained by madame Clement, who gave him to understand, that Fathom was already overtaken by the vengeance of heaven: for she had traced him in all the course of his fortune, from his first appearance in the medical sphere to his total eclipse. She represented the villain as a wretch altogether unworthy of his attention; she said, he was so covered with infamy, that no person could enter the lists against him, without bearing away some stain of dishonour; that he was, at present, peculiarly protected by the law, and sheltered from the resentment of Renaldo, in the cavern of his disgrace.

Melvile, glowing with rage, replied, that he was a venomous serpent, which it was incumbent on every foot to crush; that it was the duty of every man to contribute his whole power in freeing society from such a pernicious hypocrite; and that if such instances of perfidy and ingratitude were suffered to pass with impunity, virtue and plain-dealing would soon be expelled from the habitations of men. "Over and above these motives," said he, "I own myself so vitiated with the allay of human passion and infirmity, that I desire, I eagerly pant for an occasion of meeting him hand to hand, where I may upbraid him with his treachery, and shower down vengeance and destruction on his perfidious head."

Then he recounted the anecdotes of our adventurer, which he had learned in Germany and Flanders, and concluded with declaring his unalterable resolution of releasing him from jail, that he might have an opportunity of sacrificing him, with his own hand, to the manes of Monimia. The discreet lady, perceiving the perturbation of his mind, would not further combat the impetuosity of his passion; contenting herself with exacting a promise, that he would not execute his purpose, until he should have deliberated three days upon the consequences by which a step of that kind might be attended: before the expiration of that term, she thought measures might be taken to prevent the young gentleman from exposing his life or reputation to unnecessary hazard.

Having complied with her request in this particular, he took his leave, after he had, by repeated entreaties, prevailed upon her to accept a jewel, in token of his veneration for the kind benefactress of his deceased Monimia: nor could his generous heart be satisfied, until he had forced a considerable present on the humane physician, who had attended her in her last moments, and now discovered a particular sympathy and concern for her desponding lover. This gentleman attended him to the house of the benevolent Joshua, where they dined, and where don Diego was recommended, in the most fervid terms of friendship, to the good offices of their host. Not that this duty was performed in presence of the stranger, Renaldo's delicacy would not expose his friend to such a situation; while the physician, before dinner, entertained that stranger in one apartment, Melvile withdrew into another, with the Jew, to whom he disclosed the affair of the Castilian, with certain circumstances, which shall, in due time, be revealed.

Joshua's curiosity being whetted by this information, he could not help eying the Spaniard at table, with such a particular stare, that don Diego perceived his attention, and took umbrage at the freedom of his regard. Being unable to conceal his displeasure, he addressed himself to the Hebrew, with great solemnity, in the Spanish tongue, saying, "Signior, is there any singularity in my appearance? or, do you recollect the features of don Diego de Zelos?"

"Signior don Diego," replied the other in pure Castilian, "I crave your pardon for the rudeness of my curiosity, which prompted me to survey a nobleman, whose character I revere, and to whose misfortunes I am no stranger; indeed, were curiosity alone concerned, I should be without excuse, but as I am heartily inclined to serve you, as far as my weak abilities extend, I hope your generosity will not impute any little involuntary trespass of punctilio to my want of cordiality or esteem."

The Spaniard was not only appeased by this apology, but also affected with the compliment, and the language in which it was conveyed. He thanked the Jew for his kind declaration, intreated him to bear with the peevishness of a disposition, sore with the galling hand of affliction; and turning up his eyes to heaven, "Were it possible," cried he, "for fate to reconcile contradictions, and recal the irremeable current of events, I would now believe, that there was happiness still in reserve for the forlorn Zelos: now that I tread the land of freedom and humanity; now that I find myself befriended by the most generous of men. Alas! I ask not happiness! if by the kind endeavours of the gallant count de Melvile, to whom I am already indebted for my life; and by the efforts of his friends, the honour of my name shall be purified and cleared from the poisonous stains of malice, by which it is at present spotted; I shall then enjoy all that satisfaction, which destiny can bestow upon a wretch whose woes are incurable."

Renaldo comforted him with the assurance of his being on the eve of triumphing over his adversaries; and Joshua confirmed the consolation, by giving him to understand, that he had correspondents in Spain, of some influence in the state; that he had already written to them on the subject of don

Diego, in consequence of a letter which he had received from Melvile, while he tarried at Mons, and that he, every post, expected a favourable answer on that subject.

After dinner, the physician took his leave, though not before he had promised to meet Renaldo at night, and accompany him in the repetition of his midnight visit to Monimia's tomb: for this pilgrimage the unfortunate youth resolved nightly to perform, during the whole time of his residence in England: it was, indeed, a sort of pleasure, the prospect of which enabled him to bear the toil of living through the day; though his patience was almost quite exhausted before the hour of assignation arrived.

When the doctor appeared with the coach, he leaped into it with great eagerness, after he had, with much difficulty, prevailed with don Diego to stay at home, on account of his health, which was not yet perfectly established. The Castilian, however, would not comply with his request, until he had obtained the count's promise, that he should be permitted to accompany him next night, and take that duty alternately with the physician.

About midnight they reached the place, where they found the sexton in waiting, according to the orders he had received: the door was opened, the mourner conducted to the tomb, and left, as before, to the gloom of his own meditations. Again he laid himself on the cold ground; again he renewed his lamentable strain; his imagination began to be heated into an extasy of enthusiasm, during which, he again fervently invoked the spirit of his deceased Monimia.

In the midst of these invocations, his ear was suddenly invaded with the sound of some few solemn notes, issuing from the organ, which seemed to feel the impulse of an invisible hand.

At this awful salutation, Melvile was roused to the keenest sense of surprize and attention: reason shrunk before the thronging ideas of his fancy, which represented this musick as the prelude to something strange and supernatural; and while he waited for the sequel, the place was suddenly illuminated, and each surrounding object brought under the cognizance of his eye.

What passed within his mind on this occasion, is not easy to be described: all his faculties were swallowed up by those of seeing and of hearing: he had mechanically raised himself upon one knee, with his body advancing forwards; and in this attitude he gazed with a look, through which his soul seemed eager to escape. To his view, thus strained upon vacant space, in a few minutes appeared the figure of a woman arrayed in white, with a veil that covered her face, and flowed down upon her back and shoulders: The phantome approached him with an easy step, and, lifting up her veil, discovered (believe it, O reader!) the individual countenance of Monimia.[1]

At sight of these well-known features, seemingly improved with new celestial graces, the youth became a statue, expressing amazement, love, and awful adoration. He saw the apparition smile with meek benevolence, divine compassion, warmed and intendered by that fond, pure flame, which death could not extinguish: he heard the voice of his Monimia call Renaldo! Thrice he essayed to answer; as oft his tongue denied its office: his hair stood upright, and a cold vapour seemed to thrill through every nerve. This was not fear, but the infirmity of human nature, oppressed by the presence of a superior being.

At length his agony was overcome; he recollected all his resolution, and in a strain of awe-struck rapture, thus addressed the heavenly visitant. "Hast thou then heard, pure spirit! the wailings of my grief? hast thou descended from the realms of bliss, in pity to my woe? and art thou come to speak the words of peace to my desponding soul? To bid the wretched smile; to lift the load of misery and care from the afflicted breast; to fill thy lover's heart with joy and pleasing hope, was still the darling task of my Monimia, e're yet refined to that perfection, which mortality can never attain: no wonder then, blest shade, that now, when reunited to thy native heaven, thou are still kind, propitious, and beneficent to us, who groan in this inhospitable vale of sorrow thou hast left: tell me, ah! tell me, dost thou still remember those fond hours we passed together? Doth that enlightened bosom feel a pang of soft regret, when thou recallest our fatal separation? Sure that meekened glance bespeaks thy sympathy! Ah! how that tender look o'erpowers me! Sacred heaven! the pearly drops of pity trickle down thy cheeks! Such are the tears that angels shed o'er man's distress! Turn not away: thou beckonest me to follow: yes, I will follow thee, ætherial spirit, as far as these weak limbs, encumbered with mortality, will bear my weight; and, would to heaven! I could, with ease, put off these vile, corporeal shackles, and attend thy flight."

So saying, he started from the ground, and in a transport of eager expectation, at awful distance, traced the footsteps of the apparition, which entering a detached apartment, sunk down upon a chair, and with a sigh exclaimed, "Indeed, this is too much!" What was the disorder of Renaldo's mind, when he perceived this phænomenon! Before reflection could perform its office, moved by a sudden impulse, he sprung forwards, crying, "If it be death to touch thee, let me die!" and caught in his arms, not the shadow, but the warm substance of the all-accomplished Monimia. "Mysterious powers of providence! this is no phantome! this is no shade! this is the life! the panting bosom of her whom I have so long, so bitterly deplored! I fold her in my arms! I press her glowing breast to mine! I see her blush with virtuous pleasure and ingenuous love! she smiles upon me with inchanting tenderness! O

The Heavenly Visitant, by Stothard.
(General Research Division, The New York Public Library—
Astor, Lenox and Tilden Foundations.)

let me gaze on that transcendent beauty, which the more I view it, ravishes the more! These charms are too intense; I sicken while I gaze! Merciful heaven! is not this a mere illusion of the brain? Was she not fled for ever? Had not the cold hand of death divorced her from my hope? This must be some flattering vision of my distempered fancy! perhaps some soothing dream: if such it be, grant, O ye heavenly powers! that I may never wake."

"O gentle youth! (replied the beauteous orphan, still clasped in his embrace) what joy now fills the bosom of Monimia, at this triumph of thy virtue and thy love? When I see these transports of thy affection, when I find thee restored to that place in my esteem and admiration, which thou hadst lost by the arts of calumny and malice! this is a meeting which my most sanguine hopes durst not presage!"

So entirely were the faculties of Renaldo engrossed in the contemplation of his restored Monimia, that he saw not the rest of the company, who wept with transport over this affecting scene: he was therefore amazed at the interposition of madame Clement, who, while the shower of sympathetic pleasure bedewed her cheeks, congratulated the lovers upon this happy event, crying, "These are the joys which virtue calls her own." They also received the compliments of a reverend clergyman, who told Monimia, she had reaped, at last, the fruits of that pious resignation to the will of heaven, which she had so devoutly practised during the term of her affliction: and, lastly, they were accosted by the physician, who was not quite so hackneyed in the ways of death, or so callous to the finer sensations of the soul, but that he blubbered plentifully, while he petitioned heaven in behalf of such an accomplished and deserving pair.

Monimia taking madame Clement by the hand, "Whatever joy," said she, "Renaldo derives from this occasion, is owing to the bounty, the compassion, and maternal care of this incomparable lady, together with the kind admonitions and humanity of these two worthy gentlemen."

Melvile, whose passions were still in agitation, and whose mind could not yet digest the incidents that occurred, embraced them all by turns, but, like the faithful needle, which though shaken, for an instant, from its poize, immediately regains its true direction and points invariably to the pole, he soon returned to his Monimia; again he held her in his arms; again he drank inchantment from her eyes, and thus poured forth the effusions of his soul. "Can I then trust the evidence of sense? And art thou really to my wish restored? Never, O never did thy beauty shine with such bewitching grace, as that which now confounds and captivates my view! sure there is something more than mortal in thy looks! where hast thou lived? where borrowed this perfection? whence art thou now descended? Oh! I am all amazement, joy and fear! thou wilt not leave me! no! we must not part again: by this warm kiss! a thousand times more sweet than all the fragrance of the east! we never more will part. O this is rapture, extasy, and what no language can explain!"

In the midst of these ejaculations, he ravished a banquet from her glowing lips, that kindled in his heart a flame, which rushed thro' every vein, and glided to his marrow: this was a privilege he had never claimed before, and now permitted as a recompence for all the penance he had suffered; nevertheless, the cheeks of Monimia, who was altogether unaccustomed to such familiarities, underwent a total suffusion; and madame Clement discreetly relieved her from the anxiety of her situation, by interfering in the discourse, and rallying the count, upon his endeavours to monopolize such a branch of happiness.

"O my dear lady! (replied Renaldo, who by this time had, in some measure, recovered his recollection) forgive the wild transports of a fond lover, who hath so unexpectedly retrieved the jewel of his soul! yet, far from wishing to hoard up his treasure, he means communicate and diffuse his happiness to all his friends. O my Monimia! how will the pleasure of this hour be propagated! As yet thou knowest not all the bliss that is reserved for thy enjoyment: mean while, I long to learn, by what contrivance this happy interview hath been effected: still am I ignorant, how I was transported into this apartment, from the lonely vault, in which I mourned over my supposed misfortune!

CHAPTER LXIV.

*The mystery unfolded. Another recognition, which,
it is to be hoped, the reader could not foresee.*

The French lady then explained the whole mystery of Monimia's death, as a stratagem she had concerted with the clergyman and doctor, in order to defeat the pernicious designs of Fathom, who seemed determined to support his false pretensions, by dint of perjury and fraud, which they would have found it very difficult to elude. She observed, that the physician had actually despaired of Monimia's life, and it was not till after she herself was made acquainted with the prognostick, that she wrote the letter to Renaldo, which she committed to the care of madame Clement, with an earnest in-

treaty, that it should not be sent till after her decease: but that lady believing the count had been certainly abused by his treacherous confident, dispatched the billet without the knowledge of Monimia, whose health was restored by the indefatigable care of the physician, and the sage exhortations of
the clergyman, by which she was reconciled to life. In a word, the villainy of
Fathom had inspired her with some faint hope that Renaldo might still be
innocent; and that notion contributed not a little to her cure.

The letter having so effectually answered their warmest hopes, in bringing
back Renaldo such a pattern of constancy and love; the confederates, in consequence of his enthusiastic sorrow, had planned this meeting, as the most
interesting way of restoring two virtuous lovers to the arms of each other; for
which purpose the good clergyman had pitched upon his own church, and
indulged them with the use of the vestry, in which they now were presented
with a small but elegant collation.[1]

Melvile heard this succinct detail with equal joy and admiration: he poured
forth the dictates of his gratitude to the preservers of his happiness: "This
church," said he, "shall henceforth possess a double share of my veneration;
this holy man will, I hope, finish the charitable work he has begun, by tying
those bands of our happiness, which nought but death shall have power to
unbind." Then turning to that object which was the star of his regard, "Do I
not over-rate," said he, "my interest with the fair Monimia?" She made no
verbal reply; but answered by an emphatic glance, more eloquent than all the
power of rhetorick and speech. This language, which is universal in the
world of love, he perfectly well understood, and in token of that faculty,
sealed the assent which she had smiled, with a kiss imprinted on her polished
forehead.

In order to dissipate those interesting ideas, which, by being too long indulged, might have endangered his reason, madame Clement intreated him
to entertain the company with a detail of what had happened to him in his
last journey to the empire, and Monimia expressed a desire of knowing, in
particular, the issue of his contest with count Trebasi, who, she knew, had
usurped the succession of his father.

Thus sollicited, he could not refuse to gratify their curiosity and concern:
he explained his obligations to the benevolent Jew; related the steps he had
taken at Vienna for the recovery of his inheritance; informed them of his
happy rencounter with his father-in-law; of his sister's deliverance and marriage; of the danger into which his life had been precipitated by the news of
Monimia's death; and, lastly, of his adventure with the banditti, in favour of a
gentleman, who (he afterwards understood) had been robbed in the most

base and barbarous manner by Fathom. He likewise, to the astonishment of all present, and of his mistress in particular, communicated some circumstances, which shall appear in due season.

Monimia's tender frame being quite fatigued with the scene she had acted, and her mind overwhelmed with the prosperous tidings she had heard, after having joined the congratulations of the company, on the good fortune of her Renaldo, begged leave to retire, that she might by repose recruit her exhausted spirits; and the night being pretty far spent, she was conducted by her lover to madame Clement's coach, that stood in waiting, in which also the rest of the company made shift to embark, and were carried to the house of that good lady, where after they were invited to dine, and Melvile intreated to bring don Diego and the Jew along with them, they took leave of one another, and retired to their respective lodgings in a transport of joy and satisfaction.

As for Renaldo, his rapture was still mixed with apprehension, that all he had seen and heard was no more than an unsubstantial vision, raised by some gay delirium of a disordered imagination. While his breast underwent those violent, though blissful emotions of joy and admiration, his friend the Castilian spent the night in ruminating over his own calamities, and in a serious and severe review of his own conduct. He compared his own behaviour with that of the young Hungarian, and found himself so light in the scale, that he smote his breast with violence, exclaiming in an agony of remorse;

"Count Melvile has reason to grieve; don Diego to despair: his misfortunes flow from the villainy of mankind; mine are the fruit of my own madness: he laments the loss of a mistress, who fell a sacrifice to the perfidious arts of a crafty traitor: she was beautiful, virtuous, accomplished, and affectionate; he was fraught with sensibility and love: doubtless, his heart must have deeply suffered; his behaviour denotes the keenness of his woe; his eyes are everflowing fountains of tears; his bosom the habitation of sighs; five hundred leagues hath he measured in a pilgrimage to her tomb; nightly he visits the dreary vault where she now lies at rest; her solitary grave is his couch; he converses with darkness and the dead, until each lonely isle re-echoes his distress. What would be his penance, had he my cause? were he conscious of having murthered a beloved wife and darling daughter! ah wretch! ah cruel homicide! what had those dear victims done to merit such a fate? Were they not ever gentle and obedient, ever aiming to give thee satisfaction and delight! Say, that Serafina was enamoured of a peasant; say, that she had degenerated from the honour of her race: the inclinations are involuntary; perhaps that stranger was her equal in pedigree and worth. Had they been fairly questioned, they might have justified, at least excused that conduct which appeared so criminal; or had they owned the offence, and supplicated pardon: oh barbarous monster that I am! was all the husband; was all the father extinguished in my heart? how shall my own errors be forgiven, if I refused to pardon the frailties of my own blood; of those who are most dear to my affection! Yet nature pleaded strongly in their behalf! my heart was bursting while I dismissed them to the shades of death: I was maddened with revenge! I was guided by that savage principle which falsely we call honour: accursed phantome! that assumes the specious title, and misleads our wretched nation! is it then honourable to sculk like an assassin, and plunge the secret dagger in the heart of some unhappy man, who hath incurred my groundless jealousy or suspicion, without indulging him with that opportunity which the worst criminal enjoys? or is it honourable to poison two defenceless women, a tender wife, an amiable daughter, whom even a frown would almost have destroyed! O! this is cowardice, brutality, hell-born fury and revenge! heaven hath not mercy to forgive such execrable guilt. Who gave thee power, abandoned ruffian! o'er the lives of those whom God hath stationed as thy fellows of probation; o'er those whom he had sent to comfort and assist thee; to sweeten all thy cares, and smooth the rough uneven paths of life? O! I am doomed to never-ceasing horror and remorse! if misery can atone for such enormous guilt, I have felt it in the extreme: like an undying vulture it preys upon my heart; to sorrow I am wedded; I hug that teeming consort to my soul; never, ah never shall we part; for soon as my fame shall shine unclouded by the charge of treason that now hangs over it, I will devote myself to penitence and woe: a cold, damp pavement shall be my bed; my raiment shall be sackcloth; the fields shall furnish herbage for my food; the stream shall quench my thirst; the minutes shall be numbered by my groans; the night be privy to my strains of sorrow, till heaven, in pity to my sufferings, release me from the penance I endure. Perhaps the saints whom I have murdered, will intercede for my remission."

Such was the exercise of grief, in which the hapless Castilian consumed the night; he had not yet consigned himself to rest, when Renaldo entering his chamber, displayed such a gleam of wildness and rapture in his countenance, as overwhelmed him with amazement; for, till that moment, he had never seen his visage unobscured with woe. "Pardon this abrupt intrusion, my friend," cried Melvile, "I could no longer withhold from your participation, the great, the unexpected turn, which hath this night dispelled all my sorrows, and restored me to the fruition of ineffable joy. Monimia lives! the fair, the tender, the virtuous Monimia lives, and smiles upon my vows! This night I retrieved her from the grave: I held her in these arms; I pressed her warm, delicious lips to mine! O! I am giddy with intolerable pleasure!"

Don Diego was confounded at this declaration, which he considered as the effect of a disordered brain: he never doubted that Renaldo's grief had at length overpowered his reason, and that his words were the effect of mere frenzy. While he mused on this melancholy subject, the count composed his features, and, in a succinct and well-connected detail, explained the whole mystery of his happiness, to the inexpressible astonishment of the Spaniard, who shed tears of satisfaction, and straining the Hungarian to his breast, "O my son!" said he, "you see what recompence heaven hath in store for those who pursue the paths of real virtue; those paths from which I myself have been fatally misled by a faithless vapour,[2] which hath seduced my steps, and left me darkling[3] in the abyss of wretchedness. Such as you describe this happy fair, was once my Serafina, rich in every grace of mind and body, which nature could bestow. Had it pleased heaven to bless her with a lover like Renaldo! but no more, the irrevocable shaft is fled: I will not taint your enjoyment with my unavailing sighs!"

Melvile assured this disconsolate father, that no pleasure, no avocation should ever so entirely ingross his mind, but that he should still find an hour for sympathy and friendship: he communicated the invitation of madame Clement, and insisted upon his compliance, that he might have an opportunity of seeing and approving the object of his passion. "I can refuse nothing to the request of count de Melvile," replied the Spaniard, "and it were ungrateful in me to decline the honour you propose. I own myself inflamed with a desire of beholding a young lady, whose perfections I have seen reflected in your sorrow; my curiosity is, moreover, interested on account of that humane gentlewoman, whose uncommon generosity sheltered such virtue in distress; but my disposition is infectious, and will, I am afraid, hang like a damp upon the general festivity of your friends."

Melvile would take no denial, and having obtained his consent, repaired to the house of Joshua, whose countenance seemed to unbend gradually, into a total expression of joy and surprize, as he learned the circumstances of this amazing event: he faithfully promised to attend the count at the appointed hour, and in the mean time earnestly exhorted him to take some repose, in order to quiet the agitation of his spirits, which must have been violently hurried on this occasion. The advice was salutary, and Renaldo resolved to follow it.

He returned to his lodgings, and laid himself down; but, notwithstanding

the fatigue he had undergone, sleep refused to visit his eyelids, all his faculties being kept in motion by the ideas that crouded so fast upon his imagination: nevertheless, though his mind continued in agitation, his body was
refreshed, and he arose in the forenoon, with more serenity and vigour than
he had enjoyed for many months: every moment his heart throbbed with new
rapture, when he found himself on the brink of possessing all that his soul
held dear and amiable; he put on his gayest looks and apparel; insisted upon
the Castilian's doing the same honour to the occasion; and the alteration of
dress produced such an advantageous change in the appearance of don Diego,
that when Joshua arrived at the appointed hour, he could scarce recognize his
features, and complimented him very politely on the improvement of his
looks.

True it is, the Spaniard was a personage of a very prepossessing mein, and
noble deportment; and had not grief, by increasing his native gravity, in some
measure discomposed the symmetry of his countenance, he would have
passed for a man of a very amiable and engaging physiognomy. They set out
in the Jew's coach for the house of madame Clement, and were ushered into
an apartment, where they found the clergyman and physician with that lady,
to whom don Diego and the Hebrew were by Melvile introduced.

Before they had seated themselves, Renaldo enquired about the health of
Monimia, and was directed to the next room by madame Clement, who permited him to go thither, and conduct her to the company. He was not slow in
availing himself of this permission: he disappeared in an instant, and, during
his short absence, don Diego was strangely disturbed: the blood flushed, and
forsook his cheeks by turns; a cold vapour seemed to shiver through his
nerves; and at his breast he felt uncommon palpitation. Madame Clement
observed his discomposure, and kindly enquired into the cause; when he
replied, "I have such an interest in what concerns the count de Melvile, and
my imagination is so much prepossessed with the perfections of Monimia,
that I am, as it were, agonized with expectation; yet never did my curiosity
before raise such tumults as those that now agitate my bosom!"

He had scarce pronounced these words, when the door re-opening, Renaldo led in this mirror of elegance and beauty, at sight of whom the Israelite's countenance was distorted into a stare of admiration. But if such was
the astonishment of Joshua, what were the emotions of the Castilian, when,
in the beauteous orphan, he beheld the individual features of his long lost
Serafina!⁴

His feelings are not to be described: the fond parent, whose affection
shoots even to a sense of pain, feels not half such transport, when he unex-

pectedly retrieves a darling child from the engulphing billows or devouring flame. The hope of Zelos had been totally extinguished: his heart had been incessantly torn with anguish and remorse, upbraiding him as the murtherer of Serafina. His therefore were the additional transports of a father disburthened of the guilt of such enormous homicide. His nerves were too much overpowered by this sudden recognition, to manifest the sensation of his soul by external signs. He started not, nor did he lift an hand in token of surprize: he moved not from the spot on which he stood, but, rivetting his eyes to those of the lovely phantome, remained without motion, until she, approaching with her lover, fell at his feet, and clasping his knees, exclaimed, "May I yet call you father?"

This powerful shock arrouzed his faculties; a cold sweat bedewed his forehead; his knees began to totter; he dropped upon the floor, and throwing his arms around her, cried, "O nature! O Serafina! merciful providence! thy ways are past finding out." So saying, he fell upon her neck, and wept aloud: the tears of sympathetic joy trickled down her snowy bosom, that heaved with rapture inexpressible. Renaldo's eyes poured forth the briny stream: the cheeks of madame Clement were not dry in this conjuncture: she kneeled by Serafina, kissed her with all the eagerness of maternal affection, and with uplifted hands adored the power that pre-ordained this blessed event: the clergyman and doctor intimately shared the general transport; and as for Joshua, the drops of true benevolence flowed from his eyes, like the oil on Aaron's beard,[5] while he skipped about the room in an aukward extacy, and in a voice resembling the hoarse notes of the long-eared tribe,[6] cried, "O father Abraham! such a moving scene hath not been acted since Joseph disclosed himself unto his brethren in Ægypt!"[7]

Don Diego having found utterance to his passion, proceeded in this strain, "O! my dear child! to find thee thus again, after our last unhappy parting, is wonderful! miraculous! Blessed be the all-good, almighty power, that saved thee for this hour of joy! Yet while my heart yearns towards thee; while I pant with inconceivable affection, and thus review these living features, which were so long my study and delight, I dare not ask by what mysterious means this meeting is effected; lest, in the fond enquiry, I find my present bliss unreal, and awake to misery again!"

"O ever honoured father!" she replied, "if to see your Serafina at your feet, melting with filial love and veneration, can impart a gleam of satisfaction to your breast, enjoy that pleasure, and behold her now restored to your protection and paternal will, which she never more will disobey. Alas! had heaven thought proper to reserve another parent for this interview, our joys had been compleat; but she hath already paid her debt to nature, and from the seats of bliss looks down well pleased on this interesting scene."

"Ah, my Antonia!" cried the father, interrupting her, "she is then at rest. Peace be to her unspotted soul; to have found her here, had been too much: how my Serafina hath survived my blindfold rage, I know not; but sure the guilt of fair Antonia's death, still hangs upon my soul."

"Dismiss that fatal thought," said Serafina, "my mother quietly bade adieu to life in England; she peaceably expired within these arms, and with her latest breath prayed for her hapless husband." "Her mind was ever godlike," he resumed, "she was a saint in virtue, ill bestowed on such a wretch as me; yet thy words have raised a dreadful burthen from my conscience: I am not then the dire assassin, who sacrificed his wife and daughter to an infernal motive, falsely titled honour? tho' I am more and more involved in a mystery, which I long to hear explained."

"That shall be my task," cried Renaldo, "but first permit me to implore your sanction to my passion for the incomparable Serafina. You already know our mutual sentiments; and though I own the possession of such inestimable worth and beauty, would be a recompence that infinitely transcends the merit I can plead, yet as it hath been my good fortune to inspire her with a mutual flame, I hope to reap from your indulgence, what I could not expect from my own desert; and here we present ourselves, in hope of your paternal assent and benediction."

"Were she more fair, and good, and gentle than she is," answered the Castilian, "(and to my partial observation, nought e'er appeared on earth, more beauteous and engaging) I would approve your title to her heart, and recommend you to her smiles, with all a father's influence and power: yes, my daughter! my joy on this occasion is infinitely augmented by the knowledge of those tender ties of love that bind thee to this amiable youth: a youth! to whose uncommon courage and generosity I owe my life and my subsistance, together with the inexpressible delight that now revels in my bosom. Enjoy, my children, the happy fruits of your reciprocal attachment. May heaven, which hath graciously conducted you through a labyrinth of perplexity and woe, to this transporting view of blissful days, indulge you with that uninterrupted stream of pure felicity, which is the hope, and ought to be the boon of virtue, such as yours."

So saying, he joined their hands, and embraced them with the most cordial love and satisfaction, which diffused itself to every individual of the company, who fervently invoked the Almighty Power, in behalf of this enraptured pair. The tumult of these emotions having a little subsided, and the

Castilian being seated betwixt Renaldo and his beauteous bride, he politely bespoke the indulgence of madame Clement, begging she would permit him to demand the performance of the count's promise, that he might be forthwith made acquainted with those circumstances of his own fate, which he was so impatient to learn.

The lady having assured him, that she and all the company would take pleasure in hearing the recapitulation, the Spaniard, addressing himself to Melvile, "In the name of heaven!" said he, "how could you supplant that rival, who fell a sacrifice to my resentment, after he had bewitched the heart of Serafina? for, sure, the affection he had kindled in her breast, must have long survived his death." "That rival," replied the count, "who incurred your displeasure, was no other than Renaldo." With these words, he applied to one eye a patch of black silk provided for the purpose, and turning his face towards don Diego, that gentleman started with astonishment, crying, "Good heaven! the very countenance of Orlando, whom I slew! this is still more amazing!"

CHAPTER LXV.

A retrospective link, necessary for the concatenation¹ of these memoirs.

Indulge me with a patient hearing," proceeded the Hungarian, "and all these riddles soon will be explained. Inflamed with the desire of seeing foreign countries, I disobeyed the will of an indulgent father, from whose house withdrawing privately, I set out for Italy, in disguise, by the way of Tyrol, visited Venice, Rome, Florence, and embarking at Naples, in an English ship, arrived at St. Lucar, from whence I repaired to Seville; there, in a few days, was my curiosity engaged by the fame of the fair Serafina, who was justly deemed the most accomplished beauty in that part of Spain. Nay, blush not, gentle creature! for, by my hopes of heaven! thy charms were even injured by the cold applause of that report: nevertheless, I was warmly interested by the uncommon character, and eagerly longed to see this pattern of perfection. As don Diego did not train her up in that restraint to which the Spanish ladies are subjected, I soon found an opportunity of seeing her at church; and no person here present will, I presume, doubt that I was instantly captivated by her beauty and deportment. Had I thought that don Diego's favour was unengaged, perhaps I should have followed the dictates of vanity and inexperience, and presented myself in my own character, among the croud of her professed admirers. I knew her father had been an officer of distinguished rank and reputation, and did not doubt that he would have regarded a young soldier of unexceptionable pedigree, and I will even add, of unattainted[2] fame: nor did I suppose my own father could have objected against such an advantageous match; but, by dint of industrious enquiry, I learned, that the divine Serafina was already betrothed to don Manuel de Mendoza, and this information overwhelmed me with despair.

After having revolved a thousand projects for retarding and preventing that detested union, I resolved to avail myself of my talent for drawing, and professed myself a master of that science, in hope of being employed by the father of Serafina, who, I knew, let slip no opportunity of improving his daughter's education. Accordingly I had the good fortune to attract his notice, was invited to his house, honoured with his approbation, and furnished with unrestricted opportunities of conversing with the dear object of my love. The passion which her beauty had kindled, was, by the perfections of her mind, inflamed to such a degree of transport, as could not be concealed from her penetration. She chanced to relish my conversation; I gradually acquired her friendship; pity was the next passion that she entertained in my favour. I then ventured to disclose myself, and the dear charmer did not disapprove of my presumption. She and her mother had been perplexed with some religious scruples, concerning which they appealed to my opinion; and I was happy enough to set their minds at ease.

This sort of intercourse naturally created a mutual confidence among us; and, in a word, I was blessed with the daughter's love and mother's approbation. Don Diego will pardon those clandestine measures which we took, from a full persuasion, that it was impossible to render him propitious to the views in which our hearts and hands were so deeply interested: I did not then know how little he was addicted to superstition.[3]

Without entering into a detail of the schemes we projected to delay the happiness of Mendoza, I shall only observe, that knowing the fatal day was, at length, unalterably fixed, we determined to elude the purpose of don Diego by flight, and every thing was actually prepared for our escape. When the hour of appointment arrived, I repaired to the place at which I had proposed to enter the house, and stumbled, in the dark, over the body of a man still warm and bleeding. Alarmed at this occurrence, I darted myself through the window, and rushing to the apartment of the ladies, (immortal powers!) beheld the peerless Serafina, and her virtuous mother, stretched on a couch, and in all appearance deprived of life.

The company will easily conceive what agonies I felt at such a spectacle. I ran towards the spot in a transport of horror! I clasped my lovely mistress in my arms, and finding her still breathing, endeavoured, but in vain, to wake her from the trance: Antonia was overwhelmed with the same lethargic power. My fancy was immediately struck with the apprehension of their being poisoned. Regardless of my own situation, I alarmed the family, called for assistance, and requested the servants to summon don Diego to the dismal scene. I was informed, that their master had rode forth in manifest confusion; and while I pondered on this surprising excursion, an apothecary in the neighbourhood entered the chamber, and having examined the pulses of the ladies, declared, that their lives were in no danger, and advised that they should be undressed and conveyed to bed. While their women were busied in this employment, I went into the court-yard, attended by some of the servants with lights, in order to view the body of the man, which I had found at my arrival. His apparel was mean, his countenance ferocious, a long spado[4] was buckled to his thigh, and in his belt were stuck a brace of loaded pistols; so that we concluded he was some thief, who had waited for an opportunity, and seeing the casement open, intended to rob the house, but was prevented and slain by don Diego himself, whose retreat, however, did not a little confound our conjecture. For my own part, I remained all night in the house, tortured with fear, vexation, and suspence.

My hope was altogether disappointed by this unhappy accident, and I shuddered at the prospect of losing Serafina for ever, either by this mysterious malady, or by her marriage with Mendoza, which I now despaired of being able to defeat. The major-domo having waited several hours for his lord's return, without seeing him appear, thought proper to dispatch a messenger to don Manuel, with an account of what had happened; and that nobleman arriving in the morning, took possession of the house. About four o'clock in the afternoon, Serafina began to stir, and at five, she and her mother were perfectly awake.

They no sooner recovered the use of reflection, than they gave signs of equal sorrow and amazement, and earnestly called for Isabella, who was privy to our design, and who, after a very minute enquiry, was found in a lone and solitary chamber, where she had been confined. Such was the confusion of the house, that no person ever dreamed of asking how I had entered, each domestick, in all probability, supposing that I had been introduced by his fellow: so that I tarried unquestioned, on pretence of concern for the distress of a family, in which I had been so generously entertained; and by Isabella sent my respects and duty to her ladies: she was therefore not a little surprized, when, after every other servant had withdrawn, she heard the lovely Serafina exclaim, with all the violence of grief, "Ah! Isabella, Orlando is no more!" but their astonishment was still greater, when she assured them of my being alive, and in the house. They recounted to her the adventure of last night, which she explained by informing them of the letters which don Diego had intercepted: and they immediately concluded, that he had, in the precipitation of his wrath, killed, by mistake, the person who was found dead in the court-yard. This conjecture alarming them on my account, they, by the medium of Isabella, conjured me to leave the house, lest don Diego should return, and accomplish his resentment; and I was persuaded to withdraw, after I had settled the channel of a correspondence with the confidante.

Being now obliged to alter our measures, because our former intention was discovered by don Diego, I secured a retreat for Serafina and her mother, at the house of the English consul in Seville, who was my particular friend; and next day understanding, from Isabella, that her lord had not yet re-appeared, and that don Manuel was very urgent in his addresses, we concerted an assignation in the garden, and that same evening I was fortunate enough to convey my prize to the asylum I had prepared for their reception. Inexpressible was the rage of Mendoza, when he heard of their elopement: he raved like one deprived of reason, swore he would put all the servants of the family to the rack, and in consequence of the intelligence he obtained by threats and promises, set on foot a very strict enquiry, in order to apprehend the fugitives and Orlando, who had, by some means or other, incurred his suspicion.

We eluded his search by the vigilance and caution of our kind host; and while we remained in concealment, were extremely astonished to hear, that the unfortunate don Diego was proclaimed a traitor, and a price set upon his head. This information overwhelmed us all with the utmost affliction: Antonia lamented, without ceasing, the disgrace of her beloved lord, from whom she never would have withdrawn herself, but with the lively hope of a reconciliation, after the first transports of his ire should have subsided, and the real character of Orlando should have appeared: it was not long before we had reason to believe, that Mendoza was the accuser of don Diego.—

Nay, start not, Signior; Manuel was actually that traitor: this was the turn of his revenge; when he found himself disappointed in the hope of possessing the incomparable Serafina, he took a base advantage of your absence and retreat. He posted to Madrid, impeached you to the secretary of state, of having maintained a criminal correspondence with the enemies of Spain, included me in his accusation, as a spy for the house of Austria, and framed such a plausible tale from the circumstances of your distress, that don Diego was outlawed, and Mendoza gratified with a grant of his estate.

These melancholy incidents made a deep impression upon the mind of the virtuous Antonia, who, waving every other consideration, would have personally appeared for the vindication of her husband's honour, had not we dissuaded her from such a rash undertaking, by demonstrating her inability to contend with such a powerful antagonist, and representing, that her appearance would be infallibly attended with the ruin of Serafina, who would certainly fall into the hands of the villain to whom she had been contracted. We exhorted her to wait patiently for some happy revolution of fortune, and encouraged her with the hope of don Diego's exerting himself effectually in his own defence.

Mean while, our worthy landlord was suddenly cut off by death; and his widow being resolved to retire into her own country, we secretly embarked in the same ship, and arrived in England about eighteen months ago. Antonia still continued to pine over the ruin of her house; as she could hear no tidings of Don Diego, she concluded he was dead, and mourned with unabating sorrow. In vain I assured her that soon as my own affairs should be adjusted, I would exert my whole endeavours to find and succour him. She could not imagine that a man of his spirit and disposition would live so long in obscurity; and her affliction derived new force from the death of the consul's widow, with whom she had lived in the most unbounded intimacy and friendship. From that day her health evidently declined: she foresaw her dissolution and comforted herself with the hope of seeing her husband and her friend, in a place where no treachery is felt, and no sorrow is known; confident of my integrity, and the purity of my love, she in the most pathetic terms recommended Serafina to my care.—

Ha! weepest thou, fair excellence, at the remembrance of that tender scene, when the good Antonia, on the bed of death, joined thy soft hand to mine, and said, 'Renaldo, I bequeath this orphan to your love; it is a sacred pledge which if you cherish with due honour and regard, internal peace and happiness will ever smile within your bosom: but if you treat it with indifference, dishonour or neglect, just heaven will punish your breach of trust with everlasting disappointments and disquiet.'

Signior Don Diego, I see you are moved, and therefore will not dwell on such distressful circumstances. The excellent Antonia exchanged this life for a more happy state; and so exquisite was the sorrow of the tender-hearted Serafina, as to torture me with the apprehension that she would not long survive her pious mother. How I obeyed the injunctions of that departing saint, Monimia (for that name she now assumed) can testify, until that artful serpent Fathom glided into our mutual confidence, abused our ears, poisoned our unsuspecting faith, and effected that fatal breach, productive of all the misery and vexation which we have suffered, and which is now so happily expelled."

"Heaven," said the Castilian, "hath visited me for the sins and errors of my youth; yet, such mercy hath been mingled with its chastisements, I dare not murmur or repine. The tears of penitence and sorrow shall water my Antonia's grave; as for Mendoza, I rejoice at his treachery, by which the obligation of my promise is cancelled, and my honour fully acquitted. He shall not triumph in his guilt: my services, my character and innocence shall soon confront his perfidy, and I hope, defeat his interest: The king[5] is just and gracious, nor is my family and name unknown."

Here the Jew interposing, presented to him a letter from a person of consequence at Madrid, whom Joshua had interested in the cause of don Diego; that nobleman had already found means to represent the case of Zelos to his majesty, who had actually ordered don Manuel to be confined, until the injured person should appear to justify himself, and prosecute his accuser according to the terms of law: at the same time don Diego was summoned to present himself before the king within a limited time, to answer to the charge which Mendoza had brought against him.

The Spaniard's heart overflow'd with gratitude and joy, when he read this intimation; he embraced the Jew, who, before Zelos could give utterance to his thoughts, told him that the Spanish Ambassador at London, having been prepossessed in his favour, craved the honour of seeing don Diego; and that he, Joshua, was ready to conduct them to the house.

"Then is my heart at rest! (cried the Castilian) the house of Zelos once more shall lift up its head. I shall again revisit my native country with honour, and abase the villain who hath soiled my fame! O my children! this day is replete with such joy and satisfaction, as I did not think had been in the power of heaven to grant, without the interposition of a miracle! To you Renaldo, to you illustrious lady, and to these worthy gentlemen, am I indebted for the restoration of that for which alone I wish to live, and when my heart ceases to retain the obligation, may I forfeit the name of a Castilian, and scorn and dishonour be my portion."

Perhaps all Europe could not produce another company so happy as that which now sat down to dinner in the house of madame Clement, whose own benevolent heart was peculiarly adapted for such enjoyment. The lovers feasted their eyes more than their appetite, by a tender intercourse of glances, which needed not the slow interpretation of speech; while the Spaniard regarded them alternately with looks of wonder and paternal joy, and every individual surveyed the all-deserving pair with admiration and esteem.

Serafina taking the advantage of this general satisfaction, when the heart softened into complacency, deposits every violent thought: "I must now, (said she) try my interest with Renaldo: the good company shall bear witness to my triumph or repulse. I do not ask you to forgive, but to withold your vengeance from the wretched Fathom. His fraud, ingratitude and villainy are, I believe, unrivalled: yet his base designs have been defeated; and heaven perhaps hath made him the involuntary instrument for bringing our constancy and virtue to the test; besides, his perfidy is already punished with the last degree of human misery and disgrace: the Doctor, who has traced him in all his conduct and vicissitudes of fortune, will draw a picture of his present wretchedness, which, I doubt not, will move your compassion, as it hath already excited mine."

The generous hostess was ready to enforce this charitable proposal, with all her eloquence, when Melvile with a look that well expressed his magnanimity of love, replied, "Such a boon becomes the gentle Serafina. O! every moment furnishes me with fresh matter to admire the virtues of thy soul: if thou, whose tender heart hath been so rent with misery and anguish, canst intercede for thy tormentor, who now suffers in his turn, shall I refuse to pardon the miserable wretch! no, let me glory in imitating the great example, and sollicit Don Diego in behalf of the same miscreant whose perfidious barbarity cost him such intolerable woe." "Enough," cried the Castilian, "I have disclaimed the vindictive principles of a Spaniard; and leave the miserable object to the sting of his own conscience, which soon or late, will not fail to avenge the wrongs we have sustained from his deceit."

CHAPTER LXVI.

The History draws near a Period.

Universal was the applause which they acquired by this noble sacrifice of their resentment: the afternoon was spent in the utmost harmony and good humour; and at the earnest solicitation of Renaldo, whose fancy still harboured the apprehensions of another separation, don Diego consented that the indissoluble knot should be tied between that young gentleman and Serafina in two days, and the place appointed for the ceremony, was the very church where they had been restored to the arms of each other.

The lovely bride, with a silent blush that set her lover's heart on fire, submitted to this determination, in consequence of which, the company was bespoke for that auspicious hour, and the evening being pretty far advanced, they took leave of the ladies, and retired to their respective homes; don Diego and his future son in law being reconducted to their lodgings, in the coach of the Jew, who taking an opportunity of being alone with Melvile, observed that it would be necessary on this occasion to supply the Castilian with a sum of money, in order to support his dignity and independance, in furnishing Serafina with every thing suitable to her rank and merit; and that he would willingly accommodate him, provided he knew how to propose it so as to give no offence to his punctilious disposition.

Renaldo thanking him for this generous anticipation, advised him to sollicit the Spaniard's correspondence in the way of business, and to put the whole on the footing of his own interest; by which means don Diego's delicacy could sustain no affront. Fraught with this instruction, the Israelite desired a private audience of the Castilian, in which after an apology for the freedom of his demand, "Signior don Diego, (said he) as your fortune hath been so long embezzled by your adversary in Spain, and your correspondence with that country intirely cut off, it is not to be supposed that your finances are at present in such a condition, as to maintain the splendour of your family. Count de Melvile's whole fortune is at your command; and had not he been afraid of giving umbrage to the peculiar delicacy of your sentiments, he would have pressed you to use it for your convenience. For my own part, over and above the inclination I have to serve don Diego, I consult my own private advantage in desiring you to accept my service on this occasion. Money is the chief commodity in which I deal, and if you honour me with your commands, I shall be a gainer by my obedience."

Don Diego replied with a smile that denoted how well he understood the meaning of this address; "Surely, Signior, I am bound by the strongest ties, to exert my utmost endeavours for your advantage; and I pray God this your proposal may have that issue: I am well acquainted with the Count's generosity and refined notions of honour; and too much obliged by him already, to hesitate with punctilious reserve in accepting his future assistance: nevertheless, since you have contrived a scheme for removing all scruples of that sort, I shall execute it with pleasure; and in the form of business, you shall have all the security I can give for what shall be necessary to answer my present occasions."

The preliminaries being thus settled, Joshua advanced for his use a thousand pounds, for which he would take neither bond, note nor receipt, desiring only that the Castilian would mark it in his own pocket book, that the debt might appear, in case any accident should befal the borrower. Although the Spaniard had been accustomed to the uncommon generosity of Melvile, he could not help wondering at this nobleness of behaviour, so little to be expected from any merchant, much less from a Jewish broker.

While this affair was on the anvil, Renaldo who could no longer withhold the communication of his happiness from his sister and relations in Germany, took up the pen, and in a letter to his brother in law, recounted all the circumstances of the surprizing turn of fate which he had experienced since his arrival in England: he likewise related the story of don Diego, informed them of the day appointed for his nuptials, and intreated the major to make a journey to London with his wife; or if that should be impracticable, to come as far as Brussels, where they should be met by him and his Serafina. There was now but one day between him and the accomplishment of his dearest wish, and that was spent in procuring a license, and adjusting the preparations for the grand festival. Don Diego in the forenoon visited madame Clement, to whom he repeated his warm acknowledgments of her bounty and maternal affection to his daughter, and presented to Serafina, bank notes to the amount of five hundred pounds, to defray the necessary expence of her wedding ornaments.

All the previous steps being taken for the solemnization of this interesting event, and the hour of appointment arrived, the bridegroom, accompanied by his father in law, hastened to the place of rendezvous, which was the vestry room of the church we have already described; where they were received by the good clergyman in his canonicals; and here they had not waited many minutes, when they were joined by madame Clement and the amiable bride, escorted by the friendly physician, who had all along bore such a share in their concerns. Serafina was dressed in a sack of white sattin, and the ornaments of her head were adjusted in the Spanish fashion, which gave a peculiar air to her appearance, and an additional spirit to those attractions which engaged the heart of each beholder. There was nothing remarkable in the habit of Renaldo, who had copied the plainness and elegance of his mistress; but when she entered the place, his features were animated with a double proportion of vivacity, and their eyes meeting, seemed to kindle a blaze which diffused warmth and joy thro' the countenances of all present.

After a short pause her father led her to the altar, and gave her away to the transported Renaldo, before the priest who performed the ceremony, and bestowed the nuptial benediction on this enraptured pair. The sanction of the church being thus obtained, they withdrew into the vestry, where Melvile sealed his title on her rosy lips, and presented his wife to the company, who embraced her in their turns, with fervent wishes for their mutual happiness.

Tho' the scene of this transaction was remote from any inhabited neighbourhood, the church was surrounded by a crowd of people, who with uncommon demonstrations of surprize and admiration, petitioned heaven to
bless so fair a couple. Such indeed was their eagerness to see them, that some
lives were endangered by the pressure of the crowd, which attended them
with loud acclamation to the coach, after the bridegroom had deposited in the
hands of the minister, one hundred pounds for the benefit of the poor of that
parish, and thrown several handfuls of money among the multitude. Serafina
reimbarked in madame Clement's convenience, with that good lady and don
Diego, while Renaldo with the clergyman and doctor followed in Joshua's
coach, to a pleasant country house upon the Thames, at the distance of a few
miles from London. This the Jew had borrowed from the owner, for a few
days, and there they were received by that honest Hebrew, who had provided a very elegant entertainment for the occasion: he had also bespoke a
small but excellent band of musick, which regaled their ears while they sat at
dinner; and the afternoon being calm and serene, he prevailed on them to
take the air on the river, in a barge which he had prepared for the purpose.

But, notwithstanding this diversity of amusement, Renaldo would have
found it the longest day he had ever passed, had not his imagination been
diverted by an incident which employed his attention during the remaining
part of the evening.[1] They had drank tea, and engaged in a party at whist,
when they were surprized with a noise of contention from a publick house,
that fronted the windows of the apartment in which they sat. Alarmed at this
uproar, they forsook their cards, and throwing up the casements, beheld a
hearse surrounded by four men on horseback, who had stopped the carriage
and violently pulled the driver from his seat. This uncommon arrest had
engaged the curiosity of the publican's family, who stood at the door to observe the consequence, when all of a sudden, appeared a person in canonicals, well mounted, who riding up to those who maltreated the driver, bestowed upon one of them, such a blow with the but-end of his whip, as laid
him sprawling on the ground, and springing from his saddle upon the box,
took the reins into his own hand, swearing with great vehemence, that he
would murther every man who should attempt to obstruct the hearse.

The good priest who had married Renaldo, was not a little scandalized at
this ferocious behaviour in a clergyman, and could not help saying aloud, he
was a disgrace to the cloth; when the horseman looking up to the window,
replied, "Sir, may I be d——n'd if any man in England has a greater respect for
the cloth than I have; but at present I am quite distracted." So saying, he
whipped up the horses, and had actually disentangled the hearse from those

who surrounded it; when he was opposed by another troop, one of whom alighted with great expedition, and cut the harness so as that he could not possibly proceed: finding himself thus driven to bay, he leaped upon the ground, and exercised his weapon with such amazing strength and agility, that several of his antagonists were left motionless on the field, before he was overpowered and disarmed by dint of numbers, who assailed him on all sides.

The mad parson being thus taken prisoner, an elderly person of a very prepossessing appearance, went up to the hearse, and unbolting the door, a young lady sprung out, and shrieking, ran directly to the public house, to the infinite astonishment and affright of the whole family, who believed it was the spirit of the deceased person, whose body lay in the carriage. Renaldo, who was with difficulty restrained from interposing in behalf of the clergy-man against such odds, no sooner perceived this apparition, than supposing her to be some distressed damsel, his Quixotism awoke, he descended in an instant, and rushed into the house, among those who pursued the fair phan-tome. Don Diego and the physician took the same road, while the real clergy-man and Joshua tarried with the ladies, who were, by this time, very much interested in the event.

Melvile found the young lady in the hands of the old gentleman, who had released her from the hearse, and who now bitterly upbraided her for her folly, and disobedience: while she protested, with great vivacity, that what-ever she might suffer from his severity, she would never submit to the hateful match he had proposed, nor break the promise she had already made to the gentleman who had now attempted to rescue her from the tyranny of a cruel father. This declaration was followed by a plentiful shower of tears, which the father could not behold with unmoistened eyes, altho' he reviled her with marks of uncommon displeasure, and turning to the count, "I appeal to you, Sir," said he, "whether I have not reason to curse the undutiful obstinacy of that pert baggage, and renounce her for ever as an alien to my blood. She has, for some months, been sollicited in marriage by an honest citizen, a thirty thousand pound man; and instead of listening to such an advantageous pro-posal, she hath bestowed her heart upon a young fellow, not worth a groat.[2] Ah! you degenerate hussy, this comes of your plays and romances: if thy mother were not a woman of an unexceptionable life and conversation, I should verily believe thou art no child of mine: run away with a beggar! for shame!"

"I suppose," replied Renaldo, "the person to whom your daughter's affec-tion inclines, is that clergyman who exerted himself so manfully at the door."
"Clergyman!" cried the other, "adad![3] he has more of the devil than the

church about him. A ruffian! he has, for ought I know, murthered the worthy gentleman whom I intended for my son-in-law; and the rogue, if I had not kept out of his way, would, I suppose, have served me with the same sauce: me! who have been his master for many years, and had resolved to make a man of him. Sir, he was my own clerk, and this is the return I have met with from the serpent which I cherished in my bosom."

Here he was interrupted by the arrival of the citizen for whom he had expressed such concern: that gentleman had received a contusion upon one eye, by which the sight was altogether obstructed; so that he concluded he should never retrieve the use of that organ, and with great clamour took all the spectators to witness the injury he had sustained; he entered the room with manifest perturbation, demanded satisfaction of the father, and peremptorily declared it should not be a lost eye to him, if there was law in England. This unseasonable demand, and the boisterous manner in which it was made, did not at all suit the present humour of the old gentleman, who told him peevishly he owed him no eye, and bade him go and ask reparation of the person who had done him wrong.

The young lady snatching this favourable occasion, earnestly entreated Melvile and his company to intercede with her father in behalf of her lover, who, she assured them, was a young gentleman of a good family, and uncommon merit; and, in compliance with her request, they invited him and his daughter to the house in which they lodged, where they would be disincumbered of the croud which this dispute had gathered together, and more at leisure to consult about the measures necessary to be taken. The old gentleman thanked them for their courtesy, which he did not think proper to refuse, and while he led, or rather hauled mademoiselle over the way, under the auspices of the Castilian, Renaldo set the lover at liberty, made him a tender of his good offices, and advised him to wait at the public house for an happy issue of their negotiation.

The pseudo-parson was very much affected by this generous proffer, for which he made suitable acknowledgments, and protested before God, he would die a thousand deaths, rather than part with his dear Charlotte. Her father no sooner entered the apartment, than he was known by Joshua to be a considerable trader in the city of London, and the merchant was glad to find himself among his acquaintance. He was so full of the story which had brought him thither, that he had scarce sat down, when he began to complain of his hard fate, in having an only child, who was so mean, stubborn and contumacious; and every sentence was concluded with an apostrophe of reproaches to the delinquent.

The Jew having allowed him to ring out his alarm, condoled his misfortune, and gravely counselled the young lady to wean her affections from such an unworthy object: for he supposed her favourite was a man of no principle, or liberal endowments, otherwise her father would not exclaim so bitterly against her conduct. Charlotte, who wanted neither beauty nor understanding, assured him, that her lover's character was, in all respects, unblemished; for the truth of which assertion she appealed to her papa, who owned, with reluctance, that the young man was a gentleman by birth, that he had served him with remarkable diligence and integrity, and that his accomplishments were far superior to his station in life. "But then," said he, "the fellow has not a shilling of his own, and would you have me give away my daughter to a beggar?"

"God forbid!" cried the Jew, "I always understood you possessed an ample fortune, and am sorry to find it otherwise." "Otherwise!" replied the citizen, with some acrimony, "take care what you say, Sir, a merchant's credit is not to be tampered with." "I beg your pardon," answered the Hebrew, "I concluded that your circumstances were bad, because you objected to the poverty of the young man, after you had owned he was possessed of every other qualification to make your daughter happy: for it is not to be imagined, that you would thwart her inclinations, or seek to render an only child miserable, on account of an obstacle which you yourself could easily remove. Let us suppose you can afford to give with your daughter ten thousand pounds, which would enable this young man to live with credit and reputation, and engage advantageously in trade, for which you say he is well qualified: The alternative then will be, whether you would rather see her in the arms of a deserving youth, whom she loves, enjoying all the comforts of life, with a moderate fortune, which it will always be in your own power to improve; or tied for life to a monied man, whom she detests, cursing her hard fate, and despising that superfluity of wealth, in spite of which she finds herself so truly wretched."

The old gentleman seemed to be startled at this observation, which was reinforced by Renaldo's saying, that he would, moreover, enjoy the unutterable pleasure of giving happiness to a worthy man, whose gratitude would co-operate with his love, in approving himself a dutiful son, as well as an affectionate husband. He then represented the family disquiets, and dismal tragedies, produced from such mercenary and compulsive[4] matches; and in conclusion related the story of don Diego and his daughter, which when the merchant heard, he started up with marks of terror in his countenance, and throwing up the casement, called upon Valentine with great vociferation; this was the name of his daughter's admirer, who no sooner heard the summons, than he flew to the spot from whence it came, and the merchant, without any further preamble, seizing his hand, joined it with that of Charlotte, saying, with great trepidation, "Here take her, in the name of God, and thank this honourable company for your good fortune."

The lovers were transported with exquisite joy at this sudden determination in their favour. Valentine having kissed the hand of his mistress, with all the eagerness of rapture, and acknowledged the merchant's generosity, paid his respects to the ladies with a very polite address, and with demonstrations of uncommon gratitude and sensibility, thanked the gentlemen, and the count in particular, for their good offices, to which he attributed the happiness he now enjoyed. While Serafina and madame Clement caressed the amiable Charlotte, the rest of the company congratulated her admirer upon his choice and success; though the clergyman could not help reprehending him for profaning the sacerdotal habit.

Valentine heartily asked pardon for having given such cause of offence, and hoped he should be forgiven, as it was a disguise which he thought absolutely necessary for the execution of a scheme upon which his happiness altogether depended. He then, at the request of Renaldo, unfolded the mystery of the hearse, by giving them to understand, that Charlotte's father having got inkling of their mutual passion, had dismissed his clerk, and conveyed his daughter to a country house in the neighbourhood of London, in order to cut off their correspondence: notwithstanding these precautions, they had found means to communicate with each other by letters, which were managed by a third person, and his rival being very importunate in his sollicitations, they had concerted the expedient of the hearse, which he provided and conducted through a road contiguous to the end of the merchant's garden, where Charlotte being apprized of the design, waited for its approach, and embarked in it without hesitation. Valentine thought himself sufficiently screened from discovery by his disguise, but he was unfortunately met by a servant of the family, who recollected his features, and immediately gave the alarm, upon which the father and his friends took horse, and pursued them by two different roads, until they were overtaken at this place.

He had scarce finished this short relation, when his rival bluntly entering the apartment, with an handkerchief tied round his eye, committed Valentine to the charge of a constable, who attended him, by a warrant from a justice of the peace in that neighbourhood; and threatened to prosecute the merchant on an action of damages for the loss of an eye, which he said he had sustained in his service. The company endeavoured to appease this citizen, by representing, that his misfortune was no other than a common inflammation; nor was it owing to malice aforethought, but entirely to the precipitate passion of an incensed young man, who, by the bye, acted in his own defence. At the same time the merchant promised to make any reasonable satisfaction; upon which the other demanded an obligation, importing, that he would, in ten days from the date, bestow upon him his daughter in marriage, with a portion of fifteen thousand pounds, or, in case of failure, pay him double the sum.

The merchant, exasperated at this extravagant demand, told him flatly, he had already disposed of his daughter to Valentine, who he believed was a much more deserving man; and that he was ready to wait upon the magistrate who had granted the warrant, in order to give bail for his future son-in-law. This was a mortifying declaration to the plaintiff, though he condoled himself with the hope of being a gainer by the loss of his eye; and now the pain was over, would have been very sorry to find his sight retrieved. The old gentleman, Joshua, and Renaldo accompanied the prisoner to the house of the justice, where he was immediately admitted to bail: upon their return, Valentine shifted his dress, and they supped together with great cordiality and mirth, maintained at the expence of the discarded lover.

After supper, don Diego walked a minuet with madame Clement, for whom, by this time, he had contracted an extraordinary degree of affection. Valentine had the honour to dance with the incomparable Serafina, whose beauty and attractions dazzled the eyes of the new comers, and struck her bashful partner with awe and confusion; and Melvile presented his hand to the agreeable Charlotte, who performed so much to the satisfaction of her father, that he could not help expressing his joy and pride: he praised God for throwing him in the way of our company, and engaged the clergyman to unite the young couple; after having appointed a day for the ceremony, and invited all present to the wedding. The evening having been insensibly[5] consumed in these avocations, and the night pretty far advanced, the ladies withdrew without ceremony; and the retreat of Serafina filled Renaldo's breast with tumult and emotion: his blood began to flow in impetuous tides, his heart to beat with redoubled vigour and velocity, while his eye seemed to flash with more than human splendor: now his imagination began to anticipate with the enthusiastic rage of an inspired Sybil;[6] he was instantaneously transported from the conversation, and every nerve was braced to such a degree of impatience, that human nature could not long endure the tension.

He therefore, having withstood the impulse about a quarter of an hour, at length gave way to his impetuosity, and springing from his friends, found himself in a dark passage, at the farther end of which, he perceived madame Clement coming out of a chamber with a light, which at sight of him she set down, and vanished in a moment. This was the star that pointed to his paradise: he hailed the signal, entered the apartment, and like a lion rushing on his prey, approached the nuptial bed, where Serafina, surrounded by all the graces of beauty, softness, sentiment, and truth, lay trembling as a victim at the altar, and strove to hide her blushes from his view; the door was shut, the light extinguished: he owned his lot was more than mortal man could claim.

Here let me draw the decent veil, that ought to shade the sacred mysteries of Hymen:[7] away unhallowed scoffers, who profane with idle pleasantry, or immodest hint, these holy rites; and leave those happy lovers to enjoy, in one another's arms, unutterable bliss, the well-earned palm of virtue and of constancy, which had undergone the most severe refinement: a more deserving pair night's curtain shrouds not in its dark extent.

The thoughts of Renaldo's felicity threw a damp on the spirits of Valentine, who saw the term of his probation protracted a few days longer, and could not help wishing in his heart, that he had atchieved the adventure which would have abridged his expectation, though at the expence of the old gentleman's displeasure. He filled a bumper to the health of the bride and bridegroom, and throwing up his eyes, with marks of admiration, exclaimed, "How happy is the count! alas! five days longer must I rein my impatience!" "It is but reasonable, you rogue, that your betters should have the start of you," said the merchant, who did him justice in the glass, and counselled him to drown his impatience with good claret. The youth followed his advice, and it was late before the company retired to rest.

These citizens, however, resolved to seize an opportunity of rallying the new married couple, according to custom, and with that view arose early in the morning, on the supposition of finding them still asleep; but they were not a little surprized, when they entered the breakfasting room, to see Renaldo, and his amiable bedfellow, already dressed, and waiting to do the honours of the house. The old gentleman would fain have cracked a joke upon their extraordinary dispatch, but he was so much over-awed by the dignity, and tamed by the sweetness of Serafina's carriage, that he durst not give utterance to his conception; and Valentine stood silent and abashed, as in the presence of a superior being. After breakfast, these gentlemen and Charlotte again expressed their sense of the obligations they owed to this happy family, repeated their invitation, and taking leave, returned to London in a coach that was provided over night.

Our friends being thus left to themselves, don Diego turning towards

Melvile, "Now," said he, "that I have yielded to the impatience of your love, as well as to the eagerness of my own desire to make you happy, I must beg leave to interrupt, for a little while, the stream of your mutual pleasure, and propose a melancholy excursion, which, however, will not be wholly void of enjoyment. I have too long delayed the performance of my duty at Antonia's grave: let us spend the forenoon in that pious pilgrimage: I will drop a few tears to the memory of that excellent woman, and never afterwards shall my friends be troubled with my grief."

The proposal being universally approved, they set out for the place, which had oft been visited by the gentle Serafina, who conducted her father to a black marble stone, which Renaldo had ordered to be laid over the grave, and as he kneeled to kiss the monument, he perceived this plain inscription in the Spanish Tongue: *Antonia de Zelos primera en todo lo que es ser bueno, y sin segundo en todo lo que fué ser desdichado, quedad con Dios!* that is, *Antonia de Zelos, unmatched in virtue, and unequalled in misfortune, adieu!*[8] "O faithful record! (cried the Castilian, smiting his breast, while his tears distilled upon the marble) thy goodness was the gift of heaven, but thy misfortunes were derived from the guilt of don Diego; yet his sorrow shall expiate his offence, and his penitence find favour in the sight of heaven: rest, rest, ill-fated virtue! eternal peace shall guard thy tomb, and angels minister to thy unspotted shade; nor shall thine ashes lie in dark obscurity: here will I raise a monument, more suited to thy excellence and name." Serafina melted with filial tenderness, nor were the rest unmoved at this affecting scene, which don Diego did not quit without reluctance.

CHAPTER LXVII.

The longest and the last.[1]

The nature of this visit had softened every heart, and saddened every countenance; and they walked in solemn silence to the other side of the church-yard, in order to regain their carriages; when, at the turning of the stile, they saw a young woman, in wretched attire, running out of a poor habitation, wringing her hands in all the agony of despair. Notwithstanding the distraction in her countenance, and the meanness of her apparel, she discovered a regularity of features, and a delicacy of air, which did not at all correspond with the misery of her equipage. These exhibitions of extreme distress, soon attracted the notice and compassion of our company, and Melvile's beauteous help-mate, accosting this forlorn damsel with a pity-breathing aspect, asked the cause of her disorder.

"Alas! dear lady," cried the other, with all the emphasis of woe, "an unhappy gentleman now breathes his last, within this inhospitable hovel, amidst such excess of misery, as would melt the most flinty bosom: what then must I feel, who am connected with him by the strongest ties of love and conjugal affection!" "Who is the unfortunate object?" said the physician. "He was once well known in the gay world: (replied the young woman) his name is Fathom." Every individual of the company started at mention of that detested name. Serafina began to tremble with emotion; and Renaldo, after a short pause, declared he would go in, not with a view to exult over his misery, but in order to contemplate the catastrophe of such a wicked life, that the moral might be the more deeply engraved on his remembrance. The young countess, whose tender heart could not bear the shock of such a spectacle, retired to the coach with madame Clement and the Jew, while Renaldo, accompanied by the rest, entered a dismal apartment, altogether void of furniture and convenience, where they beheld the wretched hero of these memoirs, stretched almost naked upon straw, insensible, convulsed, and seemingly in the grasp of death.[2] He was wore to the bone either by famine or distemper; his face was overshadowed with hair and filth; his eyes were sunk, glazed and distorted; his nostrils dilated; his lips covered with a black slough,[3] and his complexion faded into a pale clay-colour, tending to a yellow hue: in a word, the extremity of indigence, squalor and distress, could not be more feelingly represented.

While Melvile perused this melancholy lesson, and groaning, cried, "Behold the fate of man," he perceived a letter in the right hand of the unfortunate Fathom, which lay fast clinched across his breast. Curious to know the contents of this paper, which the young woman said he had kept in that position for several days, he drew nearer the wretched couch, and was not a little surprized to see it addressed to the right honourable Renaldo count de Melvile, to the care of Mr. Joshua Manasseh, merchant in London. When he attempted to disengage this billet from the author's hand, the sorrowing female fell on her knees, entreating him to desist, and telling him, she had promised, upon oath, to communicate the contents to no person upon earth, but to carry the letter, upon her husband's decease, to the gentleman to whose care it was directed.

Renaldo assured her upon his honour, that he was the very Renaldo count de Melvile for whom it was intended; and the young creature was so much confounded at this information, that before she could recollect herself, Melvile had opened the billet and read these words. "If this paper should fall into the hands of the noble Renaldo, he will understand that Fathom was the most execrable traitor that ever imposed upon unsuspecting benevolence, or attempted to betray a generous benefactor. His whole life was a series of fraud, perfidy and the most abominable ingratitude: but of all the crimes that lay heavy upon his soul, his being accessory to the death of the incomparable Serafina, whose father he had also robbed,[4] was that, for which he despaired of heaven's forgiveness, notwithstanding the dreadful compunction and remorse which have long preyed upon his heart, together with the incredible misery and deplorable death which by this time he hath undergone. Tho' these sufferings and sorrows cannot attone for his enormous guilt, perhaps they will excite the compassion of the humane count de Melvile: at least, this confession which my conscience dictates under all the terrors of death and futurity, may be a warning for him to avoid henceforth a smiling villain, like the execrable Fathom, upon whose miserable soul almighty God have mercy."

Renaldo was deeply affected with the contents of this scroll, which denoted such horror and despair. He saw there could be no dissimulation or sinister design in this profession of penitence: he beheld the condition of the writer, which put all his humane passions in commotion; so that he remembered nothing of Fathom but his present distress. He could scarce contain those indications which might have been justly deemed the effect of weakness and infirmity; and having desired the physician and clergyman to contribute their assistance for the benefit of that wretch's soul and body, he ran to the coach, and communicated the letter to the ladies; at the same time drawing a picture of the object he had seen, which brought tears into the eyes of the gentle Serafina, who earnestly intreated her lord to use his endeavours for the relief and recovery of the unhappy man; that he might, if possible, live to enjoy the benefit of mature repentance, and not die in that dreadful despair which he manifested in the letter.

Renaldo returning to the house, found the pious clergyman reading prayers with great fervency; while don Diego stood with his right hand upon his breast, looking stedfastly upon the agonizing Fathom, and the young woman kneeled with her streaming eyes lifted up to heaven, in an extasy of grief and devotion: the physician had run to an apothecary's shop in the neighbourhood, from whence he soon returned with an assistant, who applied a large blister[5] to the back of the miserable patient, while the female, by the doctor's direction, moistened his mouth with a cordial which he had prescribed.

These charitable steps being taken, Count de Melvile intreated the apothecary's servant to procure a tent bed[6] for the accommodation of the sick person, with all imaginable dispatch; and in less than an hour, one was actually pitched, and Fathom lifted into it, after he had been shifted and in some measure purified from the dregs of his indigence.[7] During this transaction the ladies were conducted to a tavern not far off, where dinner was bespoke, that they might be at hand to see the effect of their charity; which was not confined to what we have already described, but extended so far, that in a little time, the apartment was comfortably furnished, and the young creature provided with change of apparel, and money to procure the necessaries of subsistance.

Notwithstanding all their care, the wretched Fathom still remained insensible, and the doctor pronounced a very unfavourable prognostic, while he ordered a pair of additional vesicatories[8] to be laid upon his arms, and other proper medicines to be administred. After dinner, the ladies ventur'd to visit the place, and when Serafina crossed the threshold, the weeping female fell at her feet, and kissing her robe, exclaimed, "Sure you are an angel from heaven!"

The alteration in her dress had made a very agreeable change in her appearance, so that the countess could now look upon her, without shuddering at her distress: and as Fathom was not in a condition to be disturbed, she took this opportunity of inquiring by what steps that unfortunate wretch was conveyed from the prison, in which she knew he had been confined, to the place where he now lay in such extremity; and by what occurrence he had found a wife in such an abyss of misfortune. Here the other's tears began to flow afresh. "I am ashamed (said she) to reveal my own folly; yet I dare not refuse a satisfaction of this kind, to a person who has laid me under such signal obligations."

She then proceeded to relate her story, by which it appeared, she was no other than the fair and unhappy Elinor,[9] whom the artful Fathom had debauched upon his first arrival in town, in the manner already described in these memoirs. "Heaven," continued she, "was pleased to restore the use of my reason which I had lost, when I found myself abandoned by the count; but, all my connexion with my own family being entirely cut off, and every door shut against a poor creature who could procure no recommendation, except the certificate signed by the physician of bedlam, which instead of introducing me to service, was an unsurmountable objection to my character; I found myself destitute of all means of subsisting, unless I would condescend to live the infamous and wretched life of a courtezan, an expedient rendered palatable by the terrors of want cooperating with the reflection of the irretrievable loss I had already sustained. I ask pardon for offending your chaste ears with this impure confession of my guilt, which heaven knows, I then did, and now do look upon with abhorrence and detestation. I had already forfeited my innocence, and wanted resolution to encounter misery and death. Nevertheless, before I could determine to embrace the condition of a prostitute, I was one day accosted in the park by an elderly gentleman who sat down by me upon a bench, and taking notice of the despondence which was evident in my countenance, pressed me to make him acquainted with the nature of my misfortune. So much sympathy and good sense appeared in his deportment and conversation, that I gratified his request, and he, in return for my confidence, saved me from the most horrible part of my prospect, by taking me into his protection, and reserving me for his own appetite. In this situation I lived a whole year, until I was deprived of my keeper by an apoplectic fit, and turned out of doors by his relations, who did not, however, strip me of the cloaths and moveables, which I owed to his bounty. Far from being as yet reconciled to a vitious life, I resolved to renounce the paths of shame, and converting my effects into ready money, hired a small shop, and furnished it with haberdashery ware,[10] intending to earn an honest livelihood by the sale of these commodities, together with the plain-work in which I hoped to be employed, so soon as my talents should be known. But this scheme did not answer my expectation. The goods spoiled upon my hands, and as I was a stranger in the neighbourhood, no body would intrust me with any other business: so that notwithstanding the most parsimonious œconomy, I ran in debt to my landlord, who seized my effects; and an hosier from whom I had received some parcels upon credit, took out a writ against me, by virtue of which, I was arrested and imprisoned in the Marshalsea,[11] where I found my first seducer. Good heaven! what did I feel at this unexpected meeting, overwhelmed as I was before, with my own distress! I with a loud scream fainted away, and when I recovered, found myself in the arms of Mr. Fathom, who wept over me with great affliction. All his prospects of gaiety had now vanished, and his heart was softened by his own misfortunes, to a feeling of another's woe, as well as to a due sense of his own guilt. He expressed the deepest sorrow for having been the occasion of my ruin, endeavour'd to comfort me with promise of assistance, and indeed, by practising medicine among the prisoners, made shift to keep us both from starving. But surely, no sinner underwent such severe remorse as that which he suffered during his imprisonment. From the day of our meeting, I never once saw him smile; a melancholy cloud continually overhung his countenance. He numbered the minutes by his groans, he used to start with horrour from his sleep, and striking his breast, would exclaim, "O Elinor! I am the worst of villains!" Sometimes he seemed disordered in his brain, and raved about Renaldo and Monimia: in a word, his mind was in a dreadful situation, and all his agonies were communicated to me, whom by this time he had married, in order to make some attonement for my wrongs. Wretched as he then was, I remembered the accomplished youth who had captivated my virgin heart, the old impressions still remained, I saw his penitence, pitied his misfortune; and his wife being dead, consented to join his fate, the ceremony having been performed by a fellow prisoner, who was in orders. Though his hard-hearted creditor had no other chance of being payed, than that of setting him at liberty, he lent a deaf ear to all our supplications; and this cruelty conspiring with the anguish of my husband's own reflection, affected his health and spirits to such a degree, that he could no longer earn the miserable pittance which had hitherto supported our lives. Then our calamities began to multiply. Indigence and famine stared us in the face; and it was with the utmost difficulty that we resisted their attacks, by selling or pledging our wearing apparel, until we were left almost quite naked, when we found ourselves discharged by an act passed for the relief of insolvent debtors.[12] This charitable law, which was intended for a consolation to the wretched, proved to us the most severe disaster: for, we were turned out into the streets, utterly destitute of food, raiment and lodging; at a time when Mr. Fathom was so weakened by his distemper, that he could not stand alone. I supported him from door to door, imploring the compassion of charitable christians, and was at length permitted to shelter him in this miserable place, where his disease gaining ground, he lay three days in that deplorable condition, from which he hath now been rescued (tho' I fear too late) by your humanity and benevolence."

She shed a flood of tears at the conclusion of this mournful tale which did not fail to affect the whole audience, especially Serafina, who assured her, that whatever should happen to her husband, she might depend upon finding favour and protection, provided her conduct should correspond with her professions. While this grateful creature kissed the hand of her kind benefactress, Fathom uttered a groan, began to stir in the bed, and with a languid voice called upon Elinor, who instantly withdrawing the curtain, presented the whole company to his view. He had now retrieved the use of his perception, by the operation of the blisters which began to torture him severely; he looked around him with amazement and affright, and distinguishing the three persons against whom the chief arrows of his fraud and treachery had been levelled, he concluded that he was now arrived at the land of departed souls, and that the shades of those whom he had so grievously injured, were come to see him tormented according to his demerits.

Fraught with this notion, which was confirmed by the bodily pain which he felt, and the appearance of the clergyman and Joshua whom he mistook for the ministers of vengeance, he cried in a tone replete with horrour, "Is there no mercy then for penitence! is there no pity due to the miseries I suffered upon earth! save me, O bountiful heaven! from the terrors of ever-lasting woe; hide me from these dreadful executioners, whose looks are tor-ture: forgive me, generous Castilian. O Renaldo! thou hadst once a tender heart. I dare not lift my eyes to Serafina! that pattern of human excellence who fell a victim to my atrocious guilt; yet, her aspect is all mildness and compassion. Ha! are not these the drops of pity? yes, they are tears of mercy: they fall like refreshing showers upon my drooping soul! ah murthered inno-cence! wilt thou not intercede for thy betrayer at the throne of grace!"

Here he was interrupted by Melvile, who with a grave and solemn air, pronounced, "Great hath been thy guilt, unhappy Ferdinand, and great have been thy sufferings. Yet, we come not to insult, but to alleviate thy distress. Providence hath kindly defeated thy dire intentions, which we therefore now forgive and transmit to oblivion,[13] whether it be thy lot to yield up thy spirit immediately, or to survive the dangerous malady with which thou art at pres-ent overwhelmed. Suffer not thyself to despair; for, the mercy of heaven is infinite; and submit to the directions of this worthy gentleman who will em-ploy his skill for thy recovery, while we shall take care to furnish thee with necessary attendance: as too much speaking may be prejudicial to thy health, I dispense with a reply, and exhort thee to compose thy self to rest." So saying, he drew the curtain, and the company retired, leaving Fathom in-tranced with wonder.

The next step which Renaldo took for the benefit of this wretched peni-tent, was to send for the apothecary with whom he left a sum of money to be expended for the convenience of Fathom and his wife; then he laid injunc-tions upon the physician to repeat his visits; and that gentleman, together with the clergyman and Joshua, taking leave of the others till next day, the count set out with the ladies and his father in law, to the house where they had lodged the preceding night.

The reader may well imagine the conversation of the evening turned wholly upon the strange occurrence of the day, which seemed to have been concerted by supernatural prescience, in order to satisfy the vengeance, and afford matter of triumph to the generosity of those who had been so griev-ously injured by the guilty Fathom. Tho' not one of them would say that such a miscreant ought to live; yet all concurred in approving the offices of humanity which had been performed, and even endeavoured to find specious pretexts for vindicating their compassion. Don Diego said it would ill become a transgressor like him, to with-hold his forgiveness from a sinner who had wrong'd him: Madame Clement appealed to the approbation of heaven, which had undoubtedly directed them that way, for the purpose they had fulfilled: Serafina observed that the crimes of the delinquent were obliterated by his sorrow, misery and repentance: Renaldo honestly owned that, exclusive of other reasons, he could not deny himself the luxurious enjoyment of communicating happiness to his fellow creatures in distress; and each fervently prayed that their charity might not be disappointed by the death of the object.

While they amused themselves in these discussions, Fathom, after having lain some hours silent, in consequence of Renaldo's advice, could no longer suppress the astonishment of his mind, but, addressing himself to his wife, "O Elinor! (said he) my delirium is now past: tho' I still remember the phantasies of my distemper'd brain: among other reveries, my imagination was regaled with a vision so perfect and distinct, as to emulate truth and reality. Methought count de Melvile, don Diego de Zelos, and the divine Serafina, the very persons who are now crying before the throne of heaven for vengeance against the guilty Fathom, stood by my bedside, with looks of pity and forgiveness; and that Renaldo spoke peace to my despairing soul. I heard the words distinctly: I retain them in my memory. I saw the tears trickle from Serafina's eyes: I heard her father utter a compassionate sigh; and should actually believe that they were personally present, had not I long ago seen with my own eyes, the funeral procession of that young lady whose wrongs God pardon; and were I not convinced that such a meeting could not be effected without the immediate and miraculous interposition of heaven. Yet every thing I now see, corresponds with the words of Renaldo, which still sound in my ears. When my perception forsook me, I lay in the most abject misery, among straw; and thou, poor injured innocence, wast naked and forlorn. Now, I find myself reposed in a warm easy comfortable bed: I see around me the marks of human charity and care, and the favourable change in thy appearance, glads my poor dejected heart. Say, whence this happy alteration? Do I really wake from that dream of misery in which we have continued so long? or do I still utter the extravagant ravings of a distemper'd brain?"

Elinor was afraid of imparting at once all the particulars of the happy change he had undergone, lest they might leave a dangerous impression upon his fancy, which was not yet duly composed: she contented herself, therefore, with telling him that he had been obliged to the humanity of a gentleman and lady, who chanced to pass that way by accident, and who understanding his deplorable case, had furnished him with the conveniencies which he now enjoyed: she then presented to him, what the doctor had directed her to administer, and admonishing him to commit his head to the pillow, he was favoured with a breathing sweat,[14] fell fast asleep, and in a few hours waked again altogether cool and undisturbed.

It was upon this occasion that his wife explained the circumstances of that visit which had redeemed him from extremity of wretchedness and the jaws of death; upon which, he started up and throwing himself upon his knees, exclaimed, "All gracious power! this was the work of thy own bounteous hand; the voice of my sorrow and repentance hath been heard. Thou hast inspired my benefactors with more than mortal goodness, in my behalf; how shall I praise thy name! how shall I requite their generosity! O I am bankrupt to both! yet, let me not perish until I shall have convinced them of my reformation, and seen them enjoying that felicity which ought to be reserved for such consummate virtue."

Next day in the forenoon, he was visited by the physician, whom he now recollected to have seen at the house of madame Clement; and after having thanked that gentleman for his humanity and care, he earnestly begged to know by what means Serafina had been preserved. When he was satisfied in this particular, and given to understand that she was now happy in the arms of Renaldo, "Blessed be God! (he cried) for having defeated the villany of him who sought to part such lovers. Dear sir, will you add one circumstance to your charity, and bear to that happy couple and the noble don Diego, the respects and the remorse of a sincere penitent, whom their compassion hath raised to life. I have been such a traitor to them, that my words deserve no regard. I will not therefore use professions. I dare not hope to be admitted into their presence. I am indeed, ashamed to see the light of the sun: how then could I bear the looks of that injured family! ah, no! let me hide myself in some obscure retreat, where I may work out my salvation with fear and trembling,[15] and pray incessantly to heaven for their prosperity."

The physician promised to represent his contrition to the count and his lady, and accordingly proceeded to their habitation, where he repeated these expressions, and pronounced his patient out of danger: so that their thoughts were now employed in concerting a scheme for his future subsistence, that he might not be exposed by indigence to a relapse in point of morals. Renaldo being still averse to any personal intercourse with such a wretch, until he should give some undoubted proofs of amendment, and as yet afraid of in-trusting him with any office that required integrity, resolved, with the ap-probation of all present, to settle him in a cheap country in the north of England, where he and his wife could live comfortably on an annuity of sixty pounds, until his behaviour should intitle him to a better provision.[16]

This resolution was just taken, when Joshua arrived with a gentleman whom he introduced to don Diego as the secretary of the Spanish ambas-sador. After the first compliments, this stranger told the Castilian, that he waited upon him at the desire of his excellency, who would have come in person, had he not been confined by the gout; then he put into his hand, a letter from the court of Madrid, written by a nobleman of Diego's acquain-tance, who informed him that don Manuel de Mendoza having made away with himself by poison, in order to avoid the disgrace of a legal conviction, his catholic majesty was now convinced of don Diego's innocence, and granted him leave to return and take possession of his honours and estate. This information was confirmed by the secretary, who assured him that the ambassador had orders to make him acquainted with this favourable decision of the king. The Castilian having first acquitted himself in the most polite terms to the secretary and the Jew who, he said, had always been a mes-senger of glad tidings, communicated his happiness to the company; and this evening concluded the third day of their rejoicing.

Next morning, don Diego went to visit the ambassador, accompanied by Joshua and the secretary; while the physician repairing to the habitation of Fathom, signified, by Renaldo's direction, the resolution which had been taken in his behalf; and the patient no sooner heard his doom, than lifting up his hands, he cried, "I am unworthy of such tenderness and benevolence:" while Elinor shed a flood of tears in silence, unable to give utterance to her grateful thought: Melvile's bounty having so far transcended her most san-guine hope.

The Spaniard having paid his devoirs to his excellency, returned before dinner; and, in the afternoon, desiring a private conference with Serafina, they retired into another apartment, and he expressed himself to this effect. "You have contracted, my dear child, an habit of calling madame Clement your mother, and doubtless, by her maternal tenderness and regard, she hath acquired a just title to the appellation: yet, I own, I would fain strengthen it by a legal claim. I no sooner retrieved my daughter, than I gave her away to the most deserving youth that ever sighed with love. I rejoice in the gift which secured your happiness: but I left myself in a solitary situation which even the return of my good fortune cannot render easy and supportable.

When I revisit the castle of Zelos, every well known object will recal the memory of my Antonia, and I shall want a companion to fill her place, and to sympathize with me in that sorrow which will be derived from my remembrance. Who is there so worthy to succeed your mother in the affection of Don Diego, as she who interests her love for Serafina, and resembles her so strongly in every virtue of the sex? similar attractions will produce similar effects. My heart is already attached to that good lady; and, provided Serafina shall approve of my choice, I will lay myself and fortune at her feet."

The fair countess replied with an enchanting smile, that, before this declaration, she had with pleasure perceived the progress which madame Clement had made in his heart; and that she did not believe there was a person upon earth better qualified to repair the loss he had sustained; tho' she foresaw one obstacle to his happiness, which she was afraid would not be easily surmounted. "You mean," answered the Castilian, "the difference of religion, which I am resolved to remove by adopting the protestant faith; though I am fully satisfied that real goodness is of no particular persuasion, and that salvation cannot depend upon belief, over which the will has no influence. I invest you therefore with the charge of declaring my passion and proposal, and impower you to satisfy her scruples with regard to the religion which I now profess; and which I shall not openly relinquish, until I shall have secured in this country, effects sufficient to screen me from the ill consequences of my king's displeasure."

Serafina undertook this office with pleasure, because she had reason to think his addresses would not be disagreeable to madame Clement; and that same night made the count acquainted with the nature of her commission. Nor was her expectation disappointed: the French lady, with that frankness which is peculiar to virtue and good breeding, confessed that don Diego was not indifferent to her choice, and did not hesitate in receiving him upon the footing of a lover. As we have already dwelt circumstantially on the passion of love, so as perhaps even to have tired our readers, we shall not repeat the dialogue that passed, when the Spaniard was indulged with an opportunity to explain his sentiments. Suffice it to observe, that the lady's days of coquetry were now over, and that she was too wise to trifle with the time which every moment became more and more precious. It was agreed then, that don Diego should settle his affairs in Spain, and return to England, in order to espouse madame Clement, with a view to fix his residence in this island, where Renaldo likewise proposed to enjoy the sweets of his fortune, provided he could draw hither his interests and connexions.

Mean while, having for some days enjoyed his bliss with all the fulness of rapture, amidst this small but agreeable society, he shifted the scene, and conducted his dear partner to a ready furnished house in town, which, together with an occasional equipage, his friend Joshua had hired for the accommodation of him and his father-in-law, who during his stay in England, failed not to cultivate the mistress of his heart, with the most punctual assiduity. Hitherto Serafina had been as a precious jewel locked up in a casket, which the owner alone has an opportunity to contemplate: but now the count, who was proud of such a prize, resolved to let her shine forth to the admiration of the whole world. With this view, he bespoke such ornaments as befitted her quality, and while the mantua-makers[17] were employed in her service, made a tour among his former acquaintance, and discharged the obligations under which he lay to some who had assisted him in his distress. He did not, however, introduce them to his charming Serafina; because not one of them had formerly treated her with that delicacy of regard which he thought her due; and some of them were much mortified at their neglect, when they saw what a dazzling figure she made in the beau monde.

She was visited by the Spanish and Imperial ambassadors, and divers other foreigners of distinction, to whom Melvile had letters of recommendation: but her first public appearance was in a box at the opera, accompanied by madame Clement, the count and don Diego: the entertainment was already begun, so that her entrance had the greater effect upon the audience, whose attention was soon detached from the performance, and rivetted upon this amiable apparition, which seemed to be some bright being of another world dropt from the clouds among them. Then did the spirit of curiosity play its part: a thousand whispers circulated; as many glasses were exalted to reconnoitre this box of foreigners; for such they concluded them to be from their appearance. Every male spectator acknowledged Serafina to be the paragon of beauty; and every female confessed, that Melvile was the model of a fine gentleman. The charms of the young countess did not escape the eye and approbation of royalty itself; and when her rank was known, from the information of the ambassadors and other people of condition who were seen saluting her at a distance, that same evening a thousand bumpers were swallowed in honour of the countess de Melvile. The fame of her beauty was immediately extended over this immense metropolis, and different schemes were concerted for bringing her into life. These, however, she resisted with unwearied obstinacy. Her happiness centered in Renaldo, and the cultivation of a few friends within the shade of domestic quiet: she did not even forget the concerns of the wretched Fathom and his faithful Elinor, who daily enjoyed fresh instances of her humanity and care: when his fever forsook him, he was supplied with nourishing food for the recovery of his health; and soon as he found himself in a condition to travel, he gave notice to his benefactor, who desired Joshua to settle with him the manner in which he was to receive his allowance, and to pay the first half year's salary per advance.

This affair being adjusted, and the place of his retreat signified, the Jew told Elinor, that she might wait upon the countess before their departure; and she did not fail to make use of this permission. After they had made the necessary preparations for their journey, and taken places in the York stage-coach, Mrs. Fathom, cloathing herself in decent apparel, went to the house of count Melvile, and was immediately admitted to the presence of Serafina, who received her with her usual complacency, enriched her with salutary advice, comforted her with hope of better things, provided her conduct and that of her husband should henceforth be found irreproachable; and wishing her peace and happiness, presented her with a box of linen, and twenty guineas in a purse. Such excessive goodness overpowered this sensible young woman to such a degree, that she stood before her in speechless awe and veneration; and the countess, in order to relieve her from the confusion under which she suffered, quitted the room, leaving her to the care of her woman. It was not long, however, before her gratitude broke out in loud exclamations and a violent passion of tears, which all her efforts could not, for a good while, overcome. By this time the coach was brought up to the gate, for the reception of Serafina, who took an airing every day at the same hour; when Renaldo, leading her to the vehicle, beheld a man plainly dressed standing within the court, with his head and body bent towards the earth, so that his countenance could not be perceived.

Melvile, who supposed him to be some unfortunate man come to implore his charity, turned towards him, and asked, with a humane accent, if he wanted to speak with any person in the house? To this interrogation the stranger replied, without lifting up his head, "Overwhelmed as I am with count Melvile's generosity, together with a consciousness of my own un-worthiness, it ill becomes a wretch like me to importune him for further favour; yet I could not bear the thought of withdrawing (perhaps for ever) from the presence of my benefactor, without solliciting his permission to see his face in mercy, to acknowledge my atrocious crimes, to hear my pardon confirmed by his voice, and that of his accomplished countess, whom I dare not even at a distance behold; and to express my fervent wish for their prosperity."

Melvile, whose heart was but too tender, could not hear this address with-out emotion: he recognized the companion of his infancy and youth; he re-membred the happy scenes he had enjoyed with Fathom, whose voice had always such an effect upon his ear, as to excite the ideas of friendship and esteem; and he was disturbed by this unexpected meeting, which also discomposed the beauteous Serafina. Renaldo having paused a little, "It is with pain," said he, "I recollect any thing to the prejudice of Fathom, whose future behaviour will, I hope, eraze the memory of his offences, and justify what other steps I may take in his favour. Mean while I heartily forgive what is past; and, in token of my sincerity, present my hand;" which our adventurer bathed with his tears. The countess, whose mind was unison with her husband, repeated her assurances of pardon and protection; at which the penitent rejoiced in silence, while he raised his head and took a parting view of those charms which had formerly enslaved his heart.

Having thus obeyed the dictates of his duty and inclination, he next morning embarked in the stage-coach, with his faithful Elinor, and in six days arrived at the place of his retreat, which he found extremely well adapted to the circumstances of his mind and fortune: for all his vice and ambition was now quite mortified within him, and his whole attention engrossed in atoning for his former crimes, by a sober and penitent life, by which alone he could deserve the uncommon generosity of his patrons.

While he thus accommodated himself to his new system, Renaldo received letters of congratulation from his sister, who with the major had come to Brussels, in order to meet her brother and Serafina, according to his proposal. This intimation being communicated to don Diego, he resolved to accompany them to Flanders, in his way to Spain. Preparations were made for their departure; the clergyman and physician were honoured with valuable marks of friendship and esteem from the countess, Renaldo, and the Castilian, who were convoyed[18] to Deal by madame Clement, to whom, at parting, don Diego presented a diamond ring, as a pledge of his inviolable love.

Here the travellers hired a vessel for Ostend, which they reached in a few hours; in two days more they arrived at Brussels, where mrs. Farrel and her husband were struck with admiration at the surprizing beauty and accomplishment of their sister-in-law, whom they caressed with equal tenderness and joy.—In a word, all parties were as happy as good fortune could make them; and don Diego set out for Spain, after they had agreed to reside in the Low Countries 'till his return.

FINIS.

Title Page

"Every meeting with his own kind gave him food for laughter. He laughed at the troubles and at the joys of the crowd; and sometimes he also wept." Smollett repeats this epigraph, drawn from lines 47–52 of Juvenal's Satire 10 ("The Vanity of Human Wishes"), on the title page of the second volume of his novel. By adding the word *fundebat* to the Latin original, he changes the meaning of the passage: Juvenal's wise but cynical Democritus laughs at all he sees—troubles, joys, and tears; Smollett does likewise, but he is able as well to share in the tears.

Dedication

1. "TO DOCTOR ******": Here Smollett adopts the unusual practice of dedicating his work to himself (on the certainty of this claim, see Knapp, 154–55). His purposes are multiple. Obviously he means to sneer at the accepted practice of writing slavish dedications to patrons or to other worthies whose favor an author wishes to court; just as obviously he intends to mock the patronage system itself, from which he had suffered during his earlier attempts to have his tragedy *The Regicide* produced and published. But there is, additionally, an attractively self-reflective quality about portions of this dedication reminiscent of the autobiographical elements in *Roderick Random* and anticipating the self-portrait drawn many years later in Matthew Bramble of *Humphry Clinker*. The satire of self here is quite severe, but the portrait as a whole serves as a vindication of Smollett's character against those who had maligned him for the "lowness" and personal satires of *Roderick Random* and *Peregrine Pickle*. Finally, this dedication contains Smollett's most extensive and memorable statement of a theory of fiction.

2. "Mæcenas": Gaius Mæcenas (d. 8 B.C.), friend and counselor to Caesar Augustus, who trusted him for his ability and his vigilance in state service despite his reputation for riotous living. Mæcenas was admired by eighteenth-century writers as the honest, generous patron of Horace and Virgil.

3. "The author of the SEASONS": This is Smollett's note in reference to James Thomson (1700–1748), the best known Scottish writer of his day, whose poem *The Seasons* had been widely celebrated ever since its initial publication in four parts ("Winter," 1726; "Summer," 1727; "Spring," 1728; "Autumn," 1730). According to Knapp (82–84), Smollett knew Thomson at least reasonably well and admired not only *The Seasons* but also his *Castle of Indolence* (1748) and his tragedy

of *Coriolanus* (produced posthumously in 1749). As this paragraph of the dedication suggests, Smollett seems to have possessed private information about a plan his friend had conceived to expose the unworthy among his patrons. The most important of Thomson's benefactors was George Lyttelton (1709–73), who had gotten the habitually feckless poet a sinecure in 1744. Smollett bore a deep resentment against Lyttelton and had recently attacked him severely in *Peregrine Pickle* (chapter 102), where he also praised Thomson for his refusal to submit slavishly to his patron's suggestions about his work. The remarks here, in the dedication, seem to carry a further reflection upon Lyttelton (see also chap. 1, p. 10 and n. 21). The reflection is unjust, for Lyttelton was a good friend and patron to Thomson, even providing for payment of his considerable debts after his death and arranging for production of *Coriolanus*, to which he contributed the prologue. For the details of these benefactions see *James Thomson (1700–1748): Letters and Documents*, ed. Alan Dugald McKillop (Lawrence: University of Kansas Press, 1958), 178–80, 208, 212. For the background of Smollett's antagonism to Lyttelton see Knapp, 126–29; and for full details of Lyttelton's many years of patronage and literary friendships, including his important relationship with Henry Fielding (who dedicated *Tom Jones* to him), see Rose Mary Davis, *The Good Lord Lyttelton: A Study in Eighteenth Century Politics and Culture* (Bethlehem, Pa.: Times Publishing, 1939), especially pts. 2 and 3.

4. "severity of my reproof": As Knapp has observed (155–56), Smollett was painfully conscious of the personal defects enumerated in these two paragraphs and strove all his mature life to overcome or at least control them. Just as interesting here is his mocking way of upending the conventions of dedication-writing by criticizing instead of fulsomely praising his "patron."

5. "occurrence": Concurrence. These two words were almost synonomous when used in the context of a discussion of purposeful design (*OED*).

6. "A Novel . . . his own importance": This paragraph contains the most important of Smollett's surprisingly few statements about the principles of appropriate formal design in a work of fiction. For discussion of the statement see the introduction, pp. xxvii–xxviii.

7. "deep impression of terror": Smollett, in this and the following three paragraphs, actually reflects his age's growing interest in the psychological and aesthetic significance of the emotion of terror, or fear. Shaftesbury was among the earliest to inquire into the subject (in the *Characteristics*, 1711; rev. 1713), and more recently Francis Hutcheson (*An Essay on the Nature and Conduct of the Passions and Affections*, 1728; 3d ed., 1742) and Henry Home, Lord Kames (*Essays on the Principles of Morality and Natural Religion*, 1751) had given it major attention in their works. Smollett's remarks here, brief and moralistic as they are, at least tentatively anticipate some of the aesthetic arguments of Edmund Burke's *Philosophical Enquiry into the Origin of our Ideas of the Sublime and Beautiful* (1756). The most deliberate and conspicuous exploitation of the emotion of terror in *Ferdinand Count Fathom* comes in the extended Gothic episodes (chapters 20–21 and 62–63), where Smollett

actually prefigures the appeal of the Gothic novels that were to captivate English readers a few decades later.

8. "RICHARD . . . MASKWELL . . . BEVIL . . . EDWARD": Smollett refers to Shakespeare's *Richard III*, a popular play often seen at the time in Colley Cibber's adaptation of 1700; to William Congreve's *The Double-Dealer* (1694), whose darkly comic villain is the cunning, cynical Maskwell; to Sir Richard Steele's *The Conscious Lovers* (1722), whose hero is the virtuous Bevil; and (probably) to William Shirley's *Edward the Black Prince*, staged at Drury Lane in 1750 to considerable applause. In 1753, prose fiction in general still did not enjoy the respect accorded to older and more established forms of literature, and surely one of Smollett's rhetorical purposes in his allusions to celebrated plays was to suggest a qualitative parallel between them and his own narrative. Another purpose, perhaps, was to point out that what was permissible in the drama (that is, a primary focus upon wickedness) ought to be allowed in a work of fiction too.

9. "irremeable": Permitting no return; from, by, or through which no return is possible (*OED*).

10. "by surveying . . . FATHOM": The claim made in this paragraph repeats a commonplace in contemporary literature of roguery. The anonymous author of *A Full and Particular Account of the Life and Notorious Transactions of Roger Johnson* (London, 1740) observed in defense of his own narrative that natural human curiosity provokes a "Desire of enquiring into the Lives and Actions of those who have, in any Shape, render'd themselves famous or infamous in the World: when a Jonathan Wild, or a Macray, meet the just Reward of their Villanies, tho' we approve their Punishment, and abhor their crimes yet, at the same Time, *it is a secret Satisfaction to hear an Account, how such Men have perpetrated those Villanies*, and gull'd the Unwary, as it may, in some Measure, enable us to be upon our Guard, if any such Attempt should be made upon us" (p. 3). Smollett's defense of the narrative of low life here in the dedication should be read in conjunction with the concluding three paragraphs of his first chapter. See also chap. 49, p. 239 and n. 9.

11. "the most delicate reader": The statement of moral purpose with which Smollett concludes his dedication has usually been repudiated by critics as insincere and of no real or serious substance; see, for example, Damian Grant, *Tobias Smollett: A Study in Style* (Manchester: Manchester University Press, 1977), 49–52. But Thomas R. Preston has argued that in *Ferdinand Count Fathom* Smollett portrays the man of feeling in need of disenchantment with the deceptively alluring appearances of the world, and that in the dedication he purposefully overturns the sentimental exemplary formula, invoking fear instead of the attractions of virtue as a deterrence to vice; see "Disenchanting the Man of Feeling: Smollett's *Ferdinand Count Fathom*," in *Quick Springs of Sense: Studies in the Eighteenth Century*, ed. Larry S. Champion (Athens: University of Georgia Press, 1974), 223–39. Joel J. Thomas offers a contrary view in "Smollett and Ethical Sensibility: *Ferdinand Count Fathom*," *Studies in Scottish Literature* 14 (1979): 145–64. In the very last

paragraph of the dedication, following the discussion of his moral and ethical aims, Smollett repudiates the pious platitudes of most prefaces and dedications to popular works of fiction. In content if not quite in tone, this paragraph echoes Samuel Johnson's final *Rambler* paper (no. 208, 14 March 1752), which appeared in print just as Smollett was probably planning or even beginning to write his novel.

Chapter 1

1. "Cardinal de Retz": Jean François Paul de Gondi (1614–79), named cardinal in 1651. His several years of exile in England, caused by his political activism, made de Retz a familiar figure there. In 1723 his *Mémoires* (first published in Amsterdam, 1717) were translated into English and were thereafter widely read and quoted in letters, journals, and newspapers.

2. "through the mists of prejudice and passion": Smollett distrusted the autobiograpical writing so popular during his period. This entire paragraph, in its broader concern with the writings of "historians," or biographers, reflects attitudes shared by many of Smollett's contemporaries, including Henry Fielding, who repeatedly raised similar issues in *Joseph Andrews* (1742), *Jonathan Wild* (1743), and *Tom Jones* (1749). On the large question of historical truthfulness, Smollett had very strong feelings. He believed that the novelist was at liberty to reshape and re-create the facts of history, but that the historian was obliged to record them faithfully (see the introduction, pp. xxxiii–xxxvi). In a letter written five years after the publication of *Ferdinand Count Fathom*, Smollett echoed words used in this paragraph of his novel when he professed to look upon the historian who "willfully suppresses any Circumstances of Importance that may tend to the Information of the Reader, as the worst of Prostitutes" (*Letters*, 69). The occasion of this letter was the hostile response of some readers to Smollett's *Complete History*, which was charged with expressions of Tory, Jacobite, or Scottish biases; see, for example, Thomas Comber, *A Vindication of the Great Revolution in England in A.D. MDCLXXXVIII* (London, 1758), and the anonymous commentary (the author is possibly Owen Ruffhead) in the *Monthly Review* 18 (April 1758): 289–305.

3. "from whose loins our hero sprung": Smollett unmistakably mocks the conventions of romance by introducing Fathom with a parodic account of his lineage. Fielding had done the same in the early chapters of *Jonathan Wild*, and indeed such reductive beginnings were commonplace in the period's more lighthearted literature of roguery. On Smollett's general attitudes toward romance, see Jerry C. Beasley, "Romance and the 'New' Novels of Richardson, Fielding, and Smollett," *Studies in English Literature* 16 (1976): 437–50.

4. "ascertaining . . . birth-place of Homer": The continual debate concerning Homer's place of birth originated in classical times. Seven Greek cities claimed the honor: Smyrna, Rhodus, Colophon, Salamis, Chios, Argos, and Athens.

5. "the last year . . . Marlborough's command": John Churchill (1650–1722), duke of Marlborough and celebrated commander-in-chief of allied forces during the War of the Spanish Succession (1702–13), was dismissed from all his offices in 1711. The Tory ministry prevailed over strong opposition by embarrassing Marlborough with charges of graft in the administration of the financial affairs of his command. Marlborough nonetheless remained exceedingly popular among the English people, who regarded him as a great national hero. He died before the magnificent monument to his achievements, Blenheim Palace, could be completed. Some years after Marlborough's death, the grammarian and historian Thomas Lediard published the first important biographical study of his life and career: *The Life of John, Duke of Marlborough*, 3 vols. (London, 1736).

6. "geneva": Gin; a spirit originally made in Holland, flavored with juniper berries, and variously called Hollands Geneva, Hollands, or Geneva (*OED*).

7. "the milk of human kindness": *Macbeth* 1.5.17.

8. "adventures of a waggon": Here Smollett is apparently alluding to the critical reception accorded *Roderick Random* and *Peregrine Pickle*, both cried down by some readers as low and base (see Knapp, 96–100, 118–20). The phrase "adventures of a waggon" doubtless refers specifically to *Roderick Random*, chapters 11–12, where Smollett describes the comic experiences of the hero and Strap aboard the cart taking them to London.

9. "Petronius Arbiter": Titus Petronius Niger (d. A.D. 66), "arbiter of elegance" at the court of Nero and author of the earthy *Satyricon*.

10. "amorous sallies of Ovid's pen": Probably a reference to the *Ars Amatoria* (*Art of Love*), a didactic poem completed about 1 B.C. and designed to teach the ways of seduction and intrigue.

11. "Lucian's ass": *Lucian and the Ass*, a brief comic romance possibly written by Lucian (c. A.D. 120–80), the Greek rhetorician, satirist, and popular philosopher. The same story was told at greater length in the more famous *Golden Ass* of the Roman poet Apuleius (born c. A.D. 123).

12. "Guzman d'Alfarache": *Guzman de Alfarache*, by Mateo Alemán, was published in 1599–1602 and is a splendid early example of the Spanish picaresque romance. First translated into English (as *The Rogue*) in 1622, it enjoyed a steady popularity for many years after.

13. "Don Quixote and his squire": Among English readers and writers of the first half of the eighteenth century, *Don Quixote* (1605–15), by Miguel de Cervantes Saavedra, was one of the most popular and influential of all works of fiction, native or foreign. It went through as many as nineteen editions in various translations between 1700 and 1750, some eight of these appearing in the 1740s alone. Smollett's own translation was published in February 1755.

14. "ragged troop of strollers": The reference is to *Le Roman Comique* (1651), by Paul Scarron, which was first translated into English in 1665 and remained widely popular for many years thereafter. A fifth English edition of Scarron's *Whole Comical Works* (1700), which included the *Roman Comique*, had appeared in 1741.

15. "Gil Blas": *Histoire de Gil Blas de Santillane* (1715–35), by Alain René Le Sage, was very popular in English translation; by 1746 it had appeared a half-dozen times in its various stages of completion. Smollett published his new translation of *Gil Blas*, dated 1749, in October 1748; just months before, in the preface to his first novel, *Roderick Random*, he had identified Le Sage's work as a model for his own performance. *Ferdinand Count Fathom*, the story of a thoroughgoing villain, introduces some striking adaptations from the picaresque tale as practiced by Le Sage and others. For discussion of these adaptations, see the introduction, pp. xxviii–xxx; see also Robert Donald Spector, *Tobias George Smollett* (New York: Twayne, 1968), chap. 4.

16. "Swift or Pope": Smollett greatly admired both of these writers, and here invokes them as precedents to justify the mannerisms and subject matter of his novel.

17. "jakes of Rabelais": François Rabelais (1494?–1553), author of the earthy *Gargantua and Pantagruel* (5 parts, 1532–64), was known—and, by some (including Swift), admired—for his vigorous treatment of low subjects. *Jake*, meaning privy or latrine, is an archaic term dating from the late Middle English period (*OED*).

18. "a lady's dressing-room": Smollett here refers to Swift's racy, somewhat Rabelaisian debunking of romantic convention and female costuming in his poem "The Lady's Dressing Room" (1732).

19. "china chamber-pot": Probably a reference to an episode in chapter 14 of *Peregrine Pickle*, where Peregrine employs a chamber pot as the instrument of a practical joke at the expense of Commodore Trunnion and his bride. Smollett eliminated this episode when revising his novel for its second edition (1758).

20. "Catullus, Juvenal, Persius and Lucan": Smollett refers to four of the greatest and most admired of Roman authors: Gaius Valerius Catullus (c. 84–54 B.C.), satirist and poet of love, noted for lyrical intensity and technical brilliance; Juvenal, or Decimus Junius Juvenalis (c. A.D. 50–127), author of fierce satires against the failings of human nature and the corruptions of Roman society, and widely imitated by eighteenth-century English writers, including Samuel Johnson in "London," 1738, and "The Vanity of Human Wishes," 1749 (Smollett's epigraph for the title page of *Ferdinand Count Fathom* is taken from Juvenal's Satire 10); Persius, or Aulus Persius Flaccus (A.D. 34–62), satirical poet of the school of Horace who wrote little but was appreciated by English readers and writers for his vividness and eloquence (John Donne took his work as the model for some of his own verses); and Lucan, or Marcus Annaeus Lucanus (A.D. 39–65), satirist and political rebel whose *Civil War* (also known as *Pharsalia*) was especially honored in eighteenth-century England, partly for its portrayal of the arch-republican Cato the younger, heroic figure of the war between Caesar and Pompey (49–48 B.C.).

21. "a Pseudo-patron": Smollett doubtless refers to George Lyttelton, whom he had cruelly lampooned in chapter 102 of *Peregrine Pickle* as a man of small talent and dubious judgment and character. Some of his readers were outraged by this swipe at a man so widely admired for generosity and taste. The reference to Lyttelton here is much more blatant than that introduced earlier into the dedication (see p. 3 and n. 3).

22. "individuals . . . their ancestors": Smollett refers to the increasingly familiar (and, to many, very objectionable) practice of conferring peerages on commoners as rewards for their sometimes dubious services to crown or state. Sir Robert Walpole, the brilliant but notoriously corrupt prime minister whom Fielding pilloried as the hero-villain of *Jonathan Wild*, was vilified as a "monster" and a "criminal" throughout his long years in power (1721–42) but was named earl of Orford before his death in 1745.

23. "inoffensive pen . . . soul-sweeting praise": This entire paragraph echoes the critical argument advanced in the concluding section of Smollett's dedication. His ironic pronouncement on the current state of English satire all but attacks the readers of *Ferdinand Count Fathom*, challenging them to abandon their entrenched prejudices in favor of the vapid moral posturing typical of so much contemporary fiction. There is no statement quite like this one in any other novel of the day. Clearly, it represents an attempt on Smollett's part to justify an extension of the range of subject matter and approaches to character available to the novelist writing in English.

Chapter 2

1. "leathern zone": A leather girdle, or belt (*OED*). The "delicious nectar" is gin. Smollett's comic reference to the nourishment of the infant with gin reflects lingering widespread concern over the effects of cheap liquor on the families of the poor. In 1751, both Fielding (in *An Enquiry into the Causes of the late Increase in Robbers*) and Hogarth (in *Gin Lane*) had made the victimization of children a specific theme of their general attacks on the "gin craze." Legislation passed in that same year did little to break the pernicious connections between poverty and drunkenness, both of which contributed greatly to the alarming crime rate.

2. "cag": A small cask, or keg.

3. "with simple element": With water.

4. "a German trooper": During the War of the Spanish Succession several German states joined the Grand Alliance, whose armies were under the command of the duke of Marlborough.

5. "at the drum-head": A marriage performed in impromptu military style, the ceremony conducted round an upturned drum, much in the manner of a drum-head court martial held for expedient dispatch of offenses during military operations in the field.

6. "Ferdinand de Fadom": The name Ferdinand refers perhaps to the great kings who ruled over vast reaches of Europe (notably Bohemia, Hungary, and Spain) through much of the sixteenth and early seventeenth centuries. Shakespeare had used the name twice, for the son of the king of Naples in *The Tempest* and for the king of Navarre in *Love's Labour's Lost*. Whatever its source, the unmistakable irony of Smollett's choice of "Ferdinand" lies in the discrepancy between the regal

grandeur of his hero-villain's Christian name and the reality of his low birth and evil nature. The surname Fathom is more obvious in its function. One common eighteenth-century definition of the word, in its verb transitive form, is "to grasp, or reach"; another definition, common both to the eighteenth and the twentieth centuries, is "to sound," or measure for depth. Ferdinand's life is devoted to grasping for what is not his; those who encounter him in the course of his adventures typically have some difficulty in sounding his character, while he generally (though not always) penetrates others with great ease.

7. "*natale solum*": Native land; a reference to a theme in Horace's *Satires* and *Odes*, though the phrase itself is not Horatian. Smollett may have misremembered his classics here, confusing Horace with Ovid (see *Metamorphoses* 7.52 and *Epistolæ ex Ponto* 1.3.35).

8. "the peace of Utrecht": A reference to the treaties of peace and commerce signed at Utrecht 31 March–11 April 1713, bringing the War of the Spanish Succession to an end.

9. "a suttling-tent": A makeshift place for the sale of drink and food to the soldiers (*OED*).

10. "Bohemia": In the early eighteenth century, a small principality in the western region of what is now Czechoslovakia, forming part of the Austrian empire.

11. "cabaret": A common eighteenth-century name for a drinking house.

12. "the emperor": Charles VI, Austrian emperor 1711–40. The imperial army employed many mercenaries, among them a large number of Scottish and Irish soldiers whose Jacobite sympathies may have attracted them into the service of the Catholic Hapsburgs. For discussion of the role of Bohemia in the empire and of the importance of Irish and Scottish nationals in Bohemian culture and its military, see Robert Joseph Kerner, *Bohemia in the Eighteenth Century* (New York: Macmillan, 1932).

Chapter 3

1. "the renowned prince Eugene": Prince Eugene (or Eugen) of Savoy (1663–1736), commander of the Austrian armies. During the summer of 1716 the Turks, provoked by Austrian refusal to promise neutrality in their war against the Venetian state, began a march against Hapsburg strongholds. Prince Eugene ran a brilliant campaign that brought the Ottomans to their knees, and the war itself to an end, within exactly two years. Eugene was a military genius who had joined forces with Marlborough during the War of the Spanish Succession, and the two men were regarded by all Europe as the greatest military commanders and strategists of their day. In England their praise was widely broadcast in such works as *The Lives of the Two Illustrious Generals, John, Duke of Marlborough, and Francis Eugene, Prince of Savoy* (London, 1713). Subsequent celebratory books included *The Military History of the Late Prince Eugene of Savoy, And of the Late John Duke of Marl-*

borough (London, 1736), printed in two volumes and lavishly illustrated by Claude Du Bosc; and *Memoirs of the Lives and Conduct of those Illustrious Heroes Prince Eugene of Savoy, and John Duke of Marlborough* (London, 1742). Eugene was himself the subject of several early and quite ambitious biographies by Englishmen, the two most important being *The Life and Military Actions of His Royal Highness Francis Eugene, Prince of Savoy* (London, 1735) and *The History of Francis-Eugene Prince of Savoy* (London, 1741). Smollett was an admirer of Eugene, and praised him highly in his *Complete History*, 4:572 as "an invincible hero and consummate politician." The events of Fathom's youth detailed in chapters 3 and 4 coincide with Eugene's campaign against the Turks; and later, in chapters 18 and 19, Fathom's soldiering adventures occur during the War of the Polish Succession (1733–35), when Eugene commanded the Austrian forces for the last time.

2. "one hundred and fifty thousand Turks": Smollett exaggerates, but only slightly, the triumph of Eugene's army at the battle of Peterwardein, on the Danube, 5 August 1716. The Austrians, sixty thousand strong, defeated an Ottoman force more than twice their number, and the great victory was celebrated throughout Europe. See Henderson, 223–25. In this chapter and the next, Smollett displays considerable knowledge not only of the battles fought during the war against the Ottomans but also of Turkish battle regalia and weaponry. Probably he acquired most of his information from such works as the popular biographies of Prince Eugene published in 1735 and 1741 (see above, n. 1) and perhaps from Count Luigi Ferdinando Marsigli's *L'Etat Militaire de L'Empire Ottoman* (Amsterdam, 1732), which, like many books printed in Dutch cities during the eighteenth century, was available to English readers.

3. "distressing the enemy": The mock-heroics of Fathom's mother as recounted in this and the next chapter reflect widespread interest in the battlefield exploits of a number of real-life camp followers whose stories had been written and widely read. The character of Mrs. Fathom may be based in part on the famous "Mother Ross," subject of a popular biographical narrative entitled *The Life and Adventures of Mrs. Christian Davies, the British Amazon, commonly call'd Mother Ross* (London, 1739–40). The story of Mrs. Davies was sensationalized by J. Wilson, "formerly a surgeon in the army," who revised and abridged the original *Life and Adventures* and then published his new version under the title *The British Heroine* (London, 1742; 2d ed., 1744).

4. "poignard": A dagger; variant of *poniard* (*OED*).

5. "mussulmen": Moslems or Mohammedans.

6. "hussars": Light cavalrymen; the term originated in the name for Hungarian cavalry but became common throughout Europe.

7. "Temiswaer": The six-week campaign to capture Temiswár, a fortified Hungarian city held for some 164 years by the Turks, was completed successfully by Eugene in the early fall of 1716 (see Henderson, 225–27).

8. "count Melvil": According to John Macky, in *A Journey through Scotland* (London,

1723), the Scottish family of the earl of Melvil (or Melville) was of Hungarian descent but had been prominent in Scotland for more than four centuries. During the reigns of William III and Queen Anne the earl of Melville held high commands in the military, achieving no great distinction. There is nothing to suggest that Smollett based his count on any actual person, but as a gesture of national pride he may well have projected a deliberate association between his homeland and the figure of the supremely benevolent Melvil (or Melvile, as Smollett often spells the name).

9. "Presburg": Pressburg, an ancient city about thirty miles east of Vienna; until 1784, the capital of Hungary. Today the city is called Bratislava.

10. "celebrated battle of Belgrade": The siege of Belgrade in August 1717 was probably Prince Eugene's greatest campaign, and the city's capture his greatest triumph. There his army of fifty thousand troops routed an Ottoman force of more than two hundred thousand. The victory heralded the peace that was to come in the following summer, and the news of it was joyously received all over the Austrian empire and in England as well. Eugene himself was extravagantly praised for his rescue of the Christian world from the Mohammedan threat. The anonymous author of *Belgrade. A Poem* (London, 1717), expressing what many felt about Eugene's heroism, characterized him as both great and good, as a man

> By Heav'n deputed to assert its Laws,
> And vindicate Religion's injur'd Cause:
> Whose rising Fame has with the circling *Sun*
> Round the wide Globe in swiftest Paces run;
> Who next to Heav'n Commands, and his Commands are done.
>
> (p. 5)

For an account of the siege of Belgrade see Henderson, 227–30.

Chapter 4

1. "spahis": Turkish cavalry (*OED*).

2. "Penthesilea": In Greek mythology, the mighty Amazon queen who came to the aid of Troy after the death of Hector at the hand of Achilles. Her female warriors fought bravely but were at last overcome when Achilles slew Penthesilea in combat. His contemplation of her youth, beauty, and courage threw him into deep mourning.

3. "Camilla": A beautiful maiden of Volscian legend. When Camilla was a baby her father, the despotic King Metabus of Privernum, fled with her from his kingdom and, to elude angry pursuers, fastened her to a javelin, dedicated her to Artemis, and hurled her across the Amisenus River to safety. He then trained her to be a huntress and a warrior, and she grew up to fight heroically in Italy alongside Turnus before his defeat by Aeneas and the Trojans. Virgil tells Camilla's story

in book 7 of the *Aeneid*. In *An Essay on Criticism* (1711), Pope evoked Camilla as an image defining grace and fleetness of movement in verse:

> When *Ajax* strives, some Rock's vast Weight to throw,
> The Line too *labours*, and the Words move *slow*;
> Not so, when swift *Camilla* scours the Plain,
> Flies o'er th'unbending Corn, and skims along the Main.
>
> (lines 370–73)

4. "the utmost disorder": Smollett's description of the battle of Belgrade as a rout is quite accurate, though of course the part played by Fathom's mother is entirely a product of his imagination. The account given here is corroborated by Prince Eugene's early English biographer in *The Life and Military Actions*, 179–81; and see Henderson, 229.

5. "caparisons": Coverings, usually of cloth and often brightly ornamented, to be spread over the harness or under the saddle of a horse (*OED*).

6. "Atropos": In Greek mythology the oldest of the three Moirai, or Fates. Atropos was particularly associated with the idea of death and inevitability, or the "Irresistible."

7. "perdue": In an exposed, hazardous position, but waiting in ambush to attack (*OED*).

8. "beneath his covert": Beneath his covering.

9. "the golden crescent": The image prominently displayed on the Turkish flag in which the fallen officer has wrapped himself.

10. "Semiramis, Tomyris, Zenobia, Thalestris": Semiramis, the legendary daughter of the Syrian goddess Derceto, is said to have ruled Assyria, founded Babylon, and, at her death, changed into a sacred dove; Tomyris, a Massagetean queen, is remembered as the slayer of Cyrus during fierce combat in 529 B.C.; Zenobia, the beautiful, ambitious ruler of Palmyra (A.D. 267–c. 271) during her son's minority, was conqueror of Syria and Egypt; Thalestris, a legendary Amazon warrior queen, is supposed to have flourished during the period of Alexander the Great.

11. "ninth year of his age": The mother's death occurred during the siege of Belgrade in August 1717 (see chap. 3, n. 10). Fathom, born in 1711, must have been in his sixth or seventh year, not his ninth. Here is an early instance of Smollett's lack of interest in chronology. For general discussion of his approach to the novelistic uses of time and historical fact, see the introduction, pp. xxxiii–xxxvi.

12. "insinuation": Smollett uses this word in its archaic sense to suggest a quietly and subtly ingratiating manner (*OED*).

Chapter 5

1. "the peace of Passarowitz": The treaty concluding the war between the Austrian and Ottoman empires was signed 21 July 1718; it excluded the Turks from Hungary, ended the Turkish threat to western Europe, and left the Austrians in posses-

sion of Temesvár, the Bánát, Belgrade, and parts of Bosnia, Serbia, and Wallachia. See Henderson, 230–31.

2. "a right pedagogue": The incompetence of schoolmasters was one of Smollett's favorite targets in his early novels. Both *Roderick Random* (chapters 2–5) and *Peregrine Pickle* (chapters 12–13) treat the subject at length and with considerable satiric vigor.

3. "like a true flogger": Like a typically ignorant, brutal pedagogue. The derisive term *flogger* was commonly applied to schoolmasters who hid their incompetence behind a show of severity and harsh physical discipline.

4. "the days of his puerility": Literally, the days of his childhood.

5. "fives": A game of handball, especially popular among schoolboys, played against the front wall of a three-sided court.

6. "draughts": A game very similar to checkers, played on a chessboard; see Strutt, 255–56.

7. "a meer adept": A complete or perfect adept (*OED*).

Chapter 6

1. "a german flute": The German or transverse flute first began to appear outside Germany in the fourteenth century; it was commonplace in England by the sixteenth century, and Henry VIII owned several of the instruments. See *The New Grove Dictionary of Music and Musicians*, ed. Stanley Sadic (London: Macmillan, 1980), 6:669–71.

2. "the method of sap": A military metaphor referring to a stealthy or insidious way of attacking a target; literally, a process of constructing covered trenches to allow approach without detection or danger (*OED*).

3. "Her behaviour . . . her pride": Smollett makes Fathom look rather foolish by the playful description of his expectation that Mademoiselle de Melvil will respond to his advances like a heroine of romance, or like the blushing girls of silly amatory novels by such popular writers as Eliza Haywood.

4. "Secundum Artem": According to the rules of the art.

5. "like a true graduate": Fathom's physician is Hungarian, but he performs in the expected manner of one holding an English medical degree—incompetently, stupidly, and avariciously. Smollett here introduces what is to be a recurring theme in his novel, the widespread quackery and corruption of the medical profession (see chap. 35, pp. 164–65 and n. 5; chap. 51, pp. 248–49 and nn. 5, 6; and chap. 52, pp. 254–56 and n. 5). Smollett had a high estimate of the best physicians and medical theorists (see Knapp, 141–42) but little tolerance for incompetents or frauds. In many places throughout his novels he joined the attack on corrupt and unqualified medical practitioners; see, for example, his treatment of the stupid, drunken, avaricious, and physically grotesque Dr. Launcelot Crab in chapter 7 of

Roderick Random. The fullest discussion of Smollett's attitudes toward the medical profession may be found in George S. Rousseau, "Doctors and Medicine in the Novels of Tobias Smollett" (Ph.D. diss., Princeton University, 1966). See also Claude E. Jones, "Tobias Smollett (1721–1771)—the Doctor as Man of Letters," *Journal of the History of Medicine and Allied Sciences* 12 (1957): 337–48.

6. "his prescriptions": Physicians commonly received paid commissions from apothecaries (pharmacists, or "chemists" in British parlance) to whom they sent patients for preparation of medicines; the arrangement was mutually lucrative and therefore jealously guarded.

7. "the usual forms": Smollett refers to common treatments for a variety of ailments, including fevers. The purpose of the treatments was to remove contaminants from the body: blood was drawn by incision or by the application of leeches; vomiting and purging of the bowels were induced (usually) by the ingestion of some virulent liquid concoction; blisters were raised by the action of plasters or ointments placed upon the skin. The effects were often violent and debilitating to the patient, especially when the treatments were carelessly prescribed. Smollett shows his skepticism by subsequent reference to the Hungarian physicians as men quite the equals of their counterpart "leeches" elsewhere. The treatments were in themselves respectable if judiciously applied, as Smollett believed; they continued in England by the authority of such medical men as the venerable Richard Wiseman, Serjeant-Surgeon to Charles II, whose medical papers were often printed throughout the seventeenth and early eighteenth centuries. Smollett probably acquired a copy of Wiseman's *Eight Chirurgical Treatises* (1676; 6th ed., 1734) while he was apprenticed to the Glasgow surgeons John Gordon and William Stirling (see Knapp, 25). In chapter 7 of *Roderick Random*, the hero mentions Wiseman's book as one of only two (the other is an edition of Horace) he takes with him on his journey to London.

8. "bolusses, draughts and apozems": See Barrow, whose *Dictionarium Medicum* of 1749 quickly became a standard reference work and was probably known to Smollett. The bolus was an internal medicine, sometimes in the form of a small pill but sometimes (as described by Barrow) in a form "soft, coherent, a little thicker than honey, and whose quantity is a little mouthful"; draughts were internal medicines in liquid form; the apozem (from *apozema*) was a "decoction" from boiling.

Chapter 7

1. "intendered": Made tender, full of tenderness; variant of *entendered* (*OED*).

2. "latitudinarian": In theology, a body of unofficial Pelagian doctrine associated with English divines like Isaac Barrow (1630–77) and Archbishop John Tillotson (1630–94), who insisted less on strict conformity to established Church dogma

than on adherence to such Christian social principles as chastity and benevolence. Here, Smollett uses the term pejoratively in its loose generic sense of tolerance toward free thinking and laxity of belief in the articles of Christian faith and the Anglican creeds. For full discussion of latitudinarianism and related issues see Roland N. Stromberg, *Religious Liberalism in Eighteenth-Century England* (Oxford: Clarendon Press, 1954).

3. "in defiance of all decency and law": Smollett refers to the practice of irregular marriages performed without banns, license, or legal sanction and called "Fleet marriages" because the vicinity of the Fleet Prison in London was the scene of thousands of such ceremonies each year. Fleet marriages were not always faithfully recorded (though they were tacitly recognized), and so they were easy for either party to escape at any time, without legal permission or penalty. The controversial Marriage Act passed in 1753, the very year of the publication of *Ferdinand Count Fathom*, put an end to the Fleet marriages by declaring void all ceremonies conducted irregularly. See Timbs, 2:302–3.

4. "reversionary hope of heaven's forgiveness": In this passage Smollett repeats, with ironic suggestiveness, a commonplace about the rarity of genuine piety and faith in the age. There is also at least an oblique reference to the persistent antinomian doctrine of salvation through grace associated with certain nonconformist groups, most conspicuously George Whitefield's "enthusiastic" branch of Methodism. It is impossible to know with any certainty just what Smollett's personal religious convictions were (see Knapp, 307–8), though he clearly believed in the standard Christian virtues and he seems tolerant enough of Humphry's Methodism in *Humphry Clinker*. But he did scorn antinomian orthodoxy, especially as espoused by vocal religious enthusiasts. "For my part," he wrote in his *Travels* (Letter 5), "I never knew a fanatic that was not an hypocrite at bottom. . . . Enthusiasm and hypocrisy are by no means incompatible. The wildest fanatics I ever knew, were real sensualists in their way of living, and cunning cheats in their dealings with mankind" (p. 39).

Chapter 8

1. "Zoilus": Grammarian and cynic philosopher of the fourth century B.C., residing in Amphipolis. Zoilus was notorious for his savage attacks on Plato, Isocrates, and especially Homer; his name is proverbial for a bad critic.

2. "elocution": Eloquence, beauty of style (*OED*).

3. "subscription for the author": This anecdote is possibly based on some real episode Smollett knew about, but there is no evidence that it is autobiographical. Its primary purpose, it seems, is to continue the novel's recurring minor theme of attacks against the capriciousness of the patronage system (see the dedication, p. 3 and n. 3; and chap. 1, p. 10 and n. 21).

4. "certain dangerous books . . . young people": Probably Smollett refers to "nov-

els," a specific kind of brief amatory fiction still regarded in the mid-century period as frivolous, morally impoverished, and dangerous to the young. Many popular "novels" by writers like Eliza Haywood did in fact give justification for this attitude. Richardson, Fielding, and Smollett all conspicuously avoided the label in naming their works. Smollett was the only one of the three to use the term *novel* in a serious way, in the dedication to *Ferdinand Count Fathom*, where he introduced it into the strictly literary context of a definition of genre and narrative form. The most important contemporary comment on the hazards of novel-reading, and on the proper moral function of prose fiction as a guide to youthful minds, is Samuel Johnson's famous *Rambler*, no. 4 (31 March 1750). For an account of the quality and status of "novels" in the period see Jerry C. Beasley, *Novels of the 1740s* (Athens: University of Georgia Press, 1982), chaps. 1 and 6.

5. "mischievous preparations": Aphrodisiacs.

Chapter 9

1. "make hay while the sun shone": Past tense version of a familiar English proverb dating back at least to 1509 (*ODEP*).
2. "escrutore": A writing desk constructed to hold stationery, documents, and papers; variant of *escritoire* (*OED*).
3. "Abigail": Generic name for a servant maid, popularized by Beaumont and Fletcher, who gave the name to the "waiting gentlewoman" in *The Scornful Lady* (1616); see also 1 Samuel 25:24–31, for Abigail the Carmelitess and wife of David, who styles herself the "handmaid."

Chapter 10

1. "florins": The English name for various coins of gold or silver used on the Continent; in 1741, a Genoan silver florin was valued at about 8¼*d.* sterling. The diamond earrings are thus worth the equivalent of some £16–20 sterling.
2. "at the academy": At the Militärakademie, an institution for the training of future officers in the Austrian army. There hopeful young gentlemen were instructed in the polite arts, in the social graces, and in the rudiments of fighting, battlefield strategy, and combat command.
3. "resent": Feel strongly about; an archaic usage (*OED*).
4. "seeking whom he might devour": 1 Peter 5:8: "Be sober, be vigilant; because your adversary the devil, as a roaring lion, walketh about, seeking whom he may devour."
5. "talent . . . in his possession": Smollett allows Fathom to type himself as a criminal version of the Volpone character, thus echoing (if only faintly) Ben Jonson's perennially popular play of that name. In the course of this self-definition,

Fathom undertakes a conventional misanthropic representation of bestial human nature drawn quite directly from Hobbes and Mandeville, and especially from the latter's celebrated *Fable of the Bees* (1714). Later, in chapter 25 ("the last") of *Sir Launcelot Greaves*, Smollett echoes himself when he permits the misanthrope Ferret to speak in a very similar way, citing Hobbes as the authority for his view that every man has the right to use his natural talents at the expense of other people.

6. "executive part of gaming": That is to say, the execution of the games of chance. Fathom avoided actual play.

7. "Tyrol": Alpine province of western Austria, much of it controlled by the Hapsburgs in the eighteenth century; location of the city of Innsbruck.

Chapter 11

1. "pass-dice": Alternative name for "passage," a difficult game for two players throwing three dice (Strutt, 247–48). Pass-dice was risky for the amateur and was therefore a particular favorite of sharpers.

2. "FERDINAND de FATHOM": In this letter Fathom has challenged his Tyrolese accomplice to a duel. The bastions (usually built of stone in the pattern of an irregular pentagon) extending from the fortified walls of European cities were popular sites for dueling at early or late hours, since they protected the antagonists from view and thus reduced the risks of discovery. In Vienna "the Ramparts" was, according to a later guide book called *Picture of Vienna* (Vienna: S. Mosle, 1839), "a very agreeable walk round the walls of the town" (p. 57). The location Fathom mentions is at one of the gates to the city. Dueling was a matter of widespread concern in early eighteenth-century England. Smollett shared this concern, and he raised the issue several times again in chapters 23, 33, and 41 of *Ferdinand Count Fathom*. Roderick Random and especially Peregrine Pickle frequently find themselves embroiled in duels or threatened by challenges from would-be antagonists. Virtually the whole of Letter 15 in the *Travels* is given over to a severe attack on the folly and the moral horror of dueling. For an early history of dueling and of the controversy it caused in Smollett's time, see *The Duellist, Or a Cursory Review of the Rise, Progress, and Practice of Duelling* (London: Longman, 1822).

3. "knight of the post": Generic term for a perjuror (*OED*). Here Smollett seems to mean confidence-man as well.

Chapter 12

1. "the doux-yeux": Literally, "the sweet eyes"; a French colloquialism. In English colloquial phrase, Fathom has been "making eyes" at Wilhelmina.

2. "bashaw": A high-ranking Turkish military officer, or governor of a province; sometimes written *pasha*, though *bashaw* is the older English form (*OED*).

3. "a period to my wretched life": The extravagant theatrics and heightened sentimental language in which Fathom indulges throughout this long passage expose his shallowness and dishonesty. Smollett repeats this same tactic, though not always with such hyperbole of tone and manner, on virtually every occasion when his adventurer advances against the virtue and fortune of a respectable young woman. Aside from its effectiveness in exposing Fathom, Smollett's manner carries an implied attack on the traditions of romance and pastoral. Such attacks were not unusual in the mid-eighteenth century. Two of the *Rambler* papers, no. 4 (31 March 1750) and no. 36 (21 July 1750), had raised serious objections to the falsifications of romance and to the debasement of pastoral tradition and conventions by servile imitators. Smollett himself had vigorously repudiated romance in the preface to *Roderick Random*. Interestingly, he launched into some extravagant language of his own in a letter of 22 May 1744 lamenting the death of his friend John Ritchie: "O my dear Ritchie, little did I think at our last parting we should never meet again! . . . How has my heart throbbed at thy imaginary presence! And how oft have I conversed with thee by the indulgence of a dream! Even when I waked to my disappointment, I flew to pleasing hope for refuge, and reflected on the probability of real gratification! But now, alas, even that forsakes me" (*Letters*, 2). Apparently Smollett considered an inflated style appropriate under certain circumstances, such as those arising from virtuous love or sincere grief; hence the effusive passages of dialogue between the hero and Narcissa in chapters 56 and 65 of *Roderick Random*, and hence Renaldo's language in the sentimental episodes of *Ferdinand Count Fathom*.

Chapter 13

1. "phlegmatic habit": Phlegmatic temperament; that is, coldness and dullness of character. In earlier conceptions of the "humours" and the character types associated with them, excessive phlegm in the body was thought to produce the effects here represented in the German jeweler.

2. "the creature": Whiskey or other intoxicating liquor (*OED*).

3. "schellum's": *Schelm* is a German term of abuse meaning knave, or rascal. Smollett uses the word in a common eighteenth-century English variant.

4. "the beasts of the field and the fowls of the air": Isaiah 56.9: "All ye beasts of the field, come to devour, *yea*, all ye beasts in the forest."

5. "Dulcinea": In *Don Quixote*, the name given by the Knight of La Mancha to the peasant girl he loves and serves in the fanciful belief that she is a noble lady.

6. "in propria persona": Latin "in his own person."

Chapter 14

1. "her ruling appetite": This phrase refers specifically to a commonly shared eighteenth-century assumption about individual human character, which was thought by many to be formed under the pressure of an internal conflict among the several passions, with one passion finally prevailing. Eliza Haywood devoted a whole novel to dramatic display of this conflict, *Life's Progress through the Passions; or, The Adventures of Natura* (London, 1748). Pope had treated the subject seriously in the *Essay on Man* (1732–34); and Fielding, who toyed with the question of the passions somewhat ambivalently over a period of many years, made it a central issue in *Amelia* (1751) during the crisis of Captain Billy Booth's conversion in book 12. The idea of the prevailing passion is closely related to Smollett's interest in a typological approach to characterization in his fiction (see the introduction, pp. xxxii–xxxiii; and see chap. 10, pp. 42–43 and n. 5).
2. "lansquenet": A card game of German origin in which players bet on single cards (*OED*).
3. "quarterly meeting of the jewellers": Smollett doubtless refers to a meeting of the guild of Viennese jewelers. In Vienna as in England during the eighteenth century, business was transacted at guild meetings, and mutual commercial interests were discussed.
4. "blessing himself": Preserving himself from further danger by invoking God's blessing or favor. Probably Fathom made the sign of the cross—a manifestly impious gesture in the present context.

Chapter 15

1. "two hundred florins": Equivalent to some £7–8 sterling, a respectable sum at the time. See chap. 10, n. 1.
2. "kindled the train": Fathom has ignited the "train," or fuse, leading to the explosive charge of his plot. In this military usage, the "train" was a line of gunpowder or other combustible.
3. "mine of his craft": Smollett mixes metaphors here by shifting to the language of nautical warfare: Fathom has loaded the "craft" of his plot with a "mine" (*i.e.*, an undetectable explosive weapon) so as to ensure the success of his assault.
4. "two hundred crowns": A crown was a coin of silver or gold, either foreign or domestic, valued at about 4*s*. 6*d*. sterling; see John Hewitt, *A Treatise upon Money, Coins, and Exchange*, 2d ed. (London, 1755), 161. Thus Wilhelmina's gold chain was originally worth the equivalent of almost £50 sterling.
5. "enemies of our faith": Moslems. Presumably the knight died in a battle fought during the two-year war (1716–18) between the Austrian and Ottoman empires (see chap. 3, n. 1).

Chapter 16

1. "scrutore": A writing desk. In the third paragraph following, Smollett names the same object "escritore"; both words are variants of the more common form *escritoire* (*OED*).
2. "Diana, surnamed Orthian": Diana was a Roman goddess (called Artemis in Greek mythology) variously associated with the wood, with the moon, and with womanhood, chastity, and fertility. In her identification with Hecate (see chap. 21, n. 1) she was also linked to the awful regions of darkness and evil magic. The Spartan women worshipped her in her most severe character as Orthia, offering up songs and dances to appease her fierce vengefulness and to invoke her assistance in the battles fought by their men. Smollett is wry and ironic here; the allusion to Diana reductively associates the jeweler's wife with the archetypal figure of the hunt and of female sensuality and wrath.
3. "feather her own nest": A proverbial English saying first recorded in the year 1553 (*ODEP*).

Chapter 17

1. "duenna": Generic term for an elderly woman appointed to watch over a young unmarried girl (*OED*).
2. "the gates of mercy": Probably an echo of Thomas Gray's recent and very popular poem, *Elegy Written in a Country Churchyard*, 1751 ("And shut the gates of mercy on mankind," line 68); but the phrase is biblical as well: see Isaiah 9:10–11. Smollett turns this allusion into a sexual joke.

Chapter 18

1. "a rupture between the emperor and the French king": The War of the Polish Succession broke out between France and the Austrian empire in the spring of 1733, following the death of the Polish king Augustus II. Austria and Russia supported the succession of Augustus's son, who was eventually crowned Augustus III; France and Spain sought to restore the deposed Stanislaus to the Polish throne. Prince Eugene of Savoy commanded the Austrian armies. The war went badly for both sides, and a treaty of accommodation was signed at Vienna in October–November 1735. See Henderson, 276–87.
2. "Heilbron": German city in Swabia on the Neckar, noted for its mineral waters. The Austrian army retreated and encamped there in April 1734 following Prince Eugene's decision not to hold the line of the Rhine against the enemy.
3. "campaign . . . neither perilous nor severe": There was relatively little savage

fighting in the Rhine theater during the first year of the War of the Polish Succession, and the number of casualties was comparatively small.

4. "Philipsburg": German city situated on the Rhine, crucial to the Austrians, and site of a major siege by the French during the summer of 1734.

5. "fort Kehl": A vital fortress on the Rhine, once the possession of the French, who "invested" (i.e., besieged) it early in the campaign of 1734.

6. "Scylla . . . Charybdis": In Greek mythology Scylla, the six-headed monster, lived in a cave across a narrow sea from Charybdis, the ship-devouring whirlpool. Homer introduced Scylla and Charybdis into a famous episode in book 12 of the *Odyssey*. Variants of the familiar phrase "between Scylla and Charybdis," used to describe a difficult dilemma, first began to appear in English early in the sixteenth century (*ODEP*).

7. "capitulation . . . honours of war": Philipsburg fell to the French on 18 July 1734. Smollett describes the siege at some length in his *Complete History*, 4:561–62.

Chapter 19

1. "cantonment": A place of lodging assigned to troops for lengthy encampment (*OED*).

2. "land of promise . . . milk and honey": See Exodus 3:8, where God promises Moses that he will deliver the Israelites from their bondage in Egypt "unto a good land and a large, unto a land flowing with milk and honey." Smollett renews this biblical analogy later, when Fathom is preparing to cross the Channel to England (see chap. 27, p. 127 and n. 5).

3. "Canaan": Palestine, or the "promised land."

4. "without beat of drum": Furtively, without sounding the retreat.

5. "Alsace": Strategic French territory bordered on the east by the middle Rhine, and thus contested during the War of the Polish Succession; location of the city of Strasbourg.

6. "bedlamite": An inmate of the Hospital of Saint Mary of Bethlehem, called "Bedlam," a London asylum for the insane. The subject of madness and its treatment interested Smollett, and he was familiar with the literature in which those subjects were discussed; see Richard A. Hunter and Ida Macalpine, "Smollett's Reading in Psychiatry," *Modern Language Review* 51 (1956): 409–11. Chapter 23 and part of chapter 24 of *Sir Launcelot Greaves* are set in an asylum, though the conditions described there are hardly so squalid as those at Saint Mary of Bethlehem. This hospital, which dated from the thirteenth century, had stood in Moorfields since being rebuilt in 1674–75. Because treatment of the mentally ill was so inadequate at the time, inmates of the hospital were rarely cured, and the term *bedlam* was coined from "Bethlehem" as a reflection of the chaotic, noisy, nightmarish scenes that might be witnessed there. See *An Encyclopedia of London*, ed. William Kent (New York: E. P. Dutton, 1937).

7. "prêvot": Fr. *prévôt*, equivalent to the English *provost*; an officer of the military police in a garrison or camp (*OED*).

8. "trusses": Bundles of hay or straw. The dragoons (or cavalrymen) are foraging for feed for their horses.

9. "count Coigny": François de Franquetot, comte de Coigny (1670–1759), became commander of the French army of the Rhine as of the summer of 1734, replacing the distinguished Marshal Villars, who died at above eighty years of age. See Smollett, *Complete History*, 4:562–63.

10. "the affair of Hallch": No specific place called Hallch has been identified, but Smollett surely refers to the fighting in the Rhineland just prior to the conclusion of treaty negotiations in Vienna. According to the *Gentleman's Magazine* 5 (October 1735): 622, a series of marches and countermarches took place immediately before a bloody skirmish at Clausen Abbey in the vicinity of Trier on 18 October. Both the French and Austrian armies suffered heavy casualties on this occasion.

Chapter 20

1. "Bar le duc": A small medieval city 128 miles east of Paris.

2. "Chalons": Chalons-sur-Marne, a medieval city forty miles northwest of Bar-le-duc and ninety-five miles east of Paris.

3. "leagues": A league was an informal measure of about three miles' distance (*OED*).

4. "ducats": Gold coins in use in several European countries at the time; the Austrian ducat was valued at about 9s. 6d. Fathom's lost "two hundred ducats" would thus be worth some £95 sterling, a very tidy sum.

5. "the tenth part of his treasure": Smollett alludes ironically to the biblical admonition to tithe. Mosaic law proclaimed that one-tenth of all earthly possessions were "holy unto the Lord" (Leviticus 27:30).

6. "milkiness": Softness or weakness (*OED*).

7. "travel-tainted": Exhausted from travel.

8. "Luneville": A small city in the northeast of France, ruled by the dukes of Lorraine from the mid-fourteenth century until the War of the Polish Succession; residence (in 1735) of the deposed King Stanislaus of Poland, who held the duchy until his death. Luneville is more than one hundred miles east of Chalons, and so the Tyrolese has shrewdly set off in a direction opposite from that taken by Fathom.

9. "stretching their extravagant arms athwart the gloom": Smollett quotes inaccurately from his friend John Armstrong's poem *The Art of Preserving Health* (1744):

> And more gigantic still th' impending trees
> Stretch their extravagant arms athwart the gloom.
>
> (2.369–70)

Smollett and Armstrong, both Scotsmen and both medical men, were friends and

correspondents from the mid-1740s until Smollett's death. See Knapp, especially
80–82; and see Knapp's essay, "Dr. John Armstrong, Litterateur, and Associate
of Smollett, Thomson, Wilkes, and Other Celebrities," *PMLA* 59 (1944): 1019–
58.

10. "strange phantoms in his imagination": Here begins the important episode of
Gothic terror in the forest and the robber's den. For commentary on this and the
other major Gothic interlude in Smollett's novel (chapters 62–63), see Devendra
P. Varma, *The Gothic Flame* (London: Arthur Barker, 1957), 39–40, and Edith
Birkhead, *The Tale of Terror: A Study of Gothic Romance* (London: Constable, 1921).

11. "furlongs": A furlong was originally measured by the length of a furrow in a
standard agricultural square containing ten acres; as a statute measure it is equal
to one-eighth of an English mile (*OED*).

12. "a rush light": A long-lasting light made by burning a dried reed-stem, or stalk, as
the wick in an oil lamp.

13. "a faggot-maker": A gatherer of sticks, twigs, and branches to be bundled together for use as a fuel.

Chapter 21

1. "Hecate": A figure of Greek mythology, associated with the evil or dangerous
aspects of Artemis in her role as goddess of womanhood (see chap. 16, n. 2), but
more closely identified with witchcraft, sorcery, and alchemy. Hecate was familiarized by Shakespeare; see especially *Macbeth* 2.1.52; 3.2.41; 3.5.1.

2. "on the crupper": On the rump of the horse, behind the saddle.

3. "filip": Tossing, turning, or "flip" (*OED*).

4. "impeach": In legal parlance, to accuse or bring charges against.

Chapter 22

1. "Fauxbourg de St. Germain": The city of Paris was at the time divided into
twenty quarters (faubourgs), one of which was called Saint Germain des Prés.
Smollett probably refers to the Hotel de Montmorency on La Rue Mazarine,
where he himself stayed some years later (*Travels*, Letter 6). In *Peregrine Pickle*
(chapter 42), the hero and his entourage resort to the same quarter of Paris—and
probably to the same hotel—immediately upon their first arrival in the city.

2. "ordinary": An eating house or tavern offering public meals at fixed prices.

3. "Westphalian count . . . Bolognian marquis": The count is from Westphalia, in
Smollett's time a German duchy administered on behalf of the archbishop of
Cologne; the marquis is from Bologna, a province of northern Italy.

4. "loss of your own princes": The complicated treaty (signed October–November
1735) ending the War of the Polish Succession gave the French duchies of Lor-

raine and Bar to the deposed Polish king Stanislaus, who was to hold them until his death; the same treaty awarded the Italian province of Tuscany to Duke Francis of Lorraine. See Henderson, 287–88.

5. "Grubenhagen": A small city in Westphalia, site of a splendidly preserved thirteenth-century castle. The comparison of the Chateau with Versailles is hardly apt, and only serves to make the Westphalian look ignorant and foolish.

6. "Schenkenschans": A German fortress situated at the Westphalian city of Schenkenzell and considered vital for the protection of the Dutch.

7. "among the hundreds of Drury": Within the environs of Drury Lane. In English law a "hundred" was a subdivision of a county or shire. The area of Drury Lane was among the poorest in London during the eighteenth century, and it was rampant with crime, vice, and especially prostitution. Smollett's sentence contains a joke arising from his play with words. The term *ramble* was commonly used to describe the activities of young men in search of sexual pleasure, which was easily to be found among the crowds (*i.e.*, the "hundreds") of prostitutes in Drury Lane.

8. "ex vestitu": By virtue only of his garment, signifying his profession as a clergyman. The satirical implication of what follows is that neither the abbé's investiture into his profession nor his garment certifies him as a man of learning and wit, qualified to be a critic.

9. "petit collet": Clerical collar, or neckband. J. C. Maxwell, "French Borrowings in *Ferdinand Count Fathom,*" *Notes & Queries*, n.s., 9 (1962): 18–19, points out that Smollett's use of *petit collet* antedates the earliest citation in the *OED*. The same is true, says Maxwell, of his later use of the word *commissaire* (see chap. 23, p. 96 and n. 16) and the phrase *soupe maigre* (see chap. 28, p. 130 and n. 9).

10. "templars in London": Barristers or students of the law residing in the Inner or Middle Temple. Smollett is severe on the law in his novel; the most important instance of his satire against the legal profession occurs in chapters 36 and 37.

11. "a first rate buck": A consummate dandy, or fop.

12. "American plantations . . . public exit nearer home": The implication of Smollett's sarcasm here is that abbés and templars frequently sink either into degradation or into infamy, crime, and finally punishment by sentencing to the galleys or to transportation. Templars sometimes make a more spectacular "exit" from their station by means of a public execution.

13. "the seven United Provinces": The Union of Utrecht (1579) had brought together the seven northern Dutch provinces into one republic. Possession of the southern provinces (modern Belgium), called the Spanish Netherlands, was contested for years afterward by Spain and Austria; the treaty of Utrecht signed in 1713 (see chap. 2, n. 8) left these territories under the undisputed control of the Austrian emperor.

14. "humourist": Dominated by a bodily humor. In subsequent sentences it becomes clear that the baronet is choleric; that is, his choler (bile) makes him sour, irascible, sarcastic.

15. "the true English mould": The depiction of this baronet (he is Sir Giles Squirrel) here and in the next two chapters surely draws upon the stock figure of the dandy in Restoration comedy. It also reveals Smollett's bemused interest in the English character. His anatomy of the English people in *Present State*, 2:212–16 echoes in some important particulars the portrait of Sir Giles: the English are a collection of "originals, whose singularities break out in every occurrence of life; in their dress and address, their way of living, their clubs, societies, courtships, marriages, wills, legacies, funerals, letters, writings, and advertisements" (p. 216). These words betray affectionate regard, and they accompany expressions of admiration for the sturdy individualism marking the same people. In his *Travels* Smollett repeatedly emphasizes the attractive qualities of the English to the detriment of other peoples (the French especially), whom he often finds capricious, pretentious, and silly; this is, of course, exactly how he represents Europeans here, in chapter 22 of his novel. But Smollett also observed with amusement a strain of smugness, proud provincialism, and occasionally stupidity or *naïveté* in the English character. Sir Giles (like Sir Stentor Stile, introduced in chapter 24) seems to exemplify a kind of ridiculous xenophobia, and Fathom sees him as easily duped, a natural prey. He is wrong, of course, as events are to prove in chapter 24. Ratchkali, the Tyrolese, renews the theme of English national pride in chapter 31 and is more convincing about it than Fathom. Fathom's reactions to the English character create a set of multiple ironies furthering his portrayal as a talented knave, but finally foolish as well as depraved.

Chapter 23

1. "the form of a Turkish bow": The old woman is deformed into a shape resembling the severe arc of the bow used by Turkish archers in the Ottoman armies of the seventeenth and eighteenth centuries.
2. "rheum": Watery discharges from the mucous membranes of the eyes and nose; when profuse or otherwise abnormal, thought to cause disease (*OED*).
3. "lost her nose": A familiar sign of venereal disease in the eighteenth century; usually taken to mean the advanced stages of syphilis.
4. "Delphic sibyl": In Greek mythology, the ancient Delphic oracle of Apollo.
5. "the consort of chaos, or mother of time": According to Greek mythology, all things began with the formless and hideous nothingness of Chaos, sire of night and day and hence of time. The "consort" was part of Chaos itelf, and thus equally hideous and formless. Smollett also seems to allude very obliquely to a familiar passage in the first book of *Paradise Lost*, where Milton speaks of how "the Heav'ns and Earth / Rose out of Chaos" (lines 9–10).
6. "Urganda": The enchantress, noted for her metamorphoses in appearance, who figures importantly in the late-medieval romance of *Amadis of Gaul*, Don Quix-

ote's favorite story. Smollett had used this same allusion in *Roderick Random* (chapter 50) when describing the ridiculous Miss Withers, a wrinkled hag of seventy who had duped the fortune-hunting Roderick into believing she was beautiful and young.

7. "extemporaneous altercation": The old brothelkeeper is loud and profane, in "the Covent-Garden strain," a reference to the reputation of Covent Garden as the major London center for illicit pleasure. Mother Douglas (d. 1761) kept the most notorious house there, and her obese figure was so well known that Hogarth incorporated it into several of his drawings. She seems to have served as model for the bawd who takes in Fanny Hill in John Cleland's *Memoirs of a Woman of Pleasure* (1748–49). Smollett very likely modeled his own character on Mother Douglas, whom she strikingly resembles in appearance and manner. See E. B. Chancellor, *The Pleasure Haunts of London During Four Centuries* (London: Constable, 1925), chap. 8.

8. "cordelier": A Franciscan friar of strict rule, so called because of the knotted cord worn at the waist. Smollett is ironic here at the expense of the Franciscans, but his real target is Catholicism itself. In chapters 42–43 of *Roderick Random* and in chapters 56–62 of *Peregrine Pickle*, he had displayed the lust and avarice of the Capuchins; his portrait of the abbé in *Ferdinand Count Fathom* continues his satire against the Roman Church. The reference to the Franciscan who absolves the whores after hearing their confession, thus preparing them for new sin, is a very severe expression of Smollett's contempt for Catholic theology and clerical practice. During his career as a writer he rarely expressed anything but such contempt. Perhaps the most important exception involves the character of Father Patrick Græme (or Graham), a Scottish expatriate and former officer in the army of James II who had taken vows as a Capuchin friar and had risen to become superior of his order's convent at Boulogne. In *Peregrine Pickle* (chapter 40) and again in the *Travels* (Letter 3), Smollett mentions Graham favorably as a kindly man of learning, refinement, and exemplary habits.

9. "Amanda": Generic name for an eligible young lady of beauty and virtue. The name, Latin in origin, means "worthy of love"; it was popular among writers of romance. Characters called Amanda figure prominently in two popular plays, Colley Cibber's *Love's Last Shift* and Sir John Vanbrugh's sequel, *The Relapse* (both 1696). In *Peregrine Pickle* (chapters 56–62), Amanda is the lovely young married woman whom Perry, assisted by her Capuchin chaplain, pursues and attempts to seduce.

10. "chevalier": French equivalent of the English *cavalier*. Smollett uses this term derisively in two of its familiar meanings: the blustering Westphalian ridicules his English rival's knighthood and, simultaneously, his pretensions to gallantry.

11. "ebriety": Drunkenness.

12. "rixdollars": Dutch and German currency. A rixdollar was worth about 4*s.* 6*d.* sterling (Hewitt, *Treatise upon Money*, 76). The Englishman thus speculates that

the Westphalian count's annual income might be valued at about £75, a very small sum for a member of the European nobility.

13. "fine Holland sleeves": Sleeves made of fine Holland linen.

14. "brocard": Brocade, a fabric woven with raised figures or designs.

15. "Westphalian hog": Westphalia was known in Smollett's time (and still is known) for its bacon and hams, hence for its hogs.

16. "commissaire": An officer of the law. Smollett's use of this French word antedates the earliest citation in the *OED*; see chap. 22, n. 9.

17. "myrmidons": Hired ruffians. In the eighteenth century the term *myrmidon* was also applied contemptuously to certain inferior officers of the law, such as bailiffs and watchmen (*OED*). Originally it referred to a warrior race of men from Thessaly led by Achilles to the siege of Troy (Homer *Iliad* 2.684).

18. "cross-buttock": A throw over the hip in wrestling (*OED*).

19. "the whole ban of the empire": Samuel Johnson, in his *Dictionary of the English Language* (1755), defined "ban of the empire" as a public censure by which the privileges of a German prince might be superseded. But here the *ban* is the whole muster of French troops for war, summoned by the king from throughout his dominions; in feudal times *arrière-ban*, a term used more recently to refer to older citizens constituting a reserve, while *ban* is the term for the younger men likely to be called into active service. (*OED*).

20. "forest of Senlis": The wood outside the ancient French town of Senlis, located approximately twenty-eight miles northeast of Paris. This forest was the site of frequent duels because of its remoteness and the protection it gave to antagonists.

21. "rhodomontade": Rodomontade, or vainglorious bragging and boasting (*OED*).

22. "madam la Maquerelle": *Maquerelle* is a feminine form of French *maquereau*, which corresponds to the English *mackerel*. In eighteenth-century usage both the French *maquerelle* and the English *mackerel*, as phonetically similar words, were slang terms to describe a procurer, procuress, or brothelkeeper.

23. "Pepin . . . de Fumier": The abbé's name is a grotesque, reductive joke combining several noble Christian names with the surname "de Fumier," which means dung, manure, or stable-litter.

24. "quadrille": A fashionable card game for four persons, played with forty cards (Strutt, 263).

25. "twenty louis' clear gain": A louis d'or was a French coin of gold valued at about 17s. sterling (Hewitt, *Treatise upon Money*, 152). Thus Fathom had winnings of £17.

Chapter 24

1. "such a figure . . . in that place": The portrait introduced here represents an adaptation from the conventional character of the bumpkin in popular stage comedies of the Restoration and after. Sir Stentor Stile (or Stiles, in a variant spelling

Smollett uses later, in chapter 37) cuts a truly ridiculous figure, especially considering the setting in which he makes his entrance. His language, with its amusingly tortured mixture of country dialect, foxhunter's cant, and nautical slang, is equally ludicrous. Even Ralph Griffiths, whose generally unfavorable notice of *Ferdinand Count Fathom* appeared in the *Monthly Review* for March 1753, seems to have recognized the merits of this portrait; about half of his lengthy essay is devoted to quotation of chapter 24 very nearly in its entirety. Sir Stentor's Greek name, of course, suggests his bombast (see Homer *Iliad* 5.785). His dress, by flouting all standards of taste and custom in a most outrageous way, makes him truly laughable; see Cunnington and Cunnington, 183–265, for description and illustration of styles in men's dress during the 1750s and after. Despite his manner and apparel, Sir Stentor is not the fool Smollett's adventurer imagines him to be. The first hint of Fathom's mistaken estimate of his English prey is planted in the next paragraph of this chapter, when the dandified baronet Sir Giles Squirrel makes himself known to his old friend. In the eighteenth century, *gile* was a variant of *guile* (*OED*).

2. "jockey": Smollett uses this term quite literally in its most familiar sense as the name given to one who rides in horse races. Sir Stentor is dressed as a country jockey, hence the crudeness of his apparel. There is a latent irony here, however. In the eighteenth century, *jockey* also meant "cheat" and "fraud" (*OED*), and Sir Stentor later proves to be both of those things.

3. "fustian": A coarse cloth of cotton and flax.

4. "buff": Stiff ox-hide leather, dressed with oil and thus made fuzzy in texture and yellowish in color.

5. "cohorn": A cohorn (or coehorn) mortar was a small weapon for firing grenades (*OED*).

6. "the cry of mackarel or live cod": Probably a reference to a common cry of a Billingsgate fishmonger (see chap. 28, n. 11). But there is a sexual joke: *mackerel*, a slang term for a procuress, is here combined with *cod*, a slang term for the scrotum.

7. "frigasee and ragooze": Fricassee and ragout, two similar kinds of meat stew, the latter of which was usually more highly seasoned.

8. "some savage monster or maniac": Sir Stentor's strange dialect, which makes him sound both crude and crazy to his listeners here, suggests the language of west-country England (probably Somersetshire); it is very close to the dialect spoken by Fielding's bumpkin Squire Western in *Tom Jones*.

9. "Waunds": An oath; variant of "Zounds," or "God's wounds."

10. "Odds heartlikens": An unusual form of a common oath meaning "God's heart"; "heartlikens" is a diminutive form, as in "babykins."

11. "pulville": Pulvil or pulvilio, perfumed powder for the wig or body.

12. "bedizened": Dressed out, as with vulgar finery (*OED*).

13. "squire Snaffle": A snaffle is a bridle bit for a horse, but in eighteenth-century slang usage the word also referred both to the manipulations of one person by

another and to devious acts of purloining or thievery (*OED*). Sir Stentor has been "snaffled," it appears, by the squire at home; as a confidence man he will now seek to snaffle others during his stay in France.

14. "bodikins!": An oath meaning "God's dear body."

15. "Odd's heart!": An oath meaning "God's heart."

16. "doublets": Upper-body garments, or jackets, worn by men.

17. "fob": A small pocket in the waistband of the breeches, used to hold a watch or money.

18. "belly timber": Nautical slang for solid food.

19. "Apize upon them!": "A pox upon them." This was a common imprecation; the "pox" referred to is syphilis.

20. "Bully": Boiled lean beef.

21. "the flesh of Pharaoh's lean kine": Genesis 41:18–21. In a dream described to Joseph for his interpretation, the Pharaoh had seen seven fat kine, or cattle, and seven kine "poor and very ill favoured and lean-fleshed, such as I never saw in all the land of Egypt for badness."

22. "rabbet them!": A meaningless imprecation, now archaic; "rabbet" was usually written "rabbit" (*OED*).

23. "dividing spoon": Literally, the spoon used for transferring (or "dividing") soup from the bowl to the mouth.

24. "Blood!": An oath meaning "God's blood."

25. "a word to the wise, as the saying is—": A reference to a common proverbial expression derived from the Latin *Verbum sapienti sat est*: "A word to the wise is sufficient" (*ODEP*).

26. "leveret . . . fumet": The second course is a young rabbit of highly gamey odor, in this instance because it is spoiled.

27. "to discuss it": To sample or taste the food.

28. "auberge": An inn.

29. "the Early Horn": A popular hunting song, rendered as follows in *Songs of the Chace* (London: Thomas Simpson, 1811), 296:

> The early horn salutes the morn,
> That gilds this charming place;
> With cheerful cries bid echo rise,
> And join the jovial chace.
> The vocal hills around,
> The waving woods,
> The crystal floods,
> All, all return the enliv'ning sound.

30. "Odd's flesh!": An oath meaning "God's [or Christ's] flesh."

31. "all fours . . . chuck-varthing": The first three of the simple children's games named by Sir Stentor are played with cards; tetotum is played with dice, and both hussle-cap and chuck-varthing (or chuck-farthing) are played with coins, which are tossed (Strutt, 223, 262, 266, 305–6).

32. "cross or pile": Heads or tails. The guinea coin of the mid-eighteenth century featured a cross on one side and, on the other, the king's portrait together with a die mark, or "pile," from the mint where the coin was impressed. The guinea took its name from African Guinea, source of the gold from which it was minted beginning in 1663. Originally worth 20*s.*, it was valued at 21*s.* from the reign of George I to the reign of George III. See C. H. V. Sutherland, *English Coinage 600–1900* (London: B. T. Batsford, 1973), 174–77.

33. "hazard": An ancient dice game of medieval origin; so called because many arbitrary rules restrict the player's chances of winning (Strutt, 248).

34. "the face of Lewis": The image of Louis XV on the louis d'or coins Sir Stentor is winning.

Chapter 25

1. "remarks": Notice or observation (*OED*).

2. "come abroad . . . country": An ironic euphemism; in actuality, Sir Stentor and Sir Giles had most likely left England in flight from the law or from the vengeance sought by angry victims of their frauds and deceptions.

3. "complimented . . . Pas": The Persian courteously allowed Fathom to pass by first.

4. "out of order": Indisposed.

5. "outlandish": In the literal sense, out-of-land, foreign.

Chapter 26

1. "*The history of the noble Castilian*": The digression, or interpolated "history," was a convention of early romances, including *Don Quixote* and the narratives lampooned by it; the "history" became a fixture in French heroic romances of the middle and later years of the seventeenth century. English writers adapted the convention freely, using it to create analogues to their central story lines, to underscore their moral purposes, or—in many instances—to flesh out their works to greater bulk. Fielding introduced major digressive interludes into *Joseph Andrews*, *Tom Jones*, and *Amelia*, successfully integrating them into his plots. Smollett interrupted the main narrative of *Roderick Random* for the histories of Miss Williams (chapters 22 and 23) and the poet Melopoyn (chapters 62 and 63); and he stopped the movement of *Peregrine Pickle* to offer the sensational "Memoirs" of Lady Vane (chapter 88) and the history of the celebrated case of James Annesley (chapter 106), the supposedly disenfranchised nobleman. See John M. Warner, "The Interpolated Narratives in the Fiction of Fielding and Smollett: An Epistemological View," *Studies in the Novel* 5 (1973): 271–83.

2. "the honour to own myself a Castilian": The region of Castile, formerly a Spanish

kingdom, extends from the Bay of Biscay in the north to Andalusia in the south. In the eighteenth century, the Castilian nobility was still noted for a fierce and haughty pride of class and tradition.

3. "Don Diego de Zelos": Smollett comes very close to the Spanish *celos*, which means jealousy. The root form of the same word (*celo*) also means religious fervor, piety. As was often the case among eighteenth-century novelists who used the interpolated tale for ostensibly moral purposes, Smollett here chose a name that imparts an almost allegorical quality to his character.

4. "Don Gonzales Orgullo": The Spanish word *orgullo* means pride, haughtiness.

5. "battle of Saragossa": On 9 August 1710, at Saragossa (or Zaragoza) in northeast Spain, the allied forces scored a major victory over King Philip V in the War of the Spanish Succession. Smollett described the battle as follows in his *Complete History*, 4:371: "the enemy was totally defeated: five thousand of their men were killed, seven thousand taken, together with all their artillery, and a great number of colours and standards. King Charles [of Austria] entered Saragossa in triumph, while Philip with the wreck of his army retreated to Madrid."

6. "Portuguese horse": In the War of the Spanish Succession, Portugal had joined the Grand Alliance with England, Holland, and Austria.

7. "treaty of Utrecht": See chap. 2, n. 8.

8. "reducing the Catalans to their allegiance": Catalonia is a hilly and rugged region in the northeast corner of Spain, noted for its rich mineral deposits and fertile valleys and coast lands. Proud of their traditions and freedom from domination, the Catalans sided with the Grand Alliance against King Philip V in the War of the Spanish Succession; when the Treaty of Utrecht awarded the region to Philip, the Catalans resisted but were at length subdued and obliged to submit to Spanish rule.

9. "Seville": A great medieval center of culture and trade located on the Guadalquivir in southwest Spain; in the eighteenth century, still a major inland port, though gradually being eclipsed by nearby Cadiz.

10. "allay": Alloy.

11. "mechanic": A laborer in a manual occupation or trade (*OED*).

12. "ORLANDO": Since the very earliest medieval times, when the fame of Charlemagne's great paladin Roland spread all over Europe in ballads and tales (most notably in the eleventh-century *Chanson de Roland*), the name Orlando (Italian for Roland) had been associated with heroism and romance. In the *Orlando Innamorato* (1487) of Matteo Maria Boiardo, in the *Orlando Furioso* (1516; 1532) of Lodovico Ariosto, and in Shakespeare's *As You Like It*, the name was made almost synonymous with the ideals of courage, love, and gallantry. Orlando is very nearly an anagram for Rinaldo (or Renaldo), the name for a cousin of Orlando in the *Innamorato* and the *Furioso*, and the real name of Serafina's lover in Don Diego's history.

13. "Plebeian": Commoner; from Roman plebs, or commoners (*OED*). In the eigh-

teenth century the term also suggested vulgarity, meanness of birth, lowness of character.

14. "St. Lucar": The seaport city of Sanlucar de Barrameda, located at the mouth of the Guadalquivir and thus on a direct route to the sea from Seville.

15. "Gallicia": Anglicized name for Gallaecia, an ancient kingdom in northwest Spain bounded on the north and west by the Atlantic and on the south by Portugal.

16. "Vigo": A seaport in northwest Spain located on the Estuary of Vigo, an inlet of the Atlantic.

17. "corregidor": Chief magistrate.

18. "physiognomy . . . character and disposition": Smollett uses the term *physiognomy* somewhat loosely, suggesting the possibility of reading character in the face. This is consistent with his view of human nature, which he divides into types, each type revealing and defining itself through appearance as well as conduct (see chap. 10, pp. 42–43 and n. 5; and chap. 14, pp. 54–55 and n. 1). The importance of physiognomy as an index to character is as old as Theophrastus and Aristotle's *Nicomachean Ethics*; it is closely related to the seventeenth-century tradition of the humors character as represented in the plays of Ben Jonson or the *Characters* (1614) of Sir Thomas Overbury. Smollett's reference to physiognomy here, and in many other places in *Ferdinand Count Fathom*, reflects increasing interest in the subject among scientists and some philosophers of his day. See John Graham, "The Development of the Use of Physiognomy in the Novel" (Ph.D. diss., Johns Hopkins University, 1960); and Graeme Tytler, *Physiognomy in the European Novel: Faces and Fortunes* (Princeton: Princeton University Press, 1982).

Chapter 27

1. "a thousand crowns": Almost £250 sterling. See chap. 15, n. 4.

2. "fix the standard of his finesse": Erect the banner of his triumphant manipulations and artifice. The basic metaphor here is military, but the context suggests other frames of meaning. In the eighteenth century (and earlier), as now, the term *finesse* referred to artful stratagems in games of cards; but it also carried connotations of sinister deception, as practiced by confidence-men like Fathom.

3. "Boulogne": A seaport city in northern France, located on the English Channel, with a considerable British population in the eighteenth century.

4. "poulard": A young hen, spayed and fattened for the table.

5. "another Moses . . . mount Pisgah": See Deuteronomy 3:27, 34:1–4. Earlier, Fathom had dreamed of England as a "land of promise, flowing with milk and honey" (see chap. 19, p. 77 and n. 2).

6. "Calais": French seaport city located on the Strait of Dover; a usual place of departure for boats and ships sailing to England.

7. "Deal": A small English seaport situated in Kent on the Strait of Dover. Deal was

a frequent destination for boats and ships sailing from France, and reputedly it was the site of Julius Caesar's landing in 55 B.C.

8. "difficulty . . . swelling surf": Smollett ironically compares Fathom to Julius Caesar, who is also supposed to have had difficulty landing because of rough seas; see *Caesar's Commentaries* 5.8.

9. "cutter": A small, single-masted landing vessel.

10. "Scipio's behaviour on the coast of Afric": Scipio Africanus (236–184/3 B.C.), the great Roman general, invaded Africa in 204 B.C. with an army of thirty-five thousand men; by the year 200 he had totally defeated Hannibal and was proclaimed conqueror of the continent. When first approaching the African coast, Scipio is supposed to have prayed to the gods for blessings, whereupon he learned that he was about to land on a promontory called "Cape of the Fair God" (Livy *History* 29.27.5–15).

11. "insolence": Pride, but here not exclusively in the negative sense of haughtiness.

12. "another conqueror of the isle": Fathom is compared to Julius Caesar for the second time in this chapter. Here, however, the irony runs deeper, for the comparison is Fathom's own and not his author's.

Chapter 28

1. "fat Wapping-landlady": Wapping, a section of Stepney extending from Smithfield along the north bank of the Thames, was in the eighteenth century a bustling, noisy place noted for its fishermen, fishmongers, ship and boat builders, chandlers, rope-makers, nautical signs, taverns and inns (see Timbs, 2:749–50). By the middle of the century, the phrase "fat Wapping landlady" had become almost a generic term for a particular type of familiar London character. Goldsmith made fun of the bulging actress Mrs. Hannah Pritchard, who, he said, might "act the part of the Wapping Landlady without a Bolster" (*The Bee*, no. 1, 6 October 1759). There were drawings of the character by the illustrator Francis Hayman, and she appeared in several works for the stage, including a farcical dance called *The Wapping Landlady* performed at Covent Garden on 26 April 1768. In *Humphry Clinker*, Jery Melford writes laughingly from Bath of a lady who reminds him of the character type as she struggles through the crowd in the pump room to reach her brandy merchant (Jery Melford to Sir Watkin Phillips, Bath, April 30).

2. "Obadiah": A minor Old Testament figure, author of the book of prophecy bearing his name. Smollett used Obadiah as the Christian name of Lieutenant Lismahago in *Humphry Clinker*. The name was perhaps most familiar in the eighteenth century as a slang term for a Quaker.

3. "children of vanity, like thee": The Quakers believed in the reality and power of the "Inner Light" of the spirit, and hence came to be called the "Children

of Light" (as here amusingly opposed to the "children of vanity"). The name "Quakers" was given to members of the Society of Friends by the magistrate Gervase Bennett when George Fox, founder of the sect, exhorted him to *tremble* at the word of God. Smollett admired the honesty, simplicity, and courage of the Quakers, but he was nonetheless deeply suspicious of their fervid religiosity (see *Present State*, 2:189–93). He felt much the same way about other "enthusiastic" or fanatical groups of Christian believers (see above, chap. 7, n. 4). Many people shared Smollett's doubts about the Quakers in the extreme, and members of the sect suffered much persecution throughout the early years of its history. For full discussion of the Quakers during the formative period of the seventeenth and eighteenth centuries, see W. C. Braithwaite, *The Beginnings of Quakerism*, rev. Henry J. Cadbury (Cambridge: The University Press, 1955).

4. "corporation": A vulgar colloquial name for the abdomen, or sometimes for the body itself (*OED*).

5. "pretend to have a motion . . . preach nonsense": The reference is to the Quaker custom of all present sitting quietly in worship service until someone is moved by the spirit to stand and speak. The mockery here is obvious, for the "motion" of the spirit is equated with an involuntary action of the bowels.

6. "Mr. Goose-cap": Presumably this is a reference to the curled brim of the Quaker's hat. The effect was achieved by the hatter's use of a tailor's goose, or smoothing iron.

7. "Mr. Yellow-chaps": A reference to the derisive eighteenth-century English stereotype of the Frenchman (or the Frenchified fop), who was fancied to be effete, ill-nourished, bilious, and therefore yellow (or jaundiced) in the face.

8. "learning to cabbage": The eighteenth-century tailor's notorious habit of charging for oversized pieces of cloth and then surreptitiously appropriating the shreds (*i.e.*, the large leftover strips) for future use was called "cabbaging." The word *cabbage* was sometimes used as a slang term for a tailor (*OED*).

9. "soup maigre": French *soupe maigre*, a thin vegetable or fish soup. Smollett's anglicized use of this phrase here, and earlier in *Peregrine Pickle* (chapters 13 and 48), antedates the earliest citation in the *OED*. See chap. 22, n. 9.

10. "atomy, . . . rat's tail . . . tinsy jacket": The man looks like a skeleton, has a long lock of hair depending from the back of his wig, and wears sparkling (tinseled) clothing. This is a very derisive description of a Frenchified fop.

11. "Kate Brawn . . . Thames-street": Thames Street extended from Blackfriars to the Tower of London and was noted for its taverns, butcher shops, fishermen, fishmarkets, and shops and suppliers serving the fishing trade; the Billingsgate fish market stood in lower Thames Street. The peculiar loud, vulgar language of the fishmongers in Billingsgate was known as "Billingsgate discourse"; and the familiar figure of the coarse oyster woman was stereotyped as a "Billingsgate," a "scolding, impudent slut": "She wore a strong stuff gown, tucked up, and shewing a large quilted petticoat; her hair, cap, and bonnet flattened into a mass by

carrying a basket upon her head; her coarse, cracked cry, and brawny limbs, and red, bloated face, completing a portrait of the 'fish-fag'" (Timbs, 1:45–46, 2:711). Smollett has added dimension to his initial characterization of this female as a "fat Wapping-landlady" in the first paragraph of the present chapter. The name Kate Brawn is intended to suggest shrewishness (most likely after the example of Shakespeare's Kate in *The Taming of the Shrew*) as well as bulk, strength, and vulgarity.

12. "Bear key": A reference to the key (or quay) opposite the endings of two streets, Great and Little Bear Key, which led directly from Thames Street down to the waterside; nearby stood the Custom House. On this quay were landed great quantities of corn, and formerly of bear, a kind of small barley brewed into ale and beer, especially in Dublin; hence the name "Bear Key." The area of the quay was frequented by merchants and shipowners, but it was also the haunt of low-life types and thus a fit place for the "education" of such a female as the gentleman takes his vulgar antagonist to be.

13. "take up arms against such seas of trouble": Smollett paraphrases a line from the most famous soliloquy in *Hamlet*:

> To be, or not to be, that is the question:
> Whether 'tis nobler in the mind to suffer
> The slings and arrows of outrageous fortune,
> Or to take arms against a sea of troubles,
> And by opposing, end them. . . .
> (3.1.55–59)

The implied comparison between the foppish passenger and Hamlet is, of course, ludicrous.

14. "disgraced": Put out of countenance.

15. "the best orators on the Thames": Smollett probably refers to the familiar contests of invective carried on among watermen on the river; but he may also allude mockingly to debates among the members in Parliament.

16. "Eleusinian mysteries": The most secret and important of the religious ceremonies of ancient Greece, celebrated at Eleusis, near Athens. Originally a feast of purification and fertility in honor of Demeter and Persephone, the Mysteries at some point became associated with ideas of Hades and the future life. The celebration culminated in a ritual held in a darkened hall, where the worshippers were shown visions in flashes of light. In the latter part of his sentence Smollett seems to allude to a scene in *The Frogs*, by Aristophanes, where the chorus of Initiates into the Mysteries is introduced as accompanied by a train of boisterous female worshippers.

17. "an Hungary-water bottle": A bottle containing a medicinal liquid, distilled from rosemary flowers infused in spirits of wine and named from an unidentified Hungarian queen supposed to have used it. The mixture was prescribed for treatment of "the Wandering and Hip-Gout," for "Disorders of the Head, Brain, and

Nerves," and for "Convulsions, Cramps, Palsies, Lethargies, and hysterical Disorders"; see Richard Brookes, M.D., *The General Dispensatory, Containing a Translation of the Pharmacopoeias of the Royal Colleges of Physicians of London and Edinburgh*, 2d ed. (London, 1755), 155. Ladies typically carried Hungary-water bottles; often, as is the case with Smollett's Wapping-landlady, the bottles were filled with something of more than medicinal powers.

18. "Sal volatile": An aromatic solution of ammonium carbonate used to revive those suffering from fainting fits (Brookes, *General Dispensatory*, 308–9).

19. "the Downs": A rendezvous for ships off the east coast of Kent, within the Goodwin Sands.

20. "monument . . . this island": Fathom's (and probably Smollett's) scornful attitude here adds a significant qualification to his previous estimation of England as a luxuriant place of beauty and wealth (see chap. 27, p. 128).

Chapter 29

1. "the young pretender": Smollett here introduces a very interesting anachronism, the first of many to follow in succeeding chapters. By the most liberal calculation of the events in the narrative to this point, the date of the present episode cannot be later than 1735–36. Fathom is now in his early twenties, and the Young Pretender (or Young Chevalier), Prince Charles Edward Stuart (1720–88), is just fifteen or sixteen. The Jacobite Rebellion of 1745–46, with all its long aftermath of public speculation concerning the whereabouts of the prince, is still ten years in the future. Smollett's obvious purpose in this episode is to place the experience of his character against the specific background of the 'Forty-Five. Fielding had already made excellent capital of a similar incident in book 11 of *Tom Jones* (chapters 2–6), where a silly provincial landlord mistakes Sophia Western for Jenny Cameron, Charles Edward's Scottish mistress. See the introduction, pp. xxxiii–xxxvi, for discussion of Smollett's historical anachronisms in *Ferdinand Count Fathom*; see also Jerry C. Beasley, "Smollett's Novels: *Ferdinand Count Fathom* for the Defense," *Papers on Language and Literature* 20 (1984): 165–84.

2. "the protestant succession": The German Protestant Hanovers succeeded to the English throne in 1714 following the death of the last Stuart monarch, Queen Anne.

3. "reward . . . that famous adventurer": In August 1745 the House of Lords "issued a proclamation, offering a reward of £30,000 to any person who should apprehend the prince-adventurer" (Smollett, *Complete History*, 4:662).

4. "trundled": Literally, rolled.

5. "leash of hares": Three hares.

6. "one of the Quorum": The gentleman is an appointed justice or magistrate. No hearing could be conducted without the presence of such an official person.

7. "mittimus": A warrant, given under the hand of a justice of the peace, for the detention of an accused offender in prison until trial (*OED*).

8. "next size": The justice has decided to remand Fathom to prison until the county's next assize, or periodic session of the criminal court.

9. "some sinister intent": The suspicions against Fathom lead to a gross travesty of justice, quite like the torment suffered by Roderick Random when he is tried on board ship by officers who cannot read the Greek in his diary and thus suspect him of conspiracy (chapter 30). The present scene continues Smollett's criticism of the legal system begun in chapter 22 and to be renewed in chapters 36 and 37.

10. "refectory": Refractory. This bumpkin justice, besides being ignorant of the law, is portrayed as something of a malapropist. Smollett repeats this same device of mockery when developing his character of Justice Gobble in chapter 12 of *Sir Launcelot Greaves*.

11. "composition": The justice appears to mean "competition."

12. "extinguished": Distinguished.

13. "accrues": Occurs.

14. "two hundred ducats": About £95 sterling. See chap. 20, n. 4.

15. "Perruquier": Besides cutting hair, the eighteenth-century barber very often served as a perruquier; that is, he made, dressed, and sold wigs.

16. "shalloon": A closely woven woolen fabric used primarily for linings (*OED*).

17. "surtout": A greatcoat or overcoat. The buckram was a heavily sized cloth of cotton or linen introduced between the outer fabric and inner lining of a coat to give it an elegant stiffness—or, in the case of the wine merchant, to provide a hiding place for smuggled goods.

Chapter 30

1. "Rochester": A cathedral city in Kent located twenty-eight miles southeast of London on the Medway River; an important coaching stop for travelers from the coast.

2. "the Black Bull": One of the major coaching inns in Rochester during the eighteenth century.

3. "Amanda": See chap. 23, n. 9.

4. "Gravesend": A town in Kent located twenty-two miles east of London on an estuary of the Thames.

5. "his beauteous Helen": Smollett compares Fathom's prey to Helen of Troy. The name Helen means "the bright one"; it is sometimes used as a diminutive of Elinor or Eleanor.

6. "Dartford": A Kentish port town located about fifteen miles east of London on the Darent River estuary of the Thames.

7. "wresting": Twisting, distorting by false interpretation.

8. "Canary": A light, sweet wine imported from the Canary Islands off the coast of Africa.

9. "fishing in troubled waters": An old English proverbial expression dating back at least to 1568 (*ODEP*). As used here, the proverb hints at an obscene sexual joke.

10. "hysterical affection": Certain symptoms of distraction, dizziness, delirium, and fainting were thought by medical diagnosticians of the day to proceed from hysterical affection; in its worst form, this malady was apoplectic and often fatal. See Richard Brookes, M.D., *The General Practice of Physic*, 2d ed. (London, 1754), 1:15–16. Dr. George Cheyne devoted nearly two-thirds of his important medical study *The English Malady: or, A Treatise of Nervous Diseases of All Kinds* (London, 1733) to description of the many varied nervous distempers known to him and to discussion of their treatment; the other one-third of Cheyne's book is given over to case studies and includes an account of "The Case of the Author" (pp. 325–64). Dr. Cheyne is best remembered now as the friend and physician of Samuel Richardson, who for many years suffered from sometimes acute disorders of the nervous system.

11. "sapping": Advancing surreptitiously; undermining. See chap. 6, n. 2.

12. "concentred": Brought together, concentrated in a center; here, as in a heap of combustibles ready to be ignited.

Chapter 31

1. "ought": Anything whatever, or at all; variant of *aught* (*OED*).

2. "Ludgate": According to legend, this great gate at the western extremity of the old city of London was built by the British King Lud in 66 B.C. Rebuilt in the thirteenth century and restored many times thereafter, its quarters had by the eighteenth century become a prison for debtors; the entire gate was pulled down 1760–62. Probably Fathom has walked from Fleet Street, location of many taverns and coffee-houses, through Ludgate, on his way up Ludgate Hill toward Saint Paul's Cathedral.

3. "in the toil": In the net, or trap (*OED*).

4. "two heads are better than one": "Two heads are better than one, even if the one's a sheep's," a Cornish proverb first recorded in 1864 (*ODEP*). G. L. Apperson, *English Proverbs and Proverbial Phrases: A Historical Dictionary* (London: J. M. Dent, 1929) traces other forms of the expression back to Homer; but Smollett's use of the proverb in its most familiar wording must be one of the earliest literary repetitions of it.

5. "Franckfort upon the Maine": Frankfurt am Main, located at the site of a Roman military establishment, was the scene of the coronation of most German emperors from 1152 to 1806.

6. "my operations . . . enemies of our religion": Ratchkali the Tyrolese is surely

Roman Catholic, and he especially enjoyed his schemes against Protestant here-
tics, who (in Frankfurt) would have been Lutherans.

7. "one of the fraternity": The purchaser of Ratchkali's stolen jewel was a member of
the fraternity (or guild) of Frankfurt jewelers.

8. "a Saxon pebble": Probably an agate, polished to resemble a valuable diamond.
Such stones were commonly found in England, Scotland, and northern Europe,
and they were often passed off by sharpers as valuable gems.

9. "a lapidary": One who cuts, polishes, or engraves precious stones; a connoisseur
of such work (*OED*).

10. "these islanders": The English. Here Smollett renews the subject of the English
character introduced earlier by Fathom's reflections upon his impressions of Sir
Giles Squirrel (see chap. 22, p. 92 and n. 15). Ratchkali's anatomy of the Englishman is Smollett's lengthiest treatment of the national character in any of his
novels.

11. "*the great the unbounded prospect lies before me!*": Smollett slightly misquotes from
Addison's *Cato. A Tragedy* (1713), 5.1.13: "The wide, th' unbounded prospect,
lyes before me." It is of course ludicrous for Ratchkali to compare himself with
Addison's Stoic hero; perhaps the joke is on Ratchkali, for Smollett surely expected that some readers would remember the next line: "But shadows, clouds,
and darkness, rest upon it."

12. "let": Hindrance (*OED*).

13. "least penalty of the law": London was without an effective police force in the
eighteenth century, and only the army stood between authority and anarchy.
Crime was rampant, and thieves acted almost with impunity. Riots were night-
mares; during the Gordon Riots of 1780, the situation was saved only by the
king's demand that the military be pressed into service. In *Amelia*, Fielding lamented the deplorable state of the London constables, who, "being appointed to
guard our Streets by Night from Thieves and Robbers, an Office which at least
requires Strength of Body, are chosen out of those poor old decrepit People, who
are from their Want of bodily Strength rendered incapable of getting a Livelihood
by Work" (*Amelia*, ed. Martin C. Battestin [Middletown, Conn.: Wesleyan University Press, 1983], bk. 1, chap. 2, p. 20). In 1751, Fielding published *An Enquiry into the Causes of the late Increase of Robbers*, which was essentially a plea for
some system of effective law enforcement. For discussion of this general subject
see Turberville, 1:69–70, 327–28; and see especially M. Dorothy George, *London
Life in the Eighteenth Century* (1925; reprint, New York: Harper Torchbooks,
1965), chaps. 1, 2, and 5.

14. "*Capriciosos*": Italian *capricciosos*, improvised musical flourishes played in a free and
fanciful style.

15. "the court end of the town": At this time, the area between Kensington and Saint
James's Palace and Park. The environs of Kensington Palace and Gardens had
become fashionable when William III took up his residence there (see Timbs,
2:434).

16. "Monmouth-street": A center for shops selling fashionable secondhand clothing. The street is now part of Shaftesbury Avenue but was originally named after the duke of Monmouth, illegitimate son of Charles II and leader of Monmouth's Rebellion, 1685.

17. "the hospital of Bethlem": The Hospital of Saint Mary of Bethlehem, for the insane (see chap. 19, n. 6). It was relatively easy to confine someone to the insane asylums of eighteenth-century England, where conditions were typically unfit for human habitation. Until 1770 members of the public might, for a fee of 1d. each, visit Bethlehem Hospital to gape at the inmates (Timbs, 1:43–44). In *Peregrine Pickle* (chapter 106) and *Sir Launcelot Greaves* (chapter 23), Smollett dramatized the horrors of unjust confinement in an asylum for the insane.

Chapter 32

1. "his engine": His instrument, Ratchkali.

2. "juggler": A pejorative term for one who deceives by conjuring or acts of deception (*OED*).

3. "confutation of Sir Isaac Newton's philosophy": Fathom appears foolishly pretentious and bold here. He does not seem to realize (or perhaps he does not care) that, both in England and on the Continent, Newton's physics, mathematics, and natural philosophy were by the middle of the eighteenth century almost beyond challenge except from orthodox or evangelical churchmen. See E. W. Strong, "Newtonian Explications of Natural Philosophy," *Journal of the History of Ideas* 18 (1957): 49–83.

4. "savage Hottentot in Afric": The Hottentots were a primitive southern African race of small stature and dark, yellowish complexion. In the eighteenth century the term *hottentot* was almost proverbial for a person of inferior intellect or culture (*OED*).

5. "remarks": According to the *OED*, one familiar eighteenth-century usage of *remarks* referred to the compiling of written notes or commentaries on one's experiences. It would have been unlike Fathom to take such trouble as this; but he must have mastered the art of recalling nearly everything he had witnessed or heard that might be useful to him.

6. "the *Dilettanti* club": The Dilettanti Society was formed in 1734 by a group of young self-styled connoisseurs who had completed the Grand Tour and wanted to encourage the arts in England. Weekly meetings of this club, for the first fifty years or so, were rather frivolous affairs of eating and drinking; but the society accomplished great good by subsidizing artists with money for study in Italy and with commissions for income. Charles Fox, David Garrick, and Sir Joshua Reynolds were among the most prominent members. See Turberville, 2:21–22, and Robert J. Allen, *The Clubs of Augustan London* (Cambridge: Harvard University Press, 1933), 100–101; and see below, n. 20.

7. "Oroondates": The hero of the French romance *Cassandre* (1642–45), by Gauthier de Costes de La Calprenède. This work had been popular in England for three generations despite its extravagances of length (ten volumes), language, character, and sentiment. Oroondates was seen, often mockingly, as the archetypal romantic hero, full of fine sensibility and gallantry. *Cassandre* is named by Addison as one of the works included in "Leonora's Library," *Spectator*, no. 37 (12 April 1711).

8. "the two squires": Sir Giles Squirrel and Sir Stentor Stile. See chaps. 22–24.

9. "art of gaming . . . regular system": Gambling was a national obsession among English people of all classes in the eighteenth century, and the effects upon the fortunes of young men victimized by sharpers were often ruinous; Smollett's picture of Roderick Random in decline after heavy losses (chapter 60) reflects one of the grim realities of eighteenth-century social life. Wealthy players often lost or won huge sums in a single evening at cards; see Turberville, 1:354–55, for reference to staggering losses suffered by some important people. Public outcry against excessive gambling, especially with dice, had been more or less continuous from the fourteenth century, but to little real avail. A series of harangues in the *Gentleman's Magazine* during 1750 and 1751 (20:196, 552, 567; 21:165) urged the condemnation of gaming as a national vice but failed in an attempt to persuade Parliament to outlaw it. Smollett renews his attack on gambling periodically throughout *Ferdinand Count Fathom*; see especially chap. 50, pp. 240–41 and n. 3.

10. "Indian Brachman": A Brahmin, or member of the highest priestly caste among the Hindus in India.

11. "Pythagoreans": In Greece, followers of the sixth-century mathematician and vegetarian in the practice of an ascetic life; in eighteenth-century England, followers of the strict vegetarian diet prescribed and popularized by Antonio Celestino Cocchi (1695–1758), physician and author of (in the English title) *The Pythagorean Diet of Vegetables only Conducive to the Preservation of Health* (London, 1745).

12. "glyster": Variant of *clyster*: an injection, enema, or suppository, introduced into the rectum to empty or cleanse the bowels.

13. "brilliant": A diamond of the finest cut or brilliancy.

14. "water": Natural luster, or purity.

15. "Fort St. George": The original East India Company settlement (founded 1639) on the southeastern coast of India.

16. "bespoke the refuse": Asked for first refusal, or first opportunity to purchase.

17. "indultos": Spanish derivation from medieval ecclesiastical Latin *indultum*. In Roman Catholic practice, an *indult* granted by the Pope to a bishop or other ecclesiastical official permitted a deviation from the common law of the church. In European economic history an indult or indulto was a duty paid on imported goods to the Spanish or Portuguese king (*OED*). Smollett uses the word *indultos* in a related sense meaning indulgences, thus hinting at Chaucer's Pardoner, who sells indulgences to people as easily duped in their zeal for salvation as Fathom's victims are in their desire to be fashionable.

18. "the Cremona mark": Cremona, a town in the northern Italian region of Lombardy, produced the finest violins in Europe during the seventeenth and eighteenth centuries. Both of the Amatis, and likewise Stradivarius and Guarnerius, lived and worked there. The Cremona mark added great value to the instrument bearing it, as it was thus assumed to have been made in the shop of one of the masters.

19. "vamped": Revamped, restored.

20. "virtuoso": Dilettante. Smollett uses the term *virtuoso* here in a way that reflects its contemporary debasement. This entire episode mocks the fashionable trifling of self-styled connoisseurs and virtuosi, thus anticipating what Bonnell Thornton, George Colman, William Cowper, and the other members of the Nonsense Club were shortly to do in their periodical *The Connoisseur* (1754–56). See Lance Bertelsen, *The Nonsense Club: Literature and Popular Culture, 1749–64* (Oxford: Clarendon Press, 1986), chap. 2.

21. "intaglios": Engravings or cuttings, usually in stone (*OED*).

22. "barber's bason . . . Etrurian Patera": Smollett alludes obliquely to the episode in *Don Quixote*, part 1, chapter 21, when Cervantes's knight errant mistakes a barber's brass basin for Mambrino's helmet. Etruria was an ancient country in central Italy (now Tuscany); a patera is a broad flat saucer or dish used for pouring libations, especially during ceremonies of sacrifice.

23. "Ancus Martius": The legendary fourth king of Rome in the very early history of the city; supposed to have ruled 640–616 B.C.

Chapter 33

1. "incog": Incognito.

2. "the nursery in Hyde-park": The area of the park just north of the Serpentine and near the Ring, a fashionable place for riding or walking. A circle of trees enclosed the space, making it safe and private. Many duels were fought here, including that between Captain Billy Booth and Colonel Bath in Fielding's *Amelia* (book 5, chapter 5). Timbs (2:589) provides a catalogue of Hyde Park duels involving important people.

3. "as a malefactor bound for Tyburn": Tyburn, located north and west of the old city of London near the site where the Marble Arch now stands, was the place of public execution for London and Middlesex from the mid-fourteenth century until 1783, when the site was changed to Newgate Prison (see chap. 36, n. 4). Grandstands or galleries accommodated the throngs who came to watch on hanging days, and the condemned prisoners were brought to the gallows in carts. Crowds gathered along the way when a celebrated criminal was being transported to Tyburn. Timbs (2:744) lists a great number of famous criminals and other noteworthies put to death there. Fielding's Jonathan Wild dies at Tyburn, and Tom Jones nearly comes to the same end. State criminals and other political

prisoners sentenced to death were usually executed not at Tyburn, but at Tower Hill.

4. "Hyde-park-corner": One of the main entrances to the park, located just opposite the present Buckingham Palace where Picadilly, Constitution Hill, Grosvenor Place, and Kensington Road converge. The "nursery" was only a short walk from this corner.

5. "winked and held out his cold iron": Smollett misquotes slightly from *Henry V* 2.1.7–8: "I dare not fight, but I will wink and hold out mine iron." Shakespeare's Corporal Nym, who speaks these lines, is an amusing cowardly rogue and a follower of Falstaff in *Henry V* and *The Merry Wives of Windsor*.

Chapter 34

1. "a certain great man": Possibly an allusion to Sir Robert Walpole, introduced to suggest a context for Fathom's newest adventure. The phrase "great man" was applied ironically to Walpole during his years as first minister by those who opposed him; it was used to mock him both for his supposedly corrupt ways of governing and for his scandalous private life as the keeper of a mistress and as the father of illegitimate children. Though Walpole fell from power in 1742 and then died in 1745, the phrase "great man" remained current as a satiric reference to public and private corruptions among wealthy and influential people.

2. "Celinda": Smollett seems to have had no particular literary allusion in mind when choosing this conventional name, which suggests that its owner is young, beautiful, and virginal, like a typical idealized heroine of romance.

3. "cherished": Fostered, nurtured (*OED*).

4. "projector": One who forms or designs an enterprise or undertaking. The word was often used to give a derogatory name to a schemer or, in some instances, to describe a planner of public projects of doubtful value, as in the "Projectors" of the Academy of Lagado in the third part of *Gulliver's Travels* (1726).

5. "the harp of Æolus": The Aeolian harp, a wooden sound box about three feet long and three inches deep, fitted with catgut strings to be sounded by the wind. Versions of the wind harp were ancient in tradition; King David's lyre, or kinnor, is supposed to have been played by the wind when hung above his bed at night. The "ingenious musician" Smollett refers to is his fellow Scotsman James Oswald (1711–69), who brought the instrument to a new perfection of design in the eighteenth century, making it very popular. James Thomson praised Oswald's version of the harp in *The Castle of Indolence* (1748), canto 1, stanza 40; and on 29 October 1751 *The General Advertiser* announced the following: "By Authority This Day is Published Aeolus's Harp—A new-invented musical instrument, which is played by the wind, as described by Mr. Thomson, in his *Castle of Indolence*. Sold only by the Inventor, J. Oswald, at his music-shop in St. Martin's church-yard."

Smollett knew Oswald (*Letters*, 6), who set to music several of his lyrics, including *The Tears of Scotland*. See Lewis M. Knapp, "Smollett's Verses and their Musical Settings in the Eighteenth Century," *Modern Language Notes* 46 (1931): 224–32; see also Otto E. Deutsch, "Poetry Preserved in Music: Bibliographical Notes on Smollett and Oswald, Handel, and Haydn," *Modern Language Notes* 63 (1948): 73–88.

6. "guittarres": Guitars. Smollett uses the term loosely here, apparently as a general name for stringed instruments played without a bow, whether with the fingers or by the wind.

7. "Philomel": Philomela; in Greek mythology, the daughter of Pandion, king of Athens. Tereus, king of Thrace and Philomela's brother-in-law, is supposed to have raped her and then cut out her tongue to prevent her from telling of his crime; the gods changed her into a swallow (in Roman tradition, a nightingale) whose song became famous for its sweetness and beauty.

8. "decayed": Faded, decreased, weakened.

9. "certain cordials": Fathom gives Celinda narcotics, probably laudanum or some other concoction derived from opium.

10. "philtre": A drug or potion.

11. "Bristol . . . near the Hot-well": Bristol, an important merchandising and shipping center located on the Avon in western England, was in the eighteenth century a spa noted for its warm springs, which were thought to have great value in the cure of consumption and other ailments. The Hot Well was located at the beginning of Saint Vincent's Parade in the village of Clifton, on a hill overlooking the city. Wealthy Bristolians had moved to Clifton to escape the bustle, noise, and odors of the streets below. According to Pierce Egan, *Walks through Bath* (Bath: Meyler, 1819), the air of Clifton was "remarkably pure and salubrious" and the village itself was justly known as "the Montpelier of England" (p. 248). Smollett, in *Present State*, 3:114, observed that "Nothing can be more pure and salutary than the air of these downs." But Smollett was doubtful about the medicinal value of the waters, here as well as in nearby Bath. In *Humphry Clinker*, Matthew Bramble writes from Bristol to complain that the waters, which contain nothing more than salt and calcium, have little or no effect on the human constitution (Matthew Bramble to Dr. Lewis, Hot Well, April 20); see George S. Rousseau, "Matt Bramble and the Sulphur Controversy in the XVIIIth Century: Medical Background of *Humphry Clinker*," *Journal of the History of Ideas* 28 (1967): 577–89. The medicinal properties of the waters at spas like Bristol and Bath were a subject of great controversy, to which Smollett made a significant contribution with his skeptical *Essay on the External Use of Water* (London, 1752). In 1822 the Hot Well and Pump at Bristol were demolished; the spa had always been plagued with pollution of the waters caused by the tidal movements of the Avon, and Bath had long since eclipsed Bristol as a center of fashion. See Keith Brace, *Portrait of Bristol*, new ed. (London: Hale, 1976), 100, and Egan, *Walks*, 244–45.

Chapter 35

1. "Æsculapius": The mythical sacred snake, incarnating the god of medicine, brought to Rome from Epidaurus in 293 B.C. following a plague; a cult of worship was established in the temple built in 291.

2. "victory . . . an old physician": See the similar episode in *Humphry Clinker* when Matthew Bramble meets "the famous Dr. L————n [Linden]" (Jery Melford to Sir Watkin Phillips, Hot Well, April 18). Dr. Diedrich Wessel Linden was a German physician and self-proclaimed authority on the medicinal uses of mineral waters, a subject about which he wrote extensively. Widely regarded as a quack during his eleven-year residence at Bristol, Linden participated along with Smollett (see chap. 34, n. 11) in the sulphur controversy of the 1750s. The ignorant, jabbering doctor mocked by Fathom (and Smollett) in the present scene may be a glancing portrait of Linden. For biographical information on this controversial physician see R. C. B. Oliver, "Diedrich Wessel Linden, M.D.," *National Library of Wales Journal* 18 (1974): 241–67.

3. "waters . . . moderate warmth": Fathom did not actually invent his theory concerning the heat of the springs and wells at English spas. The specious argument he develops reflects mockingly on a popular controversy over the nature of the elements first provoked by Thomas Burnet in the 1680s and afterward carried on by two groups of antagonists known as Vulcanists and Neptunists. See Marjorie Hope Nicolson, *Mountain Gloom and Mountain Glory* (New York: Columbia University Press, 1962), chap. 6.

4. "an Ægyptian fog": In Exodus 10:21-22 God commands Moses to inflict upon Egypt the plague of darkness, "even darkness *which* may be felt . . . ; and there was a thick darkness in all the land of Egypt three days."

5. "the character he thus acquired": By his victory in this episode Fathom establishes himself as a quack physician, a character of particular abhorrence to his author. Smollett has momentarily renewed his satiric attack against the medical profession, first launched in chapter 6 (see pp. 28–29 and n. 5). In chapters 50–53 he will take up the same attack again, but at much greater length.

6. "Materia medica": The principles and theories of diagnosis and treatment of diseases, as usually published in physicians' treatises.

7. "hypochondriac": Hypochondria was considered seriously as a real affliction in Smollett's time, though it was assumed then (as now) that the activity of the mind might be an effective part of its cure. Several times in his *Essay on the External Use of Water*, Smollett refers to the large number of hypochondriacs taking the waters at Bath, with good results arising largely from faith in the treatment. The "hypochondriac disorder," according to Barrow in the *Dictionarium Medicum*, is "of the spasmodic kind, incident to the nervous system, and principally exerts its tyranny under the ensiform cartilage . . . ." Dr. George Cheyne, in *The English Malady*, is more precise. Among the types of "nervous distempers," says Cheyne, are those "attended with *Spasms*, Cramps, Convulsions, or violent Contractions of

the Muscles. Of this kind are all of the Convulsive Tribe from *Hypochondriacal* and *Hysterical* Fits, or the Convulsions of the *Epileptick* kind . . ." (p. 17). See also chap. 30, n. 10.

8. "a toy-shop": A curiosity shop selling trinkets and knickknacks.

Chapter 36

1. "Mrs. Trapwell": The name is obviously theatrical, but no specific source for it has been identified. In his comedy *The Modern Husband* (1732), Fielding had made successful use of the same device of entrapment in a criminal conversation suit that Smollett employs in the present episode.
2. "bagnio": A bathing house used as a place of rendezvous by illicit lovers.
3. "legally divorced . . . woman he detested": In the eighteenth century a divorce could be granted only by Parliament and only to a man after adultery had been proven against his wife, usually in trials before the ecclesiastical and temporal courts. The number of divorces was small; only four had ever been granted before 1720, and between 1720 and 1750 one was granted only about every three years. After the middle of the century the number of divorces increased slightly, and by the 1770s there were four a year. See Randolph Trumbach, *The Rise of the Egalitarian Family: Aristocratic Kinship and Domestic Relations in Eighteenth-Century England* (New York: Academic Press, 1978), 155–60.
4. "Newgate": Newgate Prison. Located on the east side of the Old Bailey, or criminal courts building, the prison housed debtors as well as felons until 1813. Newgate was rebuilt after being burned in the Gordon Riots of 1780; the burning occurred partly because of the prison's history of unspeakably horrid conditions: "the prisoners crowded together in dark dungeons, where the foul air caused the 'gaol distemper,' of which they died by dozens in a day; and in 1750 the effluvia created a pestilence in the Sessions House, by which sixty persons died" (Timbs, 2:634).
5. "attorney . . . further delay": The charades and delays carried out by Fathom's attorney probably parallel those endured by Smollett in the Peter Gordon affair during the weeks preceding the publication of his novel. See the introduction, p. xxii and n. 17; and see chap. 37, p. 175 and n. 10.

Chapter 37

1. "whist": A popular card game, known as the "essentially English game of essentially English origin" (Strutt, 263). Edmond Hoyle's *Short Treatise on Whist*, first published in 1737, helped to popularize the game; this little book was many times reprinted (10th ed., London, 1750). Whist is played by four persons using fifty-

two cards dealt evenly in hands of thirteen. Cards are played in rotation; the object is for players to take tricks, thereby earning points.

2. "piquet": Or picquet, a popular card game for two persons using thirty-two cards, with points scored on groups or combinations of cards taken in tricks.

3. "hazard-box": The container used for playing the dice in the game of hazard; see chap. 24, n. 33.

4. "by the canal": By the means; literally, by the channel.

5. "trample upon . . . fellow-creatures": Smollett seems to refer to the damage his own reputation suffered as a result of gossip and slander sparked by his assault upon Peter Gordon and the ensuing lawsuit and trial. See below, n. 10.

6. "drum": An assembly of fashionable people, held in a private house. In *Advice* (1746), Smollett mocked this kind of social evening (lines 30–31); and then, in a note, he approved the term *drum* as appropriately descriptive of the "noise and emptiness of the entertainment." Fielding shared Smollett's scorn for such assemblies. In *Tom Jones* he defined a drum as a gathering of "well dressed Persons of both Sexes, most of whom play at Cards, and the rest do nothing at all; while the Mistress of the House performs the Part of the Landlady at an Inn, and like the Landlady of an Inn prides herself in the Number of her Guests, though she doth not always, like her, get any Thing by it" (*The History of Tom Jones, A Foundling*, ed. Martin C. Battestin [Middletown, Conn.: Wesleyan University Press, 1975], bk. 17, chap. 6, p. 898).

7. "blown": Slang, meaning "exposed" (*OED*).

8. "Westminster-hall": The eleventh-century hall of the old royal palace of England, where the following courts sat: Common Pleas, King's Bench, Chancery, and Exchequer (Timbs, 2:447). From the time of Henry III until the nineteenth century, Westminster Hall was a principal seat of justice; many famous trials were held there, including those of Charles I and Warren Hastings. Smollett himself was tried at the King's Bench in the Peter Gordon affair during January and February 1752. See below, n. 10.

9. "caitiff": A base, despicable villain (*OED*).

10. "endeavours . . . mislead the jury": In an angry letter of 23 February 1753, addressed to the lawyer Alexander Hume Campbell following the conclusion of the lawsuit lodged by Peter Gordon and Edward Groom, Smollett quotes this passage as the one likely to have offended Campbell most, thus provoking his vicious treatment of the novelist in the King's Bench (*Letters*, 25). Smollett's attack upon Gordon and Groom occurred during early November 1752, but the matter apparently did not come to trial until January 1753. The entire Trapwell episode of Smollett's novel (chapters 36 and 37) surely registers his worry and anger over the postponements, over the behavior of the attorneys in the case, and over the embarrassment and the financial hardship threatened by the suit. See the introduction, p. xxii and n. 17; and see chap. 36, p. 172 and n. 5.

11. "played booty": A gambling term meaning to play or act doubly and falsely, to

join secretly with confederates so as to victimize an unknowing participant in the game (*OED*).

12. "cast in fifteen hundred pounds": Fathom's offense, following his conviction, was reckoned at the value of £1500. This is the amount of the suit filed jointly against Smollett by Gordon and Groom.

13. "pettifogger": Technically, an attorney whose practice deals in petty cases; but the word also suggests the practitioner's use of rascally means.

14. "upon his parole": Upon his word of honor.

15. "goal": An uncommon but accepted eighteenth-century spelling of *gaol* or *jail*. Smollett later bases a clever pun on his choice of this same spelling; see chap. 40, p. 190 and n. 27.

16. "be puzzled": Be at a loss, confused, or bewildered.

17. "White's": White's Chocolate House, located in Saint James's Street, London, was founded in 1693 by Francis White, an Italian. The building burned in 1733 as King George II looked on; it was rebuilt in 1735 by Robert Arthur, whose father had taken over the business from the family of the original owners. White's had a reputation as a place for betting and gambling, and can be seen in Plate 4 of Hogarth's *Rake's Progress* (1735). White's Club was formed in 1736, and in years after, chess seems to have been the favored game for wagers. Robert Arthur removed the club to another building in 1755, and the Chocolate House was closed. See Bryant Lillywhite, *London Coffee Houses* (London: Allen and Unwin, 1963), 639–43.

18. "TROMPINGTON": Smollett derives this name from the French verb *tromper*, to deceive, cheat, impose upon.

Chapter 38

1. "East-India bonds": Bonds purchased as an investment in the East India Company. The sale of such bonds, or shares, was regulated by the government, and only those companies holding their charter from the state were allowed to raise capital in this way. This policy was established in the early 1720s by Sir Robert Walpole, following the nearly disastrous "South Sea Bubble." It was sound policy and it made for sound financial practice, partly because it assured a stable system of credit upon which the government depended heavily for the financing of the national debt.

2. "Garraway's": Garraway's Coffee House, situated in Exchange Alley, Cornhill, was founded as early as 1657–58, and by the mid-eighteenth century was best known for its association with the world of London business and banking. It was in use as the business address of traders, merchants, stockbrokers, exchange brokers, and bank directors. The old building, put up in about 1670 following the Great Fire of 1666, burned in 1748 but was quickly rebuilt. The House became

known for its real estate and commodity auctions in the later eighteenth century; it remained popular with wealthy clientele through most of the nineteenth century. See Lillywhite, *London Coffee Houses*, 216–24.

3. "deuce": The word is used here as the slang expression of an emphatic negative.

4. "ticket porters": Hired bearers of messages or warrants.

5. "the bills of mortality": The precincts of metropolitan London. Records of baptisms and burials were kept by parish clerks and published weekly. The "bills of mortality" included all metropolitan areas within and without the old city walls except the parishes of Marylebone, Saint Pancras, Paddington, Kensington, and Chelsea. See M. Dorothy George, *London Life*, 21–28.

6. "worth powder": Worth rushing after.

7. "quit cost": Equal the cost, thus clearing it.

8. "first table of the skull": The outer bony layer of the skull.

9. "trepan": A surgical saw used for removing small pieces of bone, especially from the skull.

10. "catchpole": A petty officer of justice (*OED*); here, a subordinate to the bailiff charged with executing the court writ against Fathom.

11. "premunire": Predicament. The word in its vernacular usage derived from the statute of Præmunire enacted in 1353 as a means of reducing the power of the French popes in English courts. By this statute, civil law took precedence over ecclesiastical law.

Chapter 39

1. "Bess Beetle": This servant's name implies that she is heavy, dull, and marked by prominent brows (*OED*); that is, she is beetle-browed.

2. "mountain": Mountain wine, a variety of Malaga, made from mountain grapes (*OED*).

3. "Pimlico": In the eighteenth century a fashionable area of London, located between Chelsea and Saint James's Park and noted for its pleasure gardens, ale breweries, and taverns (Timbs, 2:616). The "fat widow gentlewoman" has not been identified.

4. "hasty pudding": A pudding made of flour or oatmeal stirred in boiling water to the consistency of a thick batter.

5. "small beer": Weak beer.

6. "French hang-tang-dang": A comic mispronunciation of *intendant*, meaning steward or bailiff.

7. "eat his white feather . . . morsel of bread": The feather was a fashionable accessory for men's hats in eighteenth-century England and France (see Cunnington and Cunnington, 88). Here Smollett jokes at the expense of the Frenchman, a chevalier, by introducing a variation upon the expression "show the white feather," that is, show cowardice. This mad fellow is one of several eccentrics introduced

in the opening paragraph of the chapter whose portraits Smollett will develop later. The identities of these characters are discussed in subsequent notes to the portraits themselves.

8. "captain Minikin . . . great solemnity": *Minikin* was a familiar eighteenth-century term for a diminutive person (*OED*). No real-life model for the eccentric Captain Minikin has been identified, though it seems likely from context that Smollett had some specific person in mind. The figure of Minikin, the manner of his introduction of Fathom to the other inmates, and the scrupulous protocol he observes and recommends all suggest that Dickens may have taken Smollett's prison episode as the model for his opening chapters in *Little Dorrit*, where William Dorrit (the "father of the Marshalsea") behaves much as Minikin does here.

9. "*have seen . . . engendered*": Closely adapted from *As You Like It* 2.7.120–23:

> True it is that we have seen better days,
> And have with holy bell been knoll'd to church,
> And sat at good men's feasts, and wip'd our eyes
> Of drops that sacred pity hath engend'red.

10. "the *Canaille*": The mob, or rabble; French form of Italian *canaglia*.

11. "*profanum Vulgus*": "Odi profanum vulgus et arceo": "I hate the uninitiate crowd and keep them far away" (Horace *Odes* 3.1).

12. "*Stage . . . players*": Adapted from *As You Like It* 2.7.139–40:

> All the world's a stage,
> And all the men and women merely players . . . .

13. "*Vix ea nostra voco*": "I call these in no true sense our own" (Ovid *Metamorphoses* 13.141).

14. "spontoon": A combination spear and battle-axe, similar to a halberd, carried by English infantry officers beginning in about 1740 (*OED*).

15. "My only comfort . . . and mend": Smollett misquotes (deliberately, it appears) from Samuel Butler, *Hudibras* 2.1.39–42:

> His onely Solace was, That now
> His dog-bolt Fortune was so low,
> That either it must quickly end,
> Or turn about again, and mend.

This passage reflects upon Hudibras's plight as he is thrown into prison. Butler's "dog-bolt" means wretched, contemptible (*OED*); Smollett plays with the expression, giving it the added meaning of "doubled."

16. "our club . . . a sovereign prince": The time of the prison chapters of the novel (39–42) must be calculated at about 1738–39; but Smollett here begins to portray as members of Minikin's "club" a number of characters (Theodore of Corsica, Sir

Mungo Barebones, the French chevalier) whose interest dates from several years later. In these same chapters he makes topical reference to political events, popular controversies, and literary works of the late 1740s and early 1750s. These very obvious anachronisms, like the one introduced earlier in the novel (see chap. 29, p. 132 and n. 1), can hardly be the result of outright carelessness; instead, they underscore Smollett's indifference to any conventions of exact historical chronology in a fictional narrative.

17. "Theodore . . . a few hundred pounds": Theodore de Neuhoff (1690–1756) was an adventurer, a former king of Corsica, and an ally of England and Austria in the War of the Austrian Succession (see chap. 40, n. 26). Theodore traveled about Europe for several years attempting to raise money to restore his monarchy and assure his little country's independence. He failed in both endeavors. While in England he fell deeply into debt and was thrown into the King's Bench Prison for debtors in 1749. He languished there until his release less than a year before he died (see chap. 42, n. 4). Theodore's plight touched the popular imagination, and Smollett, who truly pitied him, apparently went to visit him in prison (Knapp, 157–58). In this and the following chapters of his novel, Smollett makes a sincere appeal on Theodore's behalf. Just a week after the appearance of *Ferdinand Count Fathom*, Horace Walpole (writing under the pseudonymn "Adam Fitz-Adam") published a call for public action to relieve the deposed, destitute, and imprisoned king (*The World*, no. 8, 22 February 1753). Six years later, in chapter 26 of *Candide* (1759), Voltaire caused his hero to meet Theodore in a Venetian lodging house where, though a free man, the hapless monarch still had found no release from squalid penury. The best treatment of the Corsican's life and misfortunes is André Le Glay, *Theodore de Neuhoff Roi de Corse* (Monaco: Imprimerie de Monaco, 1907).

18. "*Heu! quantum mutatus ab illo*": "Ei mihi, qualis erat! quantum mutatus ab illo": Ah me, what aspect was his! what changes now from his former self" (Aeneas, upon Hector's appearance to him in a dream, Virgil *Aeneid* 2.274).

19. "Spectator . . . thinking aloud": *Spectator*, no. 225 (17 November 1711): "for indeed the Talking with Friends is nothing else but thinking aloud."

20. "his Corsican majesty . . . a certain administration": The Pelham government had refused to support Theodore or grant him any kind of amnesty.

21. "*bienseance*": Fr. Good manners, propriety, decorum.

22. "few words are best": Proverbial; a variation upon "a word to the wise is sufficient" (see chap. 24, n. 25).

23. "major Macleaver": The major has not been identified; he is a stereotyped portrait of an Irish soldier.

24. "*mauvaise honte*": Fr. Self-consciousness or bashfulness.

25. "*derangée*": Fr. In disarray, disarranged, discommoded.

26. "a gentleman . . . grand scheme": Here Smollett initiates a satirical portrait of the Yorkshire-born theologian John Hutchinson (1674–1737), who had argued in

treatises and tracts that the Pentateuch was the source of all truth and all knowledge and that Newton's physics was therefore wrongheaded, even something of a sacrilege; the "certain Hebrew word" subsequently referred to is *Elohim*. Hutchinson's followers collected and published his works by subscription in 1748–49, generating a storm of controversy. Both Earl Wasserman and Tuvia Bloch have shown conclusively that Sir Mungo Barebones is a caricature of Hutchinson and his ideas; see Wasserman, "Smollett's Satire on the Hutchinsonians," *Modern Language Notes* 70 (1955): 336–37, and Bloch, "A Source for Smollett's Sir Mungo Barebones," *Notes & Queries*, n.s., 17 (1970): 95–96. Smollett's attitudes toward the character of Sir Mungo are actually quite complex, as the allusiveness of his name (Celtic for "my dear one") suggests. Saint Mungo (518?–603) was an evangelizing churchman and bishop of the Strathclyde Britons; the crypt at Glasgow Cathedral, where he is buried, is called Saint Mungo's in his honor. Smollett was no doubt aware of this association; and he must have known, too, that in the eighteenth century *mungo* was both a slang variant of *mongoose* and a pejorative term for a primitive, or Negro (*OED*). He seems deliberately to have used the name in yet another familiar sense to suggest the shabbiness of his character's appearance and the disordering of his mind: mungo was a kind of cloth (also called shoddy) made from deviled, or shredded, woolen rags.

27. "Lazarillo de Tormes": Smollett refers to *La Vida de Lazarillo de Tormes* (1554), the prototypical Spanish picaresque novel. The French chevalier resembles Lazarillo in that he is a beggarly outcast.

28. "Caricatura": The Italian *caricatura* is the term for grotesque visual portraiture, but by the middle of the eighteenth century the same term had been adopted in English to name verbal portraiture of a similar kind. Fielding refers directly to both meanings in the preface to *Joseph Andrews*. Smollett does likewise here, quite playfully if somewhat obliquely: the chevalier, in his physical presence, is a visual "Caricatura" in the eyes of Captain Minikin; Smollett's (or Minikin's) description of him, however, is a verbal caricature. For detailed discussion of Smollett's interest in this kind of portraiture see Milton Orowitz, "Smollett and the Art of Caricature," *Spectrum* 2 (1958): 155–67; and see also George M. Kahrl, "Smollett as a Caricaturist," in *Tobias Smollett: Bicentennial Essays Presented to Lewis M. Knapp*, ed. George S. Rousseau and Paul-Gabriel Boucé (New York: Oxford University Press, 1971), 169–200.

29. "long beard . . . verses": Probably this "chevalier" is Michel Descazeaux du Halley (1710–75), who was imprisoned for debt in the Fleet in 1746. The Swedish miniaturist Charles Banks drew his portrait, a ridiculous picture of Descazeaux as soldier, musician, and poet. From this fanciful rendering prints were made, and its subject's bearded face was very likely quite familiar to the public. A separate and quite popular satirical print by James MacArdell, the disciple of Sir Joshua Reynolds, was occasioned by Descazeaux's reputation for composing verses while he sat in prison. Like the Banks portrait, the MacArdell print suggests an element

of madness in the man, or at least disoriented folly. See F. G. Stephens, *Catalogue of Political and Personal Satires Preserved in the Department of Prints and Drawings in the British Museum* (1978), 3: pt. 1, no. 2852 (the Banks portrait) and no. 3092 (the MacArdell print). See also chap. 40, p. 190 and n. 23.

30. "under the shade . . . hours of time": *As You Like It* 2.7.111–12:

> Under the shade of melancholy boughs,
> Lose and neglect the creeping hours of time . . . .

31. "*degagée*": Fr. Easy freedom of manner.

32. "modern authors . . . Betsy Thoughtless": Thomas Mozeen's *Young Scarron* (London, 1752) is a farce written in imitation of Scarron's treatment of the strolling players in *Le Roman Comique*. The rest of the "modern" works mentioned are all fictional narratives; all had appeared recently and earned considerable popularity, and all had been noticed in the pages of Ralph Griffiths's *Monthly Review*, the first periodical to give real and consistent attention, serious or otherwise, to works of fiction. Smollett himself wrote at least three reviews for the *Monthly* between October 1751 and July 1752, and so he was no doubt familiar with the more important titles being handled by other members of Griffiths's stable (see Knapp, 134–36). The novels offered to Fathom by Captain Minikin, some of them possessing special interest to Smollett, are as follows:

> John Hill, *The Adventures of Mr. Loveill, Interspersed with many Real Amours of the Modern Polite World* (London, 1750). Sir John Hill, like Smollett a physician and man of letters, was among the early reviewers for the *Monthly*. The two men were acquainted and appear to have despised each other. Smollett, for his part, thought of Hill as a wretched, talentless hack. In an essay probably from Smollett's pen, the *Critical Review* for September 1758 dismissed Hill as "contemptible" (6:239). For full details of Hill's career, reputation, and relations with Smollett see G. S. Rousseau, ed., *The Letters and Papers of Sir John Hill, 1714–1775* (New York: AMS Press, 1982).
>
> John Hill, *The History of a Woman of Quality: Or, The Adventures of Lady Frail* (London, 1751). This is a spurious version of Lady Vane's scandalous story; the very day before it was published on 8 February 1751, Smollett arranged to have a notice inserted into the *General Advertiser* (7 February 1751) protesting that the only authorized memoirs of the "Lady of Quality" would be included in his own *Peregrine Pickle*, shortly to appear.
>
> John Hill, *The Adventures of Mr. George Edwards, a Creole* (London, 1751).
>
> Edward Kimber, *The Life and Adventures of Joe Thompson* (London, 1750).
>
> *An Apology for the Life of Bampfylde-Moore Carew* (London, 1749). The subject of this book was a real person whose life had already been written several times since 1745, always with aggrandizements and fictional embellishments. A notorious gypsy traveler, Carew was also known as the "King of the Beggars"; he

probably supplied the model for the gypsy monarch in an important episode of Fielding's *Tom Jones* (book 12, chapter 12).

Eliza Haywood, *The History of Miss Betsy Thoughtless* (London, 1751). Haywood, one of the most prolific and important minor novelists of the early eighteenth century, had begun her career with the passionate, throbbing *Love in Excess* (1719); the novels of her later phase, including *Betsy Thoughtless*, are more sober, reflecting the influence of her contemporaries Richardson, Fielding, and of course Smollett.

All of the titles mentioned by Captain Minikin were published more than a decade after the date of the events recorded in this chapter (see above, n. 16).

33. "contrast with his own": Smollett develops an obvious irony at Minikin's expense; the remainder of this sentence reveals that it is the captain's wardrobe (in a foppish style fashionable through the 1720s and 1730s, but not after) that is out of date, not Fathom's.

34. "the fashion of the cock": The fashion of the turned-up (cocked) brim of the hat.

35. "landing troops . . . disembarkation": Corsica had suffered under Genoese rule since the fifteenth century, and the island was in a state of revolt throughout the second quarter of the eighteenth century. The Corsicans received the support of the empire during the War of the Austrian Succession. The Austrians took Genoa in 1746, but their tyrannical impositions upon the people fomented rebellion and they were quickly expelled following an extremely bloody campaign. This action left Corsica at the mercy of the Genoese once again. See Smollett, *Complete History*, 4:681–82. In the present episode, King Theodore fantasizes about capturing Genoa, thus making possible the restoration of his kingdom in Corsica.

36. "a deal board table": A table made of board planks, usually of fir or pine, joined together in lengths of about six feet.

37. "ambuscades": Forces lying in ambush.

38. "battalia": Order of battle.

39. "Arrah!": An Irish interjection used by Smollett on other occasions as a sign of stereotyping; see, for example, the Irish characters of Rourk Oregan in *Roderick Random* (chapter 49) and O'Clabber in *The Reprisal* (1757).

Chapter 40

1. "unsaddled his nose": Removed his spectacles.

2. "half-penny ballads": The cheapest of the variety of song sheets and broadsides sold on the streets, most of them crudely printed and adorned with much-used woodcuts. This detail of the decor of Theodore's room suggests its squalor, though certainly his surroundings are superior to those of an ordinary prisoner.

3. "a truckle-bed": A trundle bed. Such a bed was provided with wheels that permitted it to be moved under another bed when not in use. In Theodore's prison

apartment, the bed is probably rolled into a corner so as to give more space during the daylight hours.

4. "Belisarius": A great general under the Byzantine emperor Justinian (see below, n. 6). Belisarius recaptured most of Italy from the Goths (A.D. 535–40), went successfully to war there again when the same enemy threatened once more, and was covered with glory for his triumphs. In 563 he was accused of plotting to overthrow Justinian and was imprisoned, blinded, and then reduced to beggary; he died at Constantinople in 565.

5. "*Date obolum Belisario*": The precise source for this proverbial phrase is unknown. Horace Walpole used the same words as the epigraph to his paper on Theodore for *The World*, 22 February 1753 (see chap. 39, n. 17). For an account of the legend of the disgrace and death of Belisarius, see Edward Gibbon, *The History of the Decline and Fall of the Roman Empire*, ed. J. B. Bury (London: Methuen, 1909), 4:459, n. 109. By the eighteenth century it had become commonplace to evoke the name of Belisarius in condemning the ingratitude of rulers or governments to their faithful servants. See, for example, *The Life and History of Belisarius, who Conquer'd Africa and Italy, with an Account of his Disgrace, The Ingratitude of the Romans, and a Parallel between Him and a Modern Heroe* (London, 1713), 56. This same work was reprinted in 1722 as *The Life of Belisarius A Roman General under Justinian the Great. With Some Parallels to the Late Duke of Marlborough.*

6. "Justinian": Byzantine emperor A.D. 527–65, praised by historians for his land and tax reforms and for his codification of law. He died at Constantinople in 565.

7. "their former friend . . . their own service": Again Smollett severely criticizes the Pelham administration for cruel treatment of Theodore (see chap. 39, p. 184 and n. 20). Horace Walpole, in his paper for the *World*, echoes Smollett's words: "This island ought to be as much the harbour of afflicted majesty, as it has been the scourge of offending majesty."

8. "scullion": The domestic servant assigned to menial kitchen duty and thus considered of the lowest order in a household or other establishment.

9. "differences between the emperor and the queen of Spain": For years after the signing of the Quadruple Alliance in 1718, Philip V of Spain and his Italian consort Queen Elizabeth Farnese conducted negotiations with Charles VI of Austria, attempting to guarantee the reversion of Parma and Tuscany to Spanish rule in exchange for the granting of Sicily to the Hapsburgs. Since Elizabeth Farnese wished her son Don Carlos to have the rule of Parma (her native country) and Tuscany, she was actively involved in the diplomacy and was apparently quite unscrupulous. There was also an unsuccessful campaign to marry Don Carlos to the emperor's daughter, the Archduchess Maria Theresa, who was Charles VI's designated successor. The territorial diplomacy was more productive, and both countries had their wishes; but when the War of the Polish Succession ended in 1735, Don Carlos reversed matters and exchanged Parma and Tuscany for the two Sicilies (*i.e.*, Sicily and Naples). See Williams, 172–73, 206. A spurious volume called *Memoirs of Elizabeth Farnese* (London, 1746) had intrigued English

readers by its supposed revelations of the queen's machinations during the long seesaw negotiations with the Austrian emperor; judging from the allusion, Smollett may have been assuming his audience's familiarity with this sensational book, which was several times reprinted.

10. "a jockey straight boot": A high-topped boot for riding.

11. "an half jack": A short jacket.

12. "trunk breeches": Or trunk-hose; full, baglike breeches extending from the waist to the lower thighs and sometimes stuffed with wool or other fabric. Trunk-hose were commonly worn by European men in the sixteenth and early seventeenth centuries, but by Smollett's day were rarely seen in England and were considered very old-fashioned.

13. "disordered his brain . . . temporal affairs": Smollett here renews his mocking attack on the theological controversialist John Hutchinson (see chap. 39, pp. 184–85 and n. 26). Hutchinson had crazily maintained that the Hebrew word *Elohim* proved the unity of the Trinity, that it was the primary source and repository of the divine promise to redeem all mankind, and that the proper understanding of the word he had reached through philological analysis revealed its centrality to Christian doctrine. Hutchinson's disciples, principally Alexander Catcott and Julian Bate, vigorously promoted his argument in a series of pamphlets answered with equal vigor by more orthodox divines and controversialists. See Wasserman, "Smollett's Satire on the Hutchinsonians."

14. "Moses on the Mount": Moses received the Ten Commandments from God on Mount Sinai (Exodus 20:2–17; Deuteronomy 5:6–21). Smollett possibly refers simultaneously to this great biblical event and to the account of the moment when Moses, standing atop Mount Pisgah, was told by God to look over the land of Canaan, where the promised deliverance of the Israelites would be fulfilled (Deuteronomy 3:27, 34:1–4). Both allusions seem to suit the character and the ambitions of Sir Mungo; the latter allusion carries an implied ironic comparison with the ambitious schemer Fathom, who had earlier looked upon England as his "promised land" (see chap. 19, p. 77 and n. 2; and chap. 27, p. 127 and n. 5).

15. "malaxed": Softened.

16. "bouillé": Fr. Gruel. Smollett probably meant to write *bouilli*, the proper word to describe the dish Sir Mungo has made with his mutton chops, which he appears to have boiled.

17. "a brindled hue": Mixed tawny and brown, but with the colors appearing in streaks.

18. "like Aaron's, to his middle": The chevalier's beard resembles that of Aaron, as described in Psalms 133:2: "Aaron's beard: that went down to the skirts of his garments."

19. "blue drab": Linen or woolen fabric, dyed blue.

20. "vellum button-holes": Buttonholes cheaply repaired with vellum, a tailor's cloth (or sometimes parchment) used for tracing.

21. "rusty": Shabby, worn.

22. "ramellie": Ramillie, a style of tying the hair or wig into a long plait or tail with a bow at the top and bottom; so called after Ramillies in Belgium, the scene (in 1706) of one of Marlborough's great victories during the War of the Spanish Succession. See Cunnington and Cunnington, 90.

23. "a white feather": See chap. 39, n. 7. By adding the details in this paragraph, Smollett expands upon the caricature of the chevalier Descazeaux begun earlier (see chap. 39, p. 185 and nn. 28, 29).

24. "cardinal Fleury": André-Hercule Fleury (1653–1743), powerful chief minister and diplomat during the reign of Louis XV, his former pupil. Together Fleury and Sir Robert Walpole, prime minister of England, pursued joint policies that kept both France and England out of any major wars for more than two decades. Walpole was severely criticized for pursuing such a close working relationship with his French counterpart.

25. "like the prophet . . . in his own country": Following a hostile reception upon his return to the synagogue in Bethlehem, Jesus said to his disciples: "A prophet is not without honour, save in his own country, and in his own house" (Matthew 13:57). The chevalier's allusion to Christ's words carries with it an unconscious irony that underscores his folly.

26. "agreement . . . a single combat": Smollett alludes to the War of the Austrian Succession. At the time during which the events now unfolding may be judged to occur in Fathom's career (see chap. 39, n. 16), the "late emperor" referred to (Charles VII) would not yet have been crowned. The war erupted after the electors of Bavaria, Prussia, and Saxony broke pledge with the Pragmatic Sanction of 1720, an agreement that Charles VI had hoped would guarantee the uncontested succession of his daughter Maria Theresa to the imperial throne of Austria. When Charles died in 1740, the German princes challenged Maria Theresa's title as empress, though they could not dispute her claims as queen of Hungary. They invaded the Hapsburg dominions, and soon all of Europe was embattled in a bloody conflict made exceedingly complicated by the collision of many dynastic interests. France and Spain joined on the side of the Germans; and a reluctant England, already engaged in a trade war with Spain (begun in 1739 as the "War of Jenkins' Ear"), sent funds and troops to the aid of Maria Theresa. On 12 February 1742 Albert, elector of Bavaria, was proclaimed Emperor Charles VII, but the tide was already running the Hapsburg way. When Charles VII died in 1745 the crown reverted to Austria, and Maria Theresa's husband, Francis, duke of Lorraine, became emperor. By 1748, after huge expenditures of life and money, the antagonists were unanimous in their readiness for peace, and a treaty was concluded at Aix-la-Chapelle during the final months of that year. This agreement ended the war but left all of the involved powers dissatisfied. (See Williams, 207–70 passim, for accounts of the participation of the English government and armies in the war.)

27. "the author's never-failing goal": Smollett alternates freely between the common

eighteenth-century spellings of "jail," or "gaol," or "goal." Here he obviously chooses the slightly less familiar form of "goal" so as to introduce a pun on the fortunes of writers.

Chapter 41

1. "the art of transmuting baser metals into gold": Alchemy. In this paragraph Smollett further satirizes the Hutchinsonians (see chap. 39, pp. 184–85 and n. 26; and chap. 40, pp. 188–89 and n. 13). Hutchinson and his followers answered Newton's *The Chronology of Ancient Kingdoms Amended* (London, 1728) with a chronology of their own, based on the Pentateuch instead of Newton's astronomical data; see Frank Manuel, *The Eighteenth Century Confronts the Gods* (1959; reprint, New York: Atheneum, 1967), especially 85–103, for discussion of Newton's theories of time and ancient history. The somewhat mystical Hutchinsonians did not dabble directly in alchemy, though they speculated about the alchemical powers arising from a right understanding of *Elohim* and the Pentateuch. Newton had attempted experiments with the properties of metals; see R. J. Forbes, "Was Newton an Alchemist?" *Chymia* 2 (1949): 27–36.

2. "*Argumentum ad hominem*": Latin. Literally, an attack directed at an antagonist's character instead of an argument refuting his ideas. Smollett plays with the phrase, using it in the context of a challenge to mortal combat.

3. "the sword of Guy earl of Warwick": Guy of Warwick was the subject of a popular verse romance of the early fourteenth century, much admired in the eighteenth century. A soldier and crusader, Guy was supposed to have performed many heroic deeds before becoming a hermit. His sword, or the weapon thought to have been his, was on display in Warwick Castle. The legend of Guy was accepted as largely true, and the earls of Warwick claimed descent from him. See Ronald S. Crane, "The Vogue of 'Guy of Warwick' from the Close of the Middle Ages to the Romantic Revival," *PMLA* 30 (1915): 125–94.

4. "the sword of the Lord and of Gideon": Judges 7:18, 20. Gideon, an unwilling servant when called by God, led the Israelites to triumphant victories over the Midianites. The greatest of these began with the cry quoted here but was actually fought by a tiny army whose only weapons were empty jars, flaming torches, and trumpets. Sir Mungo's apparent ignorance of the facts of Gideon's story, which is not told in the Pentateuch, doubles the irony of the comparison he proclaims in his oath.

5. "By Heaven . . . the locks—": Quoted from *1 Henry IV* 3.3.201–5. Captain Minikin's implied comparison between himself and Hotspur is ludicrous, though the two characters do share something of the same extravagant conception of honor.

6. "*je ne sçai quoy*": "je ne sais quoi": "a certain something," "I don't know just what." The French phrase was popularly associated with Pope's definition in the *Essay on*

Criticism: "*Grace* beyond the Reach of Art" (line 155). Captain Minikin is thus being unintentionally ironic.

7. "a simper": An affected smile, or smirk.

8. "morceau": Fr. A short composition, either literary or musical.

9. "in *cuerpo*": Literally, bare from the waist up; but sometimes (as here) used humorously to mean entirely naked.

10. "birth-day suit": According to the 1933 and 1972 supplements to the *OED*, this is the first recorded use of a now proverbial expression.

11. "bagnio": In this context, simply a public bath house; but see chap. 36, n. 2.

12. "negro": In this usage the word means crude, stupid, primitive.

13. "an English carman": A chairman. The men who bore the sedan chairs of fashionable people through the streets were a rough, argumentative breed noted for their brawling.

14. "funk one another": Blow smoke upon each other.

15. "*Assa fœtida*": Variant of *asafœtida*, the gum used medicinally as an antispasmodic; also known as "silphium" in the eighteenth century. See below, n. 18.

16. "lieutenant's": Smollett slips here; Minikin is a captain, not a lieutenant.

17. "the succedaneum": Latin. The substitute. Smollett puns here, for in eighteenth-century medical parlance the term referred to the practice of replacing one drug of superior potency with another of inferior effects.

18. "drug . . . hypochondriac disorder": Barrow observes that "silphium" or "*assa foetida*," which he also calls "Devil's dung," has "a very strong fetid smell" and is "an excellent remedy in all hysteric disorders, whether only smell'd to, or mix'd with what is taken inwardly. It is, also, reckoned a good sudorific [*i.e.*, a diaphoretic, causing sweats] and strengthens the stomach."

19. "rotten": Corrupt, or low.

Chapter 42

1. "Champaigne": A province in northeast France; noted for its sparkling wines during the eighteenth century, but still more important as a commercial center. France held this territory safely throughout the War of the Polish Succession. It was during this war that Fathom and Renaldo had become separated in chapter 19.

2. "coarse": Variant of *corpse*. Smollett's spelling of this word perhaps reflects eighteenth-century pronunciation; the *p* may still have been silent, as it was originally (*OED*).

3. "janitor": In the eighteenth century this term still retained its original meaning as a name for a doorkeeper or porter (*OED*).

4. "act of parliament . . . insolvent debtors": The number of debtors held in prisons during the eighteenth century was enormous. By some accounts the figure

reached sixty thousand in 1716. The next decades brought a decline in the total, following minor reforms and the passage of several Insolvent Acts; but Dr. Johnson's estimate of twenty thousand in 1759 (*Idler*, no. 38, 6 January 1759) was probably much too low. The principal reformers, beginning in the 1730s, were William Hay and General James Oglethorpe. Oglethorpe pressed very hard for more liberal laws in 1754, and new acts of Parliament were subsequently passed, but without great effect; see Williams, 135–36. A measure approved in April 1755 permitted the release of Theodore of Corsica from the King's Bench Prison just months before his death; see chap. 39, n. 17.

5. "canvassing": Discussion, bargaining.
6. "*penetrable stuff*": Hamlet speaks the following lines to his mother the queen upon finding that it is Polonius he has killed behind the curtain in her apartment (3.4.34–36):

> Leave wringing of your hands. Peace, sit you down,
> And let me wring your heart, for so I shall
> If it be made of penetrable stuff . . . .

7. "the court of Vienna": At the time of the publication of *Ferdinand Count Fathom* in 1753, the court of Francis I, the Austrian emperor. But the events unfolding at this point in the novel must be dated in the late 1730s, when Charles VI was in the final years of his long reign. See chap. 39, n. 16.

Chapter 43

1. "*What's bred . . . the flesh*": An old English proverb, first recorded in the late-fifteenth-century period of Caxton and Malory (*ODEP*).
2. "Monimia . . . orphan situation": Monimia is the beautiful, ill-fated heroine of Thomas Otway's verse tragedy, *The Orphan: or, The Unhappy-Marriage* (1680). This play was among the most frequently performed during the middle years of the eighteenth century. It was also extremely popular in published form during the same period. William Strahan's ledgers for the years 1738–85 record the printing of nine thousand copies in three editions; see William B. Todd, *New Adventures Among Old Books* (Lawrence: University of Kansas Press, 1958), 16. Over the next several chapters, Smollett develops numerous broad parallels with the melancholy, dramatic story of Otway's orphan. The original Monimia is loved by two brothers, the twin sons of her guardian; she secretly marries one of them and then is deceived by the other into a fatal assignation, following which all three lovers die by their own hands as a desperate consequence of mistakes, deceit, and jealousy.

3. "every feature . . . ravishing and delightful": Smollett's idealized description of a virtuous young woman is most conventional, though rhetorically it achieves a certain effect by presenting the clearest visual picture the novel affords of pure, complete physical and spiritual beauty. Smollett had done much this same kind of thing with the introduction of Narcissa in chapter 39 of *Roderick Random*; and see Fielding's description of Sophia Western in *Tom Jones*, book 4, chapter 2.

4. "no difficulty . . . had he alone been concerned": In letters dated about a year before the publication of *Ferdinand Count Fathom*, Smollett had approached friends with anxious appeals for assistance closely paralleling Renaldo's. To his fellow Scottish physician Dr. William Hunter he wrote, sometime in late 1751 or early 1752: "I am at present, in consequence of little Demands which I have put off to the last day of Procrastination, in absolute necessity of eight or ten pieces [*i.e.*, guineas], without which I can no longer answer the Occasions of my Family. This Declaration is by God himself! like wormwood and Brimstone to me, and were myself alone concerned, I would rather perish than have Recourse to such beggarly Sollicitation" (*Letters*, 17).

5. "equity": Fair-mindedness and sense of due recompense. The emperor referred to so favorably here is probably Francis I, though at the time of the events treated in this chapter (1738–39) Charles VI was still alive.

Chapter 44

1. "hap": Luck, or fortune.
2. "infringe": Frustrate, or defeat.
3. "monied men . . . their club": This "club" is of the sort that regularly met at Garraway's Coffee House, which may be the setting Smollett had in mind for the scene described here. See chap. 38, n. 2.
4. "mortgage at cent. per cent.": Borrow money at interest equal to the principal.
5. "obumbrated": Overshadowed or darkened (*OED*).
6. "varlet": A low, mean, knavish person; a rogue or rascal (*OED*). By Smollett's time, the word was archaic.
7. "Mr. Ferret": A ferret is a red-eyed, long-snouted rodent; the same name is also given to a European species of half-tamed polecat used to drive rabbits and rats from their holes. In the eighteenth century the name was conventionally applied to pawnbrokers and usurers in order to characterize them as low and mean. The knavish quack physician of *Sir Launcelot Greaves* is called Dr. Ferret.
8. "*Bray a fool . . . never be wise*": Proverbs 27:22: "Though thou shouldest bray a fool in a mortar among wheat with a pestle, *yet* will not his foolishness depart from him." Here, *bray* means "to pound" (*OED*).
9. "on the back of": After, as a consequence of.

Chapter 45

1. "denouncing": Announcing, declaring.
2. "nice": Delicate, requiring tact and caution.
3. "blew the coals of her jealousy": The malicious ingenuity of Fathom's relentless manipulations of Monimia and later Renaldo, and especially his alertness to their capacities for jealousy, suggests that Smollett may have had in mind as a model Shakespeare's Iago, the villain of *Othello*. Robert Donald Spector, *Tobias George Smollett*, 92–94, argues that Smollett deliberately conceived his "anti-hero" Fathom as a spiritual descendant of Iago.
4. "an air of disgust": An appearance of serious dissatisfaction, as opposed to expressions of sorrow or despair.
5. "cordial": A medicine, usually in the form of a beverage, given as a restorative. Smollett continues the medical metaphor through the remainder of the sentence, referring obliquely to the insidious dangers of certain popular drugs and medicines such as Dr. Joshua Ward's "Drop and Pill," which was made from an extremely virulent concoction called Glass of Antimony; see Brookes, *The General Dispensatory*, 332, 367–68. See chap. 53, p. 259 and n. 2 for a more specific allusion to Ward.

Chapter 46

1. "deprecate": Avert by pleading, as with a prayer (*OED*).
2. "a magazine": A provision or supply, as kept in a magazine or storehouse. The metaphor is a military one, which is very often the case in Fathom's (and Smollett's) language of love and sentiment.
3. "the fatal pledge": The reference is to the picture of Monimia's father, who is later (chapter 64) revealed to be Don Diego de Zelos, the noble Castilian whom Fathom had robbed upon departing from Paris (chapter 27). In the picture Don Diego is without the Persian disguise worn in Paris, and this perhaps accounts for Fathom's failure to recognize him.
4. "the poisonous sight of the basilisk": The basilisk, a fabulous reptile of classical mythology, drove away all other serpents with its hissing and, more to the point here, killed with its look.
5. "avenging minister of heaven": This phrase cannot be certainly identified, but possibly it alludes to Saint Paul's description of Christ in Romans 13:4: "For he is the minister of God to thee for good. But if thou do that which is evil, be afraid; for he beareth not the sword in vain: for he is the minister of God, a revenger to *execute* wrath upon him that doeth evil."

6. "I will mangle . . . fowls of the air!": Throughout this speech Renaldo plays Othello to Fathom's Iago; the picture of Monimia's father recalls Desdemona's handkerchief. See chap. 45, pp. 210–11 and n. 3.

7. "Mentor": Generic name for a guide or adviser, derived from Greek mythology. In the *Odyssey* of Homer, Mentor is friend and counselor to Odysseus and teacher to his son. The name gained new currency from Archbishop Fénelon's prose romance of *Télémaque* (1699–1700), an extremely popular work frequently translated into English. Smollett himself seems to have prepared one translation, published posthumously in 1776; see Lewis M. Knapp, "Smollett's Translation of Fénelon's *Télémaque*," *Philological Quarterly* 44 (1965): 405–7. Fénelon developed the character of Mentor as wise teacher and surrogate parent to the young Telemachus during his travels in search of his father.

8. "skirts": Outskirts.

9. "madam la Mer": The French word for sea is *mer*; an English variant is *mere* (*OED*). Smollett may be using the word in its obsolete sense as "mother" (in the variant *mere*), a common eighteenth-century term for a bawd or madam.

10. "a certain noted coffee-house": Smollett appears to mean White's Chocolate House. See chap. 37, n. 17.

11. "the part of Monimia . . . on the stage": Probably Smollett refers to a performance at the Haymarket Theatre on Thursday, 18 October 1750, when (according to published announcements) the parts of Polydore, Serina, and Monimia were taken by "a gentleman and two gentlewomen who never appeared on any stage."

12. "the Huguenot": A French Protestant. The Huguenots, as Calvinists or members of the Reformed Communion, threatened the French Catholic Church and were often embattled or even persecuted in retaliation. The Edict of Nantes (1598) had guaranteed their religious freedom and rights of worship, but Louis XIV signed a royal order revoking the edict on 18 October 1685. Thereafter the Huguenots were subject to fierce persecution; many were driven into exile and found refuge in the neighboring Protestant kingdom of England.

13. "damp": Dazing, or stupefaction.

Chapter 47

1. "whet": A dram of liquor, taken as an appetizer; but also an inducement, as to desire or action as well as appetite (*OED*). In the present context of scenes introducing rapacious usurers, Smollett puns by allowing the word to be understood in both senses.

2. "Plutus": In Greek mythology, the son of Demeter and god of wealth; also associated with Hades, or the underworld.

3. "congees": Ceremonial bows; an archaic anglicism derived from the French word *congé* (*OED*).

4. "*petit maitre*": Fr. *petit maître*. A dandy or fop; an effeminate man.

5. "roll": Enroll or enlist.

6. "half-pay": The reduced allowance paid to military officers no longer in active service or permanently retired. This man probably had followed a common practice of selling his commission to another who then began to draw the half-pay allowance.

7. "my endeavours . . . successful": Smollett may have had in mind some particular person as the model for this foppishly genteel usurer. If so, the identity of the person is unknown. The kind of career described in the brief history here concluded was uncommon in the eighteenth century, but not unheard of.

8. "*sine qua non*": Latin. Literally, "without which nothing"; as used in this context, the phrase only underscores the moneylender's absolute requirement that Renaldo remain in the country.

9. "blessed himself": Swore, as in an impious prayer that he might be preserved.

10. "descendants of Judah": The Jews.

11. "Tho' they lie . . . avarice, fraud, and extortion": Renaldo's words reflect attitudes inflamed by controversy over the imminent proposal in Parliament for the naturalization of the Jews. In England at the time, Jews still suffered from severe religious, political, and legal discrimination; the traditional barriers to their ownership of land drove them into commerce, hence their high visibility in the trades of money-lending and stock-jobbing. As early as 1690 Sir Joshua Child, chairman of the East India Company, had called for the naturalization of the Jews, arguing (in his *Discourse about Trade*) that such a change would promote the economic health of the nation. John Toland's *Reasons for Naturalizing the Jews* (1714) humanely urged more liberal laws concerning property and inheritances. A Naturalization Act was finally passed in June 1753 following a great storm of protest both in the Parliament and on the streets of London and other cities. The new law provided more generously for foreign Jews seeking citizenship than for British natives and it left religious disabilities in place, but it did ease the statutes governing property and the legal privileges of citizenship. Reaction to the measure led to a move for its repeal in 1754. See Cecil Roth, *A History of the Jews in England*, 3d ed. (Oxford: Clarendon Press, 1964), chaps. 8 and 9, for full discussion of the movement toward naturalization from the Restoration onward.

12. "salt rheum . . . without intermission": The Jew weeps, a certain sign of his good heart. Ian Campbell Ross, in "Smollett and the Jew Bill of 1753," *American Notes & Queries* 16 (1977): 54–55, argues unconvincingly that Smollett's sympathetic portrait of Joshua Manasseh has little or nothing to do with the naturalization controversy. The treatment of Joshua actually seems to represent a benevolent contribution to debate over the issue. Certainly Smollett's picture of a Jew shed-

ding sentimental tears is most unusual in the literature of his day, and it marks a considerable departure from his negative treatment of the Jews in *Roderick Random* (chapters 7 and 52) and *Peregrine Pickle* (chapters 53–56); see Tuvia Bloch, "Smollett and the Jewish Naturalization Bill of 1753," *American Notes & Queries* 6 (1968): 116–17. The character of the munificent Joshua, as developed in the remaining chapters of the novel, may have been inspired by a similar figure in Christian Gellert's *Das Leben der Swedischen Gräfin von G****, which appeared in English translation during March 1752 and received favorable notice that same month in the *Monthly Review* (6:231–32); see Knapp, 154, and H. R. S. Van Der Veen, *Jewish Characters in Eighteenth Century English Fiction and Drama* (Groningen-Batavia: J. B. Wolters, 1935), 41–46.

Chapter 48

1. "Her countenance . . . *smiling at grief*": *Twelfth Night* 2.4.112–15:

> . . . she pin'd in thought,
> And with a green and yellow melancholy
> She sate like Patience on a monument,
> Smiling at Grief. Was this not love indeed?

2. "sensible": Perceived or registered by the senses.

3. "Perhaps . . . once happy Monimia": It is not clear why Smollett causes Monimia to make such a remark as this, since she has apparently never discussed the identity of her father with Fathom, not even when handing over his picture to be pawned; see chap. 46, pp. 216–17 and n. 3. This is apparently another instance of haste or carelessness on the author's part; Smollett compounds the blunder later (see chap. 67, p. 348 and n. 4).

4. "his mediatrix . . . her lodger": Many of Smollett's first readers would doubtless have recognized a parallel between Fathom's use of Madam la Mer and Lovelace's arrangements with Mrs. Sinclair in Richardson's *Clarissa*. The sturdy resolution of the languishing Monimia recalls in a more general way the pious resistance of Clarissa Harlowe to the wiles and threats of Richardson's demonic libertine, while Fathom closely resembles Lovelace in the role-playing and deceptions of his campaign against Monimia's virtue. Smollett may well have been deliberately trading on the continued popularity of Richardson's acclaimed novel, first published in 1747–48. See also chap. 49, pp. 234–35 and n. 2.

5. "several persons of note": Samuel Pegge, in *Anonymiana; or, Ten Centuries of Observations on Various Authors and Subjects* (London: J. Nichols, 1809), 287–88, identifies the four self-made men described in this paragraph as Philip Yorke, earl of Hardwicke; Henry Fox, Lord Holland; Mr. Aislabie; Mr. Mann. Yorke (1690–

1764), the son of a Dover attorney, rose to become lord chancellor during the administration of Sir Robert Walpole and was created earl of Hardwicke in 1754. Fox (1705–74), younger son of Sir Stephen Fox of Chiswick, held several high cabinet appointments under Walpole and his successors and in 1763 was named Baron Holland. John Aislabie (1670–1742) was the son of the principal registrar of the archiepiscopal court of York; he became a commissioner of the admiralty, treasurer of the navy, and chancellor of the exchequer before being expelled from the House of Commons for his disreputable part in the South Sea Bubble disaster. Horace Mann (1701–86), whose father was a London merchant, became envoy to Florence and was knighted for his service in 1755; he carried on a voluminous correspondence with Horace Walpole.

6. "consumptive condition": Almost a medical pun, suggesting only that Monimia's funds have been nearly exhausted or consumed.

Chapter 49

1. "young Tarquin": Legend has it that Sextus, son of the tyrannical Tarquinus Superbus, supposed seventh king of ancient Rome (c. 534–510 B.C.), ravished the beautiful Lucretia; she then took her own life, and public outrage caused the expulsion of the Tarquins from Rome.

2. "his sword . . . the point to his breast": This episode echoes and reverses the scene in Richardson's *Clarissa* when the heroine, pressed by her would-be seducer Lovelace, threatens to kill herself with a pen-knife (Mr. Lovelace to John Belford, Esq., Saturday, June 24).

3. *"they suffered not . . . too roughly"*: Adapted from *Hamlet* 1.2.139–42:

> So excellent a king, that was to this
> Hyperion to a satyr, so loving to my mother
> That he might not beteem the winds of heaven
> Visit her face too roughly . . . .

4. "England . . . the house of God": Possibly an oblique reference to the Test Act of 1673, which denied certain privileges of worship as well as citizenship to those not confirmed in the Church of England. The strictures of the act were applied with especial force to Roman Catholics. The context suggests, however, that Smollett may also be referring to the familiar practice, begun in the sixteenth century, of letting pews to families, who then held exclusive possession of them.

5. "Madam Clement": This name appears to have no connection with Saint Clement the martyr; rather, it simply suggests mildness, humanity, and mercy.

6. "marriage at the Fleet": See chap. 7, p. 32 and n. 3.

7. *"warble their native wood-notes wild"*: Adapted from Milton's lines on Shakespeare in *L'Allegro* (133–34):

> Or sweetest Shakespeare, Fancy's child,
> Warble his native wood-notes wild.

8. "Kensington Gravel-pits": The ground in the Notting Hill Gate area of Kensington had been dug for superb gravel since the early seventeenth century, and some of the pits remained as ponds until well into the nineteenth century. A chalybeate spring, producing water with high iron content, was much valued for its supposed medicinal value. See *Survey of London*, ed. F. H. W. Sheppard et al., vol. 37, *Northern Kensington* (London: Athlone, 1973), 38; and see John Bowack, *Antiquities of Middlesex* (London, 1705), 20.

9. "such monsters . . . public view": For the second time in this novel, Smollett repeats a conventional apology for rogue narrative; see the dedication, p. 5 and nn. 10, 11.

Chapter 50

.. "the jail infection": The "gaol distemper" or fever; see chap. 36, n. 4. Smollett is punning here.

2. "a certain gaming-house": White's Chocolate House; see chap. 37, n. 17.

3. "spirit of play . . . like a pestilence": Smollett here echoes his earlier attacks on gambling as a disastrous and disgraceful vice; see especially chap. 32, p. 148 and n. 9. *The Connoisseur*, no. 15 (9 May 1754) reported several extravagant wagers similar to those described in the next paragraph.

4. "Malacca in the East-Indies": A region of what is now Malaysia, located on the west coast of the South Malay Peninsula. An early center of the East India spice trade, Malacca was held by the Dutch in the eighteenth century and was a center of shipping and wealth. The frenzied behavior described subsequently in this paragraph is known as running amok; it is indigenous to Malayan culture and was the subject of much curiosity among Westerners in Smollett's time.

5. "ancient Lacedemonians . . . way": Lacedæmon, or Sparta, the ancient Greek city-state of Dorian origin, engaged in the Peloponnesian Wars (460–404 B.C.) with Athens. In describing the practice of the Malayans in the beginning of their frenzy, Smollett alludes to the Spartan soldiers' habit of combing their hair before battle, as noted by Thucydides in his history of the Peloponnesian Wars.

6. *"run a muck"*: From Malay *amok*; mad, frenzied.

7. "Tunbridge": A fashionable spa in Kent, rivaling Bristol and Bath in the eighteenth century. The chalybeate waters at Tunbridge had been discovered prob-

ably by 1606, and their high quality was widely praised by physicians and visitors. Henrietta Maria, royal consort to Charles I, especially favored the wells, which came to be popularly known as the Queen's Wells. In the eighteenth century fashionable people were attracted not only by the medicinal waters but also by the famous Royal Walk, or Pantiles, finished in 1700. The season began in late May or early June and continued through Michaelmas (29 September); it was at its height in mid-August. See Richard Onely, *A General Account of Tunbridge Wells, And Its Environs: Historical and Descriptive* (London, 1771). Defoe, in Letter 2 of his *Tour thro' the Whole Island of Great Britain* (1724–26), describes Tunbridge as a licentious place full of sharpers, beaux, rakes, and loose women, which may help to explain why Smollett sends Fathom there instead of somewhere else. Defoe's *Tour* was frequently reprinted (a third edition, revised and emended by Samuel Richardson, appeared in 1742); it was surely known to Smollett, who may have used it as a source in the present episode.

8. "a plain suit . . . tye perriwig": This is an accurate description of a contemporary physician's dress; see also chap. 52, p. 254 and n. 2. Smollett posed in just such a costume for a portrait presumably by William Verelst, c. 1756 (see Knapp, 142); the portrait is reproduced as the frontispiece to this edition.

9. "Rouzee's treatise": Smollett refers here to the early pamphlet by Lodowick Rowzee, *The Queenes Welles, That Is, a Treatise of the Nature and Vertues of Tunbridge Water* (London, 1632). This work, many times reprinted, was widely read as an authoritative commentary on its subject; it was included in volume 8 of the *Harleian Miscellany* (London, 1744–46).

10. "taken his degrees at Padua": The university at Padua, a great medieval center of learning located twenty-two miles west of Venice in northeast Italy, was noted for its medical faculty in the eighteenth century. The splendid reputation of the university was partly ensured by the luster of its former professors Galileo and Fallopius and by the achievements of its most distinguished graduates, Dante, Petrarch, and Tasso. Padua medical degrees were the most prestigious in Europe during Smollett's time.

11. "certain engagements . . . the faculty": The apothecary refers to commission arrangements with physicians; see chap. 6, n. 6.

12. "palpitation": Quivering of the body, and (probably) quickened beating of the heart.

13. "poet . . . with a trowel!": Smollett alludes to a class of popular poets whose origins, in his view, were more interesting than their verses. The "poet from the scullery" has not been identified; the "muse in livery" is the bookseller and one-time footman, Robert Dodsley, author of a well-known collection of poems entitled *A Muse in Livery: or, The Footman's Miscellany* (London, 1732). The phrase "Apollo with a trowel" refers to the minor Irish poet, Henry Jones (1721–70), a bricklayer by trade whose patron, the fourth earl of Chesterfield, discovered him while serving as lord lieutenant of Ireland. Jones's *Poems on Several Occasions* (Lon-

don, 1749) was followed by other miscellaneous verses; in 1752 he completed a
tragedy, *The Earl of Essex*, which was performed at Covent Garden on 21 February
1753 and published shortly thereafter. Colley Cibber, possibly at Chesterfield's
urging, tried to arrange for Jones's appointment as his successor in the poet lau-
reateship. In Smollett's day the most famous among the considerable number of
figures who had risen from obscure origins into literary fame was the "Thresher
Poet," Stephen Duck, who enjoyed the patronage of Queen Caroline and who
became a minor celebrity following the publication of his *Poems on Several Occasions*
in 1736.

14. *"illustrious part'ner . . .* praise": A mocking reference to Henry Jones's celebration
of his patron as an "Illustrious Guest" in "On His Excellency the Lord Chesterfield's Arrival in Ireland," the first poem in Jones's 1749 collection of verses. In his
later *Epistle to the Earl of Orrery* (London, 1751), Jones characterized both Orrery
and Chesterfield as "Illustrious." Smollett's mockery is enriched by ironic echoes
of Shakespeare. See *As You Like It* 1.2.113: "Well said. That was laid on with a
trowel"; and see *Macbeth* 1.3.54–57:

> . . . My noble partner
> You greet with present grace, and great prediction
> Of noble having and of royal hope,
> That he seems rapt withal . . . .

Chapter 51

1. "Phillis": Or Phyllis, a conventional name for an Arcadian shepherdess.
2. "embrocations": Liquid medications, or liniments, externally applied.
3. "Biddy": Diminutive of Bridget.
4. "doctor Looby": The name means clownish, loutish, stupid (*OED*).
5. "English universities . . . instructions of foreigners": In the mid-eighteenth century, medical education in English universities was restricted for the most part to
study of such ancients as Galen, though some rudimentary acquaintance with
anatomy was required for a degree. European universities, especially Padua and
Leyden, offered better training, as did the Scottish universities at Glasgow and
Edinburgh, where students attended lectures in chemical and anatomical science.
(Fathom claimed to have taken his degrees at Padua; see chap. 50, p. 242 and n.
10.) Medical degrees from Scottish universities were vigorously depreciated by
the Royal College of Physicians in London, and a degree like Smollett's from
Aberdeen (granted in June 1750 upon payment of a fee of £28 Scots, accompanied
by recommendations from established physicians) was especially condemned,
however competent the practitioner holding it might be. Smollett resented all this
scorn, and in the present episode he turned it back upon one of its characteristic
sources. (See also chap. 6, pp. 28–29 and n. 5, and chap. 52, pp. 254–55 and n. 5;
and see Knapp, 144–46.) For a contemporary discussion of the deplorable quality

of English medical education in Smollett's day see Richard Davies, *The General State of Education in the Universities: With a Practical View to the Philosophic and Medical Education* (Bath, 1759).

6. "limit the practice . . . a corporation": There is truth in the charges Fathom makes, for indeed this doctor seems to represent the typically provincial and elitist attitudes of contemporary medical practitioners. Possibly Smollett is reacting against a movement of the early 1750s to deny membership in the Royal College to doctors not trained at Cambridge or Oxford; see Sir George Clark, *A History of the Royal College of Physicians of London* (Oxford: Clarendon Press, 1964–66), 2:556–58. This episode is of course ironic too, for Fathom is precisely the kind of impostor the doctor has accused him of being.

7. "frontal": Or frontale, a topical medication applied to the forehead; see Barrow.

8. "'squire Stub": The name implies that the squire is a blockhead.

9. "specifick": A medication or treatment prescribed directly for a specific ailment or disease.

10. "lodgement": The secure position gained, as on enemy ground (*OED*). Once again Smollett introduces a military metaphor into a description of Fathom's amorous adventures.

11. "the river *Lethe*": In Greek mythology a river of Hades whose waters caused complete forgetfulness of the past. In his *Travels* (Letter 29), Smollett echoes his comments here upon this variety of fashionable snobbishness: "When you arrive at Rome, you receive cards from all your country-folks in that city: they expect to have the visit returned next day, when they give orders not to be at home; and you never speak to one another in the sequel. This is a refinement in hospitality and politeness, which the English have invented by the strength of their own genius, without any assistance either from France, Italy, or Lapland" (p. 252).

12. "this oblivious principle": This principle of obliviousness.

Chapter 52

1. "*the sons of Pæan*": The sons of Apollo, known as Pæan in his capacity as physician to the gods.

2. "a large periwig with three tails": The "physical" wig, worn by members of the learned professions and especially by doctors, was a full periwig swept back from the forehead to hang below the ears on the sides and below the nape of the neck in the back; see Cunnington and Cunnington, 243. Some physicians wore three ties to their wigs to distinguish them from other professional men. See also chap. 50, p. 241 and n. 8.

3. "dancing the hays": Traveling about in the patterns of a country dance having a winding or serpentine movement. Hogarth, in his *Analysis of Beauty* (London, 1753), described the hay as a pleasing series of motions in a "cypher of S's, or a number of serpentine lines interlacing, or intervolving each other" (p. 150).

4. "coachman . . . supply his place": Here Smollett mocks those medical practitioners who falsely set up as successful by undertaking to purchase coaches. Forced to return the vehicles to their coachmakers because they could not pay for them, they feigned terrible accidents, arranged to have the accidents publicly announced, and thereafter determined always to go on foot.

5. "in this manner . . . performed": This entire paragraph contains one of Smollett's most fierce reflections upon the exclusive London medical fraternity of his day; it is, despite its tone, a generally accurate description of relations among the various kinds of practitioners. See also chap. 6, pp. 28–29 and nn. 5, 6.

6. "venæsection": A blood-letting by the opening of a vein; see Barrow.

7. "his rest": His place of rest, or lodging.

8. "Charing-cross": Charing Cross, the large area south of Trafalgar Square, at the meeting of the Strand and Whitehall. Part of the name refers to the cross erected in this place by Edward I in memory of Queen Eleanor (Timbs, 1:71).

9. "the medical coffee-house": Possibly Child's Coffee House in Saint Paul's Churchyard near the Royal College of Physicians in Warwick Lane; or Batson's Coffee House in Cornhill. Both houses dated from the late seventeenth century, and both attracted physicians (and quacks); see Lillywhite, London Coffee Houses, 110–11, 156–57.

10. "cheapen an urinal": Bargain for the lowest price on a glass vessel used to collect urine specimens. Smollett indirectly develops a scatological joke in this sentence as the concluding reference to the urinal returns back upon the preceding clause.

11. "usquebaugh": Usquebaugh, or whiskey, was sold in small draughts, or drams; the actual measure of a dram was one-eighth fluid ounce, but the term was often used figuratively (OED). Usquebaugh was most familiar in the Scottish Highlands until about 1750; see Henry G. Graham, The Social Life of Scotland in the Eighteenth Century (London: A. and C. Black, 1901), 529.

12. "sculler": A sculler is an oarsman in a small boat; but here Smollett seems to use the word in a loose colloquial association with scullery and scullion, both of which suggest lowness and baseness of servitude.

13. "those sage Sibyls": In antiquity a sibyl was a prophetess, but in the eighteenth century she was also a "fortune-teller" or "witch" (OED). Here Smollett uses the word in reference to those waiting-women and nurses who, by prior arrangement, informed physicians of illnesses in the households they served or in the families of their employers' acquaintances and connections.

14. "lock": A hospital for treatment of venereal disease. The most prominent such institution was the Lock Hospital in Harrow Road, established in 1746 by contributions from eminent people. There were several other locks in the city; see Timbs, 1:383–84.

15. "remains to be proved . . . indigent": Smollett certainly had strong humanitarian impulses, as manifested (for example) by his treatment of Joshua Manasseh in this novel. But he objected to government policies and private philanthropic projects

that seemed to encourage laziness and thus indigence among the poor. He had, of course, risen above the poverty of his own youth by very hard work. In the mid-eighteenth century, existing laws and institutions for the poor seemed to have little effect, and the early 1750s brought a flurry of pamphlets urging reform. Henry Fielding's *A Proposal for Making an Effectual Provision for the Poor* (1753) was among the most important of these, and it suggested among other things a new Middlesex County Workhouse, to be built at a cost of £100,000, where the poor might be employed in useful labor. See Williams, 137–38. For some examples of contemporary philanthropic institutions see Turberville, 1:328–34. Smollett's attitudes toward his own boyhood poverty are summarized in Knapp, 302–3.

16. "young people . . . amours": A reference to venereal diseases unluckily contracted during love affairs.

Chapter 53

1. "a medicine of such rough operation": Fathom probably has decided to prescribe Ward's Pill; see chap. 45, p. 211 and n. 5.

2. "a certain famous empyrick": Smollett very probably refers here to Dr. Joshua Ward (1685–1761), though Robert Adams Day has suggested another possibility in "When Doctors Disagree: Smollett and Thomas Thompson," *Etudes Anglaises* 32 (1979): 312–24. Ward's "Drop and Pill" made him rich but notorious. Familiarly known as "Spot," Dr. Ward was a kindly man, or so many people thought, including a dying Henry Fielding, whom he treated and who paid him a fond tribute in the introduction to his *Journal of a Voyage to Lisbon*. Many others attacked Ward for quackery, as Fielding himself had once done in *Tom Jones* (book 8, chapter 9). Pope mocked him in his *Imitations of Horace*, Epistle 1.6.56 (1738) and Epistle 2.1.182 (1737); Hogarth did likewise by portraying him in Plate 5 of the *Harlot's Progress* (1732). In *Peregrine Pickle*, chapter 102, Smollett sneered at Ward in the opening lines of a poem burlesquing George Lyttelton's *Monody* (published in 1747, following the death of Lyttelton's wife): "Where was thou, wittol Ward, when hapless fate / From these weak arms mine aged grannam tore . . ." (*The Adventures of Peregrine Pickle*, ed. James L. Clifford, rev. Paul-Gabriel Boucé [Oxford: Oxford University Press, 1983], 654).

3. "moral sense . . . philosophers": Smollett alludes disparagingly to the ideas of Shaftesbury and his followers, who believed that man possesses an innate moral sense dictating benevolent action and leading to happiness for anyone able to harmonize daily living with the truths discoverable to moral reason. Among the "modern moralists" mentioned toward the end of this paragraph Smollett may mean to include Henry Fielding, certainly no Shaftesburean but nonetheless a man openly committed to the doctrine of benevolence, as reflected most recently in *Tom Jones* and *Amelia*.

4. "tide . . . leads on to fortune": Smollett paraphrases, with some irony at Fathom's expense, the famous words of Brutus in *Julius Caesar* 4.3.218–21:

> There is a tide in the affairs of men,
> Which taken at the flood, leads to fortune;
> Omitted, all the voyage of their life
> Is bound in shallows and in miseries.

Chapter 54

1. "phlebotomy": Venasection, or blood-letting.
2. "præmunire": Or premunire; a predicament. See chap. 38, n. 11.
3. "riding . . . for the plate": Riding for the trophy prize or "plate" awarded to the winner of a horse race. In eighteenth-century horse-racing parlance, the plate was actually a gold or silver cup.
4. "deposited": Laid aside or given up (*OED*). The context here exploits as well the more common reference of the word, which is monetary. Smollett is punning.
5. "Graham": George Graham (1673–1751), Quaker mechanician and watchmaker, inventor of the extremely accurate mercurial pendulum and numerous important astronomical instruments, and fellow of the Royal Society. Graham's impressive achievements were widely praised in his time, and a watch of his making was considered the finest available. In contemporary tributes published shortly before and then just after his death on 16 November 1751, Graham is called "the best Watchmaker in Europe"; see *The British Magazine* 5 (September 1750): 372, and *The London Daily Advertiser*, 18 November 1751.
6. "tye-wig . . . a major": Fathom's three-tailed "physical" wig has degenerated into a two-tailed wig resembling the "major" worn by military men; see Cunnington and Cunnington, 242–43, 250–51.
7. "a second day's shirt": A shirt worn for a second day without laundering.
8. "a soap-boiler": A soap maker.
9. "from the hundreds of Drury": From the environs of Drury Lane, London; see chap. 22, n. 7. Fathom has chosen a prostitute as a housekeeper.
10. "Doctors Commons": A college for Doctors of Civil Law, and for the study and practice of civil law, located in Great Knight-Rider Street south of Saint Paul's Churchyard. The various courts sitting in the College Hall had jurisdiction over marriages and divorces, the registration and proving of wills, the admiralty, and those ecclesiastical prerogatives and dispensations under the control of the bishop of London and the archbishop of Canterbury. See Timbs, 1:257–59.
11. "Hounslow Heath": An area in Middlesex some dozen miles from the center of London on the Great West Road, near Hounslow Village; prized for its many

acres of open grazing land but noted as a haunt of highwaymen lying in wait to rob travelers going to and from the city. See H. C. Darby, "The Age of the Improver: 1600–1800," in *A New Historical Geography of England*, ed. H. C. Darby (Cambridge: The University Press, 1973), 344.

Chapter 55

1. "jack-daw": Or jackdaw, the common name for a chattering, thieving species of small crow most commonly seen around old buildings and church towers.
2. "money in the funds": Investments in such trading corporations as the East India Company.
3. "nonsuited": The plaintiff's suit was dismissed for insufficient cause or evidence (*OED*).
4. "Fleet . . . married": This is a "Fleet" marriage of the kind outlawed by an act of Parliament in 1753; see chap. 7, p. 32 and n. 3.
5. "a counsellor of the Temple": A lawyer residing in the Inner or Middle Temple, London.
6. "buroe": Phonetic variant of *bureau*; a writing desk with drawers for storing letters and documents (*OED*).
7. "numbplush": Slang variant of *nonplus*, meaning bafflement or perplexity (*OED*).
8. "a siserary": A writ of Certiorari, by which a case at law was transferred to a higher court, usually on appeal. *Siserary* was a popular corruption of the legal term (*OED*).
9. "a primmineery": A Præmunire or premunire; here, a legal entanglement.
10. "the posse of the Fleet": The small body of armed men that could be summoned by prison authorities to provide assistance or protection. The clergyman probably refers instead to a gang of his fellows in the streets.

Chapter 56

1. "Hicks's-hall": Hicks's Hall, built in 1612, stood in Saint John's Street, Clerkenwell, Middlesex. Here the County Sittings, or Sessions, were held until the new Middlesex Sessions-House on Clerkenwell-Green was completed in 1782.
2. "his cheeks . . . penitence and sorrow": Here Smollett announces the beginning of his narrative's moral and dramatic resolution, which is not completed until the final chapter. The introduction of Providence is conventional in contemporary stories of criminals and other deviants, and many such tales ended with the redemption of the wayward character by a providential interposition leading to self-

knowledge and, finally, to reformation. Smollett himself had already used this familiar ending in *Roderick Random*, though in a very original way; *Peregrine Pickle* modifies the same pattern, bringing its roguish hero's mercurial adventures to a rapid conclusion in tranquillity and happiness. Misanthropic though he was in his general view of human nature, Smollett did believe in the role of Providence in the world of men and women, and he accepted the Christian idea of the ultimate progress of the redeemed part of humanity toward a restored paradise; see Thomas R. Preston, *Not in Timon's Manner: Feeling, Misanthropy, and Satire in Eighteenth-Century England* (University: University of Alabama Press, 1975), chap. 4. For full discussion of the importance of providential vision in early eighteenth-century literature see Martin C. Battestin, *The Providence of Wit: Aspects of Form in Augustan Literature and the Arts* (Oxford: Clarendon Press, 1974); and see Beasley, *Novels of the 1740s*, chap. 4, for treatment of the conventions of rogue narrative and the interpositions of Providence in *Roderick Random*.

3. "Contraries . . . each other": Probably a reference to the *Phaedo* streph. 70–71, where Plato records Socrates's argument that everything having an opposite must inevitably be generated from its opposite and from nothing else.

4. "turn over a new leaf": An English proverbial expression first recorded in 1540 (*ODEP*).

5. "the Borough of Southwark": Fathom had not traveled very far, for the Borough of Southwark lay just across London Bridge from the city of London.

Chapter 57

1. "Irish officer . . . Austrian service": The Austrian armies of the early eighteenth century included numerous Scottish and Irish mercenaries; see chap. 2, p. 12 and n. 12.

2. "the last war": The War of the Austrian Succession (1740–48); see chap. 40, n. 26. Smollett continues his habit of introducing anachronisms, for the date of the present episode could not possibly be as late as 1748, when the Treaty of Aix-la-Chapelle brought the long war to an end. He also seems to have forgotten that the most recent military action in which he had engaged Renaldo was the War of the Polish Succession (1733–35); see chaps. 18 and 19.

3. "a partizan . . . the late war": "Partizans" were irregular troops, or plundering lawless bands, that fought in support of the Hapsburg claim to the throne of the Austrian empire following the death of Charles VI in 1740.

4. "Presburg": Pressburg, the home of the Melvile family; see chap. 3, n. 9.

5. "the empress queen": Maria Theresa, who remained queen of Hungary when her title to the throne of the Austrian empire was contested in 1740, occasioning war. She was called empress after her husband, Francis, duke of Lorraine, was crowned emperor in 1745.

Chapter 58

1. "travelling Savoyards": The name given to bands of itinerant gypsy musicians playing cheap instruments (including the hurdy-gurdy, a kind of hand-turned barrel organ) and accompanied by tame monkeys or marmots.

2. "magic lanthorn": Or magic lantern, a lighted device that creates an optical illusion by projecting the magnified image of a picture onto a screen or wall in a darkened place; a popular amusement in the eighteenth century, frequently featured in performances by itinerant entertainers.

3. "a paultry viole": A cheaply made viol. The instrument, of five, six, or seven strings, was especially popular in the period with bands of traveling musicians and was sometimes played by the monkeys accompanying them.

4. "the scream of Savoy and the howl of Ireland": Presumably a reference to the shrill cries by which traveling Savoyards attracted an audience, and to the shriek of the Irish banshee. Farrel is Irish.

5. "conductor to madam Catherina": Madam Catherina was apparently a generic name for the performing monkeys, or marmots, typically accompanying bands of itinerant musicians. The bands themselves were so familiar in England that in the 1740s and 1750s numerous entertainments, comic dances, and pantomimes were named after them. A theatrical piece called *The Savoyards, or Madam Catherina* was staged at Covent Garden on 15 April 1763.

6. "buttery": A room for storing liquor or other provisions (*OED*).

7. "his princess": Farrel is attended by a monkey, or perhaps a marmot, who presumably entertains by playing its viol and dancing, dressed in the garb of a gypsy "princess."

8. "jealousy": Suspicion.

9. "postern": Gate.

10. "a hussar officer": An officer of cavalry; see chap. 3, n. 6.

Chapter 59

1. "Wilhelmina": See chaps. 12–17.

2. "well protected . . . the realm": It was a commonplace of early-eighteenth-century political rhetoric to proclaim the English constitution as the great protector of individual liberties and to hold it up as a proper object of envy among all nations. Here Smollett is blatantly ironic, however, for the reader already knows how little protection the law has provided to Monimia. In *Amelia* (book 1, chapter 2), Smollett's fellow novelist Fielding had launched a similar but more extensive ironic attack on the workings of the constitution, which he equated with a machine excellently designed but unable to perform its function because of the incompetence or ill intentions of those appointed to make it go.

Chapter 60

1. "like a downright Swiss": Plainly, directly, bluntly, in the manner of a Swiss. The phrase also suggests the sharp bargaining and good financial sense for which the Swiss were widely noted.
2. "convulsions . . . pathetic complaints": Renaldo appears to suffer from a severe attack of hysterical affection; see chap. 30, n. 10.
3. "exasperated": Harsh, violent, and worsening (*OED*).
4. "the solids": The solid parts of the body; that is, the flesh and organs.
5. "the manes": The spirit or shade of a dead person considered as an object of homage or reverence, or as demanding to be propitiated by vengeance or sacrifice (*OED*).
6. "elude": Baffle or divert.

Chapter 61

1. "the Austrian Netherlands": The approximate area of modern Belgium; until 1713 the Spanish Netherlands, but the territory was ceded to the Austrian empire by the Treaty of Utrecht in 1713 (see chap. 22, n. 13).
2. "the fortress of Luxemburg": The garrison fortress of Luxembourg, principal city of the Grand Duchy of the same name, at the time part of the Austrian Netherlands.
3. "terrene parts": Earthly parts, or body. Ratchkali seems to be predicting a kind of secular "sainthood" for Fathom if he is able to continue uninterrupted in his course of brilliant adventuring.
4. "import": Be of consequence to.
5. "Harwich": A small city in Essex on the North Sea, sixty-eight miles to the north and east of London; an important port of departure for small ships sailing to the Continent.
6. "pacquet-boat": Or packet-boat, a passenger vessel carrying packets or parcels as its cargo; a mail-boat.
7. "Helveotsluys": Hellevoetsluis, a small Dutch port on the island of Voorn, and the usual destination of English packet-boats sailing from Harwich.
8. "the Flemings": The inhabitants of Flanders, an ancient countship or duchy now divided among Belgium, France, and Holland.
9. "*ne plus ultra*": Latin "not more beyond." This phrase was allegedly inscribed on the Pillars of Hercules as a warning to mariners.
10. "Mons": A small Flemish city located southwest of Brussels in what was at the time the Austrian Netherlands.
11. "Tournay": A small Flemish city on the Schelde River forty-five miles southwest of Brussels, and near Mons.

Chapter 62

1. "subaltern": A junior officer below the rank of captain.
2. "equerry": The officer charged with the care of horses.
3. "Ostend": A seaport in West Flanders, and an important point of departure for passengers traveling to England.
4. "ill-omened isle": England. *Isle* also means burial grave, and that meaning is implied here. In a related sense the word can refer to an enclosed area, as within the walls of a churchyard; Smollett uses it in this way later in the chapter.
5. "During this pause . . . sorrow": The second of the novel's major Gothic episodes begins here (the first occurs in chapters 20 and 21). In this and the following chapter, Smollett clearly trades on the continued popularity of "graveyard" poetry, especially Edward Young's *The Complaint, or Night Thoughts on Life, Death, and Immortality* (1742–45). Catherine L. Almirall, in "Smollett's 'Gothic': An Illustration," *Modern Language Notes* 68 (1953): 408–10, has argued persuasively that Smollett based the scenes at Monimia's tomb on Congreve's sentimental tragedy *The Mourning Bride* (1697), a work extremely well received upon first performance and many times revived and reprinted. Garrick had staged the play successfully (for a total of fifteen nights) at Drury Lane during the seasons of 1750–51 and 1751–52.

Chapter 63

1. "the phantome . . . countenance of Monimia": The ensuing scene of reunion between the lovers strikingly parallels the similar scene in act 2 of *The Mourning Bride* (see chap. 62, n. 5), except that in Congreve's play it is the hero who returns from the grave instead of the heroine. See Almirall, "Smollett's 'Gothic,'" 409–10, for full identification of Smollett's direct echoes of Congreve.

Chapter 64

1. "collation": A light meal, usually of fruits, sweets, and wines, and sometimes including cold meats or other delicacies (*OED*).
2. "vapour": In this usage, a fancy or fantastic idea.
3. "darkling": Succumbing to gloom and dark despondency.
4. "his long lost Serafina!": The discovery that begins here echoes the similar scene in chapter 66 of *Roderick Random* when Providence reunites the hero with his father. In *Ferdinand Count Fathom* the providential resolution of the two main narrative lines of the story (*i.e.*, Fathom's and Renaldo's) actually commences

some eight chapters earlier, when Fathom first arrives at a moment of self-recognition forced upon him by the power of divine justice (see chap. 56, pp. 274–75 and n. 2).

5. "the oil on Aaron's beard": Psalms 133:2: "*It* is like the precious ointment upon the head, that ran down upon the beard, *even* Aaron's beard: that went down to the skirts of his garments."

6. "long-eared tribe": Genesis 49:14: "Issachar is a strong ass." Smollett here develops an irony from the traditional association between the Jew and the ass, converting it from a mocking association to a favorable one. He had used a comparable allusion for the more familiar purpose of mockery in chapter 57 of *Peregrine Pickle*.

7. "Joseph . . . Ægypt": Genesis 45:5–15. This is the paragraph chosen by Albrecht B. Strauss as the focus of attention in his essay "On Smollett's Language: A Paragraph in *Ferdinand Count Fathom*," in *Style in Prose Fiction: English Institute Essays 1958*, ed. Harold C. Martin (New York: Columbia University Press, 1959), 25–54. Strauss sees the paragraph as representing Smollett's characteristic style, not at its best certainly, but nonetheless revealing his manner of portraying intense emotion, his use of the dramatic tableau, his frequent dependence upon stylized and quite conventional diction, and his habit of undercutting and thus balancing sentiment with humor.

Chapter 65

1. "*concatenation*": Joining together in a unity.
2. "unattainted": Untainted.
3. "superstition": Bigotry, especially as practiced among Roman Catholics, whose religion (Smollett thought) was founded upon ignorance and superstition.
4. "spado": A sword designed for cutting and thrusting (*OED*).
5. "The king": King Philip V of Spain.

Chapter 66

1. "an incident . . . evening": The ensuing story of the tyrannical father who threatens the happiness of his daughter and her lover is another digression in the manner of the earlier "history" of Don Diego in chapter 26, though not nearly so lengthy. Smollett clearly intended the story as a dramatic counterpoint to the lately revealed benevolence and wisdom of Serafina's father, who had himself been a domestic tyrant with nearly disastrous results.

2. "groat": A coin of common currency from about the thirteenth century in several European countries. The English groat, valued at approximately 4*d*., was not

issued for circulation after 1662; hence the figurative meaning of the expression "not worth a groat," that is, not worth anything.

3. "adad!": A meaningless imprecation; possibly a variant of "Egad" (*OED*).

4. "compulsive": Compulsory.

5. "insensibly": Gradually, imperceptibly.

6. "imagination . . . inspired Sybil": Renaldo's passionate foresight of the ecstasy awaiting him is like the divinely given vision of an ancient prophetess.

7. "Hymen": In Greek and Roman mythology, the god of marriage.

8. "*adieu!*": A more literal translation of "*quedad con Dios*" is "rest with God."

Chapter 67

1. "*The longest and the last*": This concluding chapter is actually not the longest in the novel. That distinction belongs to chapter 26, which contains the "history" of Don Diego de Zelos and runs to a length exceeding that of chapter 67 by several hundred words.

2. "wretched hero . . . grasp of death": Smollett has now brought Fathom to the nadir of fortune, a characteristic development in his early novels of roguery, and one which always immediately precedes redemption and resolution. The picture here may be compared with Roderick Random's description of himself at a similarly low point while he is in prison (chapter 64); Peregrine Pickle loses his money, clothes, appetite, health, and spirits under almost identical circumstances (chapter 108).

3. "a black slough": An encrustation of dead, dry tissue, here probably mucus and blood.

4. "father . . . robbed": In the earlier episode when Serafina/Monimia gave her father's picture to Fathom for pawning, he showed no sign of recognition (see chap. 46, pp. 216–17 and n. 3; see also chap. 48, pp. 230–31 and n. 3).

5. "blister": An application to raise a blister; a vesicatory. See below, n. 8; and see chap. 6, p. 29 and n. 7.

6. "a tent bed": A bed with arched canopy and covered sides, designed for warmth and for protection against drafts.

7. "shifted . . . indigence": Fathom has been stripped of his rags, the refuse of his poverty, and his body has been cleansed and freshly dressed.

8. "vesicatories": Plasters or ointments applied to the skin for the purpose of raising blisters; such treatment, which was very painful, was thought to promote withdrawal of contaminated body fluids. See Barrow, "Vesicatio" and "Vesicatorium."

9. "Elinor": Or Elenor (Ellenor), as she is called when Fathom first meets her in chapters 30 and 31.

10. "haberdashery ware": Needles, thread, ribbons, possibly small articles of fabric, and caps or hats.

11. "the Marshalsea": This prison stood in the High Street, Southwark, across London Bridge from the city; it mainly housed convicted pirates and others guilty of crimes at sea, as well as certain debtors and Nonconformists who had committed punishable offenses. In *Roderick Random*, chapters 61–64, the hero languishes in the Marshalsea following his arrest for the crime of swindling a tailor, and it is there that he meets the poor poet Melopoyn before descending into the despair that precedes his rescue and redemption.

12. "act . . . insolvent debtors": See chap. 42, n. 4.

13. "Providence . . . forgive and transmit to oblivion": Renaldo's assurance of forgiveness and redemption completes the providential pattern of the conclusion to Fathom's career begun much earlier (see chap. 56, pp. 274–75 and n. 2). Smollett's rogue-adventurer is a true penitent, and the representation of him as such is consistent with the familiar eighteenth-century Christian typological pattern of sin and repentance; see Paul J. Korshin, *Typologies in England 1650–1820* (Princeton: Princeton University Press, 1982), 251–55.

14. "a breathing sweat": A sweat that breaks a fever by the profuseness with which it allows heated body fluids to escape through the skin.

15. "work out my salvation with fear and trembling": Philippians 2:12: "Wherefore, my beloved, as ye have always obeyed, not as in my presence only, but now much more in my absence, work out your own salvation with fear and trembling." Either Smollett or Fathom has misremembered the context of the words paraphrased from Saint Paul, and the result is ironic.

16. "settle him . . . a better provision": In *Humphry Clinker*, Count de Melvile and Serafina reappear to meet Matthew Bramble and his entourage in Yorkshire, the "country" (or county) where Renaldo had apparently decided that Fathom might live within the means he has provided. Fathom, now called Grieve, reappears also with his wife, Elinor, and their beautiful daughter, Seraphina Melvilia. Fathom has turned Renaldo's annuity of £60 to good account, has lived modestly and circumspectly, and has established himself as a respectable country apothecary known for learning and virtue. Fathom and Renaldo are brought joyously together when the humble apothecary rescues Melvile from highwaymen, and Matt Bramble concludes the episode by proclaiming his belief that Grieve will at last be reunited with the count's family (Matthew Bramble to Dr. Lewis, Harrigate, June 26).

17. "mantua-makers": Makers of dresses and gowns.

18. "convoyed": Escorted, conducted.

TEXTUAL COMMENTARY

PUBLICATION HISTORY

Little is known of the circumstances surrounding Smollett's composition of *The Adventures of Ferdinand Count Fathom*, but the manuscript must have been sufficiently complete in early November 1752 for William Johnston to purchase the copyright for £120. Although the agreement is lost, William Strahan indicates that he purchased a one-third share in the novel for £40 from Johnston on 8 November.[1] Since Strahan became a partner in the book he would seem to be the obvious choice for printer, but there is no record of his having printed it and the evidence gathered from comparing *Ferdinand Count Fathom* with other books known to have been printed by him at about the same time is inconclusive.[2] By 8 January 1753 printing and, perhaps, binding were far enough advanced to warrant a preliminary announcement in the *Public Advertiser*:

> Speedily will be published, In Two Volumes, Twelves, Price 6s. bound, THE Adventures of FERDINAND Count FATHOM. *By the Author of* Roderick Random. . . . Printed for W. Johnston, at the Golden-Ball in St. Paul's Church-Yard.

The notice was repeated in the issues for 9, 12, and 13 January. Then on 14 February the same newspaper announced that the novel would be published the next day, with confirmation of publication on 15 February, followed by the usual "This day is published" advertisements on 16 and 17 February.[3]

In the *Dublin Gazette* for 27 February–3 March, and repeated in the next six biweekly issues, is an announcement for the publication of an edition by Robert Main at Homer's Head in Dame Street. Main had published an edition of *The Adventures of Peregrine Pickle* in 1751. The appearance of a Dublin edition of *Ferdinand Count Fathom* less than a fortnight after the London edition suggests that an agreement had been made with Main to receive advance sheets from the London publisher. This is confirmed by an entry under "William Johnston" in one of Strahan's printing ledgers: "For ⅓ Fathom money from Main £5–5–0."[4] Main must have paid the London proprietors £15–15–0 for the privilege of printing the novel in Dublin, and the £5–5–0 represented Strahan's one-third share.

Another edition of *Ferdinand Count Fathom*, dated 1753 and clearly pirated, bears a parodic imprint, "T. Johnson," substituted for "W. Johnston." It is possible that this pirated edition, set from the 1753 first edition, actually appeared in 1753 to capitalize on the initial sales of the novel; but the date in the imprint may be false. A copy in the Rothschild Library (1914) carries the signature "James Paull 1777 $\frac{20}{2}$" on each title page. The piracy could not have been produced after that date, which in fact suggests that the edition supposedly pirated in 1753 may have been meant to compete with the 1771 second edition.[5] The 1753 first edition is set in Caslon Long Primer Roman No. 1, widely used by London printers, but the type in the pirated edition is distinctive. The font appears in *A Specimen of Printing Types by John Baine & Grandson in Co.*, *Letter-founders* (Edinburgh, 1787), and, although the type was sent to many parts of Great Britain, Ireland, and North America, it was very common in the north of England and in Scotland.[6] Evidence, admittedly slight, indicates Edinburgh as the most likely source for the pirated edition. The edition is a duodecimo in half sheets with the first three leaves signed, a practice common in Edinburgh. In some copies obelisks are printed near the signatures, another feature found in books printed in Edinburgh.[7]

Ferdinand Count Fathom did not sell well. After its publication in 1753, more than seven years passed before the *London Chronicle* of 8–10 April 1760 announced that a second edition would be published in "a few days." An identical notice appeared in the next issue, but it was not until 29–31 May that this advertisement appeared in the same newspaper:

> *This day was published*, In two neat Pocket Volumes, Price 6s. bound, The SEC-
> OND EDITION, of The Adventures of FERDINAND Count FATHOM. By
> the Author of RODERICK RANDOM. Printed for W. Johnston in Ludgate-
> Street.

After the repetition of this announcement in the issue for 5–7 June, the edition is not heard of again. Perhaps remaining copies of the first edition were reissued with new title leaves. Another possibility is that the advertisement was an attempt to ascertain whether there was sufficient demand for a new edition. Smollett's name appeared frequently in the newspapers, associated with his extraordinarily popular *Complete History of England* and with the *British Magazine*, which was then publishing *The Adventures of Sir Launcelot Greaves* in installments. In mid-May of 1760 the first number of Smollett's *Continuation of the Complete History of England* was announced as ready. Johnston may have hoped that Smollett's popularity would find new readers for *Ferdinand Count Fathom*; apparently it did not, as an extensive search has failed to trace a copy of a 1760 second edition.

A second edition was printed by Strahan in November 1771. In his ledgers, under "William Johnston," appears the following entry: "Count Fathom. 2d Edit. 25 Sheets. No. 1000 @£1–8–0 £35–0–0."[8] Johnston does not appear to have advertised this edition separately, preferring instead to capitalize on the popularity of *The Expedition of Humphry Clinker*. In the *London Chronicle* for 8–11 February 1772 is an advertisement announcing the publication of the "Second Edition" (actually the third) of *Humphry Clinker*, "Printed for William Johnston, No. 16, Ludgate street Of whom may be had, by the same Author, A New Edition of The Adventures of Ferdinand Count Fathom, in Two Volumes, Price 6s."[9]

EDITORIAL PRINCIPLES

As is the case with so many other eighteenth-century novels, the autograph manuscript of *Ferdinand Count Fathom* has disappeared. In fact, no printer's copy for any of Smollett's works has survived. The nature of the manuscript can only be deduced from letters, never intended for publication, and from an examination of manuscript revisions the author made in a copy of the 1766 first edition of *Travels through France and Italy* for a new edition that did not appear.[10] The revisions for the *Travels* include additions, translations of passages in foreign languages, and corrections to the printed text. It might be argued that Smollett, by the mid-1760s largely free from his numerous editorial tasks, had new leisure to correct the *Travels*; but an examination of other works he saw through the press shows much the same care, for he left uncorrected only the kinds of errors that none but the most exacting proofreaders might have caught.[11]

The revisions to the *Travels* are written in Smollett's neat hand, which, after more than two centuries, can be read with ease. A compositor, then, would have had no difficulty reading the author's manuscript of *Ferdinand Count Fathom*, but in the process of setting the type an overlay of normalization no doubt occurred. As John Smith notes in *The Printer's Grammar* (1755), "By the Laws of Printing, indeed, a Compositor should abide by his Copy, and not vary from it. . . . But this good law is now looked upon as obsolete, and most Authors expect the Printer to spell, point, and digest their Copy, that it may be intelligible and significant to the Reader; which is what a Compositor and the Corrector jointly have regard to, in Works of their own language." The compositor peruses his copy but, before beginning to compose, "should be informed, either by the Author, or Master, after what manner our work is to be done; whether the old way, with Capitals to Substantives, and Italic to Proper names; or after the more neat practice, all in

Roman, and Capitals to Proper names and Emphatical words," and nothing "in Italic but what is underscored in our Copy." When composing from printed copy and "such Manuscripts as are written fair," we "employ our eyes with the same agility as we do our hands; for we cast our eyes upon every letter we aim at, at the same moment we move our hands to take it up; neither do we lose our time in looking at our Copy for every word we compose; but take as many words into our memory as we can retain."[12] Since *Ferdinand Count Fathom* and the *Travels* are printed in what Smith describes as "the more modern and neater way," numerous changes must have occurred between the manuscripts and the printed books, including some normalization of spelling.

In the lengthy manuscript additions to Letter 11 of the *Travels*—the English translation of a Latin letter to Antoine Fizes and of the professor's reply in French—Smollett followed the old practice, though somewhat inconsistently, of capitalizing nouns and some adjectives. Schooled to capitalize substantives, he continued in his habitual way.[13] But he certainly knew that his capitalization and his use of the ampersand for "and" would be brought into conformity with the rest of the book. He seems to have accepted the new style, or at least acquiesced. In the printed text of the *Travels* he corrected such small matters as a transposed letter, "muscels" (the bivalve mollusc) to "muscles," and a verb tense "affords" to "afford"; at the same time he allowed to stand variant spellings such as "paltry" – "paultry," "ake" – "ach," and so on.[14] Smollett was not consistent in his spelling, although he did have a preferred spelling for some words; but the compositors, by taking as many words into their memory as they could retain, sometimes introduced their preferences. Smollett appears to have been content with the resulting inconsistencies in spelling as long as they were correct, and he did not attempt to restore his capitalization and punctuation.

The 1753 first edition of *Ferdinand Count Fathom*, in all likelihood printed from Smollett's lost autograph manuscript and seen through the press by the author, is the only authoritative text and has been chosen as copy-text for this edition. The Dublin edition and the pirated edition, both with independent descent from the first edition, correct a few errors while introducing the textual corruptions common to reprints. Only the Dublin edition has a table of contents, compiled on Main's initiative from the chapter headings. Readings from these unauthoritative editions have not been included in the textual apparatus.

The 1771 second edition, also set from the first edition, provides a number of useful corrections. Compositors, paid according to the amount of type they set, in general were not interested in emendation and improvement. They normally followed their copy with some care since they knew they would be penalized for failing to do so. Hence the normal assumption is that substantive revisions are authorial. An alert compositor or proofreader might have corrected typographical errors such as "expeded" for "expended" (202.28) and "ovious" for "obvious" (218.35), and might rarely have made an emendation such as "couch" for "coach" (236.12). But the compositor would not have introduced more than a few emendations at most, and several of the revisions seem beyond the powers of a compositor: "deprecate" for "depreciate" (215.7), "importunity" for "opportunity" (224.17), and, particularly, "Douglass" for "D--gl--s" (94.8). Someone read carefully a copy of the first edition for the printer. Was it Smollett?

The second edition of *Ferdinand Count Fathom* was entered in William Strahan's printing ledger in November 1771 and was first advertised the following February. Smollett died 17 September 1771 in Italy. He seems to have left England for the last time in the fall of 1768, and was certainly in Pisa by the spring of 1769.[15] He must have had a friend in London willing to assist him in arranging publication and in correcting his works for the press. Whoever it was had a sense of humor, since he persuaded John Almon and George Kearsly (or Kearsley), both political opponents of Smollett, to become involved in the publication of *The History and Adventures of an Atom*. Dr. John Armstrong seems the most likely person to have seen this work through the press; at least he knew about it before it was finally published 1 April 1769.[16] More important, someone in London supervised the printing and publication of *Humphry Clinker*. The best conjectures suggest that this novel was put in final form in early 1770, and it is possible that when Armstrong visited Smollett for two weeks in July 1770 he carried the manuscript back to London.[17]

Be that as it may, *Humphry Clinker* appeared after some delays on 17 June 1771. According to a note in Benjamin Collins's printing ledger, reprinting of the novel "was begun in July 1771, and ended the August following."[18] Publication was announced in the *Salisbury Journal* on 16 September, the day before Smollett died. It is unlikely that Smollett's ten complimentary copies arrived in Italy early enough to permit him to make revisions for the second edition. Yet the second edition of *Humphry Clinker* contains corrections and emendations similar to those found in the second edition of *Ferdinand Count Fathom*. The seven instances where "Humphry" is misspelled "Humphrey" are corrected, and "Smollet" is corrected to "Smollett." "Laddies" is changed to "Leddies," "scorocconi" to "scrocconi," and "bighetti" to "biglietti," all corrections beyond the normal ability of a compositor. Someone had a zeal for accuracy in the second edition of *Humphry Clinker*, but it was not the author. Smollett shows little concern for chronological inaccuracies in any of his novels, so the change of the date of one letter from "8" November to "14" November is inexplicable, except as the work of a person unfamiliar with the time scheme of the narrative.[19] For by changing the date of this letter, presumably to allow the proper time to elapse between the publication of banns and the marriages that followed, another chronological inaccuracy was introduced. The corrector of the second edition of *Ferdinand Count Fathom* demonstrates this same kind of unfamiliarity with the nuances of the text when, for example, he changes "vision" to "visage" (225.22). Smollett is unlikely to have spoiled his own dialect jokes, as happens in *Ferdinand Count Fathom* when "refectory" is changed to "refractory" (136.12), and in *Humphry Clinker* when "fatherbed" is changed to "featherbed."

The possibility that Smollett left a corrected copy of *Ferdinand Count Fathom* with a friend in London cannot be entirely ruled out. Perhaps he made some corrections for the abortive second edition of 1760, and William Johnston still had access to the copy. But given Smollett's need to earn a living with his pen, he could not afford to spend time on unprofitable enterprises. *Ferdinand Count Fathom* was not a commercial success, and only the enticement of a second edition is likely to have called forth revisions, as in the case of *Peregrine Pickle*, for which he made extensive revisions seven years after the appearance of the first edition. No compelling argument can be made, however, for the existence of a revised copy of *Ferdinand Count Fathom*. As we have seen, the corrections in the second edition, like those in the second edition of *Humphry Clinker*, show a greater concern for accuracy than for the kind of sensitivity to the text that the author, familiar with the work from having written it and gone over it numerous times, might be expected to have.

A more telling argument against authorial responsibility for the revisions in the second edition of *Ferdinand Count Fathom* is their lack of resemblance to the revisions made in subsequent editions of *The Adventures of Roderick Random* and *Peregrine Pickle*. Smollett was very proud of his ability to write quickly, but there are the inevitable signs of haste in the first editions of his earliest novels: verbosity, run-on sentences, awkward and redundant phrases, faulty pronoun references, and so on. By the time Smollett began *Ferdinand Count Fathom* he was a more experienced writer, but the work contains many of the stylistic faults of the first two novels, though fewer in number. Evidence drawn from his revisions for the two earlier novels suggests that, had Smollett chosen to revise *Ferdinand Count Fathom*, he would have attended to several long, confusing sentences, such as the one at the very end of chapter 15 (61.39–62.3) containing a faulty pronoun reference, or the one in chapter 45 ("He informed her . . . construction.") held together with a colon, three semicolons, and nine commas (211.7–14). It seems likely that he would have corrected such sentences and broken them into several separate sentences. In the second edition of *Ferdinand Count Fathom* not one of the numerous rambling sentences has been broken in two. The lack of interest in style is uncharacteristic of Smollett.[20] It must be concluded that the corrections and emendations introduced into the second edition of the novel were not made by Smollett but by some well-intentioned friend.

In the present edition no attempt has been made to achieve a general consistency in spelling, punctuation, or capitalization, because in the absence of the manuscript one cannot determine whether Smollett or the compositor was responsible for their variations. Hence the spelling, punctuation, and capitalization of the 1753 first edition have been retained except when they are clearly in error, or when they obscure meaning or distract the attention of the reader. All emendations to the copy-text have been made on the authority of the textual editor. Hyphenated words at a line-end have been adjusted according to the usual practice of the first edition insofar as that practice could be ascertained from other appearances or parallels. Only the following changes have been made silently: all turned letters or wrong fonts have been corrected, the long *s* has been replaced by the modern letter *s*, and "ae" and "oe" have been treated as digraphs. The abbreviation "Chap." has been expanded to "Chapter" in headings, and the display capitals that begin the first paragraph in each chapter have not been exactly reproduced. Quotations have been indicated according to modern practice, and the punctuation in relation to the quotation marks has been normalized. The length of dashes and the space around them have also been normalized according to modern practice.[21]

APPARATUS

A basic note in the list of emendations provides the page-line reference and the emended reading in the present text. Except for the silent alterations described above, every editorial change in the first edition copy-text has been recorded. Following the square bracket is the earliest source of emendation and the history of the copy-text reading up to the point of emendation. The historical collation follows the same form, except that after the square bracket is given the subsequent history of the substantive variants in the texts examined. This historical collation is confined to substantive variants in the first and second editions whether these are emended first-edition readings or rejected unauthoritative readings. Emendations not found in the first two editions are marked "W" and are the responsibility of the present edition, whether they originated here or with a previous editor. A wavy dash (~) is substituted for a repeated word associated with pointing, and an inferior caret (∧) indicates pointing absent in the present text or in one of the editions from which the variant was drawn. The form of the reading both to the right and the left of the bracket conforms to the system of silent alterations, and there is no record of any variations except for the instance being recorded. When the matter in question is pointing, for example, the wavy dash to the right of the bracket signifies only the substantive form of the variant, and any variation in spelling or capitalization has been ignored. Emendations from catchwords are indicated as *cw*. A vertical stroke | indicates a line-end.

Some emendations and decisions to retain the copy-text reading are discussed in the textual notes. All hyphenated compounds or possible compounds appearing at line-ends in the copy-text are recorded in the word-division list. The reader should assume that any word hyphenated at a line-end in the present text, but not appearing in this list, was broken by the modern printer.

COLLATION

The present edition has been printed from the copy of the 1753 first edition in the University of Iowa Library (xPR3694 A16 1753). This copy was compared on the Hinman Collator with copies at the University of Texas at Austin (Am Sm79 753a), Yale University (Im Sm79 753), and the British Library (C. 60. e. 18). No press-variants were discovered. The 1771 second edition was sight-collated against the Iowa and British Library copies using a photocopy of the British Library copy (12611. f. 12).

Notes

1. *List of Copies*, BL Add. MS 48805, f. 1.
2. Albert H. Smith, "The Printing and Publication of Early Editions of the Novels of Tobias George Smollett, with Descriptive Bibliographies" (Ph.D. diss., University of London, 1975), 2:5–13. I am grateful to Margaret Smith for the gift of her late husband's valuable Smollett archive.
3. Similar advertisements appeared in the *London Daily Advertiser*, although forthcoming publication was not announced until 15 February and actual publication

not until 21 February; the notice of publication was repeated on 22, 23, and 24 February and on 2 and 3 March. The *London Gazette* included advertisements in the issues for 3–6 March and 21–24 April. Preliminary advertisements appeared in the *Salisbury Journal* on 15 and 22 January and 5 February; publication was not announced until 9 April, by which time the novel was on sale at the shop of Benjamin Collins. Collins and Johnston were to be joint publishers of *Humphry Clinker* in 1771.

4. BL Add. MS 48800, f. 148. The receipt of the money cannot be dated precisely. The previous entry is dated 27 April 1753 and the following entry 1754, suggesting that Strahan received payment sometime between late April 1753 and the end of the year.

5. The first volume of the pirated edition was set from a copy of the 1753 first edition. Most of the second volume follows the first edition but includes a few readings also found in the second edition of 1771: "step" (217.36), "importunity" (224.17), "charge" (225.8), and "couch" (236.12). These readings fall in gatherings H, I (2), and K. The first edition reading "vision" (225.22), which also falls in signature I, is retained. The pirated edition further parallels the second edition in reproducing the plurals "accomplishments" (245.35) and "acclamations" (339.6). No conclusion can be drawn from the use of the two plurals, especially since the pirated edition introduces a number of "corrections" and corruptions of its own, including other plurals. Gathering E of volume two of the first edition, however, contains a high incidence of error and may have been set by an apprentice or a fuddled older compositor. In this gathering appear "depreciate" for "deprecate" (215.7), "stop" for "step," "opportunity" for "importunity," "change" for "charge," and "ovious" for "obvious" (218.35). Only "coach" for "couch" appears in the following gathering (F9^v). Perhaps the compositor of the pirated edition had a copy of the first edition with gathering E in a corrected state. Otherwise, unless one is willing to accept the remote possibility that the compositor of the pirated edition independently made emendations which also happened to appear in the second edition, he must have had access to the second edition, and the pirated edition could not have appeared before 1772.

6. A copy of the *Specimen* is in the library of the American Antiquarian Society. Baine was in partnership with Alexander Wilson and spent some time in Ireland managing the Irish branch of the business. He emigrated to America with his grandson and established a type-foundry in Philadelphia on 18 August 1787. See Talbot Baines Reed, *A History of the Old English Letter Foundries*, rev. A. F. Johnson (London: Faber and Faber, 1952), 259, 340–41, and Rollo G. Silver, *Typefounding in America, 1787–1825* (Charlottesville: University Press of Virginia, 1965), 4–8. See also James Mosley, "A specimen of printing types by William Caslon, London 1766: A facsimile with an introduction and notes," *Journal of the Printing Historical Society*, no. 16 (1981/82).

7. In some copies of this edition obelisks are printed near the signatures. In volume 1 a single obelisk appears to the left of signatures a, A–U, and Y; a double obelisk

to the left of signature X; and no obelisk with signature Z. In volume 2 an obelisk is printed to the left of signatures A–D, F–H, K–S, U–2D; to the right of E and I; and a double obelisk to the left of T. Albert H. Smith, "Printing and Publication," describes a 1791 edition of *Roderick Random* printed in Edinburgh with an obelisk to the right of the signatures (1:49, 2:19). Hugh Amory reports that he has observed obelisks in the signature line in a 1791–92 Edinburgh edition of *Tom Jones*. The full significance of the use of obelisks remains to be discovered. What can be said about these particular volumes of *Ferdinand Count Fathom* is that the signatures with obelisks represent reimpressions from standing type. Perhaps after the first impression was worked off, type was left standing, and when a second impression was printed the obelisks were added to indicate a different press or different printers. Changing the name in the imprint from "Johnston" to the English form "Johnson" may have been an attempt to make a Scottish edition appear to have been printed south of the Tweed. The Harvard University copy has a Scottish provenance.

8. BL Add. MS 48800, f. 148.
9. The advertisement is repeated in the *London Chronicle* in the issues for 13–15 and 15–18 February 1772. A similar advertisement appears in the *Salisbury Journal* for 13 April 1772.
10. This copy of the *Travels* is in the *British Library*, shelf mark C.45.d.20, 21. Apart from the manuscript revisions of the *Travels* and a relatively small number of holograph letters, what survives in Smollett's hand is very little: a one-leaf holograph note on the reign of Edward III in the Berg Collection, New York Public Library, and about a dozen signed receipts and documents. See *The Letters of Tobias Smollett*, ed. Lewis M. Knapp (Oxford: Clarendon Press, 1970), xvi–xvii.
11. Smollett was content to make small changes because the *Travels*, written at a relatively slow pace, did not require the extensive stylistic revisions of the earlier works. In the works of his later career, revision seems to have been carried out before publication. He was also a more experienced writer. For discussion of the composition of the *Travels*, see the introduction by Frank Felsenstein, ed., *Travels through France and Italy* (Oxford: Oxford University Press, 1979), xxxv–xli.
12. John Smith, *The Printer's Grammar* (London, 1755), 199, 201–2, 209.
13. Bertrand H. Bronson, *Printing as an Index of Taste in Eighteenth Century England* (New York: New York Public Library, 1958), 17.
14. *Travels*, ed. Felsenstein, 88, 160, 279.
15. Lewis M. Knapp, *Tobias Smollett: Doctor of Men and Manners* (Princeton: Princeton University Press, 1949), 279.
16. In a letter of 28 March 1769 written from London to his friend Smollett in Pisa, Armstrong refers to "your *new Comedy*," almost certainly making a cryptic reference to the *Adventures of an Atom*. A few copies of this work were issued by John Almon as early as December 1768, but it does not appear to have been available in any substantial numbers until it was published by Robinson and Roberts on 1

April 1769. For the complicated printing history of this work, see O M Brack, Jr., *"The History and Adventures of an Atom, 1769," Papers of the Bibliographical Society of America* 64 (1970): 336–38; and see Robert A. Day's introduction to the work forthcoming in the Georgia Edition. Armstrong would have particularly relished seeing through the press a work that attacked John Wilkes. Like Smollett, Armstrong considered Wilkes a valued friend until political events made Wilkes violently anti-Scot. Armstrong wrote a letter to Wilkes on 17 September 1763 formally terminating their friendship. See Lewis M. Knapp, "Dr. John Armstrong, Litterateur, and Associate of Smollett, Thomson, Wilkes, and Other Celebrities," *PMLA* 59 (1944): 1041.

17. Armstrong returned to London in the fall of 1770, in plenty of time to have arranged for the printing of *Humphry Clinker*; see Knapp, "Dr. John Armstrong," 1051. Armstrong also had the leisure for this work, unlike Smollett's friend the printer Archibald Hamilton, for example, who was active in trade.

18. Charles Welsh, *A Bookseller of the Last Century* (London: Griffith, Farran, Okeden & Welsh, 1885), 358.

19. It is even less clear why the letter of "28" September was changed to "22" September. See Thomas R. Preston's introduction to *Humphry Clinker*, forthcoming in the Georgia Edition. For a discussion of the chronological inaccuracies in *Ferdinand Count Fathom* see above, the introduction, pp. xxxiii–xxxv.

20. For a discussion of Smollett's revisions in *Roderick Random* see O M Brack, Jr., and James B. Davis, "Smollett's Revisions of *Roderick Random*," *Papers of the Bibliographical Society of America* 64 (1970): 295–311. For the revisions in *Peregrine Pickle* see Howard S. Buck, *A Study in Smollett, Chiefly Peregrine Pickle* (New Haven: Yale University Press, 1925), 1–19, 123–207; and see O M Brack, Jr., "Toward a Critical Edition of Smollett's *Peregrine Pickle*," *Studies in the Novel* 7 (1975): 361–74.

21. I am grateful to John G. Morris for his assistance with preparation of the text and with proofreading. I also wish to thank the graduate students who worked in the University of Iowa Center for Textual Studies for their help with sight collations and tabulation of variants.

LIST OF EMENDATIONS

[The following sigla appear in the textual apparatus of the Georgia Edition:
1 (the first edition; London, W. Johnston, 1753), 2 (the second edition; London, W. Johnston, 1771), W (present edition).]

44.36	Renaldo] 2	Rinaldo 1
62.1	her] W	his 1–2
65.2	had] 2	had had 1
72.31	Fathom's] 2	Fathom 1
88.20	to] 2	*omit* 1
95.2	have∧)] 2	~:) 1
120.12	solemnly] 2	so-|lemly 1
130.1	Flesh!] W	~: 1–2
179.4	XXXVIII.] W	XXXV. 1–2
181.33	many] 2	may 1
182.18	and stop] 1(*cw*)	stop 1(*text*)
187.19	difficulty] 2	dif-|culty 1
188.28	come;] 1(*cw*)	~, 1(*text*)
189.14	seaman] 2	seamen 1
196.1	XLII.] W	XLIII. 1–2
197.28	Trebasi] W	Trevasi 1–2
202.28	expended] 2	expeded 1
211.10	chagrin,] W	~∧ 1–2
215.7	deprecate] 2	depreciate 1
217.36	step] 2	stop 1
218.35	obvious] 2	ovious 1
224.17	importunity] 2	opportunity 1

225.8   charge] 2   change 1

236.12   couch] 2   coach 1

241.10   the] 2   the the 1

242.33   the] 2   the the 1

242.35   circulated] 2   criculated 1

245.20   gentleman,] 2   ~∧ 1

245.35   accomplishments] 2   accomplishment 1

248.28   unluckily] 2   unluckly 1

261.16   caution.] 2   ~: 1

272.14   Tuesday] 2   tuesday 1

275.34   Sunday] 2   sunday 1

275.35   Monday] 2   monday 1

279.25   sufficiently] 2   suf-|ciently 1

299.16   his] 2   her 1

314.10   ravings] W   raving 1–2

317.28   in reserve] 1(*cw*)   reserve 1(*text*)

339.6   bridegroom] 2   brim-|groom 1

16.3   Melvil] The name also appears frequently as "Melvile." As is often the case with names, Smollett shows no preference for one form over another; hence the name has not been normalized. When the young woman Fathom seduces and later marries is first introduced she is "Elenor" (139.38), but she is dismissed at the end of the next chapter as "Ellenor" (146.22). When reintroduced in the final chapter, she is "Elinor" (349.30). The surname of Smollett's country bumpkin sharper, Sir Stentor, is given in two forms, as "Stile" (101.6) and "Stiles" (174.11). In only two instances have names been emended to bring them into conformity with the clear preference of the copytext. The single appearance of "Rinaldo" (44.36) has been emended to "Renaldo." Count Trebasi is first introduced as "Trevasi" (197.28), spoiling the meaning of his name; and the variant spelling has therefore been emended.

62.1   her] Certain signs of haste in Smollett's writing are run-on sentences and faulty pronoun references. These specific problems occur at 299.10–17. When Smollett revised his two earlier novels, *Roderick Random* and *Peregrine Pickle*, he divided longer sentences and cleared up faulty pronoun references, changing some to nouns.

177.10   goal] To avoid confusion for the modern reader, it might normally be good policy to emend this variant spelling for "jail" to "gaol," a spelling used elsewhere in the novel; but to do so in *Ferdinand Count Fathom* would spoil a pun Smollett makes on "the author's never-failing goal" (190.38).

211.10   chagrin,] Although the restrictive comma is necessary, the language of the sentence is awkward, a product of Smollett's haste.

215.7   deprecate] For comments on the high incidence of error in gathering E of the first edition see the textual commentary, p. 442, n. 5.

271.23   buroe] This phonetic spelling of "bureau" and that of "resine" for "resign" a few lines below (271.30) have not been discovered elsewhere in Smollett's works; nevertheless, they may be remnants of the manuscript.

WORD-DIVISION

1. LINE-END HYPHENATION IN THE GEORGIA EDITION

[The following compounds, hyphenated at a line-end in the Georgia Edition, are hyphenated within the line in the 1753 first edition.]

14.7	house-|keeping	187.31	half-|penny
22.20	fellow-|scholars	191.33	grass-|hopper
36.16	well-|instructed	203.17	wrong-|headed
44.16	day-|break	229.31	all-|perfect
49.40	tender-|hearted	252.8	chit-|chat
62.12	well-|nigh	274.21	fellow-|creatures
79.26	ill-|usage	276.7, 281.1	law-|suit
82.33	travel-|tainted	302.16	post-|chaise
101.36	back-|side	304.1	pacquet-|boat
153.24	right-|hand	310.1	noble-|hearted
170.5	family-|dishonour	324.29	ever-|flowing
171.11	self-|interest	347.2	pity-|breathing
177.24	to-|morrow	358.8	stage-|coach
187.2	muscle-|shells		

2. LINE-END HYPHENATION IN THE 1753 FIRST EDITION

[The following compounds or possible compounds are hyphenated at a line-end in the first edition. The form in which each has been given in the Georgia Edition, as listed below, represents the usual practice of the 1753 first edition insofar as it may be ascertained from other appearances or parallels.]

11.1	first-born	189.15	nightgown
14.17	eye-witness	219.7, 324.5,	
22.31	sheep-stealer	325.35, 331.8,	
		352.21	overwhelmed
28.36, 262.21	bed-side	225.13	compting-house
37.24	help-mate	225.21	eye-brows
50.30, 51.5	step-mother	239.13	overshoot
60.20	sealing-wax	243.40	over-looked
66.15	overheard	254.29	coachmaker
86.27	lurking-place	256.10, 263.26,	
89.27, 127.21	post-chaise	271.15	coffee-house
109.25	chamber-door	263.24	mal-practice
112.11	to-day	282.12	castle-gate
114.1	overacted	297.32	overcome
150.39	paper-hangings	304.27	fellow-soldier
152.1	foot-soldier	306.28	overcame
161.7	tender-hearted	316.4	overtaken
174.7, 244.21	fellow-creatures	319.11	awe-struck
181.7, 286.38	overblown	325.37	withhold
189.6	saucepan		

3. SPECIAL CASES

[The following compounds, or possible compounds, are hyphenated at a line-end in both the Georgia Edition and in the 1753 first edition.]

80.5	counter-|marches
104.27	chuck-|varthing
188.27	over-|come
189.15	night-|gown
344.30	with-|drew

HISTORICAL COLLATION

10.29	bespoke]	bespoken 2
17.4	inspiriting]	inspiring 2
34.29	lady's natural love]	lady's love 2
44.36	Renaldo]	Rinaldo 1
62.1	her]	his 1–2
65.2	had]	had had 1
72.31	Fathom's]	Fathom 1
79.10	led]	leads 2
88.20	to]	*omit* 1
94.8	D--gl--s]	Douglass 2
95.2	should]	shall 2
105.32	insisting]	insisted 2
115.19	these]	those 2
130.1	Flesh!]	~: 1–2
136.12	refectory]	refractory 2
148.19	This]	The 2
150.26–27	extended]	extending 2
159.32	deep-toned]	deep-tuned 2
161.3	asked]	asking 2
179.4	XXXVIII.]	XXXV. 1–2
181.33	many]	may 1
187.19	difficulty]	dif-|culty 1
189.14	seaman]	seamen 1
191.10	should]	shall 2

191.18	those]	these 2
194.4	over-strained]	over-straining 2
194.37	this scheme]	the scheme 2
195.17	a window]	the window 2
196.1	XLII.]	XLIII. 1–2
197.28	Trebasi]	Trevasi 1–2
202.28	expended]	expeded 1
214.36	Tho']	Though 2
215.7	deprecate]	depreciate 1
217.36	step]	stop 1
218.35	obvious]	ovious 1
224.17	importunity]	opportunity 1
225.8	charge]	change 1
225.22	vision]	visage 2
236.12	couch]	coach 1
241.1	gaming]	gaining 2
241.9	fortune]	fortunes 2
241.10	the]	the the 1
242.33	the]	the the 1
243.18	should]	shall 2
245.35	accomplishments]	accomplishment 1
248.28	unluckily]	unluckly 1
272.3	proved]	had proved 2
273.14	alas,]	~! 2
281.11	apprehension]	apprehensions 2
282.3	those]	the 2
290.23	commotion]	commotions 2

299.16   his]   her 1

314.10   ravings]   raving 1–2

339.3   demonstrations]   demonstration 2

339.6   acclamation]   acclamations 2

339.6   bridegroom]   brim-|groom 1

BIBLIOGRAPHICAL DESCRIPTIONS

1. THE FIRST EDITION

THE | ADVENTURES | OF | Ferdinand Count Fathom. | By the Author of
RODERICK RANDOM. | [13 mm. dash] Materiam risus, invenit ad omnes | Oc-
cursus hominum. [two 10 mm. dashes] | Ridebat curas, nec non et gaudia
vulgi; | Interdum et lachrymas fundebat. [7 mm. dash] | IN TWO VOL-
UMES. | VOL. I. | [68 mm. double rule] | LONDON: | Printed for W.
JOHNSTON, at the Golden Ball | in St. Paul's Church-yard. | MDCCLIII. |

Volume 2: Title page as in volume 1 except "VOL. II." substituted for "IN
TWO VOLUMES. VOL. I."

Collation: 12° (178 x 114 mm. uncut). Volume 1: π¹ a⁴ B–M¹². Title page,
verso *blank*, *i*–viii dedication, 1–262 text, *263–264 blank*. Volume 2: *A*¹ B–
O¹² P². Title page, verso *blank*, 1–315 text, *316 blank*.

Press figures: Volume 1: 15–3 52–4 63–3 86–4 111–2 141–5 152–4 154–5 *or
none* 184–3 190–2 194–2 238–2 254–3 261–6. Volume 2: 15–4 37–2 38–5
70–2 83–3 84–5 141–2 143–6 159–2 168–3 192–5 216–6 220–3 231–4
262–6 276–5 279–2 304–2.

Typography: Volume 1: Page 242 = 422. Catchwords 33 order,] ~; 96 re-
spect∧] ~, 259 sort] ~, . No catchword viii, 213. Volume 2: Catchwords
23 and] stop 34 come;] ~, 37 time∧] ~, 78 sion] fusion 123 tion ∧] ~, 244
in] reserve.

Copies: Textually collated IaU (xPR3694 A16 1753), TxU (Am Sm79 753a),
CtY (Im Sm79 753), and BL (C. 60. e. 18). Additional copies bibli-
ographically collated IU (x823 Sm7f 1753), CSmH (77367), CLU–C
(*PR3694 F31), WU (CA 2957), MH (*EC75 Sm792 753f (A) and (B)),
CaOTU (B–10 5120), Bodleian (Don. f. 149–50), Trinity College, Cam-
bridge (Rothschild Library 1912, 1913), National Library of Scotland
(NG. 1557. c. 12), Victoria and Albert Museum (Dyce 9239).

2. THE SECOND EDITION

THE | ADVENTURES | OF | Ferdinand Count Fathom. | By the Author of
RODERICK RANDOM. | [13 mm. dash] Materiam risus, invenit ad omnes | Oc-

cursus hominum. | [two 9 mm. dashes] | Ridebat curas, neo non et gaudia vulgi; | Interdum et lachrymas fundebat. [6 mm. dash] | IN TWO VOL-UMES. | VOL. I. | [72 mm. single rule] | THE SECOND EDITION. | [72 mm. double rule] | LONDON: | Printed for W. JOHNSTON, in Ludgate-Street. | MDCCLXXI. |

Volume 2: Title page as in volume 1 except dashes vary. "VOL. II." is substituted for "IN TWO VOLUMES. VOL. I." and "neo" is corrected to "nec" in the third line of the epigraph.

Half-title: [70 mm. row of Caslon Long Primer Flowers 3] | THE | AD-VENTURES | OF | Ferdinand Count Fathom. | VOL. I. [II.] | [70 mm. row of Caslon Long Primer Flowers 3] |

Collation: 12° (178 x 104 mm.). Volume 1: A⁶ B–M¹². Half-title, verso *blank*, title page, verso *blank*, *i*–viii dedication, 1–262 text, *263–264 blank*. Volume 2: *A²* B–O¹² P². Half-title, verso *blank*, title page, verso *blank*, 1–315 text, *316 blank*.

Press figures: Volume 1: iii–8 15–2 34–3 37–7 58–1 60–7 95–6 100–3 132–3 167–7 168–7 178–6 189–7 206–6 213–7 220–6 226–2 254–3. Volume 2: 22–2 40–7 47–2 61–3 94–9 96–5 117–7 144–1 158–1 165–7 178–9 202–2 209–3 218–5 228–6 252–5 262–6 277–5 287–6 309–4 310–2.

Typography: Volume 1: Catchwords 97 informed] ed 183 in] my 250 in-chant-] nchantment,. No catchword viii. Volume 2: Page 166 = 666. Catchwords 44 pipes] ppes 92 bour's] neighbour's 171 saw] the.

Notes: William Strahan printed 1000 copies of this edition; see above, the textual commentary, pp. 442–43.

Copies: Textually collated BL (12611. f. 12). Additional copies bibliograph-ically collated CtY (Im Sm79 753c), MH (17432. 18. 10), IU (823 7f 1771), Bodleian (12. Θ. 1595–96), National Library of Scotland (Hall 209. i), University of Edinburgh Library.

INDEX

Names, Places, and Topics in Introduction, Text,
Notes to the Text, and Textual Commentary

(Reference to topics is necessarily selective. Location of some places is indicated according to eighteenth-century geography.)

TABLE OF CORRECTIONS

This reprint edition of *Ferdinand Count Fathom* is in every way identical to the original clothbound edition, except that the editors have taken the occasion of its preparation to correct certain inaccuracies. The table below will enable the reader to locate all corrections by page and line numbers. The index to the volume has been silently corrected, as necessary, to reflect revisions to the notes. A record of additions to the original list of emendations and historical collation follows the table.

xxiii.34, 39	132.10	192.34	379.28	426.26−28, 31−34, 35
xxxix.8	136.23	193.19	381.1−2	430.1−5
46.15	144.28	210.31	386.14−20	434.32
77.21	145.25	219.39	394.7−14	435.1−3, 6−7, 8−10,
88.39	159.32	229.11	400.1	11−13, 14−19,
90.11	165.13	235.2	421.24−28	21−23
101.17	182.10	290.31	424.7	
105.3	184.30	296.33	425.28−34	
117.38	185.11	365.26		

List of Emendations

26.20	sallacious]W	fallacious 1−2
49.29	re-echoed]2	re-ecchoed 1
76.30	*career*]2	*carreer* 1
96.13	putting]2	put-|ing 1
155.15	where]2	were 1
184.30	*bienseance*]2	*beinseance* 1
219.39	Orphan]W	orphan 1−2

Historical Collation

26.20	sallacious]	fallacious 1−2
49.29	re-echoed]	re-ecchoed 1
76.30	*career*]	*carreer* 1
96.13	putting]	put-|ing 1
155.15	where]	were 1
184.30	*bienseance*]	*beinseance* 1
219.39	Orphan]	orphan 1−2